About the Author

Zoë Beesley was born and raised in Scotland, and now lives in New Zealand. She has a Master's degree in International Relations and Arabic and a Postgraduate Diploma in Education. *A Sinner's Gift* is her first novel, a book that has been inspired by her love of the mountains and their secrets.

Dedication

In memory of Christopher W. Bell
And for Rob.

Zoë Beesley

A SINNER'S GIFT

AUSTIN MACAULEY PUBLISHERS™
LONDON • CAMBRIDGE • NEW YORK • SHARJAH

A CIP catalogue record for this title is available from the British Library.

ISBN 978-1-78693-189-4 (Paperback)
ISBN 978-1-78693-190-0 (Hardback)
ISBN 978-1-78693-191-7 (E-Book)

www.austinmacauley.com

First Published (2017)
Austin Macauley Publishers Ltd.™
25 Canada Square
Canary Wharf
London
E14 5LQ

Acknowledgments

Thank you to all of those people who never doubted. Your support and belief made this book possible in countless ways, every day. Thank you to Ruth Rankin, for your kind words and attention to detail. And to Rob, ever optimistic and patient, thank you for your honest and generous attention.

Opening

Present Day

"Sir?" He hesitated, nervous. "Did you hear me?"

Fergus Toop grabbed for his jacket.

"Don't touch anything. I'll be twenty minutes."

Without waiting for a reply, Toop chucked the phone onto the couch and headed out of the door.

Chapter 1

Present Day

What had she done?

Lucy closed her eyes and cast the image from her mind, knowing that her life depended on it. She had to stop rehashing the past. No, more than that, she had to erase it.

She sat back with her spine rested against the wall and her eyes shut, increasingly aware of the sharp throbbing in her lower leg, conscious of the pain that was now a part of her.

Maybe, she reasoned, tragedy was something that embedded itself, festering in live flesh even when the event had passed.

An incurable virus that lays dormant in the soul.

Someone had told her that once, a man, his face and name lost to a life that she had long outgrown. But it was only now that she understood what it meant. Now it made perfect sense.

How ridiculous she'd been. How naive. Treating it like it was all some game, a pastime intended to entertain children. The thought brought tears to her eyes, and she felt suddenly stupid.

Lucy Roy had not grown up with a normal family. There was no mother to tuck her in at night, no father to teach her right from wrong. Her life amounted to one mishap after another, a chain of regrettable events that started, most unfortunately, with her birth. But this time it was different. This time it had been her choice.

Lucy sat on the hostel bed and let her mind wander. In the grand scheme of things, her being, her very existence was trivial, barely worth noting really. She repeated the notion in her head and took a strange comfort in it.

You are one fleeting being in a vast universe, nothing more than a pinprick in history.

Yes, there had been a plan. Calculated and deliberate. She had always known how it would end, how it had to end, and to wish for anything else would have been childish. But then, retrospect was a beautiful thing. Lucy wiped the tears from her cheeks and allowed herself a moment in the past, taking refuge in the words of her old Philosophy teacher, listening as his voice ricocheted around the walls. *Pick yourself apart with tweezers and you would be little more than a pile of atomic dust... a mound of tiny, dead particles.*

No one.

She clung to his words, her thumb nail caught between her teeth, as she pictured her body disassembling into a mass of tiny atoms, dissolving limb by limb into coloured flecks that floated across the room. A sudden chill broke the air and Lucy opened her eyes. The words of her teacher faded and she was left staring at the ceiling, the wooden beams bearing down on her like a guilty conscience. A crushing weight spread across her chest and she struggled to fill her lungs. She gasped at the air, trying to swallow, as her field of vision grew hazy.

"One, two, three..."

The rhythmic recital of numbers helped to slow her pulse and she sensed the first sign of release.

"Four, five, six..."

But the reprieve was short lived, her breaths reverting to short desperate gasps. She cupped her hands over her nose and mouth to create an air pocket but nothing happened. Two words hung in the air, robbing all the oxygen from the room.

What now?

Her fingers ripped at her shirt fabric. It was too tight. She couldn't breathe. The grip around her heart stiffened and her arms and legs turned to lead. Then it hit her with a merciless clarity. She was alone.

As the seconds slipped away the urge to throw up slowly passed, but it did pass. Seconds turned to minutes and panic turned to exhaustion until Lucy managed to drag her mind from the murk. She had to keep moving.

It wasn't safe to stay still.

In one fluid motion, she moved her legs so that they hung over the edge of the top bunk and looked down at the nothingness between her feet, studying her limbs as they swung weightless in space. Her right ankle had started to swell. Lucy reached down and ran her fingers over the faint patch of purple bruising.

It was going to hurt. A lot.

She removed her hand and looked out across the room, thinking of a time when ghosts were defeated by a switch of the light and monsters were a work of fiction. Then she drew a deep breath and slipped to the floor. The pain was instant, shooting through her ankle joint like a hot poker, daring her to cry out.

Just keep moving.

The communal bedroom was deserted. The other lodgers having departed early, eager to make the most of a sunny day in the Scottish Highlands. It took a moment for Lucy to absorb her surroundings. She glanced at the array of books and clothes that cluttered the beds, the contents of each bunk offering an insight into the life of a stranger. A canvas bag had been chucked onto one of the bunks and the contents spilled out onto the duvet; a tattered Lonely Planet guide to Scotland, a worn diary, a toothbrush and a pair of green walking socks.

"Keep moving," she whispered.

Lucy averted her eyes and looked over at the weathered rucksack on the floor. It was covered with numerous badges and attached to the strap she recognised one of the identification labels that they handed out at the airport. She could just make out the letters LHR.

Lucy wrapped her blanket around her shoulders and limped across the room, the wooden floorboards creaking under her bare feet. The electric heater in the corner emitted a continuous buzzing sound that made her whole body flinch. Each dull buzz wedged itself inside her head and produced a pulse that pounded behind her eyes. She tucked the blanket under her arms and shuffled towards it. As she inched across the floor her reflection moved with her, caught in the mirror on the opposite side of the room.

Lucy stared back at her face.

Pick yourself apart with tweezers and you would be... dust... dead... no one.

Tears singed the rims of her eyes and she held out her arm, beckoning the reflection closer with her hands. She touched the mirror with the tips of her fingers, half expecting the reflection to brush off. Her thin arms shook and her chest protruded further as her breaths deepened.

What if everything that she had ever dared to want had just cost her everything that she had?

The desire to turn away was a solid thing, a tangible force that pulled at her muscles, but she found herself moving closer to the mirror. Lucy devoured every detail, the blood red hair that framed her face and the freckles that were splashed across her nose. Crimson curls fell over her pale skin, the loose coils sweeping across her vacant expression.

Lucy had waited years, a lifetime, for this moment. But as the reality of daybreak shone through the window she felt numb. She was completely on her own. She wanted to dissolve into her duvet, to lie there and let the world forget her. It would be so easy, she thought, to slip away like sand through open fingers.

But those eyes.

They burned into her, glaring back with an unspoken purpose. A shiver ran through Lucy's spine and she hugged her arms. Her nails dug into her skin as she stared back at her reflection, her own image a perpetual reminder of the past. Lucy didn't notice the blood that formed under her finger nails, numb to the pain of her own grip. She started to move backwards, sliding her feet across the floor to create distance between herself and her reflection, from everything that she knew. Everything, all of it, was captured in that small, unassuming frame.

Her blue eyes darkened, and before she had time to process her actions she grabbed a mug from the table. It struck the mirror with a piercing crash, smashing the glass into a thousand uneven shards. Lucy didn't flinch. She stared ahead at the empty frame, eyes vacant, and listened to the familiar voice echoing inside her head.

At some point every rose has to die.

Lucy lowered her gaze and checked her watch.

There was a bus leaving in an hour and she had every intention of being on it.

Chapter 2

Fergus Toop had the look of a man who understood that the night would be long. And he had good reason to believe so. Death, he had learned, was never simple. It grew more elusive with each passing minute.

He stared at the corpse, clenched his hands behind his back and bit his lower lip. The dead body was dwarfed by jagged walls of scree, a limp mass of limbs propped up against the rocks, seated as if in ceremony. Toop thought of a rag doll and found himself envisioning the lifeless cloth figure, the arms and legs stuffed with spare scraps of material and the face painted with the same unsettling smile.

Remnants of the day just gone still lingered in the sky, offering a couple of hours of light before the rocks turned to black shadows. The mountains held an eerie quiet, broken only by the howls of wind. Not a tree in sight. Even in the summer months the Scottish weather remained changeable. While the warmth of the sun captured the day, winds brewed over the Atlantic Ocean and gathered moisture. The first faint warnings of rain had started to fall, beading in isolation on Toop's jacket. He stood in unvoiced thought, watching as the evening mist toyed with the body. It caressed each patch of exposed skin, snaking silently round the lifeless extremities. The damp fog darkened the sky and grey clouds gathered over the mountains, threatening to break. Toop zipped up his jacket, blinking away the beads of rain as they landed on his eyelashes.

The rain grew heavier.

Toop stared out at the peaks of the Torridon hills, nature's judge, jury and executioner, his mind wandering, veering from the image in front of him to memories of a forgotten childhood. A life before everything was taken from him.

His father's words echoed through the mist.

"Don't let her fool you lad, she's a fickle mistress that."

Toop was nine years old again and his Dad's hand rested on his shoulder. For a fleeting moment, he was that small doting boy, holding on to his father's every word.

"Ferg, for what are men to rocks and mountains?"

"Nothing." The whisper of a child.

The huge boulders blotted the sky, rocks that had been beaten by the weather and left in battlement ridges across the horizon.

"Son, is it the mountains that teach us how truly small we are."

Toop felt his Dad ruffling his hair, pushing his head away in jest.

The police officer heaved a sigh, bringing himself back to the present before looking over at the crime scene. He stood and faced the dead body, one hand on his waist, the other cupped round his chin. The words formed in his head without effort.

Male, white, deceased.

His mind formalised the scene into a simple tick list.

Middle aged, alone, slim.

Gun present.

Toop drummed his fingers against his cheek, focused by the rhythmic vibration and glanced up at the sky. The words continued without effort.

Brown hair, city clothing, small rucksack.

Toop sensed something strange in the man's features. Was it relief? Was he pleased to be dead?

Toop had never seen a crime scene like it. It was haunting, beautiful somehow. He could recall a number of murder cases during his time in London but none quite so salient. So peaceful, he thought. Toop gazed out at the fortress of rocks, unable explain it, perhaps it was irrational but he couldn't ignore what he was feeling.

Something was out of place.

Absorbed in his own thought process Toop failed to notice the flash of blue, catching sight of it at the last moment. He stretched out his arm and grabbed the sleeve of his partner.

"Bailey, stop!"

Toop planted his feet on the rocky ground as his fingers connected with soft fleece. Bailey's lanky arm extended in the direction of the dead body, his eyes lost in a look of hesitant determination. The strength of Toop's grasp jolted him from his stupor, causing his boots to slip in the mud. Bailey tried to resist the momentum, grasping at the air but his feet went from under him.

"Ouch. Stupid boots," spluttered Bailey, his words distorted by a thick Scottish accent.

Toop watched in disapproval as his partner attempted to regain his footing. Humour was not one of Toop's strong points. Not anymore.

Toop leaned forward and offered his partner a strong hand, lifting his gangly frame from the ground in an effortless movement. The motion propelled Bailey upwards with such force that it threatened to unbalance him a second time. Bailey just managed to extend his arm and prevent his face from colliding with the hard ground. The young police officer picked himself up and stumbled over to Toop.

"Sorry sir, my fault, wasn't thinking."

Toop looked blankly at Bailey. He was not the greatest advocate of the local lad and his relentless enthusiasm but, bound by a sense of professionalism, he masked the exasperation in his voice.

"Would you like to explain what you were trying to do?" he asked.

"Sorry sir, it's just I've never seen one before. You know, a dead body, I just wanted to see if it was cold."

"Cold... You have got to be..."

Toop closed his eyes and took a deep breath.

"Never mind, just don't touch anything."

Bailey nodded.

"Got it. No touching."

Toop stared at the young lad's face and realised how far he was from London. He turned away, caught by a sudden feeling of sadness. Not because he missed the capital, he had hated the city, but because at some point in the last decade the Scottish Highlands had become foreign to him. Toop wondered briefly what he would have been like if he had never moved south of the border. If the accident had never happened.

But the moment of nostalgia didn't last, interrupted by the drone of Bailey's voice.

"What do you think happened?" he asked. "I reckon he topped himself, poor fella probably just wanted a peaceful place to say his goodbyes. Quite eerie mind with all those mountains round him, bit like Mordor up here don't you think, especially when those dark clouds roll in."

Bailey wrapped his arms round his ribcage and shivered.

"You wouldn't catch me up here on my own, even if it was to end it."

A look of deep concentration grew upon Bailey's face, two deep lines appearing between his eyebrows as he pressed his lips together.

"There's just something that I can't wrap my head around. How is it that he can still be sitting up like that, like in a chair or something?"

He turned to Toop, waiting for an answer. But Toop stood silently next to his young colleague, unsure if the boy's unlearned naivety infuriated him or if in fact he was envious of it.

Chapter 3

Late 80s

Jonathan Swan sat at his desk.

The spring air was warm and oddly sticky for Glasgow, causing an uncomfortable heat to hang throughout the library. Sunlight fell through the large windows in wide beams, the warm rays stifling the unfortunate few. The ill-placed students wriggled in their chairs, their bare skin sticking to the waxy fabric and leaving sweaty imprints on the leather.

The university library was clogged with bodies, each floor of the building indistinguishable from the next. The only perceivable difference between them was the large black numbers that were printed on the doors. The third level, as with all the others, resembled a large cube-shaped shoebox, identical desks and identical chairs. The same grey walls and beige carpets. Every floor, without exception, contained rows of pimpled faces. Perfect imitations, their faces distorted in expressions of concentration and confusion.

Spring, and the approach of exams, had coerced students through the library doors in their hundreds. A bleary-eyed battalion armed with textbooks that amassed upon the ugly, seventies-style construction. Mounds of books lay claim to the most prized seats, each tower of paper a testament to the accepted notion that location was the key to effective study. These seats were secured by the first light of day when the library opened its doors at 7 o'clock, when the academically eager and the socially challenged fought for those priceless locations.

Jon, who sat quietly in a booth in the corner, had yet to decide which of these categories he fitted in to.

Both most likely.

He watched as the girl across from him slipped her hand beneath her skirt. Her fingers disappeared beneath the folds of yellow cotton and rose up her outer thigh. He imagined her fingers as they slipped under the seams of unseen white lace, playing with the elastic of her underwear. He pictured the sweat on her skin, envisaging the cool release of air on her flesh.

The thought, forbidden and wrong, aroused him.

Jon turned away, ashamed.

He returned to his textbook, the roots of a frown claiming a path across his forehead. He read the passage for the third time, taking care to absorb each sentence, breathing in the words as if they might offer a new understanding.

...the light blue tinge given to the lips and the pale, bloodless skin indicates that the subject is suffering from syphilis. What makes this painting most controversial however is the fact that it is a self-portrait of the artist. Caravaggio embraces all evidence of sexual liberation, unashamed in his praise of sexual exploration and desire.

The artist, self-portrayed as a Greek god, was pictured resting upon a table, a vine of grapes held in his right hand. The image pulled Jon in, drawn like the fingers of a child to a flame. Guilt and disobedience both excited and confused him, his body responding too quickly to his thoughts. He felt the reaction between his legs and quickly moved his torso forwards against the desk.

His cheeks burned.

Jon eyed the room nervously and brought the jacket of the book closer together, hiding his shame in the crevasse of paper, before sneaking a look at the girl in yellow.

She was oblivious, absorbed in her work.

She rested her elbow upon the desk, her right hand cupping her face as she tilted her head to the side. Strands of hair escaped from behind her ears and fell upon her book, encircling the page in strawberry blonde curls. Jon watched as the fingers of her left hand rose to her mouth and she stroked her lips, unaware of the effect that it had on her doting observer.

Jon tried to focus his thoughts. He wondered what she might be reading and whether she would approve of his choice of text. He looked at the title of his book, *Art and 16th Century Society.*

It was at that moment that a voice pierced the silent library.

Multiple pairs of eyes turned in unison, as if rehearsed, to locate the offending noise. A few muffled complaints clouded the air as disapproval of the disturbance was made clear.

It was his name.

"Jon!"

Jon watched as his friend manoeuvred between the seated bodies, tactless and unrefined. His muscular six-foot frame squeezed through the narrow slips that separated the desks, advancing to a chorus of disgruntled comments and angry glares.

But the spirit of Jesse Jenkins remained undamaged.

The boys had been friends longer than Jon could remember, knotted together like two pieces of rope. In truth, Jon had but a handful of childhood moments that were his alone. His childhood memories were filled with Jesse Jenkins, Jesse and his tomato-red cheeks. On one occasion, when Jon was about three, childish intrigue had gotten the better of him. The boys had been sitting, squished together on the sofa, their little legs curled beneath them, elbows rested on the arm of the chair. They sat, wide eyed and open mouthed, clutching toy cars in their chubby fingers. Then, in a moment of unbridled curiosity, Jonathan's tongue had peeked out from his lips and he proceeded to lick Jesse's left cheek- just to see. A young Jesse had frozen in complete bewilderment.

He never let Jon live it down.

There was nothing that Jon and Jesse didn't share. The two little boys used to pull their small stools, one green and one red, up to the bowl of the toilet where they would stand in deep conversation, sharing stories as they went about their business.

But their differences were as strong as their friendship.

Jesse was taller, faster, stronger, and he was confident, growing more popular with each year at school. Girls doted on him, wagging their tails in frenzy as he spoke. He lost his virginity at fifteen and had since lost count of his conquests. Jon's sexual experiences amounted to an awkward, clichéd fumble at High School, devoid of any imagination or gratification. There was a drunken incident during his first week at university but he wasn't sure that it counted.

Jonathan's gift was his intelligence, an ability that had preserved their unlikely friendship. At ten years old Jon was awarded a grant and enrolled at a private school in the city. He attended Boys High, twenty miles away, away from the social expectations and circles of hierarchy that governed the school hallways. Jesse and Jon were left to enjoy each other's company at the weekends, far from the judging and expectant eyes of youth. Then University offered a new world, one where the gods of adolescence were moralised and intelligence was praised, where Jonathan, a timid Art History student, was best friends with the university swim team captain.

The great weight of Jesse's hand fell on Jonathan's back and he noted the faint smell of chlorine.

"Hey buddy. Whose arse did you kiss to get this spot?" smiled Jesse.

Jon grinned, the expression not quite natural on his face. "The list is long but distinguished." He replied, quoting Top Gun.

"Yeah so is my Johnson," laughed Jesse. "Damn, you gotta love that film. Think I'd make a good Maverick. You could be that geeky sidekick, hey Goose!?"

Jon snorted, forgetting where he was, a loud grunt escaping from his nasal passage. He quickly drew his fingers to his lips and returned his voice to a whisper.

"We shouldn't be talking in here," said Jon, "It's against the rules." He looked down at his book. "The rules are very strict. No talking. No eating."

"You are a right pansy you know that," laughed Jesse, not lowering his voice. "Plus, you've done enough reading to get a degree for both of us. Come on, let's get out of here."

Jon started to gather his things. He tilted his head to the side, motioning in the direction of the girl who was glaring at them.

"We must be quiet," he said, "People are looking."

Jesse turned and blew her a kiss. The girl visibly recoiled and tutted out loud.

"I don't think that you should do that," said Jon. "'I don't think she likes it."

Growing redder, Jon placed his books in his bag and got up to leave. As they reached the stairs Jesse turned and whispered to him.

"Check her out."

Jesse grinned and waved at the girl in yellow.

Chapter 4

Present Day

Lucy woke up and looked out of the bus window. She didn't know where she was, not exactly, somewhere north of Glasgow.

The bus wound its way through the Scottish countryside encased by rolling hills. The barren mounds of heather extended into the distance and flowed down to the road. Even in the height of summer the land was the colour of autumn, the coarse whiskers of yellow grass beaten down by the wind.

Rain stained the window, streaming down the glass like the roots of a tree. The droplets made their way slowly at first, building in force as they merged together. Then, without warning, the beads of water picked up speed and plummeted into the thin rubber ledge where they were stopped dead in their tracks.

Lucy placed her hand against the glass and followed a single droplet as it sped towards its inevitable demise.

Only two hours, she thought, and she would be home in Glasgow. Back to the beginning of the rest of her life, a raindrop at the top of the window.

"Are you ok hen?"

Lucy turned to the elderly woman sitting next to her. Her face was kind, adorned with a fine tapestry of lines and creases. The most prominent, Lucy noticed, were the lines around her mouth and the sides of her eyes. Delicate smile-lines that had been etched into her skin, the result of a lifetime filled with laughter.

"Yes, thank you."

The lady smiled, her eyes disclosing a learned wisdom, as ten years fell from her face.

"My dear," she said, placing her hand on Lucy's thigh. "Can I let you in on a wee secret?"

Lucy nodded.

"Men, you see, have never been very good at multitasking. Truth be told, they're terrible at it. It is why it was such a ghastly mistake when God decided to give them both a brain and a penis. I should know. I've been married for nearly sixty years."

For the first time in what felt like days Lucy smiled, a genuine untainted smile.

"Now that's better." The lady patted Lucy's leg. "We can't have a pretty thing like you getting all upset over some boy. As my mother said, you can't grow roses until you get rid of the weeds."

Lucy smiled, her eyes not quite meeting the old lady's.

"I'm afraid I don't like roses," replied Lucy.

"Lilies then," she said, her watery grey eyes creasing at the corners. "Red lilies, like the colour of your hair."

The lady squeezed Lucy's forearm and turned back to her book. Her aged skin was surprisingly soft against Lucy's, the fine leaves of tissue paper covering her hands like loose silk.

Tilting her head discreetly, Lucy tried to focus on the title of the woman's book, intrigued by the plain black cover, but her eyes grew heavy and her mind filled with the sound of nothingness. Exhausted, and unable to fight it any longer, she found herself drifting off, not waking until the bus pulled into Buchanan station.

The driver killed the engine, his hand disappearing from sight as the folding doors sprung open. Then, without looking back, he dislodged his body from beneath the steering wheel and waddled from the bus. Lucy stepped off a few moments later, pushed her hair behind her ears and glanced around at the constant flow of people. Part of her was glad to be back in Glasgow. Part of her was terrified. She rubbed her hands across her face, tired, and went to collect her bag from the back of the bus.

Despite the throb of her ankle she decided to walk. She tightened the straps of her rucksack and jiggled on the spot to allow the contents to settle, the weight falling evenly upon her hips.

The walk was slow and every step hurt but the fresh air was good. She had always enjoyed people-watching and inventing their stories. She watched as an exasperated mother pulled her child along by the arm. The young girl, five or six, clutched the handle of a scooter in her free hand, dragging it along behind her. A teenager shuffled past, head lowered as the soles of his trainers scuffed the ground. He looked back at Lucy, a brief glance, before he turned away to be diluted by the crowd.

Lucy wondered what people might think about her. She looked down at her muddied walking boots and felt the rub of her rucksack on her hip bones.

Not that it mattered, she thought. What mattered was who she was going to be from now on.

Lucy stopped and glanced at her watch. 11 am. She needed caffeine.

The cafe she chose was sandwiched between two travel agents, the prime location on Great Western Road ensuring a steady flow of customers all day and every day. Lucy pushed the door open and stepped inside. Most of the patrons, students and young professionals, were drinking coffee from tall glasses and eating pastries from white plates. Lucy loved everything about the place, the smell of roasted coffee, the acoustic music and the huge windows that filled the room with sunlight. In winter, she would sit by the glass and watch the flurries of snow, admiring the way that they danced along the pavement.

Had danced, she thought. Before.

Now the snow would simply fall, lifeless and cold. She cast the image aside, not allowing the memory to grow roots, and walked to the counter.

She couldn't live in her memories. The lure of the past was too dangerous. It had the potential to get under her skin and break her.

The barista, Clare, flicked her fringe from her eyes and flashed Lucy a smile. Her hair smelled of vanilla and almond.

"What can I get you hun?"

"Just the normal," replied Lucy.

"We haven't seen you here in a while. Have you been..."

She cut her sentence short, refusing to compete with the piercing scream of the steamer. Her hands navigated the machine with ease as the shrieking faded and she placed two take-away cups on the counter.

"There you go. Two skinny cappuccinos, extra hot with cinnamon."

Lucy stared at the cups and she felt her pulse quicken. The feeling was instant, suffocating. It gripped her lungs, choking the words in her throat. Lucy pulled her shirt from her chest. *Where was all the air*?

"Lucy? Are you ok?"

The barista's words didn't register.

A moment passed before Lucy replied.

"Just one..."

"Sorry?" asked Clare.

"Just the one coffee," managed Lucy.

"My mistake," laughed Clare, shaking her head, "I just assumed. No worries." Clare took the extra mug and offered a friendly smile. "Don't worry about it. I'm sure one of the girls will be appreciate an extra coffee. So, where's..."

Lucy's heart stopped. Not here, she thought, not yet. She wasn't ready to hear her name.

"Gone," said Lucy, "she's gone."

She walked out before Clare had time to respond.

Air. Sweet, fresh air.

Lucy gulped it into her lungs. Oxygen pumped back into her brain and rational thought started to form, reclaiming a sense of calm. Lucy sat on one of the outside chairs, raised the cup to her lips and took a long sip. She took a few moments to collect her thoughts, getting back to a point of control. The rhythmic and mundane motion of lifting the drink to her lips helped to calm her and she sat there until her heartbeat slowed to a normal beat, until she no longer felt like she was drowning.

There was no radical change. The moment hadn't been particularly special or revolutionary in any way. But, Lucy thought, she had regained control. She was okay.

Small steps.

She stood up, finished the last sip of her coffee and left the cup on the table. Then she turned and hobbled off.

Maybe you can do this.

Chapter 5

Present Day

That was the first mistake.

Toop folded his arms as his teeth made a play at his lower lip and the thought repeated.

The body, it was too perfect.

The scene was immaculate, faultless, just a single hole to the torso.

It was clear how the man had died, the gun wound to the chest was fatal, but what wasn't obvious was why he had died. Toop stood alone and stared down at the corpse. No visible signs of a struggle. Nothing. The ground around his feet was visibly undisturbed. And yet, Toop's gut wouldn't settle. There was something.

Someone else had pulled the trigger.

He was sure of it. Definitely. Maybe.

It had been two hours since Toop first received the phone call and he now had full control of the investigation. The scene parameters were set up and all non-essential personnel had been removed from the site. To his great relief only two of the local officers had been involved in the initial response. For Toop this meant two things, minimal hassle and fewer potential cock ups for him to sort out.

"Aye, just me and Roberts sir, we came straight up after we got the call. I took one look at the body and called you right then. We've been standing about here ever since, making sure that no walkers came passing through."

"So you talked to them?" asked Toop.

Bailey offered a blank expression and his eyebrows veered down towards his cheekbones, distorting his eyes as the rain drove into his face.

"Who sir?"

"The couple who found the body."

"Aye them, yes. I spoke to them. Right shook up they were."

"And who let them leave the scene?"

"Nobody sir, they phoned us from the village. Said there wasn't any signal up there, had to come down first. Bloody wise decision given the weather."

"I'm going to need their address and a recording of that phone call. Get Roberts stationed in the Major Incident Room."

"Sorry?"

Toop didn't bother to reply. He would do it.

Toop was satisfied, in part, that the scene hadn't been compromised. However, his reasoning had nothing to do with assumptions about an adherence to protocol. His expectations about the professional standards of his colleagues were low at best. Toop was working on the more probable assumption that they were scared of him, their new boss from the big lights of London.

Toop rubbed his forehead and groaned. Sometimes he wished that he could be left to handle things on his own. No, that was wrong. He always wanted to be left on his own. For the past ten years he had worked by himself, refusing to be partnered up or to accept help. He was better alone, he preferred it that way. Babysitting a team of amateurs was not what he had signed up for. He took a deep breath, ran his hands through his hair and returned to staring at the body.

The second mistake, he thought, was the way that it was positioned. It was all wrong, too calculated. He strained his mind, going back over the details. Bailey's flippant comment kept coming back to him.

Perhaps the lad had a point.

Toop focused on the man's face. The body was propped upwards, seated as if he was awaiting a sentence.

So, what did you do?

Toop took a step closer.

The image fitted all the prerequisites of a suicide. It was picture perfect, textbook. The location overlooking the loch was faultless, a mixture of tragedy and romance. The man's legs hung over the boulder, hopeless and heavy, long void of any life source to support them. His arms fell limp from his torso, dangling like anchors, two foreign weights that had been sewn into the skin of his shoulders.

Toop tapped his fingers against his cheek. Something in his gut told him to keep digging. His thoughts didn't line up and his premise was unsubstantiated, but something told him that it wasn't suicide. He was missing something. Toop crouched down, a slight reprieve from the wind.

The bend in his legs caused his trousers to tauten, pulling tight over his thighs and around his calf muscles. He balanced his weight upon his heels, forming two crescent moons in the mud. Water seeped through the seams of his boots and his toes sunk further into the soft ground. He leaned in to examine the man's jacket. His clothes, a budget windproof and heavy trousers, were completely inappropriate for the weather conditions.

What the bloody hell were you thinking?

Most confusing were his shoes. Toop peered at the casual slip-on shoes and noted the buckle at the front. The material was frayed from the rocky ground and a layer of wet dirt had settled between the soles of the man's feet and the bottom of the sandals. The original colour had been distorted by the mud and there was a visual line above the man's ankle bones indicating where the water had been soaked up by his socks.

It didn't make sense, thought Toop. It would have taken him hours to get to the loch, a hard day of walking over rough terrain, navigating through deep bog and heather. The discomfort of doing it in sandals would have been excruciating.

There was more.

The windproof jacket that he had on was grossly inadequate, shower proof if that. Toop had spent enough years in the Mountain Rescue Team, and had wasted enough evenings guiding ill-prepared tourists off the hillside, to recognise an ignorant pundit when he saw one. But pundits didn't tend to venture into the mountains on their own. And, he reasoned, there was no camera.

But Toop couldn't put his finger on what was missing.

"Bailey." Toop called out, raising his voice against the wind. "Get over here."

The seconds went by and Toop wondered if the boy was going to respond. Finally he appeared, his arm raised in front of his face to protect his eyes from the horizontal rain. Toop noted that Bailey was shivering, his clothes soaked through. He looked at the lad and handed him his hat.

"Put this on."

Bailey thanked him as he slipped the hat over his wet hair. He rubbed his palms together, brought his hands to his mouth and blew warm air onto his fingers.

"Why do you think that he is dead?" asked Toop.

Bailey looked back at him, confused by what seemed to be a trick question.

"You mean the hole in his chest sir?"

Toop took a long breath. "Yes. But who shot him?"

Bailey hesitated a moment, stumped by another obvious question.

"He shot himself sir."

"And why do you think that?" asked Toop.

"You want to know what I think?"

"Yes." Toop replied matter-of-factly. "What makes you, Boyd Bailey, so certain that he killed himself?"

"A couple of things," replied Bailey.

Toop nodded again.

"Well," said Bailey, "there's the location. That's how it is, isn't it, people head up to these remote places, you know when they're feeling depressed. A nice quiet spot to say your goodbyes. And, well, his clothes. Nobody in their right mind would head up here dressed like that unless, well unless they he had no intention of coming back."

Toop rubbed his hand across his mouth and bit down on the end of his thumb.

"And," Bailey hesitated, scared to state the obvious. "There's the gun."

"What about it?" said Toop.

"Surely you wouldn't just leave the murder weapon for the police to find. It wouldn't make no sense that, especially when you could just chuck it into the loch."

Toop rested his hand on Bailey's shoulder. "You did good," he said, "Many officers would agree with you."

Toop handed Bailey his phone. "Find me some signal. I need to get in touch with the pathologist."

"Pathologist?"

"I asked for her to be flown in from Inverness. The helicopter can't be far away now and we need to get the body moved before the weather gets worse."

"But I thought pathologists only attended homicides."

Toop looked back at him without comment and walked away. He had just worked out what was missing.

There was no tragedy in the dead man's face.

Chapter 6

Late 80s

Jon waited outside the Bute Hall. He wasn't expecting anyone. There was no-one making their way to join him. He was simply waiting. Jon sat in the same place that he chose every Wednesday morning, in the very centre of the bench, just so, with the heel of his right foot rested on his left knee.

The university grounds were empty.

Jon unscrewed the lid of his thermos, tilted the container to the side and poured himself a cup. He filled the small plastic beaker that doubled as a lid and drew it to his lips, breathing in the smell of fresh filter coffee. He sat alone in the ancient undercroft and admired the Gothic-style crypt. The grand sandstone cloisters stood in silence, a forest of cylindrical columns that rose up from the ground like lily stalks. The tall stone pillars splintered the rays of early morning light casting shadows across the hall.

Quiet.

It was something that he did every Wednesday without fail, a routine that had turned into an addiction, a need. On the odd occasion Jesse would join him. He would sit and smoke, but his friend didn't care for the silence or the early start. In truth, it was the silence that Jon craved. He would sit beneath the pointed arches for hours, leaving at the first sight of another human being.

An hour passed.

Jon had smoked two cigarettes and his flask was empty. He twisted his arm so that his palm faced upwards and his elbow moved in towards his ribs, another age-old habit that he completed without thinking. He always wore the face of his watch on the underside of his wrist, hidden from view, with the strap on display. His reasons were simple. He did it because, in his mind, the beauty of a watch lived in the worn creases of the leather, in the lifelines.

It was 10 o'clock.

Shit.

The nerves convulsed in his stomach. He should never have listened to Jesse.

Jon picked up his satchel and hung it over his shoulder. He wore a white t-shirt tucked into his jeans with the ends of the sleeves rolled up an inch. Using his middle finger, he pushed his glasses further along his nose, the large black frames extenuating his skinny, angular face.

He lit another cigarette.

How bad could it be? One coffee.

He walked out onto the street, paused, and gave the pavement a tentative scan but the gesture proved to be unnecessary. He heard her before he saw her. She was already there, waving at him from across the road. Jon looked up and offered a cautious smile.

Just breathe.

He stepped out to cross the road, adjusting his pace so that it would take him a few additional seconds to reach her. Heather, his blind date. She was jumping on the spot with her arms waving above her head.

Jon watched as her palms waded through the air. He felt like the victim of an ambush.

It was stupid of him to have agreed to it.

No. His answer should have been no.

But it hadn't been. He had come because Jesse had suggested it.

Four seconds, two seconds. She was close enough that he could smell her, a strong floral aroma mixed with citrus, slightly soapy.

She was wearing a blue blouse with a white leather jacket. The jacket was cropped short, cut just below her chest with a curtain of long tassels that fell down the arms. The padded shoulders protruded outwards making her look top-heavy. Jon didn't know where to look and he felt almost relieved when she ended the predicament for him by throwing her arms around his neck, plunging his face into a mist of curls and hairspray.

Jon's body tensed as she pressed up against him and he became overly aware of his own arms. They hung motionless at his sides as Heather secured her arms around his neck, her breasts pushing into his body. The crotch of her shorts rubbed against his thigh, inches from where his fingers hung. Jon started to sweat. He was getting hard. Panicked, he pulled back from her, his feelings of hesitation going unnoticed.

"You came," she beamed. "I'm so glad that Jesse suggested we do this."

She linked her arm through his and pulled him in the direction of the cafe.

"My name's Heather but of course you already know that, silly me. Jesse was hardly going to send you on a blind date and not tell you my name. How would you know who I was if you didn't know my name or have any idea of what I looked like? Anyway, sorry I'm babbling, must be nerves. It's Heather."

She turned to look at him, pausing just long enough to smile.

"My friends call me Vi, short for violet. Original, I know," she rolled her eyes, "with heather being purple and all. But my Mum had it in her garden when she was growing up and she thought it was pretty. Anyway, you can call me Vi. Jesse calls you Jonny sometimes. Should I call you Jonny? I like it, it's cute."

She stopped and stared at him with huge, expectant eyes.

Jon pinched his lips together, aware that the moisture had evaporated from his mouth. He had no words. Every word in the English language had vanished from his vocabulary. His lips parted, hanging open for a moment and exposing the whites of his teeth before he managed three syllables.

"Jon is fine."

Heather stared back at him, her eyes accentuated by black liner, and waited for more.

"I don't like being called Jonny."

"Oh," she replied.

Her eyebrows drew closer together as if she was contemplating a thought.

"You should tell Jesse."

Heather clung to his arm and continued to steer him along the pavement, caught up in her own monologue. Jon let her talk. In truth, he was dreading the moment when she would stop and it would be his turn.

The walk took five minutes. Jon managed to navigate the conversation with a couple of acknowledging nods and a few murmurs of agreement. When they reached the cafe Heather freed Jon from her grasp and pushed against the blue of the door with her palm. The door swung open, releasing the sound of Berlin's latest single out onto the street. The lyrics of 'Take My Breath Away' blasted out from the stereo system, the hit love song of the moment made famous by the erotic montage in Top Gun. The image of Tom Cruise and Kelly McGillis engaged in an aggressive French kiss flashed into Jon's mind and he pictured Cruise dipping his tongue into her open mouth. As he contemplated the exchange of saliva, Jon found himself considering the possibly of kissing Heather. He wondered what she would taste like.

Maybe it wouldn't be so bad, he thought.

He pulled out a seat opposite her and sat down, their knees almost touching. Maybe he should just go for it, that's what Jesse would tell him to do.

"Coffee?" The waitress hovered above him, rooted by an impatient boredom.

"Black," replied Jon.

The waitress didn't bother to write it down. She turned her head and looked at Heather.

"And you?"

"A strawberry milkshake please with everything, cherries, chocolate, cream and sprinkles. Pile it all on. I have a bit of a sweet tooth!"

The waitress gave her a weak smile and walked away, feeling no obligation to indulge Heather's enthusiasm.

Heather leaned her body across the table towards Jon, sandwiching her hands between her chest and the red table cloth.

"I'm trying to make myself drink coffee." She whispered it as if it was a treasured secret. "I want to like it. All students should like coffee don't you think? It's so romantic, the idea of sitting amongst a pile of books and sipping coffee. But it just tastes so bitter."

Her nose crinkled and she stuck out her tongue.

"And black, the way you have it, no sugar or anything, yuck!"

Jon studied her face as she talked, mesmerised by the movement of her lips. And as he watched her it occurred to him that she was quite pretty. No, not pretty, sexy. Heather was sexy. Her face was drowned in make-up and her nose had a slight rise in the centre but she was far from unattractive.

The waitress ambled over and discarded two drinks on their table. Jon was grateful for the mug, welcome for something to do with his hands. He realised that he had never before been so conscious of his arms, where to put them and what to do with them.

"So what do you study?" asked Heather. She looked up at him through her dark eye lashes and took a sip through her straw.

It took a moment for Jon to register the question.

"Art history," he replied.

"Really?"

The question was rhetorical, her curious tone prompted more by surprise than genuine enquiry. She removed the straw from her lips and continued.

"Do you know that you're the first guy I've met who studies art history. My friend Denise, she says that it's the most useless degree in the university. But what does she know?"

Again rhetorical, but this time she drew breath and paused long enough to take a sip of milkshake.

"She studies words, or the form of language, or some nonsense. Linguistics, that's it. But I think that art history is a wonderful subject, so dreamy, like a love story drawn on paper. Well not paper, canvas, or material. Sorry I must seem so ditzy."

She stared into her glass, her cheeks reddening beneath a thick layer of foundation.

"So anyway," she continued, "tell me, why would someone choose to study art history?"

She looked right at him, waiting.

"You wouldn't understand," said Jon. The words just blurted out.

Jon bit down on his lower lip and turned away, embarrassed. His eyes focused on the rim of his mug and he rubbed his thumbs together. A pause, then he looked up at her. She was staring directly at him.

"Try me," she teased.

"Sorry," replied Jon, "I just mean that art is very complex. It isn't something that you can just reach out and touch." He dipped his gaze, focusing on the handle of his mug. "Art history, the story behind each painting, is about human events, things that have passed."

Jon dared a second glance at her face. This world of non-verbal expression, it made no sense to him. It seemed to Jon that an entire language had been built upon a set of incomprehensible signals. But, from what he could decipher, she seemed to be listening to him.

"A piece of artwork," he continued, "is the tangible evidence of something far deeper." Jon's hands had left his mug, forming an imaginary sphere in front of him as he said the word tangible.

"It represents something much more intriguing. When I see a painting I think about the artist who painted it and I ask myself, what made him pick up the brush? What was he thinking?"

Heather remained still with her elbows rested on the table and her face cupped in her hands.

"That's beautiful," she said. "Those things would never even occur to me. I suppose I just thought that art history was about..." she paused. "To be honest, I'm not sure what I thought it was about."

Heather smiled. "You're not like other boys, are you?"

"Sorry," stuttered Jon, "I didn't mean to bore you."

"No no, you're not boring me in the slightest. That's not what I meant at all. It's interesting, really. It sounds fascinating. Please, go on."

Jon stalled.

"Tell me what you mean about human events?" asked Heather. "I'd like to know."

Jon studied his mug. Red and smooth and still, sat on a small saucer. His hushed words fell onto the table.

"Art provides a different way of looking at human history. It is the only real picture we have of history, you know, before cameras."

"Do you paint?"

"Yes," he replied.'

"Well, what kind of things do you paint?" she urged.

"Things I see." His thumbs fondled the rim of the mug. "I see things, people and places, I dream them and then I paint them."

He talked and Heather listened. It was almost going well.

Then he felt it, like a switch flipped inside him. Heather's bare knee rubbed against his leg, perhaps it was intentional. It didn't matter. Jon's mind started to race and his palms began to feel clammy. He removed his hands from the mug and wiped them down the sides of his jeans. Heather's leg pressed further into his. This time he was certain that she had done it on purpose. He could feel the moisture leaving the insides of his lips. His tongue was too big for his mouth. He felt pale, nauseated.

"Jon, are you ok?" Heather placed her hand on his knee. "You look a little white. Wait there, I'll get you some water." She got up.

Jesse's words rang over and over in Jon's head.

Girls can smell inexperience, it's like dog shit.

Jon gathered his fingers in tight fists under the table.

Shut up! Shut up!

So what if he was nervous? Who cared if he didn't screw a new girl every night? He didn't have to do everything that Jesse did. He couldn't help it if the mere sight of a girl gave him a hard on. Jon stood up and grabbed his jacket from the back of the chair.

"Jon, where are you going?"

Heather stood with a glass of water in her hand, her face lost in confusion.

Jon didn't hear her.

He was already out of the door, fighting back tears.

Chapter 7

Today

Lucy looked at the mounds of clothes on her bed, the 'old' Lucy and the 'new'. She stared at them, two disconnected worlds, two separate lives that had been stripped down and left depicted as a couple of neat piles.

Nice and simple, she thought, no room for hesitancy. No hoarding of the past.

The 'unsure' pile had been revaluated and divided up. Indecision, she decided, wasn't productive.

She wore no makeup and she was dressed in a matching set of pyjamas, pale blue shorts with a tight strappy top. Her red hair was gathered in a messy bun on top of her head and fluffy slippers covered her feet. Her task was simple. Every shelf and drawer had to be emptied of the past.

The foundations of the 'old' mound were comprised of the walking trousers that she had removed earlier, still muddied around the bottoms, and the rucksack that she had lugged from the bus station. She hadn't bothered to remove the contents. The memories stored inside were not ones that she wanted to keep.

She had contemplated burning the rucksack but she soon realised that she didn't have the slightest idea about how or where to burn something of that size. She had never had to worry about those sorts of things before, the 'man' tasks. Those had always been, well it had never been her responsibility. The bathtub had seemed like a reasonable idea at first but then Lucy had grown concerned that it would set off the fire alarm and the last thing she needed was firemen tramping through her apartment. So the bag lay at the bottom of the pile, covered by two thermal tops and a pair of running leggings.

The new Lucy didn't run.

Not recreationally.

Lucy joined her hands behind her back and pushed them forward until she heard a comforting click. She sighed. It was dark and drizzly outside and a gentle breeze tapped against the old tenement window. She turned her head to the source of the noise, regretting it at once. There it was. Her face, looking back at her from the glass. The image shot Lucy's mind backwards and her eyes grew wide with fear. The scene played itself out in her head and the piercing echo of a woman's cry filled her head.

"Go!"

It was a scream that would stay with her forever, an order that scraped against her eardrums like shards of glass.

"Go! Leave, just leave!"

Lucy had hesitated then. Feet cemented to the earth.

"NOW!"

The desperate scream sent Lucy running. And she had kept running, tears burning her cheeks, not once looking back.

Standing there, in pyjamas and slippers, the memory owned her. It became her.

What finally brought her back was the sound of a car alarm, a long, shrill drone that broke into a high-pitched monotone. It polluted the entire street, leaking through the windows. Torn back, and thrown into the present, Lucy lunged forward at the window and pulled the curtains closed.

This is stupid, she thought, you can't avoid mirrors forever.

But maybe just a little longer.

She slumped onto the bed and hung her legs over the edge. Lucy looked down at her slippers, tilting her toes up towards the ceiling so that they didn't slip off her feet.

"You're innocent," she whispered, "you've done nothing wrong."

In one swift motion Lucy pushed herself up from the bed and walked, still with a visible limp, through the door. She returned a few moments later with a black bin bag. It took her another two hours but she filled two bags, not including the box that she had used for recycling. It was crammed with old magazines and loose sheets of paper, receipts, leaflets and other miscellaneous items that she hadn't looked at. There was no point. The only item that she had queried over was an old scrap book. It rested in her hands just long enough to indicate its significance before falling unceremoniously into the rubbish.

The doodles and ramblings of children, thought Lucy, dreams of the young and naive that were best thrown away.

She removed her right slipper, massaged her ankle and lifted her foot into the box, compressing the contents beneath her toes. Her right heel stuck to the cover of the scrap book, a photograph sticking to her clammy skin and peeling off. She lifted her leg, bending her knee and angling her body so that the sole of her foot faced upwards. Two little girls smiled up at her, their heads poking out of the sea. Lucy removed the picture from her heel and crumpled it in her hand.

No tears.

Lucy stood back and surveyed her room. It was as if a part of her had never existed, a part of her past had been bagged and discarded like unwanted junk. If someone was to walk into Lucy's bedroom they wouldn't find a single trace of Alexandria. There was nothing to attest to the fact that Alex had once been a part of her life. She might just as well not have existed.

Alexandria was gone.

It was the only way.

Lucy knew that if she was to keep on living she had to get used to being alone. She understood that. She just hadn't realised how painful it would be. She walked into the kitchen and pulled out a fourth bin bag from under the sink. Hesitating, she picked up the plastic roll and ripped off a further handful.

She was going to do this properly.

The next room she entered was smaller than her own and the double bed consumed most of the floor. The bed was unmade, still littered with various items of clothing. Jeans and sweatshirts fell from the hanging canvas wardrobe. Lucy thought that having an open closet made the room look unkempt and messy. But Alex said that it made the room looked lived in. Crumpled receipts and loose coins had escaped from pockets and were gathered on the bedside table. The tiny cluttered surface was covered by an empty tissue box, surrounded by tissues, a mini portable speaker and numerous electrical cords. A huge stereo system occupied the only available floor space. Alex had spent more than a month's wages on it.

Everything went into a black bin bag.

Everything apart from a single piece of jewellery, an inexpensive trinket that Lucy had made for Alex's twenty-first. She had spent three evenings hidden away in her room with a selection of Alex's tools, instructions printed from Google, and a table of random objects. A petite mustard spoon, a plastic mallet, pliers, wire cutters, socket wrench and a file. Lucy had never heard of a finger-sized socket wrench but their neighbour had been happy to help, also giving her a piece of heave fabric to prevent scratches. It had taken Lucy three long sessions but she made a ring, a spoon bent into an almost perfect circle.

The intricate mustard spoon had belonged to Alex's foster parents, the only family that she ever liked. The Calhouns were an elderly couple who lived on the West side of Glasgow. Their house was small, nothing fancy, and the garden backed out onto Mugdock Country Park offering an endless playground of wilderness and adventure. Alex loved it. It was the one place that Lucy had heard her refer to as 'home'. Alex spent two Christmases there and each year she was put in charge of polishing the silver cutlery, a sixteen-piece set that was kept inside a red velvet-lined box.

When the fostering agency took Alex away, deeming the couple too frail to support a child, Alex stole a single spoon. Each Christmas, until she died, Mrs Calhoun took the box out and traced the empty velvet space with her fingers. She never used them again.

It was years later that Lucy found the spoon, stored in a shoebox under Alex's bed. The only other item in the box was a letter, a single piece of paper that had been concealed in Alex's bassinet, crumbled beneath the tiny legs of an abandoned baby. Alex had taken the letter when she left but the ring had been sitting by the bathroom sink, hidden under a green face cloth.

She disappeared without it.

Placing the green cloth to the side, Lucy had slipped the ring on her right ring finger. It fitted perfectly. One little memory couldn't hurt.

Lucy paused in the doorway and stared at the room. It was empty, no longer lived in. As she stood there, with her arms hugged round her stomach, Lucy allowed herself a smile. The letter wasn't the only thing that Alex had taken with her. Just to be sure, Lucy scanned the room with her eyes another time.

It definitely wasn't there.

The soft bear, with faded fabric and worn ears, was gone. It had been a Christmas present from Mrs Calhoun.

Maybe, thought Lucy. Maybe there was a part of Alexandria that could still be saved.

Chapter 8

Today

Toop stepped forward against the wind but his gaze remained on the helicopter. He tucked his chin into his chest and grimaced. He wasn't about to admit it to his partner but Toop was anxious.

In a few minutes, she would step out in front of him and he had no idea what he was going to say.

Had she forgiven him?

Toop lifted his hand and shielded his eyes from the rain.

Why would she?

He buried his face in the bend of his elbow as the helicopter approached, planting his feet firmly into the ground. Bailey stood next to him with his unzipped jacket flapping around his body like a cape.

"As if it wasn't windy enough," yelled Bailey, taking a step backwards.

The gusts of wind ploughed straight through the young officer and he waved his arms around attempting to maintain his balance.

The helicopter hovered a few feet above the ground. The huge rotor blades competed with the harsh weather conditions and sent a sheet of waves across the surface of the loch. Toop lifted his arm away from his eyes and looked out at the mountainous terrain. His mind worked through each and every angle. Even in calm weather it would have been almost impossible for the pilot to assess the ground conditions. Any holes or uneven patches would have been concealed by the thick heather and long grass. Toop considered the possibility of the helicopter rolling and calculated the significant chance of the wind causing a tail boom strike.

The pilot needed to get it right.

Toop squinted against the rain and watched as the helicopter inched lower, his gaze held on the approaching tail rotor. It was evident that the man sitting in the cockpit was experienced. Rather than landing pointed into the wind, the pilot had his tail into it with the wind at a 7 o'clock position. Toop had witnessed the same landing approach when he was the mountain rescue team. His teammate, a well-seasoned pilot, had read the wind conditions perfectly and prevented the rotor blade from flapping down in powerful gusts. Toop watched as the pilot in front of him executed the same manoeuvre. The helicopter rested down safely and the landing skids sank into the heather.

Toop lowered his gaze. Not bad.

"Should we get up closer sir?" shouted Bailey.

Toop responded by extending his right arm and pointing to the spot where Bailey stood.

"Stay," he shouted.

A few moments passed before the cabin door opened and Toop caught his first glimpse of her.

Sally Gillespie.

Sally bowed her head and stepped out of the helicopter. She held one hand out across her forehead to keep her fringe from her eyes, not that it did much good, and her free hand gripped the collar of her jacket to stop the cold air from leaking down her neck.

She looked different, thought Toop, different and yet just the same.

Toop walked towards the grounded helicopter, his body bent into the wind. He still didn't know what he was going to say. She looked straight up at him and mouthed something but the noise of the wind, coupled with the sound of the slowing blades, made it impossible for her to be heard. Giving up on verbal communication Toop reached out his arm, laid his hand on the small of Sally's back and guided her in the direction of the cordoned-off area.

"Your hair, it's short?" he shouted, his voice diluted by the wind.

Sally smiled. "It's nice to see you too Fergus!"

"Sorry," yelled Toop, "I mean you look different, good, you look good."

She yelled back, smiling with her eyes this time. "It's been ten years, people change. Can't look twenty-five forever you know!"

"I meant to phone."

Toop grimaced, ashamed by his feeble attempt at words. It sounded even more pathetic out loud than it had in his head.

Sally raised an eyebrow and pressed her lips together, hiding the bright red colour that she had applied two hours ago.

"I wanted to call," Toop kept digging, sinking. "It just got harder and I wasn't... I... What I mean to say is I'm sorry."

She squeezed his arm and leaned in towards him. The intimacy of her touch jolted him and Toop felt a lump lodge itself in his throat. "I am more than happy to listen to your apology," said Sally, "I may even enjoy watching you try and dig yourself out of this one. I mean, what woman doesn't like a good grovel! But I'm pretty sure that a crime scene is neither the time nor the place. Wouldn't you agree?"

"I know but..."

"No buts... you have dragged my ass out in this weather, which by the way is bloody awful. You can count yourself damn lucky that Jimmy has a bit of a sadistic streak. I swear that man actually enjoys a good hurricane. Me however, not so much. You should think about adding a few IOU beers to that apology of yours!"

Toop didn't meet her eyes but he managed a grin. "Pale ale?"

"Till the day my liver betrays me!" She linked her arm through his. "Right show me this body of yours. You had better have a good reason for dragging me out in this miserable weather."

"There's just something about it that doesn't fit," he replied, "Just doesn't feel right Sal."

She glanced over at his face but Toop looked away, ashamed by the intensity of her gaze.

"No one has called me that in a long time," she said.

When Toop glanced back up at her, her face was already tilted away and she was looking out at the landscape. But there had been something in her features. Was she actually pleased to see him?

"It's not like you to go over-thinking things, is it Ferg?" Sally looked back at him and smiled. "It's nice to know that there are some things that will never change."

Sally unlinked her arm and walked towards the yellow police tape. "Oh, and I should mention, I'm staying at yours tonight."

"With me?"

"'Well there's not a hope in hell that I'm getting back into that flying death trap. Jimmy is flying home solo this evening."

Toop's eyes hung on her back as she walked over to Bailey. He could just make out the crease of her shoulder blades.

"Hey kid," said Sally and she extended her arm, "you hanging in alright?"

"Aye thanks, bit cold."

He shook her hand.

"Sally Gillespie, pathologist and go to girl in suspicious cases." She smiled. "Don't worry, we'll be off this mountain soon. He can't keep us up here all night. "

"Boyd Bailey. Sorry, suspicious... I..."

"Something about this one has given your boss the heebie-jeebies. He won't admit it but he is about as stubborn as a mule. If in doubt, investigate as homicide. So here I am."

"But I thought..."

"Sometimes it's just best not to kid." She offered him a wink. "You'll learn how to deal with him."

"But this isn't a homicide investigation."

"You sure about that?" she smiled, her question met by a look of confusion. "Did he get you to ring it in with the coroner yet?"

"Em, yeah, it was the first thing he asked me to do. How'd you know that?"

Sally rested her hand on his shoulder.

"Don't look so worried," she laughed, "your boss, he has his ways. You can take the cop out of London but you can't take London out of the cop. The worst part of it, these suspicions of his, more often than not they're right. Not that we have to let him know that." She patted Bailey on the arm. "Come on let's have a look."

Bailey frowned and glanced back at Toop. His boss was staring into the distance with his hands buried deep into his pockets. The young officer spoke in a low voice, "He doesn't like me much."

"Give him time."

They approached the body and Sally got to work. She bent down on her knees and held her face a few inches from the corpse. She moved with a small camera held in her hand, working around the dead man as she documented every detail. Sally had been through the procedure a hundred times, never faltering in her attention to detail. For her, every death deserved an explanation, no corpse should be put in the ground without a reason for why it was there.

Sally stood up, photographed the surrounding area and slipped the camera back into her pocket. She stretched out her neck, massaged the top of her spine and rolled her head backwards. Then she walked around the body, logging the scene to memory. Sally made a mental note of the position of the corpse, his physical condition and the blood stains around his chest.

She felt Toop's presence before he spoke.

"So?" he said.

"The weather's too bad to do much now," Sally replied. "We're risking contamination if we don't get him wrapped up and removed. Do I have your permission to package him up now? I'm afraid the full body examination will have to wait."

"I thought that would be the case," said Toop. "But I want as little trace evidence to be compromised as possible. That means clothes off, hands and head bagged separately. Same goes for the physical evidence. I want the gun and rucksack to the MIR immediately."

"I'm quite capable of doing my job thank you very much." The sharpness in her words was barely detectable. But it was just enough to have the desired effect.

"It's going to be difficult in these conditions though," she added.

"Do what you can," replied Toop, all condescension gone from his tone.

"It's really got to you this one, hasn't it?" Sally stood next to him. "What is it?"

Toop held Sally's stare.

"Someone once told me that the sight of a dead body can linger in a man's thoughts for years. It lodges itself in the mind, revealing itself at unforeseen moments."

He turned away and glanced at the upright body.

"I don't know. It's just something. What do you think, do you think that he killed himself?"

"Fergus, if I'm being honest I can't see how it could be anything else. It just seems like he knew that he was walking to his death."

Toop looked away.

"Knowing that you're going to die isn't the same as suicide."

Chapter 9

Late 80s

"You're an arsehole!" Jon kicked the side of Jesse's locker.

"Calm down buddy, what's gotten you so worked up?" Jesse tightened the towel around his waist and placed his swimming cap on the bench.

"I'm not your buddy." Jon threw his fist into the locker door, leaving a dent. "What the fuck! What the fuck! That's what I'm meant to say isn't it. Screw life and everyone in it! Everyone should just be like the fucking perfect Jesse Jenkins."

"Jesus Jon! What's gotten into you?"

Jesse reached for his t-shirt.

"Is it that Heather chick I set you up with? Come on mate, it was just meant to be some fun. Loosen you up a bit."

"Fun, that's all you care about, screwing around and having fun. It's all about Jesse having fun!"

"God damn it Jon! Shit! I'm not going to apologise for enjoying my life while you bury your head in the sand and let it pass you by." He paused, pulled the t-shirt down his body and lifted his head. "Is that what this is about, you being jealous?"

For the first time in his life Jon looked like he might punch his friend.

"You really are full of yourself aren't you! You think we all bloody worship you from down here in the dirt. All hail the mighty Jesse and his words of wisdom." Jon threw his arms in the air. "Say screw it to the world."

Jesse grabbed his swim bag from his locker and threw it over his right shoulder. "I don't have to put up with this bullshit."

"Of course, you don't. You just do who and whatever you bloody well please. Just piss off then. Good luck finding yourself a new best mate."

Jesse stood still with his back to his friend. "You've been saying that since primary school."

"I always was a fucking bright eight-year-old." The words fell from Jon's mouth but his voice had lost its vigour and he looked exhausted.

Jesse slipped off his shoulder strap and placed his bag back on the bench. Both sets of eyes rested on it like an abandoned body. Jesse hesitated, uncertain of what was meant to happen next. He'd never seen his friend like this before.

"Jon buddy, what's happening here? Talk to me."

The air escaped from Jon's open mouth in a defeated sigh and his body deflated, the energy wisped out of him. He sank on to the bench and rested his head against the locker, the dull thud breaking the silence. He looked up at the ceiling with lightless eyes, his head tilted upwards as he spoke.

"Next to you I'm nothing."

Jesse sat next to him. "Come on mate, that's bullshit."

"Bullshit? So you do give a damn about me, is that what you're saying?" Jon gripped his fingers around the lip of the bench, his knuckles white. "You give a fuck about what goes on in my pathetic, boring life? Is that it, I'm the tragic friend that you keep around to feel good about yourself."

"Don't be an arsehole Jon. You are the only real bloody friend I have. My parents' divorce, remember? You were the one who told the other kids that I was crying because I had conjunctivitis or some crap. You said that it gave me blotchy eyes and that it prevented me from talking. Even at eight years old you were my fucking hero. So don't give me any of this bullshit about me not caring."

Jon was silent. His head was drowning in words but he couldn't select a single one. Silence was the only certain way that he could avoid crying. He wouldn't cry.

The door swung open and Byron, one of Jesse's teammates, strolled into the changing room. He threw his bag onto the bench and inserted a key into his locker. Byron looked over at Jesse and nodded in acknowledgment, choosing not to remove his headphones. He hummed along to his music, bobbing his head, oblivious to the tension in the room. He clasped his hands behind his back and raised his arms up towards the ceiling, his shoulder blades protruding beneath his t-shirt. Jon heard a gentle crack as Byron's shoulders responded to the stretch. The left pocket of his shorts sagged, weighed down by the portable cassette player. Jon

47

glanced over as Byron peeled off his shirt, the Athenian physique of the swimmer making Jon feel even more inadequate.

Byron changed, locked his belongings away and headed towards the pool.

"Catch you later Jenkins."

Jon and Jesse sat in silence. It was Jesse who eventually broke the quiet, his voice was kind.

"Look Jon, maybe I don't know what you're going through, or I don't understand and maybe I do get a bit wrapped up in the whole uni thing. But we're meant to be having the time of our lives here. You can't get mad at me for that. The dates, the girls, it's just human bloody nature, I'm a victim to my own urges."

He smiled but Jon wasn't looking at him, his eyes were pointed at the ceiling.

"Right sorry, I get it, less focus on Jesse. Sorry, I'm used to being the fuck up. You do the whole supportive thing, not me. Bit out of my depth here mate. But that doesn't mean I'm not trying." Jesse sat back against the locker door and ran his hand through his hair. "You've got to give me something though buddy, something to go on. You know me, head ten metres up my own arse. Fuck, I've never even done this before, chat about important stuff, not even with a chick. I tend to leg it before breakfast. But you're my best mate, Jon. Hell, I'd stick around and cook you a full fry up, with black pudding and those gross half-fried tomato things. Can't promise it would be any good, but still."

Jon stood up and smiled weakly. "You're right."

"Really? Because in situations like this that almost never happens."

A relieved smile tugged at the corners of Jesse's mouth, slipping away just as quickly. "Look even now I'm making inappropriate attempts at humour. So, was it me, did I do something to piss you off?"

"You're right Jesse." Jon's voice adopted a subdued monotone. "You don't understand me."

Jon turned his back on his friend and walked away. He didn't quicken his pace or attempt an impressive exit.

"Nobody understands me."

The door closed, leaving Jesse alone on the bench.

Chapter 10

Clean slate, thought Lucy, as she turned on her laptop.

It was an old, second-hand device that took about ten minutes to load up. Lucy didn't mind. In truth, she liked that it was slow. It offered her a few stolen minutes to make a cup of tea and to run to the toilet before settling in front of the small screen. But in the past week, with her mind on other things, she had forgotten about its elderly tendencies. Her hot chocolate was already made and she was nestled into the chair with a pink blanket wrapped around her legs and a fluffy pillow supporting her back. So, she sipped at her mug and waited. She had her legs curled up, her chin on her knees, as she peered over at the screen, trying not to let her thoughts wander.

Forwards, not backwards, thought Lucy.

She focused her attention on her action list, a single piece of paper with three bullet points scribbled in black biro.

Job. Flatmate. Friends.

She read them out loud, pausing between each word, deciding that the modest length of the list in no way reflected its hugeness. Maybe she should have written it in bold or underlined it. Lucy picked up a pen and drew three lines under each of the words, glanced at it, then replaced the dot in friends with a small heart. But the words were the same. She sighed and let the note drop onto her desk.

"New job. New Flatmate. New friends."

Lucy had spent most of the day in bed. She was still in the same pair of blue shorts and strappy top that she had slipped into the night before. The thought of having a shower had crossed her mind at some point but she had decided that having slightly cleaner hair wasn't worth the effort. She certainly wouldn't be having visitors and besides, she would just throw her red hair back up into a messy bun the moment she stepped out of the bathroom.

Packing away Alex's things had been exhausting. Lucy had anticipated the emotional tiredness but she had not considered the effects of missing a night of sleep. Her eyelids struggled with the persistent pull of gravity and her arms still hurt from all the heavy lifting. Moving the huge stereo system had not been an easy task. While lowering it down the stairs, tentatively sliding it over the lip of each step and releasing it in centimetre increments, it had occurred to Lucy that Alex must have had help hauling it up the three flights. The thing was ridiculously heavy.

Maybe the neighbours had helped her.

Lucy was not built for manual labour. She would stop to catch her breath on the second floor when it was warm outside or when her handbag felt heavy. Alex was the exact opposite. The hallway was always filled with various toys of hers, bikes, kayaks, skis, snowboards, climbing gear. Last summer, at Lucy's instruction, Alex had obtained a small storage space at a nearby warehouse and Lucy had gotten her hallway back.

Lucy was glad that she didn't have to worry about the storage space. Alex had taken the key to her locker and Lucy had no intention of ever going to it, in fact, she wasn't even sure where it was. And, more importantly, she didn't want to know. The less she knew the better. She couldn't be held accountable for things that she didn't know.

Naivety is just another form of innocence, that's what Alex had told her.

Her computer made a chiming sound and the password box appeared. Lucy placed her mug on a coaster and typed in the author of her favourite book, her screen saver lighting up as she typed in the final letter. It displayed a photo that she had taken the previous winter when she and Alex had gone to visit the Christmas market in Edinburgh. A red cappuccino mug filled the screen, the thick layer of foam not yet touched, something that Lucy had insisted on as she rummaged through her handbag looking for her phone. The photograph appeared on Lucy's Facebook feed a few moments later, a perfect cinnamon rose dusted on top of the thick white milk. Alex's fingers could be seen hugging the mug, her ring half covered by the bright handle.

It was the same ring that clinked against Lucy's mug as she clicked the mouse. A split second and her Facebook page popped up.

Delete profile? Yes.

Lucy opened up her emails, mostly junk, one email about the next book club meeting, which had been last Friday, and a couple of newsletters from the museum. Three from Patrick.

Lucy loved her job at the Museum and she hated that she had to leave. She didn't like deceiving Patrick and seeing his name in her inbox filled her with guilt. He was a wonderful boss and she felt awful about the fact that last Monday, she simply hadn't turned up. Half past nine had come and gone, no Lucy. Lucy frowned, maybe she should email him, just a quick message to let him know that she was ok, tell him not to worry. She held the cursor over the reply button. Guilt won over. She had to apologise.

'Dear Patrick.

I want to apologise for last Monday and for not giving you any notice. I'm fine, everything is fine but I'm afraid that I won't be back to work at the museum.

It's a family matter.

Again, sorry for the lack of explanation.'

Lucy bit her lower lip and sunk her head into her hands. She had to say something or it would seem too suspicious. She lifted her head and brushed her fingers over the keys as she processed her thoughts. Her ring tapped against the mouse as her mind ticked over, thinking over a number of possible replies. She went with the third.

'I can't say too much, just that there was a family emergency, it all happened so quickly and I had to leave Glasgow at a moment's notice.'

Almost true.

'Sorry again. I loved my time at the museum. Regards Lucy.'

Send.

That's enough, decided Lucy. He was the curator and Alex was his protégé, it was too complicated. She would miss it though, taking the school children around the exhibits, acting out stories from the past and playing on their active imaginations. She smiled as she thought about little Logan Lightfoot. He had been convinced that the floating heads in the main stairwell were real. Lucy had found him looking up at the display of famous heads, fifty-three faces each cast in white plastic and hung from a length of clear string. The poor child had been rooted to the spot in shock. Nothing Lucy could say would convince him that they were models. In the end, she had to tell him that they were very naughty people and that nice little boys didn't have to worry. The child had smiled at Lucy and then he ran off to play, his mind at ease. It occurred to Lucy then that Logan Lightfoot must have been a well-behaved child.

That or he was the youngest known advocate of capital punishment.

Capital punishment. Lucy felt sick.

She closed her eyes and shook her head, ejecting Logan Lightfoot from her thoughts. She tried to recollect her thoughts.

"Right, focus," she spoke to herself. "Flatmate, job, friends, new, new, new."

The google search bar sat empty in the middle of the screen as Lucy deliberated, job or flatmate first. She looked around the room, very aware of the distinct lack of noise. No tapping of computer keys, no remnants of music being played through the wall, no clattering from the kitchen. Nothing. The silence made the decision for her.

Flatmate it is.

Lucy frowned and stared at the screen. She didn't know where to start. Her hands hovered over the keyboard. Surely the internet wasn't the best way to find a potential flatmate, only weirdos and computer geeks would advertise themselves online. The idea of posting an online biography of herself did not appeal to Lucy at all and she mentally crossed off the possibility of creating a personal profile. Lucy often thought that she would have done well in the 1800s, living in the romantic world of Jane Austen. And yet a few of her friends had met their partners online.

Maybe it wasn't so bad, she thought. She could always vet people and say no. If she didn't like someone then she could ask them to leave.

Lucy typed 'flatmate Glasgow' into the search bar and clicked on the top website, *Buddy Up*, concluding that the first hit had to be legitimate. Two columns filled the screen, a selection of faces matched with a short description. She bent in towards the screen and scrolled down the page, examining each of her potential house mates. Lucy thought quickly, vetoing males, smokers, animal lovers, sports enthusiasts and anyone over thirty-three. She logged her preferences into the search engine and waited as a new, Lucy-approved screen loaded.

Twelve female images appeared in front of her.

Lucy browsed through the profiles, carefully reading the biographies. As she checked over them a second time her legs started to cramp and she straightened out her knees, sitting forward in her chair with her elbows resting on the desk. Her right thumb nestled between her teeth and she supported her head with her other hand. Her eyes hurt from staring at the bright screen. With Alex, it hadn't been a case of choosing, it had just been. It felt strange to Lucy, selecting people like a pair of new shoes. She frowned. Could she return them if they didn't fit or was there some sort of no returns policy? What if she chose someone who was socially inept or who liked playing the drums at 3am?

Lucy started reading from the top of the page. Best just to get it right the first time, she thought. Her finger followed the faces, moving downwards and her lips parted as she spoke to herself.

"Too young, too alternative, too intense, too into gardening, seriously... a puppeteer, that can't be a real thing."

The laptop made a sharp, high pitched dinging sound and a notification box appeared at the bottom right hand corner. Lucy's eyes drifted towards the message before it sunk away from the screen.

One new e-mail.

It was from Alex.

Lucy sat up in her chair and double clicked on her name, there was no subject. It was short and to the point, like a blade entering her stomach. There were just two sentences, each on a separate line.

We are done.

I did love you once, you know that. Sorry.

Lucy stared at the laptop with intense purpose, her nose hovering a few inches from the screen. She read it twice, following the words with her fingers and then she read it a third time. Just to make sure. She fell back, releasing all of her weight onto the chair.

There was nothing she could do, nothing but try to forget, to forget and move on.

It was done. Finished. The finality of it all was oddly surreal. Lucy felt numb all over, as if her whole body was rejecting reality, like she was awaking from a dream.

"Forward, not backwards," she whispered, and started typing up her own profile.

Six hours passed and Lucy's smartphone chimed. One new email from Buddy Up. She clicked on the caption of the sealed envelope and the message opened up.

Congratulations Lucy, you have received a Buddy Up request from Circe McGraw. Buddy-ability match 89%.

That was quick, thought Lucy.

Chapter 11

Present Day

"I don't think I've ever had coffee this strong."

Sally sat at Toop's kitchen table. Her words presented themselves as a statement. It wasn't an attempt to initiate polite conversation. In fact, any notion of a reply was somewhat beyond her expectations. It was just her way of injecting life into the silence and confirming her presence.

Fergus stood at the sink with his back to her. He hadn't spoken since they had walked through the front door, wordlessly discarding their soaked jackets and boots in the porch before heading to the kitchen. He turned off the tap, returned the cleaned plate to the cupboard and forced himself to gather his thoughts.

He turned around.

"Can I get you something to eat?"

He stared at the table for a moment or two before he sat down and raised his eyes to meet hers. She smiled back at him and for a brief instance he had a recollection of what his life used to be like. Sitting in the pub, the local band playing in the background as pint glasses clinked and voices blurred. A different life. One before the accident. Fergus closed his eyes, willing himself into the past, to another time, another place.

A time when she was there and he was happy.

"It's ok, Fergus." Sally moved her chair closer, no more than an inch, and rested her hand on his arm. "We don't have to talk about it now."

"Thanks Sal. I know it's been ten years, it's just. I'm not."

"I know." She pushed her chair back and squeezed his shoulder as she stood up. "Wee midnight dram?"

Toop nodded and pointed towards the cupboard next to the sink. "Glasses are on the shelf, above the mugs."

Sally moved around the kitchen as if it was her own. Toop had been in the place for less than six months and his boxes were still stacked in the corner, filled with surplus plates and kitchen utensils. He wondered if

Sally noticed that he had unpacked the whiskey glasses while most of the pots and pans remained wrapped in newspaper. He hadn't cooked a proper meal in the best part of a decade. In London he was working ninety-five hour weeks, forty of them unpaid, and since moving up to Scotland he had been living on toast and Weetabix. The sound of running water followed by clinking china indicated that Sally had found the unwashed evidence in his sink. It occurred to Toop that he hadn't eaten anything all day and that it was unlikely that Sally had either. The feeling of shame crept up on Toop but he remained silent, not even turning his head. Since the moment that she had stepped off the helicopter something had changed. Toop had spent the last ten years running from his past and now it was standing in his kitchen placing bread in his toaster.

"There you go," said Sally, handing him a plate of toast and marmite. "I'm going to go out on a limb and guess that it's been quite some time since you had a home-cooked meal." Sally placed two whiskeys on the table and took a bite from her bread and honey. "I still don't know how you stand that stuff, it's like eating tar."

Toop stared at the piece of toast in his hand. "It was my Dad's favourite."

"Have you spoken to him lately?"

The words washed over Toop without a flicker of recognition, the complete lack of response making Sally nervous. She would have preferred him to curse and launch his toast across the room.

"Sorry. I didn't mean," she whispered.

Neither of them spoke, the room filling with silence. It was the type of silence shared by friends and lovers, an entire conversation that passed without the utterance of a single word. The moment passed leaving two old acquaintances sat side by side, two bodies united by an unspoken agreement to leave the past undisturbed.

Tonight was not the night.

"So Sal, are you married?" Toop looked directly at her, taking a bite from the toasted bread.

She relaxed.

"Not even close. Well, unless you include a drunken proposal from my boss at the last staff night out. But I'm afraid I had to decline his kind offer." Toop watched as the spark returned to her eyes. "I believe I said something wonderfully eloquent and witty like not over any of my dead bodies."

Toop smiled. A real smile. "How a classy woman such as yourself hasn't been snapped up? The mind boggles!"

She punched him in the arm. "Thin ice my friend, very thin ice."

A weight lifted from Toop's shoulders as he tilted his head back in an effortless chuckle.

"No one able to meet your impeccable standards then?"

Sally lent back in her chair and offered a dramatic sigh. "Oh, you know, there's been a couple over the years. But it's the same old story that's been rehashed in a hundred chick flicks. Girl meets boy, girl plays hard to get, boy battles with his internal demons until one day they fall madly in love, followed by lots of sex and heated arguments about nothing. Then the boy gets frustrated that the girl spends so much of her time cutting up dead bodies. Maybe, possibly he gets a little freaked out when a bagged hand accidentally makes it home in her work bag. You know, same old!"

For the first time in six months, the small kitchen filled with laughter.

But there were no sentimental smiles or lingering glances, neither of them thinking the gesture necessary. Normality was the far greater sentiment. The absence of tears was what made their relationship real, making the passage of time irrelevant, and Toop realised that he loved her for it. She really was happy to see him, he thought. And, despite a decade of assuming otherwise, he was relieved that his past had caught up with him.

One night, he decided, he would be ready to talk about it. Not tonight, or the next one but one day he would talk about her again.

Toop put down his whiskey glass, leaving it unfinished, took out his pen and opened his note pad.

"Right, while it's still fresh, just a few notes. Then bed."

Sally smiled. "You can take the workaholic cop out of London. But you can't take the workaholic out of the cop!"

"Well at least when I take work home with me it doesn't come with four fingers and a thumb!"

"Touché."

Sally got up from the table and returned with her own notepad, in which time Toop had filled a page with scribbles. The softened appearance had gone from his face and his mind no longer operated within the confines of the kitchen, he was somewhere else. It took Sally three attempts to be heard, eventually drawing her hand to her mouth in a deliberate cough.

"So you're still convinced that it's not a suicide?"

"What?" Toop glanced up. "Yes. I mean no, it's not suicide."

"But what makes you so certain?"

Sally pulled out a seat and positioned her body so that she was sitting side on to him.

"The location," she said, "the clothing, the shot to the heart, it's a textbook case. A lonely man who found a remote place to die."

Toop returned his eyes to his notepad, adding to his notes.

"Are murderers not just as likely to choose a remote location?" he said distractedly.

Sally pursed her lips but she didn't answer. She folded her arms and sat back.

Toop noted this, aware of the sudden change in her posture. Fingers tapping off her arms, legs crossed, her lips pressed together in a thin line, waiting for him to stop and pay attention.

Toop put his pen down and closed his notebook.

"Sorry Sal."

He sat straighter, knitted his brow in a frown and considered how best to phrase it.

"Think about how often the mountain rescue team is called out to rescue tourists or to pick up amateurs who have been stranded in their skinny jeans and flip flops, trying to navigate using those bloody smartphones. They are morons and these ill-prepared idiots are becoming commonplace in the Highlands. But this man was not a tourist. He was there for another reason."

Toop stopped, bit his thumb nail between his teeth and forked his fingers through his hair. A second thought caught his attention, the first forgotten and he wiggled his pen in Sally's direction.

"You are assuming that remote places offer a romantic and peaceful place to die."

"Well not romantic exactly, but lonely, quiet."

"Precisely. Quiet and unpopulated, unobserved. No witnesses."

"I'm not questioning your logic. But how do you convince a man to willingly walk up a mountain to be shot. There were no visible signs of disturbance on the ground, no evidence of a struggle. Tell me, why would he simply stroll up, take a seat and wait for the bullet? It doesn't make sense."

Toop's eye's fell on his note pad. "I don't know yet."

"Ok, well what about the gun. You have to admit that Bailey had a point. You don't kill someone and leave the murder weapon lying around as an early Christmas present for the first cop that happens by. It was inches from the loch, why not just throw it in or ditch it in a bog?"

"I don't know that yet either." Toop didn't look up. He flipped the pad open and jotted down a new thought, stopping occasionally to tap his fingers against his right cheek.

This time Sally was undeterred by his lack of engagement. "But it's definitely not suicide."

"Not suicide."

"Shot to the heart. Very symbolic don't you think, a common choice for suicide victims."

"Wrong."

Sally crossed her arms and turned her body towards him. "Excuse me?"

Toop picked up on her tone and lifted his head. "It's a common misconception that gunshot suicides will always choose the heart. In truth, only one in five people are willing to hold a gun to their chest. So, statistically speaking, you are wrong." He smiled, the gesture returned.

"Well I can't go arguing with statistics now, can I?" said Sally, resting her hand on his shoulder. "Right, I'm off to bed."

She turned back as she was leaving the kitchen. "I will be in your room. You're on the couch."

Toop didn't hear her. His fingers were already tapping on the table.

Chapter 12

Late 80s

Jon could feel the force of his pulse beating against his neck. His arteries pumped with blood, drumming under the surface of his skin and hammering at a vein near his temple. Each of his senses responded to the onset of fear, functioning on overdrive as his lungs strained for air. Jon stood motionless. He was no stranger to the violent increases in heart rate. The sensation of being smothered was nothing new.

But he wouldn't lose control this time.

Jon counted in his head, his lips betraying the slightest hint of discomfort.

...four, five.

The front of his shirt filled as his stomach expanded under the soft fabric.

Six, seven.

He denied his body the delicious refreshment of air, disciplining his subconscious and blurring the edges of the room until they faded from reality. Each background sound distorted in turn like ink bleeding into porous paper, the words resting on the canvas before settling into the deep holes. Jon stayed rooted to the spot, frozen, apart from the slight twitch of his right hand. The tips of two fingers twitched involuntarily beneath the arm of his jacket, brushing against the settled fabric. He mentored himself, denying the desire to relinquish control. Stagnation and cognitive control were his only weapons. Only his mouth hinted at any sense of movement.

Relax your mind. Acknowledge, guide, replace. It's all about control, nothing more.

Varying streams of people joined him, middle-aged housewives and retired art lovers, treading inches from his passive body. An elderly woman knocked his elbow with her handbag, offering a reflexive apology, but not one person offered him a second glance. The visitors to the gallery sauntered around him as if he were a piece of art, too wrapped up in their own thoughts.

...Twenty-six, twenty-seven.

Jonathan Swan had suffered from panic attacks since he was five years old. He knew how to conceal them. Time had taught him to disguise the intense and suffocating apprehension from the world. His face remained void of emotion, hiding the fear that paralysed his body. He would not cede. Not when his best friend, his only real friend, had been the cause.

Jon had been standing in front of the painting for ten minutes, seeing what no-one else did, what no-one else wanted to see. The imperfection was visible only to Jon, his eyes drawn to the undetectable flaw because he knew where to look. To Jon, the concealed disfigurement was the work of art. The disguised lesion had more depth and meaning to it than a thousand brush strokes.

A subtle defect.

Jon traced over it with his eyes, the L shaped incision cut deep into the fabric.

A vicious stab into the heart of the artist.

Laboured efforts had been made to restore the canvas but at that precise angle, in line with the light, the scar was made visible. Jon looked through the stitching, feeling calmed, watching as the painting ripped open before his eyes and curled limply from the canvas, leaving a black, imageless hole. His fingers stopped twitching as his mind drifted, considering the hostility in the blade. He closed his eyes, feeling the intimacy of the stitching that had returned life to the vandalised image. It was the evidence of something far more powerful than artistic genius. It was proof of humanity, of imperfection, the very state of being human.

"The infamous Christ of St John of the Cross." The voice came from behind Jon. "Quite something isn't it, a painting that's shed a thousand tears they say."

Jon felt the presence of the man next to him. The man stared at the painting, observing the bowed head of Christ. "A thousand tears," he repeated. "I've often wondered, is it sadness or appreciation that brings people to tears when they see images of the crucifixion? Guilt perhaps?"

Jon slipped his hands in his pockets and looked down at the floor. The stranger smiled. "Not much of a talker then?"

As they stood there, neither man looked at each other. Jon lingered over a number of sentence openers but none of them materialised into words. The silence was oddly comfortable. The two men stood in front of the oil masterpiece, their feet paddling in the sea at the edge of the canvas with Jesus as the great pendant hanging above their heads. There was not a single religious disposition between them.

"So tell me," the man asked, "what do you see? Art or vandalism?"

The question took Jon by surprise and the response escaped his mouth without effort.

"Neither."

"He does talk." The man's smile was relaxed. "So, I have to ask, what is it exactly that have you been staring at for the last forty minutes?"

Jon stared down at his shoes. He didn't need to think about his answer but he wanted it to come across the right way. He wanted the man stood next to him, this stranger, to understand him.

"Salvador Dali," replied Jon, voicing the artist's name.

The man's expression didn't alter, his eyes waited, empty of cynicism.

"When I look at the painting," continued Jon, "I see the life of the artist". A painting is like an autobiography, a personal insight into another human being." Jon stopped. What was he thinking, why would a stranger care about his frivolous notions on art.

The man held out his hand, "I'm Thomas, Tom. Please go on."

Jon shook it. "Jonathan." What was he saying? Nobody used his full name. "Jonathan Swan."

Stop saying your name. Ask him something.

"The port painted beneath Christ's feet," he blurted, "do you know it?"

"I can't say that I do."

"It's Port Lligat, Dali's hometown in Spain," offered Jon. "Dali had a dream in which he saw Christ floating in a black sky above his house. That's what inspired the painting. The image is a literal depiction of the artist's subconscious."

"So he's a fanatic."

Jon felt a surge of disappointment. The man's ignorance irritated him. "No, not at all, there weren't any religious incentives behind Dali's art. In fact, his decisions to omit nails from the palms and to leave out the crown of thorns were based on personal preferences. It was a matter of taste not belief. Dali praised aesthetics and it was because of his love of beauty that he chose not to blemish his subject."

Jon couldn't stop himself. He wanted the man to understand him. "Dali modelled Christ, not on a depiction from the bible, but on Russell Sanders..."

"Shhh!"

The breath of disdain came from a lady in a mustard coat. Jon recoiled but his new acquaintance laughed with his eyes. "Russell Sanders, you mean Gene Kelly's body double in Singing in the Rain?"

"Yes," whispered Jon, shocked, impressed. "Dali strapped Sanders to a gantry so that he could view the pull of gravity on his body. The whole image is based on scientific calculations. Dali himself said the painting championed science, combining it with religious belief."

The man turned to Jon. "Nuclear Mysticism."

"Em yes. Exactly." It wasn't often that Jon looked jolted by someone else's intellect.

"Sorry, I've been messing with you kid! I know exactly who Salvador Dali is. Mr Melting Clocks himself." That warm smile again. "The father of surrealism, isn't that what they call him, more Freud than Father almighty."

Kid, thought Jon, they were the same age. "Then why?"

"I'm intrigued. You intrigue me. This place, the art gallery, it means something to you, doesn't it?"

Jon felt uneasy.

"This must be your fifth visit this month." A look of interest crossed his face, bringing his eyebrows closer together. "And always this room, an interesting choice for someone who is clearly unconvinced by religion. So what is it about Dali that's gotten you so hooked?"

Third time this month, not fifth.

Jon's fingers started twitching. "Look, I don't know what you want but I think I need to leave." He lowered his arm, grabbing the bag that was resting by his legs. His hand gathered a fistful of material, allowing the bag to swing beneath his knuckles.

As he turned, Jon felt a hand catch his elbow.

"Sorry, I'm being an asshole. Let me explain," said the man, "you see my Dad, he works here, so I'm often around and well I've seen you a couple of times, that's all. Thought I'd say hi."

Jon eyed him cautiously. Five seconds passed before he replied. "Someone once told me that Dali enjoyed playing with logic, an observation that is pretty obvious when it comes to his surrealist works." Jon turned to look at the painting. "But this isn't one of his surrealist pieces, so what is he trying to say here? I don't know, it sounds stupid, but thinking about it calms me down." The words formed before Jon had time to think about them. It felt strange, not bad. Never before had he admitted such intimate details about himself.

The man placed a hand on Jon's shoulder.

"I think that we are going to be good friends, Jonathan Swan."

Chapter 13

Present Day

Lucy peered through the cafe window, the tip of her nose reflected in the glass. There she was, Circe McGraw. Her future flatmate sat a few metres away nursing a glass of water, legs crossed, waiting for Lucy.

Circe McGraw had her ankles entwined, her legs hugged by denim jeans as she skimmed through a magazine. Her slight frame was hidden beneath a loose fitting jumper. It was green and gathered around her elbows exposing her pale forearms. She was both effortless and feminine, the suggestive rise and fall of her chest observed by more than one of the male customers.

Shit!

Circe McGraw looked straight up at the window, her long hair falling down her back in a ponytail. Lucy stumbled backwards in a fluster, adopting a futile pretence as her eyes browsed over the contents of the window.

Wonderful first impression, thought Lucy, very smooth.

Gathering herself, she pushed the door open, her limbs and clothing interweaving in a distorted shuffle. Lucy cursed as she wrenched her handbag through the doorway, disentangling the strap from the door handle. The tinkling of a copper bell signalled her entrance and the door swung on its hinges. Lucy reddened, but no one in the cafe seemed to notice. No one except Circe who sat smiling back at her, all smoky eyes and white teeth.

Lucy wanted to turn and leave.

But instead she walked to the table and offered her hand, complete with a smile. "Hi, I'm Lucy." Circe's hand felt warm against her ice-cold skin. Lucy flinched in response, ashamed of her poor circulation. She had Raynaud's, a hereditary disease apparently, not that it mattered to her.

"Circe, but everyone calls me Cece. I recognised you from your Buddy Up photo."

Lucy lingered behind the chair as she removed her coat and sat down. "It's hard to mistake the little mermaid hair."

"I love it." Cece's smile was infectious. "I always wanted red hair as a child, I wanted to be like Lady Hamilton. She was so elegant. My Dad actually named me after her. She was..."

"You mean George Romney's muse?"

Cece nodded, "You know her?"

"Know her?" Lucy paused in a gapped mouth stare. "I volunteered on the Romney exhibition at Kelvingrove Art Gallery, I know everything that there is to know about Romney's affair with her. The man was so obsessed that he once described her as the divine lady, superior to all womankind. From their first meeting she became his most devoted muse, in fact he became so infatuated that it ruined his career."

Cece giggled, "I'm impressed."

Lucy inhaled a sharp breath and leaned into the table. "Of course, Circe, your name." Lucy captured her head in the palm of her hand, resting it there as the revelation washed over her. "Romney often combined the features of ancient Greek sculpture with Lady Hamilton's beauty; he painted a portrait depicting her as Circe, the Greek goddess of magic."

Cece laughed. "That's me. My Dad is a bit of an art buff, as it would seem are you. I can't believe that you know all of that stuff."

Lucy reddened.

Maybe, she thought, this flatmate thing wouldn't be so bad after all.

Time slipped away unnoticed and a continuous turnover of customers passed through the cafe. But the two girls remained lost in their own conversation, oblivious to the screech of chair legs on the cement floor and the screams from the coffee machine. An hour later they ordered a second coffee, scanned the menu and selected two warmed apple and cinnamon scones with cream.

Cece took a bite of her scone and dabbed her mouth. "So did you have someone else living with you before?"

The mug stopped halfway to Lucy's mouth and she hesitated, wondering if she should mention Alex. "Just a student from the university," she said, "but she didn't stay long."

"How come?"

"She was doing a semester overseas," Lucy said. "To be honest I didn't see her much, she kept herself to herself."

"Well, it sounds like a change of housemate will do you good," smiled Cece.

"That's the plan."

They finished their coffees and Cece excused herself, taking a few minutes to freshen up in the bathroom.

Lucy watched her as she disappeared from view, rounding the corner at the far end of the room. Then, when she was sure that Cece had gone, Lucy leaned over and picked up Cece's empty mug. The handle was still warm. She could feel Cece in the porcelain. It was all real.

With the mug held in her hand, Lucy realised that she had never felt more normal.

Her philosophy teacher had once told her that normality was repulsive; "normality is one of society's great inhibitions, it suffocates the living." At the time his words had comforted her, but sitting holding Cece's mug, Lucy could not disagree more. From the minute that Lucy had entered the world, nothing about her had been normal and nothing about her life had been easy. Pain, death and heartache had made her abnormal, her life drowned in secrecy. Now, for the first time, she was breathing fresh air.

Normal was good, painless.

Cece reappeared from the bathroom and Lucy couldn't help but watch as she walked towards the table. The easy motion of her long arms and the sway of her ponytail made it hard not to look at her. Lucy's eyes hung on her body a fraction too long and Cece feigned embarrassment as she sat down.

Lucy's face went pink beneath her blusher and she bit her lower lip.

"Sorry, I was just thinking about Lady Hamilton and how much you look like her."

"But without the red hair." Cece twisted a stray slip of hair and wrapped it behind her ear. "Do you want to trade?"

Lucy appeared startled. "What? Why? Your hair is gorgeous."

"I like you," smiled Cece, dipping a hand into her handbag. "Consider coffee my treat."

"You don't have to," persisted Lucy.

"But I want to." She stood and strolled over to the counter to pay.

Contented and full, they stepped out onto the street. But Lucy stalled, paused on the pavement. Her lips parted, saying nothing, as the confidence drained from her face.

She had been let down by people her whole life. All the relationships that she had known had been complicated and painful. So what reason did she have to think that this one would be any different?

Cece placed a hand on her forearm.

"What is it? You can ask me anything."

Lucy cast her eyes down, focusing on the ground around her shoes. "Even if it may seem a little strange?"

"Stranger the better."

"I do want you to move in. It's just..." Lucy didn't look up, her words falling upon the side of the road. "I'm looking for a fresh start. This year hasn't been easy for me and I want to start anew, no looking back." Lucy risked a glance at Cece's expression. She was smiling, the edges of her mouth lifted ever so slightly. "And I have a sort of proposition."

"A proposition, I'm intrigued."

"I was thinking that we could each have a no-go area, a subject that we can take off the table, something that can't be discussed or questioned. Then we don't have to lie about it."

Lucy's voice was barely a whisper. "Does that sound crazy?"

"Not at all, in fact I think it's a great idea. So, what's your deep dark, forbidden subject?"

Go on.

The words crawled from her dry mouth. "My family."

"Done," said Cece, sweeping her arms wide. "And I'll choose my family too. No questions, no lies, right?"

"Right." Lucy replied.

Then a thought hit Lucy. She knew what she was hiding but why didn't Circe McGraw want to talk about her family?

Now she would never know.

Chapter 14

Present Day

He was suffocating.

Toop's eyes flashed wide open in panic.

The end of the sofa was covered in objects that crushed down upon his legs, now two paralysed lumps of flesh. He could see bones and teeth and rings and bracelets. He saw a turquoise pendant, the green stone reflected in the moonlight as the silver casing floated in a pool of red blood. He saw them and willed his body awake, wanting it to be a dream. He wanted it to be a nightmare but reality had him pinned to the couch in a cold sweat. Panicked, he plunged his fist into the tangle of bones and jewellery, his fingers dripping with warm, red liquid as he raised his hand to his face.

The feeling of death drowned him and his lungs filled with ice cold snow. The urge to gag threw his torso over the edge of the sofa where his head hung limply above the carpet. But no amount of dry heaving could clear the white power from his windpipe. There was no escaping it.

Death lived in him.

It was a Saturday when Death had first knocked on Toop's door, ramshackling his life with a single blow. Death's lifeless eyes had flooded with glee as He ripped the paper from the walls, leaving it hanging in long uneven shards, his hollow laugh echoing through the halls. Death came for a second time the next day. He dismantled the foundations, burning it all to the ground with two syllables and Toop was left standing in a pile of ash, surrounded by Death's confetti.

Toop knew of only one way to escape the images.

Gasping, he fell from beneath his duvet and landed on the floor with a violent thud. His helmet and bike shoes were ready at the foot of the sofa. The digital clock on his bedside table shone a dull yellow. 04:23. Toop tumbled through the living room, collecting his mountain bike from its hook on the wall, and headed out into the darkness without hesitation. He switched on the light that was mounted on his handlebars and drove his tyres through the thick gravel.

The snow inside him started to melt.

Sally watched him through the open door, lingering long enough to feel the cold round her ankles. Then she pushed against the wooden panels and the door clicked shut. She turned, letting her palm rest against the wood as she walked back to the warmth.

* * *

The clock in the kitchen hung above the AGA cooker, the two hands falling on top of each other. Six thirty-three.

"Coffee?"

Sally was waiting for him as he walked in. She held a steaming mug in the direction of the opening door.

"Thanks."

Toop took the mug from her hand and started towards the bathroom, not looking her in the eye.

"I'm going to grab a shower."

Toop cast his eyes quickly around the living room. His duvet was folded neatly at the end of the sofa and the cushions had been smoothed out.

"I'm making poached eggs, you keen?" Sally shouted, half hidden behind the fridge door.

"Yeah, thanks." The snow had all but gone from his lungs. "There should be some bread in the freezer."

He paused halfway up the stairs. "What time is the post mortem?"

"Examination room is booked for four." Toop nodded to himself, wordless in his response, before turning back to the stairs.

Sally smiled as she heard the bathroom door close. In spite of everything, she couldn't deny it.

She had missed him.

* * *

The whiteboard in Toop's office was decorated with a hand-drawn diagram of all the known access routes, a map of local knowledge courtesy of the Mountain Rescue Team.

69

Toop stared at the illustration, bringing one hand to his face, while Bailey observed. Toop wasn't in uniform. Not yet. The back of his t-shirt still held the sweat from his bike to work. He would shower again later; right now his mind was on other things.

Bailey was not yet awake, his eyes clouded over with sleep. He sat at the desk with a coffee, watching Toop's back. His boss's face was concealed but Bailey had a relatively good idea what his expression might be. It had always occurred to the young officer that Toop's eyes and brain were disturbingly out of sync, as though his mind anticipated that his pupils would see things that weren't there, or before they happened. Bailey was convinced that Toop's brain processed information before his eyes had registered it. Bailey sipped from his coffee, glad that Toop had his back turned. He had also learned, the hard way, not to interject until his superior had stopped tapping his fingers against his cheek.

So Bailey waited and Toop stared at the board. The arm of the clock ticked with each second.

It was Toop that spoke.

"Loch Coire Fionarack is accessible from two main directions..."

"You mean Fionnaraich." The words escaped Bailey's lips without mediation and he cursed himself for the tactless outburst.

"Sorry sir." His voice faded in the silent room.

Toop cleared his throat and continued, not retracing his words, but the correction left a small wound. A reminder that he had forgotten how to speak his own language.

"Most will choose to walk up to Loch an Eion and then continue on to Loch Coire Fionnaraich. This means leaving from the hotel on the main road. Alternatively, according to the Mountain Rescue, some walkers go from Coulags and follow the river up. This route passes by a number of cottages and a small bothy."

Toop paused. Bailey didn't know if he was meant to speak. He decided against it.

"Do you have any local knowledge to interject on the subject?"

Bailey straightened in his seat. He could feel the plastic beneath his bony arse cheeks.

"Aye. I've been up both paths many times, been walking these hills since I was a nipper. There's no groomed tracks up there, not like the ones down south, it's all rough single-track up here. Definitely not meant for those flimsy sandal things the guy had on."

Bailey rose from his chair, walked over to the white board and held his finger over the cross marking the hotel.

"The walk up from the hotel on the Annat side makes more sense if you are just going up to Loch Coire Fionnaraich and back down. Most walkers approaching from Coulags tend to head up to the MBA bothy and continue up Maol Chean-Dearg." He paused and frowned. "Unless you are doing the whole loop round Maol Chean-Dearg, then you would go via the bothy." Another pause. "So basically, he could have come up from either way, no real way to tell which. There are numerous stalker's paths in the area with it being on the Beinn Damh deer estate, so people can do what they please, go wherever they want."

Toop held his hand up to stop him, pulled his phone from his pocket and held it to his ear, addressing Bailey as he waited.

"We need to speak to the staff at the hotel and find out who has stayed at the bothy over the last couple of..."

The call connected. Toop turned on the spot and focused his eyes on the whiteboard.

"Officer Toop with the Gairloch police force." Pause. "I need the names of all of the people who have stayed at the MBA bothy over the last three days." Pause. "Right, yes. I understand."

He hung up.

He turned his arm and glanced at his watch, the calculations in his head visible on his face. As Bailey watched him he imagined the numbers floating across Toop's corneas. Without losing focus, Toop walked past Bailey and opened the cabinet at the far side of the room, sliding the top drawer out on its rails. The drawer hung in the air, a metal arm that held numerous OS maps, crammed in side by side. Toop extended two fingers, methodically working his way to the back of the drawer. His body bent further into the industrial structure and the metal handle pressed against his flat stomach as he brushed the spine of each map. Numbers passed silently across his lips until he reached 429. Toop slipped it from the drawer and placed it on the table, smoothing it out with the palm of his right hand, his face lost in deep concentration as his fingers moved across the detailed sheet.

Bailey stood and gazed at his boss, a man who, he was fairly certain, had forgotten that he was there. Sometimes he didn't get Toop. No, that was wrong. It wasn't so much a lack of understanding that he felt, as a feeling of awe.

Toop folded and pocketed the map and headed for the door. Then, as an afterthought, he stopped in the doorway and turned back around. Bailey stood at the far wall, staring back at him.

"Can I help?"

Toop looked at his eager colleague with expressionless eyes, pokerfaced, giving Bailey nothing. His face was illegible, not a single twitch indicative of his thought process.

"I need to go to the bothy to check the log book," he said, "the mountain rescue doesn't have any electronic records. I'll be quicker going myself."

"What can I do for you?" asked Bailey, under no illusions that he would be accompanying Toop to the bothy but with his enthusiasm intact.

Toop hesitated.

"Go to the hotel and speak to the staff, ask about any new faces. I will be back by 4." He half turned but his body jerked backwards. "Take detailed notes."

"Yes, boss," said Bailey. "Watch out for water bars, you don't want to be getting punctures."

A smile caught Toop's mouth as he walked out. Bailey was sure of it.

Chapter 15

Late 80s

They headed southwest towards Kelvin Way, fringing the edges of Kelvingrove Park.

"An art gallery encased in greenery and flanked by water. Rather poetic wouldn't you say?"

Tom turned to Jon as they passed over the river Kelvin and Jon felt the scent of his cologne wrap itself around his face, recognising the fragrance. It must have been one that Jesse used. Jon discarded the thought, not wanting to dwell on it, not wanting to think about Jesse.

The two boys stopped to rest on a park bench. Tom leant back with his hands clasped behind his head, the occasional breeze bringing the noise of traffic from Argyle Street.

"It's not all as it seems," said Tom as he curved his head from left to right. "This. The park. The perfect flowers and the trees." Tom gave a bold smile. "Let me enlighten you with a little tale."

His legs were stretched out straight in front of him, two long lanky limbs poured into tight denim.

"In the mid-1800s our dear old Glasgow laid victim to the rapidly slumming depths of the city centre. Can you imagine it, the poor, haughty middle classes forced to fraternise with the deadbeats from the east side?" He paused intentionally, winning a smile from his companion. "And so came Kelvingrove Park, a gift from the town council, a sanctuary for the wealthy that could provide relaxation opportunities away from public squalor." His sentence concluded abruptly, absent of any rising inflection or an obvious change in tone. He didn't demand a response or fish for a reaction. He just smiled, leant his head back so that it rested in his hands and closed his eyes, the sun casting a shadow in the space between his nose and lips.

Jon felt comfortable around Tom. It was an odd feeling. He had grown up with Jesse but the dynamics were completely different. While he had never admitted it out loud and he wasn't entirely sure what it meant, Jon had always known that there was an unspoken desperation in their friendship, a friendship born out of the naivety and innocence of children. With Tom on the other hand, well, it was different. He inspired a confidence in Jon that he didn't even know he had.

"I wish I had bumped into you earlier," said Jon, the composed tone supporting his words feeling quite foreign to him.

"You too kid," replied Tom.

Kid?

"You realise we're the same age? We could even be in the same year."

"I doubt that?"

"Why?"

"Well, I never went to university, in fact I dropped out of school at sixteen. Not a single qualification to my name."

In that split second, Jon couldn't help but wonder if he judged him; it was a question that Jon revisited a number of times over the years. He liked to think that he hadn't because Tom, as it turned out, was one of the smartest people that Jon would ever know.

"You surprised, Jonathan Swan?" Tom's question came with a knowing grin. "Have I shattered your societal expectations? An uneducated drifter lurking in the shadows of the much admired and prestigious Kelvingrove Gallery, quite scandalous!"

"No. Please don't think..."

"Relax kid. I'm winding you up. You make it too easy, you know that. Did anyone ever tell you that you should unwind a little?" His voice was soft, kind, but the image of Jesse's face flooded Jon's eyes and Jon's mouth choked with a dry sensation.

"Sorry... I..."

"Hey, don't apologise to me," said Tom. "It keeps you interesting." Then Tom did something, said something, unexpected. He looked Jon straight in the eye, his breath falling on his face, his tone was stern, no smile this time.

"I'm serious. Stop apologising. Stop making the assumption that you are the one who is wrong."

Then Tom uttered two sentences, voicing the two sentences that would repeat in Jonathan Swan's mind on the day that he died. Tom held Jon's gaze, not faltering until he had finished. His words were carefully placed and appropriately separated by pauses, a statement of such precision that it could have been rehearsed.

"Of all the words of mice and men there are some words that hold a particular sadness, and for me, those words are unmistakable." He shook his head, just enough. "No man, not you, not me, should ever have to utter the words, it might have been."

He placed his hand on Jon's shoulder, an unusual gesture for two boys who had just met but Jon didn't question it. "So just be, and be you." Tom turned back to his former position, legs out, hands behind his head while Jon sat in silence, making the quiet transition from acknowledgement to understanding.

Jon had always nurtured the idea that he was different but he could never voice the internal feelings that troubled him. Shame, revulsion, fear. In truth, Jon believed that there was a dormant blackness inside of him, a darkness that he would much rather conceal than confess to. Less shame in it, he thought.

Just be, and be you.

It should have been one of those turning points in his young life, a moment of clarity in which Jon took charge and accepted who he was.

But, unfortunately for Jon, it wasn't.

And so the moment passed in silence.

Jon felt a surge of sadness for his new friend. He could feel Tom accepting his silence, mistakenly believing that Jon was experiencing some sort of epiphany. Perhaps, decided Jon, if he continued to stare at the worn knees of his jeans then he wouldn't disappoint Tom.

He wants to fix you, thought Jon.

He can't.

He can't, thought Jon. But he could let him believe that he could.

Just stay silent.

The noises of the park drifted into Jon's ears, the songs of birds and the boisterous laughter of university students. With eyes held on his knees, Jon pictured the young women prancing across the grass, skipping in a flirtatious and infantile manner. Their amorous, high-pitched shrills stirred the crotch of his jeans, stroking him with the tenderness of bare fingertips. The sensation of an impending erection stole the oxygen from the air, leaving it thin and insubstantial and his breathing quickened. Jon felt trapped, helplessly caught between a feeling of excitement and the burden of his deficiencies. He tried to concentrate on the faded denim that concealed his knee caps.

Focus.

He felt nauseated.

You can't ever tell.

You can't let anyone see how shameful you are, he told himself, how revolting. They'll judge you, he'll look at you with a damning disgust. You're not normal Jonathan Swan. Normal men don't get aroused listening to girls in the park. Don't tell, keep quiet.

Silent.

Four words. *It might have been.* They should have been a turning point. Jon should have trusted in his friend. But he didn't, he sealed his lips and buried the darkness deeper. It was a grave mistake, a mistake that would cost him everything. One day, in the not too distant future, the darkness would stir and his life would be changed forever.

So there they sat, two young men resting on a park bench. Anxious and protective, Jon waited, watching for a gesture or expression that would allow the wordless moment to pass. He wasn't sure how much time was expected; how long did Tom expect him to reflect? Then, as the question engaged his thoughts, Tom coughed, holding his clenched fist to his mouth.

Oh God, thought Jon, maybe he wants me to talk now. Jon felt queasy. It was easy to lie mutely, but lying with words, that seemed far more deceitful.

"Shall we get moving?" Tom's long body unfolded as he rose from the bench, his arms bent backwards causing his ribcage to protrude against his jumper. His words held the hint of sleep. Jon let out a silent, undetectable breath of relief and the darkness in him settled.

It was left undisturbed, unchallenged.

"It's only a fifteen-minute walk to my Granddad's shop." Tom nodded ahead. "Come on, we've got to head down towards Argyll Street."

Chapter 16

Present Day

It was beautiful.

Lucy had expected a flood of emotions when she returned to the flat that night. Her fingers had paused over the door handle, hovering in a state of suspense, knowing that Cece would have had more than enough time to unpack and move in. Packing up Alex's things had been one thing but someone else unpacking in her room was something else entirely. Lucy had paused at the door, her nose crinkled in contemplation, picturing Cece on the other side of the door, her scent flooding through the flat like a coat of fresh paint. The former shades of Alex never to return.

Doubt crept up on her then as she stood with toes pressed against the door. She knew that Cece was inside, placing her clothes in drawers that weren't hers and lying on a bed that still held the indent of Alex's body. The pressure of Lucy's hand on the door had pushed it forward and the latch flipped open, a homely aroma escaping through the small opening.

The radio was playing. Alex never played the radio.

"Great, you're home!" beamed Cece.

Even her voice was welcoming. Cece's face appeared at the door, blocking Lucy's view. "I hope you like it," she said, moving to the side and pulling the door open.

It was beautiful.

Lucy's eyes scanned the room and she realised that until that very moment she had never been quite sure of what she liked. If she had, it would have been this, it would have been the willowy art sculpture in the corner and the vibrant pillows that lined the window seat. How had she lived without the grand tulip sculpture in the corner, with its skeletal frame head sinking towards the floor. No, not sinking, bowing. And the patchwork of mismatched pillows, would they not have been there previously? The notion of a cushion-less couch, sitting naked and exposed, seemed almost impolite, vulgar even.

Shifting her feet, Lucy's eyes caught on the far wall. The brushes of paint soaked into her vision, leaving her drunk on the image.

Lady Hamilton hung above the vacant fireplace, presented as the goddess Circe. Lucy gazed at the haunting interpretation of the George Romney original, drinking in the over-valiant brush strokes and the crude use of red paint, death-white skin drained by the twines of bloodied curls. It was sensational.

Lucy could feel Cece's anticipation.

"Staging houses for a living has its perks," smiled Cece, "and I should mention, the smell of brownies coming from the kitchen, all part of the homely facade."

Cece lifted her weight up, balancing upon her toes, and cupped her hands behind her back so that her body swayed with the anticipation of a child. Her lower lip disappeared beneath her teeth, enveloped by her wet tongue.

She smiled, bashful and kittenish. "So, are you sold!?"

"It's amazing," said Lucy, pleasing herself with a genuine laugh. "You must be good at your job, you've almost convinced me to buy a flat that I already live in!"

"I was hoping you'd say that." Cece turned on her heels in one single, fluid motion and faced the kitchen. "Can I offer you a brownie?"

"Yes, please, I'd love one."

Lucy listened to the creak of the oven being opened, followed by the dull sucking sound of the freezer seal breaking. Ice cream, thought Lucy absent-mindedly as she walked towards the painting. She had just assumed that it wasn't the original but as she stared at it frown lines started to congregate between her red brows. It couldn't be, could it? Surely, the cost, the rareness, obviously it was a copy. It was just so perfect, thought Lucy. Her lips parted without instruction, carrying her words through to the kitchen. "Where did you get it?"

"Sorry? What did you say?" Teaspoons clattered against side plates.

"The painting, where is it from?"

"Oh, it was a gift." The kettle sprung to life. "I got it years ago." Cece was shouting. "It's a family piece."

"Who was the artist?"

Cece's head appeared through the doorway.

"Believe it or not," she said, "it was originally painted by a woman in her late seventies called Mary Troon, or Tod I think. She used to produce puppet films, as in proper, dancing from strings, puppets! Crazy huh? Apparently, a number of them were even shown on TV. Anyway, when she retired she started painting all sorts of obscure, largely erotic, images of women. And well, she decided to vamp up one of Romney's paintings." She slid out of view once more but her voice drifted through the archway separating the kitchen from the living room. "You should look her up online. Let's just say that Lady Hamilton was one of the few ladies that she choose to dress so generously."

"Now that you mention it, there does seem to be a greater emphasis on shading in certain provocative areas", Lucy spoke through a lingering smile. "So, this isn't the original painting by the artist then?"

"Oh gosh no, just a painting that's been in the family since..." The last few words in her sentence were lost in the open cupboard as Cece reached forwards to fish out two mugs from the back. "I think that we need to invest in some new mugs," she shouted.

We, thought Lucy. It was all happening so fast. Lucy had never expected to find a flatmate in such a short space of time. It was all a bit overwhelming.

I suppose anything in the West End is prime real estate.

Cece called out from the kitchen. "Can you pop the TV on, there's a cooking programme starting in a few minutes and I have to confess, I'm slightly addicted."

Lucy did a quick scan of the room from where she was standing and her eyes caught on a sliver of black plastic wedged between the couch pillows. Alex, though Lucy. Her left hand, she had always been ambidextrous, delved amid the tough fabric, producing the device and bringing the monitor to life with a press of the red button.

"What channel?"

A rustling from the kitchen preceded Cece's entrance and she offered Lucy a steaming mug of tea. "Em, I'm not entirely sure. Let me have a flick." She held her arm out straight, her slender limb gliding through the air like silk, and directed the remote at the small box beneath the television.

A bleak picture of the Scottish Highlands filled the TV, the lower third of the screen blocked out in red with a white text overlay. Lucy noted that the graphics department had gone to the effort of drawing shadows under each individual letter, giving the impression that the two white words were raised above the red background.

Breaking News.
Cece left the channel on.

Chapter 17

His tyres moved over the rocks like water racing through a stream.

Toop's body hung low and central over the frame, using his arms and knees to throw the bike round each corner. The steel frame moved freely beneath him as he shifted his weight from side to side, navigating the wheels around rutted twists and turns. His mud-streaked shorts hovered over the saddle, occasionally brushing the hard leather seat but without applying any firm pressure.

The barren wilderness rose up on each side of the glen forming a cloak of dull, weathered greenery. The vast landscape was stained by a sole speck of orange as Toop slipped through the mist on his bike. Toop unweighted his body with ease, a readjustment that allowed him to peddle smoothly over the jarring rocks and funnels of soft mud. The rough single-track continued on for a few kilometres before it forked off to the left and down a set of steep rock steps. Toop's weight fell back naturally and he released all pressure from the brakes, leaving a single gloved finger hovering over each lever. The hard-tail floated down the two foot drops like liquid.

The front tyre bit into the wet ground with vigour as Toop turned on the shoulder edge, the rubber tread cutting into the rough earth. The overcast sky spotted with rain as the rutted track started to ascend. Wet rocks camouflaged the trail, bucking his tyres as he pedalled along the east side of the burn. He did not slow to mull over the narrow bridge but shifted down a gear, locked elbows and ploughed through the water. The first concealed rock, lying dormant in the sand, connected with the front wheel as it severed the stream. Toop gripped the handlebars and moved out of the saddle, his feet dragging through the freezing water with each down stroke of the pedals. He didn't notice the cold seeping into his socks. The rear wheel started to lose traction on the smooth stones, sucking the bike backwards. Without hesitation, Toop shifted his weight and forced power through the cranks. The stream relinquished its hold, the bike unbeaten.

The only sound was the wind and the gentle tapping of rain on his helmet. The air was no different down in the village but to Toop it felt fresher, purer. He breathed in deeply, taking in the smell of the Highlands.

Of home.

The steep gradient burned in his thighs like a drug and his chest felt like it was being constricted in a vice. Toop relished the sweat that collected at his temples and he took deep, powerful breaths, finding salvation in his lungs. He felt alive. His eyes rested about forty feet ahead of him, assessing the rough terrain. Then it appeared, Coire Fionnaraich Bothy, a patchwork of stones against the landscape.

The modest hut was accompanied by a solitary ash tree, its roots buried deep beneath the doorway making it an integral part of the settlement. It was not the first time that Toop had rested his bike against the elderly trunk and as he stood there looking out into the cool summer morning he glanced down at his feet and felt her fingers interlock with his. Her skin was cold, soft but cold.

You're here.

Her voice echoed through the air and her face appeared around the side of the green door, curls of hair playing in the breeze. "Come on slow coach, get your ass inside. It's incredible in here, they even have wooden panelling. Correction, freshly painted white wooden panelling! It's luxury. Come on, no one's going to steal the bikes. There's nobody around to steal them even if they wanted to. Get in here. I'll make it worth your while." Her smile.

Toop followed her to the door and pushed against it, his shoulder jutting backwards with the sudden impact. Closed. Of course, it was closed. Toop lowered his weight on the handle and turned it.

You're dead.

A cold breeze kissed his cheeks and the door creaked open revealing a well-known image. It was just as he remembered. A little less light perhaps but the memories punched him hard and fast in the gut, a solid steel fist that dented his internal organs in one swift, targeted motion. He winced.

The place that time forgot, thought Toop. The place it freed.

They were still there, the freshly painted wooden panels, an off-white colour this time, no longer pure snow. Sock-less pegs hung on a line of string above the fireplace with two wooden chairs, side by side, looking upon unborn flames. Timeless and forever. The shelves were cluttered with various items, matches, books, mugs, candles. Toop contemplated taking a rest on one of the seats, a very long, permanent rest.

He resisted.

Remote, desolate places were not a reason to give up, thought Toop. There was more to it than that.

"A lot more," he whispered.

Toop sighted the open log book on the table beneath the window, a large body of water visible through the squares of glass. Loch Coire Fionnaraich. Or was it? It irritated him that Bailey would know. Acting on his first impulse Toop retracted his bare fingers as they moved towards the aged pages, not wanting to contaminate evidence. Veins protruded from the underside of his wrists as he gripped the edge of the table, retaining the majority of his body weight in his hands and forearms. You're being an idiot, he cursed, hundreds of people have leafed through this book. Concentrate, don't lose focus just because you're here.

He adjusted the book and applied pressure to the inner binding joint, using his palm to keep the pages flat. Toop was under no illusions, any potential suspect with even half a brain was hardly going to sign his autograph in a log book. Toop almost smiled, although you could never underestimate the modern criminal halfwit, and well, there were always those who were just plain cocky. But Toop was looking for something else, clues, records of any witnesses who may have stayed in the bothy.

The last entry was two weeks ago, written in blue biro. He read it in his head, a few unintentional words escaping his lips in a whisper. *July 28th. Great day on the hill, topped off by a welcoming cup of tea in this fantastic wee bothy. Nothing like stealing a few hours of solitude from the wife! Thomas Burns.*

Toop couldn't help but feel a little disappointed. Nonetheless he made a note of his name and started leafing backwards. Neatly written accounts of day trips, scrawled messages left after a dram or two, a few attempted illustrations and sketches. Even a couple of poems and a rather personal insight from a man detailing his midlife crisis with subsequent comments included, some supportive, others, well others not so. Toop's finger hovered over a lengthy reply from a girl who had not so politely told the man that he was a cheating sleaze bag who deserved anything his wife threw at him.

Toop turned the page.

Thomas Burns' name appeared a few more times. Could be interesting, thought Toop, or just a local guy who enjoyed a few nights away from the wife. Toop sat down with the book open on his lap. The entries back dated by five years. He couldn't escape the question. What happened to the previous log book? The thought twisted the steel fist further into his abdomen. He hated that he couldn't remember what she had written that day, as with many of his memories, it had rotted away piece by piece.

Get it together.

Toop twisted his wrist round to reveal his watch. He was cutting it fine if he was going to get back in time for the post-mortem. He glanced back at the assortment of handwritten notes. Five years back wasn't going to be of much use to him anyway. He went to close the book.

As the pages folded in on each other, he saw it.

"Shit."

Chapter 18

Late 80s

Jon manoeuvred his body through the chaotic assortment of shelves, benches and tables. He fumbled with his jacket and satchel, using a hand to withhold them from the rows of lawless arrangements, with his bag pressed tight against his right leg. Without intention or conscious thought, he pictured an old, brown sedan, a bulbous, three box design. He watched it negotiating the narrow side streets of Paris, aimlessly navigating its way along roads that didn't lead anywhere.

Jon's eyes squinted to make up for the absence of natural light. The sole window made idle by the facade of disorganised books. Then he did a double take.

It couldn't be.

Jon arched his neck forward with an unnatural twist, avoiding the object by his head. He didn't know what it was, a cooking utensil perhaps. It didn't matter. Jon stepped, inched forward. It couldn't be, he thought, his view obstructed by a worn jacket. Wait. He paused. Surely it wasn't being used as a coat stand? Forgetting his surroundings, he reached out, the satchel dislodging and hitting against a three-string guitar, and grabbed the jacket. The wrinkled leather weighed heavy in his hand as he peeled it from the statue. Eyes wide, lips estranged, he knew that it couldn't be. But damn it was impressive.

The dusty, chesty laugh caught him by surprise. "I see you've found my Oviri. Quite something, isn't she?"

Embarrassed, Jon held his hand out to the old man. "My apologies sir, I'm Jonathan Swan." Jon noted the defiant strength in the man's grasp and the warmth of his cracked, weathered skin. He offered Tom's grandfather the jacket. "This must be yours." He could feel Tom's smile latched onto him. "It's not..."

"Real! Don't be soft lad!" The dry laughter had rooted itself deep in his lungs. "Just a bloody good fake." A coy, knowing smile mimicked

Tom's, making the old man seem surprisingly youthful. "Don't mention that to the customers mind. White lies are what keep this old bugger in business! Jimmy isn't above a couple of wee untruths, isn't that right, Tommy boy?"

"Well you nearly had me fooled," said Jon. "Can I?"

"Inspect away boy. My pleasure."

Jon placed a hand on the waist of the ceramic sculpture, the goddess of life and death. Beautiful, he thought. The glazed stoneware welcomed his fingertips as they brushed round her hips, caressing the snout of a blood-stained wolf cub nestled at her waist. Jon couldn't feel a single condemning crack. A second wolf was curled in submission at her feet. "Oviri, the savage," Jon's words diluted in the air beneath his chin, unheard. He had studied photos of Gauguin's work in class. He had even seen the original 1894 sculpture in the Musée d'Orsay during a school trip to Paris.

Incredible, thought Jon.

Tom stood next to him. "Gauguin," he said, "the self-confessed civilised savage."

The inclination in his voice was intended to exaggerate his point, rendering the question rhetorical.

"Aren't we all?" Jon didn't mean to voice it, the thought slipped out against his will.

Tom stared at him.

Feeling the physical expectancy created by his words made Jon feel faint. The anticipation leaked into the dark room and panic seeped into him, a white-hot poker direct to the chest. The familiar, deep seated internal impulse brought his hand to his neck and he applied pressure, willing his arteries to stop filling with blood.

Acknowledge, guide, replace, acknowledge.

Jon's mind wouldn't relent. The voices screamed at him. "You are a dirty, filthy savage, black and broken." Jon felt the sweat pooling in his palms and on his lower back. "A blackness, restrained and shackled by social compacts. Jon Swan the civilised savage, filthy and broken."

"Jon. Jonathan can you hear me?"

Jon's world, observed through two slits, was filled by Tom's face. The fine edges of his peripheral vision were coloured brown by Tom's hair, preventing any further details from reaching his eyes. Jon searched Tom's face with urgency, his eyelids flickering in response. But he couldn't find it. No panic, no fear.

No pity, thought Jon.

Tom's voice was reassuring but firm. "Come on, let's get you up." He didn't tell Jon to calm down, but equally, he didn't dismiss his fear.

"Tom, I'm... I'm really."

"I bloody well hope that sorry isn't going to be the next word out of your mouth."

Tom directed Jon to a small chest, releasing his weight and allowing the wooden surface to take the burden. Jon noticed that a space had been cleared on the floor where he must have collapsed. A small, tiered verge of antiques created a moat around the area in question.

Tom continued. "You can go with dizziness or thirsty."

Jon noticed a changing lightness in Tom's voice and he started to feel the return of colour to his face.

"Even tell me that you are fucking pleased with yourself for breaking that ugly china basket thing that you landed on."

Tom's grandfather entered the room. He held out a glass of water and a plate with toast and marmalade. Jon accepted it in silence.

"An interesting chap you've found yourself, Tom."

Tom's grandfather smiled and sat opposite Jon, resting a hand on each overhanging knee, elbows bent and chest bent forward. His voice was strong. Not a hint of condescension.

"Allow me tell you a story about my father. You see, while there was only one good thing that I learned from that idiotic drunkard, it was a pretty cracking piece of advice. Six I was when he sat me on his lap, whiskey weeping from his pores. He looked right at me. I can remember it damned clear, remember thinking the stink of his breath was going to burn me eyes out right there and then. Wild imagination of a six-year-old. I can also mind that, as he spoke, the saliva hanging on his lips wet my eyebrows. He was right serious too." Jimmy paused, sealing Tom and Jon's attention. "Then my father said to me, he said, boy, just you remember that an arrogant mind is the height of genius." Laughter flogged Jimmy's chest as he spoke, retribution for a lifetime of smoking. "Didn't have a bloody clue what it meant at the time! But it seems to me son, that brain of yours, is quite the son of a bitch!"

Jon managed a weak smile but his eyes were directed at his shoes.

Oil-less joints creaked as Jimmy shifted his unwilling body into a standing position, the stilted performance defined by a staggered sequence of stages, each slow and strenuous. Jon watched. The magnitude of effort demanded from the old man shook through his limbs and knees. Ageing, observed Jon, was neither kind nor graceful.

Life was neither kind nor graceful.

"Come back to visit kid," said Jimmy. "I've taken a liking to you." He gave a coy, youthful smile and staggered through the shop and out a door at the back.

"Panic attacks?" Tom was still sitting next to Jon.

"Yes."

"They hereditary?"

"Don't know," he replied. "Never told anybody that I get them."

"What? That's crazy," said Tom. "But even so, surely your Pops noticed something strange when you collapsed into your plate of mince and tatties?"

"You're the first person to see me have one."

"So you didn't get them as a kid?"

Jon looked at him, his eyes tilted upwards while his head remained bowed.

"Oh. Right." There was a kind acknowledgment in Tom's voice and for the first time he sounded affected, pitying. "But how does a kid hide that kind of thing?"

Jon blinked back tears. "Necessity I suppose. My father didn't condone weakness." The delivery of his statement rendered the conversation closed. Jon had already shared more with Tom than with anyone else in his entire life.

People don't want to hear about the abused kid, thought Jon. Not really.

The silence hung weightlessly between them. Time continued on regardless and Jon's breathing returned to normal.

"So if you're not a student," asked Jon, "what is it that you do with your time?"

"You're looking at it."

Instinctively, Jon's eyes surveyed the room, looking for it. Stupid really.

Tom laughed at his quizzical expression. "The shop, numbskull! I help my granddad out with the shop."

Jon reddened, "Of course." His cheeks tingled and he cast his gaze downwards to conceal his embarrassment.

As he dipped his eyes they caught on Tom's watch, noting the large solid gold case and the recognisable blemish free dial. It was the second time since walking into the little shop that Jon was taken by surprise. The contemporary shield motif was clearly visible, changed from the distinctive rose that had been used on earlier watches. Jon squinted, achieving a clearer inspection of the piece. The word "Tudor" was well-defined in clear black, not a trace of bleeding into the white background. It was a new Tudor Rolex Gold, Jon was sure of it.

But obviously it couldn't be.

A watch like that would cost Tom two months' wages at least. Like the statue, concluded Jon, it had to be a good fake. Impressive, he thought.

"Shall we get something to eat?" Tom asked as Jon lifted his head.

"Sounds good." Jon went to stand up. "Should I head through the back and thank your grandfather?"

"No." The reply was instant. "Sorry. I mean he's probably busy and he doesn't like to be disturbed." Tom placed a hand on Jon's back and guided him towards the front door. "Best get you some fresh air."

He guided Jon out, steering him away from the black door at the back. Jon twisted his head back round, taking a final glimpse of the back of the shop. He hadn't noticed it before, but it was there, a small sign on the door. He could just make out the white lettering.

Danger. Asbestos. Keep out.

Jon felt a sudden hint of concern followed by instant confusion. Tom's grandfather had walked in without any hesitation.

Strange.

But the thought vacated his mind the moment they hit fresh air and he didn't give it any further consideration.

The answer would find him later.

Chapter 19

Present Day

The images flickered from the television across the room, accompanied by the controlled, monotone voice of the reporter. The continuous flow of words crawled across the bottom of the screen, indicating the breaking news story. Lucy's eyes scanned the easy-to-read font with the square-looking s' and narrow t's.

Body found in the Scottish Highlands.

A familiar sensation debilitated Lucy's body as she stared at the screen. It took a minute for her to place it, the feeling of frailty. She was fourteen, reluctantly dragging her heels on a Duke of Edinburgh expedition, she couldn't remember the name of the school but the three days of solid walking and two freezing nights in a tent were embedded in her memory.

Lucy felt that same desperate brittleness as she stood in her living room. Her limbs were watery, anaemic almost, and she had a surreal feeling that her entire body, every sensation and reaction, was trapped inside her head. Her arms and legs felt like foreign objects, like disconnected lumps of flesh that didn't belong to her.

Exhausted, she fell onto the couch and gathered her eyebrows together in a pained frown. The TV, it was loud, why was the news reporter shouting?

"Can you turn it down a little?" she managed.

Cece's expression gave away her confusion, but she didn't question it. Lucy watched her raise the remote to the box and counted the yellow lines as they disappeared from the screen.

Lucy found that she couldn't concentrate on the solitary sounds of the words, they all merged together. She adjusted her position amongst the pillows, tucking one beneath her chin while strangling it with her arms. She listened to the monotone narration, questioning how the news broadcaster could remain so self-contained, not wavering from that same emotionless tone.

Someone's dead, doesn't he know someone's dead?

"Local police are investigating the circumstances surrounding an unnamed man's death in Torridon in the Scottish Highlands. The body was discovered late Saturday evening, however investigators believe that a few days had passed before his body was found."

The picture changed to show a white police building and the noncommittal voiceover continued.

"Gairloch police received a call from two walkers after they came across the body. Officers arrived on the scene shortly afterwards to find a loaded gun abandoned by the body. However, the cause of death has not been released."

The two girls watched in silence. Two anaesthetised expressions, indistinguishable in all but motivation, one born of shock, the other of apathy.

"Police are withholding the name of the man while his identity is investigated and relatives can be notified."

The image of the Torridon hills returned, flickering from the small screen in the middle of the room.

"Gairloch police force is asking anyone who might have information on the case to contact their local station."

The image of a small speaker, cancelled out by two diagonal lines, materialised as Cece hit mute. The symbol covered the weather map, blocking out a quarter of Wales.

"Shit," Cece placed an emphasis on the initial two letters, letting it hang in the air before she pushed herself up from the couch opposite Lucy. "Poor guy."

She bent over the coffee table and picked up the empty mugs, hooking a finger through the handles, leaving a distinctive, residual circle on the out-of-date TV guide. "Why can't there ever be anything happy on the news? You know, I read somewhere that the only reason that cats are happier than us is that they can't read newspapers. And do you know what, every time I watch the news I am inclined to believe it." Lucy's stagnation didn't register with her and Cece continued to speak through it, oblivious. "You don't find many cats shooting themselves."

Cece brushed against Lucy's legs as she passed her, her face distorted in a gentle frown. "I must have got the days wrong."

"Sorry?" Lucy said, blinking finally.

Lucy swivelled on the cushion and draped her arm over the couch in an attempt to feign normality. "What did you say?"

"My cooking programme, it must be tomorrow."

"No, what did you mean about the cats shooting themselves?"

"Oh right. I mean I've never heard of a depressed cat committing suicide. Have you?"

"Suicide. So you think the man on the news..." Her voice faded out as she turned her head back to the muted screen.

Cece lowered her knees and twisted her body to catch a glimpse of Lucy's face, the mugs hanging limply in her right hand. "Hun are you ok, you look pale, really pale actually." She moved to sit on the chair arm by Lucy. "You feeling alright?"

Lucy's voice was weak. "It's nothing. It's just..."

She felt Cece's hand on her arm and looked up at her as she said it.

"I was there."

Chapter 20

Toop was out of breath.

He strode straight up the hallway, followed by a baffled Sally, and flung open his office door. Grabbing for a pen, he wrote a single sentence on the whiteboard. His helmet was still clutched in his left hand and his shoes capped in mud. No hello.

"I think we've found our motive." He let the statement hang in the air as Sally's eyes drifted from his face over to the board.

Sally took it in slowly, a faint twitch at the right side of her mouth giving her away as she appreciated the moment, savouring the anticipation that needled at her colleague. Her eyes flickered as she scanned Toop's hurried handwriting. His hand had left damp smudges on the board, rain water or sweat she couldn't be sure. She read it twice, slower the second time, her lips forming the sounds of the words as she processed them.

Toop stood next to her. There was a chair inches from his left knee but the adrenaline pumping through him prevented him from sitting. As Sally's lips flirted with the passage he found it difficult to remain still. Toop's fingers tapped impatiently against his muddy thighs. It had been that way as long as he could remember, it wasn't so much nervousness as a desire to think out a riddle. When he was on a case part of his brain was constantly working it through, finding details and fixing them.

Toop watched her read it a third time. He knew she was baiting him.

"What are you thinking?" Sally posed the question.

Toop looked straight at her. "How long have you been involved in investigating murder cases?"

She thought about it. "Longer than I'd like to admit."

He nodded. "And would you agree that there is a thin line between murder and retributive justice."

"I'm not sure I understand what you're getting at, Fergus."

Toop ran his hands through his damp hair and down the back of his head, pausing them briefly around the nape of his neck.

"Almost every sixty seconds, every hour of the day, a murder is committed somewhere in the world. Without fail men shoot, stab, poison and pummel one another."

He paused, mulling over his words. Sally watched him.

"But what we need to ask is why? Is there some universal reason given for murder? No of course there isn't. Murder is an act born out of emotion, it is a situation that affects all sorts of criminals, the accidental drunkard, the situational opportunist, the idiot, the neurotic, the insane, even the professional. But murder does have a constant."

Toop stopped himself, a sudden injected pause in his dialogue as the apprehension hit him. He had a natural disinclination to share with people, a natural disinclination towards oral communication in general. Talking, sharing, wasn't his strong point. But his subconscious mind it seemed had made an exception for Sally. Toop let the realisation sit a second longer before he continued.

"Murder involves malice aforethought, an intention to do harm." He slowed his words. "And where there is intent there is also a motive."

"Ok..." Sally knew a question was coming.

"Find the motive. Find the murderer." He held Sally's gaze. "You have had a front seat to countless homicides. So let's say I asked you to give me one word to describe the most common motive for murder, what would it be? One word."

The silence was short-lived. In truth, she knew the answer before she said it.

"Revenge."

"Exactly."

Toop eased into the chair, the legs scrapping on the floor. He pointed at the whiteboard. "I give you the murderer, right there in block capitals."

Toop recited the quote from memory. "And he repents in thorns that sleeps in beds of roses."

"I've heard it before, I read it somewhere I think. It's a famous quote."

"Correct. But in this case it was written with one very important purpose."

Sally didn't respond. She let him continue.

"Punishment."

"Revenge?" she said.

94

"Yes, but it's more than that." He leant forward towards Sally, gesturing with his fingers. Sally handed him a piece of paper and Toop placed it flat on the table, his fingertips weighing heavy on the pen as he wrote it out again. "The poetic, almost romantic choice of words is testament to the inherent feelings of personal interest, but the offer of repentance implies that a real wrong has been done." He circled the word *thorns* twice. "Justice must be carried out."

Sally's forehead gathered in a frown. "I'm still not sure that I entirely understand what it means... Sleeps in beds of roses?"

"If you repent but you do not mean it, then you will never be forgiven."

"But even if this is what you think it is, why does the punishment have to be death? You said that the note offers the condemned an opportunity to repent?"

"It's quite simple really," he replied. "Men lie, yes?"

She nodded.

"So," he continued, "how can you tell if someone has truly repented and that they are not simply lying to be forgiven for their wrongdoings? Would you not lie, confess anything, true or not, so that your life would be spared?"

"I suppose."

"So, in what instance could you guarantee with reasonable belief that those words of repentance were true?"

The thought stole the air from her. She spoke slowly, more to herself than Toop. "If you know for certain that you are going to die. If you will die regardless of your answer."

He smiled, not a happy expression but a smile. "If you know that you are on your deathbed, why try to seek forgiveness unless you genuinely want it?"

Neither of them spoke.

Toop's mind moved on, working through the details while Sally's remained stagnated, immobilised by the image of bloodied thorns. She stared at Toop's resolute expression, unsettled by his theory.

"It's still not sitting well with me, Fergus," she said, "I don't know. Could it be that you are looking at it the wrong way? I mean, rather than it giving us a motive for murder couldn't the message be giving us a motive for suicide? We don't actually know who wrote it, you're just assuming that there was another person involved. But what if he wrote it himself?

What if it's a suicide note of sorts, evidence that he killed himself. Proof of his own personal repentance? Perhaps it's about his guilt rather than revenge."

Toop turned, oblivious to Sally's words, and continued with his train of thought.

"The last entry in the log book was written by a man named Thomas Burns," he said. "And it seems that he may be a local, looks like he went up there a lot. Do you recognise the name?"

The question jolted Sally out of her reflection. "Wait. You mean that someone has been there since the roses quote was written?" The life had returned to her cheeks. "Why didn't you lead with that rather important morsel of information?"

"What? No. Burn's entry was a couple of weeks ago."

"Ok, now I really am lost. When was the rose quote written?"

"It was dated July 2011."

Shock caught and stuttered in Sally's throat but her response was interrupted by a loud knock on the door. Bailey's hand appeared round the edge of the door, followed by his head. It hung suspended in mid-air, the only part of his body that was visible from inside the room.

"Is it ok to come in? That's me just back from the hotel."

"Yes, come in Bailey," said Toop.

Bailey walked in and closed the door behind him. He sauntered into the room, slowing his stride as he sensed the tension around Sally. He took a strategic step behind the desk, under the impression that whatever conversation he had interrupted, it wasn't over. He didn't talk, deciding to just wait.

"Excuse me." Sally fired at Toop. "Two thousand and bloody eleven? You got me riled up over a note written over six years ago."

"I said dated 2011," Toop replied, too calmly.

Bailey looked at his boss with wide eyes, aware that he was heading into dangerous territory.

"Dated? You want to explain yourself on that one?"

Toop eased himself up from the chair and slipped his hand into his pocket. The black material of his shorts bulged as he rummaged in his pocket. Sally folded her arms across her chest, waiting.

Toop revealed a folded piece of paper.

"That's not?" she said.

"The quote from the log book."

"You can't... You can't just rip pages out from..."

"She's right, sir." Toop glanced over and Bailey shut his mouth tight.

"Just take a look," said Toop, holding the paper out to Sally. The words were written in his own handwriting, scribbled over the faint contour lines of a dog-eared OS map. He had copied it exactly, a careful replica of the real thing, the scrawled characters seeping off the bottom of the paper.

She took it, without comment, and read it over. Her eyes fell on the writing but her focus was on Toop's voice.

"It first caught my eye because of where it was positioned. It's on the very bottom of the page with the last few words squished beneath the final line. If you look closely you can see that the p in 'sleeps' has lost the end of its tail, it disappears off the end of the paper as if the words have been made to fit into the available space." He paused. "But if the page was full why wouldn't you just turn over, or why not just start on a new page?" He pointed at Sally's hands. "Unless of course the next page was already filled and the next and the next. Five years' worth of comments had already been written."

"Or maybe they didn't want to be wasteful," replied Sally, not willing to roll over just yet.

Toop stared straight through her, ignoring the comment. Bailey's eyes widened at his boss' risky gesture.

"But it's the writing itself that provides the tell," said Toop, retrieving his phone from his pocket. He clicked on a photograph of the log book and offered it to Sally.

She examined the screen, continuing with her line of questioning. "Ok then, but why aren't the surrounded comments faded in comparison? It's biro, yes? Surely the newer ink would be clearer?"

"That's something that throws a lot of people," Toop stated.

Bailey's eyes stayed wide, daring a glance at Sally's expression.

"But today," continued Toop, "the composition of contemporary ink in biro pens has reduced the likelihood of fading, especially when the pages of a book are not exposed to light. Therefore, because sensitivity to light is unpredictable, fading cannot be relied upon to provide an indication of time." He held his finger in Sally's direction. "But, zoom in, look at the thickness of the ink."

Sally couldn't deny it. The quote in question was written in noticeably thicker ink.

"The ink is thicker than that of standard ball point pens, a consequence of newer erasable ink."

"But they had erasable ink when I was at university."

"True. Erasable ink pens have been around since the late 70s. But it took about thirty years for them to succeed in perfecting a modern ink that was completely erasable. 2008 to be precise."

"Impressive history lesson," Sally retorted. "But if it is completely erasable how do you know the writer rubbed anything out? Maybe it is an old, bog standard erasable pen and there were just no mistakes." She knew he would have an answer, but she couldn't help herself.

"That." Toop pointed at the end of quote. It didn't reach the end of the page. There was an obvious space. "Why leave a gap when you had such little space to begin with?"

The question circulated the room in silence. Sally answered. "Because someone signed it off, thought better of it and rubbed it out."

Toop smiled, "precisely."

Sally smiled back, turning to walk to the door. Her words followed her out. "I have a post-mortem to do and I'm already late." The door clicked shut.

Bailey watched Toop as he picked up his pen and started writing. Bailey feigned a cough, hinting at his presence and stepped forward.

"Sir, I thought you would want to know. I was speaking to the barman and he said that a man came into the hotel about ten days ago, he wanted to know where he could sell his car."

Toop nodded to show that he was listening and continued making notes.

"2012 Ford Focus, mint condition, nice car. The barman bought it."

Another nod. His pen manoeuvred its way across his pad, a quiet scratching.

"For £500."

Toop looked up.

The scratching stopped.

Chapter 21

Late 80s

Silence but for the lecturer's voice.

Over one hundred pubescent bodies hooked on the words of a single man with longish, unkempt hair. His cable knit sweater was worn under a light brown tweed blazer with the elbows reinforced. Jon liked this professor.

A quiet clicking was heard as the projector revealed the next image.

His voice bellowed from the stage, powerful and engaging. The eloquent, perfectly articulated words rose up with ease, reaching Jon in the final level of tiered seating. Jon had his note pad open with the module name penned as a title, Art, Society and Politics in Europe c. 1790 - 1900.

There was an empty seat to his left. And right.

"Tell me," the professor had no need of a microphone, "are you shocked and appalled, perhaps even scandalised?"

He spoke to the whole room, addressing each individual. Jon focused his eyes on the painting of a female farm worker standing in a field, her figure a little plump. The brush strokes were light, gentle.

"Who in this room feels personally violated and challenged by this painting?"

Jon took a moment to observe the confused expressions, a few tentative hands rose into the air, wavering in their decision.

"An oil on canvas by Pissarro, France circa late nineteenth century." Pens scratched furiously on paper. "It is a prominent example of an artist breaking away from the juste milieu and making a stand, in this case a political one."

He paused, allowing the hurried pens to catch up with him.

"Anarchism." The word was shouted and Jon underlined it twice in his notes. The flare in the man's voice endured. "At the time, Pissarro's 'Farmer' was at the height of controversy. He had chosen, with vicious intent, to paint a dignified peasant. The figure before you is not destitute or subhuman as many of Pissarro's more privileged patrons would have believed." He turned to address the image on the back wall. "I give you a peasant of importance." He threw his arms in the air. "The anarchy, the controversy, for an artist to show such a blatant, no, such a perverse disregard of preconceived ideologies."

Jon grinned. The man knew how to hold an audience.

"But alas." He offered a kind smile. "Such controversies do little to stimulate the apathetic, worldly youth of today." He offered a dramatic bow of defeat, teasing a laugh from his audience. He straightened his body, his hand left hanging until the final moment. "Let me have one more try."

The projector clicked.

"Gustave Courbet, France, 1866," he stated, the jesting now absent from his voice.

The room drowned in a sudden silence. Not a single pen connected with paper. Mouths agape.

"So, it would seem that you're not entirely apathetic yet." The corners of his mouth stirred.

Jon's heart raced and his crotch stirred, blood quickly redirected towards his groin as it filled with heat. Guilt, panic, disgust. He wanted to stand up and leave but he couldn't, everyone would see the shame protruding from beneath his jeans.

Excited mutterings eclipsed the silence and the lecturer stood to the side of the stage, arms crossed as he let the image speak for itself. Jon couldn't drag his eyes away from the image, a vivid close up of a woman's genitals. Jon listened to the shocked murmurings around him, taking note of the whispers of excitement as his heart palpitated beneath his ribcage.

The lecturer continued. "*L'Origine du Monde*, or, Origin of Life. Quite apt wouldn't you agree?" The room settled and he took three steps forward. "Here we have a rather more obvious example of an artist challenging societal expectations. Take a moment to look at the way in which he has framed the nude body, a task that I'm sure the young gentlemen among us won't object to."

This is hell. I'm in hell.

"Look at the way Courbet has deliberately framed the naked body, choosing to omit the head, arms and lower legs from the painting. By only revealing the genitals and abdomen he has emphasised the eroticism of the work."

Jon tried desperately to remain conscious but each breath was an effort. He lowered his gaze, focusing on the back of the chair in front of him. The fabric was worn from years of students resting their feet against it. He started counting, one, two, three. Then out of the corner of his eye he caught a glimpse of her. God no, please no, thought Jon. It was the girl from the library, the one in yellow. She couldn't see him like this.

He had to get out.

Gathering his satchel Jon rose from his seat and made his way along the aisle. Feet moved inwards and thighs tilted to the side as he hunched his body, curving his lower back and secured his bag round his lower torso.

Two more seats and he was free.

Isle. Door. Stairs. Fresh air.

Jon started running.

He ran in the direction of Jesse's flat. On this occasion he needed Jesse, someone to teach him how to be normal. All you have to do is go along with him, thought Jon.

Just copy.

***

"I'm really glad you decided to come tonight, mate." Jesse's voice was sure but tentative.

He took two beers from the fridge, handing one to Jon.

Jon sat on the sofa.

Jesse's student flat was small, a modest open plan living space equipped with the bare necessities. The standard design was functional, uncomplicated by interior sprucing or aesthetic embellishment, just the necessary seating, table space and an assortment of mismanaged shelves that were laden with books and folders. Unwashed dishes piled up next to the sink, the remnants of two days' worth of consumption. The fridge contained a pint of full milk, half a block of cheese and a partially opened packet of bacon. Numerous beers chilled in the door.

His flatmate was out at the gym.

Jon stared into the neck of his bottle. "Sorry about my outburst the other day."

Jesse made an arch with his right hand. "Bridge..." He slipped his left hand through it. "Water. Don't worry about it. I get that I can be a bit of an arsehole sometimes." He tilted his half-full bottle in Jon's direction. "That's why I need you around."

Jon surveyed the room. "Where's Timothy?"

"Late night gym session with some of the guys from the swim squad."

"You not joining?"

"Friday night. You've got to be kidding!" There it was, the Jesse Jenkins winning smile. "Uni has far greater things to offer than the grey walls of a dreary gym!"

He means no harm, thought Jon, it's all just good fun.

"Friday is skirt getting night!" Jesse necked the remaining dregs from his bottle. "What's your poison this evening Jonny, brunette or redhead?"

Jon bypassed the question. "Doesn't it bother you, sleeping around? Isn't it a bit..." he lowered his voice, "a bit disrespectful?"

"You really crack me up, you know that! Look, I've done pretty much all there is to do with a girl, including a few experimental things that I've no intention of doing again. Screwing isn't about respect." He let his body drop onto the sofa next to Jon. "I think that's the difference between you and me mate, you're all high and mighty and noble. You know what they say about the nice guy right?"

Jon looked away and nodded.

"Right, and last isn't where you belong Jonny boy. Come on, let's have a good time tonight, live a little."

Jon closed his eyes and took a deep breath before he spoke. "I've never been very good with girls. I don't think I even know how." Jon focused on the label of his beer, his fingers picking at the edges as he peeled the paper away front the glass. "How do you speak to a girl without, without... you know?"

Jesse's face softened and for a moment they were two young boys, sitting side by side with toy cars grasped in their little fat fingers. Jesse with his tomato red cheeks.

"Look buddy, when it comes down to it, girls are put on this earth to tease us. We are helpless victims to a parade of pert boobs and cleavage, all sent to test us. Our challenge is to resist, select and conquer."

"But, the resist part, how..."

Jesse manoeuvred onto his left hip, giving him access to his right jean pocket. "Here." He handed Jon an elastic rubber band. "This is yours for the evening."

Jon stared back at him blankly.

"Wear it round your wrist and when little Jonny decides to make an appearance just pull the band and let the rubber snap against your skin. The sharp nips of pain will keep him at bay."

Jon took it and slipped it over his hand.

"Right." Jesse stood up. "We've a party to get to."

Chapter 22

Present Day

"What do you mean you were there?" Cece asked.

Lucy looked troubled by the question, her face caught in an expression somewhere between apprehension and guilt. She filled her lungs, drinking the air as it dripped into her.

"Lucy?" Cece repeated. "Where is there? Do you know something about the guy who died?" Her voice became less calm.

You can do this, Lucy thought, steady voice.

"I was in Torridon."

"When?"

"Then." Lucy's eyes flickered towards the TV. "When it happened."

"I don't understand. You saw him die?"

"No, no I didn't see anyone die." True, thought Lucy.

"Then what?"

"I was on holiday in Torridon, just before you moved in."

"So? I'm sure loads of people happen to be visiting Glasgow when a body is found. It's not unheard of, just unfortunate timing, wrong time, wrong place. It's not something that you should beat yourself up about..."

"You don't understand." Lucy played with her hands, knotting her fingers together. "Torridon is a tiny village. There are only a few hundred people living there, there's one hotel, one pub and the Youth Hostel where I stayed."

Lucy's face was the sole focus of Cece's gaze. "What are you saying Lucy?"

"I probably met him."

You mean you did meet him, didn't you Lucy? She pictured his eyes as clear as a photograph.

"Maybe I bumped into him in the pub, or the hotel restaurant." Calm and steady, just as you practiced it, thought Lucy.

"But you don't know for sure?" Cece sounded concerned. "I mean the police haven't released a picture, so you can't be certain. Do you remember seeing anything that might be of use to the police?"

"No." Lie, thought Lucy.

"Why were you visiting such a tiny village in the first place?" asked Cece.

"I needed to get away from things." Her eyes damped at the edges, her tears were genuine. "My flatmate and I had a falling out. It got a bit, well a lot messy and she moved out." Not a lie. "I needed to be alone."

Cece ran her hand down Lucy's arm. "I'm sorry." She glanced back at her room. "Is that who you were living with before I moved in?"

Lucy just nodded. "Yeah, she left pretty quickly afterwards."

"Look," said Cece, taking control with her confident tone. "You don't need to worry yourself with anything at the moment. We can keep an eye on the news and if the police release a photograph, well, then we will cross that bridge when we come to it. And Lucy..." she sat next to her, knees touching, "...chances are that it was just some poor guy who had lost his want to live. And any unfortunate, lost soul who drives to the hills with no intention of coming back is unlikely to stop for a drink at the pub. So, you probably didn't meet him. It will be ok." She looked up at the face of the clock. "Let me make us something to eat, maybe a full stomach will make you feel better."

Cece patted Lucy on the thigh, letting her hand linger for a few seconds, and stood up.

"Just you sit," she said, motioning to the pillows on the sofa.

Lucy eased into the couch. She was about to say something then decided better of it, choosing to glance back at her entangled fingers. It taken a lot out of her. New beginnings were draining, thought Lucy. The past just kept trying to claw its way to the surface.

Is this what it will be like from now on, a constant battle to stay afloat, trying to stay one step ahead of the truth?

Her philosophy teacher's voice settled her once more.

A fleeting pinprick in history.

Lucy's attention shifted and she caught sight of Cece hovering by the bookshelf in the hallway. She watched as her flatmate flicked through the pile of mail that had come through the letter box that morning. Lucy had seen it but she hadn't had the time to read it. Cece looked up and smiled back at Lucy, her hand disappearing into her pocket, unnoticed.

"This reminds me," Cece shouted from the hall, "I need to change my address with the bank." Then she disappeared into the kitchen, reappearing a few moments later.

"No milk. I'll pop out and get some. Won't be long."

The door shut and Lucy snuggled deeper into the pillow.

***

Cece had the phone pressed to her ear as she descended the first flight of stairs, the dialling tone ringing into her ear. She quickened her step, the balls of her feet tapping on the stone as she passed the second floor then the first.

Her heart was pounding by the time she reached the ground floor. She took a moment to compose herself and to steady her breathing, bending over with her left hand rested on her knee.

The postcard was clasped between her fingers.

Another few seconds and the dialling tone came to an abrupt end, interrupted by the sound of a deep voice.

Cece was still catching her breath when she started to speak.

"It's me." Her heartbeat slowed. "I think you're right."

She pushed the door open with her free hand, requiring some effort to sway the heavy fire door into motion, and stepped out onto the pavement.

"Yes," she answered, "I'm outside the flat now."

"She's upstairs."

"I don't know. I'm working on it. It's only been a couple of days, although, if the last hour is anything to go by, secrets are not her strong point. If she's hiding something I'll find out."

The man on the line interrupted, asking questions.

"Something to do with a suicide in Torridon," replied Cece, "but that's not why I called. I found something."

Cece craned her neck upwards, checking for any sign of Lucy at the window. It was empty.

"A postcard arrived at the flat this morning with a picture of a beach." She turned the card over in her hand. "It doesn't say which beach." Cece lowered her voice to a whisper and pushed the phone closer to her mouth. "But it's from him."

Cece listened to the silence on the other end of the line and pictured him thinking.

106

"Yes," she said, "I'm sure. It has to be him, right?" The question was rhetorical. "It means that your suspicions were right, either Lucy knows something or her flatmate did."

Cece listened, tapping the insides of her feet together as she stood on the curb.

"That could be more difficult," she answered. "They had an argument and she moved out. I'm not sure if they're talking anymore."

She listened.

"I'll see what I can find out. Speak soon."

Cece ended the call and headed back up the stairs, turning around before she reached the first floor.

"Milk," she mouthed to herself.

***

Lucy was unmoved, curled up on the same spot on the couch.

She swivelled round as Cece walked in. "Thanks," she said, noticing the plastic milk carton in Cece's left hand.

"No problem."

Cece headed into the kitchen. "Any thoughts on what you would like to eat?" Her voice carried from the other room, shortly followed by her head.

"I'm not particularly hungry. I don't mind, whatever you fancy."

"Beans on toast it is then," Cece smiled. "Oh, and here's the mail. All for you I imagine." Cece walked further into the room and leaned over the back of the couch. Her arm stretched outwards with one foot raised slightly off the ground as she dropped the letters on Lucy's lap.

The postcard sat on top.

Cece watched Lucy as her eyes scanned over the white sand beach and she turned the card over in her fingers. Lucy glanced at it and placed it at the back of the pile. Her expression didn't change.

Cece frowned and walked back into the kitchen, the words on the postcard playing over in her head.

My Rose Jaune, I'm so sorry. I know that means nothing but my apology comes without an excuse and I do not expect, or deserve, to be forgiven. Please know that the guilt is mine alone. You are innocent. You are free.

Signed Jonathan Swan.

"Who's Rose?" Cece whispered to herself. "What did you do Jon?"

Chapter 23

Toop looked at his watch, almost five. Sally would be at least another two hours, more likely three.

He started tidying his desk and slid his notes into his rucksack. The motion of his arm stirred the air and Toop caught a whiff of himself. He looked down at his shorts. The mud had dried a pale sandy colour.

Shower.

"Bailey," Toop said, "you can head home."

"Sorry sir?"

"You did a great job today. At the hotel."

Come on, communicate with the lad.

"Thanks for your help," he added, "I'm going to head over there now."

Bailey eyed his boss, raising an eyebrow.

Toop looked up from his desk and smiled, he couldn't help it. "Yes, I plan to shower first. But you should head home, get some food and a good rest. Sally, Dr Gillespie, will have some results by the morning."

"Sure you don't want me to come? I could butter up the locals for you."

"Thanks but I'd rather go alone, it'll just be a quick visit. Not worth you driving out."

It was a forty-five-minute drive out to Torridon from Gairloch police station on an unlit country road.

"And I'll be heading back to my place in Badachro." Toop liked being out of Gairloch, even if it was only by a few miles, less people. Almost none in fact. The remote hamlet made Torridon seem big.

"I don't understand why you choose tae live out there, in the backend of nowhere. Why haven't you got a place in town? I know Gairloch isn't exactly a metropolis but there's more happening than in that wee fishing hamlet of yours!" Toop's lack of response didn't faze him. "London to Badachro, that's got to be a bloody big shock to the system."

Bailey's face caught in a look of contemplation as he pictured the change, his hands drawn to the ledges above his hips.

"I like the old harbour. It's quiet," said Toop.

"Each to his own." Bailey turned to leave. "You should grab a beer or two at the hotel, the Wildcat makes a good pint." His voice carried through the corridor as his footsteps faded. "Say hi to Jimmy for me."

Jimmy?

***

Twenty minutes later Toop was in the shower at home, grit circling the drain. The six-mile cycle back to Badachro had helped to clear his head. He hadn't passed a single car on the road, both expected and fortunate. No lights meant a £30 fine, a penalty which he should have administered himself.

Perks of the job, thought Toop, had to be at least one.

Quick bite of toast and marmite and he was out the door. Car this time.

Toop stood in front of the Torridon Hotel, a former shooting lodge for the privileged one percent. The timeless structure rose up in front of him, eloquent turrets and stone towers. Toop gave the building the once over, up down, side to side, a natural observation embedded with years of police training. All the twirls and trimmings of a proper Scottish castle, thought Toop. The fifty-eight-acre estate was wedged in between the shores of Loch Torridon and the Torridon mountains.

The bar was located in the Inn; a more modest building situated about a hundred metres from the hotel. Toop noted the solid block partitions and archways. Most likely it had been the old stable block. He pushed open the heavy door, his face warmed by the heat from the fire.

Inside it was cosy. Homely.

Toop stood in the doorway of the pub and looked around the dimly lit room. The act was not premeditated by police training but something that was done by most tourists who crossed the threshold. He was greeted by a quaint, old-fashioned interior, reminiscent of a Jane Austen set or a princely hunting cabin. Open fire in the middle, encircled by leather thrones and small, wooden tables. The bar was situated along the back wall, a long, mahogany panelled bench that curved with the natural shape of the walls. Two of the oak bar stools were occupied, making up half of the total occupancy of the bar.

Toop walked over and took a seat. A fair haired, Scandinavian-looking boy welcomed him from the other side of the bar. He couldn't be more than twenty, thought Toop. The lad was unusually tall and he still had the thin, gangly frame gifted by adolescence. He held a white towel, using it to clean a wine glass.

"Evening Officer, what can I get for you?" He reached up and hung the blemish-free glass from the rack above his head. His arm paused as he withdrew it, noting the obvious question on Toop's face.

"It's a small place, everybody is knowing who everybody is." He smiled with the enthusiasm of youth. "It took me some time the getting used to it. I am on my gap year from Stockholm. My name Stefan." He offered his hand across the bar. Toop shook it. A good, firm grip, thought Toop, warming to the lad.

"I'm actually looking to speak to..."

"You want to speak to Jimmy, the head barman." Another smile. "Like I said, it is a small place and Boyd Bailey, he is very much enjoying talking. I'll go and get Jimmy. He was just eating his dinner."

Toop was waiting at the bar, drumming his fingers on the bench, when she spoke.

"The famous police officer, come all the way from London." The voice came from the girl three stools to his right. "I'm putting my money on business rather than pleasure."

The girl was about twenty-five, maybe a little older, with long red hair that escaped from beneath a striped bobble hat. She wore tight, faded blue jeans, ripped at one knee, and a green t-shirt with an owl stencilled on the front. The letters DC were printed on the side on her trainers.

"I'm Eve." Her tone was confident.

"Fergus."

"I know," she said, quite nonchalant. "It's not every day that we get a cop venturing up from the big city. You do something wrong to get sent up here?"

Her blunt, direct manner caught Toop off guard but it felt familiar somehow. He stared at her, unsure of how to respond, his lower lip hanging low in the anticipation of conversation.

The girl smiled. "Not much of a talker then."

Eve ran her fingers up and down her glass leaving streaks in the condensation. She was about five eight and in good shape, athletic, not an ounce of extra weight.

"So what brings you to the pub, I'm assuming it's not the alcohol." She paused, frowning as she looked at him. "Do you ever drink? Or is that against your rules?" Eve took a sip of her own beer, her eyes fixed on the row of whiskey bottles behind the bar. "It's the body they found, isn't it? You're out doing the door to door thing, questioning and querying."

She turned towards him.

"Any luck with that?"

Toop felt lost for words. But it felt different. It wasn't a conscious decision to avoiding talking.

"Yes," he replied. "To your first question, I do drink. The second, I can't answer."

She smiled. "Not at liberty to talk about it, fair enough, but you can't blame a girl for trying. Not much excitement around here, dead body kind of tops it for the year."

"So, you're a local?"

"Recently, longer than you anyway, I moved up before Easter."

"Up?"

"Glasgow."

Eve readjusted her position on the bar stool, the padding not quite sufficient for her bony figure. As she moved Toop caught a glimpse of a tattoo, part concealed by red underwear. He couldn't make out what it was but the brief flash of skin stole his attention. Eve caught him looking but she didn't say anything.

"So what brought you this far north?" he asked.

"The mountains," she said matter-of-factly. "Torridon has some of the best mountain biking trails in the world." Eve smiled at him, more with her eyes. "But I'm sure you know that." She took another sip. "So I converted my van. Bed, bike storage, small cooker and headed up this way. I've been parked out at Golden Sands caravan park ever since. Paul lets me use the showers and occasionally I stay a couple of nights in the youth hostel when I'm in need of a proper bed."

Toop sat and listened to her. "Do you work?" he asked.

"No, I just steal things," she teased, "maybe you should arrest me, officer."

"I didn't mean..."

"Relax. I saved up enough to go travelling on the cheap for a year." She turned her beer glass so that Toop could see the distinct red T for Tennent's. "Meaning drinking cheap lager at a cheap price. Not too bad if you don't dwell on the taste."

Toop stared at the glass.

He had interviewed countless people over the years, both liars and truth tellers. Liars had their tells, the amateurs were like open books but the old timers, more experienced in the art of deception, they took a little more work. The interview process was not dissimilar to poker, the same nervous, inconsistent eye contact and unnatural breathing patterns. Toop couldn't count cards, but when it came to reading people he was spot on. Liars were easy. Hands clasped together, trapped between closed thighs, arms crossed in front of the torso, those were the first tells.

Eve didn't do any of those things.

But there was something. Something that had Toop convinced, almost convinced, that Eve was lying to him. To what extent he couldn't be sure.

You're being paranoid.

Then it hit him. The familiar feeling, he knew what it was. Eve reminded him of her.

"You ok?" asked Eve. "You're kind of staring and not in a fun flirtatious manner, more psycho stalker."

Toop blinked and averted his gaze. "Sorry. You just remind me of someone."

"Anyone special?"

Eve didn't get a response.

The door at the end of the bar swung open and Jimmy walked in, a sizeable beer gut followed by an even more sizeable beard.

"Evening, officer," he bellowed. "I hear you've come to talk to me about my car." His huge hands landed on the bar in front of Toop, ginger hairs decorating his weathered knuckles. "I hope you've no plans to take it away. I paid for that vehicle fair and square. It may have been pennies but money's money!"

"You have no need to worry," said Toop, "you can keep the car."

"Grand. In that case, how can I help?"

"I wanted to ask you a couple of questions about the man who sold you the car and to have a look at the vehicle."

"I can see no problem with that."

"Do you have an office where we can talk?" asked Toop.

113

Jimmy gestured past the bar. "Follow me."

Toop gathered his things and stood up. He turned to his right but Eve's seat was already empty. He hadn't even noticed her leave. That wasn't like him. Her glass was left half full, pinning a piece of paper to the bar. He lifted it up.

A phone number and a short message.

Let me know if you want to break the rules.

Was she?

Surely not, thought Toop, she was too young. Far too young for him. He read it over once more and slipped the card into his pocket.

"This way, officer." Toop followed Jimmy to his office.

Eve who? thought Toop, realising that he hadn't asked her second name.

Chapter 24

Late 80s

All things considered, thought Jon, it had been a relatively successful evening. He allowed himself a smile as he recalled the night's events.

Jesse's sofa offered a welcome bed, improved by the arrangement of blankets and a pillow that Jon had taken from Jesse's room. Jesse wouldn't be doing much sleeping.

Jon had returned around 2am, alone, and Jesse stumbled through the front door an hour later, cursing when he tripped over a marooned sports bag. Not alone. The high-pitched giggling ricocheted around the walls of the small flat, falling over Jon's makeshift bed like beads of shrapnel, piercing straight through his skull. For twenty minutes the creaking of Jesse's bed kept Jon awake. He pictured what his friend was doing, feeling both excited and repulsed as he eventually found sleep.

Jon stretched and rose from the sofa before tiptoeing through to the kitchen. He had no desire to awaken the high-pitched creature currently passed out in Jesse's bed. Staring at the kettle, it occurred to him that the noise could be problematic. Worth the risk, he thought, pulling a mug from the cupboard. He needed coffee. He switched the kettle on and smiled to himself.

He was the proud, successful procurer of a girl's address.

Jon closed his eyes, he could still smell her.

She had been looking in his direction when Jon sauntered through the door. He entered the party, instantly dowsed by the palpable dew of oestrogen and testosterone, his eyes taking a few moments to adjust to the dull lighting. She was the first person that he saw, the girl from the library. She stood at the entrance to the living-room talking to a girl with pigtails. Unlike most girls she did not look away when he caught her eye, she smiled back at him through the throng of hormone-fuelled bodies, her expression playful, flirtatious even. Jon focused on her face, struck by how delicate it was, sculpted like a china doll and painted with flecks of untamed freckles. Then she vanished, engulfed in a group of girls. Jon continued to stare at the vacant space long after she had gone. She had smiled at him, him, Jon. His eyes found her again. There was no yellow this time, she wore denim shorts and a pink, cropped top. Jon's heart raced, calmed by the sharp sting of elastic on skin.

Jon's skin tingled as he recalled the surreal feeling that she had aroused in him, a heightened awareness of the space occupied by their bodies. Her body seemed to radiate at a higher temperature than her surroundings, a glowing white light in a room of darkness. Jon had studied her face, watching as she fabricated scenarios, ensuring that their bodies were brought into close proximity. Not once did he touch her, content just talking. More than content, relieved. Hours were spent in conversation, the type of conversation that excluded the rest of the world. Art was the focal point and art he could talk about. And, as it turned out, she was taking two of the same modules as him.

The kettle boiled, emitting telling streams of steam. Jesse's door remained closed, no indication of movement. Jon smiled and slipped the piece of paper from his pocket for the umpteenth time, a ritual that confirmed its authenticity. The skin around his wrist was red raw from the elastic band. He didn't care. Jon was grateful for the biting pain.

He read the note.

Jenny Pingleton. Room 209. Queen Margaret Halls. Bellshaugh Ct.

He ran his thumb over the first two words, worth more to him than gold. The girl in yellow had a name and she had given it to him.

The first twitterings escaped through the seams of Jesse's door. He could hear Jesse groaning, picturing his friend stretching his arms towards the ceiling, stalling as he tried to recall the name of the girl next to him. Jean, if Jon remembered correctly. Maybe he should leave Jesse a note, he thought. The notion hung in his head for a brief moment before it sieved away like sand.

Jon threw back a long gulp of coffee and slung his bag over his shoulder, still in the previous day's clothes. He had just had an idea for the perfect first date.

He had to find Tom.

The door shut behind him, the couch abandoned in disarray. He hadn't bothered to fold the blankets. His mind was on more important things.

***

"I'm looking for Tom."

Jon stopped, embarrassed. It occurred to him that he didn't know Tom's surname. It had never come up in conversation, it hadn't seemed necessary.

He started to panic. There had to be tens of Toms working at the gallery.

The man at the front desk stared back at him, his expression blank, withholding any information. His taut lips proving themselves to be impenetrable.

Jon leaned against the desk and rapped his fingers on the wooden surface.

"His Dad works here," he said nervously, unsure of how to proceed, not knowing what department his Dad worked in or whether he would be in that day.

"My height," Jon held his hand out in demonstration. "Dark hair, skinny, quite pale."

The man at reception rubbed the back of his hand across his mouth and looked up at Jon through bored eyes.

"Jon!" Tom's voice echoed through the gallery and the relief resonated through Jon's shoulders, easing down his back.

Tom greeted his friend with an enthusiastic thump on the arm. "What brings you to these hallowed halls?" he smiled, "me or Salvador?" He feigned jealousy as he spoke the second name.

Jon felt the man at the front desk watching him as Tom guided them towards the stairs. "Em, neither actually. Well, not exactly. I was kind of hoping that you could introduce me to your Dad."

Tom made no attempt to hide the surprise in his expression. "My Dad? What the bloody hell do you want with that old codger?"

Jon's cheeks flushed. "I was wondering, hoping that he could help me with an idea I had. For a date." His voice quickened, rushing on from the last word. "With him working at the gallery and all."

"A girl," beamed Tom. His smile grew. "I'm sure he'll jump at the chance, well not literally but my old man's quite the romantic." Tom increased his pace, "Come on, I think he's up in the Study Centre, top floor." A boyish spark crossed his eyes, "He's trying his hand at technology."

117

"Tom?" Jon asked as they ran up the stairs, managing two at a time. "What's your surname?"

"McGraw. Thomas McGraw." He turned to look at him. "Somewhat unfortunate wouldn't you agree?"

Thomas McGraw, the name rang a bell. McGraw, McGraw, Jon turned the word round in his head. Thomas McGraw was one of the most wanted men in Glasgow, in the country. Drugs, violence, thought Jon, and wasn't there a murder accusation?

Tom laughed at the concern etched between Jon's brows. "Don't worry, I'm a little too young to have amassed such an impressive rap sheet! And don't worry he's not a third cousin or anything. It just one of life's cruel little jokes, completely ruined my chances of being Prime Minster, well that and the fact that I don't have a single qualification!"

Jon smiled. Tom's irrepressible gusto made him feel lighter somehow. Jon liked it.

Tom inched the door ajar.

The hunched form of a cripple came into view preceded by a medley of colourful vocabulary, choice obscenities that poured from the man's lips. His unstable frame crouched in front of a computer screen, leaving spittle on the monitor as he cursed at it. Jon noted how his distorted, unnatural posture added a certain mileage to his natural age.

"He's not entirely taken with the wonders of technology," Tom whispered as they walked through the door.

"Having fun Pops?"

"Bloody thing's no good." He swore, without averting his eyes. "As if I give a rat's arse about computer-generated imagery." He continued squinting at the screen, his nose grazing the glass. Jon wondered if he was using it to lean upon. "Virtual reality they're calling it. Virtual bollocks I say. Exquisite pieces of art rehashed and displayed on one of these fancy computers. It's a god damn violation." He spat the words. "I'm Assistant Curator, not a fucking..." The screen froze. "Fuck, fuck, fuck. Tom give us a hand and throw this bloody thing out the window will you?" He turned to look at the boys for the first time, showing no sign of embarrassment when he caught Jon gawking at him.

Tom chuckled, "How did you get roped up in this anyhow Pops?"

"Something to do with enhancing public experience, the big suits want me to pick a selection of pieces for their new virtual reality program.

Computers in art galleries, complete bollocks I tell you." He hung his head and shook it between his hands. "Bloody nonsense."

Tom let the moment pass and turned to Jon. "Pops I'd like you to meet Jon."

Jon held out his hand, regretting it immediately. He felt queasy with guilt as he watched the man struggle out of his chair and shuffle across the floor to meet his hand. The room held in silence but for the scraping of his walking stick. Jon held his hand out for an eternity, convinced that stepping forward would further wound the man's pride.

"Mr McGraw."

Jon shook his hand, acknowledging the strength in his grip and the unmistakable youth buried in the man's confident stare.

"My Tom tells me that you're quite the painter."

Jon flashed a look at his friend, confused. He'd never shown Tom any of his work.

Tom smirked, slipped his lower lip beneath his front teeth, and raised his hands in mock surrender. "You got me," he exhaled. "Those visits that you made to the gallery, well, I may have been a tad nosier than I originally let on." He lowered his arms, placed one hand in his pocket and used the other to point at Jon. "That first time that I saw you, must be a good few months ago now, you had a painting tucked under your arm. Initially, I thought that maybe it was one that you'd bought, like a replica from the gift shop or something. But the next time you turned up with one I noticed the rather shoddy homemade canvas frame and I realised that you must have painted them yourself." Tom's face broke in a smile and he threw an arm around Jon's shoulders. "I mean Jesus Jon! I thought that I was technically up there, that I could produce a pretty painting when I wanted to. But shit man, you've got something else. I can't quite quantify it but whatever it is that those great artists have, you've come pretty damned close."

Jon turned red at the comment and stooped to look down at his feet, but the slight raise of his mouth betrayed how much it delighted him.

"I..." he stuttered. "Thank you."

Tom laughed and gave him a friendly nudge. "Well, are you going to ask my Dad or not?"

Mr McGraw turned and spoke directly to Jon. "So young man, how is it that I may help you?"

Jon felt Tom nudge his arm a second time. "Go on Romeo!"

***

Jon left Tom and his father to discuss the intricacies of virtual reality. He smiled, noting the changing tones of their voices as the door swung behind him.

He had a date planned, a private night time gallery viewing, and in that moment Jonathan Swan allowed himself to feel happy.

Now she just had to say yes, thought Jon, contemplating when he should ask her. Was tomorrow too soon, too desperate? Lost in his own world Jon walked straight past the exit and sauntered into the next room on his right.

All thoughts of Jenny Pingleton dissipated in an instant.

Jon froze.

The blood pooled inches from his toes. He couldn't not look at it. The body was rigid, stained with purple-red blotches.

Jon threw up.

Chapter 25

Lucy awoke to the sound of Cece in the kitchen.

She cast her eyes around her bedroom. It was small and uncluttered. Her few belongings were neatly placed on shelves and tucked away in drawers. She had not been left with many possessions after the clear out, her wardrobe was the only item left unaltered. Their fashion tastes had been different. Diametrically opposed, thought Lucy, Alex not having any. She gathered her eyebrows in a frown, regretting thinking her name.

Light evaded the curtains. What time was it, thought Lucy, feeling in no way replenished. She looked at her watch, as long as she could remember she had worn one in bed, frightened little girls woke often in the night and time was a comforting companion in the darkness. Lucy counted on her fingers, another childish habit. A full twelve hours of sleep.

She pulled the covers back in a seamless motion, allowing her bare legs to drop to the floor. Soft carpet met the soles of her feet and Lucy afforded herself a reflexive sigh, a brief moment of normality. It was a routine moment at the start of a routine day. Except that it wasn't, she thought, no day would be normal again. The thought followed her to the window and she pressed her face against the cool glass. The sky was a dreary grey, a haze of clouds penetrated by high tenement buildings. A normal day in Glasgow at least, she contemplated, aware of the cool beads of condensation contacting with her flushed skin.

It didn't seem real.

Lucy couldn't believe that he was dead. The stranger, whom she had met little less than a fortnight ago, was lying lifeless on a metal tray somewhere. Lucy pictured men in white coats prodding and poking at his cold body. The unconscious thought made little sense. But then, neither did any of it, concluded Lucy.

Half an hour passed. Lucy had showered quickly, dressed and was standing in front of the mirror. She wore jeans and a grey, loose fitting jumper layered over a check shirt, the untucked hem visible. Lucy's bent elbows were raised above her head as she back-combed her unwashed hair. She ran her fingers through the thick tousled strands of red, twisting sections before securing her hair in a messy ponytail, the crimson waves falling half way down her back.

Cece had gone out so Lucy went straight to the kitchen. She put a piece of bread in the toaster and clicked the kettle on. As she waited she walked into the living room and picked up the stack of letters.

She only had one in mind.

Lucy had recognised the beach at once. She held the card in her fingers, her thumb following the stretch of red-hued sand to the edge of the postcard. Lucy knew that she wouldn't cry anymore, she was empty. She just stared at the photograph. It was the last place that she had seen Alex. Or, more accurately, it was the last time before their lives had changed forever. Red Point beach, the calm before the storm.

She frowned as she looked at the circular postage stamp. It was dated over two weeks ago.

Impossible.

***

Cece slipped into the driver's seat and slotted the keys into the ignition. She knew exactly where she was going. She started the engine, threw the car into gear and pulled out into heavy traffic. West End traffic at the weekend was never fun.

Twenty minutes later and the flow of cars had started to clear and she was headed northwest, a six-mile drive from the city centre. Cece had spent half of her childhood in Bearsden, the middle-class suburb was a home from home. As a young teenager, she had decided that her Dad's house in Lennoxton was equivalent to living in the sticks, the ten miles to the city felt like a lifetime. Cece smiled, recalling her many hormone-fuelled tantrums. Her poor Dad, it couldn't have been easy bringing up a teenage girl on his own. Her time in Bearsden with her uncle must have offered a welcome respite. The car revved, protesting the change into fifth gear. Well, her honorary uncle. What teenage girl wouldn't want to live in Bearsden, the seventh wealthiest area of Britain, a fact that Cece reiterated to her defenceless father countless time over breakfast. "Why can't we leave this desolate wilderness and move to somewhere more affluent, with things like shops and civilisation." Her words distorted as she shovelled down toast and marmalade. "Bearsden is like totally nice, it's one of the wealthiest places in the country you know."

Cece grinned to herself as she checked the side mirror and changed lanes. You were quite the little madam weren't you, she thought.

She slowed her speed.

Bearsden was as pleasant as always, quaint cafes offering a bustling trade and old ladies walking their dogs along the pavement, far from the dangerous streets of the inner city. Cece took three turns and parked the car in front of the house. She stepped out and walked round to the boot, popped the lock and pulled out a small bag packed with essentials. A screwdriver, with a slotted head, two plastic cards, a selection of rubber bands, a wire hanger and a hammer, just in case. Cece wasn't planning on using the last item. She didn't want to have to explain anything to the police.

The car locked automatically, Cece heard the beep as she approached the door. The bag swung against her leg.

"Ouch!"

Exposed wire from the hanger nipped her thigh through her jeans. She wedged the bag into her side with her arm, preventing it from swinging. Her Dad may have been inept when it came to girl problems and ballet lessons, and his parental insights were less than conventional, but Cece thanked him for it as she rang the doorbell.

The old woman was short and frail, her height reduced by two inches over the last ten years.

"Circe honey!" Her eyes filled with youth as she held out her arms. "Come in pet, come in. I'll pop the kettle on." She gestured Cece in with one hand, the other clutching the top of her walking stick. Cece looked at the lady, convinced that Mrs Irvine had aged in the last month. The wrinkles clustered around her eyes were deeper and she looked unsteady on her feet. Cece kissed her on the cheek. Behind that brittle body, she thought, was a feisty lady with the heart of a lion.

"I'm afraid I can't stay, Mrs Irvine, I need to pop in next door."

The woman's expression changed, showing concern. "In truth, I was beginning to worry hen. I haven't seen him at all this month. Not like him to just up and leave, didn't even give me his key." She glanced down at her feet, thinking. "He always leaves me his key. Those Chinese evergreens of his need watering."

Cece jumped on the lady's words. "That's why I'm here, the plants. He phoned me and asked me to drop by and water them. He said that he had been in a rush and forgot to see you before he left?"

"Left?"

Cece lowered her voice and delivered her words carefully, pausing often. "I'm not meant to say." She smiled gently at the elderly lady. "But I'm sure he won't mind me telling you." She placed a deliberate emphasis on the last word. "There's been death in the family. Tragic." She shook her head. "He had to take off at a moment's notice." Cece let the sadness hang in her eyes.

Mrs Irvine raised her hand to her mouth. "My gosh. I had no idea, how awful."

Cece offered a consoling hug. "You weren't to know."

The two women stood on the doorstep in silence until Cece chose the appropriate moment to interject. "I just wanted to let you know, so that you wouldn't be alarmed, but I am going to have to break in next door. I don't have my keys either. And, well, the plants..."

"Of course dear, of course."

Cece felt bad lying to the old lady but she didn't want the police turning up, one foot in the door of her uncle's house and the cops would have a field day. Breaking and entering, even with Mrs Irvine's blessing, would still be risky. Any nosy passer-by could blow the whistle on her. But Cece was willing to risk it. She hadn't seen her uncle for almost a month.

Something wasn't right.

Chapter 26

Toop sat alone at the bar. He didn't want to go home, he didn't want to be around people. Not even Sally.

Small circular motions released the tension from his temples as he revisited the same question over and over. A man sells his car for a fifth of its value and a few days later he winds up dead. Toop strained his mind for possible scenarios, other than the obvious.

He nursed a pint of Wildcat ale, on the house. The offer had been non-negotiable. Jimmy, it turned out, was quite persistent when it came to ale. "I'll tell you one thing lad. Beer is made by man, ale by God." Deadpan certainty.

Toop contemplated the untouched pint, his thoughts offering him little solace.

A professional?

He regurgitated the words in his head. It wasn't impossible, he thought, there were people who killed for a living and those people were different, calculated, masters of precision and misdirection.

He mulled it over, his mind ticking without pause. When murder is premeditated the executioner cannot be overestimated, he concluded. He is not mad, nor does he reveal his internal rantings across a slur of low-budget websites. Professional killers plan and prepare each detail. Textbook perfectionists, thought Toop. There is a pragmatic nature to killing; murders don't fulfil an emotional or psychological need. In which case, a staged suicide could be conceivable. He tested the theory in his head. What better way to ensure a closed file than to kill the prime suspect? Toop leant forward on his elbows, the weight of his head supported by his thumbs. The space between his eyebrows reddened with the localised pressure.

How else could he justify a car like that being sold for peanuts? A contract killing, engineered to look like suicide? Toop sighed. It was laughable.

Maybe you've just been wrong all along.

Admit it, he thought, it's just suicide. He rubbed his hands over his face and stopped, his chin in his palms, fingers framing his jaw. And if his theories about revenge and punishment were accurate then the whole thing, all of it, was about fulfilling an emotional need. Toop groaned. Which would rubbish the notion of a calculated and staged suicide. And then there was the obvious fact that kept slapping him across the face. Jimmy had provided a more than accurate description of the body who was now lying on Sally's table. The dead man had sold Jimmy the car, no questions.

Toop lifted his pint.

An hour and three drinks later she slipped into the seat next to him.

"I stand corrected," said Eve, "he does drink."

She hauled her bag up and planted it on the bar.

He might have smiled at her but Toop wasn't certain. He didn't answer. No eye contact.

Eve turned to him and, registering the mood in his features, she softened.

"Tough day at the office then?"

"Had worse." Toop had no plans to discuss it. "Your evening going well?" His unconvincing and monotone delivery reduced the question to a statement.

"Had worse." Her mouth twitched in a smile.

Toop looked straight at her. So young, he thought. It had been a lifetime since a woman, a girl he corrected himself, had captured his attention. She was beautiful and the room was empty except for the two of them. Straight away Toop regretted looking at her. It left him feeling aroused in ways that were long foreign to him. Toop turned away, too quickly, certain that Eve had noticed it.

"Do you have a surname?" he asked.

"Stone." She paused, preparing her words. "Who is she?"

He stared back at her. The question caught him off guard, a feeling that he wasn't used to. The sound of his own heartbeat surprised him and he continued to look at her with a fierce intensity. Eve didn't drop her gaze.

Eve's blank expression faded, replaced by a determined, careful curiosity. "The girl I remind you of. Who is she?"

For a moment, it seemed that the conversation was over.

"Kara," said Toop. "Her name was Kara."

The name brought the images back with it.

Toop was in his early twenties, handsome and tall with a muscular frame. His body fat wavered around the eight percent mark, an athlete with climber's arms, sculpted calf muscles and a chiselled out jaw. He wore black shorts and a plain cotton t-shirt, the material clinging to the natural raise of his chest, his uniform not yet removed from the locker. He had ten minutes until he needed to clock in. Toop was at the police station, not his normal shift. He'd come in by prearrangement, one of the boys was sleeping off the effects of a heavy stag night. Toop smiled. Harry was a good lad, he was more than happy to help him out even if he was meant to be elsewhere. Toop poured himself a coffee, the office stuff tasted like dirt but it was caffeine all the same. The girls would be fine, he thought.

He was wrong.

Nothing in the world could have prepared him for it, the phone call and the instantaneity of loss. It plunged into his chest until the hilt of the blade tore right through him, making contact with his sternum. Her dead eyes looked up at him from the snow. Shattered limbs crushed and made idle by fallen rocks, blood smeared across the white mountain. The life choked from her lungs.

"Kara was my wife." Toop looked up from his glass. "Kara is my wife," he said, not wanting to commit her to the past tense.

A decade he had avoided using her name, not saying it had kept her present.

Eve watched him and waited, but Toop was done.

They sat in silence. Two minutes. Then she reached over and placed her hand on his forearm, moving her fingers down to his wrist to rest around his clenched fist. Her eyes gave her away. Eve Stone was no stranger to the taste of death.

"Do you trust me?" she asked.

Toop studied her face.

"I don't really know you."

"You don't know me at all," she said. "Remember that."

Eve removed her hand.

"I'm not her and I never will be."

Toop continued to stare at her face, her eyes seemed old. The young, carefree girl was gone, leaving something far darker. Damaged, thought Toop.

"Can you promise me, promise that you won't forget that?" said Eve. "I'm not her."

Neither of them spoke as an Ed Sheeran song played out of the stereo.

Toop broke the silence. Eve's hand had returned to his.

"My wife died," he said. "She was killed in an avalanche ten years ago along with my mother. They both died and I wasn't there."

Eve looked shocked by his admission.

What was she doing?

She extracted her fingers in a swift, desperate movement, the act provoking a slight activity in Toop's eyes.

A barely noticeable flicker.

She didn't want to feel sorry for him, his problems were of no concern to her. Eve Stone had very little capacity for compassion, it went against her nature. It was a fierce, unconditional apathy that had kept her alive all of these years.

Eve hooked her feet behind the bar at the bottom of her stool and clasped her fingers around her glass. She took a sip of beer, her left hand drifting to her throat. The lump wasn't meant to be there, it felt foreign and obtrusive.

"Good," she managed, regretting it straight away. "Sorry, I don't mean good about the avalanche. Obviously, I just meant..." What do you mean exactly Eve, she thought. Why are you bothering to preserve this guy's feelings? Just get up and leave. You don't care about his loss. Shit happens, you of all people know that. "I meant it's good that you don't think I'm her." They both turned, locking eyes. "I'm really sorry."

"It's not something I..."

"So that's why you moved to London?" asked Eve.

"Wasn't much left for me up north."

"But you're back?"

Toop eyed her for a few seconds. "Shall we get out of here?"

Eve gave him a hard look before answering. She ran her hand round the back of her neck and up into her hair. This wasn't the plan. Toop watched her as she sat frozen in indecision. This wasn't the plan at all, thought Eve.

She's so young, reasoned Toop, his gaze hanging on her lips. Her bottom lip was slighter fuller, still wet from the touch of her tongue.

Eve's face relaxed and Toop watched the evidence of youth ease back into her features. She rose, throwing her bag over one shoulder. "I know just the place."

Toop left his drink, discarding a five pound note next to the glass. He followed Eve out of the pub, aware of a troubling premonition tingling up his spine.

Did he trust her?

He debated it as he held the door open for her, and watched as she slipped under his arm without lowering her head. She smelt like summer in France.

Yes, decided Toop, he trusted Eve Stone, And, with that, he allowed the door to close behind them.

But trust had its limitations.

Chapter 27

Late 80s

Angus McNab watched as his one-year old shovelled a tiny handful of pre-mashed banana from the surface of her high chair and smeared it across her mouth. Isla McNab had not yet been sold on the use of a spoon. Her open mouth produced an award-winning smile, revealing small chunks of yellow fruit. Laughing and eating were also regarded as simultaneous activities.

McNab loved being a dad. He relished the occasional evening when he had time to come home for dinner with his daughter. Deciding upon coffee and toast over regurgitated banana and raisins, he enjoyed the brief moment of respite. Two minutes later McNab would be in his car on the way back to the station. Crime in Glasgow didn't sleep. But for the next 120 seconds he would play the part of the proud, dotting dad. The days that involved time with his daughter were that little bit less stressful. It was a fact that would hold true for another minute.

His wife could be heard in the background. Caroline appreciated these rare evenings almost as much as McNab. The sound of running water indicated that she was in the shower, enjoying the time to use conditioner and to shave her legs. McNab smiled, he would take full advantage of that fact later. The demands of full-time parenthood had taken them both by surprise. They had read all of the books and they had been to all of the classes but that hadn't made Isla sleep any longer or cry any less.

A baby had not been on the cards, perhaps it never would have been. Isla was an accidental slip up after a work night out. Too much alcohol coupled with a condom supply problem. Caroline had been on the pill, forever prepared, but the effects of a memorable hangover had rendered the little white tablet useless. In truth, they were delighted when the little blue positive mark appeared but the timing was far from optimal. Angus, at only thirty-nine, had just been made Detective Chief Inspector, the ultimate goal in his career. It was tough, but they were making it work. Overall, they were happy.

Then the phone call came.

McNab answered and listened. The running water stopped.

"Oh God. Inside the gallery itself?" He rubbed his head, feeling tired. "The press are going to have a field day with this one."

Caroline appeared, her hair wrapped up in a towel, and gave him a knowing smile. She kissed her husband on the forehead, knowing that he had a long evening ahead of him.

McNab opened the car door and sank into the driver's seat. No silky-smooth legs tonight, he thought, as he turned the ignition.

***

One thumb clasped between his teeth, the other buried in his pocket, McNab looked around the room. More of a large closet really. He took the time to look over the entire area, taking in the scene and the one lone occupant.

A death within the walls of Kelvingrove Art Gallery, McNab couldn't believe it.

His modest flip pad filled with notes as he jotted down the contents of the room and the condition of the body. McNab included a detailed sketch. He held it at arm's length, tilted the paper, and frowned. McNab was not a natural artist, forever grateful for the advancements of photography. Peter, the photographer, would be in shortly to reproduce each detail of the room on film.

Body, check. Blood, check. Weapon, check. One bloodied utility knife.

McNab walked back out into the hall, replacing the police tape. A tight squeeze he thought as he listed off the staff, a photographer, print lifter, pathologist, too many bodies.

"Just the photographer for now," he said, addressing the nearest officer. The man nodded in response, taking a step closer to the open door, choosing to stare out towards the hall, away from the body. McNab didn't blame him. He found desensitisation far more concerning.

The kid who had found the body was sitting with his head hung between his legs. Most likely in shock, thought McNab. Poor lad.

"You holding up ok?" McNab asked, leaning his hands forward on bent knees.

Jon nodded, raising his head a few centimetres but his eyes remained on his feet. Tom sat next to him, also pale.

"He suffers from panic attacks sir," Tom interjected on his friend's behalf. "Can questioning wait a bit?"

"No problem. Just stay around here. Make sure he gets some sugar in him and a good few glasses of liquid." McNab looked down at his notes them up at Tom. "Your dad works here, is that correct? Curator."

"Yes. My dad and I were in the Study Centre further down the hall when Jon found the body. He had just left us and was heading out, must have taken the wrong door. Bit of a warren up here, officer."

"When did you find...," a quick look at his pad, "Jonathan."

"Jon. He appeared back a few minutes after leaving us. He just stood in the doorway, pale as a ghost. And..." Tom looked over at his friend, resting his palm on the top of his back. "I'm sure he won't mind me saying this but he was covered in his own, well, I mean to say, it was pretty obvious that he'd been sick."

"Did he say anything?"

"Nothing comprehensible, just led us back here."

"Us? You and your dad?"

"Yeah. Don't think there was anyone else up here. He took us back here to the janitor's office." Tom shook his head, his voice wavering. "Poor Bill."

"So you knew the deceased, Bill Anderson?"

Identification hadn't been difficult; the janitor's name was printed on his badge.

"Yeah. He'd occasionally invite me to his office for a cup of tea and some biscuits when I came to see my dad. Didn't talk much, kept himself to himself, but he always struck me as a gentle man."

McNab's eyes wandered across to the young boy, sheltered under the arm of his friend. The lad didn't look good. "You two rest up. We can have a chat later." He half smiled at Tom, the right of his mouth catching in an expression of pity. Then McNab turned and crossed the room to where the pathologist was waiting. The photographer was just finishing up.

"Any initial observations?" he asked.

The pathologist was a heavy, big-boned man, settled into the latter half of his fifties. He had deep-set, button eyes framed by circular black glasses that rested upon a blotchy, notably rotund nose. He stared at the body with avid fascination. The clothing was saturated in dark red liquid and a rancid smell contaminated the air, indicating that the man had relieved himself in his final moments. McNab had been present at enough crime scenes to know that death brought an unfortunate and involuntary relaxation of the sphincters. In death, all men became equal, dignity could not be bought from the ferryman. McNab watched the pathologist. The man made him feel uneasy. McNab flinched as he noticed the lines form and cluster around the pathologist's beady eyes, squinting to absorb each detail. It didn't seem natural to have such a blatant interest in the dead. But someone had to do it, thought McNab, and his job would be much harder without those certain people.

He walked over to the pathologist, repeating his question, "Any thoughts?"

The generously sized man manoeuvred his body to face McNab and looked at him, the tilt of his head sinking his collar into a roll of fat, his eyes revealing a childish, guiltless intrigue. McNab's skin tingled, raising the hairs on his lower arms. A deep voice accompanied the large mass of flesh.

"A determined bugger," the pathologist smiled.

"Excuse me?" asked McNab. The tactless comment took him by surprise. But he decided not to voice his displeasure. There would be no skirting around the facts, no unnecessary niceties. McNab had to accept it, move on, and work with the tasteless bugger.

"Wrist slitter. A serious one." The smile hung on the pathologist's swollen face, refusing to vacate his mouth. "Exsanguination. Blood pours from the body until the volume and pressure is reduced to a fatal level, to death and a bloody great mess."

McNab wished the man would stop smiling.

"The cut on his arm," said McNab, "so your assumption is suicide?"

The pathologist continued speaking, more to himself than to McNab. "Wrist slitting is a notoriously unsuccessful method of suicide. You need to hit the right artery, otherwise you just sit for hours waiting for an ambulance. All in all, a painful waste of time that often results in brain damage." He turned his flabby arm, exposing his forearm, and ran two fat fingers down towards his wrist. McNab frowned, imagining the man's arteries buried beneath folds of fat. "The arteries near the wrist are small and slitting them will most likely end in hours of futile bleeding. But there are two decent sized arteries that run along the inside of the forearm; the radial and ulnar arteries. Drag a blade through one of those and you'll bleed out in no time. Shock sets in within minutes, followed by extreme confusion and unconsciousness."

The pathologist turned to look at the body. "He's gone for a deep vertical slit down his forearm, almost eliminating the margin for error. A serious suicide attempt, no half-hearted cut across the wrist. Man did his research."

Peter, the photographer, stepped out through the doorway and the pathologist walked in. The victim was slumped in his chair, legs splayed out to the side of his desk, meaning that kneeling next to the body demanded a considerable effort from the pathologist. McNab watched, finding himself mesmerised by the unnatural movement that was performed in a staggered slow motion.

It seemed like his knees had barely made contact with the floor before the pathologist craned his neck to stare back at McNab. The smile. "You want the good news or the bad?"

It amazed McNab how flippant people could be when it came to death. He had never got used to the sight of a body, the way death changed people. How life could be devoured in an instant, leaving nothing but a discarded, almost unrecognisable shell. "Both would be appreciated."

"Well the good news is that he's been dead a matter of hours, not days, eight or so. As you can see, rigor mortis has moved throughout the body." He prodded at the man's throat. "Advanced stiffening of the eyelids, neck and jaw progressing now to other muscles and most likely to his internal organs." Using a single finger, he pulled up the bottom of the man's shirt, exposing a tyre of bare skin. The distinct discolouration was clear to McNab. The pathologist continued. "Livor mortis. The purplish, red blotting formed up the back of the body shows that the heavy blood cells have already settled, putting time of death at some time this morning."

"And the bad news?"

The smiled evaporated. McNab stared at the thin, lipless line that occupied the space between the man's nose and chin.

McNab already knew the answer.

He knew that his night was about to get a lot worse.

Chapter 28

Present Day

Cece pushed open the garden gate and walked up to her uncle's house.

Her uncle Jon had been around from the day that she was born, no relation but she couldn't remember calling him anything else. Family was not something that you were born with, that's what her dad always said, it's the people who walk in when the rest of the world walks out. And that was her uncle, part of the family. Memories of her mum had faded almost completely, having died when Cece was only four. A car crash. Jon had been there, he had looked after her when her dad couldn't, on those days when he was unable to face the normalities of life. Days that continued for months after it happened.

It was a short ten metre stretch from the gate to the front door.

The small garden was well kept, clean edges and well-tended grass, vacant but for the prominent statue. Cece hated it as a child, the two ceramic wolf cubs terrified her, bemused her innocent mind. Why would anyone want a dead animal sculpted on their lawn? Her eyes had held wide open, aroused by a childlike curiosity, as her Dad had smiled.

Cece glanced over at the statue and decided that she still didn't like it. Ugly thing. Stray, uneven tufts of grass were just visible beneath the heavy base. Cece frowned. Her uncle was neat, bordering on obsessive. Either her uncle's standards were slipping or he had left in a hurry. She suspected the latter.

Cece stood in front of the door and let her gaze sweep in each direction. She didn't see anyone passing the street, by car or by foot. Middle of the day, most people would be at work. Mrs Irvine had returned inside.

Cece knocked on the front door. Just in case.

No response.

Her gaze shifted right then left, no prying eyes. Why would there be? It was a well to do street in Bearsden, in broad daylight. Cece felt silly.

She tried the handle. Locked.

It was not the first time that she had broken into a house. The family business was somewhat untraditional, show and tell had not been an option at school for little Cece. She looked down at the handle clasped in her hand; the dead bolt lock was visible above it. A simple spring bolt system would have been too easy.

No fun without a bit of challenge.

The handle moved freely in her palm, cold against her skin. Damn, thought Cece. The dead bolt was locked tight in position. She knelt down on the front step, the rough mat digging into her knees, and peered through the slight gap between the frame and the door.

Moulding too.

Using her knees as leverage Cece pushed herself up. Using a card wouldn't be an option.

Plan B. Screwdriver, a little more conspicuous.

Her head turned over her shoulder and she glanced sideways, checking for unwanted neighbours. No one. She wondered if anyone walked anywhere anymore. Oh well, thought Cece, pulling the screw driver from her bag, now was not the time to complain about the health of the country.

She took a step back and surveyed the door. It had two small, rectangular windows about head level, just over a foot in length. The height wasn't ideal but there wasn't much that she could do about it. Cece looked around her, taking in the garden decor. She stared at the statue, hands caught on her hips. Contemplation crossed her brow, causing her nose to crinkle as she thought better of it. Not a good idea, he'd blow a fuse. As she studied the ground around the dead, ceramic fox cubs the decorative stones stole her attention. Some of them were pretty big, a good six inches of additional height. That was all she needed. Perfect. The painful, slow task of dragging one to the doorstep proved less ideal and she cursed herself for not bringing something.

Clearly she was out of practice.

At last, she stood atop one of the stones with the slotted screwdriver inserted into the bottom of the window pane. Her uncle kept a spare set of keys in a bowl by the door, within reach of the window. If her calculations were correct then she had a reasonable chance of procuring them through the window. If not, it would prove to be a futile waste of time.

Her mouth distorted into a grimace as she levered the screwdriver up and down, exerting a gentle upwards force. It didn't want to move. Cece slid the metal head along to the other side, tried again, and the window popped loose. Yes, she mouthed, working the pane of glass free. It came out with surprising ease, no residual shards of glass. Cece was grateful for this; a trip to the hospital was not part of the plan. Replacing the pane however was something that she would have to worry about later.

Cece craned her neck. She could just about see through the hole in the door, a respectable view if she lifted up onto her toes. Not overly comfortable but she had a clear picture of the hall. Cece's gaze turned vertically downwards, the end of her uncle's welcome mat inching into her vision, her prize rested two feet to the right. A tall, narrow cabinet exactly where it should be. She smiled. The bowl, complete with keys, was hers for the taking. Pulling her head back from the hole, she extended the arch of her feet, crushing all ten toes. The additional inch hurt but it was enough. Cece hooked her arm though the opening, grateful once more for the absence of broken glass. *Damn.* Her strained fingertips flirted with the edge of the bowl and pain shot through her armpit as the solid frame bit into her skin. She fell short by a few millimetres.

Her fingers were splayed, shaking in an act of determination. Three, rather painful, failed attempts were preceded by a choir of coloured language. Foul words for a young woman. Cece retrieved her arm and stepped back from the door, massaging her strained muscles. She paced on the spot, frustrated. The thought of not reaching them hadn't occurred to her. Real impressive Cece, she thought, great planning. The skin under her arm burned.

Cece stopped pacing and slumped on the doorstep. Without conscious thought, her foot reached out and kicked the bag, hard, the obscure, mismatched contents spilling onto the path. *Crap.* She leant forward to collect her belongings, grabbing for the wire hanger. Then she smiled. Of course, thought Cece, it was child's play really. She picked up the hanging device.

Let's go fishing.

Five minutes later she held the keys in her hand, feeling more than a little pleased with herself. The lock welcomed the thin slip of gold metal and the solid bolt turned free. Cece's nose almost collided with the large wooden door as it stopped dead, restrained by the short length of chain that had pulled tight on the other side.

"Come on!"

Cece stepped backwards, taking a few seconds to compose herself. She knew it was there, that it existed, but she had never known her uncle to fasten the chain lock. The thought was instantaneous, it didn't linger.

It should have.

Her mind and fingers were already occupied with removing the elastic tie from her hair. The chain was cheap, exposing a generous, arm-sized crack. Cece looped one end of her hair tie around the length of visible chain and through the other. A well-practiced skill. Her dad, bless him, chained their house door without thinking, unintentional wrongdoing he called it. Cece better described it as old age. During her later teenage years, the skill had proven invaluable when arriving home in the small hours of the morning. Drunk or stoned, Cece was well rehearsed. An expert. With one end of the rubber band tied taut around the chain and the other looped away, Cece slid it along to the furthest away point of the chain, a few centimetres from the handle. She looped the loose end around the handle, second nature, and shut the door. A familiar smile spread across her face. The motion of the door forced her hair tie to tug the chain to the side, releasing it. A welcome noise caught in the air as the chain fell.

She was in.

Cece stalled in the doorway. It occurred to her that getting in was the easy bit. She had no idea what she was looking for. Cece's hand pulled the door closed behind her until she was alone in the house. Her arm hung behind her, fingers frozen to the cold metal. Silence.

What now?

Seconds passed and Cece looked up from her feet. Her eyes caught on a painting on the far wall, one of his. Her uncle's careful brushstrokes gave her a reason to walk forward: if something had happened to him she would find out. She let go of the handle and moved towards the living room.

Preoccupied by thoughts of her uncle, Cece could not be blamed for her unfortunate oversight.

Chain locks, identical to the one that she had skilfully disarmed, could only be fastened from inside the house.

Chapter 29

Present Day

It went straight to voicemail for a third time.

"Ok Fergus, where are you?" said Sally as she hung up. Her eyebrows united in a look of contemplation and she pocketed the phone. It sank deep into the breast pocket of her scrubs.

Sally looked down at the corpse on the cold slab; a sheet covered the body, concealing everything but the head. She reached out and touched his cheekbone, running her finger along his skin before retrieving her hand. Dead bodies were no longer a novelty to her, the urge to throw up had long subsided and she was immune to the smell. Sally had no doubt that most normal people would question her career choice. But, in truth, she had never taken a delight in examining dead bodies and she had no interest in horror movies or with the macabre. There was no deep sense of morbid curiosity that she was aware of. Sally Gillespie was anal, bordering on unhealthy, and she had a strong visual memory, complemented by an unusual talent for pattern recognition, a skill that had been identified during art class. Pathology had just happened.

Sally ran her hands up past her elbows and rubbed her upper arms. They were cold, a consequence of the job. Dead bodies needed the cold. She took a step back and stared at the man. Who are you? she thought. From an external perspective the body, discounting the bullet wound, was in good shape. There was no sign of blows or bruising around the wrists or arms, the most common indicators of a struggle. But, inadvertently or not, Toop's suspicions had unsettled her. Sally had been meticulous, overly thorough, checking again for defensive wounds or marks. Nothing. If he had been knocked unconscious and then shot, there would have been clear evidence of head trauma. Nothing.

But it was there.

Something, just visible.

Sally looked at the clock on the wall. Midnight. She wished that Toop would pick up the phone.

***

"Where did you go?" asked Toop, breaking the silence. A little more direct than he intended.

Eve turned to look at him, her hands resting at ten and two on the steering wheel.

"Earlier, when Jimmy came through to the bar, you disappeared for two hours? I thought you'd left."

"Keeping tabs, officer?" she teased. "Or is it being kept in the dark that you don't like?" Eve smiled. "If you must know..." Her eyes left Toop's and focused on the darkness though the windscreen. "I was with a man."

Toop looked at her, noted the trace of discomfort in her eyes and turned away. He suppressed the want to say something, choosing to stare out of the passenger window and into the blackness. It was none of his business.

The next twenty minutes passed without conversation. Toop didn't utter a word when they took a left off the A832 towards his house. He held his gaze on the sign. *Badachro 3 miles*. The van jolted with the forced change of gear as it veered down the small road and crossed the narrow humpbacked bridge.

She must have changed her mind, thought Toop.

He was wrong.

Eve drove straight past his front door, her eyes fixed straight ahead, not affording it a moment's notice. As they drove past his drive it occurred to Toop that Eve had no reason to know where he lived. He stole a brief look at the modest building. No lights. Sally must be asleep, he concluded, dismissing the fierce stab of guilt. Toop pulled his head back in Eve's direction and focused on the side of her face. She had no reason to know where he lived, but Toop was in no doubt that Eve Stone knew exactly which house was his. It was a small town after all.

He also had no doubts about where they were going.

After eight miles, the road ended. Eve killed the engine and stepped out onto the verge. She slammed the door behind her, the force ricocheting through the body of the vehicle. Toop watched her in the side mirror, following her slender figure as it disappeared behind the van, and listened to the faint noise of items being hauled and shifted in the back. His eyes were still on the mirror when she re-emerged in a red puffa jacket. She had a head torch on, making it impossible to read her expression.

"Coming?" she shouted with her back already turned. She walked into the night, the dull glow from the torch exposing her position.

The wind blew against his door. It was ajar, just enough to create a slight draft around his left ankle. Well, are you? thought Toop. He sat alone in the dark, unsure of what to do. Sally would be wondering where he was. He had to be up in five hours and there was an open case file waiting for him on his desk. Toop gathered his face in his palm, forcing his nose down towards his lips. And Kara. He didn't know what he was feeling. Or, possibly, he just hadn't felt it in a long time.

He opened the door and walked out after her, the light of her torch almost lost to view. But Toop didn't need one, he knew where he was.

Toop knew the gate would be there before it appeared, emerging out of the dark. Remnants of light ebbed from the sky, disclosing the black structure against the night. Toop pushed it open, the gentle creaks drowned out by the soft wind. The contours of the muddy track felt familiar beneath his boots, the shallow uneven channels long dug out of the earth. The path wound through the field, carved out by a timeless and prolonged amble of sheep hooves. Eve was the only other person for miles. Toop watched as the light from her head torch disappeared, retreating below the horizon. He pictured her bending her knees and leaning back on her arms, palms nestled in the sandy grass as she prepared to slide down the sand dune, feet, then legs, then butt, then back, as if she were made of glue.

Toop's eyes adjusted with each step, negating the absence of light. Soon the mud gave way to sand and the smell of salt filtered through the air. It felt cooler against his skin. He lengthened his stride, planting his feet with confidence as he descended the rough terrain down to the beach.

Nothing.

Eve's silhouette stood motionless. Toop stared past her and out to sea where a dark blue band had formed above the horizon. The view had been taken by the shadow of the earth, the surface of the water discernible as a blue-grey expanse. Toop closed his eyes. The view was embedded in his memory. He could picture Applecross and the Trotternish peninsula protruding from the Isle of Skye. He allowed the past to exhaust him, expending a decade of rejected memories in a single moment. He could feel her beside him there, the presence of his wife's warm body beating through his own. She was the blood in his veins, pounding against his neck with an unrestrained fervour.

"Kara," he whispered, as her delicate fingers encased his own. The cruel reality of it teased with his thoughts. An instant and the moment shattered.

Toop closed his eyes, took a deep breath, and walked across the beach to Eve.

They sat side by side in the sand, alone, somewhere in nowhere. Silence. Not forced. Eve's mind was elsewhere. On occasion she looked over at Toop, the act in itself irrational. She looked round a third time. Could he know? Eve curled her knees into her chest and wrapped her arms around her shins. She knew that it was impossible; people couldn't be witnesses to mere thoughts. Her thoughts were hers, private and invisible. She looked over a fourth time. Weren't they? Eve quickly retracted her gaze and buried the notion, along with her chin, deep into the crevasse between her knees. There was something else troubling her. It seemed odd, she thought, although odd wasn't the right word. Insane, she corrected. Insane, that the man she had only just met, the man who she should have feared and avoided, was the same man that she wanted to confide in. Eve looked over at the officer sitting next to her. His eyes stared ahead into the dark abyss and the heels of his boots disappeared into the ground.

You can't, she thought. *Never.*

"You said that you weren't there?" she said, breaking the quiet, her words followed by instant regret. She wasn't meant to care.

Toop looked back at her. His eyes held a strange expression, somewhere between fear and expectation. Eve couldn't be sure.

"It's just a strange thing to say," she continued.

The wind caught her hair, catching three red strands that curled around her face and glued to the surface of her lips. Eve brushed them away with her finger, a futile act in the constant breeze. She didn't bother the second time, letting the auburn threads of hair flirt with her mouth.

Red on red, thought Toop, titling his gaze.

"You said it like you were meant to be there," Eve prompted.

"I was."

Toop's tone was flat, absent of any tell.

Eve stared at the sand around her toes, unsure if the conversation was over, and ran her hands down the front of her shins, gathering her fingers across her exposed ankles. The draft that circled her skin barely registered, but the natural adjustment of her body allowed her a moment to think. The muscles up her back tensed, spreading down her shoulders. She wasn't ready for the conversation to be over. Eve had never been one to avoid confrontation. In fact, conflict formed the basis of most of her relationships, including the one with herself. She rubbed the small scar, a 3cm line that crossed her knuckles, the remnants of misunderstanding with her bedroom wall. Eve had been eight. She was not known for treading on glass and she was not about to start now.

Not for him, thought Eve.

"Why weren't you there?"

"I was at work," replied Toop.

"That doesn't make sense." Eve was determined. "If you had work then you were never meant to be there?" The wind failed to conceal the bite in her voice.

"Shift change. Last minute."

Toop looked out at the black expanse of water and pulled his hands through his hair, turning his face away from her. His lips broke apart and sealed twice before he spoke.

"I was meant to be up the hill with them but a friend needed a favour. I stepped in." Little more than a whisper. "And I ended up losing everything."

The statement hung between their bodies.

"Or you denied the avalanche a third victim." Eve's voice lacked the inflection expected of compassion. "Or do you think that Kara would have preferred it if you had died with her." It wasn't a question.

Toop's first impulse was to hit her. He gathered his fists, focusing on the sharp pain that penetrated deep beneath his left ear. His jaw muscle seized.

"How old were you?" asked Eve.

Toop released the pressure from his hands, just enough, and focused on the delivery of his words. "It was the day before Kara's twenty-fourth," he answered.

"You were very young. To already be married."

"We started dating at secondary school." His knuckles still held the whiteness of anger, his nails marking his palms. "When we were fifteen."

She looked at him with a serious expression and returned her chin to the gap between her knees. It was ten minutes before she spoke again, by which time the fire inside Toop had retreated to a controlled flame.

"And what happened to you?" she asked. "Afterwards."

"London."

"Straight away?"

"No," he said.

"So?" she prompted, "First you buried yourself in a pit of depression?"

"Something like that," he said. "A lack of natural buoyancy, that's what Sally called it."

"The pathologist?" Eve had shifted her body round, her weight balancing on one hip, with her arms extended out in the sand.

"Yes. How did you..." Toop paused. "Never mind."

"Booze?"

He nodded. "It was like drowning every day. It was a strangely calming experience, peaceful somehow. The world and all the people in it just faded away."

"And Sally?"

"Apart from Sally," he repeated. "She refused to let me go, she forced me back to the surface. Again and again." Toop found Eve's eyes. "I owe her my life. And I just left her. One Tuesday, I was just gone."

"London?"

Toop nodded again. "I didn't return a single letter or phone call. Ten years." He took a deep breath. "Last week was the first time I'd seen her. Sally Gillespie is my oldest friend."

"That makes you a bit of a shit."

"Yes. Yes it does."

Chapter 30

Late 80s

McNab shook his head again. The ridge of his brow was buried deep in the palm of his right hand.

Seeing is believing, that's what they say, isn't it? he thought. But the possibility of it sent a nervous shiver across his back. Surely it couldn't.

He leant against the doorway, staring at the body, and half listened. He knew what the pathologist was going to say.

The man's voice had changed. It was stern, factual, an articulated delivery reserved for old, guttural lecturers. His words were chosen and deliberate. His gaze took refuge in his hands, which he continued to rub together, one hand clenched in a fist while the other rotated around it. McNab looked at the soft, loose skin and pictured a ball and socket joint.

The pathologist continued, "Livor mortis or post-mortem lividity is a noticeable discolouration of the skin that occurs after death; without a beating heart to pump the blood around the body, the blood pools and settles. Or, more accurately, it sinks. Gravity pulls it to the lowest parts of the body." He paused and peeled up the victim's shirt to expose the area beneath his shoulder blades. "However, as can be seen here, lividity fails to form in areas of the body that are pressed hard against a surface. Too much pressure is forced upon the capillaries and those areas are left white." He released the shirt from his sweaty hand. "This is called blanching."

McNab remembered the first time that it had been explained to him. It had been at a lecture, memorable for all of the wrong reasons. The majority of students had refrained from eating lunch afterwards, after the explicit slide show of corpses, some human, some not. It had been an endless reel of stomach-wrenching photos, each projected onto the far wall. And even when light had returned to the small room, and the projector had been turned off, McNab sat at his desk with his pen in mouth and stared at the empty whitewashed wall. It no longer seemed clean.

Now, as he stood in the doorway with his eyes on the victim, McNab rehearsed the same example that had been shown to him all those years ago. He gripped his fingers tightly round his opposite forearm causing the pressure to bite into his skin and he counted back from five, his thumb aching in protest. Two, one and he released his grip, leaving four white fingerprints.

McNab rubbed his arm and shifted his gaze to the pathologist's mouth, the lipless line still quivering beneath his nose.

"After five, maybe six hours, give or take, the livor mortis remains fixed in position. Even if the body is then moved, it doesn't affect the distribution of blood."

"And in layman terms?" asked McNab. He wanted someone else to confirm the words that had been hovering in his mind. He had been sure of it from the moment that he had seen the victim's purple and red stained back. He was sure. But it was impossible. Improbable, he thought, nothing was impossible.

"The distribution of blood along the length of the deceased's back coupled with clear evidence of blanching under the shoulder blades and under the buttocks indicate that this man was lying on his back, not sitting, when he died. Plainly put officer, this body has been moved."

McNab's features didn't respond to the information. It wasn't new to him. Just confirmed.

"Most likely in the last couple of hours," the pathologist finished.

"Thank you," said McNab. He turned on his heels, leaving the pathologist alone with the body.

McNab's head filled with questions.

He walked to the window at the end of the hall and stared outwards, his face inches from the glass. If, he thought, the body had been moved it must have occurred within a short time frame, an hour after death, maybe two. Livor mortis would have stagnated but rigor could not have rendered the body too stiff to move. He licked his lower lip, the warmth from his breath forming beads of condensation on the glass.

Flat on his back.

McNab toyed with the image. It didn't make sense. He had eyed the floor carefully. If someone had hauled a corpse, a large, bleeding corpse, across the room and up onto a chair there would have been drag marks, blood stains, spray patterns that indicated where the body had first fallen. McNab had seen no evidence, nothing obvious anyway. Forensics would do a more thorough investigation. Especially now, thought McNab, contemplating the sudden shift from suicide to homicide.

Numerous questions fought for precedence between his temples. Why move the body and why wait an hour? Did the murderer return for a particular reason, maybe they forgot something, a piece of evidence that could have implicated them? McNab sighed. Was there even a murderer at all? Maybe there was a simple explanation for the unusual blanching?

"Bill Anderson," mouthed McNab.

How many criminals, he thought, had a museum janitor at the top of their hit list? He was willing to bet that the answer was very few. But then, you only needed one. Just one.

Were you on that list, Bill?

***

Jon walked into his flat alone, despite Tom's persistence.

The last thing that Jon wanted was company.

Jon walked through to the bathroom and studied his reflection in the mirror. He was almost unrecognisable, his eyes tired and withdrawn. Jon cupped his hands under the tap, a numbness spreading through his fingers, and let his palms fill with cold water. The water hit his face and he shuddered, experiencing the shock of ice on flesh. But the cold offered no release, no refreshment. Jon scrubbed hard, using a damp flannel to grate against his cheeks and forehead until they were red raw. As he washed away the grime he surrendered to a detached stupor. His mind became a vacuum, vacant of any conscious decision and incapable of producing anything resembling coherent thought.

Mercifully the officer in charge, whose name escaped Jon, had let him leave without further questioning.

Jon bent over the sink, elbows locked. The edges of the bowl dug into the undersides of his hands. He felt a drip of water run down his nose and catch on his bottom lip, before it landed an inch from the plug hole. Jon tilted his head further and stared into the small, circular well.

Blood. So much blood.

He couldn't escape the memory of what he had seen.

So much blood.

He felt sick. Bile rose in his throat and it took Jon everything he had not to throw up. He tried desperately to stifle the panic that festered inside him, restraining it just beneath the surface. Jon scrunched up his eyes and concentrated on his breathing. The room didn't have enough air, that or his lungs were too weak. The insubstantial oxygen caused his nostrils to twitch, flaring with the beat of a pulse.

Everything was ruined.

With his hands dampened by nervous sweat and his heart punching against his ribs, Jon's mind turned to Jenny. His plan, the late-night museum tour, it was ruined. Jon looked up at the mirror feeling more nauseous. How could he look at her again? The museum, once a place of solace, of safety, had been tarnished in the worst way possible. The memories would never leave him.

Do you like to suffer, Jonathan Swan?

He spoke to his reflection. "Is that it? Are you drawn to pain, perhaps you revel in it?" The fingers on his right hand curled into a fist and without hesitation he punched himself hard in the side of his face. Jon let out a cry of revulsion and spat out into the sink, his eyes not leaving his reflection. "There isn't some inner demon that is dragging you down," he whispered, "you go to it willingly, running head first into the darkness." Jon hit himself again. There was no pain this time. The adrenaline had consumed him.

"You're pathetic," he shouted. "Pathetic!"

He stood in front of the mirror with the front of his shirt soaked through. The feelings of contempt played over in his head, again and again. He hated everything about himself.

She will never want to kiss you or touch you. You are repulsive, damaged. No girl will ever love you.

Tears threatened his eyes, a mixture of anger and self-pity. Jon lifted his hand and went to wipe his face, his eyes catching on the round handle that protruded from the cabinet mirror. He reached for it with his fingers, pulling back the door to expose a small cabinet. Inside there were three shelves lined with bottles. Jon closed his eyes and bowed his head towards the sink. For a full minute, he didn't move. It wasn't until the bottle lid fell from his hands and circled in the sink, the plastic ringing against ceramic, that he realised he was still breathing. Jon held the lidless bottle in his hand and stared down into the glass neck, peering at the selection of small pills.

He couldn't do it.

The next few seconds passed in a blur and the contents of the bottle scattered across the room. The white droplets rained down on the floor and collected in the soft fingers of the bath mat, the occasional pill rolling beneath the bath. Jon watched as two tiny capsules, which had dropped into the sink, disappeared into the darkness of the plug hole. Gone.

Coward! Coward! Coward!

He screamed until his voice faltered, clogged by violent sobs, and he slumped to the floor.

Broken and defeated.

Chapter 31

Lucy slipped the postcard back into the pile, three from the top.

You are free.

Why those words?

The postcard had caught her off-guard, she wasn't prepared for it and the date marked on the post stamp, it didn't make sense.

Unless. Could he have known?

Lucy chewed on the end of her thumb nail, unsettled, a feeling not dissimilar to remorse. The guilt pinched her gut, the sharp incision jolting her back to reality, and she sprayed the pile of letters across the table with the back of her hand.

She stood up.

You can't let his words lead you astray.

Her phone vibrated against her upper thigh, interrupting her thought process and she slipped it from her pocket without thinking. She flipped her wrist round and scrolled her thumb down and across the screen. It unlocked and the home screen lit up, a small icon in the top right corner indicating that she had one unread email. Lucy stared at the screen as the email loaded, her eyes caught on the rotating hourglass.

The subject materialised.

Alex: Things I forgot.

Alex?

Lucy's mind emptied and her body weakened, easing back into the sofa. She gripped the phone. The small screen was all that mattered to her. Her eyes absorbed the short message, blinking to keep from crying but tears came.

Sorry to trouble you. I forgot some things. Journal, helmet and compromising lingerie set. Important that I dispose of them ASAP. Very embarrassing, sorry.

Lucy traced her finger over the words, counting in her head as she read it slower and her hand rose to her lips. She grabbed the nearest piece of paper and scribbled down eight words, a fine line creasing her features and displacing any residual feelings of sadness.

Shit.

The door slammed behind her as she ran out of the flat and a silence fell over the apartment.

Twenty seconds passed before the door flew open and Lucy rushed back inside. She hurled through to her bedroom, a loud rummaging betraying her movements as she ransacked the drawer with hurried fingers.

Yes! It was there.

The front door slammed for the second time in five minutes.

Heavy traffic. Driving would take too long. Lucy sprinted for Partick station. Skinny, unprepared legs and flat soled pumps. She glanced down at her watch, doing the calculations in her head. It was a sixteen-minute walk to the train. She had seven until the next departure. Lucy sped up with awkward, unpractised strides. She could make it. Ten minutes on the train. Twenty minutes and she would be there.

She ignored the ache in her lungs, hoping that she wasn't already too late.

Chapter 32

Present Day

The van pulled up outside Toop's house. The kitchen light was still on.

Strange, thought Toop, Sally was always a morning person. Was, ten years ago, he corrected himself.

He paused, his left-hand hovering over the door handle. Toop hesitated and turned in his seat, fingers unmoved, unsure of his decision. Then he looked back at Eve.

"What does this mean to you?" he asked, handing her the paper from his pocket.

"What is it?"

"Something I read in a bothy log book, something that stuck with me."

"Why are you showing me?"

"Intrigue. People see things differently."

The note unfolded in her fingers. Creased. Toop watched her. The words passed across her face, her eyes focused on the paper long after she had finished reading.

"What's wrong?"

"I...," Eve responded. "I think the meaning's pretty clear, don't you?"

"I did."

"But?"

"Not everyone agreed."

"About what?"

"What do you think?" asked Toop, avoiding her question.

Eve thought about her words. "It's something that I would write if I was in pain." She looked up at him for the first time. "The type of pain that doesn't go away."

"What do you mean?"

"If you repent in thorn then you will sleep in a bed of roses." She spoke the words more for herself. "Poetic."

Eve stared back at him and her features stiffened. "These are the words of someone who knows that they don't deserve forgiveness. Someone who has committed a wrongdoing that is beyond pardon, beyond hope."

"Hope?"

"A hopelessness excused only in death."

"What made you say that?"

"Ending your own life, what purer form of repentance could there be? In death comes peace." Her tone was cold.

"Thank you," said Toop.

He opened the door and was halfway out of the van when his phone beeped in his pocket. Signal. He glanced down, three missed calls from Sally.

Shit.

He looked back, restrained by a single thought.

"You'd seen it before?" he asked.

"Yes, as a child." Her face softened. "A lifetime ago."

***

Sally sat at the breakfast bar, bent over an assortment of documents, both elbows positioned on the counter with her palms wedged beneath her cheekbones. The sideways pull on her face stretched her lips wider. She was dressed in pyjamas, nursing a mug of herbal tea. A short length of string wound around the handle, exposing a small square piece of paper. Lemon and Ginger.

She didn't raise her head when Toop walked in.

"Made a friend?" she said.

"Sorry, I..."

"You don't need to explain yourself to me. We're not six anymore, Fergus."

"She's just..."

"I was expecting you to appear for the post-mortem."

"I meant to, I mean, I thought that..."

"One every forty seconds," interrupted Sally, looking up at him, "eight hundred thousand a year." She held up the document that she was reading. Toop could just make out the title from across the room; it was a report on suicide from the World Health Organisation.

"Incredible isn't it," said Sally.

"What's your point?" he asked.

"No point really, I just want you to remember that people do kill themselves. It does happen."

Sally manoeuvred herself off the bar stool and raised her arms, stretching out through her back and shoulders. The kettle illuminated a pale blue colour as she turned it on.

"I found something, correction, I might have found something and I don't want you jumping to conclusions. Ok?"

"Ok."

"Tea?"

Toop looked at his watch. It was either very late or very early. "Thanks."

The post-mortem report landed on the cushion next to Toop as he settled into the couch.

"Some light bedtime reading," Sally called above the noise of the kettle, appearing a few minutes later with two steaming mugs. English breakfast, well stewed. "Builders tea," she said, handing one to Toop. "Strong and pasty, just how I like my men."

A smile passed between them.

"Do we have a name?" asked Toop.

"Nothing. Nada." She sat in the chair opposite him. "I don't have the faintest clue who this man could be, it's quite infuriating actually. I have a perfect photograph of his face but no one to verify it. Not a single friend or family member has come forward. I spent a good couple of hours searching through missing persons files and databases but no one has reported him missing."

"I looked this afternoon too," said Toop, "I had no luck either."

"A man is dead," stated Sally. "Somebody must know something, but it's like he never existed. I'd like to think that everyone has a family, you know, at least one person who would miss them. One day this man was alive, then the next day he never turned up at home and no one noticed. Or cared."

"Unfortunately," Toop turned away from Sally's weary expression, "it was often the case in London that young women without family ties, prostitutes generally, were never reported missing. It made it very difficult to find the dots, let alone connect them. But," he met her eyes, "in reality most people are reported missing sooner or later. People take trips, impromptu breaks, holidays."

Sally didn't look convinced.

Toop stared into his mug. "We can canvas the village and ask around but I have a feeling that this guy wasn't a local."

"If he was from around here, a place this small, I'm pretty sure that the police would have been the last to hear about it. You can't buy a pint of milk without someone in the village talking about it. Murder would be pretty up there."

"Murder?" A soft smile, no more than a hint.

"Death, it was just a slip of the tongue Fergus, don't go reading into it."

"What about birthmarks, scars, distinguishing features?"

"Nothing, nothing, nothing. No dental records to speak of. Although an examination of his teeth did put him in his mid-forties, not that there's any real revolution there. Preliminary fingerprint scans didn't pick up any matches, so he's not a criminal at least. Although, wait, there was something strange about his fingerprints."

Sally crossed the room and sat next to Toop. She leafed through the medical report.

"Look here. His fingertips were all hardened like little lumps of iron. Bit strange don't you think? But I'm afraid that's all I've got, I can't tell you much about his internals and it will take some time for the results to come through, could be weeks. Ballistics shouldn't take as long though, a few days if we're lucky."

Toop didn't hear her concluding remarks. His lips disappeared into a single line as he chewed on a faint memory.

"Musician," he pondered.

Sally stared at him. "Excuse me?" Her eyes widened in a look of exasperation. "Care to include me in that thought?"

"You remember Joel, the guy who sat behind you in chemistry class. He had black curls, occasionally wore eye make-up and those leather things around his wrists."

"Where are you going with this?"

"He played the guitar."

"So?"

"He used to complain about getting blistered fingers, I remember him showing me the cuts on his fingertips. So he started dipping them in white spirit to desensitise his fingers, to make them hard."

"You think that our guy was a musician?"

"I'm just thinking out loud."

"You're infuriating, you know that, right?" said Sally.

"I had my suspicions," smiled Toop before changing subject. "So, his identity remains unknown?"

"Unfortunately so, even with dental and DNA we've got nothing to compare it to. Shame we're not on CSI," smiled Sally, "one tooth filling, one kitted-out lab, the case would be closed in sixty minutes and we'd be in the pub."

Sally was smiling but Toop could see how tired his friend was, noting the dark circles that had taken up residency beneath her eyes.

"So where do we go from here?" Sally continued.

"Back tracking," replied Toop. "We need to build up a picture of the last few days and hours of his life."

"Like a mission impossible jigsaw except we're piecing together the last steps of someone's life and we don't even know who they are. Great. Not to mention the absence of a wallet, no driver's licence, no bank cards." She frowned. "And he cut all the labels from his clothes, bit weird."

"Maybe he didn't." Toop took a deliberate drink from his mug. "Maybe someone else did."

Sally looked uncomfortable.

She readjusted her position on the couch, crossing her legs and covering her feet with a pillow, as the flippancy from her voice evaporated.

"So, the reason I tried to call you." She looked concerned but Toop remained silent, listening and waiting. "Now, just remember," said Sally, "his finger nails were clean, there was no evidence of blood or skin from an attacker. There were no signs of a struggle and his prints were all over the gun. But, there was one thing." Her fingers weaved together as she spoke, "A bruise."

"Where?"

"On his right cheek. The discolouring is faint, meaning that there can't have been a great amount of force involved, and to be honest I didn't even notice it when I first examined the body at the scene. The bruise is faded but it's definitely there and given the colour and the time frame that we are working with, I'm fairly confident that it happened not too long before he died." She leant over the coffee table and reached for a folder, removing a single photograph.

"I brought you this." She handed the photograph to Toop. It was a headshot. Sally's gloved hand was just visible in the corner of the photo, her thumb pulling the hair back from the deceased's face. The photo showed that hair growth had been suppressed in two mirror image halves, exposing a v-shaped point in the centre of the man's forehead. A widow's peak, thought Toop, with a lower than usual point of intersection. His thoughts clicked over, it was an example of a dominant inherited trait.

"See here," said Sally, tracing her finger over the picture, "the bruises are all parallel, clear linear marks that are separated by a thin line of central clearing. If you look carefully, just here, the blood directly beneath the impact has been displaced to the sides which is indicative of finger marks."

"A slap mark."

"Yes," replied Sally, "which made me think that..."

"That it was inflicted by female."

"Well, yes, perhaps."

Toop placed the photo down on the table, sat back onto the couch, and drummed his fingers along his jaw.

"So, there was someone else there," he said.

Sally's voiced dipped lower still.

"It's not impossible."

Chapter 33

Late 80s

Murder or suicide?

McNab sat at his desk. The question stared back at him from a sheet of headed paper. It was written in his scrawled writing and underlined twice. The question mark had been darkened, traced over in black ink.

He twiddled the pen between his fingers, catching sight of his watch. Isla would be fast asleep, long showered and tucked up in bed. No bedtime story from daddy tonight, he thought. Caroline would be curled up on the couch reading, with smooth legs, and her clean hair smelling of coconut. He smiled. His wife had put up with a lot over the last two years. Promotion had been tough on both of them.

The pathologist's initial report was already on his desk and McNab had read it three times, the results unchanging.

Mechanism of death: Exsanguination caused by severed artery, blood loss to a degree sufficient to cause the termination of all biological functions.

Manner of death: Circumstances surrounding the cause of death are undetermined, awaiting further investigation.

Nothing that McNab didn't know already, but there was one piece of new information. It had been hand written in black biro and bordered on illegible, an end note that the pathologist had scribbled on in retrospect, squished into the additional notes box.

The finding of Lewy bodies and the degeneration of catecholaminergic neurones at post-mortem indicate that the deceased suffered from Parkinson's disease.

McNab read it and tossed the document aside, the sentence logged to memory.

He clasped his hands behind his back and stretched out his vertebrae, his spine cricking in two places. He felt tired and his eyes stung from having his contacts in too long. He berated himself for forgetting his glasses.

The calls hadn't stopped.

He had not long gotten off the phone with the lab, four calls in total. Finding fingerprints had not been difficult, the weapon was covered in them; there were clear bloodied prints all over the utility knife. McNab had been ninety-nine percent sure that they belonged to the deceased and he was right. The final call had confirmed it; the prints were indeed those of Bill Anderson. Not that McNab had time to congratulate himself. He had already issued orders for the entire room to be minutely dusted and fumed to check for additional prints, prints belonging to someone else.

Of which there could be many.

He rubbed his neck and sighed. The janitor's office doubled as a store cupboard, used by tens of employees, all of whom had fingers and all of whom he would need to talk to.

He really needed sleep but a full night's rest was a rare occurrence for a Detective Chief Inspector, never mind a new parent. It had happened two times in total, twice he had been allowed to sleep through until his alarm clock went off. Two nights of uninterrupted sleep in the best part of a year. He felt old.

It was not quite nine o'clock. An hour more and he would let himself go home.

McNab turned back to the piece of paper, thinking out loud.

"Okay, what happened to you, Bill Anderson." He leafed through the photographs that had been sent over, going through the motions once more. He lent back in his chair, balancing on two legs, and craned his head backwards in the direction of his open door.

"Davidson," he shouted.

The young officer, new enough to still be doing the late-night coffee runs, walked in. "Yes, Inspector?"

"I need a brain to pick. Take a seat." McNab gestured at the chair opposite his desk. "I'd like you to humour me, to try and convince me that a suicide happened this evening."

"Sorry sir?"

"Let's just say that I'm rather tired of listening to my own thoughts. It gets a bit tedious up there, rattling around in my head," answered McNab with a gentle smile. "So I was hoping that you could share your insight with me, a fresh perspective if you will." He leant forward, elbows on his desk. "Tell me, what evidence do we have to suggest that Mr Anderson took his own life?"

McNab's encouraging tone prompted the lad and Davidson pulled out a seat, sitting opposite his boss, his nerves dissipating as he delved into an informative and knowledgeable monologue.

Smart kid, thought McNab.

"Well," he began, "we have a weapon at the scene of the crime with the victim's fingerprints on it and it's not a gun or a machete but a bog standard commonly owned utility knife, something that the deceased would most likely have used on a daily basis. Second, the cuts inflicted by the blade were deliberately placed. There was a clear, calculated intent behind each incision whereas in examples of homicide the victim is often marked with defensive cuts on their palms and undersides of their arms, visible signs of an attempt to escape their attacker. But no such marks were found on Bill Anderson, just a single vertical slit down his forearm." He paused for a breath. "Also, while wrist slitting is often showcased in films as being a common method of suicide, it is much harder than advertised to hit the correct artery. More often than not wrist slitters fail in their goal, resulting in a painful, bloody mess which usually causes severe nerve and tendon damage. In the best-case scenarios victims are left with a weak, deformed hand but it's not uncommon for all mobility to be lost. In other words, achieving such a perfect cut that eliminates the possibility of failure would have required research and planning. This is an example of a well-prepared suicide, carefully thought out in advance. Additionally, it's not a big thing but the deceased has pulled back the sleeve of his shirt to expose his skin. In cases of homicide it's normal for victims to be stabbed through layers of clothing but in examples of suicide people rarely stab themselves through their clothes. Strange really to be concerned with mess when, well you know."

His cheeks flushed.

McNab leant back in his chair, letting the information wash over him then he nodded and signalled for the lad to continue.

"Then, of course, there is the suicide note which is with forensics at the moment, who are authenticating the handwriting. It is generally thought that about 30% of suicide victims leave a note, usually to ease the pain of those left behind or to increase it. Blame," he added, as if a side note, "can be a powerful thing when you can't defend yourself. In this case Mr Anderson's note fits into the first of those categories, an apology to his family left along with instructions as to how he wishes his body to be disposed of. Cremated."

He stopped, withholding the next few words, stalling them on his tongue.

"Yes?" asked McNab.

"It's just, I mean, don't you think it's strange that..."

McNab raised his hand to interrupt him. "I know what you're going to say. And, for the record, yes I do think it's strange." He smiled. "But your job is to convince me that it's suicide, not to doubt it."

"Yes. Sorry sir."

"But your insight is noted," said McNab. "Carry on."

"Well there are no obvious signs of a struggle, no trail of blood across the room, no broken or displaced furniture, no unexplained impressions or marks on the carpet. There is just the large amount of blood that was ejected across the room when the artery was severed. This is supported by initial reports which indicate that the blood splatter patterns fit with the body's location. Finally, the presence of alcohol at the scene could lend itself towards suicide."

The two officers sat in silence, mulling it over.

"Thank you, Davidson," said McNab. "Greatly appreciated. But you should get yourself home, it's late. Early start tomorrow."

"Thank you, sir." He got up to leave, pausing in the doorway on his way out. "Do you think..."

"A difficult question that," smiled McNab. "See you in the morning."

The pen flicked between his fingers. Based on everything that the young officer had said it had to be suicide.

But it was definitely strange, he thought, that a man would leave a letter of apology to his family.

A family that didn't exist.

McNab had not been able to find a single living relative to contact. Bill Anderson lived alone and the emergency contact information on his employment contract had been left blank.

McNab chewed on the end of his pen, a dirty habit. There were two possible scenarios. Either, Mr Anderson was estranged from his family in which case writing a final note of apology was entirely possible. McNab knew this because during his time in the police he had come to realise that in death people often expressed thoughts and feelings that they were unable to express in life. Asking for forgiveness, he had learned, required a type of bravery that was not possessed by many. Perhaps Mr Anderson was one of those people, courageous only in death.

Or, thought McNab, there was the alternative scenario.

The one in which Bill Anderson didn't write the note at all.

The question lingered with him as he reached for his jacket. He gathered the documents from his desk and locked them in the side drawer, pocketing the key in his trousers. The autopsy report went into his bag; some reading to do over breakfast. Hopefully Isla wouldn't mind her dad multitasking as he spooned chucks of mashed up banana into her mouth. The image of his daughter brought a smile to his face.

Car keys? Car keys?

McNab ran his hands over his trouser pockets and rummaged in his jacket, lost in thoughts of sleep and breakfast.

He didn't notice the man standing in his office until he was right in front of him.

McNab took a step back and looked up.

His night was not over.

Not by a long way.

Chapter 34

Present Day

The interior layout of the house was simple. It was architecturally very efficient; all the prerequisites of a modern flat divided over three compact floors and three bedrooms. Two of the bedrooms contained beds, only one of them used, the other was still decorated to satisfy the tastes of a twelve-year-old girl.

The Spice Girls phase. Cece cringed. She really needed to take those posters down.

The blueprint of the house was embedded in Cece's memory; she could navigate her way from room to room with her eyes closed. The front door opened onto a short L-shaped hall with rooms off it; a living room, closet toilet and an open plan kitchen with a large wooden table. The back door opened straight into the dining area, not that it was ever used. Her uncle always ate at the breakfast bar, alone.

Cece bit into her lower lip as she walked through the living room door, she should have visited more.

"Weird," she muttered, overly aware of the sound of her own voice.

It felt strange sneaking around her uncle's house, a house that she had grown up in.

A home from home.

The house was silent. Cece hung back, just enough to prevent her from being seen through the window. Better safe than sorry, she concluded. No suspicious neighbours, meant no cops. The heavy curtains provided a good shield. Police, she knew, would be bad, very bad.

It didn't feel homely, not anymore.

The antique clock in the corner chimed twice and Cece's heart skipped a beat, lodging itself in her mouth. The sharp intake of oxygen caught in her throat, trapping the next breath in her windpipe.

Shit, she cursed, catching her breath.

Get a grip.

She took her time to look over the room, not moving from her concealed position. Orderly as ever. No clutter. The minimalist decor exuded calm, a feature appreciated by Cece for the first time. Her heart beat slowed. The assortment of adjectives that she had used as a child had been less prudent; boring, dull, plain. Drab, that had been one of her personal favourites during her early teens. Uninspired, that became the critique a few years later.

The prevalent colour in the room was an unassuming, pastel green. More tranquil apparently. Like snot, she had retorted, displaying the tactful innocence of a seven-year-old. Cece smiled at the memory. Even as an adult, working as a professional house dresser, she had not been allowed to alter a single thing. Not for a lack of trying. But her uncle would just smile kindly at her suggestions, humouring her, while avoiding eye contact.

Cece's gaze swept across the carpet and up to the ceiling, looking for anything out of place. Nothing obvious. Everything was in its allotted spot. Just so. Cece smiled. In this instance, her uncle's frustrating habits made things a lot easier. A perfect, ordered room. Everything tidied away in drawers with doors shut tight, no visible evidence of clutter, just two large paintings on the bare walls.

She pictured him walking in and sitting in his armchair.

Growing up, the minimalistic room, uninspired or not, had been one of Cece's most favourite places. Her dad's house had been, and still was, an array of chaos. Stuff everywhere, an anarchy of art work, collectables, books and antiques, some of them genuine, some not so genuine. True, she loved the pandemonium of her father's house but her uncle Jon's offered a welcome haven, miles from the bedlam. Cece looked around once more and noted how the decor failed to reflect her uncle's financial gains, unless of course you knew the true value of the two paintings hanging on the wall. Originals. Both Monet. Her uncle wasn't a boastful man. He'd most likely outlive his money.

Cece regretted the thought straight away. She turned swiftly and headed upstairs. She had no proof that anything had happened to her uncle. Just a feeling. Well, that and his chosen area of work. Cece frowned. Any enemies that he did have would be powerful. Wealthy individuals with significant resources. She didn't like the implication in her own words.

Stairs led up to the second floor; a bathroom, master bedroom and a small reading room.

A quick scan of the bedroom. Everything just so. The corners of the bed folded and tucked, sheets smoothed. There were three pairs of shoes lined up beneath the window and a long, mirrored walk-in wardrobe. Closed.

It would help if you had the faintest clue what you were looking for, thought Cece, as she went to open the wardrobe. She hesitated, taking note of her hand as it hovered an inch from the handle. The doubt could be read in her features. It felt intrusive. Ironic, smiled Cece, given that you've just broken into the bloody place. Her fingers moved forward. Stopped. But going through his clothes, that was personal.

"Too weird," she said, the words spoken in a whisper. It didn't feel right.

She took a step back, her eyes catching on his bedside table before she walked out.

Third floor.

Entering her old room was like taking a step back in time. On the far wall, Baby Spice promised, in large pink font, to spice up the life of every boy and every girl. Cece turned to look at the nonsensical, vaguely euphemistic phrase that had been cut out by her and stuck onto her mirror. "I wanna zig a zig ah." Oh God, thought Cece, not withholding a smile.

The two shelves were occupied by a selection of photos; it was the only evidence of clutter in the whole house. Cece held her face up to each image, recalling the memories one by one; ice-cream in the park, Thursday cinema nights, slush puppy and popcorn, always mixed, sugar and salt, her first day of primary school and her first day of secondary school. Cece caught sight of her own smile reflected in the glass. It receded slowly, snagged on a recurring notion. Cece had always wondered, thought of it as strange, that her uncle had never had a family of his own. Not once had he gone on a date or introduced her to a special lady friend.

What was that?

Cece froze instantly, her body rejecting all movement.

She had definitely heard something. Hadn't she? Her mind raced. There were many things that could have caused the house to creak. Innocent things.

She waited. Silence.

The mind can play tricks, she thought. Maybe it was nothing. You're just on edge, that's all.

Cece released her body and let out a long breath. "You're going crazy," she whispered. Disappearances, conspiracy theories, creaking houses. Note to self, consider watching less TV.

Feeling composed, if not a little embarrassed, Cece slipped into the en-suite bathroom. The door clicked shut behind her and the room lit up. Sensor switch. She raised her hand to shield her eyes from the harsh glare. White floor, white sink, white walls. Clean, clean, clean, thought Cece. A door, identical to the one that she had just come through, occupied the opposite wall. It led to the third bedroom; a Jack and Jill bathroom, two doors, accessible from both rooms.

At least that was the original design.

Cece stood in the middle of the third bedroom. Her uncle had made no attempt to hide it. If the police were to happen upon it, he would be behind bars within hours.

***

The woman's nose hovered inches from the wardrobe door. She could smell perfume ebbing through the tiny gaps, through the marginal spaces created around the hinges.

She didn't move, remaining silent. Dark filled the cupboard, black but for the faint ribbon of light that leaked in along the carpet. The light was quickly drowned out, futile in its attempts to infiltrate the blackness.

Two feet, untouched by light settled into the carpet and compressed the twisted tufts of soft wool. Two feet, separated from the narrow strip of daylight by a single inch. The woman held one hand pressed against her lips, the intrinsic urge to breathe burning deep into both lungs with a fierce pain. The other hand was clutched onto her prize, her fingers sweating.

Her silent pleas remained muttered in the dim air. The house should have been empty, she thought, willing the person on the other side of the door to turn around.

Please. Just turn around and walk away.

Two sets of eyes burrowed into each other, separated by the width of a single mirrored door. One was met by her own reflection, the other by complete darkness. The woman could see nothing but darkness and the imagined depiction of an unknown face.

Time stopped.

"Too weird." The feminine whisper was followed by footsteps.

Wordless thoughts counted in silence.

Eight, nine, ten.

Then the woman allowed herself a delicious intake of air.

That was close. Too close.

Chapter 35

Present Day

It wasn't a hot night. A draft crept along the living-room floor.

Toop tossed and turned on the couch. His skin stuck to the sheets with fresh sweat. Part conscious, he ripped the saturated cotton sheets from his body and threw them to the floor. His t-shirt followed, peeled from his moist back.

He closed his eyes.

The noise of collapsing snowpack filled the silent room and thunder ripped through his ear drums, white powder compressing and shifting in violent thumps, the mortal rumble encasing him from all sides.

It's too late, it's too late. The words sent a wave of panic through him.

Her lips were blue. Her skin was bloodless and pale from the cold: ghostly white from fear. He held her in his arms, embracing her tiny numb frame. She felt so cold. He held her there for a long time until his arms hurt and his clothes were drenched. She was melting. There was no warmth left in her. He held her tighter. But she was dissolving in his arms. Puddles of red snow formed at his feet.

He kissed her head again and again. Desperate. Almost violent. He begged her not to leave, tearing at her skin with his nails and digging his hands into her back.

Please. Please.

Toop awoke to the sound of his own voice and it took him a minute to get his bearings, his eyes straining as they adjusted to the darkness. He surveyed the room: couch, table, pillows. The larger objects started to come into focus as indistinct, black masses. Had he been shouting? He glanced around the room to check that he hadn't woken Sally. The sweat had gone cold and goose pimples covered his arms. He didn't notice.

Toop sat up on the couch and looked at his watch. Four forty-five. Two hours' sleep, he calculated. He stood up and walked to the window, pulling the curtain aside an inch. He could hear the gentle drizzle of rain. It would be light soon.

In ten minutes, he was dressed. Shorts, t-shirt and a light waterproof jacket. He grabbed his helmet and stepped outside. The rain felt good on his skin. Clean.

Sally lay in bed listening to the sound of bike tyres carving through gravel, followed by the swing of the garden gate. She turned over and pulled the duvet up around her shoulders. In two hours, he would be back for breakfast. She would make eggs.

Poached, she thought, before falling back to sleep.

Chapter 36

Late 80s

The man took up most of the doorway, his chest almost level with McNab's nose.

How the hell had he failed to notice this man entering the office, thought McNab. The man had to be at least six foot five, maybe six.

McNab adjusted his footing and stepped back, annoyed that he had been caught unawares. The figure towering in front of him didn't seem to notice, or care, noted McNab. At a glance, McNab placed him in his mid-sixties although there was nothing other than a head of close-cropped white hair that was remotely ageing about him. He had broad shoulders and an athletic build, and his short-sleeved shirt was stretched to capacity. He looked like a retired Marine sergeant, thought McNab, or one of those action men figures that he used to play with as a kid.

"Angus McNab?" The man was soft spoken.

McNab looked up, physically upwards. He was the biggest man that he had ever seen. McNab straightened his back and stared into the man's eyes, wondering how he got in the building. It suddenly occurred to McNab that it was late, very late, and the office was deserted. Davidson had hit the main lights on the way out and the huge man was blocking McNab's only exit. McNab held out his hand.

"Yes. How can I help you?"

No response. The man's eyes darted around the room and McNab's hand hung in the space between them. The visitor didn't acknowledge it. He stood in silence, wringing his shovel sized hands together in a fluid and continuous motion like clogs on a wheel. McNab's eyes caught on the man's hands as they withdrew from their mesmerising cycle, rising to touch the back of his neck. The man touched his face, his forehead, his earlobes. Finally, he ran his fingers through his hair where they hesitated, twitched, and returned to his pockets.

Then it hit McNab, the reason why he wasn't intimidated. It was the man standing in front of him, he was the one that was frightened.

McNab didn't let the realisation show on his face but the question tugged at the back of his mind. What scared a man of that size?

"Would you like a seat?" asked McNab, turning his body and extending his arm to expose a desk and two chairs. Although, reasoned McNab, the man probably had a clear view of his office straight over his head.

"Thank you." He sat down.

McNab walked around his desk and pulled out his own chair.

"What was it that you wanted to talk to me about?"

***

One photo. That was all he had.

Jon lifted the frame from his bedside table and hugged it into his chest, cocooning the precious item in the depths of his crumpled body with his back rested against the side of the bed. A broken man.

Jonathan Swan had never met his mother. She had died bringing him into the world.

Eclampsia.

His father had made it his life's objection to ensure that his son knew the meaning of the word from a young age. It was a word that had plagued his entire childhood, a childhood that he didn't deserve. Worthless, unwanted boy.

Murderer. That was another word.

The peak in blood pressure had been too much for his mother's delicate body. As with some rare cases there had been no convulsions, no visible signs of a seizure. She had simply fallen into a deep coma, into an endless and fatal sleep. The last thing she heard was the cry of her baby boy, a virgin sound that leaked from his tiny lungs.

Jon closed his eyes, reciting an old memory. He knew it off by heart. The note that she had left him, tucked at the back of his sock drawer, away from his father's prying eyes. *John 15:13. Greater love hath no one than this: one who lay down one's life for another.* His mother had chosen his name before he was born. Jonathan. She was not a naive woman, his mother was aware of her odds. She knew that she would die.

The bed creaked under the weight of his body. "How could you," mumbled Jon, the words barely audible. "I hate you!" His head fell between his knees and he felt his lungs writhing beneath his rib cage. Why did it hurt so much? How could he miss her so much, someone he'd never even met?

Pathetic, unwanted boy. The cruel, gritty voice of his father burned into his skin.

From day one his father had thought of the pregnancy as a vicious poison. It was too dangerous and uncertain, he pleaded with his wife but she held his weathered face in her palm and smiled. She wasn't a well woman. She suffered from both diabetes and hypertension, increasing the risks tenfold. But she had wanted nothing more than to bring a child into the world, it was what God put her on this earth to do. And her husband had never been able to say no to her and so her wish was granted. Jon's mother fulfilled her reason for being and she paid for it with her last mouthful of air.

A life for a life.

There had been no question of guilt, no judge or jury, just a single executioner. Jon. Jonathan Swan would forever be a butcher in the eyes of his father. It was a view that was reiterated to him again and again, a sentiment delivered with great precision and reinforced by the power of his father's fists.

Jon hadn't spoken to his father in over two years. The old man had long been defeated by the bottom of a bottle, drowned by a broken heart.

Jon jerked his head up. He needed to get out, out of this room, out of this house, out of his head. He released his arms from his body and wiped his sleeve across his eyes, the photograph sliding to the carpet. He wanted to run and never stop, away from the flat, down the street, and the next, and the next. He couldn't bear to be in the room one moment longer. It was trapping him. The panic stared to rise in his throat.

"Stop it! Stop it!" he begged. *Acknowledge, guide, replace, acknowledge.*

He tried to focus his mind.

The smell of his own vomit slapped him hard across the face and brought him back to reality, causing him to recoil with a violent jar of his neck. Clothes, clean clothes, he needed to change. A party, yes, Jesse had mentioned something about a party. Jon convinced his body to move from its dejected position and walked through to the shower. His hands trembled as he dried and dressed himself. Jeans, white t-shirt. He gazed at his reflection. He looked quite normal from the outside. Jon stood in front of the mirror for the next four minutes, his hands nervously rubbing up and down the sides of his thighs. Perhaps he could persuade her that he was normal. A normal, young man with a crush.

The thought of her developed without censorship. He pictured her naked body, firm thighs, flat stomach, and small, perfectly formed breasts. The delicate touch of her hands moving closer and closer to his stiffening groin. He closed his eyes. The sensation brought him to a point of familiar dread, sweaty palms, twitching fingers, his heart pounding in his throat. Jon hurried the thought to the back of his mind, afraid that he would arrive as he stood there in front of his mirror. Jon cast his eyes towards his feet, ashamed. He could picture the look of disgust in her face. What if he finished the moment her lips touched his skin?

He felt physically sick.

Then the answer caught him. The band. He still had the elastic band. It was stuffed into the back of his wallet.

Steadied, Jon collected the essentials from around his room. Keys, wallet, a small flask filled with whiskey and, after a moment of hesitation, a condom. A gift from Jesse. Jon slotted the transparent packaging between the leather dividers in his wallet. He was a normal boy, a normal man with normal male urges, urges that deserved to be satisfied. The thought was his but Jon heard it in Jesse's voice. Direct. Absolute. It's a game, Jesse's words this time, you've just got to understand the rules, simple as that buddy. Play it right, and you're guaranteed to score. A Jesse Jenkins smile.

He headed out the door. Jon had already decided that he would find Jesse, get drunk, and let the night take him wherever it wanted to. He would drown his ghosts in hard spirits.

Darkness had set in and the street was lit up by rows of identical lampposts. Jonathan Swan could not have known what his decision would cost him.

Jon had not been born with the foresight of his mother.

174

Chapter 37

Present Day

The young woman stepped out of the cupboard. She had what she came for.

"Shhh." The hinge emitted a loud oil-less screech. She froze still and waited, listening as the sound fought against the silence. It weakened before it was engulfed in still air.

Her heartbeat slowed, returning to an almost normal pace. She wasn't out of danger yet.

"Don't be scared," she whispered to herself.

How did it get to this? she thought as she eased her way down the stairs, grateful for carpets. But then, what exactly had she expected was going to happen. A man was dead.

The bottom of the stairs. Almost there. She had met him only once and now he was dead.

She glanced back behind her. Someone was up there. A relative of his perhaps or maybe just the cleaner? The place was immaculate, she reasoned. She turned her head, maybe it was best not to know. She secured her prize under her arm, wanting to put the whole thing behind her.

Then she saw it. At the end of the hall. It caught in the corner of her vision as she turned on her heels and fear grabbed at her windpipe. The glass had been removed from the window. Someone had broken in. It wasn't a relative that was snooping around upstairs.

The woman ran on tiptoe through the kitchen and towards the back door. She slipped the key from her pocket and carefully inched the door open. She pushed it shut, pressing her palm flat up against the glass and guiding it closed with gentle precision. It shut without a sound. She returned the key, concealing it under a stone. He had left it there for her. Just in case, he had written.

She was almost two hundred metres down the street when she stopped. Who was upstairs? Her feet stayed glued to the pavement. The woman's back remained turned away from the house but intrigue prevented her from taking another step. Heartened chants and raised voices interrupted the quiet of the street and she looked around. A school football match was being played on one of the pitches across the road. She could make out the animated cheers of parents, their tempers roused by the sound of the referee's whistle. A small boy had just been caught offside, penalised for an offence that he had no understanding of. The bemused six-year-old, thwarted in his moment of penitential glory, was close to tears.

She turned away. Not once had her parents come to stand and shout on the sidelines. They hadn't come to a single dance recital, not one school talent show. They couldn't. She didn't have any.

The woman turned round and started walking back towards the house. She didn't know why but she had to know who was inside the house.

She would watch and wait. Out of sight.

***

"Come on, you've got to give me something to go on," said Cece, looking around the room. "I'm shooting in the dark here."

Cece had known about the hidden room in her uncle's house from a young age. Neither of the father figures in her life had chosen to hide it from her, it was the family business after all and one that she had bought into for a while. However, after the incident three years ago, she had decided to get out. The memory still caused her heart to race. It had been too close. In truth, if it hadn't been for her uncle's quick thinking and his willingness to part with a significant sum of money she would have been looking at a decent stint behind bars.

"I owe you," she whispered.

There was no secret code or security system to the room. Anyone could have walked through the bathroom, pushed the handle and uncovered her uncle's secret. Although, as a man who rarely entertained, wandering visitors weren't a large concern. Cece could count on one hand the number of people that had made it as far as the living-room. Her father and she made up two of the total count.

The room had been transformed into a workshop before Cece was born. As a child, she thought of it as her own magical hideout, hidden from the rest of the world. "Like Narnia Daddy! But it's not a wardrobe you go through, it's a bathroom." Her little hand tugged on his shirt and she gave a delighted smile. "And I'm Lucy, you remember Daddy, the little girl and Uncle Jonny is Mr Tumnus." A serious frown. "Although he has legs not hooves." Her dad hoisted her up in a single motion and planted a kiss on her nose. "You are most wise little one."

Even now as a grown woman, Cece couldn't think of her uncle as a criminal. His world was still magical to her, a glamorous fairytale. His workshop was a temple to his artistic talents. She walked around the perimeter of the room, brushing random items with the tips of her fingers; resins, powders, paints, brushes, knives, pots, pallets and frames of all shapes and sizes. Her uncle had spent over two decades creating masterpieces from inside this small room.

Fake masterpieces, she thought.

The walls were a living tribute to art forgery. Fake paintings hung from every available space. Cece's favourite, an unfinished sketch, rested against a small table. The oil painting was intended as a gift for Cece's firstborn daughter; a portrait of the seventeen-year-old Lady Hamilton portrayed as the tempting sorceress Circe. The fall of her white drapes exposed her pale throat and chest, her auburn hair gathered in a knot with loose strands teased free by the wind, staring outwards, lips just parted.

Cece smiled and continued to look around the room. She knew that her uncle cared little for the money. He was a very rich man but money had never been a primary goal. It was simply a consequence of his hobby, of his way of life, money and the risk of a criminal record. On a few occasions, he had suffered from cold feet, attacks of morality her dad called them. But her father would console him with gentle unforced words, reminding him that he was creating things of splendour, nothing to feel ashamed about. "Not everyone can see beauty the way that you do and so it's up to you to make them see."

Glancing round the walls Cece was propelled back to a period in her life when little girls were princesses and fathers were kings. Her uncle was the magician. Everything he touched was transformed into a thing of beauty. It was the same every time, for days in a row he would lock himself away in the tower devoured by an intense focus. Cece would wait patiently. Quite content. She later learned that what he achieved in those

177

few days would have taken most normal people months. Pieces of magic. She would sit admiring his paintings, watching for hours at a time, her little legs folded on the hard floor of his workshop. A child in awe.

"Where are you, Uncle Jon?" she asked.

Cece spent the next half hour searching through his things, carefully returning everything to its allotted space. She paused once or twice to leaf through papers and to read notes that had been scribbled into jotters. Lots of lists; paint colours, dimensions for paintings, ideas for future pieces. As minutes accumulated into an hour, she started to crave information. She wanted to find something, anything, even the smallest clue as to her uncle's whereabouts.

She was starting to question her search, doubting a favourable outcome.

Cece sat back in the old chair and rubbed her hands down her thighs. Her legs stretched out beneath the wooden desk. It held a well ordered, systematic clutter of items. She pulled on the handle of the first drawer, reaching right to the back and removed a small, red address book. Cece knew that it only contained a handful of personal addresses; it was filled with the contact details of potential buyers. Not that her uncle had much to do with that side of the business, her dad and her grandfather dealt with the clients. They were the true cons artists, thought Cece. Like her dad said, Uncle Jonny just made beautiful things.

She didn't entirely approve of her dad's profession. In truth, her abrupt removal from the family business had worked out for the best. Cece enjoyed staging apartments. It paid the bills and it was legal. But she had to admit, her dad was brilliant at what he did. More of an artist than a con man really.

She had never met anyone as talented as her father; a born conversationalist, who could sell God to an atheist. On a number of occasions, she had watched in awe as he took an intense interest in a client, worked to understand them and played them like a game of chess. He studied their physiology and body language. "To con is simple, just two steps," he had told her, "work out what they desire, then convince them that what you have will fill that void." His smile was always playful, childlike. "In the art world, all you have to do is convince the buyer by validating his need to believe that he has the edge on other people."

In poker terms, her father played the people rather than the cards and he made millions from it.

Cece cast the thought aside and flicked through the pages. She knew that it would be there but seeing it still came as a surprise. The address wasn't under the name that Cece expected, it was listed under A for Alexandria. No surname.

Alex.

It was the third time that she had seen the address in her uncle's writing. Each of those previous occasions it had been on sealed envelopes. Left in the kitchen, glued closed, no name, no stamp, waiting for Monday when the post office would open. "Letter boxes are unreliable, far too risky," her uncle reiterated to a young Cece.

Cece stared at the address.

The letters were printed, not joined, identical to the writing on the two envelopes. She touched the words with her fingers and thought of her uncle, a gifted artist who had always struggled with the mechanics of writing. Cece pictured the letters sitting in the kitchen, waiting to be posted.

They were the reason that she was now living in Alex's, or Alexandria's, empty room.

It started more than four weeks before, twenty-three days since she had heard from her uncle. No phone calls or texts, no invites for tea, no visits. True, his situation wasn't what most people would consider normal and although it pained her to admit it, they didn't keep in touch like they used to. Weekly dinners had dwindled and eventually stopped now that she was working in the city. In the last few years Cece noticed that he shut himself away for longer periods, often hibernating in his workshop for a week, sometimes two. But after three weeks Cece and her father had grown concerned. One night, as she had been browsing the Internet, an opportunity presented itself.

Work had been going well for Cece and she had some money saved. She wanted to move to a more central location, ideally in the West End, but buying her own place was still out of the question. That night, while searching online for a flatmate, Cece struck lucky. The exact address, the one that her uncle had been sending letters to, appeared on Buddy Up. Jon was missing and this was their chance to find him. The address was the only thing they had to go on. Cece had to get that room. It hadn't been difficult to find Lucy online and gather information about her. Current employment, bands she liked, films she'd seen, her favourite food, hobbies, activities, likes and dislikes, and even her preferred clothing brands.

Manufacturing a high Buddy-ability match had been child's play. Less than a week later, Cece had moved in.

Chapter 38

"You seem preoccupied."

Sally looked back at Toop as he followed her into the morgue. They had eaten their eggs in silence and driven into town in separate vehicles. He wouldn't be staying for long.

"Don't I always?" He managed a smile. "Sorry Sal, I had a restless night."

"You can talk to me you know."

"I know."

"I just wanted to make sure that we are clear on that point." She paused in the doorway, forcing his eyes to meet hers. "I never needed to forgive you Fergus, because there was never anything to forgive." She placed her hand on his forearm then walked into the room, not waiting for a response.

Toop appreciated it.

The smell hit him with his next step and the moment was over.

He had been in more morgues than he could remember but it was always the same. Two thoughts. It was never as cold as he expected. True, the chill succeeded in rousing the hairs on his arms but it was nothing like the freezing walk-in fridges that he had imagined as a child. Toop felt his gut contract. That smell. It was the second thing. First the potent aroma of antiseptic cleaning products, then an underlying scent of death and decomposition. An almost alarmingly sweet stench that broke in dense, wet waves. It seemed to dissipate only to strike again, returning with excelled vigour. The vile odour made Toop want to retch. It smelt like the vomit that pooled on pavements outside nightclubs.

"Sorry. I often think about how nice it would be to work in a bakery." Sally smiled. "Come have a look."

Toop walked over to the body. It was still covered. Sally pulled the sheet back to reveal the man from his shoulders up, withholding the fatal hole that occupied his chest. The man looked inexplicably sad, thought Toop. He leaned in and followed Sally's finger with his eyes as she traced across the man's cheek. With careful inspection, it was possible to see the discolouration.

"There. Every contact leaves a trace. Just like every foot leaves a footprint."

"Footprint," mouthed Toop.

"Fergus?"

But he was already out the door.

***

"Bailey?"

"Morning boss," he answered, "nice to see a bit of sun this..."

"Where are you?" The phone was pressed between Toop's right ear and his raised shoulder. His hands held the steering wheel.

"Just got to the office the now, had to stop in..."

"I'll be there in three minutes. Be ready at the front door."

"Do I need any..."

The phone went dead.

Toop was waiting for him as Bailey piled out of the station door. The engine was still running as Bailey opened the passenger door and jumped in. The vehicle was thrown into gear before he had time to speak.

Bailey tilted an open box in Toop's direction.

"Muffin? I've got blueberry and chocolate chip. Wasn't sure what you'd like."

"I'm fine. Thanks."

"Thought you'd say that." He smiled and closed the lid. "But you never know. So where are we going?"

"The car Jimmy bought, there were sandy footprints on the floor."

"Yes?"

"I assumed they were Jimmy's."

"Jimmy at the beach! You've got to be kidding. Don't think anybody's seen him outside that pub for months."

"Exactly."

"Oh." Bailey said. "You think that they belong, I mean that they belonged to the dead guy?" He stared down at the box of muffins and pursed his lips before looking up with interest. "Can we use the prints to identify him?"

"No."

Bailey's face fell.

"But," Toop continued, without removing his eyes from the road, "sand is a valuable piece of trace evidence that we could use to link him to a certain location, help us build up a picture. The beach, like you said." He turned to look at his partner. "And you're a local; you know all of the beaches."

"Yes," Bailey beamed. "Yes, I do."

"Great because I'm counting on you to find me an answer quicker than forensics can."

Bailey offered him a blank stare.

"It will take too long for the lab to process," Toop explained. "So, you tell me, where are we going?"

***

Bailey sat in the car and fumbled with his shoes, his fingers caught up in the knotted laces.

He gathered his eyelids into a deliberate squint, straining to see through the windscreen. The salty sea air gusted through the open door and filled his nostrils. Bailey wiped his fringe from his face and scanned the Big Sands beach, searching for his boss. He could just make out a blurred figure.

Toop tightened his jacket round his body and headed across the sand. He stood looking out across the sea, the mountains of Skye and Torridon filling the horizon. He was sheltered from the sharp onshore wind by the small and uninhabited mass of land known as Longa Island. The huge looming sand dunes that enclosed the beach provided an additional release from the relentless breeze.

A pocket of still.

Toop didn't look too hard, he didn't force it. He hoped that whatever he was looking for would reveal itself. He just needed a foothold, something that made sense.

But there was nothing. Nothing made sense. It was all strange to him now. The remote landscape that he had grown up in was alien to him. He understood high rise buildings and dark alleys. He closed his eyes, the realisation unsettling him. Kara was in the sea, she was in the mountains.

Toop offered an upward glance as Bailey approached.

"What were you doing?" asked Toop.

"Sorry, my laces, I had to..."

"Never mind, let's go." Toop walked straight past Bailey as he finished his sentence, his mind already on the next location. "Gruinard Bay you said?"

"Aye," Bailey ran after him, stumbling in the soft sand, "the pink beach."

It proved to be pink and fruitless.

Three hours later they were parked up at Gairloch beach and Toop was starting to lose hope of finding anything. Five beaches, ten tons of sand, and countless miles of coastline. Nothing. They sat in Toop's car and stared out at the grey water, the windscreen wipers left on. The weather had worsened to a persistent, dreary drizzle and Bailey's enthusiasm was wavering. But he was still smiling, making Toop wonder if an alternative facial expression was even an option.

"So, what's the plan now?" asked Bailey, delivering the question between mouthfuls of chocolate chip muffin. He balanced the box on his knee, grateful for the sugary content. Bailey doubted that his boss had a stopping point, or a braking point for that matter. He would need the additional calories.

"We keep checking beaches," replied Toop. "One of them has to be the right one."

"But, what I don't understand is how will you know which one is the right one? It's not like there will be nice footprints left lying for us."

"I'll know when I see it."

"See what exactly? It's all the same, just piles of sand." He raised the muffin to his mouth, producing a spray of crumbs when he spoke. "Although my pop and I did find an unexploded bomb at the beach once when I was a boy, even made it into the news. It could have been there for months before we came across it."

"Unlikely," replied Toop, absentmindedly. "Someone else would have picked it up. Was probably just a big storm the day before, they tend to churn up unusual objects."

"Nah. No storm. Nobody else went there, it was our secret beach. We used to go there to play marooned pirates!"

"Sorry?" asked Toop.

"Like on a deserted island..."

"I mean the secret part," interrupted Toop, not smiling.

Bailey stared back at him, a chunk of chocolate held in his mouth.

"And have we been to this secret beach yet?" asked Toop, struggling to reign in his annoyance.

"Not exactly..."

"Well?" Toop spat the single syllable.

Bailey was lost for words, a lifetime first. The remains of his muffin sat limply in his suspended hand.

"Just give me the directions," said Toop as he put the car into reverse.

***

The view stopped Toop in his tracks and feelings collided at once.

Awe and triumph.

He had found what he was looking for.

Mellom Udrigle beach.

The turquoise water stretched out against the horizon, the clean white sand set against a backdrop of ashen dunes. Toop caught himself as he stared out at the rocky headland. It was beautiful.

However, it was not the horizon that held his attention.

His mind was focused on one thing.

Toop sunk his feet into the sand, leaving large footprints as he walked towards it.

Chapter 39

Late 80s

Bill was murdered.

McNab sank back into his chair, relaying what the man had just told him. His body slouched into the leather, the posture knocked from his torso by the three words.

A quiet contemplation fell over the room; two men silent, both unsure of how to progress. Hesitant.

"That is quite an accusation Mr..." McNab paused, moving his elbows forward to meet his desk. "Sorry, I didn't catch your name."

"Alec. Alec Allaway." He adjusted his broad shoulders and shifted uncomfortably. "Although I would appreciate it if that information was kept between us."

"Of course, Mr Allaway."

"Alec."

"I take it, Alec, that you knew Mr Anderson. In which case, please allow me to offer my condolences." McNab made to stand up. "Can I offer you a coffee or..."

"I would prefer not to waste your time officer," Allaway interrupted. "I did some digging on you, asked around, talked to a few friends that I still have in the police force. Word is that you are a decent cop, still straight and honest." He leaned in towards the desk. "You need to understand that my friend didn't kill himself."

"You seem quite sure of this."

"I am."

"I'm assuming that you've seen the news and that you are aware of the situation," said McNab. "No evidence of a struggle, a knife covered in fingerprints and a suicide note found at the scene. It doesn't look good."

The man ignored the comment.

"Operation Boot," he said. "Have you heard of it?"

Politics was not McNab's strong point. He rubbed his left temple, coaxing the memory to the front of his mind. He had heard the name before.

"1953. Iranian coup d'état," offered Allaway.

The coup, McNab had read about it. He recalled a modern studies lesson at secondary school.

"Start of the Cold War," he replied, "the democratically elected leader in Iran, he was overthrown."

"Mossadegh, yes," said Allaway. "Operation Boot was the name that was given to the British intelligence plot, a covert operation intended to overthrow the Iranian Government. The whole thing was a conspiracy, orchestrated and staged in a joint mission between the CIA and MI6. Britain needed assistance and it was in the interests of the US to restore the Shah of Iran to his throne."

McNab wasn't sure of the relevance or about how to respond. In truth, he didn't have a clue what the man was getting at.

"Oil?" McNab asked.

"Yes. It was all about getting a share of Iran's oil wealth and ensuring that the country remained under the command of an allied dictator." He paused. "Iran, in the fifties, was not a nice place to be. Bill and I were posted in Tehran at the time. And when shit hit fan we got covered."

"You're an MI6 agent?" asked McNab. That explained his physical condition, he thought, shifting in his seat. McNab's evening had taken an unusual turn.

"Was. We both got out after Iran."

"What happened?"

Allaway's expression hardened, his tone wasn't friendly. "What I am about to tell you, it's not something that I like to talk about. I don't talk about it." His eyes betrayed a hint of weakness. "But Bill was a friend and he did not kill himself."

McNab offered a slow nod.

***

Jon recognised one of the girls who was laughing in the corner.

She had long, mousy brown hair and looked drunk. Maybe high. She was swaying on her five-inch heels and kept gripping onto the arm of the boy next to her. A piercing giggle carried across the room. Jon noted the hunger in the boy's eyes, a greedy look each time she fell into him, her pert breast pressing against his chest. Jon pictured the boy getting hard beneath his jeans, the blood rising up in his crotch. His gaze held, fascinated by the incriminating bulge between the boy's pockets. He continued to stare as a hand, nails painted pink, entered the image. A single, extended finger ran its way across the sinful mound in slow teasing stokes.

Another high-pitched giggle.

Jon averted his eyes, remembering where he had seen her. She had been talking to Jenny, that night at the party, the night that she gave him her address.

Jenny Pingleton. Room 209, Queen Margaret Hall, Bellshaugh Court.

He repeated the address in his head, unaware that he was smiling. The alcohol had numbed his face.

"Jonny Boy!" Jesse's voice rose above the music and he appeared through the crowd, arms raised in the direction of his friend. "Are you ready for it? Because tonight my friend, we are getting fucked up!"

His arms collapsed round Jon's neck. "What do you say Jonny, babe!" Jesse grinned and waved a clear plastic bag in front of Jon's face. Jon's eyes followed the little coloured pills as they swung back and forth.

A mixture of spirits and beer pumped through Jon's veins and he felt the room start to spin.

"I'm in." He nodded, unable to stop.

"Bloody brilliant."

Jesse threw his arm around Jon's neck and they headed for a bedroom.

Jenny Pingleton saw the door close as she walked into the party. She was wearing yellow, a polka dot mini skirt, high-waisted with a strip of pale skin visible beneath her white crop top.

***

"August 19th, 1953," Allaway's face darkened. "It was the day that changed Bill Anderson's life forever. The man I knew was never the same again."

McNab remained silent. He rubbed a hand across his face, fighting sleep deprivation. He could sleep later. Now, he would sit and listen. He said nothing, the act prompting the man to speak.

Allaway's large hands extended into the vacant space between them, his body revealing more than his tone. The movement of his vast palms stirred the cool air, producing a gentle draft. More than once he paused to look around, as if he expected someone to stop him.

"It started in 1952 when the CIA and MI6 came up with a strategy, a propaganda mission. They intended to supply Iran with arms and trucks, a so called selfless act that would allow Iran to save itself from the dangers posed by a godless communism. Weapons, mainly rifles and sten guns, began pouring into the country. The British flooded the arms market, using RAF aircraft to fly the guns into Iran via Baghdad. First, they armed the tribesmen in the North and then they paid the mobsters in Tehran to fight for them."

Allaway was standing now, his huge frame towering over the desk. McNab noticed that the colour ebbed from his knuckles as he gripped the edge of the wooden table.

"The Americans and the British were knowingly putting guns into the hands of thugs. These were official orders, orders approved at the highest levels of government."

The sentence robbed the energy from his body and he sat back in his chair, dejected.

Ashamed.

"On 19th August, pro-Shah riots backed by the CIA broke out. Our government paid gangsters and hooligans to take to the streets and fight, to protest against communism by using force and violence. What ensued can only be described a vicious bloodbath. Crowds of civilians, ordinary people, gathered outside their homes armed with makeshift weapons, just like lambs to the slaughter. Hundreds of innocent people were killed that day."

He looked straight at McNab.

"There are certain things that you cannot un-see officer, things that will haunt you forever."

"I'm sorry, I can't imagine..." McNab didn't know how to finish the sentence.

"Bill never recovered."

McNab watched as a vacant haze caught on the man's face. A moment and it was gone.

"After Iran," continued Allaway, "Bill developed haemophobia, an extreme and irrational fear of blood, which the doctors believe was caused by the repeated and direct trauma that Bill witnessed that day."

"So..." McNab's mind was racing, formulating questions quicker than he could articulate them. "You're saying..."

"Bill's condition was severe," said Allaway. "A significant increase in blood pressure could occur hours, sometimes days before an upcoming encounter with blood. He went through a number of cognitive behavioural therapy sessions and experimented with various medications but nothing worked. The mere thought of blood caused Bill's heart to race and more often than not he passed out cold."

Pause. McNab chose not to talk.

"It is inconceivable that Bill could have slit his own wrists. Medically impossible," reiterated Allaway. "He would have been unconscious before he lifted the knife. Just the idea of cutting his wrists would have paralysed him."

Everything seemed to speed up in McNab's head. All of it, the results from the post-mortem, the forensics report, the fingerprinting, the blood spatters, if Allaway was to be believed, then everything, all of it, had just been blown to shit.

Both men sat in silence, looking at each other, their features not giving anything away. Both thinking the same thing.

The game had just begun.

It was McNab that broke the silence. "Was Mr Anderson close to his family?"

As though reading his mind, Allaway replied, "You don't believe that Bill wrote the suicide note."

McNab didn't say anything.

"The contents of the note made it into the news," Allaway said, deciphering McNab's thoughts a second time.

"Shit."

"And no," said Allaway, "he wasn't. Close. Bill lost contact with his family over twenty years ago. He had a wife and a young boy. Although I guess the boy would be in his late thirties now, William I think. It got to the point that Bill couldn't bandage his boy's wounds, couldn't be near the lad if he hurt himself. Bill lost all sense of perspective, he was sending the poor kid to the emergency room twice a week. Over time Bill's behaviour got too extreme and his relationship with his family suffered.

That's why he became a janitor, he could shut himself away, work at night and talk to as few people as possible." Allaway let out a sigh as he stood up. "Like I said, he was never the same again." He paused, his eyes meeting McNab's. "The government took something from him. He sacrificed everything, his family, his health and his mind. And what did he get in return?" It was rhetorical. "Bill didn't deserve what happened to him."

He towered over McNab and offered his hand. "He was a good man."

McNab shook it before Allaway turned and headed towards the door.

"One question," McNab rose from his seat as he spoke. "Do you know of anyone who might have wanted Mr Anderson dead?"

Allaway continued to walk out the door.

"I've already said too much."

He glanced back.

"The suicide note," said Allaway, "were there any abnormalities in the handwriting, small letters or cramped words?"

"Not that I'm aware of but we're still awaiting the official results."

"Strange," said Allaway, "given that Bill had Parkinson's disease."

Then he was gone.

Chapter 40

Present Day

Cece gave herself a second or two to take it all in before she left. The walls were covered with paintings, two more resting on easels, several already covered in bubble wrap, stacked together and waiting to be sold.

Her uncle's little secret, she thought.

Cece closed the door feeling deflated. She hadn't learned anything new. She had been so sure that there would have been something.

The house was silent; she could just make out the faint fall of her own footsteps. Her soundless treads were absorbed by the soft carpet as she moved down the stairs, dragging her feet and running her hand along the wall. Her mind was elsewhere. Cece reached the bottom step and paused, closing her eyes and letting out a defeated sigh, before she opened them again.

Her hand jumped straight to her mouth. It was all she could do not to swear out loud.

The wardrobe.

She stared straight into her uncle's bedroom. "What the..." she whispered, halting her words.

Cece hesitated, took a step forward then ran through the open door. She looked quickly around the room; squatting to peer under the bed and slamming the door wide open, eliminating any concealed space behind it.

Nothing, just furniture.

The expression on her face turned from one of fear to curiosity. She frowned. The wardrobe door was wide open. Cece pushed it closed with her palm, the creak of the hinges breaking the stillness.

"Doors do not open themselves," she said to herself.

Cece took a step away from the closet and sat back onto the bed, her arms extended behind her to support her body. Ten minutes later she was still sitting in the same spot. Cece eyed the room, walking her eyes back and forth. She had a distinct feeling that she was missing something, that there was something she wasn't seeing. Her thoughts raced ahead of her, exploring possible scenarios and asking countless questions. It was getting her nowhere. She needed to write it down, to organise her thoughts. It was harder to ramble on paper.

"Paper, paper," she mouthed, her eyes searching the room.

Then her stare fell on a single spot on the bedside table.

It's gone!

Cece jumped up and pounced on the small table, running her hands over the smooth wooden surface and opening each of the drawers. Her uncle's journal. It had been there just before, when she had been in his room. She had seen it. Hadn't she? It was lying next to the lamp little more than hour ago. At least, that's where he always kept it.

"You idiot," she shouted in a whisper, "why wasn't it the first thing that you looked for, how could you be so stupid?"

Cece pushed the drawers closed, quickly smoothed out the bed with her arm and walked out. She hurried to the front door, tossed the key back into the bowl, and stepped outside. The door locked behind her.

The broken glass would have to wait.

She half walked, half jogged to the street and slid into her car as she heard her phone ringing. The device vibrated against her groin. Cece slid her hand into her jeans pocket, tight, slim fit. She raised her hips off the seat to get a better angle. A picture of Lucy's face flashed on the screen as Cece pulled the phone free.

"Hi Lucy."

She listened to her flatmate's voice.

"Yeah that sounds great, thanks," replied Cece.

Pause.

"I don't mind, whatever you cook I'm sure it will be great." Cece managed a juvenile tone, followed by silence as Lucy questioned her.

"I'll be back in an hour or so. I just popped into town for a coffee."

More questions.

"I was catching up with an old friend from university." Cece didn't have trouble lying, it was a family trait.

"See you soon."

Cece hung up.

***

The woman watched as the intruder walked out of the front door and hurried along the garden path.

Only this intruder, she knew.

The woman's attention was captured the moment that she saw the young, familiar face.

She ducked down behind the bus stop, hiding her identity in one of the free timetables. She waited a few seconds before peering over the laminated leaflet so that she could watch the woman walk to her car, following her every step.

"Impossible," she whispered.

She felt sick.

Chapter 41

Present Day

Sally had one thought on her mind.

Who had slapped him and why?

Sally sat at Toop's desk, frowning as she leafed through her report yet again. The room was completely untouched, bare walls, bare desk. Not a single photograph or personal trinket cluttering his work space. Apart from the pair of dirtied mountain bike shoes that sat in the corner, the office could have belonged to anyone. Or no one, thought Sally as she opened a side drawer in searched of a pen. Her hand swept over the few contents of the compartment, removing a single biro from an unopened box.

She understood why Toop hadn't decorated his office or unpacked his house. He had memories. Many of them. And most of them, she reasoned, were tainted by loss and tragedy. She sighed and trapped the pen between her teeth to release the lid. It held briefly between her painted red lips before falling to the desk with a dull tap. Sally twisted it between her fingers, occasionally scribbling a few words in the margins.

The phone rang.

Sally reached for it, extending her unoccupied hand, without lifting her eyes from the page.

"Officer Toop's phone. Dr Gillespie speaking," she mouthed into the receiver.

"Oh hi Sally, it's Fraser. McGlone."

"Hi Fraser, we've been expecting your call," she said with a smile, placing the pen down. "Sorry Fergus is out. I'm just using his office. It's nice and quiet, he doesn't get many visitors. So how's life over at the lab, ballistics treating you well?" Her tone was friendly, casual.

"Not too bad, can't complain. I needed the change. And, well, I'm not missing the Friday night shifts, that's for sure! I've arrested enough drunken idiots to last me a lifetime."

"Two I'd say," laughed Sally. "So, what have you got for us?"

"Well, I've had a look through your report." He paused, reading from his notes. His voice altered, prolonging the words. "It states here that the cause of death is a bullet wound to the heart but the means of death has been left undetermined."

"Yes. That's correct."

"Sorry, the ex-cop in me can't help but ask. You don't..."

"We can't be certain," Sally cut him off. "What do you think?"

"What do *I* think? Hum, well, how about I tell you what I do know," he said. His voice changed then, an acquaintance turned professional. "According to your report, the shot to his chest was a close contact wound, fired from a distance of less than 20cm but not touching the victim. Ballistics evidence backs this. The photos show a degree of blackening around the wound but less than would be expected from a contact shot. If the weapon had been in direct contact with the body there would have been intense sooting around the bullet hole." He paused. Sally could hear the shuffling of paper. "Based on the inconclusive evidence regarding the means of death, I took the liberty of test firing a replica weapon into pork skin."

"Excuse me, did you just say pork, as in pig?"

"Yes, I have found it to produce the most similar characteristics to human skin."

"Oh..." Sally pictured a bloodied pig corpse swinging lifelessly from a large hook, her bowels twisting in response. Ironic, she managed a smile, given that she wouldn't have been the least bit put out if it was a human corpse.

"The shot fired from 200mm left marks on the pig's skin, and produced black powder residue, that were similar to those found on the deceased. A distance such as you would expect in a suicide."

"What about a shot fired from further away?" asked Sally.

"When shots are fired from a distance, most often in homicide cases, the black powder is sprayed more widely and sparsely around the entry point. But in the case of John Doe here, the powder was most predominant in the wound track by the pericardial track and there was a fissure in one of the ribs where the bullet had exited the body."

"And the angle?"

"I test fired the pig from three different positions to try and identify the angle at which the gun was shot. I did this based on the assumption that he was orientating the weapon towards his own torso." He cleared his throat. "Evidence suggests that the gun was most likely held horizontally at rib height and aimed at the chest area. The low positioning of the gun indicating that it was held by the victim."

"So he pulled the trigger himself."

"Yes. It would seem so."

* * *

Bailey sat in the car. His hands were trapped under his thighs, resisting the urge to move. He was under strict instructions not to leave.

He watched as his boss paced across the beach, his shoulders dipping from side to side as each foot sank into the sand.

Boyd Bailey was confused.

The cause of death was a given; a gunshot to the chest. You didn't need a pathologist to figure that one out. And the motive, well that seemed just as obvious, lonely location and a lonely man. Suicide.

The thought brought about a tightening of his brow and three creases etched into his skin as he looked out of the windscreen, focusing on his colleague. Bailey counted down, the words just loud enough to hear.

"Three, two, one."

Toop disappeared out of view.

A few moments later Toop stopped and bent over, his upper body descending into the porch of the tent. Toop bent forward on all fours, his knees bedded into the groundsheet with his head and arms protruding forward into the main body of the tent. He pinned back the fly sheet, the air inside the tent feeling instantly warmer on his skin. A forceful breeze battered the outside walls causing the canvas to flap inwards. Toop brushed the material with two outstretched fingers, his eyebrows raised. It was traditional 100 per cent cotton. He hadn't seen a cotton fabric tent in years. True, cotton was still used to make luxury tents but it was rare to see it used for contemporary mountain gear. It was simply too heavy compared to modern, man-made fabrics.

He closed his eyes, taking in the smell. Nothing could beat the warm smell of a cotton tent. It took him back thirty years, to another life, to a childhood of adventures and camping trips. He thought back to a particular trip with his dad. They had just bought a new tent. Cotton.

197

It had rained hard that night, the clouds opening in torrential waves of water. Damp pools of rain leaked through the material, seeping into the tent and soaking the end of his sleeping bag. "Sorry lad," his dad chuckled, the laugher comfortable in his eyes, "I forgot to mention that brand new cotton tents tend to leak! You have to weather them, give them a good soaking or two first. Beds in the material, seals it." He ruffled Toop's hair. "You're a tough lad though, you don't mind a wee bit of water do you boy?"

"I'd sleep outside if you'd let me, I ain't scared of no rain," he boasted, beaming back at his dad.

Toop opened his eyes, stepping out of the memory, and scanned the tent walls. The thin weaves of cotton fibres were visibly turgid, swollen from the drips of water that had leaked through. Strange, thought Toop, the design of the tent was decades old and yet the evidence of leakage suggested that it couldn't have been used more than once or twice. An old, unused tent, unsuitable clothing and sandals. The owner, thought Toop, was clearly not at home in the outdoors. He wasn't a local, not by a long stretch.

Toop looked around the tent, left, right, up and down. His body penetrated the small space while his feet remained outside, tops rested flat on the grey ground sheet, attempting not to disturb the scene. At first there was nothing obvious that he could see. Although, what struck him was how organised it was. Every item was neatly in its place. Sleeping bag packed away and stored in the corner. A small selection of clothes folded and piled, three books stacked one on top of the other sat next to the pillow, their edges aligned and spines parallel. A single pen had been placed on top.

Toop pulled his entire body into the cramped compartment, his approach slow and methodical, taking mental notes of his surroundings. He was forced to hunch his shoulders, tilting his head to avoid hitting the roof. He pulled a pair of white gloves from his jacket pocket, slipped then on, and lifted the pen with great care. He picked up the first book, turning the hardback copy over in his hands to read the title, handling the article as little as possible. "*What?*"

Toop read the cover in disbelief. *The Floral Offering: A Token of Adultery and Deceit*. He frowned as he scanned the ancient and crumbling hardcover. It was a dictionary, a very old dictionary, about flowers. He opened the first few pages, fingering only the periphery of the paper, and leafed through several sheets of yellowed manuscript until he found the publication details. 1863. The pages turned in his hands, revealing scraps of poetry and scribblings collected by previous owners. Two dried flowers fell onto his lap, slipping free from the grasps of the pages. He had never seen a book like it.

Two chapters in, he stopped.

Page fourteen.

It was marked.

Toop ran his finger under the folded edge, gently flipping it up to reveal a faint diagonal crease across the top corner of the page.

A new crease.

The thought brought back memories of his mother. She had yelled at him as a child, scolding him for folding back the pages of his book. Toop could hear her voice. "Fergus! You mustn't do that! Stop, come here. Sit." She pulled out a chair, opening the book between them. "Look at this. Every page is made up of a weave of fibres and these are very brittle." She brushed her fingertips over the page. "When you crease the paper the fibres break forever. A page never forgets a crease Fergus, not even a hot iron can remove it. It's damaged forever."

Toop looked at the crease, inspecting it. This crease was new, superficial. The fibres had only been bent, distorted, not yet fractured.

There was a single flower on the marked page, a yellow rose. And written underneath, was what Toop could only assume was the meaning. Toop squinted, raising the text closer to his face. The script type made the words almost illegible to his modern eye. It looked, he reasoned, like the writer had been in a great hurry, running the letters together and trailing threads of ink from one character to the next. He struggled to decipher even the first letter, whittling it down to either 'n', 'i' or 'u', possibly 'm'. The second word was little easier, either a 'J' or a 'T'. "Shit," he whispered. Maybe it was an 'F'.

He sat back on his heels and laid the book down on the pillow, letting out a frustrated sigh. The distance distorted the words even further. The skinny, pinched up style seemed to dissolve the individual letters into a single elegant wave, each of the characters flattened into almost identical shapes. His fingers migrated to the centre of his thighs and drummed gently. The repetition funnelled his thoughts into circles, twisting his mind and allowing it to peer round corners.

In a moment the tapping stopped and he leaned forward. There were no visible dots or cross-strokes. No 'i's or 't's, he thought, triumphant. Although the feeling was short-lived. His eyes caught on it; just visible was a single horizontal line. Faint to the point that it was almost non-existent but there all the same.

His fingers twitched.

Toop stared at the page.

He had it.

Hurrying his hands into his pocket he pulled out an old receipt and a black biro. It was something that they had done at school once when they were studying the Victorians. An old trick of the trade, that's what his history teacher had called it. Toop laid the paper lightly over the script, his hand resolute as he traced each letter. Careful and steady, listening to his teacher's instructions. "Historians used this method to help them decipher old, illegible texts. They found that the act of writing the words themselves, with their own hand, actually unravelled the problem."

Toop smiled as the words revealed themselves and he spoke them out-loud.

"Infidelity. Jealousy."

Toop closed the book and placed it, along with the pen and flowers, into one of the large cellophane envelopes that he'd brought. Then he backed out of the tent. The adrenaline caught in his pulse as the realisation hit him.

A motive insinuated murder.

And now he had one.

Chapter 42

Late 80s

Jon took a step back, then another one, putting distance between himself and the body.

The vomit rose in his throat. Bitter.

He crouched down towards the floor, his knees failing him as he sank into a defeated ball. Sickened. A clear bile released from his small intestine and the muscles in his stomach tightened, inducing a wave of violent contractions. He hung his head to the side of his knees, retching repeatedly as the spasms gripped his body, reducing him to a shivering mass. His voice remained trapped in his chest.

Jon grasped his legs into his torso and rocked back and forth in a nervous tempo.

What had he done?

The enormity of it made him want to throw up.

He held his hand up to his face. Blood.

The sticky liquid covered his fingertips, seeping into the creases of his skin and drying in blotches across his palm. He averted his gaze, forcing himself to take in the rest of the room. As he looked up his body heaved, reacting as his eyes adjusted and her body came into focus.

She was lying on her back with her arms and legs splayed at an unnatural angle. Her neck fell limply to one side, flaccid and unresponsive just as if she were sleeping. Jon's eyes grew damp as reality encroached upon him, the memories building in his head one piece at a time. He stared at her face. She didn't look peaceful or content, he thought. The muscles in her features seemed to have failed, leaving her hollowed face drowning in skin and her eyes gasping for air.

A clear fluid leaked from her nose.

The blood had started to pool, staining the carpet beneath her left ear.

Jon started to cry.

***

McNab was exhausted, that he knew.

He rolled over and back again, readjusting his pillow before throwing the covers from his upper body. It was futile. His mind refused to release him, denying him much-needed sleep.

McNab leaned over to the other side of the bed and kissed his wife on the forehead, the fresh smell of cucumber and avocado shampoo filling his nostrils. So peaceful, he thought, looking at her face. Her nose twitched as he withdrew his lips and she snuggled deeper into the crevasse of her pillow. McNab sighed and slipped his feet into a pair of slippers. He crossed the floor on his tiptoes, leaving the door ajar so as not to risk the squeak of the handle.

The hall was still, enveloped in a quiet darkness and penetrated by a single bulb of light; a small nightlight plugged into the wall at ankle height. The shape of a bumble bee.

McNab paused outside Isla's room, listening to the faint rise and fall of his daughter's breathing. His face broke into a smile, a subconscious reaction that befell all new fathers. He loved his little girl more than anything in the world. She was his world. And, as long as he was alive, no harm would come to her. Not to a single strand of hair on her beautiful head.

A single flick of a switch brought the kitchen into a pool of brightness. The sudden interjection of artificial light stung McNab's eyes, his pupils retreating to half their size. It took him a few seconds to adjust to the glare as he ambled around the kitchen. Mug. Coffee, the cheap instant stuff. Milk. Sugar. He switched the kettle on and pulled out a stool at the breakfast bar. He leaned forward on his elbows, catching his head in the palms of his hands, and rubbed his trembles in continuous, concentric circles.

A thought trickled to the forefront of his mind.

A man incapacitated by the mere thought of blood, making a perfect clean incision into his own arm. Alec was right, it didn't add up. And, thought McNab, what about the kid, William wasn't it? Did he even know that his father was dead? He needed to get in contact with him. McNab lifted his head and rose from the stool, motivated by the noise of the boiling kettle.

He filled his mug. World's Best Dad. But his mind elsewhere.

202

The question remained; if Anderson hadn't done it, then who had? If Bill had been murdered, reasoned McNab, then whoever had pulled it off had staged the perfect suicide, not the job of an amateur. The perfect murder, thought McNab, and for the first time in almost five years he wanted a cigarette. He wanted the momentary calm brought on by nicotine and the quiet clarity of mind. The case was becoming increasingly more muddled and he felt that he knew little more than nothing.

McNab stirred in the instant brown granules, watching them circle on the surface before dissolving. He brought the mug to his lips, opting for caffeine instead of tobacco. Then he lifted the case file from the counter with his free hand and sauntered through to the living room, gripping the loose sheets of paper between his left elbow and the side of his torso. The curtains had been left open; Caroline must have forgotten to close them before bed. The residual glow from the street lights ebbed through the glass and cast a faint taper of light across the room. McNab walked over to the chair nearest the window and eased his body into the leather cushions. He collapsed the last few inches, his tired thighs giving way beneath him.

He let out a deep sigh.

His wife had bought the chair as a gift for his last birthday. She had seen it advertised on television. The Restful Recliner, a revolution in comfort and functionality. McNab leant back, feeling the glide system adjust as it responded to his slightest movement. He smiled. It really was a very comfortable chair. Resting his eyes, he located the lever and arched his body backwards, causing the system to slide back into a more horizontal position.

He was awoken thirty minutes later by a familiar sound. But it took him a few seconds to place it, his mind half lost in sleep.

The house phone. He twisted his neck. The rotary dial phone sat on the table next to him, the finger wheel vibrating with each ring.

At this hour, thought McNab, never good.

He lifted the black handset and held it to the side of his face.

"McNab speaking."

Silence but for a distant static.

"Hello?" No response. McNab returned the receiver to the cradle.

Strange.

Yawning, he rubbed his hands over his face, circling his fingers around his eyes. He stretched out his legs and looked down at his feet. The file had slipped from his lap and sheets of papers lay strewn across the floor. He crouched over, gathering up the assortment of documents and photographs.

McNab felt himself frowning. He turned one of the photos around in his hand, bringing it closer to his face. It was a picture from the post-mortem. McNab had attended the autopsy, as detective he had no choice. It was a prerequisite that came with the promotion, a condition that he remained uncomfortable with. Watching someone tinker with human flesh was not an experience that he relished. McNab always stood at a distance, listening, the distinctive aroma that was sealed in the walls thwarting his ability to concentrate. He preferred to examine the photographs at a later point, in a less unsettling environment.

McNab turned on the side lamp to get a clearer look, speaking out loud as he organised his thoughts. "Blood settles at the lowest point, fixed in position after six hours." He ran his finger across the photo, tracing the purple colouring along the deceased's back. "Fixed, even if the body is moved."

McNab reached for a second photograph. The crime scene.

He studied Bill Anderson, who was sat upright in his chair, soaked in his own blood. No drag marks, no irregular blood patterns on the walls, his rigid body comfortable in its seated position. McNab balled his fingers into fists and drummed them off his forehead. What was he missing? Recumbent when he died, sitting a few hours later. It didn't make sense.

Wait. McNab's eyes widened in an instant.

He snatched back the photo. The answer had been right in front of him the entire time. Beneath him.

Of course.

Bill Anderson, reasoned McNab, was a janitor. He worked long shifts on his feet, mostly at night. It would have been a tiring job for a man of his age, and therefore entirely logical that his office chair would have been a recliner. The gallery wasn't short on cash; they could have provided the state of the art model, the new push back ones that operated without a lever. They were more stylish than the home range, almost identical in appearance to a standard desk chair and they required less space.

Perfect for a small office.

There was only one give away. McNab squinted at the photo. The angle made it difficult but he could just make it out. Folded back and concealed under the seat was a leg rest. Without hesitating, McNab leafed thought the photographs. He found it within a matter of seconds. The photo showed Anderson's naked body pictured from above with the effects of blanching clearly visible. Clear white patches, absent of blood, were present on the back of both calves, evidence of where body had been in contact with the leg rest.

"So," said McNab, "he was lying down and someone pushed the chair back up hours after he died." But, if Bill Anderson was indeed murdered, why did the murderer come back? What did he leave behind? McNab filed the question away at the back of his mind. But for the first time Angus McNab felt that the trail was warming up.

His body twitched involuntarily, shocked by the sudden ringing of the phone. His hand reacted on instinct, lifting the receiver for a second time that night.

"Detective McNab speaking."

"I know who you are, detective."

The voice was distorted, muffled by a piece of material. It was a technique that McNab was familiar with, simple but effective.

"And who may I be talking to?" he asked.

"That's not important."

"I'm afraid I disagree."

A brief pause.

"In that case, we will have to agree to disagree. Or would it make you feel better if I humoured you? A white lie perhaps."

"Perhaps." McNab straightened in his chair.

"Then you can call me Harry."

"Ok, Harry. And what is it that you want?"

"Such a tragedy, isn't it?" he said, discounting McNab's question. "What a waste."

"Waste?" questioned McNab.

"To throw away your life like that. A terrible waste."

"I'm sorry if what you have seen on the news has upset you, Harry," said McNab, choosing each word with care.

"Suicide is upsetting."

"It is."

"Have you ever lost anyone close to you, Angus?" the man asked.

McNab didn't respond. The man knew his first name.

"I lost my wife years ago," the voice continued, "but sometimes it feels like just yesterday." Silence. "How is Caroline by the way and that sweet little girl of yours? Isla isn't it?"

McNab tightened his grip on the receiver.

"What do you want?" he demanded.

"There's nothing worse than losing a loved one, Angus, nothing at all, especially when it can be prevented."

McNab felt his gut tighten. He didn't like being threatened.

The man continued.

"A tragedy like I said, but if someone chooses to end their own life then we should respect their decision. Wouldn't you agree, detective? Best not to meddle, meddling can be dangerous."

Then the line went dead.

Chapter 43

A second bus pulled away but a single figure remained. She sat hunched down on the ground with her back leant up against the glass, her weight balanced on her heels with her legs tucked up towards her chest.

The woman had one thought.

Revenge.

It had consumed her entire life. It had driven her every decision for as long as she could remember.

And now that he was dead she felt nothing. A numbness.

Particles lost in space, empty and alone.

Her thoughts turned to a night almost two decades ago.

Her ninth birthday.

Thunder cracked through the heavens, the small bullets of rain lying siege upon the single paned windows. Tiny, bare feet carried her across the cold floor and she crawled into her sister's bed. There were no presents or cards, no birthday wishes from Mum or Dad. Her sister took care of them. She didn't mind though. She loved her sister more than anything in the world.

Their small room was a dump; just darkness, no light to banish the nightmares. There were switches that could be flicked back and forth but the girls no longer tried. They knew that the electricity bill had not been paid; houses with stained mattresses that served as beds did not deserve light. Better left hidden in the shadows, she decided. The innocent reasoning of a child.

"I'll make it right," her sister whispered, hugging her close. "You'll see. I'll make it right."

The next day the two little girls walked down the stairs, opened the front door and ran. They kept running with nothing to stop them. Two little girls and a single pillowcase stuffed with their worldly belongings.

Twenty-eight hours of freedom passed before they were returned to the foster care system, to another house and another family. One foster home to the next; a few nights huddled under bridges and curled up on iron benches. But this time it was different. At nine years old they chose revenge.

They chose revenge above everything. Above happiness, thought the woman, wiping her eyes with her sleeve. She had given up everything and for what? To be alone and frightened, continually looking over her shoulder, repulsed by her own reflection.

And now someone was on to her, she thought, picturing the familiar face that had emerged from the house.

Could she know?

***

"Lucy?"

Cece stuck her head into each room as she searched their flat but Lucy wasn't home. Cece pulled her phone from her pocket. No messages. She swiped the screen and it unlocked, her fingers tapping in the number from memory.

Three rings before the connection went through.

"I just got back to the flat, no Lucy," Cece began. "I did what you asked but I didn't find anything helpful. Although..." She cupped the device closer to her mouth and glanced over her shoulder. "I'm pretty sure that someone else was at the house."

Pause.

"His wardrobe had been opened," she replied. "Yes. When I was upstairs. I didn't hear anything. I was in his office and the door was closed." Cece let the statement hang for a moment. She could hear him breathing on the other end.

"And Dad," she said. "I think that they took his journal."

Cece listened, pressing the phone tighter against her ear as she wandered through to the living room, falling back onto the couch in a slow motion. She followed his every word. He only repeated himself once. Deliberate.

Cece frowned. Her father sounded different, more serious, and it made her feel uneasy.

Without waiting for her reply, he hung up.

His instructions were clear. Unsettling.

Cece held her fingers to her lips, resisting a strong desire to gag, and a vile taste rose up in her throat. She couldn't believe what her dad was asking her to do. But he was her dad and she trusted him, above all others. He wouldn't have asked unless it was important. But it was that exact thought that bothered her the most. She gathered her fingers in a fist and swallowed hard, knowing that she didn't have a choice.

Cece stared across the apartment in the direction of Lucy's bedroom. There wasn't much time. She had to act fast.

***

The woman picked herself up and stood to face her reflection in the glass.

The tinted panes of the bus shelter acted like a mirror; a floor-length looking glass that returned her eyes to her. Two pools of blue on white skin. Her fingers lingered on her face, her freckled cheeks bordered by a mane of blood-red curls. Mascara leaked from her eyelashes, tarnishing her white complexion. She ran her fingers beneath her eyes and wiped the circles of black paint on her fingertips.

No tears.

If someone knew, she thought, if someone had found out what she'd done, then her life was over. The thought held, circling at the front of her mind as the evening played over in her head. The same image again and again. The same familiar voice pleading, begging, with her.

Go, leave. Just leave. Now!

"Naivety is just another form of innocence," she whispered.

With the words still dry in her mouth, she allowed her eyes to close for a moment, weary. But then, she thought, she was neither, she was neither naive nor innocent. Those virtues had been lost the day that she turned nine.

Now she was just guilty.

Tainted.

She reached into her pocket and pulled out her phone. There was only one person that she could speak to. One person who would understand. She drew a long breath and switched her phone on. There was one person whose hands were as bloodied as hers.

Alex. Her sister.

Alex. The one person that she couldn't speak to.

Not now, not ever.

Lucy slipped the phone back into her pocket.

Chapter 44

Present Day

Toop saw it, clocking it from the moment that his car came into view. He started running, counting the paces as he struggled to gather speed. Toop cursed as the sand robbed him of his momentum.

Twenty-five, twenty-six...

He fell upon the bonnet of the car, propelling his body towards the windscreen with his right arm outstretched. The piece of paper fell into his fingers.

Bailey woke up with a jolt, hearing Toop before he saw him. He listened to the sound of his boss as he thumped the bonnet of the car, his fist connecting with metal.

"Shit!" Toop shouted, his eyes locked on the note as he read the single sentence that had been scribbled on the paper.

Plant roses and be prepared to grasp the thorns.

Toop ran his hand through his hair.

"Shit!"

Chapter 45

Late 80s

Jon sat on the floor shaking.

He couldn't take his eyes off her; her neck was twisted at such an unnatural angle. His body trembled, conceding to each convulsion as his mind relived it. He pieced it together, one memory at a time; a haze of images merging like white polka dots in a sea of yellow.

He could feel the pressure of Jesse's arm wrapped around his shoulders. The weight had been exaggerated, increased by the alcohol that intoxicated his limbs, rendering them useless. Jon could smell the booze on his friend's breath. He watched in slow motion as Jesse's free arm entered into his blurred vision, pushing open the door in front of them.

A bedroom. Empty.

"In here." Jesse's words were slurred and he continued to monologue as they stumbled towards the bed. The words lost on Jon.

They sat on the mattress, side by side. Jon hung his head over his knees. He felt nauseous, overly aware of the room that was rotating around him. The walls pulsated, expanding and contracting in regular bursts, entering in and out of his personal space.

"Now you got to chew," Jesse said, "You got it. Like this." He opened and closed his jaw, spitting small droplets of saliva into the air. Jon watched, transfixed by the vile display of tongue and tonsils.

"Or else it's a bloody waste. If you want to be rolling off your face you got to chew, ok, don't swallow. Right?"

Jon nodded. Not stopping. His head continued to bob as his eyes focused on Jesse's hand, a blur of fingers suspended inches from his face. His pupils adjusted, concentrating on the small pill. Blue. Jon squinted. He could make out an image printed on the side. It was a tiny dolphin.

Jesse's hand connected with Jon's back, a forceful thud right between his shoulder blades.

"It's all about balance, mate. The taste is all part of it. Bliss through suffering." A smile. "Bit of poetic bullshit for you, to help with the fucking taste."

A foul, bitter sensation lined Jon's mouth. He fought the urge to gag and spit up as saliva collected in the roof of his mouth, the fine power spreading over his tongue and gums. It burned.

"Drink." Jesse handed him a beer. Jon sealed his lips around the glass and tilted his head back. The cool liquid eased from the neck of the bottle, soothing the inside of his cheeks.

The boys waited in silence. Minutes passed as seconds, seconds as hours. All sense of time lost in hard spirits and beer. A couple of heads peered round the door allowing the noise from the party to drift into the room. A quick, uninterested look and the door would close. The room quiet once more. Still but for the dull constant bass that ebbed through the walls.

Jon slouched from the bed onto the floor, landing with an awkward thud. He stretched out his gangly legs, his knees straightened out in front of him. His head hung down around his chest, all strength gone from his neck. His eyes flickered from side to side, absorbing each colour in isolation, drawn in by the blue of his jeans. Intoxicated, Jon began to rub his legs, running his hands up and down his thighs. He did it again and again, the friction causing his palms to overheat. He started to grab at the material, his fingers clutching at the tight fabric in an attempt to merge with it. Jon watched his hands, the whole event occurring in slow motion. He smiled. Everything in that moment was perfect. Everything was correct.

A warm chill crept up his spine in pleasing waves and his scalp broke out in tingles. Jon's grin widened, the toothy smile settling on his face. He held his hand out in front of his body, grasping at the air, suddenly confused when his fist returned to him empty. He frowned. The distant bass beats seemed to be in touching distance. His hand snatched at the air a second time and he caught a glimpse of his friend. Jesse's face was scrunched up like a tissue, his head tilted backwards, staring at the ceiling, mesmerised.

Memories bonded together, neither one distinct from the other, the only constant being the feeling of purity, of perfection. Tears stung Jon's eyes as he relived the past few hours, the random images and sounds playing back to him. Water, he remembered water. Jon looked down at his jeans. Wet hand prints. There had been a sink. He glanced round the room, his brain pumping. There. Of course. Most student bedrooms had sinks. He'd put his hands under the warm water from the faucet. He remembered it feeling amazing. Jon recalled the sensation, recalling how he'd let the liquid run for minutes. Then, as he drew his hands to his face, reality punched him hard in the gut.

Blood.

The creases of his fingers were stained red and no amount of water could make him clean. Not after what he'd done. He could still hear her begging and her piercing scream pulled him back, forcing him to relive it.

The drugs pumped through his body. Jon sat grinning, unaware of the serotonin that was leaking into his system, disrupting the dangerous and delicate balance of chemicals in his brain. He continued to grin, ignorant that Jesse had left. In a moment his world turned yellow, brightening as she entered the room. White dots floated towards him, blurred in a perfect glow of yellow.

Yellow sunshine, thought Jon as he reached out to touch the soft fabric, all inhibitions lost.

His fingers hovered above the warm skin of her thighs, her long smooth legs standing inches away from him.

"Jon?" Her voice sounded like honey. "It's Jenny. Are you ok?"

She bent down next to him, leaning forward on her knees. Jon watched as she leant back to sit on her heels, her mini skirt riding up and exposing her upper legs. Jon could smell her.

"I just saw Jesse outside," she said, "and he didn't look good."

Jon's response, if there was one, never found its way back into his memory.

He felt her hand on his forehead as she brushed a stray sweaty strand of hair from his eyes. The feeling of her skin on his thrilled him, the excitement growing in his groin. He was unable to pull his eyes away. He stared at her chest, at the two distinct mounds that hovered just inches from him, rising and falling beneath her top. The thin, white material did little to quell his imagination. Her breath fell across his eyes, a gentle rhythmic sound that escaped through her nostrils.

Jon could sense it coming, the feeling of disgrace building between his legs, only this time he made no attempt to scramble the thought away. It lingered, bolstered by a new sense of confidence. Jon stole a look at her lips, wanting to slip into her soft, beautiful mouth. The sexual desire stifled him. Then a thought entered his clouded mind, something that Jesse had said. *They always want it mate, they just don't always know it. A little persuasion goes a long way.*

Jon's thoughts felt muddled, cloudy. Jon scrunched up his eyes in protest, the contents of his brain seeming to pour together. He felt confused, unable to process the reality of the situation quick enough. But he reasoned, she had found him, she was the one stroking his forehead, it was her naked legs that penetrated into his personal space. She wanted him.

Do it.

Jon's fingers reached out and touched the warm skin of her inner thigh. She tensed but didn't resist; a reaction that added to his confusion and served to fuel his sexual desire. The hormones surged through him. He wanted to be closer to her. He needed to be closer to her.

His tongue slipped past her teeth, violating the sanctity of her mouth and she accepted. It was warm. Jon could feel her tongue under his, pushing it against the roof of his mouth then sliding back and round, generating a shared pool of saliva. His hand migrated towards her underwear and his fingers succeeding in finding cotton. At that moment her hand closed around his wrist with a light but deliberate touch.

"Stop," she said in a kind voice, her lips retreating just far enough from his to utter two words. "Not now."

But Jonathan Swan didn't want to wait. He didn't want to stop.

Waves of serotonin flooded his brain, poisoning his already weakened mind. The desire owned him. He grabbed her forearm and, in one quick violent movement, he forced her to the floor, crushing her ribcage with the weight of his body.

She wants it, Jon thought.

It was his final memory before his world turned black.

That night Jenny Pingleton begged, she screamed. She cried until her own tears refused her and her eyes filled with a haunted sadness.

But the loud bass droned on and Jon didn't stop. With his eyes departed and his mind lost beyond return, Jon stole it from her.

He robbed her life of light.

Ripped back to the present, Jon looked at the body and threw up.

He'd killed her.

Chapter 46

Present Day

Cece stopped frozen to the spot.

She stood in Lucy's bedroom with her feet cemented to the carpet, her body crouched over her findings.

There had been a noise.

Footsteps. She could hear them ascending the stairs, delicate steps on stone. The noise wasn't a total surprise to her; she knew that Lucy would be back soon. They had arranged to eat together after all.

Just keep calm, she thought.

She moved quickly, sealing up the bag and slipping it into her pocket. Cece figured that she had about twenty seconds until the next sound, the familiar jingle of keys. She swept her hand across the floor, collecting a pile of tissues and a used mascara tube before returning them to the bin.

She crept out of the room, pulling the door closed behind her.

Cece was sitting on the arm of the sofa when she heard the lock disengage and the front door opened. Lucy eased through the opening, her eyes cast downwards.

No shopping bags, noted Cece.

"You're back." Cece smiled, fingering the little plastic bag in her pocket.

"Sorry, I'm not feeling very well all of a sudden. Migraine," Lucy added as she edged past Cece, not lifting her gaze.

"Do you want me to whip us up something simple?" asked Cece, "beans on toast?"

"No thanks," Lucy answered and disappeared into her room.

Cece sat for a few seconds, staring at the spot where her flatmate had been a moment earlier. Something felt off. She stood up and grabbed her handbag. It wasn't a feeling that she had time to sit and contemplate. Her dad would be waiting for her. Without thinking she drifted her hand to the seam of her pocket and traced over the stitching with her finger tips. The small cylindrical item felt heavy in her pocket and she wanted to be rid of it as soon as possible. A tampon. Used.

Cece wasn't naive, she knew what her father wanted it for.

DNA.

Fingernail clippings, hair pulled from the root, they would have been difficult to get. And taking a toothbrush, she reasoned, would have been too obvious, Lucy would have noticed that it was missing. Also most people rinsed their toothbrushes, so the sample would have been unreliable anyway. Cece crinkled her nose in a grimace. It was futile. No amount of logic, viable or not, would make her feel less weird about the item that was currently stashed in her jeans.

"So gross", she mouthed, moving towards the living room.

There was one more thing that she needed.

As Cece stepped forward she listened. She could make out Lucy moving around in her room. The sound of sinking bed springs and shoes kicked across the carpet. Cece continued into the middle of the room, counting on her flatmate staying in her room for the next few moments. Cece sank down, tucking her knees under the coffee table and leant back on to her heels. She waited another twenty seconds, just to be sure. She needed the room to herself. The pile of letters in front of her were placed on the corner of the table where Lucy had left them the previous evening. Except, thought Cece, the postcard was no longer on top, it had been moved. She leafed through the mail, stopping three from the top.

The beach.

She didn't waste any time, quickly pulling out her phone and taking a picture of it. Two, to be safe. Then, with a quick glance at the inscription she returned the card to its place in the pile and stood up.

Rose Jaune, thought Cece, what could it mean? Maybe it wasn't a name at all. Jaune, wasn't that French for young or youthful? Or was that jeune? She made a mental note to look it up. Right now, she had something else that she needed to do. Cece looked at her watch; he would still be at work. It wasn't far to Argyll Street. She would just walk. The fresh air would do her good.

Cece hurried down the stairs, unable to shake a thought that had been needling away at her, a question about blood. She was reasonably certain, positive almost, that her dad wanted it for DNA purposes. Cece had always been perceptive, even as a child she had been able to read a lot from a little. But on this occasion there was something that troubled her. Her mind kept drawing a blank.

What possible reason could her dad have for wanting a sample of Lucy's DNA?

***

Lucy sat on the bed, her fingers clasped around the phone. Her knuckles were white. Alex had been very clear; they were to have no contact. None. It could ruin everything.

Lucy stared at the journal. It lay just beyond her toes, sunken into the duvet where it had fallen, lifeless and abandoned.

She had listened to Cece leaving. The door had swung shut and the flat had fallen silent, all that remained was the sound of her heartbeat. She rocked back and forth with her knees bent up under her chin. It was all that she could do to keep from screaming. She wanted to shout it out loud, to make a confession for the entire world to hear but the words refused her, clinging to the end of her tongue.

He was murdered.

Jonathan Swan was murdered. And I know. I know who did it. I know who killed Jonathan Swan.

Lucy looked around the room. There was nothing except her desk and her open wardrobe. Even if she did scream it from her lungs, there was nothing. The furniture alone would hear her omission. She couldn't take it anymore. Lucy pounced forward and grabbed the journal in her hands.

She needed to know.

The book fell open and the pages fluttered out without a sound, before finding a natural parting, settling halfway through the text. Lucy stared at the text, choosing not to flick the pages backwards. The middle was as good a starting point as any. She gathered her body into a seated position, her legs crossed beneath her with her back bent into a gentle curve, and balanced the journal against her upturned feet.

As her eyes skimmed over the exposed page a quiet realisation captured her, gripping her throat He had held this very item. She was touching something that had belonged to him. They were his words, his thoughts. Lucy ran her fingers over the page. Despite everything, she couldn't deny it. She was grieving.

He was gone and his journal was all that she had.

His writing was printed, all written in pencil. Not pen. Very small, printed words. Each individual letter perfectly formed. Lucy could make out patches where the paper had been thinned, worn away by the repeated use of a rubber. She recognised the marks from something that she had done as a child. A perfectionist at primary, Lucy had hated her writing to look messy. All of her work was edited and re-edited until it was just so. The teachers had soon given up trying to make her write in pen. Ten year old Lucy would erase each mistake regardless of how minimal it was, ensuring that no imperfect letters were left committed to paper.

Unwanted mistakes. *Discarded, just like me.*

She started to read and for the first time in her life she felt the possibility of closeness; the chance to connect with a man that she had never known.

She wiped a single tear away with the back of her hand.

She wouldn't waste her tears on a stranger.

Even if he was her dad.

Chapter 47

Present Day

Toop was sitting alone at his kitchen table. His coffee had gone cold.

It was getting late and he knew he should eat but he wasn't hungry. His mind was working too fast to think about food. Copies of the notes lay on the table in front of him and as he read over them his mind kept coming back to the same conclusion.

Someone was leaving him a message.

Toop's mind started to move through possible scenarios. Two separate notes, one recurring theme. Flowers, or more specifically, he thought, roses. He squinted as he placed the two pieces of paper side by side. It was undeniable. The handwriting had distinctive similarities. He leant back into the chair and tilted his eyes towards the ceiling, the back of his head cradled in his hands. It was possible that the note in the bothy log book could have been written by the victim, the scribblings of a guilty conscience like Eve said. But dead men didn't leave riddles on car windscreens. And Toop didn't believe in coincidences, two different writers with an unusual fondness for flowers. He wasn't buying it.

But, he sighed, there was the issue of the book, the one that he had found in the tent. A book he could only assume had once belonged to the victim. To the unnamed man, thought Toop. A dictionary, a rare and antique reference book devoted to the descriptions of ancient flowers. An odd choice of bedtime reading, especially for a middle aged man. Toop tapped the end of his pen on his note pad. There was only one possibility. There had to be some connection between the victim and the killer. He must have known the man who killed him. Or woman, Toop corrected himself as he circled two words with his finger.

Infidelity. Jealousy.

"A motive", mouthed Toop, pulling a photograph out of a pile of documents.

"And intent", he finished, looking at the faint slap mark.

A crime of passion?

But something just didn't add. There was no sign of a struggle, the car had been sold for nothing and the gun had been left there. Either he was missing something or he was thinking it through the wrong way, approaching it from the wrong angle somehow. Toop was about to open the dictionary when he heard the springs on his garden gate. He stood up and walked to the window, pulling the curtain back with two fingers.

Sally.

She walked through the front door a few seconds later. Toop noted her casual wear, the scrubs gone. Jeans and a jumper with a heavy bag slung over her shoulder. Her short hair was unbrushed while choppy bangs, swept to the side, were held in place by natural grease. It had been a long day, stressful. Sally had a habit of running her fingers through her fringe when she was stressed.

Toop followed her movements as she walked in, dumped the bag in the corner and went straight to the fridge to get a cold beer.

"Want one?" she asked, raising the bottle in Toop's direction.

Toop shook his head and returned to his seat. "I'm good. Head's foggy enough as it is."

"That's not like you. Maybe the alcohol would do you good, loosen you up a bit. It works for me anyway."

Sally moved round the kitchen, opening cupboards and fishing through the cutlery drawer. She finished making herself a piece of toast and honey and pulled up a chair.

"So what was it? The epiphany you had earlier," she asked. "In the autopsy room, I said something about footprints and you were gone in a shot."

Toop held up the dictionary and handed it to Sally.

"I remembered seeing sand in the car that Jimmy had bought."

"Trace evidence?"

"Yes. I've been driving around beaches all day with Bailey."

"That must have been fun for him," smiled Sally, already leafing through the old pages.

Toop ignored the comment. "We found an abandoned tent that was pitched at melon, melon something beach."

"Mellom Udrigle," she said and looked up from the text. "So you think the tent was his?"

"Yes. And I found that inside."

221

"It's beautiful, if not a bit odd. Why on earth would he have something like this?"

"Look here," Toop held the book open with the side of his hand, "page fourteen has been marked. A yellow rose. Apparently each flower represents something, a code that the Victorians used to communicate in private. Yellow implies infidelity and jealousy," he said pointing to the inscription.

"You're thinking a motive?"

"Perhaps." Toop rummaged through the mess on the table and produced a piece of paper. "And there's this. It appeared on my windscreen when I was down at the beach." He handed the note to her. "What do you make of it?"

"You mean that someone was actually at your car?"

"It would seem that way."

Sally held it up in front of her. "This is creepy Fergus. I don't like it. I mean, what are we dealing with here exactly, a mentally unhinged florist or some twisted bloodthirsty gardener?"

"Don't forget the note in the log book," he said, slipping a photo of the quote onto the table in front of her.

"The handwriting is the same. But then..." Sally paused, her concentration diverted by the implications of her statement, "then maybe it wasn't a suicide".

They stared at the two messages.

And he repents in thorns that sleeps in beds of roses.

Plant roses and be prepared to grasp the thorns.

"What does it all mean?" asked Sally.

"I'm not sure," answered Toop. "But I'm beginning to think that they could both be threats."

"But to who?"

"Sorry?"

"Well," said Sally, "let's say that we go with the current working theory. Infidelity, a crime of passion in which a woman discovers that she is being cheated on and so she decides to put a bullet in his chest. In which case, the first note I can make sense of. If you cheat you're toast, a clear threat. But, the second one was written after he died. So who is the threat meant for?"

Toop held Sally's gaze for a moment.

"Me," he replied. "I think it means that if I continue to investigate the case then I must be prepared to face the consequences."

"Well," said Sally rising from her chair, "now I really don't like it." Her brisk tone betrayed her casual manner. She placed her dirtied plate in the sink and continued to talk over the noise of running water.

"What are you going to do?"

He twisted his wrist and glanced at his watch. "There's somewhere that I need to go in the morning."

"I'm guessing that you don't mean the hairdressers."

He turned his shoulders to look back at her. "There's a small antique's book shop in Gairloch. At least there used to be one. It was run by an old Swiss gentleman." Toop paused. "Although he was nearing eighty the last time I was in there and that was ten years ago."

"You want him to look at the book."

"I'm hoping he'll be able to make sense of whatever it is that I'm missing."

"Missing?"

Toop took a few seconds to answer. "There's something that just doesn't fit," he replied, more to himself.

Sally finished washing the dishes and stacked them on the draining board. "Ok, well I'm knackered." She drew her palms to her mouth in an attempt to conceal a deep yawn, the dramatic intake of air filling her parched lungs. Satisfied, she balled up her fists and rubbed her eyes, raising her arms above her head in a long stretch.

"Good night, Fergus."

He wasn't listening.

She walked towards the bed, her tired mind forgetting about all about her phone call with Fraser McGlone and his pig.

***

It was almost midnight and Toop had skimmed through the dictionary for the second time. A useless exercise given that most of the writing was illegible. He contemplated lying down on the couch and closing his eyes.

He didn't.

Long experience had taught him that he would just lie there staring at the ceiling. Toop got up, paced around the living room and walked across to the window. It was black. There were no street lamps in Badachro; no lights leaked from neighbouring houses, there was just the empty night and his reflection. Toop slipped his hand into his pocket and pulled out his wallet. He had a feeling that he wasn't the only one who wouldn't be asleep. He opened the small leather pocket; the original design was intended to hold coins but Toop didn't like the bulk of loose change against his leg.

He removed a folded scrap of paper from the leather pouch and traced his thumb over the ten digits. Then he entered them into his phone and opened up a new message box. He paused with his thumb hovered over the touchscreen, the pang of guilt stopping him. He felt uneasy about wanting to see her again.

He started typing and pressed send before he could reconsider.

You awake? Fergus.

The reply was instant.

Meet me at the bottom car park. 30 mins. E x.

Toop knew exactly where she meant and he knew what she was implying. Mountain bike tracks were the one area where his local knowledge excelled.

35 mins.

Her reply was instantaneous.

Sweet x

***

Eve was waiting for him when he pulled into the car park; a gritty passing place just off the road.

Toop had changed into biking shorts and cleats. Eve was dressed in similar sports gear, a long-sleeved base layer, loose-fitting shorts and knee pads. Toop noted that the night air was unusually warm for Scotland which probably accounted for her lack of jacket or wind proof shell. He wore a t-shirt, his muscular forearms left bare.

The summer sky still held the remnants of light, complete darkness rare so far north. The head torches mounted on their helmets were almost unnecessary.

"Come on then," said Eve.

Toop followed her as she spun off, his gaze drawn to the backs of her legs.

The track ascended before them and her bike floated over the rocks, navigating the trail with ease.

Eve glanced back at him just long enough to meet his eyes.

"Think you can keep up?" she smiled.

Toop leaned out of his saddle and bore down onto the pedals. The sweat soon worked its way out from his body, clearing his thoughts as they bled out onto the dirt. Time disappeared from beneath them as they peddled into the shadows, evaporating into the night.

Their two lights flickered against the sprawling horizon, indifferent to the gentle drizzle that ebbed over the hills.

Chapter 48

Late 80s

"Jonathan. Jonathan"

He was only partly conscious of his name. Jon frowned; the words seemed to be coming from the inside of his own head. They were loud, too loud. He lifted his palms to his ears in an attempt to quiet it.

"Go away," he said, his voice feeble, barely audible.

Jon looked down at his legs, they felt motionless. He let out a quiet sob, unable to muster the energy to move them. All he saw were two dead lumps, useless and broken. He started to panic and paranoia set in. What if he could never move them again, what if he rotted and died on this very spot? They would find him crippled and covered in blood. Condemned right there and then on the bedroom floor, his life over.

His head started to spin, one incoherent thought after the other battling in a torrent of confusion. His mind was destroyed, mangled, yet he couldn't switch off. The inside of his head pounded. He wanted to die.

"Jonathan. Jonathan."

That voice again. He thought that he recognised it. Then he blacked out.

***

He couldn't move.

Jon opened his eyes and stared straight up at the ceiling. It took him a moment to come to. The delay in his brain left him debilitated, unable to relay the messages to his limbs quick enough. He lay awake in a cold sweat, incapable of movement.

The first reaction to hit him was one of confusion. Where was he? What day was it? Then, without warning, his lungs contracted. They were seized by a feeling of despair, of complete and utter hopelessness. Jon started to cry in deep consuming sobs that stifled his windpipe. He began ripping at his chest, clawing into his own body with his fingers. He wanted it to end.

"You're ok, boy."

Jon's fingers froze. He jerked his head round, two more thoughts digging into his mind. It was a different voice this time. And he wasn't alone. The man stood just to the side of his bed. He was bent over a small table, his wrist twisting back and forth. Back and forth. Jon watched as the man massaged the curved head of the spoon into the plate, crushing two white pills. Then he lifted the plate and scraped the fine power into a full glass.

"Drink this. It will help."

Jon didn't recognise him straight away. Even when he stared into the man's confident eyes there was no immediate connection. True, his mind was fuzzy and he couldn't focus but it was something else.

"You're coming down," the man continued, extending the glass to Jon. "You have experienced a significant surge of serotonin and as a result your brain's supply has been depleted, effectively turning it into a dry sponge. I'm afraid that it will take time but this should help you sleep."

Jon drank. Not caring if he lived or died. He just lay there, listening and waiting.

The man walked around the room, manoeuvring around a myriad of tables and boxes, pausing to attend to certain items. Jon followed him, watching him through wearied slits, his eyes half closed. There had been something about the man's voice, and a familiarity in his eyes, that had sparked a memory but there was something in his stance, a certain relaxation about his posture that weakened the same memory.

The drugs kicked in and released Jon into a deep sleep.

***

Angus McNab watched as his daughter played with her breakfast. Her tiny hands mashed clumps of kiwi into the plastic table of her highchair, moving the pieces of fruit around in concentric green circles. Her big blue eyes looked up at him and she smiled. He couldn't help but smile back.

No one threatens my family.

McNab leant forward and kissed his daughter on the forehead. "Daddy loves you," he whispered.

An hour later McNab was at his desk, content in the knowledge that there was a police car positioned outside his house. He wasn't taking any risks, not when his wife and baby girl were concerned. If his home phone number could be traced then so could his house address.

McNab worked hard for the next three hours, searching official databases, making phone calls and scouring through a number of websites. There was someone that he needed to find. It took him another hour but he got the call that he had been waiting for. The woman on the end of the line confirmed that William Anderson, son of Bill Anderson, was living in Edinburgh. McNab allowed himself a smile. The man could have been living anywhere by now. The world had shrunk since McNab was a kid. With immigration, work opportunities abroad and foreign incentive schemes there had been no guarantee that William Anderson would still be based in Scotland. Yet, as it turned out, he was only an hour away by train ride.

Small victories, thought McNab.

He made notes on a small pad, using his shoulder to balance the phone against his ear. William Anderson worked in construction, had done for most of his adult life. The woman on the phone verified that Mr Anderson was employed by an Edinburgh-based company. Jones & Jones Construction, she said.

McNab thanked her and hung up. He ran his hand through his hair. There was something familiar about the name, he had read it somewhere. *Something recent.*

McNab eyed the weekend edition of the Scotsman on a colleague's desk. He reached over and lifted it, spreading the newspaper out across his desk. The large broadsheet covered the majority of his workspace. Page two. *A Commonwealth Brought to its Knees*. McNab skimmed through the article, his index finger passing over the main details; rumours of crippling boycotts, Thatcher's refusal to impose sanctions, racial segregation, massive financial losses. He paused, stopping to read out loud.

"A lack of Government investment, coupled with a gross miscalculation of costs by the host city, has put the Games under great threat. However this almost certain downfall has been avoided by the work of Edinburgh's own knights in shining armour. Volunteers have signed up in their thousands, local people determined to see their city succeed."

McNab scanned over the next few sentences until he found it.

'Local construction company Jones & Jones Construction have promised to subsidise all additional labour costs, ensuring that deadlines will be met on time and within budget. In an interview with the BBC, business owner Steve Jones commented that, 'Jones & Jones feel that it is our responsibility to assist our beloved city in producing yet another world-class Games and therefore the company has decided to foot the bill for any overtime that is incurred. At present we are involved in the restoration of the Royal Commonwealth Swimming Pool in Edinburgh, a project that is going smoothly and that will produce a first-rate venue.'

McNab smiled. A few hours ago he had nothing and now he knew exactly where William Anderson was. He returned the paper and picked up the phone. A quick call to directory enquiries and he had what he needed. Things seemed to be going his way.

He dialled the number.

"You have reached Jones & Jones Construction. How may I help you?" answered a female voice. Young, friendly, noted McNab.

"Good afternoon. Officer McNab, Strathclyde Police, speaking. Sorry to bother you. I was just hoping to reach one of your employees, a William Anderson. I believe that he is working on a project at the Commonwealth Pool in Edinburgh."

"Certainly officer, I'll patch you straight through to Mr Jones. All employee matters are dealt with him directly. One moment please."

She put him on hold and an inoffensive harmony played in the background, filling the silence. McNab listened. He leant back in his chair, wondering if he would be put through to the first or second Jones of Jones & Jones Construction.

He straightened out his legs, appreciating the stretch, unaware that in forty-eight hours his world would fall apart.

Chapter 49

Present Day

It took half a page, fifty words maybe. Lucy's eyes widened as she grasped the reality of what she was reading.

Half an hour passed, not a sound, just a single emotion that settled on her brow.

Sadness.

She put the journal down and let out a small sigh. After all of this was over, and that seemed like a big if, she would learn how to be normal. She would live an ordinary life, free from revenge, free from loneliness. No pain. No death.

As a child she had often run away, her tiny fingers clutched in the steering grasp of her sister, two girls escaping to the ends of the earth. The sound came back to her, the swift, anxious patter of fleeing feet. For hours they would sit side by side. Free. Occupying park benches, perched on walls, just looking. People watching, her sister called it. The act of observing strangers and guessing their story, a game Lucy loved, excelled at even. She invented the most scrupulous and wonderful tales. The endings were always happy, no exceptions. Alex told her that she was silly, a foolish little girl. But Lucy didn't care. Firstly, they were the same age so calling her little was stupid. Secondly, she believed that people looked content going about their daily business, normal people doing normal things. Every time, without fail, Lucy's eyes were drawn to their hands, the entwined fingers of couples, a palm rested on the back of a wife, mothers guarding their children. Lucy's own hands would sit nestled into her lap, fingers intertwined, her wrists bent back at right angles, giving the impression of being held.

The memory started to fade and Lucy continued reading. She shook her head from side to side, the slightest movement made without conscious thought. Twice she lifted her fingers, pressing them against her parted lips in disbelief. His words leaked like confessions from each page;

the writings of a man condemned and completely exposed. A single thought kept repeating in her head, over and over.

She was the daughter of a criminal.

Any hopes of an emotional connection with her father had been short-lived, traded for something quite different. What she held in her hands was the first person narrative of a felon. As she read over his words, her father emerged from the pages, a man who far surpassed any of her childish preconceptions. The contents of his journal could have seen him locked up for years. If he hadn't been punished already that is, thought Lucy, flicking to the next page.

August 21st 2011
Tom is pleased.
He has a potential buyer from Japan.
Wants to see the painting in two weeks. Arrives in Glasgow 4th September.
August 28th 2011
Tom is worried.
Two forgers have been charged in the last month. Sentences of 6 and 4 years. Both exposed by irregularities in their paintings. Black lighting revealed floating signatures.
Tom must not worry. I will not let him down. Non-fluorescing paints can be used to counter this effect.
Order more masking varnish.

Each entry was the same, concise and intentional.

It was far from a conventional diary, short of the predictable outpourings of feeling and sentiment most often expected. Jonathan Swan had not wasted time with the frivolous, finer points of speech, only writing the details that he considered worthy of permanent importance, offering simple recounts. His recounts were factual.

Lucy noticed that the entries were often days, sometimes weeks apart. Such inconsistencies, she noted, weren't uncommon. She skipped back a few pages to reread. An idea or an event would be mentioned once but then he wouldn't reference it again. There was no logical progression to his writing, no consistent train of thought. It was almost like each entry was written in isolation. Not all, but enough to make it noticeable, she reasoned. Also, his use of punctuation and grammar, it was irregular, erratic almost and his sentence structure was poor. Lucy frowned. It was as if he made sense of the world differently; saw things in a different way.

Who are you?

Who were you, Lucy corrected herself as she read ahead.

November 6th 2011

Power illuminated pocket microscope arrived yesterday.

Revealed bleeding on the Degas. Assess and fix hairline age cracks.

Problem with stretcher bars. Inconsistencies in the date, canvas too old.

Experimenting with aging: staining wood, re-cutting old frames, surfacing painting with yellow-toned varnish.

Fake dust.

November 15th

Tom made a big sale today. My latest. £18,000.

He told the client that new stretcher bars could no longer support the weak canvas.

Lucy placed the book down and rubbed her temples. Her mind was fuzzy. The more she read the more questions were left without answers. She wanted to stop. What good was it doing her, she thought, he was dead. But intrigue kept pulling her back. He was her dad after all. Her blood.

Like father, like daughter, she thought.

Her left foot had gone to sleep and the sensation of pins and needles made it impossible to sit still. Lucy adjusted her position on the bed, stretching her legs out and pointing her toes. She pulled her toes in towards her then lengthened them out again. The third attempt offered a release. What time was it, she thought, stealing a glance at her bedside clock. Hours had passed since she had shut herself away. True, she no longer wanted to scream until her lungs exploded across the room. She did feel calmer. Less on the edge of a breakdown, she decided. More rational perhaps, that was it. She settled back into a comfy position and reopened the diary.

Maybe this time, she thought, she should start at the beginning. She turned to the first page and let out a sharp gasp.

No.

It couldn't be.

***

She was pissed off.

Cece sat in the corner of the shop with her face contorted in a childish pout. She kicked the table in front of her and cursed.

Fuck!

She scowled and retracted her wounded toe. Her dad knew something, something important, and he wasn't telling her. She cradled her injured foot in her hands and watched her dad out of the corner of her eye.

He was standing at the end of room talking to her grandfather. They were both hunched over looking at the screen on her phone, at the picture that she had taken of the postcard; the unnamed beach. If it hadn't been for the worried look on her dad's face Cece would have marched over and given him what for. It was her phone after all. Her careful snooping. But something in his expression stopped her.

Fear.

Cece cast her eyes down, realising that she was scared. Scared about what he might say.

Anxious, she turned her body so that she was facing away from the two men.

The shop hadn't changed since she was a child. It was an organised disarray of items, hundreds of shelves covering each wall. The floor was concealed by tables and various inanimate items; rows of antiques, some genuine and some not so genuine. But Cece loved it. It felt like home.

She listened to the low mumble of conversation, not quite audible. Then she heard one distinct word, her name.

"Cece?"

She sat up straighter and turned to face her dad. He gestured her over, clearing his throat as she neared. Cece looked across at her grandfather and their eyes caught in a moment of understanding. Something had happened, something bad, and her dad couldn't protect her any more, his little girl or not, it was time that he told her. Her dad looked first at his own father then back at her before pushing the door open to reveal a large room. The old sign remained, *Danger. Asbestos. Keep Out,* but the white lettering was less prominent against the faded red background.

Cece had been inside her father's office many times. It was much less ordered than her uncle's, more chaotic, more in tune with the twenty-first century. Her eyes caught on the row of computers at the back of the room, the screens in hibernation. The monitors were hemmed in by piles of paperwork; lists of clients, upcoming exhibitions, gallery showings. A tower of illegal documents had been left out in full view. Cece glanced over at the disarray realising that the contents of the papers held enough evidence to see her family locked away twice over, as would the two fake paintings which hung on the wall: a Rembrandt and a Degas. Two of her uncle's earlier works. They were good, outstanding, but just not quite outstanding enough. The flaws were minute, undetectable to the naked eye, but they were there. Subtle tells that would have raised suspicions within certain art circles. The Rembrandt was technically perfect, there were no discernible errors. In fact, her uncle's oversight could have remained concealed for years, a complete mystery until one day a maid was instructed to clean it. The moment the cleaning fluid came into contact with the canvas the paint layer would have disintegrated before her eyes. Not ideal. It was a problem that her uncle later solved, applying a layer of glycerine under the paint; a simple but effective trick.

Now the paintings had pride of place in her dad's office. Flawed but no less exquisite, he said. Her dad, a romantic at heart, reasoned Cece, was a sentimental old man who was harbouring a room full of incriminating evidence.

Cece had been eight when he told her the truth. He had taken her into this very office and offered her a seat. She sat, legs folded, with her little hands gathered in a basket on her lap just like school had taught her. Her eyes followed her dad's hands as he reached into his pocket and pulled out a small trinket. He tossed it to her. The key to his office.

"Sweetheart," he started, "I think that you are old enough to learn about your family."

For twenty minutes she didn't speak, she just nodded along to the sound of her father's voice. It was a day that changed her life. Most people would have denounced their family as criminals, lawless crooks. But they were her family. And she loved them.

She would do anything for them.

Almost two decades later Cece sat in the same chair with her father opposite her. But this time she sat while he paced, followed by her eyes. Finally he paused, pulled out a chair and moved it next to her. His features were impassive but Cece could sense the concern in her father's eyes. She didn't look away.

She was ready.

Tom McGraw brought his fist to his mouth and cleared his throat. Two sharp coughs. Then he leaned forward and took her hand.

And there and then, in a soft voice, he told her that her uncle Jon had been murdered.

***

Lucy stared at the inner cover.

It couldn't be.

But the inscription was there, written as clear as day in blue ink.

Dear Uncle Jonny, Happy Birthday. Thank you for introducing a little girl to a world of magic. She still believes. Love Cece x

"Uncle", whispered Lucy.

That made Cece her cousin.

Chapter 50

Present Day

The light of dawn started to leak into the sky as they lay side by side in the heather, heat rising from their naked bodies, the steam visible against the cool air.

Toop felt her fingers lingering against his bare chest. The sensation sent the blood straight back to his groin which had only recently recovered. Eve turned over next to him, her body pressed against his for warmth.

"Again?" she teased, playing with the hairs on his chest.

He didn't wait to be asked again. Toop secured her slight frame in his left arm and threw her on top of him. Eve returned his gesture with a coy smile, leaning forward with a soft laugh. Her young breasts hung before his eyes, left exposed before she pressed them down into his chest. She kissed him. It was forceful, almost violent. Toop gripped her hips in his fingers, digging his nails into her skin. Eve let out a groan of pleasure and pulled at his lower lip with her teeth. Desire pulsed through his veins and Toop raised his head off the ground allowing him to consume more of her. His lips fell upon hers and she kissed him back, desperate and determined. Her tongue moved round the concaves of his mouth, running along the underside of his upper lip.

Toop tightened his grip around her hips and, without any effort, he manoeuvred her onto him. He could feel the warmth flowing from between her legs and over his aroused body. The invitation was explicit, they both knew it. Toop let his head fall backwards, moaning as he eased inside her.

***

Toop stood in the shower and let the water run over his face.

He had left Eve less than two hours ago. They had dressed and driven off in separate directions, separate cars. No parting kiss. No lingering glances.

Just sex, Toop told himself.

He dried himself off, dressed and headed down to the kitchen. Sally was already up. She was sitting at the breakfast bar, halfway through a bowl of muesli. The coffee was on.

"Morning sunshine," she smiled, looking over her shoulder. "Good ride last night?"

"Yes, thanks," he replied.

"You were gone a while. I heard you head out around midnight, you must have done a good few miles on the bike."

"Uh-huh." He kept his back to her.

"You don't mind it then, being on your own in the hills at night."

Toop muttered a reply as he poured himself a mug of coffee. He wasn't in the mood to chat.

"You're an open book you know that," laughed Sally, "hard to shut you up sometimes." She turned back to her breakfast and started flicking through the pages of the newspaper, leaving Toop to mope around the kitchen. He joined her a few minutes later, setting down a plate of toast and marmalade.

Sally turned over the last page of her newspaper to the football results. She folded it up, not interested. Her mug was halfway to her mouth when it stopped, suspended mid motion. In an instant she spurred from her seat and disappeared from the room, returning a few seconds later with a collection of papers.

"There was something that I forgot to mention last night," she said, placing them down on the table.

Toop picked up the first page and started to skim through it without a word.

"Ballistics called your office when you were out," said Sally, "and I had a chat with Fraser. He faxed these through for you to see." She paused and added. "I'm not sure that you'll like it."

Sally watched Toop as he reached the bottom of the first page. She tried to read something deeper in his expression, waiting for him to react, but Toop didn't give anything away. His face held in a still, impassive stare. He finished reading in silence then turned to look at her, letting the pages fall limply from his grasp.

"A pig. You're saying that I should close the investigation based on the findings of a pig."

"Well, technically it wasn't the pig that..."

Toop interrupted her, not listening. "Is this a joke? Some guy shoots a couple of rounds into a carcass and it's a suicide. Case closed."

Sally held up her hands in surrender. "Look, I'm just passing it on. No need to shoot the messenger."

She lifted her bowl and mug, swung down from her stool and walked over to the sink, placing her dishes in the basin. Her hand paused over the tap and she turned back to Toop, leaning her body up against the counter.

"Ok, so forget the pig. But I checked the body too Fergus, and I'm inclined to agree with him. It was a close contact wound. The powder residue left around the entry point was too diluted for it to be a direct contact shot. The gun was aimed at him, not pressed into his chest. You can't deny that. And I've been thinking, it's possible that we could have interpreted it all wrong, the notes and the bruise I mean. Maybe we are so eager to find something that we are overlooking the simplest explanation."

Toop didn't respond so Sally continued.

"I'm not saying that all suicide shots are at close contact range but more often than not that is the case. There was no burn mark, nothing. One bullet angled slightly upwards and shot straight through his shirt. It's textbook, Fergus."

"What about his hands?"

The question caught Sally off guard.

"Sorry?"

"His hands. If he shot himself then the unburned carbon would have left powder residue on his hand."

"You know that there wasn't anything on his hands, Fergus," she snapped. "Even with the hands bagged there wasn't a hope in hell of getting any viable trace evidence from them. The rain would have washed any powder away within minutes. You know that."

He said nothing and Sally returned to her dishes. Toop listened to the sound of running water followed by the clink of ceramic on ceramic. Sally closed the front door behind her as she left, using a little more force than necessary.

Toop knew that he was being unreasonable but he didn't have time to worry about social niceties. His mind was elsewhere. He grabbed his coat and car keys.

Screw the pig, thought Toop.

A man had been murdered and now someone was threatening him.

**

"Well now, what have we here?"

The old man turned the book over in his hands, his accent untouched by time. Each word carried a romantic Swiss French inflection, a subtle weight that was left on the last syllable of each sentence. Toop watched the man's lips as he spoke, his 'i's morphed into something more like an 'ee' and each 'h' left silent. The lasting remnants of a childhood spent in Sion, a sleepy town in the West, French-speaking part of Switzerland.

Toop stole a quick glance around the shop. Nothing much had changed. If anything, he thought, there were more books and more shelves.

"Most interesting," the man continued, talking to himself.

He hunched over the text, pacing in concentric circles as his fingers worked through the pages. Toop took a sudden step backwards, preventing the old man from colliding with him. He stood back watching as the rotund little man compassed his shop, circumnavigated the clutter with impressive ease. The resemblance he bore to a tortoise was uncanny. His head peered out from his round body like a tiny pinball perched on an ageing neck. The skin hung loose, all the effects of elasticity long gone.

"You may go," he said.

"Sorry," replied Toop. "I haven't told you what..."

A pair of bespectacled eyes stopped him mid-sentence.

"Come back in an hour."

"But?"

Two beady eyes peered out over the frame of his glasses.

"One hour."

"I don't mean to be rude," said Toop, with little attempt to be polite. "But I am here for a specific reason, so if you wouldn't mind I have a few questions."

A smile cracked across the man's face. "I know why you are here boy." He turned his back on Toop and ambled across the room, showing no urgency. Then he settled into a chair by the window.

Boy. Toop was not in the mood to deal with a senile old man. He opened his mouth to protest but was cut short.

239

"What's in a name?" The man asked, with no want of a reply. "That which we call a rose by any other name would smell as sweet."

He winked. "Shakespeare. Quite beautiful don't you think?"

"Well yes," replied Toop, "but..."

"A rose by any other name would still be a rose," the old man continued, "names are meaningless, the creation of man, but colours dear boy. Yellow for example," another wink, "now that's God's doing." The old man smiled. "God and the telling mark of a newly creased page."

Toop was unable to find a response. He had to admit it, the old man had impressed him. Perhaps, thought Toop, senile was a little harsh.

"One hour." The man lowered his head and returned his attention to the book, adding a final few words. "You'll get a good cup of coffee next door."

Toop stood outside the shop, baffled. A minute passed. Questioning his decision to leave he turned around and reached for the handle but it was locked. The 'closed' sign already hung from the window.

Coffee it is then, thought Toop.

***

Five pairs of eyes watched him as he walked to the counter.

"What can I get you hen?"

"Coffee," replied Toop. "Black."

"Nothing sweet for you today. Scone? Teacake?"

"No. Thank you."

He walked to a small table in the corner and sat down, followed by the whisperings that came with living in a small town.

Chapter 51

Late 80s

McNab hung up the phone. Things, he thought, might just be going his way.

He rummaged through his desk for a pen and noted down the address. Meadowbank Stadium, Edinburgh. He checked his watch. Two o'clock. That gave him plenty of time. With any luck, he would be back to put Isla to bed.

McNab smiled to himself. True the case wasn't exactly clear but, thanks to the second of the Jones', certain elements of it were falling into place. At least now there was someone that he could talk to.

William Anderson was still living in Edinburgh and he was working at Jones and Jones Construction. He had been with the company for the best part of a decade, employed as a builder. Not overly intelligent or ambitious but reliable, a hard worker who clocked in at 8am each morning without fail. It was explained to McNab that the company had finished work on the Commonwealth Pool and that it was now focused on preparing Meadowbank Stadium. McNab would be able to find Anderson there.

It took McNab all of fifteen minutes to grab his coat and run to the nearest train station. He bundled onto the platform in time to see the two thirty train pulling in. McNab paused to catch his breath and he leant forward, resting his hands on his bent knees. Having a one year old was not conducive to exercise.

The train journey from Glasgow Queen Street took just over an hour. McNab stepped down onto the new platform at Meadowbank Stadium railway station and turned his head to peer over each of his shoulders. It was deserted. A small, unopened coffee vendor occupied the central island. No signs of graffiti. There was not a single piece of rubbish littering the platform. McNab frowned. He was used to the great bustle of Glasgow, to the crowds and the noise; hordes of impatient commuters who weaved like ants, the insults coughed from their lips in spits of saliva. He was used to the drunkards who stumbled along without aim or intention. It had taken McNab a while to adapt to the charm of Glasgow but now he was a Glaswegian through and through, loyal to the end. He would sell a limb before moving to Edinburgh.

"Bloody Edinburgers," he smiled to himself.

Meadowbank station had been completed a week previously. It was all part of the hype around the Commonwealth Games; an expensive development that allowed spectators to travel directly to the stadium. McNab shook his head. It didn't make sense to him. The capital's obsession with the Games was pushing it further and further into economic ruin. He couldn't complain, he thought, it had proved very handy for him today. He walked along the immaculate pathway as the train moved off. Only two other people followed him.

McNab walked outside. The air was warmer in Edinburgh than back home. It was one of those bluebird days that you rarely got in Glasgow, not a cloud in the sky. The capital city had always been a bull's eye on the weather map. Systems on the east coast had a knack for catching the sun and holding it hostage, leaving Glasgow in a constant grey drizzle.

It didn't take long for McNab to find the stadium. The building rose out of the ground across the road from where he was standing. He had to admit, Edinburgh or not, it was damned impressive.

William Anderson was there waiting for him.

At least McNab assumed that it was him. He squinted to get a better look. The man standing at the entrance was huge. Well over six foot, he thought, as he began walking towards him.

McNab was still a few steps away when Anderson held out his hand. The man showed no signs of embarrassment as he waited for his gesture to be returned. McNab quickened his step, desperate to close the gap and connect with the human shovel that was suspended between them. Anderson locked McNab's hand in a vice-like grip. He shook it once, hard, before releasing him. It required a conscious effort on McNab's part not to lower his eyes to assess the condition of his crumbled fingers.

"Boss mentioned that a copper was coming by to see me. I assume your wanting to talk about my Pops."

His abrupt tone caught McNab off guard.

"Well yes, I was hoping... I wanted to make sure that you knew."

"About my Pops being murdered, aye I ken."

McNab shuffled his feet as he located his words. "Nothing has been confirmed, Mr Anderson but we are investigating all possible angles."

"My Pops didn't kill himself."

"I understand that it must be difficult for..."

Anderson stopped him with a raised hand.

"Look officer." His voice softened. "I'll be straight with you. Yesterday I got a call from Alec Allaway. He said he'd spoken to you, told you all about my Pop's condition. He said you seemed decent enough. Made me agree to help you. So what do you want to know?"

"Well..."

"And no pussying around, I don't have time for bullshit. Every minute I'm out here with you is a minute that I'm not getting paid. So have at it."

McNab didn't need to be told twice. No bullshit, that's what the man said.

"Sorry," said McNab, "but you don't seem overly distressed about the death of your father."

Anderson raised an eyebrow and eyed McNab. For a moment McNab thought that he was going hit him, but to his great relief Anderson chose to level his brows and answer.

"We weren't close. Not since I was a lad."

"Did you speak much after he left?"

"The odd birthday card when I was growing up. But mother didn't approve, she didn't think that it was right for a kid to be exposed to that." He paused just long enough for it to be noticeable. "Cancer got her four years ago. She was dead within the year."

"I'm sorry."

"Her funeral was the first time I'd seen him since I was six. He kept himself to himself, didn't say a word to me then. But not long after that, that's when the letters started, one a month like clockwork. Came straight to my front door."

"So he knew where you lived?"

"I asked him about that in one of my letters. Said he got the address from my mother before she died. Apparently she sent him parcels a couple of times a year, photos, school marks, you know the like."

"What did he write to you about?"

"Nothing really. Didn't say much, didn't ask much. Just pleasantries."

"Did he seem..."

"Suicidal?" said Anderson. "No." He held the officer's gaze. "But towards the end he was different. Scared."

"Of what?" asked McNab.

"Of who."

***

"Jon, can you hear me?"

The voice was all around him, faint. It was the kind of distant echo that Jon had experienced in dreams. But it was clearer somehow, more real. Almost as if there was a substance to the words.

"Tom?"

"Yes mate, it's me."

Jon opened his eyes, taking a moment to orientate himself. He was lying down, flat on his back, with a wall to his right. Jon released his arm from the blanket and pressed his hand against the cold plaster. Yes, the wall was there. Groaning, he positioned an arm on each side of his hips and pushed himself up into a sitting position. The feeling of despair still lingered, drawing the energy from his body but it no longer consumed him.

Tom sat on a chair by his bed. Jon looked over at his friend. His face was different; there was no lightness in it.

"Tom," said Jon, "I don't understand. Where am I? Why are you here?" He paused, straightened, and glanced around the room. "There was a man. He gave me something."

"It's ok, Jon." Tom laid a reassuring hand on his friend's shoulder. "Just take it easy. You've been out of it for almost two days. You feeling any better?"

"Yeah, bit." His head was foggy.

"You had me worried Jon, running off from the gallery like that. I shouldn't have let you leave," he cast his eyes downwards and focused on his hands. "I'm sorry."

Jon was confused. Why was Tom apologising, he hadn't done anything wrong.

"I went past your flat," Tom continued, "but you weren't there. Eventually I tracked you down to the party."

The party.

Oh God. Jon felt sick. He grabbed at Tom's arm, digging his fingers into skin.

"Tom. I did something bad, something unforgivable." Jon's eyes held wide in desperation. He started to sob.

"She's ok, Jon." Tom met his eyes for the first time, "Jenny is going to be fine."

"What? I don't understand. I... I... There was so much blood. I saw her Tom. I killed her."

Tom straightened up and inched his chair closer to the bed. He forced a lightness back into his voice but his eyes betrayed him. "The moment I got you out of the house, I called an ambulance and she was taken straight to Southern General."

Jon nodded to show that he had heard the information.

"I brought you back to my granddad's place, made sure you were ok, then I went back to check on her. I wasn't allowed in to see her, family only but one of the doctors filled me in. I think he felt sorry for me, that or it pays to be persistent." The right side of Tom's mouth almost managed a smile. Then it was gone. "Apparently she suffered a fracture to the base of the skull. The doctor couldn't say for sure but he reckoned that it was caused by an impact with the edge of a table."

"But there was so much blood. It was everywhere, Tom."

"I know. I saw."

Jon shifted uncomfortably. Despite everything, he couldn't help but wonder what his friend might think of him. Was he disgusted?

"The doctor said that with skull fractures it is not uncommon for a mixture of clear fluid and blood to drain from the ears and nose. And because she was lying in the same spot it would have started to pool around her head."

"But she'll be ok?"

"Yes." Tom paused. "Because of the fracture there were initial concerns about brain damage but she was lucky. They just need to keep her in for a few days, rest mainly and to make sure that the fluid stops leaking. If it doesn't heal on its own then they drain it. If that fails then she will have to have to have surgery to get it closed up."

"Did she say anything?" asked Jon. "About me." His words were stuttered. "I didn't mean to hurt her."

"I know," replied Tom. "And I think that Jenny knows that too. She was still slipping in and out of consciousness when I left but as far as I'm aware she never mentioned your name."

The way that he said it made Jon look at him, his eyes caught somewhere between expectancy and hope.

"I don't think that she blames you," said Tom.

"Do you?"

Tom stared past Jon's shoulder to where there was a slight tear in the wallpaper. Three long seconds passed between them.

"I think that you need help, Jon." Tom pulled his eyes away from the wall and looked at his friend. "I've talked with my dad. And we would like to help you, to make you an offer."

"I don't understand."

"You will." Tom rose from his seat. "But you need to sleep now. It is not an offer that you should consider lightly."

Jon's body slipped back in a horizontal position, defeated and weak. The conversation had wiped him of all his energy. In truth, he was relieved when Tom shut the door and the room filled with darkness and as he drifted off his mind battled with a single thought.

How did Tom know who Jenny was? They had never met.

Chapter 52

Her uncle was dead.

Her dad had stopped speaking for a moment and Cece sat next to him with her head hung in silent contemplation, lost for words. She was grateful for the pause in conversation, anything to stop the painful torrent of words.

Jon was dead.

Cece could feel her dad watching her. She stared down at her hands and pinched her lower lip with her teeth to stop it trembling, not ready to meet his eyes. The touch of his hand on her knee made her jump and for the first time she noticed that she had been crying.

Her lips disappeared as she pursed them together and contorted her eyebrows into a frown.

Stop it Cece.

"How do you know?" she asked.

Tom hesitated for a moment and then he withdrew his hand. His hesitation caused Cece to lift her head and she wiped the moisture from her eyes with the back of her hand.

"Tell me." Her voice was resolute. "I want to know."

He glanced over at his daughter.

"Please." She reached over and placed her hand on his, squeezing his fingers.

Tom reached into his pocket with his free hand and retrieved Cece's phone. He held it out to her. Cece took it and looked at the photo. It was the picture that she had taken. The white sand beach.

Cece looked up and handed it back. "I still don't understand. I don't know where this is."

"Think." He lowered his voice. "Don't look with your eyes."

Then it hit her, punching the air from her chest with a single crushing blow.

"No," gasped Cece.

She slumped back in her chair and held her hands over her mouth. The monotone voice from the television whirled around her head, repeating the same two phrases over and over.

Body found in the Scottish Highlands.

A loaded gun abandoned by the body.

Then her ears dialled in to the sound of her own voice, her words, she had been so flippant, so detached. "Poor guy must have lost the will to live." That's what she had said, wasn't it?

Cece didn't move. Her brain raced ahead, trying to process the reality that was unfolding in front of her. The unnamed man on the news, the one that she had dismissed so cruelly, was her uncle. One question formed after another, causing her eyes to flicker back and forth.

"He didn't," she said finally. Cece closed her eyes, taking a moment to regain her breath and to get her nerves under control. "He didn't kill himself."

"I know."

"Then someone killed him."

"Yes."

"Who?"

"I can't say for sure."

"But you have an idea?"

"Yes."

Cece slipped her hand into her pocket.

"Does it have anything to do with this?"

She held up the small bag, watching as the red cylinder swung from her fingers.

***

The more she thought about it, the more worried Lucy became.

She wasn't stupid. It wasn't chance that had brought Jonathan Swan's niece, her cousin, to her door. Not now.

There was only one explanation that made sense.

Cece had to know.

The thought tightened in her gut and made Lucy want to throw up. She walked to the corner of her room and pulled open the heavy tenement window.

Air. Fresh air.

A second question niggled its way into her head. If Cece did know the truth, why hadn't she said anything? What was she waiting for?

Lucy didn't like it. She took a deep breath, filling her lungs with the scent of Glasgow, and made a decision. She had to contact her sister. In this instant, she decided, it was more dangerous not to.

She felt herself hesitate, something that had become a recent habit, then she jumped to her laptop and flipped it open before she could reconsider. Uncertainty had never been an issue as a child, she thought, Alex had made all the decisions. Lucy increased the pressure on the keypad, allowing her fingers to type in the new password. Eight characters.

Rose1988.

Her open inbox flashed up onto the screen. She had four new emails, one from the museum, the rest were junk. Lucy spared a quick thought for her old boss before hitting delete. The new Lucy didn't know a Patrick. She drifted the cursor down and clicked on the last email from Alex. Her lips moved as she re-read it.

Sorry to trouble you. I forgot some things. Journal, helmet and compromising lingerie set. Important that I dispose of them! ASAP. Very embarrassing. Sorry.

Lucy's eyes searched the desk for a pen. Then her hands moved down over the drawers, locating a blue biro on the second attempt. She scribbled the message on to a piece of paper, circling every third word. She rewrote it, inserting the full stops herself.

Trouble. Forgot Journal. Compromising. Important. Dispose ASAP. Sorry.

The message wasn't anything new to her. Lucy had deciphered the email earlier and the journal was now safely in her possession. She just needed to confirm something; the code. Every third word, that's what they had agreed on. The pounding in her head was getting worse. Lucy rubbed her temples with her fingers, her eyes automatically flicking to the time at the bottom of the screen. Gone midnight. There was a chance that Alex would still be up.

She hesitated again then started typing.

Delete. Type. Delete. Type. Delete.

Lucy leant back and rubbed her eyes with balled fists. She opened and closed them a number of times, struggling with the bright glare from the screen.

"Come on Lucy. Focus."

She sat up, straightened out her back and brushed the hair from her face. Her fingers moved across the keys as her mind ticked over.

Got your journal. Helmet not found. Hope you have settled in. Big hugs. No problem finding new flatmate. Girl called Cece moved in, knows some of our friends. Her plan is to stay six months, away after that.

Satisfied with her work, Lucy held her arms up in a Y shape and allowed herself a deep yawn. The pounding hadn't stopped but at least she had written something; seven completely normal sentences that could have been exchanged by two completely normal ex-flatmates.

She re-read it, voicing every third word.

"Journal found. Have big problem. Flatmate Cece knows our plan. Stay away."

Send.

Chapter 53

Present Day

The old man hunched over his desk with an array of opened books spread out in front of him. He had his back to the door. Toop could just make out the small turtle head that protruded from his shoulders. The man made no attempt to move when Toop walked in.

"Did you have a scone?" the man asked. His words fell onto an open text. "Flora makes a grand scone."

"No, I..." Toop paused. He didn't have time for idle chit chat. Correction, he never had time for it. His tolerance for frivolous conversation had died with his wife. "Sorry," he continued. "But I don't believe that I caught your name."

"Professor Fehr." He waved Toop over without turning his head. "Come look."

Twisting his body to avoid a large stack of books, Toop made his way across the cluttered shop.

Fehr ran his fingers across a faded picture, not quite touching it. "Fascinating, just fascinating," he said, his words not directed anywhere in particular. "Most delightful."

He turned the page and Toop waited.

"The Language of Flowers," stated Fehr, his thin lips caught in a smile. "I don't believe I've ever seen a first edition copy. This is quite the treat."

He mulled over his treasure, skimming through the next two pages while showing little regard for Toop's presence. Twenty seconds passed before he spoke again.

"Have you much knowledge on the subject, officer?"

"No," said Toop impatiently, dipping his hands into his pockets.

"Wonderful." Fehr beamed and gestured towards a chair. "Take a seat."

Toop lifted the pile of books that were sitting on the soft leather and placed them on the floor. He had the feeling that he wouldn't be moving for some time.

"The language of flowers can be found within the pages of many of the great classics," began Fehr. "William Shakespeare, Jane Austen, the Bronte sisters, all of them have used it in their writings. Even today it has a place. Most recently Prince William's bride, Kate Middleton, insisted that her bouquet carried a sprig of myrtle and not just any sprig, but a fresh cutting taken from the original bush planted by Queen Victoria's mother-in-law. Myrtle, you see, is used to symbolise good luck and love in marriage. It is a tradition that has followed royal brides since 1858."

Fehr looked distinctly pleased with himself, his round head bobbing up and down with excitement.

"I first discovered the language of flowers when I was a boy," continued Fehr.

His eyes drifted to the ceiling as he located the memory. "Yes, it was autumn, that's right. My grandmother had come to holiday with the family. She spent most of her time in the garden you see. Roses, she loved roses. But one morning she appeared holding a poppy. It was bright yellow. I remember watching her from the kitchen window. She stopped at the bottom of the garden where she bent over to gather up her skirt. Then she strolled up the grass hill and into the kitchen. She kissed me on the head and slipped the flower into the breast pocket of my shirt."

Professor Fehr let out a fond sigh.

"Even now I can recall standing perfectly still as she lowered her head and cupped her hands around my ear. The softness of her voice tickled against my skin and in a whisper she said, yellow for my petit garcon, a yellow poppy to bring him wealth and success."

Toop listened. Agitated. He shifted his weight and bit back a retort.

Fehr glanced over at the officer. His wide grin broadened.

"During the reign of Queen Victoria flowers were used as part of a symbolic language. They presented a way of communicating that, in those days, was as important to society as being well dressed. Each flower had a silent meaning of its own, allowing people to say what was not dared to be spoken. A language of love that defied the strict propriety of the times."

He paused to clear his throat. The smile returned.

"Each colour of flower was assigned a particular, although often debated, meaning which opened up a world of possibility for young lovers. Feelings that could not be proclaimed in public could be shared with the simple exchange of a rose."

As though in answer to Toop's thoughts he said, "However sending and receiving flowers was not just a way of showing love and affection."

Fehr handed Toop the book. He held it open at the chosen page.

"Flowers could be used to send death threats, warnings of dangers or messages of hatred. This flower here, the petunia, is intended to illustrate feelings of resentment or anger. But..." He waved his finger in front of Toop's face. "The same flower could also mean that your presence soothes me. Two messages that you don't want to confuse."

"But how do you know the correct one?" asked Toop.

"Both are correct. But which of the messages was intended, that required a degree of guesswork on the part of the receiver. In 1884 a book was published in London titled, The Language of Flowers. The author, Jean Marsh, became vastly popular and her interpretations became the accepted source for flower meanings. But you must remember that her dictionary was only one of many and it was not uncommon for miscommunications to ensue. Inconsistencies can even be found in works written by the same author."

He pointed at the book held in Toop's hands. "Take your book, for example. If you look in the table of contents at the beginning..." He waved his finger at Toop. "Go on have a look. What does it say about the common marigold?"

Toop read directly from the text. "Marigold (common): a symbol implying affection."

"Good. But hundreds of pages later in the very same book the marigold appears again. This time it appears as sorrow." He took the book from Toop and stared at the cover, his smile replaced by a perplexed squint. "I looked through the book again but I could find no explanation for the discrepancy. In an attempt to determine the correct meaning I searched through a couple of the books that I had in my collection. But instead of reaching a conclusion, I found that the problem was not specific to the marigold. I'm afraid that most flowers appear to have multiple meanings."

Toop, annoyed at the apparent waste of time, said curtly, "And the yellow rose?"

"Well, according to the dictionary that you found, a yellow rose can mean either infidelity or jealousy."

"Thank you," said Toop, struggling to conceal his impatience. "I am aware of that. Could you perhaps tell me, with regard to the accusation of infidelity, would it apply to the receiver or the sender?"

"That depends."

"On?"

"Well, it's quite a complex language to interpret. I'm not entirely sure..."

"It's important." Toop leant forward and held his face in front of the old man's. "Tell me. Is it possible that a woman could send a yellow rose as a threat, a warning perhaps, to inform her lover that she has learned of his infidelities?"

"I suppose. But..." He drew his brows together, forming a single white hedge, "...she could also be sending it as an admission of her own guilt, or to show disdain at her lover's jealous nature."

"There must be a way to decipher the message."

"As I said, it's a very delicate and complex language."

"Try me."

The old man pursed his lips, tutting at Toop's disregard for common decorum, before continuing.

"It's impossible to tell unless you have the rose in question. You wouldn't by any chance..."

"No," interrupted Toop. "But let's say I did have it."

"Well, in that case, the message is concealed within the positioning of the bow or the way that the flower is bent."

"Meaning?"

"If the bow or the flower is bent to the left then the message refers to the receiver. You have been unfaithful. But if it is positioned to the right then the message refers to the sender. I have committed adultery."

Left equalled a motive, thought Toop.

"Thank you," said Toop, rising from his chair.

But his appreciation fell on deaf ears, Fehr having already returned to the book.

Toop watched the old book keeper and considered leaving the text with him; Toop had no immediate use for it after all.

"You should keep this flat," said Fehr, smoothing out the fold that marked page fourteen. The yellow rose. His fingers stroked the paper with a careful intimacy, his eyes betraying a sense of sadness. "Just as a face is blemished by wrinkles," he said, "a book is blemished by creases.

Horrible things. And on a first edition." His shook his head. "Disgraceful, utterly disgraceful."

Toop was about to offer him the book when the old man let out a childish wail.

"No," he murmured. "It can't..." The dew in his eyes was instant.

"What's wrong?" asked Toop.

Fehr's small eyes blinked repeatedly and his fat hands waved.

"It's gone! Gone. Ripped out." He stuttered over the 'r' in ripped, unable to control his trembling lips.

"What's gone?"

"Page fifteen." More stuttering. "It's been torn out." When he looked up his cheeks were flushed and his lips were wet.

Toop lifted the book from the man's shaking fingers. He held it open and stared down the spine. Fehr was right. Small tuffs of white protruded from the gully of paper; the remnants of a stolen page.

It was a page that he needed to find.

Now.

Toop headed for the door, leaving a distraught Fehr staring at his empty hands, his head slumped forward like a Dali clock.

Toop was willing to bet that the meaning on page fifteen was the one that he needed. And he knew just how to get it.

Chapter 54

Late 80s

"Scared of who?" said McNab, repeating Anderson's statement.

"He never mentioned names."

"Names? There was more than one?"

"I can't say for certain. My pops was kind of cryptic, not much of a talker. But there was something in his letters." He stopped to light a cigarette. "Something odd."

He offered the packet to McNab. The officer shook his head.

"At first I didn't give it much thought. Pops had always been a bit dramatic, it came with his condition, he tended to make a fuss of nothing."

Anderson took a long draw on his cigarette and blew the smoke over his right shoulder.

"What changed?" said McNab, prompting the conversation.

"He started asking questions. Not the usual shit about the weather and football and the like but more personal, asking if I had a missus or any kids of my own."

"Isn't that normal?" responded McNab, his own daughter popping into his head. "Don't most fathers want to know those things?"

"Not mine."

McNab didn't question it. He let Anderson continue.

"Didn't matter anyhow, my lady up and left over a year back and I've no kids. Well, none that I'm aware of. That seemed to please the old man that, knowing that it was just me."

"What makes you say that?"

Anderson took another drag.

"He stopped asking questions, went back to talking about the Celtic scores." The cigarette rose to his lips a second time. "Couple months passed and I decided that it might be nice to meet the old fellow face to face, you know, see how he was getting on. But he dismissed the idea straight off."

"Did he say why?" asked McNab.

"Nah, no really, couple of bullshit excuses. But he was different after that."

Anderson brought his hand to his mouth and caught a chesty cough in his fist.

"Paranoid," he said, clearing his throat.

"Paranoid?"

"Each letter was the same; there would always be a reminder that I wasn't to visit or to turn up unannounced. No visits. No phone calls. It was like he didn't want anybody to know I existed, like he was scared of people finding out that he had a son."

"Do you think he was concerned about your safety?"

Anderson gave an 'it would seem so' shrug, raised his hand to his face and filled his lungs with smoke.

McNab's response caught on the end of his tongue, escaping as little more than a release of air.

Something was bugging him.

He watched as Anderson put the cigarette to his lips, expertly ridding his mouth of air. Smoke held between his cheeks for the next few seconds.

McNab took the opportunity to sort through his thoughts, letting Allaway's words play over in his head. *That's why Bill became a janitor. He could shut himself away. Talk to as few people as possible.* That fitted, reasoned McNab. New job, new start. Bill Anderson had no reason to mention a son to his colleagues.

Perhaps it was just too hard for him to talk about it.

Or, thought McNab, perhaps Bill was protecting his son from someone? Keeping him hidden.

You can't threaten someone if they don't exist.

McNab's mind turned to thoughts of Isla and the police car that was parked outside his house. He would do anything to protect his little girl, even if it meant concealing her existence.

Was that what Bill Anderson had done, he thought, a scared man who chose to hide his son.

McNab's thoughts flicked to the suicide note and the apology that Anderson had written; an apology written to a family that didn't exist. *Didn't exist.* Those were the words that he had used before learning that Anderson had a son. But son or no son, Bill Anderson had died alone. Not a single living family member had come forward to confirm the identity of the body. In fact, if it wasn't for Alec Allaway's appearance, he wouldn't have met Anderson's son. Perhaps that was the intention, reasoned McNab, for William not to be found.

But then there was the obvious question. Why did Anderson need to protect his son? Who was he hiding him from? The questions lined up without a single answer. Was Bill Anderson murdered? And if so, why would someone want him dead?

McNab rubbed his head. He felt old. The more he thought about it the more frustrated he got about how little he knew. There were too many question marks.

A second notion stalled his thought process.

If Bill Anderson had been trying to conceal his son then why had he apologised to his family in a suicide note? Something didn't add up. Why, thought McNab, would he go to the effort of hiding his son and then expose him with his final words?

Technically, it was a manageable question, there was one simple answer. The problem, realised McNab, was that it wasn't a good one.

Someone else must have written the note.

The thought didn't have time to settle, diluted by the thickening of the air. McNab's nostrils twitched. Acid, must, and a slight tinge of damp urine. The pungent smell violated McNab's nasal passages and jolted him back to the present. Cigarette smoke.

"You still with us there officer?" asked Anderson, flicking the glowing head of his tab. McNab watched as the discarded particles found their way to the pavement.

"Sorry," said McNab, "I was just thinking a few things through."

Anderson didn't question him and McNab didn't feel an evaluation was wanted.

"It was his last couple of letters though," continued Anderson. "Weird like. I started to think that the old man might be losing a few screws. I can't mind exactly what they said but the gist was the same. The old man kept making these weird references about the devil."

He took another draw and McNab waited. He didn't know if Anderson was going to continue.

"Can you elaborate?" asked McNab.

"He kept going on about the devil breathing down his neck. Didn't mean nothing to me."

"Do you still have the letters?"

"Aye. Back at the house."

"Do you think that it would be possible for me to have a look at them? I understand of course that they are personal and I don't want to intrude but your father could have written something that may help us."

"Doesn't bother me. I'll post them when I'm home."

McNab left his business card, thanked Anderson and headed back to the train station.

The devil.

Why on earth would Bill Anderson be writing about the devil? McNab couldn't think of a single viable answer. But as he made his way along the platform he had the distinct feeling that whatever the reason, it was important.

He checked his watch. Isla would already be in bed. He pictured his little girl's face, her tiny balled fists pressed into her rosy cheeks as she lay curled in her cot. Peaceful and safe.

How wrong he was.

***

The policeman wound down his car window.

"Can I help you?" he asked.

"Evening officer," replied the man. "You wouldn't be able to tell me if this is the McNab residence?" He pointed to the blue door. Number 18. "Mrs McNab has been so kind to my mother you see, she's in the local nursing home and I wanted to thank her." The man held up a bottle of wine.

The policeman peered through the window. He frowned.

"I wasn't aware that Caroline worked at the nursing home."

"She doesn't." The man smiled. His question had been answered.

He leant forward so that his head and shoulders filled the car window frame. His actions were swift and deliberate, the entire process taking a matter of seconds. The police officer fell back into his seat. He had served his purpose, he was no longer of any use to the man.

The stranger's grin was the last thing that Officer Donaldson remembered before he lost consciousness.

No one stopped the gentleman as he walked up to the blue door and pushed it open.

***

Eight hours later Jon woke up.

He could hear muffled voices, not quite able to make them out. He decided that they must be coming from a different room.

The darkness around him was a solid thing. Not a single hint of light made it into the windowless room. Jon grabbed at the air with his fingers, his brain trying to connect the fragments of information that were available to him. He felt no fear. The paranoia had subsided. His hand caressed the cool surface of the air as his chest rose with quiet breaths.

The memories started to form, presenting themselves in flashes.

A bed. Tom's face. The tear in the wallpaper. Tom's offer of help.

A moment of nothing followed, then there was another cluster of memories. This time the panic began to rise in his chest and Jon started to take short sharp breaths, feeling the nausea building in his stomach.

The party. Blood. Jenny. Something about a skull fracture. Southern General Hospital.

Stop, please stop.

Drawing both hands underneath his body, Jon pushed himself into a sitting position. It was impossible to penetrate the darkness, nothing registered in his vision. His pupils refused to dilate.

He was ready to hear Tom's offer. Whatever it was, he was ready.

As if on cue the door opened and light fell upon the room. Two figures appeared in the doorway; Tom and an older man. There was no mistaking the man this time. Jon watched as he approached his bed, the stranger who had nursed him back to health only a couple of days earlier. But this time, Jon recognised him straight away.

There was no walking stick, no awkward hunch. The man walked with effortless ease and authority. But there was no question.

It was Mr McGraw. Tom's father.

Chapter 55

For a whole twenty minutes Cece didn't speak. She listened and her father talked.

Her mind remained empty, accepting her uncle's story without judgment or criticism, empty but for one thought.

Pity.

Pity for a man who had spent his entire life drowning; a small fish in a big pond. A man whose life was filled with death, doomed to die from the day that he was born.

Cece focused on her father's eyes as he shared his story. It wasn't a happy one. There was no fairytale ending. No grand epiphany. The protagonist did not live happily ever after.

When her father's words dried up they sat together in silence. There was nothing to be said. Not yet. That would come. In that moment Cece just wanted to think. She needed some time to process, only then she would decide how to act.

Who to punish.

Her father's words played over in her head, starting at the beginning and finishing at the end.

His end.

The story repeated in her mind as if it was being read out loud from a book. Her father's voice faltered only twice. Two lumps that caught in his throat.

"Life was never on your uncle's side, in fact from the start it was very much against him. Some people believe that you can make your own luck but your uncle Jon never got that chance. He was never going to be a fortunate man. You see, his very first breath, the one that brought him into this earth, was also his mother's last. She died moments after giving birth, trading her life for his."

He held Cece's stare.

"But you should understand that it was a trade that she made willingly, without regret. Jon was her world, her entire reason for being and there was nothing she wanted more than to have a child."

The first falter.

"The poor woman, she couldn't have known. She had no idea what her sacrifice would cost her son." He shook his head. "Jon was left completely alone, alone in a vast, cruel world. A relative, not his father, later told Jon that he and his mother had existed together for less than nine seconds. Those were nine brief but very important seconds because, in that short moment, his mother's wish was granted. She had her child."

Pause. A brief moment of still.

"But it was also enough time for his father to look into Jon's eyes and feel hatred. In his view his son was a murderer, a thief who stole his wife from him. There was no love there. Not then, not ever."

Silence allowed the statement to settle in Cece's stomach. The first pinch of pity.

"Your uncle," Tom continued, "he wasn't born like other little boys. He was never normal, not in the conventional sense. From a young age he struggled with people, or more precisely he struggled to get people to like him. It wasn't that he was unlikable as such, just different. And different has always been something that people struggle with. As a child he tried to form friendships, craving the human contact, but Jon had great difficulty in both acquiring and maintaining them."

Cece tried but she couldn't picture her uncle as a child. In fact, not once had she given a thought to his childhood. He was one of those people who seemed to have been born into adulthood. Quiet. Reserved. She couldn't imagine him playing in a sandpit or blowing bubbles into his milkshake. Perhaps, she reasoned, that explained a lot.

"One day," her dad continued, "he just gave up. Consciously or not, not even Jon could tell you. But at some point, I believe that it was when he was in his early teens, he shut down. He withdrew, rejecting the world that had rejected him. Jon knew that he was different but he couldn't change it. From then on he threw himself into academia. Your uncle loved learning; he would spend hours locked away with great piles of books."

An image flashed into Cece's mind. She was much younger, her knees gathered to her chest, her little feet buried into the carpet. Waiting. Her chin rested on her knees with her back pressed up against her uncle's office door. She didn't make a sound. Waiting. Listening. She would sit for hours, determined. Stubborn, her father called it. Not even the rumbling in her empty stomach would move her. Eventually, following a battle of wills, her father would give in. It was the same each time. And each time he would bring her sandwiches.

Cheese, no crusts.

"Daddy, I can't eat crusts. I just can't." Stubborn. Resolute. "Sarah, in my class, she loves crusts. And Daddy her hair is like a hedge, all fuzzy and yuck like this. See? Mrs Callander says it's the crusts, and she said that birds will start to nest in her hair." Wide eyes. "I don't want birds in my head. So no crusts, ok Daddy?"

Cece smiled at the memory. Forgetting the present for a brief moment.

Then it was gone. Along with her smile.

"There was one friend," her father continued. Cece noticed a slight change in his voice. Disapproval perhaps. "His name was Jesse. Jesse Jenkins."

"Jon never really knew how to be a friend, the intricacies of such a relationship were beyond him, but with Jesse it didn't really matter. Jesse was happy to be in charge. Even at the age of four Jesse relished the attention, encouraged the fixation. To most children a passing smile is inconsequential, a negligible expression formed with little agenda, but Jon struggled to interpret the feelings behind such facial expressions, often inventing emotions that had no foundation for belief. To him, a smile from Jesse was monumental; it signified the beginnings of a lifelong bond, an obsession. In general most children are naive, blissfully unaware of their power but Jesse wasn't. In truth, he liked it. The two were inseparable. Jesse led and Jon followed."

Pause.

"The blind leading the blind."

His eyes left Cece's without looking anywhere in particular when they fell on one of Jon's paintings.

"Jon was addicted. On one of the rare occasions that he confided in me he admitted that his relationship with Jesse caused a number of problems at school; detention, punishment exercises, a brief period of exclusion. You see Jon could get quite upset and even aggressive if anyone insulted Jesse. He was blindly protective of what he considered to be his, and I have never met anyone more focused or diligent than your uncle. Later, with help, he was able to channel this skill into his work. Jon was an exquisite artist."

263

The 'was' hurt. Cece wasn't ready for the past tense.

"Jon could focus on a painting for an unnaturally long period of time and his attention to detail was inspiring, impressive to a point of painstaking extremes. Everything had to be perfect. But as a young boy, the task that he focused on was Jesse Jenkins."

Cece knew that her father blamed Jesse Jenkins for a lot. She understood that. Really, she did. But Cece couldn't help it; she kept thinking that without him Jon would have had no one. He would have been completely alone.

Wouldn't that have been worse?

She would never admit it to her father, but at that moment Cece couldn't bring herself to dislike the little boy called Jesse Jenkins. Her uncle's only friend.

"The two of them remained friends throughout primary school and when Jon received a scholarship he moved to a private school in the city. Jesse went to the local secondary school. It wasn't an easy time for Jon and like I said, it didn't take long before he withdrew from reality, becoming more comfortable in his own world. The onset of puberty made it difficult for Jon to control his anger and anxiety, something which sent him into spirals of depression. Secondary School is a challenge for most children but for Jon it was hell. Adolescents can be particularly cruel, they have little, if any tolerance for people they perceive to be different."

Yes, decided Cece, it would have been worse.

"Day by day the social demands of school became more complex and Jon grew distance. The increasing rejection and separation from his peers was too much. His only release came during the holidays when he got to see Jesse where, away from the stereotyped corridors and societal expectations of school, the boys were free to be friends. And that's how it continued for the next few years, a friendship that grew behind closed doors."

Cece watched her father's face, noticing how tired he looked. Weary, she thought. There was something different about him, his eyes weren't his own. They were grey and the spark was gone. Where, she wasn't sure.

He looked old, she realised. In that moment her dad looked old.

"Then," he continued, "when they went to university together, that's when things started to go wrong. Really wrong."

The second falter. This time the lump broke his voice. Immovable.

"Her name was Jenny Pingleton."

He blinked the moisture from his eyes and, without thinking, Cece reached her hand out and held his.

"It's ok, Dad," she said, the father-daughter role momentarily reversed.

And for the first time in twenty-seven years Tom cried, allowing the unspoken truth to burn his cheeks, releasing the secret that he had kept for nearly three decades.

Tom McGraw had loved Jenny, adored everything about her, and Jon, his best friend, had raped her.

But Tom had chosen Jon.

Willingly, without regret.

Chapter 56

From the kitchen Sally grabbed some buttered toast and put it on a plate with a poached egg and a sliced avocado. Balancing a cup of coffee in her other hand, the good stuff, she made her way to the table.

The remnants of her afternoon's work lay cluttered across the surface. Not a single new case. In truth, she had been on holiday for the past twenty-four hours. Inverness, she decided, could cope without her for a few days. The new intern needed a kick into first gear, anything to get him to shift his arse and get his hands dirty. Quite literally. Jeremy, if she was being honest, was a bit wet for her liking. No gumption.

Toop, on the other hand, she wasn't so sure about leaving him alone. Not now. Not that she had any intention of mentioning it to him. If he asked why she was still hanging around then she would tell him. Until then she would keep quiet.

Ask no questions, hear no lies, thought Sally.

It had also occurred to Sally that by not asking, or saying anything really, could be Toop's way of accepting her help. Men and their bloody egos, she thought.

She picked up the picture. It was the same one that she had been looking at a few moments earlier, before her stomach had insisted upon a trip to the kitchen. The photo showed a man with a gun wound in the centre of his chest. His name still unknown.

She squinted. Saddened.

Sally had no idea if he'd been wealthy or poor. Did he live alone or did he have a family waiting for him to come home? What were his hobbies, did he have any, perhaps he was a workaholic. A loner, a socialite, or one of those kind-natured men who could make you smile with a few choice words. She knew almost nothing about him. And what she did know, she wished she didn't.

She ran the facts through her head for the umpteenth time.

Cause of death was the easy part, a lead ball bullet straight to the heart. There was a clear, single entry point and a fissure in the bone of the rib by the exit wound. Black powder had been left in the wound track and by the pericardial sac.

Textbook: a close contact shot indicative of suicide.

Location, again straightforward: seated at the edge of a loch looking out over the surrounding mountains. Desolate. Remote. His body was tilted backwards into the rocks, his lifeless arms hung from his torso like dead weights, with his neck stretched out into an arch. Textbook. Sitting, bent over, with the gun angled into his chest. The force from the gunshot would have sent his limp body recoiling backwards into the cold stone, leaving him in his final resting place. Sally had written up the notes herself. It was almost impossible not to be suicide. Pig or no pig, she thought, the angle caused by the path of the bullet was implicit. Any attacker would have had to have been suspended in mid-air.

Not possible.

That's when the facts became less black and white. More grey. More questions, less answers.

She picked up an A4 envelope and retrieved the documents from inside. The originals, taken in colour, had been sent over to the ballistics lab but one of the lads at the station, an old colleague, had photocopied the pages for her in black and white so that she had a set of her own. The envelope contained a selection of the photographs of the deceased's clothes and the contents of his rucksack. Sally had seen them before; two water-bottles, a sandwich, a crappy waterproof, a pair of slip-on sandals with buckles and cheap trousers. Nothing exciting or revolutionary but there was one thing that stuck out above all else. No labels. Each one had been cut out as if he, whoever he was, wanted to erase all proof of his existence. No credit cards. Nothing.

Or, thought Sally, someone had wanted to make it very difficult for him to be identified. Which, she reasoned, they had done a damn fine job of.

Credit where credit's due, she reasoned.

She had been concentrating for too long and frustration was starting to set in. Hours hunched over a selection of photographs and pieces of paper, working her way through one then the next, then the next. The process was mechanical. Sample A suggestive of suicide. Sample B suggestive of suicide. Sample C suggestive of suicide.

All nice and neat.

Expect that it wasn't. She couldn't silence the niggle at the back of her mind, that and Toop's stubborn gut. Why, thought Sally, why was she putting so much bloody faith and time into his gut feeling?

She knew why.

The she spotted it, an additional piece of paper trapped against the inside of the envelope. She removed the sheet, pulling it out by the edges so as not to rip it. It seemed to be stuck. Then, lacking patience or simply refusing to feign it, she yanked it out and it released in one fluid motion. *Yes*. Sally smiled and, pleased with her handiwork, she held it up. She recognised it straight away, in fact, she owned at least a couple of them herself. Toop probably had drawers full of them, filed in order, numbers increasing left to right. It was an Ordnance Survey map. The item in itself was nothing unusual, anyone could pick one up. Except in this case, it had been cut up. Only an A4 sized panel was left, blasphemy by mountaineering standards.

Strange, thought Sally, the man didn't own a decent jacket and he had no knowledge of appropriate footwear, yet he took a map with him. A second thought, more of a question. Why would he need a map, what would be the point if he wasn't planning to return? Surely getting lost wasn't an issue.

Perhaps, thought Sally, it was never meant to be a one way trip.

Her eyes flickered across the paper and, from habit, she scanned the map in square grids; three centimetres by three centimetres, left to right, top to bottom. After a few moments her gaze settled on something. Or it seemed, they settled on the very opposite, the absence of something.

"What are you trying to tell me?" she whispered. She dipped her nose towards the map and squinted.

Yes.

It was there, a darkened fleck in the top right corner. Visible, just. The grey dot had been added to the map. Someone, she was sure, had drawn it on. Sally was certain that it had been marked on intentionally, a tiny dark smudge. She inched closer, yes it was there. Exactly there.

"Shit," she whispered.

The tiny mark had been added to the map in the exact point where the body had been found. It was no accident.

***

Eve showered and used a razor to remove the first signs of stubble from her legs. Twice she caught old scabs, the nick of new skin turning the water red.

Shit. Ouch.

The water felt like salt on her skinned elbow, tender and raw. Her bike wheel had washed out in the mud and instinct had sent her arm outwards to protect her face, causing her to impact with a rock. In truth, she was lucky not to have broken her collarbone.

After scrubbing the dirt from her wound, her face gathered in a grimace, Eve stepped out of the shower. She towelled herself down, taking care to pat around her grazed elbow, and threw on semi-clean clothes. Twice worn jeans and a week old hoody. Washing, since living out of a van, had become less of a priority. Eve nodded at the woman and her two young children on her way out. She recognised them. They were staying in one of the caravans that was parked up across from her van. Nice family it seemed, cute dog.

The quick blast on her bike had not had the desired effect. Now, thought Eve, she was just as confused as before but also had a gammy elbow.

Great, just bloody brilliant.

Holding her wet towel under one arm she used her free hand to slide open the door to her van. It was an old painter's van that she had converted, largely herself, a couple of years back. The single bed which could slide out to make a double was designed just long enough to allow for the back of the van to double as a bike garage. Big enough for three bikes, front wheels off, with storage space beneath. Her favourite item, a one ring gas cooker with a small worktop, was tucked into the far corner. Two shelves were stacked with tea and mugs.

Eve sat on the bed with her legs crossed and gathered her long hair into a pony tail. A few red strands escaped from her fingers and fell down her back, catching in the folds of her green hood. She reached for her beanie, striped with a large bobble, glad to feel the warmth trapped around her head.

You're not meant to have feelings for him, thought Eve. That had never been the plan. Despite her careful preparation and time spent tying up loose ends, she could sense that her rear flank was exposed. She didn't like it. But Eve had no idea what to do about it. There was something about Fergus Toop.

She liked him.

And she didn't like anyone. Not really.

The knock on the side of her van startled her. Three taps. Hard. She never had visitors. Eve leant forward and slid the door open.

He stood in front of her. The rain, which had been a drizzle just moments before, soaked into his t-shirt, darkening the cotton where it clung to his shoulders.

"Do you have a laptop?" asked Toop.

He stood in the entrance to her van, a hand grasped on each side of the doorframe, his eyes locked on hers. The grey cotton held fast to his chest.

"Hello to you too," replied Eve.

"Sorry. Hi." He was out of breath, as if he had been running. "Can I use your laptop?"

"Do I have a choice?" She reached across her bed, removed it from beneath her pillow and handed it to him. Toop took it from her and flipped the screen up.

"Thanks."

He sat on the bed next to her and Eve moved an inch further from him. The act, however small, was a conscious one. Too close was dangerous. Especially, she thought, after what had happened last time.

Had he thought about it? Eve shook her head, not noticeably but just enough to clear the query from her mind. She didn't care. Did she?

Another shake. Gone.

"But," she continued, "I don't understand. What are you doing here? Wait, how did you even know where I would be?"

"Golden Sands." He didn't look up. "You said that you parked your van here, to use the showers." His eyes darted across the screen. "Do you have Wi-Fi?"

"But why are you here exactly?"

"I needed to use a computer. Yours was closer." Toop looked up. "Does the caravan site not have Wi-Fi?"

"No. I use a dongle."

He stared at her and Eve rolled her eyes before holding up a small USB device.

"Here, I'll do it."

She took the computer from him. The gap diminished. No safe inch. Both of them felt it, knee against thigh, and both of them withheld eye contact.

"A dongle. Seriously you need to get out more." Eve inserted the device into the side of her laptop. "It's a form of mobile broadband or in cave dweller terms, it's an internet stick. Attach it to your computer, comme ça and boom. Wireless broadband."

Eve smiled triumphantly. She felt more relaxed, less exposed now that she had the reins.

"Now Grandpa, how can I be of service?"

Toop ignored the jibe.

"I was hoping that you could track down an electronic copy of a book."

"Sounds easy enough. What's it called?"

"The Floral Offering: A Token of Deceit. 1863."

If she wavered Toop didn't notice.

"I just need to see one page," continued Toop. "Page 15."

Eve's fingers shifted across the keys. Hesitant. She could feel Toop watching her.

Why hadn't she taken the whole book?

Idiot, Eve cursed herself. Why had she been so foolish? Was it arrogance, a cocky brazenness, what? Why had she only taken that single page? Her eyes flickered to the shelf above the gas cooker where it was folded, hidden behind a box of Earl Grey tea.

Page 15.

***

"Hi Fraser, it's Sally again. Sorry to bother you." She pressed the phone tight against the side of her face.

"No worries. How can I help?"

"The photos of the victim's clothes and belongings, the ones that were sent over from the station, you wouldn't happen to still have them?"

"Yes, I believe I do. In fact... hold on a sec."

She listened to the sound of static, picturing McGlone as he searched around his office.

"Got them right here," he said, "due to be posted back tomorrow."

Finally, a break. Sally smiled.

"Brilliant. I was wondering if you could do me a quick favour. I have the photocopies here with me but I think that something's missing."

"One of the pages?"

"Not exactly. More something that is on one of them. Although," she paused, "what that something is I can't quite tell you."

A kind laughter filtered thought her ear piece. "Ok. Well can you at least give me a clue?"

"Sorry, yes." Sally realised how crazy she sounded. "It's on the photocopy of the map."

She listened to a quiet rustling.

"Yep. Got it."

"There wouldn't happen to be anything marked on it?"

"Yes, indeed there would. Someone has drawn on it with a yellow highlighter."

Sally gathered her fingers into a celebratory fist and her lips formed the word 'yes'. A second break.

"I was hoping you'd say that. Could you possibly take a photo of it on your phone and send it to me."

"Not a problem."

"Cheers Fraser. You're a life saver."

"Happy to help."

He hung up. Two minutes later Sally's phone beeped.

There it was. Clear as day.

Chapter 57

Late 80s

Something was wrong.

McNab didn't shout or sprint across the road. He walked towards his house, approaching the police car that had been dispatched under his orders. The pool of light from the street lamp fell just short of the bonnet, leaving the vehicle hidden in shadow. Darkness was good, thought McNab, it discouraged unwanted attention.

Anyone, or more likely, he reasoned, someone could be watching.

When Officer Donaldson made no signs of movement, McNab didn't flinch or pull back, he reached for the handle and opened the door. Slowly he bent down on his knees, using the sides of the door frame to steady himself. No sudden movements.

"Donaldson, can you hear me?" he whispered.

No response. Donaldson's head had fallen to the side, a limp mass left suspended above his right shoulder, his neck twisted at an unnatural angle. Eyes open.

McNab looked over the body, more introspective than most, and assessed it from every angle. He knew it wasn't good. But worse than that, McNab was certain that this wasn't the main event. Officer Donaldson was an aperitif, a taste of what was to come.

McNab skirted over his colleague with a trained gaze. No visible wounds. Still breathing.

"Donaldson?" A little louder this time.

Still no answer. The officer's eyes had rolled back into his skull, his entire body induced into a zombie-like state, conscious but vacant. McNab leant back onto his heels, his crouched frame paused by a single thought, a thought that crushed the wind from his lungs.

Isla.

A sharp sickness grabbed his gut. It was fear, a weakness that he was not accustomed to. It was paralysing. A troubling premonition started to move up his spine and something, everything, every inch of his being told him that it was all to do with the man on the phone. The realisation worked like a slap to the face, twisting his fear into anger, and in that moment, crouched in the road, he realised that nothing would stop him from protecting his little girl. Nothing would stop him from finding and punishing that man.

He didn't know it then but he would soon learn that some things were easier said than done.

McNab rested his head against the side of the car as he debated for a moment, deciding what do to next. His instincts had served him well in the past. In his line of work going on instinct was the difference between life and... He paused mid-thought and stood up.

Just get it right.

He closed the car door and walked towards his house. As soon as he knew Isla was safe then, only then, would he call for an ambulance. Not one moment before.

The door was unlocked and McNab walked straight in, his gaze catching on the handle, no sign of a forced entry. His hallway looked as it always did, shoes lined against the wall with a row of jackets hooked above them. A small table occupied the space at the end of the rack of raincoats. He stepped towards it and cast a glance in the cluttered bowl, nothing untoward, the house keys and the car keys lay in full view.

Whoever had been in his house, thought McNab, had not been looking to rob him. But it was not a comforting notion, the very opposite in fact. A glacial cold crept into his chest, leaking outwards through his heart before accumulating in the pit of his stomach. Why was there no noise? Nothing. Silence. No clatter of mugs as Caroline pottered around in the kitchen, no drone from the wireless as Radio 4 seeped from the living-room. He had never been able to wrap his head around the concept of a spoken-word radio channel, music was more his thing. But ever since Isla had been born, Caroline had become addicted to The Archers. Some farm based drama thing. McNab wasn't entirely sure; he had never paid attention to it. But right now, he wanted nothing more than to hear the infuriating theme tune; an orchestra recording of Barwick Green that he had heard over a hundred times.

Just once more, he thought. Let me hear the radio.

The radio. Of course!

McNab turned on his heel, adjusting his position without making a sound and opened the top drawer of the side table. Where was it? His hands grasped at the empty space.

"Come on, be here," he whispered.

The spare baby monitor always lived in the top drawer. Where was it? Caroline had begged him for weeks to buy a set, the new parenting craze at the time. McNab had relented, not convinced. The thing was a nuisance; the audible interference with the signals from his police radio drove him up the wall and if ever both of the units were in close proximity the disruptive audio feedback that was produced was enough to wake Isla up. Something, he pointed out, that defeated the purpose of the bloody thing in the first place.

Nonsense, Caroline had smiled. And, once more, he had relented, surrendering to his beautiful wife.

Now where the hell was it? He searched through the second drawer, nothing. Third drawer.

Yes!

McNab pulled out the device and turned it on. His heart thumped against the inside of his rib cage. He waited, imagining the transmission of radio waves as they moved through the house.

It was the longest three seconds of his life.

***

Tom and his father stopped within a foot of Jon's bed. Tom pulled out two seats and they sat down in front of him.

"I think it's time," said Tom.

Jon turned, shifting his body into an upright position and looked at his friend. He only had one question.

"Is Jenny ok?" he asked. Nothing else mattered; Tom could say anything to him, as long as Jenny was ok.

"Yes Jon. Jenny is going to be fine."

Tom's voice held a softness, a vulnerability that Jon had not noticed before. Jon watched him without speaking and waited for further information.

"The doctors said that she is very lucky. A fast healer, young and strong, that's what he said. Apparently the fluid stopped leaking on its own, meaning that they will be able to release her within twenty-four hours. He said that there would be no lasting damage."

Jon bit his lower lip. He wouldn't cry in front of Tom and his father. He bit hard, his teeth breaking through the soft skin of his mouth.

"She didn't press charges," continued Tom. "Apparently she told the police that there was no crime committed." Pause. "She knows that you didn't mean to hurt her." He stuttered over the "h" in hurt. "But..." Tom put his hand out, placing it on the edge of Jon's bed. "You can't go back, you can't return to the university. Do you understand that?"

Jon nodded. He did.

"I think," said Tom, "that distance is the best thing for the both of you. Jenny can continue with her studies and you can stay here with us."

Jon stared at his friend. "Us?"

"My family. My dad, my granddad and me. We want to help you. And in return, we hope that you can help us."

Jon took several long seconds to think over Tom's words. "How?" It was all that he could manage.

Tom removed his hand from the bed and sat back. It was his dad's turn to talk.

"What we are about to tell you can't go beyond these walls. Is that quite clear?"

Jon nodded. "Yes sir."

Mr McGraw smiled. "Good." He eased back into his chair. "In that case," he began, "there is something that you should know." He delivered his words without a hint of shame or unease. "My family are forgers."

He let the statement sit for a moment.

"In short, we forge and sell art for a living."

Jon took a moment to glance over at Tom and his friend gave a gentle nod.

"We," he continued, "the McGraws, are a family of art forgers, making us one of, if not the, most diverse forgery team in the world."

He was smiling now, enjoying himself, and he placed his hand on his chest as he spoke.

"I'm the salesman of the operation, the front man so to speak. Tom here, although gifted as an artist, he couldn't sell candy to a five year old. His face is too honest. Look at him, the deceit all but falls out of those big brown eyes of his. Myself on the other hand, I have no problem with the art of deception. People are easy Jon, they're all the same, all wonderfully dependable, each as predictable as the next. You see lad, people are fools and fools are easily charmed by the words of a cripple. Fact is, there is nothing more trustworthy than a man with a stick and a limp. My cane has fooled experts from all of the great auction houses, buyers from Glasgow to Vienna and London to New York. Works like a charm. Nothing makes you more honest than a disability. Genuine or not."

He winked at Jon.

"A little misdirection coupled with a respectable job as curator at Kelvingrove Art Gallery. Child's play."

McGraw senior looked across at Jon, his amused features unveiling a hidden youthfulness.

"It is my job to meet face to face with potential buyers and to put on a show, a charade so to speak. My clients are treated to a delectable fanfare, a pantomime in which I weave provenances for my artist." He pressed his hand down on Tom's shoulder. "I fabricate and deliver the stories that authenticate Tom's work, a provoking history and a carefully engineered source of ownership. And ta da, I make him real. Or more importantly, I make him desirable."

Jon's gaze swivelled between the two men and he felt weightless, like he wasn't really there. His mind, if he was being truthful, remained blank. He didn't have a reaction, at least not an emotional one.

"My father, Tom's grandfather," continued Mr McGraw, "he handles the financial side of things. The old codger is quite the natural when it comes to wheeling and dealing in old things. His shop back there is full of heirlooms, treasures that people have had tucked away in their attics without a clue of their worth. The old man's got an eye for it, always buys well at auctions and appears honourable."

Mr McGraw raised his index finger and held it out straight, firm, in preparation for his next point.

"Most importantly, his position as an antiques dealer establishes a logical explanation for why the McGraw family happen so regularly upon such valuable art pieces. His discretion at auctions and his reputation within antique circles are fundamental to our success."

His animated features gave way to a more serious look.

"Absolutely paramount."

His smile returned.

"My father's knowledge of the ancient is unparalleled and his talent is revered by buyers from all over the country. This dear boy is something that we play to our great advantage."

The final statement hung between the three men as Mr McGraw leant back in his chair and put his hands together, only the ends of his fingers touching. Jon watched, counting off the seconds as McGraw tapped his fingertips together.

Seven, eight.

McGraw smiled at Jon, gentle, as if he was somehow amused by the boy. Jon didn't return the gesture. It wasn't a conscious decision, it just didn't occur to him to smile. He looked over at Tom, unable to decipher his expression. His face wasn't unkind, more unreadable.

Eleven, twelve... The fingers continued to part and touch. Separate and join.

Jon looked up at Mr McGraw, using his legs to push his body into a better position on the bed. "I don't understand," he said. "What do you need me for?"

The comment caused the corners of Mr McGraw's smile to rise further. He drew his hands together with his fingers intertwined across his knuckles and leant forward. His face now centimetres from the bed.

"We would like you to join the family, to come and paint for us."

"To forge?"

"Exactly."

***

Four seconds.

McNab's pulse began to race. He closed his eyes as he listened.

No coos, not a single laugh or cry of hunger. Silence. McNab was done waiting, done cowering in his own hallway. Isla or Caroline could be upstairs. That was all that mattered. That was where he needed to be. He measured out the direction he needed to take based on his knowledge of the house. Three paces to the end of the hall then a sharp right would take him to the bottom of the staircase, fifteen steps and Isla's was the first room on the left. McNab pictured the inward opening door and calculated his movements away from the hinges. He had been through enough training scenarios to know that surprise and speed were key. Neither of which he was sure he had. He also knew, usually insisted, that room clearing missions were carried out by a team of three or four officers. He had none. The odds, if there was a stranger camped out in his home, were not in his favour.

Screw it.

McNab made the three paces forward. He reached the end of the hall without making a sound and approached the corner. The wallpaper brushed beneath his fingertips as his hand drifted along the wall at waist height, the feeling of solid mass against his skin keeping his senses present. Alert. His fingers followed the natural contours of the room, curving around the smoothed corner. The house remained silent as the staircase came into view.

Fifteen beige carpeted stairs appeared in front of him but the bottom three were hidden from view, concealed beneath a lifeless mass.

McNab stopped dead in his tracks as his eyes caught on her slumped body. Transfixed. Fear held him there for two seconds, a lightless eternity, before he rushed forwards.

Caroline.

Chapter 58

Her uncle, a rapist.

Cece couldn't believe it, wouldn't.

But she did.

It was the first time that she had seen her dad cry. That sound, the softness of his voice trapped within his throat, was all the proof that she needed.

A few minutes passed between them and for that unbroken moment the room hung in a respectful silence. The seconds came and went as the heartache retreated from her father's features and returned to their place of hiding. He placed his hand on his daughter's knee and looked over at her. Cece continued to gaze straight ahead, lost and unaware of his kind gesture.

"Are you ok?" he asked, stealing her from her trance.

"I'm okay. It's just..."

"I know sweetheart."

"I just can't get my head around it, the fact that I won't see him again. That he'll never paint again."

Tom kissed her forehead and met her eyes as he pulled away. He started to say something when Cece interrupted.

"There's more isn't there?"

"Yes. But we don't need to talk about it now, if you're not ready."

Cece eyed him. "Dad, I'm fine."

"It's a lot to deal with in such a..."

She straightened her back and placed her hands on her hips, her voice steady. "I'm fine. Tell me." She tilted her head in the direction of the clear bag. "Tell me why you needed that." That. She couldn't manage the word in her mouth, it still grossed her out.

One soiled tampon.

Even the serious nature of the situation couldn't prevent her brow and nose from distorting into a cringe. Her father observed her reaction, noting the imprint of discomfort on her skin, and like any loving parent he sought to remedy it. Cece watched as he opened the top drawer of his desk and removed the item from sight.

Out of sight, out of mind, thought Cece as her eyes held on the antique drawer knob.

Unlikely.

Tom began.

"After the incident with Jenny your uncle was in a very bad way. He wasn't himself, not the uncle that you knew, not the gentle man who grew to love and cherish you like a daughter. He needed help so your grandfather and I took him in and nursed him back to health in this very room. The first few days weren't easy but there was nothing that we could really do for him. He just needed time, his brain needed time to recover from being drugged."

Cece chewed on her thumb nail. She had no words, there was nothing that she could say.

"You see, when you take ecstasy it increases the activity of neurotransmitters in your brain and aggravates the chemical messages that are sent between the different cells. This explosion of activity provokes the release of serotonin from within neurons and floods the brain." His fingers gathered into a first and exploded outwards as he spoke. He did it three times.

"Do you understand?"

Cece nodded.

"The surge of serotonin produces a natural high that evokes an enhanced sense of pleasure and confidence. The delicate balance of brain chemistry is completely disrupted and this in turn has a direct effect on the regulation of mood. In certain cases it can cause a sensual awaking of sorts, an increase in sexual longing. People who are under the influence of ecstasy often lose their ability to give reasoned consent to their own actions and in effect they become slaves to their own desires. They become victims, propelled by an increase in disinhibition."

Both of them knew what he was referring to but her father didn't say it out loud and for that Cece thanked him.

"By releasing large levels of serotonin the drug depletes the brain's own supply, turning it into a dry sponge. It can then take up to a week for the brain to replace its store. In the meantime, during the comedown, the user is subjected to a number of extreme after effects. Anxiety, confusion, delusions, panic attacks, psychosis," Tom counted them off on his fingers as he said them, "paranoia, extreme depression and not just a passing sadness but a bleakness that devours your very soul."

The lump grew in Cece's throat as she pictured her uncle tossing and turning in his own sweat. It pained her to think of him like that, hopeless and empty, the last remnants of a broken man. The thought made Cece feel cold, colder than the air around her. She wound her hands around her body and rubbed against her arms but it made no difference. The cold was inside of her.

"Dad?" she asked.

"Yes."

"Do you blame him?"

"For the drugs?"

"For what he did to Jenny?"

"No sweetheart. I didn't. I don't. Your uncle, he wasn't well. He didn't know what he was doing."

"Did he ever do it again?"

"Never." Tom glanced down at his hands. "After it happened your uncle never allowed himself to love anyone again, not like that. I mean he loved you and me but it wasn't the same. It was his way of paying penance for what he did. Loneliness was the punishment that he imposed upon himself."

"And Jenny, what happened to her?"

A sad smile, barely there, caught Tom's lips. His beautiful daughter, questions, always questions.

"Jenny was released from hospital after a couple of days. All of the internal tearing had healed up and the doctors were able to send her home without surgery. But after she left the hospital we heard very little and we didn't pry. A mutual friend later told me that she spent a year in Italy, an exchange with the university, and after graduating she moved out there to do her master's in art history. Florence I think. But by then it had been three years since I had seen her."

"I don't understand," said Cece.

"What's that?"

"You."

Tom glanced at his daughter and watched her, awaiting her words.

"You said that you loved her."

"I did."

"But when?"

"I first met Jenny not long before I met your uncle."

"Did he know?"

"No. I never told him."

Cece raised an eyebrow and tilted her eyes upwards.

"Dad?"

Tom let out a sigh. His voice was soft. "I'll never forget it, the first time that I saw her. I knew it then, that I loved her."

Tom turned to look at his daughter, his mind lost in the familiar scent of a memory.

"It was towards the end of December. Cold. It had been snowing for days but on that morning the sky had cleared and there was a bitter chill left in the air, it was the type of cold that seeps through your clothes and freezes the moisture on your nose. I remember because I had run through the doors of the art gallery and I was sucking on the ends of my numb fingers. And there she was, a tiny bundle of scarves and mittens, standing in front of the Cezanne."

The memory stole time from his face. Cece looked at her father, realising that he seemed younger somehow, at peace. His gaze had long left the room, it was simply drifting in the air, his eyes focused on the space behind her right shoulder.

"I must have watched her for ten minutes before I walked over there. I smiled at her and waited. Those were the longest two seconds of my life. Then, by some heavenly miracle, the corners of her mouth twitched and she smiled back. I remembered staring, transfixed, as two perfect dimples formed on her cheeks. I don't think I spoke for a good while, I didn't know how to. In retrospect, I imagine that she must have considered running a mile. But she didn't. We spent the rest of the afternoon in front of that painting. I don't think I looked at it once."

"Then?" asked Cece. "What happened after that?"

"After that," he replied, "well, we were inseparable. I don't think that a day went past that winter when I didn't see Jenny Pingleton. We were young and naive, two art lovers in love with the city, in love with each other."

"So..." began Cece. "Why didn't it work?"

"Her father. He was... let's just say that he never a fan of mine. He forbade the whole thing from the very beginning."

"Why?"

Tom raised an eyebrow. "His only daughter, his beautiful university educated daughter, the sparkle in his eye, the spring in his step, running off with a high school dropout, a shop boy? It was never going to happen. Not until his corpse lay rotting in a ditch to be picked apart by the crows, I believe that was how he put it."

The disgusted look on his daughter's face brought a moment of lightness back into Tom's voice.

"Jenny defied him at first, sneaking out, missing lectures to meet me, skipping family meals in favour of fish and chips on a park bench. It was exciting, just me and her, but it wasn't meant to last. In the end her father threatened to cut her off and to stop paying her university fees."

He paused.

"I knew what I had to do. I loved her too much to let her throw her life away. I couldn't let her do it, not for me, not for a life of lies. That's when the arguments started, great screaming matches that lasted for hours, shoes thrown across rooms and against walls. Cruel words that were aimed with precision and anger. But, in my mind, there was no choice."

"So you broke her heart."

"Yes," he said, the voice of remorse. "I had to. And she never forgave me. One day, after a particularly heated fight her father appeared. He stood outside my flat with his arms crossed and leaned against the door of his car just waiting and basking in his victory. Jenny gave me one last look and even after all the hurt I had caused, her eyes still pleaded with me, begged. "And I..." His words faltered. "I turned my back on her." He looked straight at Cece. "I heard the car door slam through the window. It was one of the hardest moments of my life."

"Did you see her again?"

"Only a couple of times. The last time was that night in hospital, the night that..." The sentence faded into nothingness.

"Did you say anything to her?"

"No. I couldn't. I was a coward."

"Couldn't you find her now? I could help you track her down, it's easy these days with the internet. Then you could tell her that you were a coward, tell her you're sorry."

"Thank you sweetheart. But I know where she is."

"Where?"

"Lamb Hill Cemetery," he replied. "Jenny died in 1997, barely thirty. She was killed in a hit and run. According to the papers she was rushed straight to hospital but she was pronounced dead on arrival, the driver never stopped and no witnesses ever came forward."

"Dad," Cece leant forward and covered his fingers in hers. "I'm so sorry. I..." Her eyes met his, "1997, that was the year..."

"Two months after your mother."

"Oh Dad." Her grip tightened. "I had no idea."

He squeezed her hand. "But I had you sweetheart. My angel, you saved me, my very own guardian angel." He kissed her on the forehead.

"Just the two of us," she whispered, "You and me, two superheroes against the word."

"Exactly sweetheart, just you and me."

Cece smiled, she was eight years old again with a red cape tied around her shoulders. They sat together, comfortable in the silence, father and daughter. Tom made no move to talk and Cece allowed him a pause before continuing. When she eventually spoke, her words stirred the air between them, returning them to the present as the red cape faded.

"It's time," she said. "You can tell me."

There was no question, they both knew what she was talking about.

"I needed a sample of Lucy's DNA," stated Tom.

Cece nodded.

"Blood from a tampon provides an excellent source of DNA, reliable and accurate with a quick processing time."

Another nod.

"I need it to verify something, a feeling, and I want to be absolutely sure before I go any further."

Nod.

He blinked, allowing his eyes to remain closed a fraction longer. Then he let out a controlled breath.

"I think that Lucy is Jon and Jenny's daughter."

Cece's head remained perfectly still.

Chapter 59

Clear as day. A route outlined in yellow.

Sally looked down at the photo on her phone again. It was there, right in front of her.

His last steps.

She smiled to herself and shook her head. A yellow highlighter, it was that simple, that easy. It was a trick that she had used many times, photocopying defaced medical journals and rehashing old lecture notes. The science behind it had been explained to her many years ago by one of the computer types at university. Yellow highlighters, as it was described to her, didn't show up on photocopies because unlike the human eye photocopiers could only look at the total brightness of a page. In other words, she was told, photocopiers were unable to distinguish the hue shift emitted by fluorescent highlighter inks. Thus yellow inks didn't copy because they didn't absorb the light that the copier could see. It was something, she recalled, about only shifting a certain amount of the invisible light into the visible range.

At least, thought Sally, that was the gist of it.

She followed the line on the screen with her finger. It started at Torridon hotel in Annat and finished at Loch Coire Fionnaraich, his final resting place. A small cross marked the spot. Quite literally. She glanced at the tiny red dot left by the nib of a biro pen, the darkened fleck that had shown up on her black and white copy.

Annat.

Something niggled at the back of Sally's mind. She reached for her laptop and opened up google. Her fingers moved over the keys without her needing to look at the keyboard. Her eyes focused on a spot on the wall and she bit her lower lip as her mind ticked over. She typed in three words: Loch Coire Fionnaraich.

Sally scrolled through the search results until she found the one that she was looking for. She clicked on the page and started to skim read. Her lips moved over the words, the occasional word escaping from her mouth with the trace of a sound. Her eyes stopped. She read it once and scanned backwards, dictating the sentences out loud to herself.

"Although it is possible to start from Annat at the head of Upper Loch Torridon, Loch Coire Fionnaraich is usually ascended from Coulags on the A890 road in Glen Carron where is it possible to follow a more gradual incline up the valley."

She let her weight fall into the back of her chair. She had been right. Sally sighed, unaware of the crease that now formed naturally between her brows, the deep line adding five years to her face. The route marked on the map was far less common with walkers; it was harder and less rewarding. She skimmed through a few more walking forums. Each one, without exception, discouraged approaching from the Annat side.

So why go that way?

The map illuminated on the screen on her phone and she picked it up to examine a further time. The route was marked out with pen. It was calculated and deliberate, not an accidental choice happened upon by a desperate suicidal man. It had been planned out. He had intended to go that way.

But why? Sally wasn't big on coincidences. Then it occurred to her.

"Shit", she mouthed. The realisation returned her fingers to the keyboard and she brought up a digital copy of an OS map. Explorer 429. The full sheet, not the cropped version that she had on her phone.

Her brain ticked ahead of her eyes as they moved over the contours of the image. Approaching from the Annat side meant that he was never anywhere near Coire Fionnaraich Bothy; the mountain hut was only passable from the Coulags side. Meaning, she thought, that Toop was right.

He was never at the bothy.

And he repents in thorns that sleeps in bed of roses.

Someone else must have written the note.

Sally's fingers froze, suspended in the space above the keys. Her body tensed as she processed the flood of information. Then it hit her. The inscription in the bothy log book, she had just worked out what it really meant. She reached for her phone, her mind looped on a single thought.

Someone had marked out the route for him. The same person, concluded Sally, who had killed him.

She tapped at the screen on her phone, recalling Toop's number from memory.

"Come on..." She tapped her fingers off the table. "Pick up, pick up."

She counted four rings before it went straight to voicemail.

Damn.

Sally hung up and tried again. Same again. Four rings. Voicemail.

"Dammit," cursed Sally, "useless Scottish phone service." She waited for the beep this time.

"Toop, its Sally. I need you to call me back. He didn't write it, you were right, someone else did. You interpreted it correctly the first time, repenting on a bed of thorns or was it in? Wait maybe it was roses, shit I don't know but that's not the point. The point is that it's not a suicide note, it's a threat, a death warrant. He didn't kill himself to prove that he had repented, someone else killed him because..."

A sharp beep and she was cut off. The line went dead. Sally groaned, resisting the urge to throw the handset across the room.

Four rings, voicemail.

"Me again. I think the killer was acting, not only as a self-proclaimed judge but as the executioner as well. It hit me, the meaning, if you lie to try and get forgiveness then you will sleep in a bed of roses, you will be stung by the person that you wronged. The message isn't a cry for forgiveness, it is a written order, a judicial decree. The jury has reached its verdict and his sentence has been passed. The death penalty."

***

"Found it!" said Toop. Triumphant.

Eve managed a weak smile but instinct pulled her eyes to the van door. Fight or flight. The impulse twitched in her neck, in her temples and in her heart. A constant beat; the consequence of a damaged childhood, embedded in the soul of a broken child. A younger Eve would have grabbed her backpack, grabbed the page from behind the box of tea and run. As she sat next to him, motionless, she pictured herself climbing out of the van door, moving so quickly that her feet caught on the lip of the steel track causing her to fall the last foot to the ground. It played out in her head as reality and she watched herself get up and sling her backpack across her shoulder before looking back to catch a last glimpse of his face. Their eyes held. Then she was gone.

She glanced down at her knuckles. White. The bed was still beneath her and the van door remained closed. Eve felt the fabric of her sheets against her skin, real, there. The cotton had been crushed between her fingers, suffocated in her tight grip.

"Listen to this," continued Toop.

Eve watched the movement of his mouth as he read from the page. It was a page that she knew off by heart, word for word.

"The yellow rose is most often used to express feelings of jealousy and infidelity. According to legend the Prophet Mohammed, while fighting overseas, was tormented by the notion that his betrothed was being unfaithful. Out of desperation he called on Archangel Gabriel for help. Gabriel agreed and told Mohammed that upon his return he must ask his wife to drop a red rose into the river. If she had been faithful then the rose would remain blood red, a token of her unconditional love. Satisfied with Gabriel's suggestion Mohammed greeted his love with a bouquet of roses. At his request she dropped them into the water and watched as the first drop of liquid turned the petals saffron yellow. Since then a yellow rose has remained as a symbol of infidelity."

Eve closed her eyes. She knew what was coming. She had read it many times, memorised it.

"However as times progressed a hidden message bloomed, a lesser-known meaning that circulated in certain choice corners of society. This meaning was absent of an underlying legend or tale but it carried a great significance among young socialites. In such company the offering of a yellow rose could be interpreted as meaning, "I am not worthy of your love.""

Toop looked up from the screen. He was no longer reciting. He was thinking.

"I never found the rose." Pause. Eve watched the lines grow on his brow. "I searched his tent but it wasn't there. Perhaps that's because he never received one. Maybe he was the one who gave the rose away. His last act before he died. That would explain why he had the dictionary."

Eve didn't respond. Toop was right. She knew that he was right, because the rose had been given to her.

He wasn't, thought Eve, he wasn't worthy.

She swallowed hard. Don't cry.

"And," continued Toop, "it also explains why the page is missing. He probably gave it away with the rose so that his message wasn't misinterpreted."

Wrong, thought Eve, you're wrong. She almost smiled to herself, caught off guard by the feeling of relief.

You're wrong, she repeated, I took it, I stole page 15. The smile tugged at her lips, she couldn't help it. He was searching in the wrong direction. She was there, sitting right in front of him and he couldn't see it.

"What?" asked Toop, dropping a single eyebrow.

"Sorry. It's nothing. I was just, just thinking..."

"I was wrong, wasn't I?" interrupted Toop. "He did kill himself, he was depressed. He killed himself because he thought that he was unworthy."

"I think so," replied Eve. "I'm sorry, Fergus."

They both stared down at the computer screen sitting on the bed. Silent.

Toop closed his eyes and for a brief moment he pictured her, his wife, her body alone and broken in the snow.

Chapter 60

Late 80s

"Caroline?"

Nothing. No movement, just a slight twitch of her left eyelid.

"Caroline darling, it's me. Can you hear me?" The words stuttered in his throat.

Her head rolled around on her neck and dropped like a doll's. Limp.

McNab knelt beside his wife and moved to take her hands.

No blood.

Doing so gently, he lifted Caroline's hands from out of her lap and turned them over in his own. Tiny and fragile. Blinking back tears, he leant forward and kissed the soft skin above each of her wrists, left then right. Her arms felt heavy.

"What's wrong, sweetheart. Please talk to me." McNab realised that he was begging. "Tell me what happened. Please."

Caroline slowly raised her head, her eyes lost in a doped-out vacancy. The weightless and childish expression that his wife so often wore was gone and a ghost was left in its place. He gripped her forearms, harder this time and without thinking he started to shake her.

"Wake up!" he demanded. "Right now."

She did.

As if responding to his command, she raised her head a fraction. Her neck muscles initiated and her lips moved. McNab watched his wife's face as she transformed, sedated and zombie-like to cognitively nimble in the click of two fingers.

"Sweetheart, you're home," she smiled, rational, normal, as if nothing was untoward.

For a moment McNab let himself believe that everything was just that, normal. Caroline was awake and she was speaking. She looked back at him with eyes that were perfectly green, perfectly there.

"Why are you on the stairs honey?" he asked. Gentle. "Where's Isla?"

"I don't know," she replied. A look of confusion fell across her face as she surveyed her surroundings with her eyes. "I'm not sure why... how I got here. I mean... I'm sorry." She stuttered. "I don't remember."

"It's ok sweetheart. I'm here." McNab leant over and pressed his lips into her forehead. He held her there for a moment before pulling away.

"I'm here. Everything is going to be ok." He lifted a strand of hair from her eyelashes, cupping the right side of her face in his hand as he pulled it away. "Caroline, do you remember seeing anyone in the house?" He stroked the tops of her hands, not wanting to let go. Something was wrong. He just couldn't put his finger on what. His wife was coherent but she wasn't quite there.

She shook her head.

"I don't think so." Caroline shook her head again. "I don't remember."

"It's ok. What's the last thing that you do remember?"

"Isla." She replied. "I remember putting Isla to bed. About seven," she added as an afterthought.

McNab looked at his watch. That was well over two hours ago.

"Wait there." McNab stood up and spread his fingers out wide, a centimetre between each digit so that his hands formed two large paddles. He pushed both palms through the air in the direction of his wife, the same gesture executed by owners and their pet dogs, ensuring that she would stay. "Don't move."

Caroline obeyed. She sat quite still with her hands cupped and fingers curled upwards. Her hands rested limply in the hollow of her thighs, frozen in the exact spot that her husband had released them. Her limbs surrendered, lifeless, like a puppet robbed of its strings. The act of obedience didn't register with McNab. He was already halfway up the stairs. It wasn't until later, when it was already hopeless, that he questioned the passive actions of his wife. No mother, especially his Caroline, would have sat idly by while he rushed to the aid of their daughter. Nothing, not even the firm command of her husband, would have kept her rooted to those stairs.

"Isla?"

McNab stood frozen in the open doorway of the playroom and looked down at his daughter. Relief poured through him.

She was there.

He pressed his hands against the sides of the door frame and let his head fall forward. Tears collected at the edges of his eyes as he listened to the gentle rise and fall of her tiny lungs. She was safe. In that moment there was nothing, nothing else in the world that mattered to him. McNab allowed himself twenty seconds before he pulled the door closed, careful not to make a sound and he brushed his fingers across the pink "I" that he had painted on the door. He returned down the stairs to find that Caroline hadn't moved. She sat as she had left him. McNab, thinking nothing of it, lowered his body into the space beside her and slipped his arm around her shoulders. Her head fell naturally into the groove of his neck.

"It's ok," he said. "Our little princess is fast asleep upstairs."

McNab looked into his wife's eyes, into the eyes of the woman whom he'd loved ever since he first saw her walk across Kelvingrove Park over fifteen years ago. He'd been at the park having a kick around with a couple of friends from the college and they were heading over to the pub. McNab had never been shy but equally he was no ladies' man, one pint was usually enough to loosen him up but on that afternoon, seeing Caroline Pepper walk across the grass in her green box dress with her hair styled in a short bob, he had walked right up to her and asked her out there and then. His knees were stained with grass and his elbows were streaked with mud. At first she declined, later explaining to her husband that it had been an issue of pride, she hadn't wanted to seem too available. But McNab was nothing if not determined. He didn't make it to the pub that day but he got his date and his wife.

His gorgeous wife, thought McNab, kissing the top of her forehead.

"Are you ok to talk?" he asked.

"Yes," replied Caroline, although neither her tone nor her manner was defiant.

"You put Isla to bed. Then what did you do?"

"The doorbell." Pause. "I heard the doorbell. I was still upstairs, I remember because I was worried that it might wake Isla up."

"That's good honey just go slowly, piece by piece."

"I closed her door and walked downstairs."

An uneasy feeling crept up McNab's spine. Isla's door had been open when he checked on her. Wide. "Go on," he prompted.

"There was a man on the doorstep." She mulled over her words for a moment. "In his fifties perhaps, maybe older, I'd never seen him before."

"And what did he want?"

"Directions. He said that he was looking for a house on this street. 66b I think it said."

"It?"

"He had a piece of paper with him. It was tiny, like a corner had been ripped off the edge of a page." Caroline used her two index fingers to trace out the dimensions in the air. "He explained that he had left his glasses at home and wondered if I could read the address for him."

"Did you?"

"Yes. But the words were minute. I had to hold it right up to my face to make sense of it."

"And what did it say?"

Caroline thought for a moment and squinted as she repeated the address from memory.

"66b Chester's Road. Bearsden."

"Then what happened?"

Caroline looked suddenly scared and she stared back at her husband with her wide eyes, displaying the vulnerability of a child.

"I don't know," she said, "I can't remember anything after that."

***

"A game of inches," whispered McNab, talking to no one but himself. There was no one to talk to. No one conscious anyway.

He didn't like it. Not being in control.

"One half step too early or too late..."

And you don't quite make it, thought McNab, it was the difference between winning and losing, living and dying.

He tapped his hands off the roof of the car waiting for backup to arrive. Donaldson was still out of it, slumped cold in the driver's seat and Caroline was asleep upstairs. He had questioned his wife, tried to tease any memory from her, but it had been useless. The past three hours of her life were lost. It was as if the memories had never been recorded, blocked somehow. Her mind was a complete blank.

Empty. Deserted like the street.

McNab looked left and right, up and down. No change, nothing out of the ordinary that he could see, nothing but the sedated police officer who was slumped inches from his left shoulder. Donaldson had yet to move, slipping deeper into a state of unconsciousness. His head hung limp on the end of his neck, five kilograms of brain and skull pulling his muscles into an unnatural sling. McNab opened the door and leaned over the lifeless body. He cupped one hand under his colleague's chin and the other he used to secure the forehead, attempting to manoeuvre his head into a more comfortable position. It was futile. Gravity won over and the solid mass fell forward in a single violent movement.

Bugger it.

McNab cursed, aware that he had probably just done more harm than good. He ducked back out of the chassis and hearing the engine of an approaching vehicle he looked up. He eyed the white car as it pulled up next to him and two men stepped out. The first was short and round. McNab placed him somewhere in his mid-forties. The other was older. He was tall with notably more white bristle over his upper lip than on his head. Both men were in uniform.

"McNab." The bald police officer offered a polite nod.

"Officer." McNab returned the gesture. "Donaldson needs medical assistance. Can you get him to the hospital?"

"Consider it done."

The three men exchanged notes. McNab offered a brief overview of the situation, concise and detached, deciding to release details on a need to know basis. The voice niggled at the back of his mind, Harry's voice.

Or whatever your real name is.

The same two sentences replayed on repeat.

Best not to meddle. Meddling can be dangerous.

"Call me as some as soon as he comes round," McNab shouted.

The two officers finished unloading the unconscious Donaldson into the back of their car. Then they walked around to opposite sides of their vehicle, their legs concealed by the open doors of the car. Moustache replied with a curt nod and the plumper officer gave a friendly wave. Donaldson remained out cold in the back seat.

"Sure thing."

McNab returned the wave and watched as the car drove off down the street. He gave the street a quick look over and checked his watch. It was late. If Harry was out there, if the man existed at all, then he would have seen the police car drive off.

No meddling. Meddling can be dangerous.

McNab wasn't afraid of the faceless voice but there was one thing that he was certain of. Someone had been inside his house. Isla's bedroom door had been left open and he was sure that it hadn't been a mistake.

295

Someone had made the conscious decision not to close it. It had been left open for a reason.

Chapter 61

Go. Leave. Just Leave.

The familiar voice repeated between her temples. It pounded like a pulse, forcing her to remember, tearing and ripping the memories from her head. Lucy sat with her legs curled beneath her on the bedroom floor. She could picture his face as clear as day, as clear as if she held a photograph in her hand. Every detail from the bony ridges of his cheeks, coarsened by age, to the deep static wrinkles that formed around his mouth, two folds that ran down from each side of his nose. Lucy felt the rain as if she were there. Each drop of water caught on his brow and carved its way down the contours of his face to his lips.

His lips remained closed, sealed without protest. Not a single call for help.

The memory filled her room and in an instant she was back standing in the wind, her eyes searching the creases of his face. The gusts whipped at her cheeks, burning her skin. But it wasn't there. Lucy had imagined what it would look like, the expression of fear. The look in a man's face when he realised that this moment would be his last on earth.

But she searched his eyes and she couldn't find it.

There was no fear in them, no anger. Standing there, looking into his eyes, she wavered. She questioned it. He wasn't afraid to die. In that moment her father looked content, at peace. He stared into the barrel of the gun and smiled at her. His mouth never moved but Lucy was sure that he smiled.

"Just leave!"

The scream pierced through the wind.

"Now!"

Lucy didn't have time to think. No final words. She dropped her eyes and ran.

297

Her feet failed her repeatedly, stumbling over the uneven terrain as they caught on the rough mounds of heather. A stray clump of grass disabled her balance and her foot collided with the ground, impacting at an angle. Her ankle fell limp as it rolled and the ligament stretched, but the pain didn't register.

She ran.

"Eight, nine..." she panted.

The water seeped into the fabric of her shoes unnoticed and Lucy picked up her pace.

"Twenty-two, twenty-three..."

The trail began to drop away beneath her feet as it descended down the hillside, a gentle flowing stream replacing the solid path. Lucy lengthened her strides, one leg cast out in front of the other, causing the water to kick up around her ankles. She wanted to be as far away as possible. Far enough from him so that she would be left with nothing but a faint memory.

"Forty-four..."

Then it happened.

"Forty-five."

The gunshot.

She stopped dead and turned to look back at where she had come from. Nothing. The dip in the land had driven the horizon forward and she was alone.

Alone, thought Lucy, looking down at her hands. Her eyes held, mesmerised by the maroon rug that lay beneath her splayed fingers and she contemplated the upright loops of yarn that twisted and knotted to form a crimson carpet.

"Blood red," she whispered.

The wind had stopped, silence, no rain and Lucy was back in her bedroom, back to reality.

She slipped a finger through one of the loops and twisted it until the skin around her nail went white. Her hands had gone ice cold and she could feel the spoon ring slipping on her shrunken finger. She made another twist and another, causing the thread to cut into her flesh. Pain didn't frighten her. The lack of feeling, the numbness, was far scarier.

Lucy had gone along with it because, despite everything, she loved Alex.

And now both her parents were dead.

**

Cece returned with two cups of coffee.

She handed one to her dad, handle first, and sat down next to him. It was getting late but neither of them were anywhere near sleep. Cece wasn't tired, the caffeine was for her father's benefit, her mind was working too fast to contemplate rest. She had attempted to formulate a response and she had come close a couple of times but her mind kept stalling with the influx of information. In the end she had left the room and walked five minutes down the road to the twenty-four hour petrol station, returning with two below average coffees. Pouring the lukewarm liquid into proper mugs had done little to improve the taste but it had given her time to think, to process.

They drank from their cups without talking, looking up at each other from time to time. After they had finished Cece sat back in her chair. She ran her hands over her face and up through her hair before sighing and leaning forward. Her elbows rested on her knees and she arched her neck to stare up at him.

"So Jenny had a child. But how?"

There was something in her manner, the lack of intonation in her voice that rendered the question rhetorical. She frowned and thought about it for a few moments.

"Italy?"

His look was enough.

"The university exchange," voiced Cece. "She never went to Italy did she?" Rhetorical. "Jenny left university to have a baby."

"I'm not sure," replied Tom. "I can't say for certain. But given the time scales involved I always had my suspicions, wondered about it."

"But you never said anything?"

"No." His eyes betrayed a sense of hurt. "Jenny had been through enough."

Cece perched on the end of her seat, her knees moving closer to her father's. The question paused on the end of her tongue.

"Do you think that Jon ever wondered about it?"

"I don't think so sweetheart, those sorts of questions never really occurred to your uncle."

They said nothing for about a minute, occupied by their own thoughts. Father and daughter each played with the empty mug in their hands. Cece stared at her hand as she ran her index finger round the rim four times.

Finally she asked. "What changed, what made you certain that Jon had a daughter?"

"The envelopes," he replied. "They were always the same, written and sealed and left out on his kitchen table. They started to appear every Saturday evening, like clockwork, waiting to be posted on Monday."

"Did you ever open one?" The sentence lost strength in her mouth, each word less defiant than the last. The final syllable was almost inaudible. Cece lowered her eyes, embarrassed.

"Sorry," she managed.

A soft smile. "I won't lie, I did think about it. I tried to convince myself that opening one could help Jon. But no matter how I justified it, I couldn't convince myself that I wasn't lying."

"So did you ever ask him about them, about who he was writing to?"

"I didn't need to."

Cece frowned, perplexed. "I don't understand."

Tom gestured with his right hand as he stood up. "Wait here." With that he stepped past Cece's legs and disappeared through the door at the back.

She listened to the gentle shuffle of drawers, counting off the seconds in her head as the noise petered out to a quiet rustle. She made it to sixteen before she leaned back in her chair, extending her chest outwards with her arms raised above her head. The stretch felt good, revitalising. Cece bent forward, placing the mug on the floor beneath her seat and returned her hands to rub her eyes. Satisfied, she let out a yawn and surveyed the cluttered office, each time her gaze hesitated on the chair vacated by her Dad moments earlier. She couldn't shake the feeling that he was holding back on her. There was something that he wasn't saying.

Multiple envelopes, thought Cece, addressed, sealed and delivered. Addressed, sealed and delivered. Every Monday week in, week out, without fail. Addressed...

Addressed...

Cece bolted upright in her chair. The envelopes were addressed to Alex, not Lucy. But, thought Cece, he wanted Lucy's DNA sample. If Lucy was Jon's daughter then who was Alex?

She looked up and saw her father walking through the door, a collection of white envelopes held in his left hand. Her eyes skimmed down his arm to his hand, focusing in on the arc in the paper, a slight crease where his thumb and index finger applied pressure. Her lips made to part but she stalled and they closed, wordless. Cece realised that the answer she craved was not nearly as simply as it appeared to be. A part of her was surprised, the other wasn't. She drew a long breath and waited.

***

Lucy remembered as a child how she had lain and listened to the wind beating against the window, the rain threatening to smash the glass above her bed. She had screamed but no one had come. It wasn't that sort of foster home. People who came to check on you in the night usually had ulterior motives, motives that soon taught her not to cry out.

23 Mitchell Street.

It hadn't been the worst, not by some way, but it was up there. Top five.

The basement wasn't so bad. Twice a day she was allowed to squeeze through the window, a two foot by two foot square opening just big enough to fit the scrawny limbs of a nine year old. It wasn't until the last few weeks that she struggled to squeeze through and the wooden frame started to carve scratches into the skin over her hip bones. She climbed out twice a day, Monday to Friday, so that she could go to school. At first school had been a haven, a glimpse of normality, but it didn't take long for the other children to notice that she was different and after that those friends who had been vital playground comrades fell like flies. Lunch times were spent alone sitting by the school pond whispering to the frogs. Then one day the school pond was ripped up, dug out by men in one-piece overalls, and covered with concrete. It was replaced with a small, one hooped basketball court. Lucy didn't make it to class that afternoon. Her tiny legs carried her home crying and she slipped through the window, tumbling onto the basement floor with a thud. Not a single hug. Lucy had curled up on her mattress, there was no frame, and listened to the patter of footsteps and the notes of laughter that leaked through the roof. Upstairs was forbidden, that was where her foster parents lived with their children. Lucy was too dirty to be allowed upstairs, she would ruin the couches and spoil the silverware.

Filthy little fingers.

She lay in silence. Never telling. That was how it worked at 23 Mitchell Street. That was how it had worked at all of them. Suffering was something that was done quietly, in silence. As a child she knew no different and she didn't question it. Children, especially dirty ones, didn't ask questions of adults. Adults knew best. The silence soon became habit, more than that, it became second nature. But the silence was easy, it was nothing compared to the times when she was separated from her sister. Separation happened on three placements in total, Mitchell Street was the second.

Eight months with no Alex.

Thirty-two weeks. Two hundred and forty days. No Alex.

Every day on Mitchell Street was the same; a cup of dry porridge in the morning followed by two peanut butter sandwiches, one at lunch, one for dinner. The bread was always white and the peanut putter was always smooth, one small tub and one pre-sliced loaf. Those were her rations for the week. Once, out of hunger, she made the mistake of eating the entire lot in one sitting. A young Lucy used her fingers to spread the brown slime, extending her tongue to clean the sticky remnants from the webs of her fingers. Her empty stomach ached for the next six, Alex empty days.

She learned after that.

Secrets to the last.

Lucy's eyes hadn't moved off the red carpet and her finger was now snow white, bloodless.

They, Alex and her, had been just children. They were children living in hell and it had affected them in ways that Lucy would never fully understand. Couldn't understand.

Just remember who the real enemy is. Alex had said it to her time and time again, a sentence spoken with a maturity far beyond the words of a child.

Our real parents abandoned us. They left us. Mum and Dad put us here, they are the ones who left us in hell and they should be punished.

Her sister's voice filled the room. Lucy released her finger and her body responded without pause. The blood began to pump violently, sending sharp throbs straight to the starved tip.

Whatever happened to you as a child, thought Lucy, good or bad, it changed you. And if what happened was something particularly bad then it moulded you absolutely and completely.

She looked out the window. Her philosophy teacher's words finding her once more.

When a child suffers severe trauma it etches a scar deep into the brain, a mark that is permanently ingrained. It neither recedes or fades, it simply exists, preventing the brain from forgetting. As an adult you are powerless to fight against it. The scar becomes a part of you, a mark that no therapy can cure.

Both she and Alex had it. They were both scarred.

Engineered from childhood, thought Lucy. There was only one difference.

Lucy craved peace.

Alex craved revenge.

Chapter 62

Toop hadn't moved. He remained sat on the bed, faintly aware of the clink of mugs as Eve hovered around above him. She hadn't said anything to him in almost ten minutes, nor had he tried. His thoughts were far away, buried with her in snow.

Toop stared at the wall of the van and it occurred to him that he hadn't felt this tired in a long time. He often functioned on little more than a few hours of sleep and a strong coffee. The long hours and stressful conditions were all part of the job, or at least the way that he did it. But this was different.

Maybe you can't do this.

He wasn't used to failure and admitting it wasn't something that sat well with him. His mind tortured him, seeping the energy from his neck and shoulders, as her face stared up at him from the snow. Her vacant eyes and blue lips were stark reminders that he was a broken man. It was a reminder that a part of him had died with her that night, frozen on the side of the mountain. Since the accident Toop had changed, he sought to punish, to make the guilty pay for what they had done. No remorse, no second chances. Debts had to be paid. All sinners had to suffer. It was a mantra that had made him an excellent and relentless London policeman.

Another five minutes passed and Toop continued to stare at the wall. No expression. Eve leaned over and placed a mug of tea down on the table next to him. She didn't ask if he wanted one or how he took it, simply sat it down, retrieved her hand, and turned to pull a raincoat from a large plastic storage box. Then she threw the jacket over her head, not bothering to slide her arms through the sleeves, and walked out into the rain. She gave no explanation.

Alone, it occurred to Toop that perhaps he should leave, go home and catch up on a decade's worth of sleep. The idea almost took root before he shook it away. He couldn't sleep even if he wanted to. The nightmares would come. Instead he slipped his fingers around the warm mug and let the liquid break against his lips, the hot steam awaking his eyes.

Maybe, he thought, maybe this time, there was no one to punish. Maybe it was time that he stopped looking for something that didn't exist and accepted what was right in front of him.

The gun.

The location.

The note in the bothy.

The yellow rose.

All of the above pointed towards suicide, to a sad man who wanted to die. To find peace. As Toop pictured his wife's face he wondered why he had ever questioned it. To die of a broken heart, thought Toop, it would be hard to find a statement with more truth in it. He returned the mug to the table, closed the laptop and slipped it back under the pillow before standing up. His arm was half extended in the direction of the door when it swung open, caught in a bluster of wind as Eve stepped in. A wild tangle of red hair concealed her face as she battled to secure the jacket over her head. She cleared her eyes with her left hand and produced a box of chocolate biscuits with the other.

She held it out, caught off guard by his sudden presence and failed to judge the space between then. The corner of the packet pressed into Toop's chest as their two bodies rested less than a foot apart. They were close enough that Toop could feel the cold night radiating from her, he could smell the sea on her. He watched as a harboured drip of rain fell from her hair and landed on the floor by his foot. Neither of them moved and neither stepped back.

Toop raised his hand to her face, her skin was cold. He slipped his fingers through her thick hair and pushed it behind her ear. He felt her hand clamp tight around his wrist, a sudden movement as if to stop him. But she didn't. Her grip loosened, allowing her fingers to hang limply from his forearm. The brush of skin and the touch of her finger tips against the inner side of his wrist sent an electric sensation straight to his groin.

He wanted to devour her.

She tilted her head up and looked at him for the first time, the biscuits falling to the floor. Toop kissed her hard, grabbing each side of her face in his hands as he explored the warmth of her mouth with his tongue. The initial force pushed her body backwards, slamming her back against the van wall and she let out a surprised gasp, her eyes drawn wide just long enough to share a glance. Toop used the wall for leverage and positioned his hands round the back of her thighs hoisting her up to his hips. The presence of clothes amplified his craving and he thrust his body into hers. Eve responded to the intense intimacy with a shallow moan, her body tensed with anticipation.

She needed to get out of her clothes.

As if reading her mind, Toop swung her round and dropped her on the bed. Without thinking, he extended his arm and used his hand to lower her head onto the duvet. She stared up at him, his body suspended over hers with his arm caught under her shoulders. Toop paused just long enough for them both to notice, both admitting the softness of his gesture. The moment passed, not forgotten, and he retrieved his arm.

Less than a minute and they were naked, each hot and breathing heavily. The sweat dripped from Toop's temples and formed droplets on his bare shoulders. He turned Eve so that she had her back to him and then he pressed the palm of his hand against the low of her back as if to lift her. Eve understood, moving forward into a kneeling position in front of him. Toop moved in behind her and slipped her bent legs between his. Grateful that she didn't have to look into his eyes Eve leant backwards, lowering herself onto him. He moved his arms around her waist, forceful but kind, and directed the movement of her hips with his hands.

Neither of them spoke, more out of exhaustion than anything else, stopping twice to settle their heart rates. His rib cage pounded against her back as he pulled their bodies together. His eyes caught on something, a blemish or a fading birthmark, but his brain didn't have the energy to process the thought.

Elation came as he tilted backwards, the intense pressure flooring them in moments.

***

Toop woke first. He twisted his wrist and checked his watch. Twenty minutes he had been out.

Eve lay sleeping next to him. She was curled in the foetal position with her bum pressed against his groin. He felt a strange, long forgotten sensation as he looked over at her.

Toop looked away, choosing to stare at the ceiling.

He mouthed the words to himself. "I am not worthy."

Eve was right, he thought, the words left in the bothy log book were nothing more than the uttering of a guilty conscience. The words of a broken man preparing to die.

"You can leave you know." Eve's voice startled him. "I don't expect you to stay the night."

She remained with her back to him. "No need to leave a note on the pillow in the morning."

Toop opened his month to respond. Then he froze, his gaze miles away.

"Idiot," he cursed.

"Excuse me?" This time Eve turned around.

"Sorry, not you. Me." He was already sitting up and had started pulling on his trousers. "I'm the idiot."

"Again, what?" asked Eve.

"I was so obsessed with deciphering the yellow rose that I forgot about..." His eyes searched the floor for his shoes. "How could I be so stupid, how could I let myself get so distracted."

Distracted. The word hurt. He might not have meant it, not consciously, but Eve knew that he wasn't just talking about the rose.

"I don't understand," she said.

"Someone else had to be involved."

"How do you know that?"

"Because they made a mistake. A huge fucking mistake that I forgot about."

"It?"

"The note on my car," he said, pulling his belt tight. "It was intended for me. It was written after he died." His eyes were focused on something beyond the present, drawn elsewhere. "Meaning that someone else wrote it."

Eve sat in silence as Toop gathered his things. She watched him, she couldn't help it. He was more than ten years older than her, and he was the last person on earth that she should have feelings for, but still there was something about him that she couldn't shake. He, like her, had survived his past and somehow he had made it through the darkness. And for that she respected him, she felt connected to him. Also, she thought, he had the most beautiful pair of eyes that she had ever seen.

Toop finished dressing and stopped to look over at her. Eve felt her cheeks growing warmer.

"Thanks," he said and left.

Eve waited two minutes then slipped off the covers and stood up. She lifted Toop's mug from the table and slid the van door open with her spare hand. It had stopped raining. She held the mug out and poured the cold liquid out onto the grass.

Toop was right, she thought, it had been a huge mistake.

She never should have written that note.

Chapter 63

Late 80s

Meddling can be dangerous

McNab played the words over in his head as he walked up the steps to his house. He knew that it had been a threat. McNab had never had any doubts about the caller's intentions. In his line of work, a policeman in Glasgow, he received threats on a weekly basis. But this one had been different from the rest for one simple reason.

It had just become real.

McNab stared ahead, one foot in front of the other, all emotion removed from his features. At work he was often commended for his patience. His gentle and understanding nature was something that was less prevalent amongst his colleagues. Such tolerances tended to waver after a couple of Friday night shifts on the job. But now McNab was pissed off. His wife and daughter had been targeted and in his mind that meant that the line had been well and truly crossed.

He climbed the stairs in silence, not wanting to disturb Caroline, and stood outside his daughter's room. The door opened with a gentle push of his hand. McNab stepped through the door frame, flicked the light switch and looked around. Isla lay sleeping on her back, her little fists balled above her head. He knew that the intruder was gone, the bogeyman had gone from behind the curtains, but caution was a hard feeling to ignore. It had been drilled into him.

The room hadn't changed. It was exactly as a child's nursery should be, nothing out of place. The walls were brightened by white clouds and blue skies and silver stars were painted on the ceiling. McNab sat in the one chair that stood facing Isla's cot, a soft throne adorned with yellow pillows. With his right hand he reached around and removed a star shaped cushion from behind his back and placed it on the floor.

The door had been left open for a reason.

But why? What should I be looking for?

He scanned over the room, his mind two steps ahead of his eyes. He looked up and stared at the window, taking note of the open curtains. The light had long diminished from the sky and the glass revealed nothing but the darkness of night, the square window converted to a murky black mirror. At least, he thought, it appeared as a mirror from his direction. He stood up, conscious that the light from the room would be visible from the pavement and that he could be seen by anyone standing outside.

"Are you out there watching?" he whispered.

He ran his hand along the wooden beam of the cot, stealing a glance at his daughter. He retrieved his hand and went to step towards the window but he never made it and the curtains never closed. What caught his eye stopped him on the spot.

What on... ?

He watched as Isla stretched out in her sleep, a slight movement that lengthened her tiny limbs and revealed a roll of skin above the waist of her nappy. There it was, a black line, just to the left of her belly button. McNab leant over and lifted up the front of her top with a single finger, exposing his daughter's skin to the cold night air. The message covered the majority of her small body. It had been handwritten across her stomach in large un-joined letters. Black marker pen, all capitals.

"JOHN 13:27".

McNab read it out loud in a calm voice, attempting to silence the anger inside him. Someone had touched his daughter, that was unforgivable, but anger would do him no good, not now. Now he needed to keep a clear head.

Focus.

He checked his watch. Damn. It was too late.

McNab knew who he needed to speak to. There was one person who he could count on to be informative and discreet. But it was too late. He would have to wait until the morning. The man in question didn't answer the phone after 10pm.

No exceptions.

***

Twelve hours had pasted since the offer and Jon hadn't slept since.

He sat on the bench outside Bute Hall, exactly in the middle. It was a Wednesday morning, the last Wednesday morning that he would spend on University grounds. No coffee this time, or any time after that. After Jenny, after what happened, he never allowed another drug to pass his lips.

Jon looked up at the towering white sandstone cloisters and closed his eyes. It was the closest thing that he knew to peace, to be alone and surrounded by the quiet of nothingness. His thoughts, as they often did, turned to Jenny. It was a habit that never left him. He didn't know it then but years later Jonathan Swan would die thinking about Jenny Pingleton, about her smile and her yellow dress. There would be no fear in his features, just acceptance.

Jon had never thought about the fairness of life before, in truth it wasn't something that he had ever thought to think about. There had been no need, no reason. But in that moment he decided that it wasn't fair. Not at all. There was nothing fair about it, he thought as the anger formed in the pit of his stomach.

Jenny was good and kind and pure.

And he had tainted her.

Tears formed in the corners of his eyes. It wasn't right. Jon squeezed his fingers into tight fists, the frustration causing his entire body to shake. He needed to fix it. His mind raced ahead, working in the only way that it knew how, applying logic to emotion.

Compute and solve.

His thought process stalled, clouded. He needed to move. Jon stood up, instinct taking over as he ran his hands over his pockets. It was still there. He didn't know what it was or rather he didn't know what it meant. He hadn't asked, there was no need, his instructions were clear. And they were instructions that he intended to follow, blindly with no questions.

It was a test after all.

Jon walked out of the Main Gate and continued down University Gardens road, stopped by a large grey building.

School of Law. Sir Alexander Stone Building.

He read the plaque a second time, his feet grounded to the pavement.

It was inside these stone walls that young minds were supposed to be enlightened, where the naive and ignorant amassed to learn about justice, about right and wrong. It was where a single message resonated within the walls, a message that was drilled into the psyche of willing students.

Justice, thought Jon, the righting of wrongs and the vindication of the innocent.

He turned and continued down the deserted street.

The punishment of the guilty.

One day he would be punished for what he had done. He was sure of it. But until then, he was sentenced to live with it. Every day. Death was too easy, death was a copout. He deserved to suffer. He was meant to endure the gut-wrenching pain of reliving it over and over.

Endless.

Jon walked for another twenty minutes, arriving at the bus stop with two minutes to spare. The sky started to cloud over, heavy and low, covering Glasgow in a murky shadow. A few spits of rain leaked through the drizzle and landed on the toes of his shoes but he didn't notice. He slipped his hands into his pockets, just to be sure.

The instructions were clear.

Make the delivery.

No questions asked and no questions answered.

The drizzle grew heavier, falling in consistent wet drops. Glasgow was hidden in grey mist as the number 17 bus pulled up. Jon flashed his student card and stepped on. He walked up the aisle, counting only two other passengers, and took a window seat near the back.

One delivery.

It was a test, a display of loyalty, his first criminal act for the McGraw family.

An act that would help a man to get away with murder.

Chapter 64

Revenge

It was Alex's craving that had been satisfied.

"Remember who the real enemy is," whispered Lucy.

She wrapped the duvet tighter around her shoulders. Her chin rested on her knees, heels buried into the warmth of her body.

It was raining outside.

There was no light in the sky, the sun had long gone but she could hear the rain against the window. It ricocheted off the glass in tiny bullets. The air caught glimpses of her breath, cool despite the lingering summer months. The old Glasgow flat with its high roof and single glazing failed to insulate the heat.

Lucy shivered, replaying her sister's words in her head.

They abandoned us, left us in hell. Our real parents are the guilty ones, no one else.

Lucy closed her eyes, conjuring up the only images that she had of her parents.

Her mother - a young, much loved woman - (that's what the newspapers said) who, on her last day on earth found herself wrapped around the scalding engine of her car. Lucy was eight, young and oblivious, in foster home number four at the time.

It was years later, a decade after it had occurred, that she learned of her mother's death. Alex, following months of searching, finally did it. She tracked down information about their birth mum. They were given an hour, that was all, but for those sixty minutes their mother was real. It wasn't complete; they didn't have the full set. But for the first time in their lives two little girls had one out of two.

They had a parent, a mother.

A mother who was ripped away from them before the hands of the clock completed a single rotation. The article, the one that took her, was hit number three on google. It was an excerpt from the Scotsman. There were two hundred words and a picture of their mother's face. She smiled back from the laptop screen with delicate doll like features, her petite nose dusted with freckles. Just like Lucy's. Just like Alex's. She wore a yellow blouse that had been unbuttoned at the top revealing a thin gold chain. The small pendant rested on her bare collarbone and just visible in the grainy image were two entwined roses. Her hair was swept back in a loose ponytail, curls of strawberry blond escaping around her ears.

Not quite as red as Lucy.

Not quite as red as Alex.

The excerpt beneath the photograph was short and concise.

Jenny Rose Pingleton, 30, was killed in a car crash on Thursday evening in Glasgow.

Lucy gripped the blanket tighter and wiped her palm across her cheek. She was crying. She closed her eyes but it didn't help. She would never forget what happened next. Her sister, a child of only eighteen years old, closed the laptop over, holding it shut with the pressure of her hand and turned to Lucy.

Callous, no emotion.

"That just leaves Dad," she said.

Alex stood up, laptop tucked under her arm and walked toward the door.

"Mum got what she deserved."

She walked out, leaving Lucy standing alone.

The blanket was wound so tight that the pressure started to constrict Lucy's lungs. Both her cheeks ran with tears.

"Engineered at childhood," she whispered, "powerless to fight against it."

***

"Here"

Tom handed a small pile of empty envelopes to Cece. She leant forward and took them from him, alternating between looking at the contents of her hands and back at her Dad.

"I don't understand. What am I looking at?"

314

"The back," he said, "I never found the actual letters that Jon received, but these were the envelopes that they came in."

Cece turned the first envelope over with her fingers, then another, then another.

Each was the same, the same identical drawing.

The image, which was not much bigger than a ten pence piece, had been hand-drawn in black biro. It was always the same, in the same place, drawn over the flap like an old wax seal, only visible when the top flap was closed.

A rose.

"Jenny Rose Pingleton," said Tom. "Rose was Jenny's middle name."

Cece thought about it for a moment.

"Ok," she said, "So the rose was a message, a way of proving her identity and by hinting at her name it let Jon know that Jenny was her Mum."

"Yes but I think it was more than that."

"Meaning?"

"It was a punishment of sorts".

"I'm not following."

"The rose was a constant reminder, one with every letter, a cruel message that Jon was forced to acknowledge before opening each envelope." Tom extended his arm and pointed to the drawing. "The rose, what colour is it?"

"It's not," replied Cece, "I mean it's drawn in pen."

"That's what I thought at first but then it occurred to me..."

"That it's meant to be white," interrupted Cece.

"Yes. A white rose."

He pulled a Smartphone out of his pocket, swiped in the pass code, and opened up a search engine. His fingers moved quickly over the touch screen, feeding in the desired key words. It didn't take long. The first hit was a match. Tom handed the device over to his daughter and Cece held the screen up to her face, using the tip of her finger to scroll down the page. It didn't make complete sense but it was enough that she could begin to understand what her Dad was getting at.

Tom watched in silence, before he voiced it for her.

"The white rose is associated with purity and innocence. It is a symbol of perfection, of a soul unspoiled and untarnished. The white rose glorifies a body that is unaware..."

315

"... unaware of the temptations of the flesh," finished Cece, reading from the screen. She stopped and looked up, her eyes saddened. The message was clear.

"With each letter," continued Tom, "Jon was forced to remember Jenny. He was forced to remember that he raped her".

"Oh Jon," whispered Cece, "why didn't you tell us?"

Tom placed a comforting hand on her knee.

"Are you ok?" he asked.

"Yeah, it's just," she looked straight at her Dad, "You know."

"I know sweetheart."

"We need to do something," said Cece. Her voice suddenly changed, resolute, the softness gone from her features. "We need to find out exactly what happened. The DNA test, let's do it now. Just to be sure."

Cece stood up.

"But first," she said, "you need to tell me who Alex is."

Tom didn't hesitate.

"Alex is Lucy's sister."

"Sister," exclaimed Cece.

"At least I think so. I think that Jenny had twins."

"But what about..." Cece stopped mid-sentence, mouth open, her mind racing backwards then forwards.

Shit.

It all started to make sense, the break up and the tears, Alex moving out and not wanting to discuss her family. Lucy and her previous flatmate hadn't been just friends, thought Cece. They were sisters.

Lucy had played her.

The thought only lasted for a brief moment, her Dad's words bringing her back to the present.

"I think that Alex murdered Jon."

Chapter 65

Eve stood in the middle of her van completely naked.

The rain had died out but the air had not lost its chill. Her bare arms were covered in goose pimples, hundreds of tiny hairs standing on end. The cold helped her think, it cleared her mind. She opened the door and leant out, taking deep breaths of the night air.

It wasn't safe. Not anymore. It was only a matter of time until her secret betrayed her.

Until he worked it out.

Eve slammed the door shut. She couldn't allow that to happen. Wouldn't.

"Get it together," she whispered.

She turned, stopped by the reflection of her naked body in the mirror. She had always been slim, athletic in build with toned arms and defined stomach muscles, a little boyish perhaps. However it wasn't vanity that stopped her. She stood in front of the mirror and ran her fingers over her hip bone. The thick liquid concealer smudged under the warmth of her touch, revealing the outline of a tattoo. She had it done on her seventeenth birthday, a sudden impulse, to be a constant reminder of her mission. It represented everything that she stood for, something to steady her in times of uncertainty or doubt.

But right now, staring at it, she felt lost.

Eve had long since given up notions of a happily ever after, she had never entertained it as a possibility. The path that she had chosen wasn't meant to have a happy ending, she wasn't a fool, she knew what was at stake. There was only ever going to be one outcome.

"In seeking revenge you must dig two graves - one for yourself."

The words clung to the soft flesh of her lips, her voice but a murmur, as she gazed at the tattoo etched into her skin. She rubbed off the remaining makeup and stroked the image with her fingertips. A rose sealed in black ink.

She blinked and averted her gaze, not allowing herself to cry.

You've come too far to fail now, thought Eve, you can't afford to lose it.

Coming back to her senses, she rubbed her hands over her face and took a deep breath. "Let's go," she whispered. She searched the van with her eyes and located clothes. She pulled on tight jeans and a green hoody with the brand *evoc* stencilled across the front in large white letters. Dressed, she stepped over to the gas cooker and reached behind the box of Earl Grey tea bags. The paper held between her middle and her index fingers as she eased it out.

Page fifteen.

Securing the single page in her pocket, she knelt down on the floor and pulled a box out from underneath her bed then she unclipped the plastic lid and set it to the side. The container was filled with a selection of pots and pans and other common camping items. It was deliberately intended to look normal. Eve rummaged around until she found what she was looking for, a blue bag originally intended for toiletries and make up. She unzipped it and emptied the contents onto the floor. Three items.

An envelope.

A hardback copy of '*Exploring the Highlands by Bike*.'

A knife.

She shook the bag again and tipped it upside down but nothing fell out. She lifted it to her face and peered inside. Empty.

Where is it?

She sat back on her heels, frowning as she began rubbing the inside of her right ring finger with her thumb. Her hand felt suddenly naked. Her ring wasn't there. She must have left it behind.

Eve discarded the thought, there was nothing that she could do about it now, and picked up the book. The pages opened in her hand, parting in the middle without assistance to reveal a hidden slip of parchment paper. The sheet had been carefully cut and folded. The contents were concealed between the non-stick surfaces, pressed and weighed down by over 300 pages. She peeled it open, eyeing the concealed item with great care.

The head of a single yellow rose, now papery and dry.

The petals were tarnished by spots, small wrinkled blemishes inflicted by rain drops. Eve stared at the tiny imperfections, reminders of what the weather had been like that night. She pressed her finger against the defaced petal, touching the finer details of a memory. It was a memory that she would never forget. He had handed it to her, without words, as the sky filled with a faint drizzle and the moist air stained the final act of a condemned man. She had accepted the rose without comment. The final act of an innocent woman.

Eve had often questioned her reason for taking it, for accepting his gesture, his white flag so to speak. On any other day she would have spat at his feet and told him to fuck off. But she hadn't. Not that day. Eve had come to think of herself as a robot, an efficient drone unaffected by emotions, programmed with one goal. And yet that night, standing in the rain, she had felt something.

A connection.

Kneeling on the van floor, the rose held in her hands, the realisation hit her. Despite her own personal misgivings, there had been one simple reason for her taking it.

She had forgiven him.

He didn't deserve to die.

Eve let the rose fall to the floor and cupped her hands around her face to conceal the tears.

What had she done?

Wiping away tears, she moved to pick up the envelope. She lifted up the top flap and pulled out a faded, A5 piece of paper. She knew word for word what it said. There were only three lines and she had read them over a hundred times. But still Eve spoke each word, her eyes not lifting from the page.

"Please take care of Lucy and Alexandria, my two beautiful girls.

They are proof that even thorn bushes can produce roses.

Tell them I'm sorry."

Three lines, unsigned. For years that had been it, everything that she knew about where she had come from. Abandoned, tossed aside on the gates of hell, left with nothing but three lines. Left to rot.

It felt strange, nostalgic, to read her real name. Eve folded the paper, the crease long formed through the middle, and placed it in her pocket. In exchange she reached under the bed and pulled out an old notepad, the unkempt pages were tired and slightly discoloured. She scribbled down three lines, careful to disguise her writing, and ripped out the page before returning it to the envelope. Satisfied, she pulled the original from her pocket and read it a final time. Then she grabbed a lighter from the box and stepped outside.

She watched as the flame devoured the paper. It was gone in seconds.

"Alexandria," whispered Eve. "Alex."

It had been a long time since anyone had called her that.

***

Five missed calls. Two voicemails. Sally.

Shit.

Toop held the phone closer to his face, squinting to see the small screen. Three bars of reception. He opened up the first missed call and hit the green call button. She answered on the second ring.

"Toop, where the bloody hell have you been? I've been calling you for hours."

"Sorry no reception, I only just..."

"Did you get my voicemails?" Sally cut him off.

He didn't have time to respond. Sally continued, not pausing to take a breath.

"It wasn't suicide, Fergus," she said, "you were right. Someone killed him. The note, the one in the bothy log book, it wasn't him. Someone else wrote it. The whole message, the bit about suffering in a bed of roses, it was a threat. He was being sent a warning Fergus, a final warning. The whole thing, it was planned out, every detail until the final execution."

"Sally slow down. An execution, what are you..."

"He was sentenced to death Fergus, murdered for something that he did. Death was the price that he had to pay for his crimes."

"How do you know he had..."

"The map, it had been drawn on. Someone marked out a route for him, starting at the hotel and heading up past Loch an Eion, meaning that he never went near the bothy. He was on the other side..."

"But I saw the map, there wasn't anything on it."

"On the photocopy, no, but the original has a clear route outlined in yellow marker."

Neither of them spoke for a moment as the implications sank in.

"Fergus," said Sally, "I'm afraid I've got some bad news."

Toop responded with a low murmur. Sally continued.

"After seeing a copy of the original map I wanted to have a second look at the ballistics evidence. I mean, after my first look at the body, I was sure that he had died from a contact or near-contact shot, the gunpowder patterns were textbook. The evidence of suicide, it was right there in front of me. But I wanted to be sure, double check. So I phoned Bailey at the station and asked him to email me through a photo of the clothing."

"And?"

"Well, when I examined the photographs for the second time I couldn't see any evidence of the original staining. The remnants of black powder that you would expect from a contact shot had quite simply vanished. My first instinct was to question my initial assessment but..."

Sally's voice lost its volume.

"When I called Bailey back to ask if I could come pop by the station, he..."

"He what?" said Toop.

"Don't be too hard on the boy Fergus, he means well..."

"He what?" demanded Toop.

"He admitted that the damp clothes had been stinking out the MIR so..." Sally took a deep breath, "so, he and Roberts decided to throw them in the machine for a quick freshen up. They didn't know what..."

"I'll kill him."

"Ferg, don't overreact, he's just a kid. It's not like..."

"Meet me in town in half an hour," interrupted Toop. "I need a drink."

"Where are you now?"

The phone went dead in Sally's hand.

She stared at the wireless handset for a few seconds before setting it down.

It was going to be a long night.

***

Eve sat crossed-legged on the van floor and checked her watch. Almost ten. Now was as good a time as any.

She pulled the box of camping equipment over to her and returned three items.

A copy of 'Exploring the Highlands by Bike', used to keep the rose pressed.

One envelope.

And page 15. I am not worthy.

She returned the plastic lid, clipped the sides down and pushed it back under the bed. The knife remained on the floor by her right knee.

She would be needing it.

Eve pulled up the hood of her jumper and tucked her hair behind her ears, hiding the strands of bright red. She lifted the knife from the floor and slipped it into the front pouch of her hoody. The loose fit of the large top hung over her slight frame, concealing the existence of the weapon.

She stepped out of the van, navigating the dark with the light from her phone, and stood by the side of the road with her thumb out. The second car stopped and she jumped in.

"Where you heading lass?"

"Just drop me at any pub in town," said Eve.

"Tough day?"

She just nodded and turned to stare out the window.

The car pulled up outside *The Old Inn* and Eve hopped out, remembering to say thank you before she watched the car drive off. She turned to look at the old white building, a favourite with locals. The rustic pub had been built next to a disused crossing of the river, an ideal spot for a beer garden and not far from the picturesque pier. The entrance to the bar was round the side of the building, facing the neighbouring art gallery, but Eve had no intention of going in. Her destination was at the other end of town, a good thirty minute walk. She slipped a hand into the front pocket of her hoody, the feeling of cold steel against her skin strangely comforting.

"Ok Alex," she whispered, and she started walking.

Chapter 66

Late 80s

"Father Alistair McNab speaking."

"Dad, it's me."

McNab held the phone to his ear as he pictured his father, the Holy Father, checking his watch. For more than thirty years he had been the priest at the local parish. His father was a stubborn man, old-fashioned and long set in his ways, immovable to the point of resentment. Many years had passed since father and son had seen eye to eye.

"It's early." No pleasantries.

"I know, my apologies, it was urgent."

McNab's father responded with a low murmur.

"I need your help," continued McNab, "but it's important that this conversation stays between us."

"I'm not willing to break the law."

"I understand that, Father. You won't be. I just need your input on something."

"Go on."

"John 13:27."

"Yes."

"What does it say?" asked McNab.

McNab waited, fingers pressed against his lips, enduring the seconds of quiet that he knew would come. The silence was meant to shame. He bit his tongue, not pushing it. Time had taught McNab that it was best to just wait. It took ten long wasted seconds. Ten seconds, that was his punishment, the penalty for not having a bible in his house.

His father recited the passage from memory.

"And after the sop Satan entered into him. Then said Jesus unto him, that thou doest, do quickly."

"Sop," said McNab. His mind ticked over, talking more to himself than his father. "Sop."

Then the memory found him.

"The crust of bread," uttered McNab, "Jesus gave the sop to Judas before Judas betrayed him."

There were some things that he still remembered from Sunday school.

"But what does it mean?" asked McNab.

Five seconds this time.

"The human body is weak," his father stated. "We are puppets to the devil, faceless dolls dancing to his pantomime. The demon is able to enter into a human body; he has the power to own it and to take control of the strings. When Judas devoured the sop Satan entered into him, possessing his body and filling his mind with darkness. The demon poisoned his heart, stirring him up more eagerly to follow his wicked design."

"With the devil in his heart Judas would betray even Jesus," whispered McNab, his words unacknowledged.

"The evil spirit pushes us to commit horrid, unspeakable acts. The possessed will pursue with vigour crimes that are far beyond the limits of their nature."

Defenceless puppets, thought McNab.

Neither man filled the silence. McNab didn't notice until the line had gone dead. No goodbye.

McNab sat staring at the phone.

It was a paralysing feeling.

Fear.

Chapter 67

Father and daughter ran side by side, silent but for the effort of their lungs.

Then without warning Cece stopped. She just stood there in the middle of the station. Not another step.

Tom turned, momentum carrying him three feet further.

"I don't understand," said Cece. "Why can't I come?"

She made no move towards her father, so he came to her and placed a hand on each of her shoulders.

"I'm sorry sweetheart. But this is something that I have to do on my own." He leaned in and kissed her on the forehead. "Jon was like a brother to me. I owe it to him."

"He was family to me too."

"I know sweetheart, believe me, I do. But I need you to stay here."

"What is it that you're not telling me? I know there's something."

Tom looked at his daughter, his expression one of genuine pain.

"I'm sorry. I have to go." He turned and ran.

Cece watched as her father sprinted down the empty platform. He reached the first carriage just as the train doors started to close.

A moment and he was gone.

Next stop Achnasheen.

He would hitch the final thirty miles.

***

Lucy punched her fist into the bed and choked back tears. She couldn't live like this.

If she was going to find a way to move on then she had to find a way to put it all behind her.

The guilt. The revenge. The fear.

Lucy refreshed the page on the computer screen. No new emails. No Alex. She leant back, cupping her hands over her bent knees, and rocked herself on the spot. She bit her lower lip, powerless as gravity pulled a single tear down towards her chin. She left it. There was no point in wiping it away.

The fear.

What did Cece know?

Lucy got up from her bed and walked to the bathroom, leaving her clothes in a pile at the door. She let the shower run for two minutes, filling the room with a cloud of steam, and stepped in. She didn't bother to pull the curtain over. The burning water fell over her in waves, beading on her arms and stomach before turning her back red. Lucy sensed every drop, willing the warmth to rid her limbs of the cold that cursed through her. She thought of everything that had brought her to this moment. Her parents. Her sister. She knew that what they had done was wrong. Murder was always wrong, even a five year old could tell you that. Yet something inside her, Alex's voice perhaps, kept telling her that it had been necessary.

Deserved.

But Alex had also lied. She had promised her that afterwards everything would feel right and that although they could never see each other again, it would all be worth it. But what Lucy felt wasn't anything close to fulfilment.

She turned in the shower, catching a glimpse of herself in the mirror. Her eyes ran up her naked torso, focusing on the wet strands of red hair that clung to her shoulders. They were the exact same shoulders that Alex had, the same stomach, the same red hair. Lucy gathered her hands in fists.

Same nose, the same eyes.

Everything was the same.

Lucy screamed, launching a bottle of shampoo across the room. It hit off the far wall and exploded on the floor. She watched as the honey-coloured liquid began seeping onto the corner of the bath mat. How, thought Lucy, how was she meant to forget someone who looked exactly like her? She and Alex were identical, dead ringers, twins matched in every detail.

Stop it Lucy. Stop it right now, she whispered.

She stepped out of the shower, wrapped a towel around her body and twisted another into a turban around her hair. She missed a few crimson strands, leaving them to fall down the back of her neck.

Now you move on.

She pulled the bathroom door closed behind her, walked through to the living room and took a seat on the couch. She took a deep breath and reached forward, pulling open the drawer beneath the table. She removed a pen and a pad of paper. If Cece wanted revenge then there was no stopping her, but she may as well know all of the facts. Some things were just worth the price and in this case the truth was worth everything. If Lucy was going to go down for the murder of her father, she would do it knowing that she was a good person.

Lucy started writing.

Dear Cece,

I thought that you should know the truth, my truth. Then it is up to you what you choose to do with it.

Here goes, from the beginning. Although I should warn you, my story is not a pleasant one. There is no happily ever after, no prince in shining armour. My life was no fairytale. In truth, it has amounted to one mishap after another, starting most unfortunately with my birth; our birth, my identical twin Alexandria, Alex, and I. We were born on the same day about twenty-six years ago. I say about because we never knew our exact birthday. The adoption agency decided on the 5th of May, the fifth of the fifth, nice and neat. I've always assumed that Alex was born first, by a few minutes or so. I don't really know why, instinct perhaps, but I always thought of her as my big sister, the leader. She was the person who I relied on and looked up to. I suppose that it wouldn't be too much of a stretch to say that I worshipped her. She was my guardian, an angel sent to lead me out of hell.

I don't suppose you have ever known hell and I pray that you never will. I'm not talking about the afterlife, about the torture chambers and fire and brimstone, I mean that feeling of complete abandonment. Hell is not something you can escape from, for there is nothing to escape to. Hell is alone. It is losing count of where you have lived and who you have lived with, moving in with family after family, home after home. Never fitting, never knowing, just floating along. You learn to act, to play a faceless part in your own life. No name, no meaning, just a mass of atoms. You become an accumulation of flesh and bones, unloved and unwanted. It does things to you, the rejection, it changes a person.

I'm not meaning to win sympathy points or to shift blame. But the crimes that I am about to share with you, they were not committed without reason.

Alex and I were dumped at only a few hours old on the steps of a primary school in Glasgow. It wasn't until the morning that the janitor came to open up and found us sleeping in the basket. Two newborns, blue with cold and struggling to breathe. Two little girls who had been deserted and tossed aside. We were left with a single note that was tucked down the inside of Alex's vest, penned in the devil's own hand.

'Please take care of Lucy and Alexandria, my two beautiful girls.

They are proof that even thorn bushes can produce roses.

Tell them I'm sorry.'

Even now the ironic beauty, the poetry of it, makes me both laugh and cry. Who knew a letter of condemnation could be so well written. The poisoned chalice, Alex called it. Although we later learned that the words were by no means an accident, they were chosen for a reason. Rose, as it turned out, was our mother's middle name. Jenny Rose Pingleton. We were her roses and the thorns, well, I'm getting ahead of myself. That comes later.

The headmistress of the school took us to the police station and we were quickly snatched up by the foster care system. I became Lucy and Alex became Alexandria. I don't know how they decided who was who. Eeny, meeny, miny, mo, Alex reckons. When we were much younger we tried swapping them around just to see, but it didn't feel right. So, who knows, maybe I was always meant to be Lucy.

Lucy Roy. Roy was something that one of the women in social services came up with, a Scottish clan name apparently. When we were a bit older a social worker explained that Roy was a medieval nickname for a person with red head, derived from the Gaelic 'ruadh' meaning red. Quite fitting.

Sorry, I'm rambling.

I don't remember our first foster home, or the second, I was too young and neither of them lasted very long. None of them ever did. On most occasions Alex and I were placed together. When we had each other, the rest of it, the beatings, the neglect, the taunts of worthlessness, they were manageable. But when we were separated it felt like a part of me had been torn out. I don't know how to explain it; maybe it's a twin thing. But *those times were the loneliest of my life. Alex was my world, she led and I followed. So when the change happened, when she changed, I never thought of questioning her.*

We were sixteen at the time.

I came home from school to find Alex sitting on her bed, the sheets were soaked through. At first I couldn't move. I stood frozen in the doorway, convinced that my sister was trying to kill herself. The blood was everywhere, and there was so much of it. I remember thinking that, that there was too much. Alex didn't notice me at first. Her head was hung down and her eyes were held in determined concentration as she carved the knife into her wrist. For a long ten seconds I just stood there, watching as my sister mutilated her arm, I didn't know what to do. Then she looked up at me. Her eyes resolute. She smiled, a horrible smile, and she held up her arm.

There were two "R"s. I can still see them now, entwined and etched into her skin. For Roses, she said and for Revenge.

From that day on she was obsessed with punishing our parents. It became her mission to track them down and I helped her. At first it seemed hopeless. We had no name, no picture to help us and after a few fruitless months Alex snapped. She started running through the streets, desperately knocking on doors around the school where we had been found. But it was futile. No one knew anything. Then by chance I saw an advert for a family tracking website claiming that it could use DNA samples to trace lineage back generations and could help track down relatives. The next day Alex made us take an ethnic DNA test which led to the discovery that we were 81% European, 9% African, 4% Arabian and 5% Siberian. Strange I know, but apparently it relates to the 18ᵗʰ century and the British involvement in the slave trade.

Rambling.

But what was most remarkable was that the website managed to match our DNA with a first cousin on the paternal side. A woman named Janet Callander. Alex sent her an email, including our picture and Ms Callander replied a few days later saying that she needed to meet us in person. At first she didn't say much, she just stared at us, gawking at us like we were dolls. The meeting, it transpired, was some kind of examination. She said that she needed to see us in the flesh before she could believe it. Her cousin Jenny, she was now convinced, had given birth to two daughters, two girls that had grown up to look just like her.

There was no doubt in Janet Callander's mind. She said the resemblance was uncanny.

However, as it turned out, the two women hadn't spoken in years, almost eighteen in fact. We sat in silence as Janet recounted her story and with each sentence she gave us a piece of the puzzle, pieces that Alex and I had been searching for our whole lives. Janet skipped details, leaving out large periods of time, and the right side of her mouth twitched nervously whenever she made reference to the 'unspeakable incident.' She refused to elaborate on it, simply stating that during the summer of 1988 her cousin changed, becoming increasingly withdrawn and distant. It continued for a few months and then she up and left for Italy. Her cousin was gone for over six months and it was only through a friend that Janet learned that she had returned to Glasgow. They hadn't spoken since.

It was all too much for Janet Callander, the lies, the hidden pregnancy, the abandoned children. After a hurried cup of coffee she scribbled on a piece of paper, slid it face down across the table, and left.

Jenny Rose Pingleton 12.06.1988.

Our mother. It was the first time we had seen her full name.

What Janet Callander couldn't bring herself to mention that day was the fact that our mother had been dead for almost ten years, her body wrapped round the engine of a car. That piece of information we were forced to find out for ourselves. The wonders of the internet.

Alex saw our mother's death as punishment for what she had done to us and we never spoke about it after that.

"That just leaves Dad." Those were Alex's words. With the flick of a switch it was his turn, our father. Your uncle. It took a lot longer to find him, years in fact. It was like we were searching for a man that didn't exist. A ghost. Then one autumn, almost two years ago, Alex managed to get us tickets to a reunion event at the University of Glasgow. She had found out, along with many other things, that our mother had been enrolled at Glasgow. (She studied History of Art). Anyway, Alex thought that the reunion would be worth a shot, even if it was a long one.

I remember feeling overwhelmed being there, walking in her footsteps, sitting on the same benches, standing in the same halls. But if Alex felt at all uneasy, she didn't show it. Alex spent the day mingling with hundreds of strangers, asking them if they knew a Jenny Pingleton. No one did of course, thousands of students had been through the university and the odds were minimal.

Then as we were leaving, I literally collided with him, tripped right over his foot. A man called Jesse Jenkins. Jesse Jenkins, it so happened, had been best friends with Jonathan Swan and he told us that Jonathan Swan had been in love with Jenny Pingleton. A small world after all, but then, you would know that wouldn't you Cece.

I remember Mr Jenkins' words exactly.

"Jonny was besotted with her but he ... well Jonny didn't really know how to handle his feelings. In truth, I think that they screwed him up a bit, poor guy. Last time I saw him we were at a house party together, summer of 1988 it must have been. Jenny was there too, that's right, I remember watching him lead her upstairs. But following that, I never saw either of them again. It was the strangest thing, after that night they both sort of disappeared. My best friend just up and gone."

I won't go into the details of how we came to piece together the events of that night. Instead, let me cut a long story short. (Just remember what I said no fairytale, no knight in shining armour. No happily ever after).

That night, in one of the upstairs bedrooms, Jonathan Swan, my dad (your uncle) raped Jenny Rose Pingleton. It was the 'unspeakable event' of the summer of 1988 and the unfortunate start to my life.

I can remember the evening of the reunion as if it were yesterday. The clouds had been building throughout the day, slowly blotting out the blue of the sky, but it wasn't until we walked out of the university gates that the first spits of rain began to fall. Alex drove us home in silence with the windscreen wipers on full as the rain grew heavier, the large drops of water attacking the glass. We got back to the flat, kicked off our shoes and both got into Alex's bed. Two sisters, identical, side by side.

We didn't sleep. We stayed up talking, planning the murder of our father.

Lucy laid the pen down and read over her work. As her eyes travelled down the page she massaged her writing hand, rubbing the small bump that had started to form on the inside of her middle finger. She stepped up from her crouched position and walked through to the kitchen. She needed a drink. She needed something alcoholic if she was going to write what happened next.

Chapter 68

Present Day

Gairloch is a sleepy town situated on the shores of the loch, surrounded by a wealth of spectacular scenery and vast beaches. Like much of the West coast of Scotland, the locals are the first to rave about the miles of picturesque coastline, the unforgettable sunsets and the secluded and sandy beaches that fill with families and tourists in the summer months. A fact aided by the Gulf Stream and the relatively warm waters that pass through during the months of July and August. It is said that the current brings the hordes of jellyfish that are often seen covering the early morning sand.

The parish lines of Gairloch were drawn up centuries ago, extending far beyond the small village community to include the hamlets of Poolewe and Kinlochewe, totalling a population of less than 1000. Since the 15th century the land around Gairloch has been under the ownership of the Mackenzies. It is said that they were a family of true Highlanders, hospitable and warm, refusing to evict a single tenant during the clearances despite their estate running at a loss. As a result, and as locals will tell you, evicted Highlanders came from all over the region and settled in the Gairloch area. The influx of skills from other settlements meant that Gairloch endured the ups and downs of the economy and was able to survive as a thriving community. The tradition of hospitality brought great benefits to the town. At least, that was the case, until a recent development in the area.

Section 66 Dispersal Mandate.

The mandate, dis-affectionately known to locals as 'The Dumping Project', was a London council initiative to eject low-income families from the inner cities, predominantly London and Glasgow, and to relocate them hundreds of miles away in a remote Scottish village. The measures, it was explained in length, were a response to cuts in welfare and a cap in housing allowance, making it impossible for disadvantaged families to afford to live in the larger cities. The answer, as locals saw it, was a game of human Monopoly, shipping homeless families to the Highlands.

Out of sight out of mind.

***

Eve walked along the pavement. There wasn't a single person in either direction. She had heard all about Section 66 when she moved up in early April. Problem families, that was the term that the locals used, dispersed and dumped throughout Highland council areas. It had been explained to her more than once that the government had tried to proceed behind closed doors, transporting families in the dead of night. No one had firm proof of these midnight shipments, no actual first person accounts, but it had come to be accepted as fact. No one in the village doubted it and it was very much true that the council houses were filling up. Three new families in two months. It was only a matter of time until the true scale of social cleansing came to light. It was the largest ever single displacement of poor people from London, an initiative designed to dilute the 'effect' that they had, a dilution that was tarring the local village's image. The number of 'nuisance' incidents had more than trebled since the spring. In other words, Gairloch was being used as a dumping ground for the government's problems.

Problem. That word again.

Except that wasn't a problem for Eve. In fact, it was just the opposite.

She walked on, lost in thought.

Three. According to the Scottish judicial system there were three acknowledged ways of being punished. A fine, the exchange of money as a form of repentance for a crime or other offence. Imprisonment, the removal of one's freedom. Lastly, non-custodial sentencing, such as community service or probation, alternatives to prison whereby the offender gives back to society. However if, like Eve Stone, you believed that complete repentance required absolute punishment, then a fourth option became available.

The only form of true justice in her eyes.

Eve stopped in sight of the house. She sat down on the opposite side of the road, balanced on the kerb of the pavement with her knees bent. She swung her bag round from her back and it fell heavily between her feet. Inside was a bottle of cheap vodka. No mixer. She didn't need one. Her intention was simple, to get drunk, so blindingly drunk that she would forget. So drunk that she'd never have to remember again.

Her throat burned with the first swig, the sharp pain distorting her features. Eve pictured her mother, Jenny Rose Pingleton. The picture of her in the newspaper, the freckles dusted across her nose and the strawberry blonde curls that fell around the corners of her mouth. The second gulp felt like razor blades cutting the insides of her stomach. She thought about her father, Jonathan Swan. The look on his face just moments before he died and the shared sense of acceptance. His final words, spoken to her over the sound of the wind, played over in her head.

Greater love hath no one than this.

The bottle rose to her lips.

Fire drowned her throat.

"Greater love hath no one than this."

The fourth gulp wasn't so bad, numb almost. Alex thought about her sister. It had always been Lucy. Lucy was the guardian angel, not her. Her sister, she was that glimmer of peace in an endless storm. Lucy was good and innocent, she deserved to be free.

Eve nursed the drink in her hand. She had to let Lucy go and there was only one way to set her free.

An hour passed and the bottle emptied. Eve's pupils seemed to grow dry and sticky while the whites turned a strained red. She could feel her body slump on the curb as she struggled to hold her back straight. The alcohol seeped through her one sip at a time, making it harder for her to locate the edges of her lips with the bottle. Eve took a final swallow and tipped the remaining vodka out onto the grass, watching as the clear liquid soaked into the soil. She needed to remain conscious. Compos mentis. She couldn't afford to pass out on the pavement, not if she was going to complete her task. She looked up, her eyes blurred, and focused her gaze on the building across the road. It was one of the three recently filled council houses and inside was her target.

All six foot four of him.

He was on probation, punishment number three.

His sentence wasn't meant to be common knowledge but secrets, Eve found out, didn't remain secret for long in a small town. According to local gossip, Kyle McPherson had been sentenced to eight years in prison after admitting to the rape of his fifteen year old niece. However his sentence was later overturned by the judge and all prison time was suspended in favour of probation.

"Prison," Mrs Mackenzie had whispered across the vegetable aisle, "can't protect those sorts. A coward and a pervert, those are the lowest of the low. The scumbag wouldn't have survived a day inside. He would have had the life beaten out of him on his first night. And quite right in my opinion but the authorities can't be having blood on their hands, so what do they do?" She waved a carrot in front of Eve's nose. "They send the filth up here."

Eve stood up, whipped her red hair from her face, and crossed the street. She held the knife up against the back of her wrist, concealed from view.

Kyle MacPherson, she thought, wasn't safe here either.

Eve walked up to the gate, unlocked the latch with her free hand, and walked towards the door.

She was unaware of the man watching her.

Chapter 69

Late 80s

It took thirty minutes. McNab arrived at the station without a single recollection of the drive.

With the devil in his heart Judas would betray even Jesus.

McNab ran up the stairs to his office, rummaged through his desk and pulled out a note pad. The pen paused against his lips for ten seconds before he started writing. Having it in ink helped him to think.

The pen moved with fury, marking a clear line down the middle of the page. The following sentences he wrote in bullet points. He made two columns; suicide on the right and murder on the left.

He started with the right. Suicide.

Suspected suicide. Cause of death - exsanguination caused by severed artery (slit wrists).

No signs of a struggle.

Suicide note.

Estranged from family.

Stress of working for the CIA in Iran.

Troubled letters to son - references to the devil.

McNab paused and bit the end of the pen before adding an afterthought.

Possible references to the devil and death could be linked to suicidal tendencies.

Guilt: thinks that he is going to hell.

Then he moved on to the left. Murder.

Blanching - the body had been moved. Bill Anderson had been lying flat when he died but his chair was found in a sitting position - someone must have tampered with the body hours after his death.

The suicide note - why try and conceal his family only to expose them with his final words?

Letters between Bill and his son - William said that Bill had sounded scared (the devil breathing down his back).

Homophobia (fear of blood): couldn't have slit his own wrists.

McNab dropped the pen onto his desk and stretched out his fingers, pumping his fist open and closed to loosen the joints. He rolled his shoulders up and back, the muscles tensing round his spine, then he tilted his head to the right, stretching his neck from side to side. Relieved, McNab clasped his hands together and cracked his knuckles. The muscle joints pulled apart, forming tiny cavities that filled with gas then collapsed, emptying with a gratifying popping noise. It was a habit that he had never grown out of.

The moment of reprieve lasted but a few seconds. McNab retrieved the pen, contemplated what he had written and created a third column.

Murder beyond doubt.

Phone call from Harry - threatening Isla and Caroline and warning me off the case.

Someone broke into the house.

Note left on Isla's stomach. John 13:27 'And after the sop Satan entered into him.'

Donaldson and Caroline's strange behaviour - memory loss

His pen stopped on the page.

Caroline. It hit him with a jerked realisation just how out of character his wife's behaviour had been. No mother, especially his Caroline, would have left her child unattended for hours. McNab leaned back in his chair and stared ahead for a full five minutes, thinking. Then he bent over his pad and jotted down her symptoms.

Placid. Docile and zombie-like. Confusion. Coherent but childlike - obeyed all verbal commands, almost as if she had no free will. Memory wiped clean - no recollection of what had transpired over a three hour period. Unable to...

"McNab?"

He didn't hear his own name. Didn't register the man's presence. Hunched over his desk, lost in his own thoughts, McNab failed to notice the man who was now hovering over him. The officer, young and fresh-faced, stood over his shoulder. It took him three attempts before McNab noticed the sound of his own name. The pen halted in McNab's hand and he looked up, the dark bags under his eyes giving him a sullen appearance.

"Sorry to interrupt..." The officer looked almost scared. "But these arrived for you this morning."

He held out three envelopes. McNab took them, thanking the lad as he stepped back, clearly eager to put distance between himself and his weary-looking superior.

McNab ripped into the first.

It can't be.

"Shit," he exclaimed, re-reading the second line.

Careful comparison concludes a POSITIVE match between the suicide note and examples of Bill Anderson's handwriting.

McNab let out a defeated sigh and ran his hands through his hair. It didn't add up. Anderson couldn't have written the note himself, not if he was murdered. It didn't make sense. He reached for the second, fuller envelope and emptied the contents onto the desk in front of him. An assortment of pages fell out, all lined, all double sided, all signed by Bill Anderson. McNab sifted through them, spreading them out across his desk, arranging them in order of date. They were the letters that Anderson had written to his son.

McNab picked up the first one. They were all dated a month apart, like clockwork. He started reading. The first few contained the normal pleasantries, comments about the weather, opinions on the football results, just as William had said. Three letters in, struggling to focus on the scrawled biro, McNab felt his eyes growing weary. The lack of sleep and the absence of coffee, or any form of breakfast for that matter, were kicking in. In an attempt to remedy one of the two he wandered through to the station kitchen, put on a pot of coffee and buttered two slices of toast. He couldn't find the marmalade. He sat on the stool by the window and noticed that it was raining. He downed his coffee and ate the toast, studying the drops of water as they made their way down the glass.

McNab poured a second cup of coffee, carried it back to his desk, and opened up the fourth letter. Again, no great insights other than the revelation that Celtic Football Club had suffered an embarrassing defeat to Rangers, 4-1 and that, according to the letters, it had been unusually warm for February. Finding nothing, and getting frustrated, McNab decided upon a new tactic. Newest letters first.

Half a page in, he sat back in disbelief.

Shit.

Everything, the tone, the grammatical errors, the hurried font, everything about the letter was completely different. The writer was writing out of fear.

But why? Bill Anderson left no indications, no names, no explanations. Just references, one every letter, to the devil.

"What are you trying to tell me Bill?" asked McNab. He reached for a pen and circled each statement, marking any mention of the devil in ink. There were three sentences that stood out, repeated more than once.

The devil's breath is tasteless and odourless.
Truth cannot hide from the Angel of Death.
The devil makes scared children of us all.

"I really hope you're not crazy, Bill," uttered McNab, but he was interrupted before he could finish his thought.

"Officer McNab?" The familiar voice came from behind him.

McNab turned round and looked up, caught off guard again. Something that had happened too many times in the past twenty-four hours. It took McNab a moment to place the man's face.

"Jonathan Swan?" asked McNab, the memory coming back to him. It was the boy from the gallery, the poor kid who had found Bill Anderson's body.

"I have something for you," Jon stated, holding out a small, wrapped box.

"Thank you," said McNab. He rose from his chair, taking the parcel with his right hand. "Can I offer you a seat? A coffee?" He gestured towards the empty chair across from his desk. "How have you been Jonathan, are you doing ok? I can't imagine how..."

"No," Jon interrupted, "no coffee." He returned his hands to his pockets. "I just needed to deliver that."

"Ok," McNab's voice was kind. "Can I ask who is it from?"

Jon shook his head.

"You don't know?"

Jon stared back at him. Blank.

"Did someone tell you to give it to me?"

A nod.

"And do you know who that someone was Jonathan?"

Jon shook his head. Slow. He lowered his eyes, his hands forming tight firsts at his sides. "No," he managed, the lie forced from his mouth. "I have to go."

No questions asked, no questions answered, thought Jon. Then he turned and walked to the door. Test passed.

McNab kept his eyes on the lad's back, not removing them until he had disappeared from sight. As he listened to the fading sound of footsteps, McNab looked down at the small box. He was certain of one thing.

Whatever was inside, it wasn't good.

He could feel it.

Chapter 70

After dropping her dad off at the train station Cece ran to the nearest chemist. It didn't take long. Glasgow was filled with them.

She threw the door open and made a beeline for the back of the shop. The word 'Pharmacy' was visible from the doorway, printed in large green letters and positioned above neat rows of prescription drugs. Cece hurried towards it, planting her palms on the counter to halt the movement of her body.

"Hi," she managed.

The pharmacist looked up from her paperwork, her face caught in an open-mouthed stare. She looked the girl up and down, taken aback by the sudden burst of excitement in her little shop.

"I need a paternity test," said Cece.

It took a moment for the woman to steady herself. Cece waited, focusing in on the lady's face, noting her sunken eyes and the visible hollowing of her cheek bones. She was so old, thought Cece, frail. The blue of her veins lined her arms, the skin thin and stretched.

Her name tag said Dot.

"I'm sorry dear, what did you say?"

"A paternity test, I need a paternity test. Do you have any?"

Dot paused and for a moment Cece thought that the woman was going to walk round the counter and hug her.

"It's not for me," blurted Cece. "I know who my dad is, I mean he's great. The test, it's for a friend."

Dot raised a single eyebrow, the expression deepening the wrinkles across her forehead.

"Really, it is," added Cece, "my friend was too embarrassed to come in so I said I would get one for her."

"Poor girl," said Dot after a moment of silent contemplation. Her expression remained unchanged, supporting the weight of quiet concern as she reached forward and placed her hand on Cece's. She gave her a gentle squeeze. "She's lucky to have a friend like you."

"She would do the same for me."

"I'm sure she would dear. Now, let's see what we have."

Dot disappeared behind the wall of drugs, returning a few minutes later with a small box that she placed on the counter.

"This is a home-kit test, very simple to use, completely confidential. Just tell your friend that she needs to take the mouth swabs then fill out the paperwork and..."

"Mouth swabs?" interrupted Cece.

"Yes, she will find two inside the kit."

"Is it possible to use alternative sample methods? It's just that, well I'm not sure her dad..."

Dot held up her hand, the gesture implying that Cece didn't need to say anything else. Her voice kind.

"Don't worry hunni, say no more." She opened the box and held out a list. "Would any of these be more appropriate?"

Cece scanned the paper with her eyes, following the words with her finger as she recited them in her head.

Fingernail clippings, plucked hair, used tampons, used condoms, Q-tips with earwax, urine, electric razor debris. The list went on.

"Yes this should be fine."

"Perfect," smiled Dot. "Well tell your friend to enclose the two samples in a paper bag or envelope and then send them, along with payment, to the address given. The DNA clinic will begin testing as soon as they receive the samples. In general the laboratory will process the samples and have the results back to you, her, within five to seven working days."

"Five to seven days!" exclaimed Cece. "That's far too long. Is there no way to speed it up?"

"Well yes, if you're willing to pay."

"How much?"

Dot pulled a folder from under the counter and found the page that she needed. She retrieved the glasses that were hung round her neck and scrolled through the information.

"There is a One Day STAT test available but it's quite pricey."

"How much?"

"£400."

"That's fine. Is all of the information inside?"

Dot nodded. "All payment options are explained in the instructions."

Cece reached for the box.

"Thank you for your help."

Cece walked out of the shop and as she made her way down the street she laid a protective hand over her handbag, pressing it into the side of her body. Everything that she needed was inside, the paternity kit, Lucy's used tampon and a small sealed envelope. Her dad had handed it to her before they left for the train station. It was a sample of her uncle's hair, debris from Jon's electric razor that her dad had collected and packaged.

It was in the post within the half hour.

***

Lucy set the bottle of wine down on the coffee table, two glasses already gone from it. She unscrewed the top and poured herself a third.

It couldn't hurt.

Using the sofa for balance, she bent down and sat on the living room floor, knees folded and tucked beneath the low table. Her stomach felt empty. But with everything that was going on, she hadn't thought to replenish the cupboards and the fridge no longer held anything edible.

She reached for the wine glass, took another sip, and picked up the pen.

Take two, she thought.

Our father; an abandoner and a rapist.

Not exactly the sugar and spice that little girls' dreams are made of.

It didn't take long for Alex to find his address. It's scary how far google can get you when you know someone's full name and, thanks to Jesse Jenkins, their date of birth. But then again, utilising the internet is something that you are quite skilled at, wouldn't you agree, roomy?

Sorry. Too much wine.

The plan was simple. Alex had four easy steps. 1. Build a relationship. 2. Arrange a meeting. 3. Put a bullet in his head. 4. Vanish.

Alex was so callous about it, removed. I tried to get through to her a few times, to find the softness that had existed in my sister when we were kids, but I never could. Alex was changed, she was hardened by it all. At first I questioned whether we were doing the right thing, but after a while

343

I started to feel guilty about questioning her. Life isn't just or fair, it is a cruel business and to survive it one of us had to be tough. Alex was tough for me. She was doing it all for me. From the day that we were born Alex has looked out for me. I would have followed her to the ends of the earth, and I did, no questions asked.

Step one; developing a relationship. That was the easy part. First we had to initiate a channel of communication, one that we could control. It had to be something that we could manipulate with complete precision. Something personal.

Letters.

Alex wrote him letters, handwritten letters that she sent every month for almost a year. She utilised her words like weapons, twisting and turning the letters more effectively than a knife. At first she wrote with anger and pain, using words that were intended to poison him, to fill him with guilt. She blamed him for everything, tarring him as the man who raped our mother and abandoned his two little girls. She condemned him for leaving us to rot in hell.

Then, as planned, came self-empowerment, the process of letting go of our anger. It was all feigned of course but Alex did it perfectly; she knew just what to say. Each word was carefully chosen. She planted every phrase, using each letter to construct a perfect web of deception and illusion, making him believe that she, sorry that we, were healing. We were ready to forgive, to let go of the past.

Finally, and most crucially, she allowed him to feel hope, to think that after all these years we could be a family.

Which leads on to step two; arranging to meet at a location of our choice of course.

Obviously he (our dad) had our address from the letters but Alex had been clear from the beginning, specifying that under no circumstances was he to turn up on our doorstep or anywhere within a five mile radius. No exceptions, one attempt and his daughters would be gone from his life forever. Instead we needed to meet somewhere remote, somewhere where no one would recognise us or see us at all for that matter. Alex and I couldn't risk being spotted together. The problem with having an identical twin is that you tend to stand out. While people may forget a face, they tend to remember seeing it twice.

So Alex chose Torridon, a remote hamlet near Gairloch.

Now Cece, this is where it gets complicated. You see Alex had already been living in Gairloch for three months. She was using a fake name and living out of her van under the pretence of being an outdoor enthusiast - a role that came naturally to her. Alex enjoyed anything that involved getting covered in mud, she loved being outside. Wide open spaces and mountains... Sorry, I'm digressing. As I mentioned, it was important that she established a legitimate story, a reason for being there, so as not to arouse suspicion when a body was found a few months later. For weeks she sent me all of the letters that she wrote him and I would forward them on, ensuring that the postmark said Glasgow.

Simple, just like Alex said. Everything was in place for

Lucy stopped and let the pen fall limp between her fingers.

She was crying.

"Stop it," she whispered.

She picked up the pen and wrote the next three words.

Step Three: Murder.

Chapter 71

Present Day

The man watched Eve as she unlatched the gate, the glint of cold metal visible beneath the cuff of her sleeve.

He crouched on the opposite side of the road, barely fifty metres from her, hidden under the cover of darkness. The line of street lights came to an abrupt end, not continuing past the last house, meaning that it wasn't difficult for him to go unnoticed.

Three hours he had been watching her.

Eve had stepped out of the white van, alone, pulled up the hood of her jumper and buried her hands in her pockets before turning on her heel and heading up the hill. He followed, tracking her across town, ducking back every now and then to avoid suspicion. It made for a good forty minute walk.

Then she stopped. He stopped, remaining silent as she knelt down on the pavement.

He knelt down on the verge. Waiting. Watching,

He focused in on the bottle as she raised it to her lips again and again. Her grimace indicated that it was something strong, vodka most likely. He squinted. She was sitting directly beneath the light but he couldn't make out the brand. She was too far away and the label design didn't register with him. Either, he thought, it was too expensive or too cheap for him to have heard of. He guessed the later.

After an hour she discarded the bottle and stood up. He noted how her legs shook beneath her, unable to balance the weight of her body.

He had recognised her the moment that she had stepped out of the van.

It was Alexandria. No question.

The nose, the hair, a little redder perhaps but it was her. He was in no doubt.

He straightened out his jacket and walked out of the shadows towards the house.

He would not watch his daughter die.

Not tonight.

***

"I had a thought." Sally broke the silence. "About the autopsy I mean."

"Yes?" said Toop, nursing a pint between his hands. Barely touched.

"You remember I mentioned that the tips of his fingers were all hardened?"

A nod.

Sally continued, "And you suggested that perhaps he played guitar, that he used white spirit."

A second nod.

"Well, it may be nothing," said Sally, "but I was doing some research on the common uses of white spirit, just flicking through the web and something kept popping up. Apparently, artists working with oil-based paints use white spirit to wash the brushes, it helps to get the oil out of the bristles. It's advised on wikiHow," she added, "that you should always use rubber gloves, something to do with the way that you have to work the spirit into the bristles. But say you didn't wear gloves, then that would cause the same toughening up of the skin that I found on the body."

"So you think that he was a painter?"

"Like I said," said Sally, taking a sip of her merlot, "it was just an idea." She ran a thumb down the stem of her glass. "And someone had to say something."

She leant over the table and placed a hand on his. Toop continued to stare into his drink.

"You were right Fergus, from the very beginning you were right, you were the only one who could see it." She squeezed his wrist. "He didn't commit suicide, I'm sure of it. It was when I was looking at the route drawn on the map that it occurred to me. The quote in the bothy log book, you interpreted it correctly the first time. Relenting in thorn, a bed of roses, it's all about repentance. But he didn't end his own life to make peace with God, he was killed as an act of punishment. Someone else was playing God just like you said."

"And where did they go?" said Toop.

"Sorry?"

"This God, this executioner? Did they just up and disappear? Someone commits a murder under our noses, leaves me messages for Christ's sake and we have no idea who they are. Not a single lead."

"Were there any fingerprints on the note, the one that was left on your car?"

"Completely clean." He sipped at his beer. "Gloves I imagine."

The two friends fell into silence. They both sat slumped back in their chairs, two minds at a loss. Toop glanced up at the bar, a thought niggling at the back of his head, one he couldn't quite place. His eyes ran across the selection of draught beer. What was he missing, there was something right in front of him, he just couldn't...

He didn't get to finish his thought.

The door flew open.

Toop and Sally turned their heads in an instant. Toop stiffened and started to rise from his seat, stopped by Sally's outstretched arm.

"Don't," she said. "Just leave it."

Bailey stood in front of them, panting heavily. He paused in the doorway, doubled over with his hands rested on his knees, as he struggled to get his breath back.

"Found you," he managed, stumbling over to their table. "I swear I've run at least 5km trying to track you two down. Didn't realise Gairloch had so many god damn pubs." He drew his fist to his mouth and coughed, a wheezy cough unsupported by his weak, recovering lungs. "No bloody wonder we've got a drink problem in this town, I must have..."

"Would you like a seat?" offered Sally.

"Yes. Thanks."

"So..." began Toop, "why was it that you needed to find us?"

Bailey held his hands up, exposing his palms. "Please don't get mad but..."

"We won't," Sally interrupted before Toop had a chance to respond. "Just tell us what you came to say."

"Okay. Well, you know how Roberts and I were first to the scene that night and it was the first..." He paused, apprehension creeping into his voice. "What I mean to say is that, well I'd never seen a dead body before, not up close and..."

"The point?" said Toop.

"Yes sorry, the point. Well, I decided... I mean at the time, it seemed like a good idea to take some photos on my phone..."

"That's completely against police protocol," said Toop, his voice notably raised. "What on earth?"

Sally stopped him mid-sentence, a gentle hand to his thigh.

"Yes Bailey, go on," she said.

"Well I was flicking through them last night, just having a look, and I found..." he reached into his jacket pocket and pulled out his phone, "here, let me show you." He scrolled down his screen with his index finger, searching through the gallery of images. "It didn't come up in the photos that you guys took, probably washed away by then. You can barely see them in these photos as it is. It's only a three megapixel, couldn't afford the upgrade."

He offered the phone to Toop as he finished his sentence.

Sally leaned in over his shoulder to see. Toop swiped his fingers over the image and zoomed in.

"Oh my god," she uttered.

They could all see them. Tyre tracks. Mountain bike tracks carved into the mud, two water filled channels sculpted in the ground only a few metres from the body.

Sally turned her head from the phone and looked over at Toop. "You didn't have your bike that night?"

He shook his head.

"You think that the tracks belonged to the killer?" asked Bailey, a touch too enthusiastic. He leaned in closer as his mind started jumping. "The person who left the note on your car, what did it say, something about roses... or touching thorns?"

"Plant roses and be prepared to grasp the thorns," Toop repeated the statement by rote, his mind elsewhere. Not lost but held, suspended in one specific place, reliving the moment of weakness over and over.

The memory of warm skin on skin.

The thoughts came at once, no separation between one and the next, silently shelling the insides of his skull. He gripped the sides of his pint as he worked through them. The tyre tracks, the note on his car, roses, thorns.

No.

The strength seeped from his limbs. The niggling thought, the one that had been trapped at the back of his mind, found its way to the surface.

"Fergus?" asked Sally. "Are you ok?"

"No," He stood up and retrieved his jacket from the back of his chair.

"What is it?"

A moment of silence passed. Toop scanned the room with his eyes, not focusing on anything in particular. There wasn't anything in particular that he was looking for. The image, the one that he could see, it wasn't on the walls of the pub, it was inside his head. The remnants of a memory.

Toop closed his eyes and tapped his fingers off his chin as the words fell under his breath. He didn't attempt to make eye contact.

"Our executioner," he said, "has a name."

"You know you he is?"

"She."

"I don't understand," said Sally, also standing.

"I didn't see it the first time," said Toop, speaking for his own benefit. "It was too dark. But in the van, I remember catching a glimpse of it. It didn't register at the time, but I can..."

"What didn't register? What are you talking about?"

Toop was miles away, consumed in his own monologue.

"There was something covering it, distorting it. It was as if she was trying to conceal it." He wagged his finger in thin air and turned on the spot. His eyes caught on the ceiling as he frowned. "I just can't quite..."

"Concealing what? Ferg... Fergus!" Sally shook his arm. "What's going on?"

The abrupt human contact brought him back and he looked directly at Sally. She stared back at him, pleading with her eyes.

"What is it Fergus?"

"She..." He faltered. "She had a tattoo on her hipbone."

A second pause.

"Of a rose."

Chapter 72

Late 80s

A child's boot

McNab stared at the item on his desk, the anger building inside of him.

It was knitted, white and pink wool with a crimson ribbon sewn into the hem.

He recognised it straight away, there was no doubt. He recognised it because his mother had knitted it. One of Isla's boots, the pair that she wore to sleep in. McNab couldn't say for sure who had sent it, there was no name but he had made the assumption the moment he'd opened it. He reached over and placed the delicate sock in the palm of his hand. This game, this twisted scheme that he was a part of, it was starting to piss him off.

Royally.

He tightened his first around the soft wool, digging his nails into his skin. Then he felt it, a slipping sensation, lubricated like silk on silk, not the harsh fabric of wool. McNab opened his fingers, the crushed boot releasing from his grasp. There was something inside, a slip of smooth paper. He pulled it out revealing a note written in black biro. One word.

Ecclesiasticus 15:14-16

Anger pulsed through him and McNab gripped the edge of the desk as he stood up. He had had enough.

"You..." he shouted across the room, a little too forcefully.

The young, fresh-faced officer turned his head, his hand still held on the coffee pot. His eyes searched the room for the voice.

"Yes you," said McNab. "Can you find me a copy of the Bible? The station should have one somewhere."

The lad stared back at him, a look of confusion crossing his face, his mug about to overflow.

"Today please," added McNab, returning to his seat.

The young officer left the mug sitting by the filter and ran off. He returned a few moments later, Bible in hand.

"Thank you," said McNab, his face hung over the book as he flipped through the pages. He paused, feeling guilty, and looked up at the officer. He managed a smile, or at least something that didn't resemble a grimace. "You might want to pour yourself another coffee, I think Brodie took yours." Pause. "And if you could bring me one it would be much appreciated."

The lad glanced at the three empty mugs on McNab's desk before answering. "Yes sir."

Fresh coffee in hand, the mug suspending an inch from his lips, McNab found it.

Ecclesiasticus 15:14-16: When God, in the beginning, created man, he made him subject to his own free choice. There are set before you fire and water; to whichever you choose, stretch forth your hand.

McNab could hear his father's voice as he read it. It sounded like something that he used to say to him as a teenager, one of his father's many lessons. The McNab household had followed an alternative approach to parenting, a more pious method of dealing with the misguided choices of a hormonal boy. His father had never been one to show sympathy. There were no second chances, no leniency.

"Other than life itself," his father used to say, "free will is the most precious gift that our Creator gives us. Our actions are our own responsibility, how we act is a consequence of free will, otherwise your punishment would be in vain."

Free will, thought McNab, searching for a pen. He reached for the nearest piece of paper, scribbling the passage down on the back of an envelope. He paused, lifted the paper and turned it over. No postage stamp, just his name. The third envelope. He had forgotten about it, distracted by Jon's visit. McNab flipped it over and ripped it open with his thumb. There was no cryptic clue this time, just three simple words.

Welcome to hell.

McNab swore and threw it across the room, ignoring the sudden turn of heads, and kicked the bin at his feet. Anger, fear, helplessness. The three emotions hit him at once. It made no sense and yet it made perfect sense. Every one of these messages had a purpose. He just didn't know what it was.

He kicked the bin a second time and took a deep breath.

"You can do this," he said to himself. "Piece by piece. Two can play at this game, you just can't let him get into your head..."

The thought froze McNab to his seat and his eyes glazed over as it hit him. The message, all of it, everything was connected.

To free will.

He mouthed three words:

"Into your head."

McNab's eyes focused and he looked down at his note pad. It was there, right in front of him, Bill Anderson's message.

The devil makes scared children of us all.

Caroline. Donaldson. Anderson. Someone, or something, was controlling their actions. Making them do things.

McNab grabbed for the phone and dialled in the number from memory. A young female answered.

"Good morning, you've reached Doctor Green's office. How can I help?"

"Is Kate in? I need to speak with her."

"May I ask who is calling?"

"Tell her it's Angus."

"Just a moment please."

The phone went silent.

"Angus, is that really you?" Her upbeat voice filled the line. "I thought that my receptionist was high when she mentioned your name."

"Yes, it's me." McNab smiled. He couldn't help it, Kate had always had that effect on him.

"How are you?" she beamed, "I mean, it's been what, eight months, more? I left so many messages that I think your assistant began to feel sorry for me! He even started trying it on, a cheeky comment here, a flirtatious hint there." She giggled. "But I understand, new dad, big promotion, no time for idle chitchat with your ageing high school sweetheart."

"Kate, I'm..."

"Sorry. I know, I know. Mr big shot Detective Chief Inspector is terribly sorry. It's a good thing that I don't hold a grudge then isn't it! How could I possibly stay angry at you, Chipmunk."

"Oh god, it's been years since anyone called me that."

"It always was a shame that you outgrew your hamster cheeks. I for one thought that they were very endearing."

"I'm afraid that the entirety of the football team tended to disagree with you, quite vocally if I remember correctly."

"Oh, come on, they only chucked you in the skip once. That's practically mandatory, all part and parcel of the secondary school experience."

"I don't seem to recall you ever being thrown into the skip?"

"Well no, but then I had cute, normal person sized cheeks," laughed Kate.

McNab smiled, twenty-five years falling away in a matter of seconds.

"When did we get so old, Kate?"

"Speak for yourself, Granddad!"

A comfortable silence passed between them, a moment of fond reflection, then Kate continued.

"Now Angus, tell me, how can I be of assistance? I'm going to go out on a limb here and say that you didn't phone to reminisce about the wonders of high school."

"Well no." The anger and fear returned in an instant. "It's about a case that I'm working on."

"Drugs related?" replied Kate. Her light-hearted manner gone, replaced by the professional tone of a world renowned pharmacist.

Kate Green was not your ordinary girl next door. She left high school at seventeen years old with a scholarship to Oxford University to study chemistry, fully funded. Her yearbook was signed, 'most likely to win a Nobel prize,' a foresight that proved to be almost accurate. At only thirty-nine she was earmarked to win the International Prix Galien for best pharmaceutical agent, an award considered to be the industry's highest accolade for pharmaceutical research and development.

An advanced clinical degree coupled with years of experience in both drug manufacturing and clinical patent management shot her to the top in her field. But that wasn't the reason that McNab had picked up the phone, well not the only one. Kate Green had a secret passion, an unusual infatuation with the lethal effects of dangerous and illegal drugs. A love of mayhem and medicine she called it.

"Maybe, well, I think so," replied McNab. "I was hoping that you could answer that question."

"Go on." He could hear the interest in her voice.

It took the best part of fifteen minutes, a couple of flicks through his notepad and an extra scan of the Bible but he managed to get her up to date on the case, on everything. He didn't leave out a single detail. He figured that he needed all the help that he could get.

She listened. Not interrupting once. He could hear her breathing, her lips held inches from the handset. McNab found himself listening to the gentle scratching of lead on paper as she jotted down notes, the sound unbroken.

The scratching paused a few moments after his finishing statement.

He waited two minutes.

"So?" asked McNab. "What do you think? Is it drugs?"

"Angus."

McNab frowned, she sounded different somehow, nervous.

"Angus, you have to listen to me very carefully," said Kate. "You need to go home, kiss your little girl on the head and pour a glass of wine for your wife. Then leave this whole thing alone. Sign it off as a suicide and walk away. Please Angus."

"I don't understand Kate. What's going on?"

"Angus, you can't win this one. Please, you have to let it go."

"Kate, what are you talking about, what are you trying to say? Why can't I win?"

"Because you're fighting the devil, Angus."

Chapter 73

Present Day

Lucy could feel the wine.

She felt confident, not quite herself. She looked down at her fingers, the words flowing more liberally from the nib of her pen.

I would have thought that getting a gun would have been the hardest part. Wouldn't you? But perhaps it's just me, naive little Lucy.

As it turns out, it is both easy and cheap to get your hands on a gun. The variety of weapons floating around the streets of Glasgow is quite extensive. Alex sorted the whole thing out, she wouldn't even let me go with her. Too dangerous she said. She made all of the arrangements, made sure that she got something light, a gun that could fit comfortably into a pocket and wouldn't feel too cumbersome in the palm of her hand. Of course, there was never any question. It was always going to be her finger on the trigger. Not mine. Not delicate little Lucy.

An 8mm Baikal.

A converted air pellet pistol, at least that's what I've heard – originally used to fire tear gas pellets. Also, it may interest you to know that according to the BBC, the Baikal is today's weapon of choice. You can find one in pretty much any poverty-stricken estate in Glasgow. Quite sad really but there are more teenage wannabe gangsters in the East End of the city than you can throw a stick at. Little crews of kids running around with these lightweight hand guns stuffed down their diapers. A good price and they'll hand one over. No questions.

It breaks your heart.

But there you have it, the murder weapon. You now have written proof that we used a Russian self-defence pistol, an 8mm Baikal, to kill our father. Condemning evidence, written in black and white that you can march straight to the police station.

Like I said, it's up to you.

But let me continue, the story has not reached its end. Far from it.

I took the bus up North just before it happened. Alex, as I mentioned before, was already living there. To be safe we stayed out of Gairloch, too many eyes. Alex picked me up from a lay-by on the side of the A890. From there we drove to Coulags, a tiny hamlet in the middle of nowhere and dumped the van in a small parking area just past the bridge. Alex took her bike but she pushed it, occasionally throwing the frame over her shoulders when it got too steep, so that we could walk together.

Two sisters on their final journey.

We stayed the night in the small bothy, I can't remember the name. Alex had instructed him, sorry our dad, she instructed our dad to come up from the other side, from the Torridon hotel. He was to sell his car for a quarter of the value and to make the walk up in sandals, no technical outdoor gear, no walking boots. Alex was quite insistent. It had to look just right, she said.

Like suicide.

I never understood why he complied with her demands. I don't know what Alex said to him, how she manipulated him, but he had to have known. He must have realised that it was a trap. I couldn't understand it. I didn't understand, not until that night, not until I looked into his eyes and the explanation became clear. It was simple. He knew that he had come to die.

He just didn't care.

I remember his face as clear as day. I don't think I will ever forget it. It's hard to explain, that feeling when you cross eyes with your father for the first time. A man, faceless and distant, that you had only ever dared to dream about. I don't think I can explain it. I mean, I was meant to hate him. He was a criminal and a rapist wasn't he? He was a bad, selfish man who had abandoned his daughters and violated their mother. I was meant to despise everything about him, to feel repulsed, sickened by his presence. But I didn't. I kept searching his face, desperate to find something, to find evidence of this horrible person that I'd grown to hate. It had to be hiding there somewhere, the evil, concealed somewhere behind those eyes. But it wasn't. I couldn't see it. And after twenty-six years, he was there. My dad was sitting in front of me. A defenceless man dwarfed by his surroundings. He looked so small. A tiny, insignificant pinprick lost in the shadows of the vast, mountainous horizon. So small.

I stood frozen, wordless, as Alex beat into him. She screamed at him through the rain, each word tearing into his flesh like a lash from a whip. There was so much anger in her. I remember feeling scared, my legs shaking beneath me and I think that I started to cry. I'd never seen my sister like that. Over time the hate had consumed her, poisoned her. There was more hurt in her than I could have imagined.

As I stood there watching her, time seemed to slow and speed up at the same time, distorted by the blasts of bitter wind. Nothing seemed real, nothing felt solid. It could all have been a show, a tasteless charade. I remember biting the inside of my mouth and willing myself from the nightmare, recoiling as she slapped him hard across the face. The crack of skin on skin seemed to echo in the hollow air, a sound now embedded in my memory. Then time stopped, a nightmare made real in an instant, a surer, more palpable reality than I have ever known. It's a strange thing Cece, but there is nothing that cements the surety of life more than the proximity of death. The image of the gun clasped in Alex's fingers is the most tangible thing I've seen. The most afraid I've ever felt.

And he just sat there. He didn't call for help or attempt to run. I stared at him, searched his eyes but it wasn't there. There was no fear in his face, no anger. It sounds crazy but in that moment it was as if he had found peace. When I looked at him all I could see was contentment. I'm not saying this to try and make myself feel better or to help ease your pain.

I have no reason to lie to you. There is nothing left for me to lose, nothing and no one.

You don't have to believe a word that I say. But I swear that standing there in the rain, a gun pointed at his chest, he smiled at me, not with his lips but with his eyes. It was the last thing I saw before I started running.

Alex was shouting at me.

"Go. Leave. Just leave."

I ran. Not looking back. Not pausing, just one foot in front of the other. I ran and I counted. I don't know why I did that, the counting. Numbers have always helped to settle my mind, calm me somehow, so I guess it was just out of habit. It gave me something, anything else, to focus on.

Forty-five. 45.

The number still haunts me. Forty-five. Four. Five. Forty-five.

That's when I heard it, a single gunshot.

The rest of the day dissolved as a blur and as much as I try I can't seem to retrieve complete memories of it, just intermittent blocks of time that are returned to me in snapshots. I remember my ankle hurting when I got in the van but I have no recollection of the drive back to Big Sands campsite, just a faint memory of leaving the van keys for Alex. I think I stashed them behind the front wheel, possibly the driver's side. Not that it matters. What did matter was that the van, it was Alex's alibi of sorts and it couldn't be left anywhere near Torridon.

The next thing I remember is waking up in a bunk bed at the hostel. I don't know how I got there or when I fell asleep. I just remember waking up alone.

Fatherless. Motherless. Sisterless. Pathetic and alone.

And do you know what Alex said, the last thing that she said to me before our father arrived? She hugged me in close and whispered, "At some point every rose has to die." I didn't understand it at the time but now I realise that she was talking about us, me and her. She was warning me that what we were doing had a price. It was her way of saying good-bye. With that sentence she fractured the sacred bond between two sisters, smashed it to smithereens.

Was it worth it, you ask? It's not a difficult question to answer. I don't need any time to think about it, no deep contemplation. The answer is simple.

No.

But if I could turn back time, if Alex asked all of those things of me once more, I would do it all again, without hesitation. I would do anything for her. Even knowing the cost, I would follow her to the end. For a while, just after it had happened, I tried to convince myself of my innocence. I didn't kill anyone, not technically. But in truth, I am no less guilty than her. The crimes were ours. Together.

Sorry, I'm almost at the end, there's just one step left.

Step Four: Vanish.

It was all planned in advance. Alex would continue to live as Eve Stone and I was to return to Glasgow. No direct contact. No slip ups. No looking back. I had to forget everything. All that I had known, all that I had been, had to be buried in the past.

New Lucy. New job, new friends, new flatmate - but of course you know that.

So dear Cece, my dear cousin (yes I worked that bit out) there it is. My life.

The true true.

One insignificant life, a mass of tiny atoms that will one day dissolve and float away in the breeze, finally finding peace.

Lucy signed her name, folded the paper, and tipped the last remnants of the bottle into her glass.

Chapter 74

"So what now, where do you want to go?"

Toop was driving with Sally in the seat next to him. Bailey was sitting in the back of Sally's silver Ford. It was less recognisable than Toop's.

Sally and Toop glanced at each other, his eyes returning to the road before he spoke.

"Big Sands Campsite."

"Where she parks up?"

"Yes," replied Toop.

"Do you think she'll still be there?" asked Sally. "Surely she knows that you'd work it out eventually. If I was her I'd ditch the van and jump on the next bus. Get the hell out of dodge."

"I'm counting on it."

Toop felt Sally's eyes on him.

"So you can search her van," she said.

Toop nodded slowly.

The car fell silent. Minutes passed as it twisted along the dark coastal road. There were no street lamps, just the black expanse of the ocean.

Sally stared out the window, her own face reflecting back at her.

"I can't believe it," she said. "Eve Stone, a killer."

No one spoke for the remainder of the drive.

Eve's van was parked in the same spot.

Toop pulled the car up next to it and killed the engine. He kept his hands held on the steering wheel, part of him not wanting to move. Right now Toop was not sure that he wanted to get out of the car. Perhaps, if he just sat there, it would all stop.

He stared at his knuckles. He could still smell her.

"Fergus?" said Sally.

The sound of his name jolted him and he looked up, a second's pause, then he glanced in the rear view mirror. Bailey was looking back at him.

"Wait here," said Toop.

As he said it he opened the car door and stepped out. Sally, he knew, would be coming with him. He didn't bother telling her to stay. He closed the door behind him. She was already out of the car and standing by the front of the bonnet.

"You ok?" she asked.

"Fine."

"That's convincing." She raised an eyebrow but didn't press it any further.

The van was dark. No lights. No signs of life. Toop reached for the door handle and slid it open. It was unlocked.

As if she knew I'd be back, thought Toop.

"It's so tidy," said Sally.

She was right. Everything was in its place, neat and tidy. Bed made, dishes washed, dried and returned to their shelf. Toop glanced at the floor, noticing that the biscuits had been picked up, then he lifted his eyes and looked across to the bed for a second time.

He stood there and stared at the smoothed out sheets, at the mattress that had held their sweaty bodies only hours ago. He was aware of noise as Sally rummaged through the boxes of clothes and cleared each of the shelves. Rain drops grew heavier on the roof. Occasionally the sound of Sally muttering to herself reached him but reality didn't seem to register, not fully. All he could see was Eve's face. Her eyes. Blue.

Blue eyes and deep red hair.

Toop thought about everything that she had told him.

From Glasgow. Moved up to Gairloch a few months ago. Saved up to travel for a year.

How much of what he knew about Eve Stone was actually true? Was that even her name? He drummed his fingers off the side of his thigh. A thought took root. Their initial meeting, when she had walked into Torridon Inn, it hadn't been a coincidence, had it? She had planned everything, all of it.

The anger built in his stomach, but it was directed at him. Not her.

His initial feeling, the one deep in his gut, he had known that she was lying. There had been something about her. But he had ignored it. Not ignored, he had chosen, he had made the conscious decision not to act on it.

And why?

Because Eve Stone reminded him of his wife, of his Kara, and he had let it blind him. Toop cursed under his breath. She had even warned him, hadn't she? *I'm not her and never will be*, those were Eve's words. But he hadn't listened, too blinded by the closeness of a memory.

Toop knew that she had played him, she had led him in the wrong direction, but he couldn't bring himself to hate her. By connecting with him, genuine or not, she had given him something precious, something priceless. She had allowed him to feel.

Eve Stone had reminded him how to be human.

He looked across at the stuffed bear, a child's memento, propped up against her pillow. The fabric had started to fade and there was visible wear around the ears. Eve Stone, thought Toop, had not been born a killer. Something had turned her into one. Something or someone, had hurt her, damaged her so badly that it had broken her. Toop pictured his face, the nameless man, a corpse now lying in a drawer at the morgue.

What did you do to her? thought Toop.

"And he repents in thorn that sleeps in beds of roses."

"What did you say?" asked Sally, turning her head. She was on her hands and knees with an arm extended under the bed.

"Sorry, nothing," replied Toop.

"Come look at this."

Sally pulled the box out from beneath the mattress and unclipped the plastic lid. Toop tore his eyes from the bed and knelt down next to her. His knees creaked, not as flexible as they once were.

"You ok there old man?" smiled Sally.

He didn't answer the question but his lips curved, just enough to return the gesture.

"Just open the box," he said, the shadow of a smile.

Sally pulled out an assortment of pots and pans.

"Camping gear," she said.

"Wait," Toop pointed at the pile by Sally's knee, "pass me that bag, the blue one."

Sally handed him the toiletries pouch, watching as he unzipped it and pulled out a book.

"Exploring the Highlands by Bike," Toop read the title. He turned the hardcover over in his hand, scanning the jacket front and back before flicking through the pages.

"Makes sense," said Sally. "She did say that..."

She stopped mid-sentence.

They watched as it fell from the pages and landed on the floor between them. A yellow rose head.

"Is that?" asked Sally.

Toop stared down at the carpet. He handed the book to Sally without raising his head. Then he picked the rose up between his fingers. He pinched it carefully between his thumb and index finger, holding it up to the light so that he could examine it.

Sally lifted the book from the floor.

"Shit," she said. "Look." The book lay open on her lap. She leaned forward and held the paper out in front of Toop. "This was tucked into the back cover."

He scanned it with his eyes, not that he needed to, he recognised it straight away.

Page fifteen. A yellow rose.

He skimmed over the second paragraph, reading select points out loud.

"… as times progressed, a hidden message bloomed... it carried a great significance among young socialites.... the offering of a yellow rose could be interpreted as meaning I am not worthy of your love."

He looked up from the paper and stared at a spot on the wall behind Sally's head, thinking.

Sally lowered the page and studied the picture of the rose.

"He gave it to her," said Toop finally. He looked straight at Sally. "He must have given the rose to Eve before he died."

"I don't understand," replied Sally.

"To apologise." Toop held his fingers up, displaying the yellow petals. "Giving her this rose was an act of repentance."

Sally frowned.

"I'm still not following, why would he apologise to her if she was about to kill him?"

"Because he meant it," replied Toop. "His apology was sincere."

Sally didn't respond. She returned her eyes to the page, needing to think about it for a few moments. She focused on the page, following the lines with her finger as she mouthed the words with her lips. She turned to see Toop watching her and their eyes held for a second before he turned and continued to sieve through the box. Sally returned to the page.

She read it through. Twice.

"But why isn't he worthy?" asked Sally without looking up, her fingertips running over the image as she spoke. "What could he have done that was so unforgivable?"

No response.

"Fergus?"

She lifted her head to find him staring at her again.

"It might have something to do with this," he said, handing her the envelope.

"What is it?" she asked, "was it in the box?"

He gave a slight nod. "Just read it."

She pulled the note from the envelope. It was old and slightly discoloured. Sally read it back to him.

"Please take care of Eve, my beautiful girl.

She is proof that even thorn bushes can produce roses.

Tell her I'm sorry."

Sally lowered the letter.

"Who do you think wrote it?" she asked.

"I'm not sure," said Toop.

His eyes returned to the spot in the wall.

"But," he continued, "I'm fairly certain that this note is the reason that a little girl grew up to be a killer."

Chapter 75

Late 80s

"The sop," said Kate. "It's all connected to the sop."

She sounded flustered.

"The reference to John 13:27. It's not just a clue. He's telling you... he's actually telling you how he did it."

"It?" asked McNab.

"How he murdered Bill Anderson."

"Slow down Kate, you've lost me."

"Sorry I..."

"Kate," McNab interrupted. He spoke softly into the phone. "Listen to me Kate. It's ok. Just take a breath and start at the beginning."

McNab pictured her closing her eyes and sitting with her forehead cupped in the palm of her hand, taking a moment to slow her breathing. He counted three long controlled intakes of air. Then he heard the rustling of paper as she collected her thoughts, flicking through the notes that she had written a few minutes earlier.

Kate recited the words from the page. The tremor in her voice was only just noticeable, gone by the end of her first sentence.

"And after the sop Satan entered into him. Then said Jesus to him, that you do, do quickly."

She took a final lungful of air, relaxing into it.

"Basically," she continued, her voice fluid, no longer reading, "it means that the demon or the devil, whatever you want to call him, entered Judas' body. The devil was the sop, he was the bread, and when Judas ate it, or him, the devil possessed his mind. He made Judas his puppet so to speak."

"That's what my dad said, something to do with the devil giving Judas strings."

"You spoke to your dad?" She said it without thinking.

"I, well, I thought..."

"Sorry," interrupted Kate, "not the time, not my place."

The moment passed.

"Like I was saying, the excerpt from John, that's what first made me think about it."

"About what?"

"I'm getting to that."

"Sorry," said McNab, "go on."

"When you mentioned the second bible reference, the one that you found inside Isla's boot, there was no doubt in my mind. Ecclesiasticus 15..." She flicked over a page. "15:14 -16, when God created man he made him subject to his own free choice. Choice or free will, it's all the same," said Kate. "It was the gift that God gave to mankind."

The line fell quiet for a moment and McNab waited, the nib of his pen suspended over the pad of paper.

"It's called scopolamine," began Kate, "or the Devil's Breath."

McNab held the phone and bit into his thumb, leaving a mark in the skin. Then he began writing.

"It's a chemical," continued Kate, "a drug that is capable of blocking free will and turning its victims into passive children. I read somewhere that people under the influence of scopolamine are turned into zombies within mere minutes of being exposed to the drug. They are left completely incapable of any independent thought. Apparently, as well as eliminating free will, the drug stops memories from forming, so that even after the effects wear off the victims have no recollection of what happened to them. Or what they did."

She let the information settle.

"The devil makes scared children of us all," whispered McNab.

He ran his hand through his hair as he recited the line from Bill Anderson's letters. As he said it he pictured his Caroline and the way that she had obeyed his every word. She had collaborated without objection or pause, following his every instruction. Coherent but childlike, he thought.

"Do you know much about it?" he asked finally.

"Some," replied Kate, "significantly more than most. Scopolamine comes from the Borrachero tree, a species common to South America. The tree blooms year round with white and yellow flowers which are deceptively beautiful. However, the word Borrachero can be loosely translated to mean get-you-drunk and it is rumoured that Colombian mothers warn their children not to fall asleep beneath it."

367

A pause.

"Wait a minute," she said, stirring her monitor into life. "I wrote up a report a few months back and I think it may have mentioned it. Nothing official, just some personal research."

McNab listened to the dull click of buttons as her fingers navigated across her keypad. It took a few moments for the machine to load.

"Yes, it's here," said Kate. "Scopolamine, colloquially known as the Devil's Breath, comes as an odourless and tasteless powder." She read on. "This most deadly of illicit drugs can erase free will, wipe a victim's memory, induce hallucinations and ..."

"And?" asked McNab.

"And," continued Kate, "in high doses the drug is lethal."

"Go on," prompted McNab.

"Devil's Breath is a muscarinic antagonist, meaning that it blocks the neurotransmitters that carry information to the part of the brain that stores memory. In other words, it depresses the central nervous system and the brain can't record anything that happens."

"With Caroline," said McNab. "It was as if her mind had been wiped. She had no recollection of what had happened to her, more than three hours of her life were just gone."

"That's the terrifying thing about it," said Kate, "the memories can't get recorded because they're never formed. It's not that you can't remember. It's that there isn't anything to remember, the memory remains blank. But..." Kate hesitated. "It gets worse."

"I'm listening."

"The hallucinogenic properties of scopolamine inhibit a person's ability to make free will choices, making victims more open to suggestions. When inhaled or consumed, scopolamine can turn any individual into a mindless projection, a robot that can be fully controlled without any inhibitions. A person on scopolamine will do whatever they are told to do. Anything. "

Kate's voice faded as she mouthed the last word and the phone fell silent.

"Kate? What is it?" demanded McNab.

"Sorry, it's just... Wait, I'll read it to you."

Kate leaned in closer to her computer screen.

"In ancient times mistresses of deceased Colombian leaders were made to inhale the powder then within minutes of taking the drug they were told to enter their husband's grave, an act that they did willingly."

Pause.

"Angus, these poor women, they were buried alive. They crawled into an open coffin and they watched as the lid was sealed shut. And they did it because someone asked them to."

McNab felt his sharp chill up his back. Fear. Hesitation.

"They committed suicide," he stated.

"Yes."

McNab waited, he knew what he needed to ask and he knew the answer. He just needed a moment.

"Okay, let's start simple, work it through," he said. "First, could someone have forced Bill Anderson to inhale scopolamine?"

"That's the thing Angus," replied Kate, "According to my research force wouldn't have had anything to do with it. You see, Devil's Breath is considered most dangerous because of the simplicity with which it can be administered. It can be blown into the face of a passer-by on the street without them having any knowledge of what has happened to them. They don't know anything has happened until hours later when it's too late and they wake up in a ditch. With no memory."

Kate bit her bottom lip. "I was thinking about the break in at your house. You said that a man came to the door?"

"Yes, Caroline said that he asked her to read out an address for him. The writing was too small for him to read."

He stopped mid-sentence. *Of course. The piece of paper.*

"That's when he must have done it," continued Kate. "The powder must have been concealed on the paper. One quick breath and he could have blown it into her face."

"66b," said McNab.

"Sorry?"

"That was the address. Caroline said that the note said sixty sixty B, her last memory. The house number, it was deliberate."

"I don't understand."

"Write it down," said McNab. "Numerals. Lower case."

He listened to the scratch of Kate's pen.

66b.

"Six. Six. Six," she said, "the devil."

"Exactly."

"I don't like this Angus," said Kate. "I'm officially creeped out. Are you sure we should be..."

"I need to know, Kate," he interrupted.

"Ok," she said, straight away, without argument. "What next?"

"Let's say that Bill Anderson was drugged. Is it feasible that a man with homophobia could be asked to write a suicide note and slit his own wrists?"

"It's more than just feasible."

***

"Close the door."

Tom did as the man instructed. He turned the key in the lock and walked across the office, taking a seat across from his father. Only the desk separated them.

"How's Jon getting on?" asked Mr McGraw.

"He's doing ok," replied Tom. "Coping."

"I'd like you to find him a flat, somewhere with a work space."

Tom frowned.

"He won't be working out of Granddad's shop?"

"No."

Mr McGraw got up and walked round the desk. He left his walking stick leaning up against the wall, the hunch gone, no need for the charade. He sat on the corner of the desk and rested his hands on his knees.

"I think it's best that Jon has somewhere private, his own place where he can get away from people."

Tom nodded.

"I know someone," continued Mr McGraw, "he's leaving Glasgow, selling up and moving abroad, America I'm told. Anyway, he has a small place in Bearsden and I've told him that you'll be round to have a look, a favour before it goes on the market."

"That's quite far out of the centre."

"I think Jon will like it."

Mr McGraw stood up and returned to his seat. He opened a drawer, pulled out a brown folder and placed it on the desk in front of them.

"This is his first job. I want you to help him out with it, show him the ropes."

Tom reached for the folder and flipped it open.

"So he passed your test then?" asked Tom, "with the police officer?"

The question was more rhetorical that analytical. Tom didn't expect a reply and besides, they wouldn't be sitting there having the conversation if Jon hadn't passed. Tom tilted his head towards the folder and started reading, scrolling across the words without commitment. Left-to-right, left-to-right, repeated on rote. He feigned the act, pretending to read, but his eyes gave him away. A restless darkness clouded his expression and his breathing was too heavy.

"It's a straightforward job," said Mr McGraw, "a watercolour. The boy needs to get his water wings established before he moves on to paint. It's a Salvador Dali. The household name should keep it simple to start with and help us to wean the money out from those clueless bidders. I've included a selection of examples to help match style but from what you've told me the boy knows Dali well enough."

Tom lifted his head. He hadn't retained a single word. He pushed the folder aside and looked straight at his father.

Now, he decided, they were going to talk about it.

Right now.

He couldn't let it go, not this time.

Someone was dead and Tom needed answers.

Chapter 76

Present Day

The feeling of claustrophobia was insufferable.

She couldn't breathe.

Air, there's no air.

The lack of oxygen built with each passing second and she could taste the carbon monoxide rising around her. Her throat itched and her lungs contracted violently, struggling to locate an oxygen source. She tried to move, desperate to find the surface, but her limbs were being crushed. Her arms and legs wouldn't respond. They were pinned to her body, constricted by the walls of her prison. She pushed then outwards with desperate bursts of energy that caused her muscles to knot and spasm. But each time her arms, two weakened lumps of flesh, were beaten back by the cold touch of wood.

Four hard unmovable walls.

She could smell trees, a musty, earthy odour, like walking through a forest. But it wasn't pleasant. It reminded her of the scent of mould or rotting wood. Her brain toyed with her. It offered fragments and disconnected clues that hinted at her location.

Wood. Mould. Dark.

She pressed her bare forearms outwards, only managing a few centimetres before they connected with the edges of her cage. The panic started to rise in her chest and she started to feel nauseous. The walls pushed back.

Smooth. Flat. Cold.

It was dark; a complete, endless dark. She couldn't see anything. She tried to peer into her surroundings but her pupils refused to dilate. The blackness was smothering; it was a solid, tangible thing. It was on top of her, pressing down on her body. Her heart started to race, tears burned into her cheeks.

Wake up! Wake up!

Her mind screamed a hysterical, high-pitched screech that bled through the insides of her skull. The fear was instant and paralysing, strangling every part of her body.

A coffin. She was in a coffin.

She cried out. Again and again. But not a single sound left her lips.

Then she felt it, a terrifying sensation that held her eyes open in wild panic. The first granule of dirt. The soil dripped into her mouth as she screamed. She couldn't close her mouth, it hung open as a crevasse, the muscles refusing to respond. Another drip, then another, then another. Soon it poured into her throat, clumps of wet mud clogging her airway.

She could feel the perspiration on her face and body. She couldn't move. She couldn't breathe. She was going to die.

She was buried in hell.

Lucy bolted upright, the sheets of her bed soaked, drenched in her own sweat.

Her mind pulsated, disorientated by her foreign landscape. She threw her hands to her mouth and clawed at the insides of her cheeks with her fingers. The sides of her mouth started to bleed and she bent over on the bed, collapsed in a heap of exhaustion.

The seconds passed as minutes and the nausea and confusion started to subside. Lucy tilted her head to the side and scanned her room through bloodshot eyes. She listed the surrounding items off in her head, taking a few moments to orientate herself.

Bed, desk, window, wardrobe.

Then she stopped, the fear gripping her stomach.

Something was wrong.

She could feel it.

Chapter 77

Eve pushed the door and walked straight in. No knock.

The smell of damp hit her first, a stale earthy scent that resonated from within the walls. The aroma of damp filled the house, masked only by the haze of cigarette smoke. She stood in the hallway and looked down at her feet. The carpet was stained with remnants of mud, dirt that had been dragged through the house by dirty trainers. It reminded her of her childhood, of a life lived in and out of foster homes. Not homes, that wasn't the right word.

She was standing staring at the floor when he called out to her.

"Hey you! What the fuck are you doing in my house?"

Eve looked up at him through her eyelashes. Her target.

Kyle MacPherson stood at the end of the hall. He was more than a head taller than her, wearing baggy sports shorts and a white singlet that failed to cover his large frame. His wide shoulders and spherical, boulder-like neck muscles completed the image. It was clear that he worked out, a lot. His left arm, full of knotted muscles, hung parallel to his body with his fingers gripped round the wooden shaft of a baseball bat.

"You deaf, bitch?"

He made a step towards her. Eve's eyes remained focused on the weapon that swung by his side.

Kyle MacPherson wasn't letting her down. He would do very nicely.

MacPherson wiped the back of his right hand across his stubbled face and pushed out his chest. An immovable mountain.

"Last time I'm asking nicely, sweetheart," he spat, "or I'll beat it out of you. I said, what the fuck are you doing in my house?"

Sweetheart, thought Eve. *Wrong move.*

She slipped the blade round into the palm of her hand and held it up so that he could see.

"I hear that you like to mess with little girls," she said.

She ran at him, not giving him time to respond, and threw all of her weight into his body. He staggered backwards, taken aback by the sudden burst of movement, but the man mountain moved no more than an inch. The impact sent a shock of pain down the right side of Eve's body, crushing the air from her lungs.

"Crazy bitch!" he yelled.

MacPherson grabbed her wrist, lifting her from the ground like a piece of bait on the end of a line. Eve kicked out with her legs, squirming as she felt the bones in her hand being snapped, crushed by the strength of his grip. She screamed out, her legs thrashing in mid-air. He bent her hand backwards, twisting it all the way back until it cracked and Eve dropped the knife.

The pain was excruciating.

He released her, dropping her body to the ground in a broken mass.

"Crazy whore," he cursed, spitting on her collapsed frame.

Eve lay on the floor in the foetal position, not moving. Seconds passed before she started to retch, the alcohol stirring in her stomach as the shock wore off. The urge to be sick was overwhelming. She hoisted her upper body from the ground with her good arm. Then in one swift movement she kicked her foot out. The end of her toe connected with the hard of his shin and he swore loudly.

"Fucking bitch!"

The full force of his foot penetrated her stomach, almost enough to make her pass out. But she refused. Screaming in agony Eve lashed out and grabbed his leg, leeching on to him with all available limbs. He tried to kick her off but Eve sunk her teeth deep into his calf and drew blood.

MacPherson looked down at the girl attached to his leg. Eve could sense the wild hatred in his eyes and she could feel the anger that pulsed through his veins. Eve managed a smile, the blood running between the seams of her white teeth. This was it. Either she had to kill him or he was going to kill her.

The first impact pierced through her body like a hot poker, the bat connecting with her right shoulder. The wave of searing pain shot through her muscles as he lifted the weapon for a second time, bringing it down on her outer thigh.

Eve clung tighter. She bit deeper.

That's it, big boy, she thought, don't let me down now.

A third blow, then a fourth.

Eve's world started to fade away from her and she felt lightheaded, drunk almost. Her head fell limp, no longer supported by her neck. It hung there heavy and lifeless as the blood dripped from her mouth. She tried to stimulate her lips, opening and closing them in slow motion but she couldn't locate each breath. The air seemed thinner somehow, out of reach. She stared down at her arms, suddenly aware of how weak she felt, too weak to hold on any longer. She was falling, slipping in and out of the present as all the strength leaked from her.

"Stop! Stop!"

The fifth blow never came.

Eve turned her head. The voice was coming from nowhere and everywhere at the same time.

"Leave her alone."

She couldn't place it. The voice, where was it coming from?

Eve didn't notice MacPherson drop the bat on the floor, run for the back door and slam it behind him. The fourth blow had connected with her abdomen and she was losing her grip on reality. She was fading in and out of consciousness when the man knelt down next to her and laid her head on his knee. Eve could see his lips moving, talking to her, but the words had no sound. She didn't feel his hand as he stroked her head and tucked her hair behind her ear. She didn't feel the warmth of his breath as he leaned forward and kissed her gently on her forehead.

Before she blanked out completely Eve made out three words.

"My precious girl."

She opened her eyes a final time. His face, his eyes, she knew him.

Her last thought was simple.

Dad.

***

Toop glanced at the caller ID as it flashed up on the screen.

Gairloch Police Station.

Toop and Sally glanced over at each other. The look gave away everything that needed to be said. A call this late, never good. Toop hit speaker and the night officer's voice filled the car.

"Toop, where are you?"

Sally held the handset. Toop drove.

"Heading back into town," replied Toop, "I was out at Big Sands, following up on a lead."

"We have a problem. A 101 call just came in. Attempted murder by the sounds of it, the girl's not in a good way. Ambulance is ten minutes out."

"What's the address?" said Toop.

"It's the MacPherson place. But he's done a runner."

"I'll be there in five. Any ID on the victim?"

"Not yet, the call only came in five minutes ago. Apparently the guy heard screaming and ran into the house. Don't know much at this point, girl in her mid-twenties. Red hair."

Red hair.

Toop pressed the accelerator to the floor.

Chapter 78

Late 80s

McNab closed his eyes and sent his mind back to the image of Bill Anderson; a corpse slumped in his chair.

The perfect murder. Neat and tidy, thought McNab, no drag marks, no signs of a struggle. He pictured the half empty bottle of whiskey that sat on Anderson's desk. A nice touch, he had to admit, drunk and suicidal.

"So," he said, "someone drugged him with scopolamine, blew it in his face presumably."

He paused mid-thought as the sentence popped into his head, another line from one of Anderson's letters.

The devils breath is tasteless and odourless.

"Then," he continued, "they asked him to write a suicide, down a bottle of Jameson's and take a knife to his own wrists."

"That would explain the positive handwriting match," replied Kate.

McNab could hear her thinking.

"And," she added, "the clean incision, no defensive marks on his palms or arms. But what I don't get is the fact that Anderson knew about scopolamine, he made references to it numerous times in his letters. It's like he knew that he was going to be murdered and he knew how they were going to do it."

"So he knew his killer," said McNab.

"Quite well I would say."

A moment of reflection passed between them.

"Anderson was scared," replied McNab. "The letters, it was his way of trying to warn his son, to protect him from someone. And Allaway, he knew something too. I'm sure of it. The entire time that he was talking about what happened in Iran, and when he spoke about Bill's illness, his whole body tensed up. Like he was afraid that someone could hear him, that someone was listening."

McNab ran his hand through his hair in frustration.

"Iran," whispered Kate, just loud enough for McNab to make her out over the phone. "Read me your notes again, the conversation that you had with Allaway."

McNab read them back to her, word for word, everything that he could remember. When he had finished she let out a hum of recognition then didn't speak for a full three minutes. McNab remained quiet, listening to the click of her keyboard.

"You said that someone sent you one of Isla's boots?" she said.

"Yes," replied McNab.

"A boot, you specifically said it was one of her boots, not a shoe or a sock?"

"Yes, she has a pair of crocheted boots that she sleeps in. Caroline likes them, thinks that they stay on better when she wriggles around in the cot."

"I think," said Kate, "that whoever sent it was making a deliberate reference to Operation Boot which would highlight Bill's link to the CIA."

"I don't understand," said McNab. "What do you mean? Why would..."

"The Search for the Manchurian Candidate?" interrupted Kate. "Did you ever read it? John. D. Marks."

"No, why?"

"Well, remember a few years back I got a little bit obsessed with Project MKUltra, the CIA mind control program? I'd studied it briefly at university when I first got into pharmaceuticals but then it came up again years later at a conference. Being controversial and dangerous it caught my attention and I became obsessed with finding out everything I could about it."

"Kate," said McNab, "you had at least two weird drug-related obsessions a year, I struggled to keep up."

"Okay, harsh but fair," smiled Kate. "Project MKUltra was an illegal program of experiments that was conducted on human subjects in the 1950s. The idea was to develop a mind control drug, something that could force people to confess during interrogations, a truth serum so to speak. It was all part of the CIA's mind control programme but it was eventually stopped in the seventies, for obvious legal issues."

"The CIA was behind it?"

"Yes. And according to John. D. Marks scopolamine was one of the drugs that was used in the behaviour-engineering experiments."

"Okay, so Bill Anderson was linked to the CIA around that time, so it's possible that he could have come into contact with the drug. But that was three decades ago, why would he have anything to do with it now? I mean he was an ageing museum janitor, not some spy."

"What if he was still getting supplies, sourcing it somehow? Old contacts helping him out."

"But I don't..."

"The suicide note, his writing, it was neat?" said Kate.

"Yes."

"But you said Bill Anderson had Parkinson's disease."

"What are you getting at?"

"Scopolamine belongs to a group of drugs called anticholinergics, a specific class of drug that works by blocking the activity of the neurotransmitter acetylcholine."

"And in English?"

"Basically they depress the central nervous system, meaning that the area of the brain that registers nausea and certain involuntary muscle movements is never stimulated. According to my notes, scopolamine actually has a few medical uses. Apparently, because of the way that it blocks the central nervous system, it can be used to treat motion sickness quite effectively, well if you are willing to ignore the life-threatening side effects that is. And," she continued, "it can also be used to control the tremors brought on by Parkinson's disease."

"So you think that Anderson was actually taking the drug himself?" said McNab.

"I don't know. It's a possibility. In small controlled doses it could have helped him and it would explain the handwriting."

"But it doesn't make sense. If he was the one with the supply, how did someone else use it to kill him?"

"I don't know," said Kate. "I feel like my head's tied in a knot."

"Unless," replied McNab, "unless that's exactly what he was, a supplier. I imagine that it would have been a nice little money maker. A little illegal business on the side, make a few extra pennies."

"His own black market pharmacy," said Kate.

"All fun and games until one day a disgruntled customer discovers the drug's darker properties."

***

"Who was Bill Anderson?"

Tom looked directly at his father.

"I want to know," said Tom. "I deserve to know."

"You know the answer to that," replied Mr McGraw, maintaining eye contact. "Bill was the night janitor, he worked..."

"Stop," said Tom. He hit his fist off the desk. "Just stop."

"I'm tired, Dad. I'm tired of you treating me like an idiot, like I'm another one of your clients, a mindless pawn in one of these twisted mind games that you like to play. This charade, this whole act that you seem to get off on, it's bullshit, all of it. And now I'm done. I'm calling it. So don't you dare sit there and lie to me."

"I haven't lied to you, son."

"Of course not, because you don't lie, do you? No, you just take liberties with the truth, ration it out as you see fit. That's what you're doing right now, isn't it? At this very minute you're willing to look me straight in the eye and feed me one of your partial truths. Just enough that it's not a lie, just enough that I'll lap it up and walk away, no questions. But not this time, Dad, this time I want the truth. All of it."

He took a breath.

"What happened to Bill Anderson?"

"You're right." Mr McGraw looked down at his hands. "I was wrong to keep you in the dark." As the final syllable left his mouth he lifted his head and stared back at his son, at his own flesh and blood.

It was time.

Father and son sat in silence and for a minute neither of them broke it, appreciating the quiet for what it was, a final moment of innocence. It was the last time that a young boy would look up at his father and see the whole world.

A final moment before the admiration of a small boy was shattered.

"I'm sorry," said Mr McGraw. He didn't drop his gaze. "But I won't sit here and pretend that I regret it, that I wouldn't do it again." He didn't look away. "You can never overestimate what a father will do to protect his family."

"Regret it?" said Tom.

His father's stare was resolute and his tone unchanged, unrepentant.

"I killed Bill Anderson."
In that moment, that little boy, naive and trusting, ceased to exist.

Chapter 79

Cece had managed to get about three hours of sleep, four if you included an hour of tossing and turning.

It had been a long, slow night.

She lifted her head from the pillow and turned over to look at the clock for the hundredth time. The two luminous hands told her that it had just gone seven. The small analogue cube was older than her by at least ten years, cheap green plastic with an ivory face. As a child she had been fascinated by the glow in the dark hands, insisted on keeping it in her room. Now it had pride of place in her dad's guest room.

Cece had decided, not that it had been much of a decision, not to go back to her new flat. Lucy, all of it, it was too much to deal with at the moment.

She pushed back the covers, showered, dressed and walked through to the kitchen. Two cups of coffee and a bowl of cereal got her to eight o'clock. The need for food was the last thing on her mind, but for lack of anything better to do she dug a piece of bread out from the freezer and put it in the toaster. Time was going painfully slowly. She turned on the radio, suddenly conscious of the fact that the house was too quiet. Music had been an integral part of her childhood and growing up, the Radio 2 breakfast show had leaked throughout the entire house. It was a ritual that occurred every morning without fail, even on Christmas when the show was pre-recorded. Terry Wogan had, without any knowledge of her existence, played a fundamental part in her upbringing. Cece got a plate from the cupboard, retrieved the toast, only partially burnt, and spread it with honey.

Part of her was glad that her dad wasn't there. She wasn't sure what she would say to him. But more of her was worried that she hadn't heard from him. On cue, as the thought caught on her brow, her pocket buzzed. Cece grabbed her phone and read the words that materialised on the screen. One new message. Dad. She swiped the touch panel before the text alert had time to disappear.

Do you have a photo of Lucy? Dad.

"That's it," Cece's frustration spilled out into words. "That all the information I'm getting."

She typed in a message.

I have a couple of pictures from the night that we met.

Send. Her fingers instantly started composing the second message.

Are you ok? Did you go to the police? Did you see the body? Her thumb hovered for a moment. *Is it Jon?*

Send.

Her phone vibrated instantaneously.

Can you send them to me?

A second buzz.

Sorry sweetheart. Will update you soon. Love Dad.

Cece attached two photos and pressed send. No words. No love Cece. Feeling angry and out of the loop, she put the phone back in her pocket.

Now back to waiting, she thought, useless and in the dark.

Maybe some light distraction would help. Maybe it would make the time pass quicker.

Grabbing a piece of fruit from the bowl, out of boredom rather than hunger, Cece padded down the hall to the living room and turned on the TV. It took her thirty seconds to flick through all of the channels, nothing of interest, before settling for one of the many breakfast chat shows. A b-list celebrity, a young woman whose face she might have seen before, was attempting to make an omelette. The catch was that the almost recognisable blonde had to do it in under one minute. Riveting watching.

Of the two potential celebrities that faced the challenge, both failed. Two eggy messes and a slur of commiserations were followed by a live performance by The Script. It wasn't bad, watchable at least. The band, a group of likeable Irish hipsters, were on their third song when Cece felt her phone vibrate against her thigh. She pulled the device from her pocket and unlocked the screen.

One new email.

Subject: DNA Test Report. Client reference: 675832fy.

This was it.

She sat cross-legged on the couch with her body hunched over the phone. She tapped her finger on the email, her heart stalling, and paused as the page loaded. Cece watched, her eyes glued to the line of purple dots that darted across the screen. A brief moment then a table of numbers and codes flashed up. The columns of data meant nothing to her, incomprehensible scientific jargon. She scrolled down until she found a paragraph written in plain English. Her lips synced with the words as she read them.

The DNA from the alleged parent was compared to the tested child. Based on the testing results obtained from the analysis of the provided DNA the probability of paternity is 99.9996%. Therefore the alleged father is not excluded as the biological father.

"Shit," said Cece.

The result was positive. Jon, he really was Lucy's Dad.

She sank back into the couch, the phone falling limp in her fingers. She sat there, unmoving. Both of her eyes stared ahead blankly, not focused on anything in particular. The sound from the TV washed over her in a mute wave. She didn't hear the reporter until he was halfway through his monologue.

One word made it through the haze.

Gairloch.

Cece grabbed the remote from the table and turned up the volume. Footage shifted from the news studio to a live feed. The scene that appeared on the screen was one that she had seen a hundred times before. The nondescript council house, sealed off with yellow police tape and a handful of concerned locals loitering on the pavement. Cece got up from the couch and sat on the floor, inches from the screen.

The TV newscaster, a pale wind-swept looking man, stared into the camera and said, "A man has been arrested on suspicion of attempted murder after a young woman was found unconscious and beaten inside his house. The woman, aged in her twenties, sustained severe abdominal injuries and pelvic injuries after being attacked.

The woman was found by a passer-by who said that he entered the house after hearing a female screaming. She has since been airlifted to hospital where she is being treated. Her injuries have been described as life-threatening.

Gairloch police arrested a 26-year-old man from Glasgow found running from the scene. A spokesperson from the police said that inquiries were ongoing and that they are trying to establish how the young woman came to be in the house late last night."

Cece spent the next ten minutes in silence, frozen to the spot by a single thought.

It was Alex.

She had no evidence, no proof that she was even in Gairloch. But the girl, the young woman beaten and fighting for her life, it was Alex.

Cece just knew.

That's why her dad had run off to Gairloch, why she couldn't go with him. It wasn't about identifying her uncle's body or saying his goodbyes. It was about Alex. He went to find her.

Cece was sure of it.

And now she was in hospital. Beaten within an inch of her life, that's what the reporter had said. A 26-year-old man arrested for attempted murder. Cece felt ashamed, embarrassed by the sudden feeling of relief that hit her. The voice inside her head telling her that it wasn't her dad, he couldn't have killed her. Her dad was too old. Cece wiped the tears from her eyes, ashamed for doubting him, even for a second.

Her dad, he wasn't a murderer. A con artist and an art forger, yes, but not a killer.

Cece stared down at the carpet. She had to get out of the house. She lifted her head and glanced out of the window. It was pouring, that constant, wet rain native to Glasgow.

She needed to find Lucy.

No one, thought Cece, no one deserved to learn about their sister's death from an anaemic looking news reporter. Grateful to have a purpose, a distraction from thinking about her dad, Cece jumped up from the floor and ran through to the guest-room, threw open the wardrobe and grabbed her shoes. She moved the hanger from right to left, sifting through the small collection of clothes that she kept at her dad's.

No jacket. Damn.

She stood up, settled her hands on her hips and rocked back and forth on her heels as she tried to conjure an image of when she had last used her waterproof.

Damn again.

She had last worn it the day that she had broken into her uncle's place. Great, she thought, a whole lot of good it was to her there. Cece turned on her heels and walked across the hall into her dad's bedroom. Plan B. Borrow one. She grabbed the first vaguely shower proof item that she could find, zipped it up and stole a quick glance in the mirror. It was far too big, but it would do. Then something stopped her. She caught a glimpse of it as she turned away from the mirror. Her dad's electric razor, the high tech one that she had bought him for his birthday, was discarded on the floor.

Strange, thought Cece, kneeling down by the bed to pick it up, her dad never shaved in the bedroom, he always used the washroom upstairs. As she reached her hand out to lift the razor she noticed a piece of paper concealed beneath the bed, a leaflet of sorts. Cece picked up the paper, unfolded it and read the title out loud.

"Home DNA Test Kit Acceptable Samples: collecting electric razor clippings."

That's when it occurred to her. Her uncle, he didn't use an electric razor. Jon didn't even own one. Impulse drew Cece's hands to her mouth and her eyes held wide in disbelief.

The envelope her dad had given her, it had been her dad's hair.

He was Lucy's father.

Cece had siblings.

She had two sisters. One who was fighting for her life and the other she had to find.

Chapter 80

Tom McGraw had let them take her.

Not a word of protest left his lips as they pulled her from his arms. She was a stranger to him. She was no one. He had to make them believe that, otherwise she had risked her life in vain.

Eve Stone.

The police kept saying it. Eve Stone. It had thrown him at first. But then, a fake name, it made sense.

He had watched as the paramedics lifted Alexandria onto a trolley, did a quick once over, then wheeled her into the ambulance. He followed her with his eyes, not once breaking the line of sight. Her head hung off to the left at an awkward angle, the stray lengths of red hair falling across her face, unsupported by her neck. Remnants of blood had dried and hardened into the cracks of her lips, leaving a line all the way round her mouth. He watched the female paramedic as she reached out a hand, concealed within a white latex glove, and slipped it under the back of her skull, lifting her head into a more comfortable position. She located a white strap with her free hand, more latex, and secured it across her forehead.

He stood on the lawn, a statue amongst the chaos. To his left, the police moved in a kaleidoscope of torch lights, a scattering of uniforms taping up the scene and wrapping it in ribbons of luminous yellow. He could hear raised voices, orders shouted across the property as the police tried to take control of the situation. Looking past the ambulance, but without taking his eyes off her, he could see the street starting to clog with cars, the array of headlights forming a dome of white in the darkness.

She looked peaceful.

As Tom stared at his daughter, a daughter who he had only known for a couple of hours, he felt a rush of mental clarity. The sense of knowing that comes when you only have one option, when the decision has been made for you.

He knew that in order to save one daughter, he had to sacrifice the other.

It was a choice that Alexandria had made for him, a decision that he had watched her make when she opened the gate and walked into that house. His daughter had walked through that door with one intention, she wanted to die. Not out of hopelessness or as a cry for help. There was another reason. He took a last glance at his daughter as the ambulance doors started to close, an inch at a time until they took her from him completely.

She was doing it to protect her sister, to save Lucy. And he would do everything in his power to honour her wish.

Tom looked up, with his hand held to his brow, and detected a small flash of light moving in his direction. The circle of light grew brighter with each pace.

The first step, he thought, would be lying to the police.

The officer walked straight up to him. He dipped the beam of his torch as he drew nearer, angling the source of light towards the grass until he was close enough that the shaft of white hung on the ground between their feet.

"Mr McGraw?" the man asked, holding out a hand. "I need to ask you a few questions."

Tom nodded.

***

Toop didn't go home.

There was only really one place for him to go, into the wild, into nothingness. He pulled his bike out from the back of his van and started peddling. He needed to put distance between himself and the rest of the world, from the cameras and the questions and the people. He had been up all night, securing the scene, talking to witnesses, communicating with paramedics, writing up reports and fending off news reporters.

Kyle MacPherson had been taken into custody, charged with the attempted murder of a woman in her twenties. No bail. He spent the night in the local custody suite, refusing to speak to anyone until he had legal representation. Eve Stone had been airlifted to hospital where she lay in bed fighting for her life. Alone but for one police guard. Toop had managed to hold the media hounds off, keeping the story out of the morning headlines, but her name would be all over the news by midday.

Eve Stone was charged with the murder of a man in his late forties, an unidentified middle aged male who had been found dead in the Torridon area.

Toop had filed the charge himself. He left the scene around sunrise and returned to his office where he sat staring at the wall, glancing up from time to time to look at the police certificate that hung by the door. Eventually he opened up his computer and compiled the report, outlining the circumstances of death and charging the accused with the offence. There was no hesitation on the part of the Procurator Fiscal, the evidence supplied by Toop was deemed sufficient and an initial charge of murder was made.

Eve Stone, suspected murderer, condemned by a yellow rose.

The weather beat into his face in constant flurries, producing diagonal sheets of rain that flooded the ground, his wheels slipping out on the loose rocks. As Toop listened to the wind he could hear her voice. She was singing to him. It was an Old Norse song that his mother had whispered to him before bed, a melody meant to soothe him as a young boy. Her voice drowned out the wind, Kara or Eve he couldn't tell. It didn't matter.

> *Land of sun and land of moonlight*
> *Land that gave us joy and sorrow.*
> *Land that gave us love and laughter*
> *We will go home across the mountains.*

Water started to run down his cheeks and he blinked back tears. Toop bore down onto the pedals, his thighs burning, and lowered his head. He opened his lungs to the vastness and screamed into the air, her voice growing fainter until finally she was gone.

***

"You're back," said Sally.

She reached across Toop's desk and handed him a coffee. His hair was still damp.

"There's a man here to see you," she said, "the witness from last night, he says that it's important."

390

"Send him in."

"Will do," Sally turned back as she reached the doorway. "You ok?"

"I'll be fine."

Sally offered a kind smile and disappeared into the hall, returning a few moments later with Tom McGraw.

Toop got out of his chair and extended his hand.

"Mr McGraw, isn't it?"

"Tom. Please call me Tom."

Toop gestured to the chair opposite him. "What can I do for you, Tom? I understand that one of my colleagues took your statement last night, you heard screaming from the street?"

"Yes that's right. I was out for a walk, clearing my head, when I heard the girl..." His sentence lost momentum and he paused. "But that's not why I'm here."

Toop didn't push it. He sensed that the man knew something and he found that not speaking was often one of the best ways of getting people to talk.

"I was in Gairloch for a reason," said Tom, "for a friend."

Toop nodded. Go on.

"The man, the one whose body was discovered by those two walkers in Torridon, I understand that he was never identified?"

"No," replied Toop, "we're still working on it."

"Do you have a photo that I could have a look at?" asked Tom.

Toop went to protest, reciting the police protocol in his head, but he closed his mouth, thinking better of it. He pushed his chair back and reached over to the filing cabinet behind him. Pulling a chain of keys from his pocket he unlocked the top drawer, sifted through the line of folders and pulled out a selection of photographs. The top two he laid on the desk, side by side, face up. Both of them had been taken at the morgue.

Tom McGraw leaned forward and lowered his nose towards the images, taking time over each one, first left then right. He repeated the action, examining the face in front of him with care. Not that he needed to. He looked up, his eyes giving nothing away. Then he placed his hand, fingers splayed, on the first photo and pushed it back across the table.

"The man in these photos is Jonathan Swan. He was my best friend."

Toop was momentarily taken aback, the surprise marked on his face.

"You're certain," he prompted.

"Yes."

Toop lifted the photos and turned them over. He waited a minute, out of respect, before he spoke.

"I'm sorry for your loss," said Toop, "it can't have been easy to learn about your friend's death over the news. I can't imagine how..." He didn't finish his sentence. Toop dipped his eyes and allowed the silence to settle for a moment before continuing. "But, if you're feeling up to it, I'm afraid I'll need to ask you a few more questions."

Tom nodded, "Like I said, that's why I came."

Toop retrieved a pad and pen from his desk.

"What made you think that the man on the news was your friend?"

Tom seemed to pause, preparing the response in his head, then he stopped.

"Can I show you something first?" he asked. "A photo."

"Of course," replied Toop, "anything that you think will help."

"It didn't register last night, not at first. I think that I was in shock, everything happened so fast and I wasn't sure, I couldn't be certain..."

"It's completely understandable," offered Toop. "Please take your time."

"There was a girl," said Tom, "back in Glasgow."

He raised his hand to his mouth so that his fingers covered his lower lip, then he continued. The lie he told was shaped with careful accuracy, one sentence at a time without hesitation.

"She was much younger than him, half his age perhaps. But Jonathan, Jon was smitten. He was obsessed with her. She led him on for a while, dragged him along with false promises. I can't say for certain how long it went on, I only met her once or twice in passing. Let's just say that I wasn't entirely supportive of the situation. Anyway one day she just up and left, I think something happened between them, a fight or a disagreement. All I know is that one morning she was gone and Jon couldn't cope with it, it broke him. When she ran off he was left in a very dark place, he spent long periods on his own, locking himself away in his house, refusing visitors and not answering his phone. Then about a month or so ago he disappeared, completely, without a word. My daughter and I were desperately worried about him but we didn't know what to do, he was a grown man after all and we had no way of getting in contact with him. We didn't know where he was or what he was doing. Then one day we got a postcard of a white sand beach. There were no words but we knew it was from him. When I showed it to my daughter she was so angry that she tore it up and threw it from the car window. She was very hurt by the whole thing. They had been very close you see, her and Jon, and she felt betrayed. After that we just waited until one afternoon I turned on the news and there was that same white beach. A body found in Torridon. I knew it then, that it was him."

Tom opened up his photo and handed the phone over. It was the picture that Cece had sent him of Lucy.

"That's her, Eve, on the right," he said, his gaze cold and steady. "The girl on the left is my daughter, Cece. It was taken the night that Jon met her. We were all out at a bar in the West End. She was put in our pub quiz team."

Toop held the screen in his hands and looked at the two faces smiling back at him. There was something different about her, something that he couldn't place. Her hair, it was different, longer. But that wasn't it. It was something else.

Toop handed the phone back. You just don't want it to be true, thought Toop, that's all it is.

Stop trying to deny what's right there in front of you.

It's her, it's Eve.

"Eve Stone," said Tom, running a nervous hand across his throat. "I didn't recognise her last night, I was in shock and the police arrived so quickly, everything happened so fast and I wasn't expecting to see her there. But the girl I found last night, that's her isn't it?"

"Yes," said Toop.

Toop stared at the man sitting opposite him. There was something unnerving about him, the rise of his shoulders and the way that his voice became shallow towards the end of his sentences. Toop looked down at his hands and interlocked his fingers. He twirled his thumbs round each other, giving himself a moment to think. The man, he reasoned, had no reason to lie.

It's all in your head, thought Toop, you have to accept it. Eve's guilty.

"Did she kill Jon?" asked Tom.

Sally popped her head around the door before Toop could answer.

"Sorry," she said, "but you need to take this call. It's the hospital."

Toop couldn't be certain, it was only brief, but he thought that he caught a glint of concern in Tom McGraw's eyes. But it was gone as quickly as it had appeared.

He got up and took the phone from Sally.

393

A male voice outlined the cause of death, internal abdominal haemorrhage caused by a ruptured liver, most likely inflicted by a kick to the stomach. Despite medical attention, he explained, the internal bleeding had proved to be fatal.

Eve Stone never regained consciousness.

Chapter 81

Late 80s

Tom looked at his father, put his hands together over his nose and mouth, and took a deep breath.

Tom McGraw didn't look up to many people but the person sitting in front of him was one man who he did admire, idolised even. Or he had until ten minutes ago. Now the man sitting in front of him was a stranger, a murderer. He had taken another man's life, killed him in cold blood with no remorse.

"Why?" asked Tom.

"It was necessary," his father replied.

"Necessary?"

"Bill knew too much," replied McGraw. "He was getting anxious and started threatening to go to the police. Somewhere along the line the fool developed a moral compass, said that he couldn't do it anymore and that he wanted out. He was becoming too much of a liability, a loose cannon, and I wasn't willing to see my family condemned to a life in prison. I wouldn't let that happen." His expression didn't change. "Steps had to be taken."

"What do you mean he couldn't do it? Do what?"

"Bill helped out with the family business from time to time. It was all off book of course, a sort of personal contractor arrangement. Over the years the services that Bill provided proved to be most lucrative. He helped us out with a few necessary precautions when things got a little tricky. All in all, he was a valuable asset to the business, helping out when deals turned sour or when a buyer required a little extra incentive. A nudge in the right direction so to speak."

"He helped you sell art?" asked Tom.

"He persuaded people to buy art," replied McGraw.

"I don't understand."

McGraw stood, deciding how best to answer. He walked across the room and stood in front of a fake Cezanne, a painting of a fruit bowl, with his arms crossed and his face turned away from his son.

"Joseph Mengele," he said, his eyes fixed on the still life painting. "The Angel of Death, that was the title that the Nazis bestowed upon him. He was an SS officer during the Second World War, positioned in Auschwitz as a physician for four years. Mengele was infamous for his tests, for the so-called scientific research that he carried out during his time at the camp. The man was notorious for conducting cruel, and frequently deadly, experiments on prisoners."

He paused, seeming to stare deeper into the bowl of fruit.

"Trauma-based mind control." He tilted his head to the side, examining the brush strokes. "Mengele wanted to create mind-controlled slaves, to breed human puppets that could be triggered to follow any given instruction."

Taking a step back from the painting, McGraw turned to see Tom looking up at him, his son's eyes cold and expressionless. McGraw, not breaking eye contact, retraced his steps and pulled out his chair before sitting down.

"One of the substances that Mengele experimented with was a drug called scopolamine, a tasteless and odourless powder that had the ability to remove the capacity for free will. It was a real-life truth serum, one that for a number of years was used by both the CIA and MI6 to help with interrogations. Morally questionable, yes, but effective. The British were also known to give scopolamine to their recruits to help reduce anxiety and stress during certain missions. That's where Bill comes into it. He was put on the drug when he was posted to Iran in the fifties, to help calm his nerves. Not that it did much good, poor fella. I'm told that he was never quite the same after that, never fully right," he tapped a finger off his temple, "up here."

He drew his hand to his mouth, taking a brief pause, and coughed.

"Shortly after returning home Bill left MI6 and started here as a night porter. He wanted a quiet job, away from people. He was managing relatively well as far as I'm aware, until a couple of years back when the tremors started. Parkinson's. He was going to have to pack it in but then one of his old contacts from the agency pulled a few strings and got him hooked him up with a supply of scopolamine, sources it from Colombia I believe. Anyway, it cleared him right up, no shakes. He's been on it ever since. Small doses of course."

"And he supplied you with it?" said Tom. "So that you could brainwash clients, get them to buy whatever you told them to."

"Simply put. Yes."

"So Bill knew?" replied Tom. "The whole time Bill knew what we were up to, the forgeries, the illegal sales."

"For a while now, yes. At first it wasn't a problem, he went along with it, kept his trap shut, not a peep so long as we kept paying him. But then something changed and he started to get nervous. He wanted to turn himself in, even threatened to hand his supply over to the cops. But of course I couldn't allow him to do that, it was too risky."

"So you drugged him." Tom's voice was cold. "And you told him to slit his own wrists."

McGraw nodded, "You must understand, the man would have ruined us."

Tom rose from his seat and went over to the window. He stared out at the rain as though the streaks of water would somehow tell him what to do. What to say.

It did and it didn't.

It did in that he accepted it; he acknowledged that there wasn't a decision to be made, not really. Standing there looking at the rain Tom realised that he would never turn his own father in to the police. The details of their conversation would never leave the confines of the room. From that moment forward Tom would dedicate his life to a lie so that his father would be kept from dying behind bars. But he wouldn't forgive him.

He turned back to look across at his father. He looked different somehow. Unfamiliar.

"Do the police suspect anything?" asked Tom. "Is there anything that could lead back to you?"

He sat down and looked his father straight in the eye, continuing before his father had time to respond.

"From now on you don't lie to me, do you understand that? If I find out that you have lied to me, even once, then I'm gone. You'll never see me again." His eyes flickered from side to side, not blinking. "So I'll ask you again, is there anything that connects you to Bill's death?"

"I moved the body," he replied.

A second of silence followed before he continued.

"It was a couple of hours after it had happened and I realised that I'd left my walking cane behind, so I went back for it. When I opened the door Bill was lying there, flat on his back. It didn't look right. His chair, the new reclining one, I'd made him tilt it back. I don't know why, it had seemed respectful at the time, like he was sleeping. But on reflection it didn't look natural, so I pushed the chair back up into the sitting position. I wasn't thinking straight, my mind was..." He paused. "I wasn't thinking. Anyway the police worked it out somehow, that the chair had been moved. And one of them, a younger fellow, McNab I think, he wouldn't let it go. He was getting too close. But I've sorted it, he won't be a problem."

"Dad," Tom's voice weakened, "what did you do?"

McGraw waited, allowing for a moment of understanding to pass between father and son. There were to be no more secrets. Then he leaned forward, resting his elbows on the table.

And he told his son everything.

The phone calls, the threats, the notes, the home visit. He explained in detail, without changing his tone, how Tom's grandfather had gone to McNab's house, drugged the officer's wife and left a message on the stomach of his one year old daughter.

Tom listened without comment as his father explained. When he was finished his father said that there was one final thing that had to be done, the nail in the coffin that would guarantee McNab's silence. Something that would ensure he wouldn't talk.

Ever.

But it was something that only Tom could do.

***

"So the question is, who wanted Bill dead?" said McNab, "and why?"

"Does it matter?" asked Kate.

"Sorry?"

"You can't pursue this, Angus," said Kate quietly, "think about your family."

For the first time the energy drained from McNab's voice.

"It's my job, Kate."

"Not anymore. It doesn't have to be. Write it up as a suicide, one report, case closed. The pathologist has already signed off on it. No one would question your judgement, Angus. Everyone thinks it's a suicide, it's practically a textbook example."

"Not everyone, Kate."

"Angus, listen to me. Bill's dead, you can't change that. But your wife and your daughter are very much alive and they're innocent. They're the ones who need you."

"I know that, of course I know that. But I can protect them Kate, I can look out for them and still do right by Bill Anderson. I'll get uniforms stationed at the house, twenty-four hours, day and night, until it's done."

"The department would never agree to that, a full surveillance operation. And based on what exactly, the riddles of a man on the end of a telephone. You've got nothing Angus, no suspects, no hard evidence. They'll laugh you out of the station."

"I can make it happen."

"It won't matter," said Kate.

McNab didn't respond. Kate gave him a few moments before she continued.

"I meant what I said before," she said, "you're fighting the devil. You won't win. You can't win this one. This man, whoever he is, he's said that he'll go after your family. And based on what happened at your house, he seems to be the type of man who keeps his word." She took a pause. "First it will be Caroline and after that Isla. He'll keep hurting you until you have nothing left. You have to let this go. It's not worth it."

"It's not that simple."

"Yes Angus, it is. It is that simple. It's your family."

McNab hung the phone across his face and pressed it against his forehead, his eyes closed. He counted to three before opening them again.

"I'll phone you back."

He hung up before Kate had time to argue. Then he leant back into his chair and tilted his head to the ceiling. It wasn't in his nature to give up.

He picked up the letter from his desk, the one Jon had dropped off, and turned it over in his hand, not really looking at it. He did the same with Isla's boot. What had Bill Anderson done? Who had he offended so badly that they wanted him dead?

His mind drew a blank. He had no answers.

McNab clasped his fingers around the woollen boot, looking at the tiny item. It felt soft to the touch, as if it had only just been washed.

Then his eyes darted upwards. The thought hit him in an instant.

Jon.

McNab whipped his head up so fast that it sent a sharp pain down his neck. He pictured Jon in his office, hovering over his desk only an hour earlier. The way the boy had shifted on the balls of his feet, the twitch in his fingers, something was off. It was his eyes, thought McNab, they hadn't left the floor once. He'd been lying. Of course he had, he cursed, a child would have picked up on it. But he'd been too distracted, too wrapped up in riddles to see what was right in front of him, and he'd just let him turn and walk straight out.

"Idiot," muttered McNab.

The kid, thought McNab, he knew exactly who'd given him the parcel.

He grabbed the jacket off the back of his chair and ran down the stairs. As he reached the exit he dipped his hands into his pockets to search for his keys. If he'd glanced up he would have seen the young man approaching through the glass panel but his head remained buried against his chest.

"Oh sorry, I..." the man spluttered as McNab walked straight into him.

McNab looked up. He recognised the face. But the name didn't come to him.

"Tom McGraw," said Tom, offering his hand, "I was just on my way up to see you."

"Tom yes, of course." McNab freed his right hand from his pocket and shook Tom's. "How are you? I'm afraid I'm actually on my way out but you can leave a message with Marie-Ann and I'll get back to you."

"It's about Jon."

McNab stopped and turned back, his body halfway out the door. His left arm was twisted round the back of his torso, partially threaded into the sleeve of his jacket. His right hand was extended in front of him, palm pressed against the door to prevent it from closing.

"Did he come to see you?" asked Tom.

"Yes, about an hour or so ago."

Tom lowered his eyes and frowned, looking concerned. "Oh."

"Something wrong?" asked McNab.

"Well, I just spoke to Jon and," he hesitated, "I realise this may sound crazy, but he didn't seem to know if he had been to see you or not. He couldn't remember. So I thought I'd come down and see you myself. I told him that he needed to go and speak to you, to ask about getting counselling. He's not been doing so well since, you know, since the incident."

McNab paused a moment before stepping back inside the building, letting the door inch shut behind him.

Didn't seem to know... couldn't remember.

"Shit," whispered McNab.

"Excuse me?"

"Sorry. Nothing," muttered McNab, "thinking out loud."

Had Jon been drugged when he saw him? McNab's expression tensed as he tried to remember the details of their conversation but he couldn't be sure. If he was being honest, he didn't know how to tell either way.

"Did Jon mention if he spoke to anyone," asked McNab, "on the way here I mean."

Tom's frown deepened, "As a matter of fact, he did," he lied, "how did you know that?"

"An educated guess. What did he say exactly?"

"Just that he couldn't remember speaking to you, or seeing you for that matter, but he did mention that he was stopped by an elderly gentleman, homeless I think Jon said. The man grabbed him by the arm and wouldn't let him go. He kept talking about the rebirth of Christ or some nonsense, just crazy ramblings. But it got to Jon, freaked him out a bit."

Neither of them spoke for a moment.

"Do you think Jon will be ok?" asked Tom, feigning concern.

If McNab answered the question he had no recollection of it. The next twelve hours of Angus McNab's life never made it to memory.

Chapter 82

Present Day

Life, she thought.

It was black and white. Only two choices.

You could give it away, without protest, or it could be taken from you, kicking and screaming.

Lucy stood on the platform with her eyes closed and listened.

She could hear voices. There were more voices than she could count, hundreds of faint pinpricks that accumulated in a dull haze. It reminded Lucy of the static of an un-tuned radio, no single voice more significant than the next. Occasionally a word made it through, a name or an apology, as people pin-balled off each other, fighting for space on the small concrete island at Hillhead subway station.

Lucy opened her eyes and looked across the sea of nameless faces, students, shoppers and businessmen. Her eyes paused on a distraught mother, her arms circling in the air as she tried to herd two young children away from the yellow line. She was pointing frantically at the ground then back up at the older looking child, scolding him from venturing too close to the edge. Both children looked up at her. They looked like two rabbits, their expressions frozen in the headlights.

As Lucy stared at the children she felt a cold breeze brush against her face and travel down her neck. The soft tingle was followed by the familiar sound of wheels turning on the track. Lucy closed her eyes as the draught grew stronger, drinking in the sudden displacement of air as the train approached. The walls shook as the machine thundered through the dark tunnel, its imminent arrival announced over the speaker system.

"The train now approaching Platform One is for all outer circle stations. Please stand back until doors open."

Lucy listened to the squeal of brakes and the slowing of the wheels, a metal on metal cacophony before the carriage drew to a halt. A sudden rush of activity caused the noise levels on the platform to soar as passengers fought their way in and out of the doors. Lucy didn't move. She stood with her back pressed up against the plastic barrier, her fingers curled around the handrail.

She watched.

Twenty seconds passed and the station fell into an eerie silence, the lull before the storm. Lucy listened. She could hear the clack of a woman's capped heels as they tapped against the concrete platform. There were just the two of them. The hush lasted eight seconds, broken by the distant click-click of spinning turnstiles. Another three seconds and the two escalators provided a new flow of people. Lucy looked up at the electronic board above her head. The next carriage was due to arrive in six minutes.

As the platform started to fill with strangers two people drew up next to her, positioning their bodies on either side of the handrail. The woman wore a tight black pencil skirt, a smart tailored jacket, black tights and stiletto heels. The man had squeezed his upper body into a tight Levi t-shirt, his arms having lost any semblance of muscle. Flesh bulged from the gaps in his clothing. He pulled a mobile from his jean pocket and started playing a game that Lucy didn't recognise.

"The next train from Platform One is due to arrive in two minutes."

Lucy glanced down at her watch and started counting off the seconds.

One minute. Thirty seconds.

She looked up towards the faint softening in the darkness, the two circular patches appearing from the depths of the tunnel. As the train lights neared Lucy released her fingers from the railings, took a deep breath and started to walk forward. One step at a time. She felt the cool rush of air against her skin, the gentle breeze pulling the strands of red hair away from her face.

Tears marked her cheeks.

Ten seconds.

Her feet moved closer to the yellow line. No one stopped her. No one noticed.

Soon nothing would matter.

Soon it would all stop hurting.

***

"Lucy?"

403

Cece peered her head into the apartment, her hands still held on the key as she pushed the door open.

"Lucy, it's me. Are you home?"

Her calls were answered by a stiff silence.

Cece closed the door behind her and walked down the hall. The temperature in the flat was a comfortable twenty-two but she felt cold. She wrapped her arms round her body and used her hands to create friction.

"Lucy." She tried it once more.

Nothing.

She walked into the living room. The sofa was littered with various cushions, all different colours, each neatly arranged and sitting in their place. Lucy's purple blanket, the one that she used to cover her legs in the evenings, had been folded and hung over the arm of the couch. Interior Decorating magazines covered a corner of the coffee table, deliberately overlapped and displayed in an open fan. Next to them was an ornate scented candle, cinnamon flavour. All the mugs and wine glasses had been removed and placed in the dishwasher. The room was neat and homely, just as Lucy liked it. The kitchen was the same. The surfaces had been wiped clean, Cece could still make out the scent of lemon, and the draining board was empty, not a single item of crockery.

Cece stepped back out into the hall, a sense of unease travelling up her spine. Shaking it off, she turned towards Lucy's room. She reached out her hand, turned the handle and pushed the door inwards.

Empty.

Cece's lungs released with a gentle exhale of air, unaware that she had been holding her breath in the first place.

The first thing that she noticed was the bed, it was unmade. Pillows lay scattered across the crumpled duvet, abandoned in various unordered locations. Cece bent down, picked one from the floor and returned it to the head of the bed as she sat down on the mattress. Lucy's laptop was perched on top of a discarded hoody with the screen tilted back, held up by one of the pillows. Cece lifted it with one hand and paused with her arm extended in mid-air. Something caught her eye. There were three sheets of paper crumpled beneath it. But it wasn't the paper itself that caught her attention; it was the sight of her own name.

Dear Cece.

Putting the laptop aside Cece picked up the letter and started reading. She read it through, absorbing every word.

Twice.

When she finished her hands dropped to her thighs, the pieces of paper falling limply in her lap. She stared up at the wall, finding it hard to breathe or to focus on anything. It took a minute for her eyes to readjust to the surroundings of Lucy's room.

Lucy, thought Cece, as she recited sentences from the letter.

A helpless baby dumped on the steps of a school.

A child tossed from one foster home to the next.

An innocent little girl beaten and neglected.

A teenager abandoned by a mother who she would never know and discarded by a father she thought to be a rapist.

Lucy, thought Cece, her sister.

Cece returned her eyes to the letter and ran her fingers over the sentence, barely touching the paper.

Fatherless. Motherless. Sisterless. Alone.

She stared at the four words. It was strange how things could change from one minute to the next. She had hated Lucy, wanted her punished for what she had done. And now, she was sitting on her sister's bed crying for her, wanting to hold her and to tell her that everything was going to be alright, that she wasn't alone anymore.

"Where are you Lucy?" whispered Cece.

She folded the letter, placed it on the bedside table and picked up the laptop. The screen burst into life with a touch of the finger pad.

Password.

"Shit."

Ok, reasoned Cece, just think, you can do this.

She ran her hands across the keyboard and typed in four letters.

Rose.

The computer spat straight back at her. Incorrect password. Too short. Try again.

Numbers, thought Cece, all passwords need numbers, eight characters, at least one uppercase, and numbers. Numbers, of course! She grabbed the letter and scanned through the first page, she knew exactly what she was looking for.

"The unspeakable incident of..." she muttered as she turned the page over, her eyes flicking from left to right, "... 1988!"

She reached for the keyboard.

Rose1988.

The screen unlocked and a web page flashed up.

"No," gasped Cece.

She drew her hands to her mouth, her nerves buzzing with a sense of apprehension as she read the headline.

Woman Murdered in Scottish Highlands.

***

"Pick up, pick up."

Cece paced across the living room with the phone pressed again her cheek.

"Cece?" he answered.

"Dad, oh my god, Dad, are you ok? Where are you?"

"I'm coming home, sweetheart."

Cece closed her eyes and swallowed back tears. She couldn't cry, not now.

"I know everything, Dad," she said, "the DNA test, Alex, who she is, what she did, I know all of it. Lucy and Alex... you're their dad."

"Sweetheart, I..."

"Don't apologise," interrupted Cece. "It's ok, really Dad, I understand. I'm not angry. I'm worried about you... you just lost a child."

The line remained quiet. Neither of them spoke for the next few seconds. The silence was enough.

"There's something that I have to do," he said, "for Alex. I know that I have no right to ask anything of you, Cece, not after everything that's happened, but I can't just walk away from this. I owe it to her. She died making sure that she would be blamed for Jon's death, she gave the police everything that they needed, left a trail of condemning evidence. She did it so that Lucy could be free. And now it's my job to make sure that happens."

"I want to help." Cece swallowed hard, the lump growing in her throat.

"What's wrong? Cece, tell me?"

"Lucy's gone." Her voice broke. "I don't know where she is, Dad. And she knows, about Alex. I'm scared, what if she does something, something stupid?"

Chapter 83

Present Day

After suffering through the rest of the day, through the endless slur of meetings and the paperwork, they had driven back to his house. Neither of them spoke.

The local police had done their bit, they had been commended for their hard work and dedication, but it was up to the higher powers now. It was no longer their job. Toop and Sally were free to leave.

They parked up on the side of the road, unlatched the gate and headed up the garden path, not a word between them. Inside they discarded their shoes and jackets, their two tired bodies filling the cramped hallway, before sharing a brief look and disappearing behind separate doors. Sally padded through to the kitchen and made herself at home. She searched through the bare cupboards, found a bag of spaghetti and a jar of pasta sauce, turned on the radio and, swaying her head to the sound of Jamie Cullum, poured herself a glass of red wine.

They ate in silence as the noise from the TV hummed in the background. The final few minutes of *EastEnders* played out before the evening headlines. Sally protested, tried to stop him, but Toop looked up at her, placed the TV remote on the table and sat down to his bowl of pasta.

She decided not to push it.

The credits rolled out and David Lowe's distinctive music theme came on, introducing the BBC News headlines. Toop reached for the remote, not looking at the screen and turned it up.

It was the fourth item.

"The sole suspect in a murder investigation in the Scottish Highlands has died in hospital. The woman in her mid-twenties passed away in the early hours of the morning. The local police have since confirmed her death but, for legal reasons, they have not yet released her name.

The woman died in intensive care as a result of injuries that she sustained during an attack last night. Police are saying that the incident, which occurred late yesterday, is unrelated to the initial homicide investigation and that it is being dealt with separately.

The shooting happened last month in Torridon and police have only just identified the victim as 49-year-old Jonathan Swan from Glasgow. The man, who sources have identified as being in a relationship with the accused, died after suffering a gunshot wound to the chest.

Local police have released new information about the ongoing investigation revealing that key evidence was found at the woman's residence that connects her to the murder of Mr Swan.

A spokesperson for Gairloch police has commented that they are confident that the individual responsible for the death of Jonathan Swan is the deceased person in question and they want the community to be assured of this so that they can feel safe in their own homes. The police believe that the 26-year-old woman was the sole suspect in this case and they have said that if she had survived then she would have been charged with first degree murder.

The camera zoomed in and for two long seconds the screen filled with a close-up shot of Toop's face. The frame paused as the reporter made a few closing remarks before the camera returned to the studio.

Toop pulled his chair out, dumped his plate in the sink and headed to the door.

"Fergus," shouted Sally, "Ferg, wait. It's late, where are you going?"

"Out."

He slammed the door behind him.

Chapter 84

Late 80s

The room was dark.

He raised his head, aware for the first time that he was lying down. The movement sent a wave of nausea and dizziness through his body and he suppressed a sudden urge to be sick. Lowering his head, he twisted his neck to the side and peered into his surroundings. It took a moment for his eyes to focus, all but blinded to his environment. His only point of reference was the vertical seam of light running down the wall to his right. Curtains, thought McNab, there was a window.

That was good.

He tried lifting his head, slower this time, and smelled something familiar, a faint sweetness like fresh dew or lavender. He tried to hold on to it, to locate the memory but his mind was confused. There was something recognisable in the fragrance, a known experience, but he couldn't connect it to an image. His brain was toying with him, offering disconnected fragments of information. It was as if the memory was neatly filed away in some unreadable corner of his mind, awaiting retrieval.

Where was he?

He splayed his fingers and drifted his hands outwards from his hips, extending his arms to three and nine o'clock. A bed. He was lying in bed. But whose, or where, he couldn't be sure, his brain lacking the mental capacity to work it out. Taking a deep breath he moved his hands, making small waves in the sheets, appreciating the feeling of softness beneath his fingertips. The feeling of familiarity was overwhelming, kept just out of reach by the paralysing state of confusion.

Minutes or hours passed, he couldn't say. All sense of time was lost on him, his mind dulled, paused in a disorganised mist. Little by little the feeling of nausea and concussion lessened. He tried lifting his head again, better this time, and listened out. He could hear voices, talking to one another. There were people on the other side of the wall.

Orientating his head towards what he thought was the source of the conversation, he stretched out his neck and strained his hearing.

McNab recognised one of the voices. He had heard it before, more than once, he was certain of it. He scrunched up his eyes, cursing under his breath but his brain was too clouded, it wouldn't let him think. Denying the waves of motion sickness, he pushed himself up into a sitting position, frustration clawing at his brain.

"Hello," he called out.

The voices stopped.

McNab held a hand over his eyes as light poured into the room. He squinted, focusing in on the two silhouettes that appeared in the doorway. One he recognised.

"Caroline?" he said.

He twisted his body, bending his legs and moving them towards the edge of the bed as if to get up. But her voice stopped him.

"Wait," she said, holding her arms out in front of her. "Don't get up."

McNab retrieved his legs, dizzy from the sudden movement, and looked up at his wife. Her eyes were cast downwards, only slightly, but enough that she could avoid direct contact. She switched the light on, the room instantly illuminated in a yellow glow, and stepped towards him. McNab took a moment to glance around, mentally checking off his surroundings, the wooden standalone cupboard and the old chest of drawers.

He was in their bedroom. It was his own bed.

Caroline paused at the end of the bed, her eyes flickering as she deliberated over her decision before she sat down, perching herself on the corner half a metre from McNab's feet. She sat gazing at her hands as she circled her thumbs around one another.

Something was wrong. Something in her expression.

"Sweetheart?" he asked.

She raised her head and forced a smile, still without looking at him. Not fully. Her smile started to withdraw, fading inwards from the edges, and her eyes darted back to her fingers. McNab stared at his wife, noticing the unnatural way that her shoulders were slouched forwards and the presence of a slight twitch in her right foot. He extended his arm and held his hand out towards her. But he quickly pulled it back, stung by her reaction. She had flinched; her whole body had recoiled at his gesture.

Then it occurred to him. The look in her eyes.

His wife was scared of him.

"Caroline sweetheart, please talk to me."

She shook her head slowly, "Oh Angus." She sounded shaky.

"What's wrong?"

"You don't remember?" she said, the words choked in her throat.

McNab wanted more than anything to say the right thing, to remember what she needed him to.

"I remember leaving the station. I bumped into someone just as I was leaving, a man involved with one of my cases..." The words stopped. He had no choice.

The rest was a blank.

Caroline drew her hands to her mouth, pressing her fingers across her lips in an attempt to stifle her tears.

"That was ... yesterday," she managed.

"I don't understand, Car. What's going on, how did I get here?" His eyes traced over her face, searching for an explanation. "And the person in the hall, I heard you talking to someone, who is it?"

"Doctor Ferguson," she replied. "It's the third time that he's been in to check on you." She paused, moving her body an inch closer. "Angus..." she placed a hand on his shin, her gaze lifting upwards and resting on her husband's face, "you've been out for nearly thirty hours."

She didn't pull away, keeping her eyes on him.

The fear still lingered in her eyes but there was also love there, he could see it. McNab wanted to hold her, to draw her body in close to his but he thought better of it. Small steps, he thought, reaching a hand down to his knee and stopping it two inches from the tips of her fingers.

"What happened," he asked. "Can you tell me?"

She nodded, filled her lungs, and wiped the tears from her cheeks.

"Yesterday, after an early lunch, I tried putting Isla down for an afternoon sleep. It's just, with you working such long hours at the moment, the housework had been piling up and the cupboards were empty."

Her eyes softened and her fingers touched his.

"It's not that I blame you," she continued, "I understand the pressure you're under at work, it's just hard sometimes, doing this on my own and

411

I just thought that if I could get Isla to sleep then I could get a wash on, zoom round with the hoover, then put her in the pram and take a walk down to the supermarket. But she wouldn't settle. Every time I left the room she started screaming. I didn't know what to do, I was so tired and she just wouldn't stop."

McNab squeezed her hand.

"I'm so sorry Car, I didn't realise. I can do more, I can be around more."

She waved the comment away with her hand, sniffing back tears in an attempt to remain composed.

"Really, it's ok," she said, "it's just taking me some time to get a hang of this whole being a mum thing. I love Isla more than anything and I wouldn't change what we have for the world, it just all a bit... overwhelming."

Their hands gripped tight now.

"I just needed a break so I gave in and phoned Sophie. Bless her, she said that she'd be happy to babysit for as long as I needed, told me to go to the shops, take my time, grab a coffee. That girl," Caroline managed a smile, "she really is a life saver."

McNab looked at his wife, wondering how it was possible to love someone so much.

"Sophie came over, got Isla from her cot and sang to her while I grabbed a quick shower. By the time I left the two of them were sitting on the sofa, Isla was fast asleep."

He continued to study her face as she collected her words. He had so many questions, a thousand things that he wanted to ask, but he knew that he had to tread carefully, to let her go at her own pace. He was toying with this thought when the words exploded from her mouth.

"Kate called me," she said. "When I was at the cafe."

He glanced over at her, noting the pained look in her eyes. Not jealousy, Caroline had no reason to be jealous of his high school sweetheart. If anything, thought McNab, she liked Kate. It was more than that.

She looked helpless.

"Kate said she was worried about you. She said that you weren't answering your phone." Her lower lip trembled. "The moment Kate said it I felt this intense physical pain in my stomach, like I was dying."

The last remnant of fear faded to nothing, leaving her eyes wet, clouded by a sheen of moisture. Caroline squeezed his hand harder and moved up the bed so that she was sitting in line with his chest.

"I was convinced that something had happened to you, Angus."

McNab ran his thumb across her cheek and leaned forward to kiss her on the forehead.

"I'm fine sweetheart. I'm right here."

She pulled back, still gripping his left hand.

"But you're not fine, Angus, something happened to you."

She stroked his knuckles.

"After Kate hung up I ran home. I swear I sprinted so fast that I thought my lungs would burst. And there you were, sitting on the front step with Isla. But you weren't holding her. She... she was lying on the cold concrete, inches from the edge of the step. Our baby girl was face down on the ground in nothing but a vest and she was crying. Crying so hard that her face had turned bright red and you were just sitting there, Angus. Sitting and watching."

McNab felt sick, unable to form a single word. He felt his gut wrench as Caroline continued.

"When I phoned Sophie she said that you appeared home not long after I'd left the house, half an hour or so. You told her that you'd finished the day early, said that it was a surprise and that you wanted to spend more time with the family. Then you sent her home. It was at least an hour until Kate called me," her voice broke, "meaning that Isla... our precious baby... she could have been out there for nearly an hour."

"Caroline... I..." McNab didn't know what to say.

"It's not your fault, Angus," she rubbed his arm, "and Isla's fine, the doctor checked her over and she's absolutely fine. It wasn't you, I mean you weren't you. It's like you were drugged, like someone else was doing the thinking for you. I got you up to bed and you fell straight to sleep. You slept for a day and a half."

Drugged, thought McNab, the image of Bill Anderson filling his mind. *A docile zombie, victim to the perpetrator's desires. Will-less.*

He looked over at his wife, the pain of the last thirty-six hours still visible in her eyes. As he squeezed her hand, McNab made a decision. He would do anything, absolutely anything, to make sure that his wife never had to experience such darkness again.

Even if that meant signing a murder off as a suicide.

He had lost.

It was over.

Bill Anderson's murderer would go unpunished.

***

Jonathan Swan sat staring at the blank canvas. It was easier for him to look at the cream coloured fabric than to focus on Mr McGraw's face.

Sometimes Jon didn't get people.

No, that was wrong. He almost never understood people. The nuances of social interaction were all but lost on him. It seemed to Jon that there was a whole world of communication that extended beyond the literal meaning of words, a foreign world that he didn't understand.

He listened to Tom's dad as the man detailed the expectations of his first job. It was to be a watercolour by Salvador Dali.

"An artist's style is unique," continued Mr McGraw, "it's like a fingerprint, a work of perfection that is created without flaws, and our job is to duplicate that print as best as possible. Experts know exactly what they are looking for and they know how to analyse it, so it's up to you to fool them."

Mr McGraw walked across the room and sat down next to Jon, moving his chair a few inches closer to him. Jon could feel the warmth of the man's breath on his skin. He didn't like it, he was too close. Agitated, Jon rubbed his hands up and down his thighs, resisting the urge to pull his chair away.

"You, Jon," he began, his knees touching the side of Jon's legs as he placed a hand on Jon's shoulder, "you have a great deal of talent."

The physical gesture made Jon feel nauseous but he didn't flinch, he was too afraid. There was something about Tom's father that made him uneasy.

"And with that talent," he continued, "there comes great responsibility. It is up to you to know the artist better than you know yourself. You must understand his work inside out, back, front, top, bottom and sides. No exceptions."

He couldn't be sure, but Jon thought that he felt Mr McGraw's fingers tighten on his shoulder, just enough to make his point clear.

Jon hesitated, "How do I do that?"

McGraw slowly removed his arm and leaned back in his chair.

"You must live and breathe them, examine examples of their art, talk with myself and Tom, ask questions and question those answers. Leave no gaps in your knowledge. No unknowns. Here..." he pulled out a pen and paper and took a couple of minutes to scribble down a list, "this will be your bible, a checklist for every piece of art that you complete."

Jon took the list and scanned through it. He could feel Mr McGraw watching him.

- Know the artist's brush stories and learn to imitate them.

- Understand the position of the artist's signature, where do they typically sign off their art, what medium do they sign in, do they use their initials or their full name?

- Research how the artist attaches their canvas to the stretcher bars and how the end piece is framed.

- Ensure that the painting looks authentic from the back.

Mr McGraw brought his arm across Jon's body and laid a finger on the final point.

"This here, the appearance of the back of the painting, is most important. It is where most forgers are caught out. Experts can often tell more from the back of the painting than they can from the front, so it is essential that this is done correctly." He turned to look at Jon, his face only a few inches from Jon's.

"Do you understand?" he asked.

"Yes sir," replied Jon.

"Good," he said, "you're a good boy. I have high hopes for you, for us."

He patted Jon on the leg.

"This is the start of a new life for you, Jon, and I hope that you realise the opportunity that you have here."

"Yes, sir. Thank you."

"I think we're going to get on just fine you and me."

Mr McGraw smiled as he stood up. He patted Jon on the shoulder. "Best get started. No time like the present."

He smiled again, returned his chair, and walked over to the door. He had his hand on the handle when the words blurted from Jon's mouth.

"Where's Tom?" asked Jon. Something told him that he shouldn't ask, but his concern for his friend overrode his personal sense of apprehension. "I thought that he was going to help me out, with my first one."

McGraw turned his head. He spoke slowly. "Tom won't be in for a few days. He needed some time away, to work through a few personal matters. But he'll be back soon enough."

He opened the door and went to step out, voicing a final comment before he pulled the door being him.

"You'll be fine."

Then the door closed with a dull thud, leaving Jon alone once more.

As Jon looked back at the black canvas he thought about Jenny Pingleton.

Jenny and her yellow dress.

And, as he lifted the paintbrush between his fingers, he wondered what she would think about what he had become.

Chapter 85

Present Day

Just arrived at Buchanan station. Will come straight to your flat. What subway station should I get off at? Dad.

Tom hit send and walked off the bus.

His phone buzzed back almost instantly.

Hillhead.

It buzzed again.

Meet u there.

And a final time.

Still no word from Lucy :-(Getting v worried.

He pocketed the phone, walked around the side of the bus to collect his rucksack from the storage compartment, then headed west on Cowcaddens Road. He decided to avoid North Hanover Street, making the split second decision that going via Sauchiehall Street would be quicker. He was right. It took him seven minutes to get to Buchanan Subway Station. The walk in the fresh air helped, it gave him time to think, to steady his nerves. But there was only one person on his mind. Lucy. His Lucy.

He hadn't decided if he should tell her or not, that she was his daughter. How could he tell her? The truth could ruin her, knowing that the man with a bullet in his chest, the man who she and her sister had sought to punish, wasn't who they thought he was.

Jonathan Swan wasn't their father.

He was.

It had happened the last time that they had been together, mid argument, a final moment of weakness before Jenny had left him for good. In truth, Tom doubted if Jenny ever knew who the real father was. Perhaps she did, deep down, but if that was the case, she never said a word. Jenny had been so angry with him, she had needed him to feel pain, needed him to know the hurt that she was suffering. And then Jon had come along. The two of them formed a connection from the first moment. For Jon, it was love at first sight. For her, it was a distraction. But Tom hadn't felt bitter about it. More than anything, he just wanted Jenny to be happy.

And now he wanted the same for their daughter.

As the rain started to soak into the shoulders of his jacket he pictured her face. An innocent child whose heart had been hardened by life's misgivings, a young spirit torn down by a misdealt hand.

She hated her parents. She despised the very people who she believed were responsible for bringing her into the world. Lucy blamed them for ruining her life. And now, that hatred and anger had taken her sister from her.

Parents killed. Sister dead.

She was the only one who had survived, thought Tom, and that suffering would never leave her. Not really. Her past was part of who she was, a second skin that she would never be able to shed.

But maybe he could save her, show her that she wasn't alone.

Tom stepped out of the rain and disappeared underground. He ran down the steps with one hand held on the handrail for balance, staying to the right to avoid the flow of bodies. A carriage, already packed with faces, was waiting for him as he reached the platform. He jumped on just as the doors were closing, the announcer's voice advising any late passengers to stand back from the platform.

He looked around at the other people on the subway, more heads than he could count. The benches along the windows were filled, thigh to thigh, hip to hip, and the handles that hung from the ceiling meant that people were standing in the middle walkway, a swarm of bodies crammed into the small space. Tom deduced that most people were students or business men. It was an easy assumption, based on the wardrobe of fashionable clothes, well ironed suits, and black briefcases. The majority of passengers had earphones in, were playing on their phone, or sat reading electronic books. Tom had nothing except his rucksack, so he stared at the adverts on the walls, his eyes pausing on a map of the subway. Fifteen stations were distributed over the 10km circuit of the West End and City Centre of Glasgow, eight stops to the North of the River Clyde and seven to the South.

He was on the Inner Circuit, four stops to Hillhead running in an anticlockwise direction.

Six minutes passed and he stepped out on to the platform, his body pushed from all directions. People shoved past him, lost in their own routines, scurrying around on the concrete like ants. Except, thought Tom, ants worked together. Here people dipped their heads and drove onwards without acknowledging another human being. He stood still, rooted to the spot, as the crowds dissipated around him.

That's when Tom noticed her.

She sat on a bench at the far end of the platform, her legs bent up to her chest with her chin rested on her knees.

As the platform emptied, deserted but for a few stragglers, his gaze fell on her fully. The resemblance to Alex was uncanny.

Lucy looked younger perhaps. Something in her posture, the way that her arms curled round her shins suggested that she was more vulnerable. She was skinny, the same boyish frame, dressed in tight jeans with holes in the knees, a large grey hoody and a knitted hat that hung off the back of her head. Her dark red hair, not a shade different, was pulled back from her face and fell down her back, dividing into soft curls. Her fingers were clasped round her ankles, a band of silver just visible, and her eyes were set firmly on the ground.

Tom inched forward. He kept his head turned and walked at an angle, not ready to be seen. As he moved closer he noticed that she was crying, her whole body was trembling. He waited for a moment, his shoulder rested against one of the pillars, near enough to make out the darkening of freckles around her nose but at enough of distance not to alarm her.

A carriage came and went, bodies flocking on and off, before the platform cleared again. She didn't move.

He walked over to the bench and sat at the opposite end. If Lucy noticed his presence, she didn't acknowledge it.

"Lucy?" he said.

Her head turned slowly and she stared straight back at him. Five long seconds, without a word, then her eyes lifted and she looked over his shoulder.

Cece was standing behind him, watching.

"Lucy?" said Cece. "Are you ok?"

Lucy turned away and looked down at her knees. Time seemed to stall, the world empty but for the three bodies that were gathered on the platform at Hillhead, bound by both blood and circumstance.

"Everyone's dead," she whispered finally.

"I know," said Cece.

Cece walked round the bench and crouched in front of Lucy, placing a hand on her feet.

"I read your letter Lucy, I know everything."

Lucy stared at her, opened her mouth to speak, but she paused. Lips still parted, she turned to eye the strange man who was sitting next to them.

"Lucy," began Cece, "this is my dad, Tom. We want to help you."

The words moved the air, not claimed or acknowledged by anyone in particular.

"I didn't want anyone to die, not really," said Lucy, ready to dissolve into tears.

"I know," replied Cece. "And we don't blame you, for anything. Do you understand me Lucy, we forgive you. Jon would forgive you."

Lucy looked at Tom, then back at Cece.

"What do you want?" she said. "I don't understand. Why are you here?"

Tom spoke, the story already worked out in his head.

"We came here so that we could tell you the truth."

"Truth, what truth?" asked Lucy. "I don't even know you."

"Jonathan Swan was one of my best friends and I also knew your mother very well." He paused and glanced over at Cece who, in turn, gave him an understanding smile.

"I was your Mum's half-brother, which makes me your uncle."

"We're family?" asked Lucy.

"Yes. You, me and Cece, we're all family," he replied.

Tom stopped talking for a moment, needing to find the words.

"When Jenny died in that accident I lost a small part of myself. You see, your mother, she meant the world to me." Tom paused to look at Lucy. "I realise that you have no reason to trust me, or to believe a word that I say, but your mother wasn't a bad person. She didn't mean to hurt you, Lucy."

Tears stung the corners of Lucy's eyes.

"She was only a child when she fell pregnant with you and your sister, a scared and confused child with no one to support her. It wasn't until years later that I learned of your existence, when you started writing to Jon. And now, here you are. A part of Jenny that lives on, precious beyond words."

Lucy wiped her eyes and glanced up at Cece. Cece smiled back at her and placed her hand on Lucy's knee.

"We want you to come home with us," she said. "To live with us."

"But why would you want to help me?" she asked. Her lip trembled. "After everything that I've done."

"Because," said Tom, "we're family and that's what family do, they forgive."

"Family," whispered Lucy.

***

Lucy lay in bed and stared at the ceiling.

Cece had made them all dinner and after a round of hot chocolates she had showed Lucy to her new room. The house was warm, and there was something homely about it, it smelt like warm orange and cinnamon.

Maybe, thought Lucy, just maybe, it would be ok.

Lucy rolled over onto her side and hugged the pillow between her arms, resting her head on the back of her hand.

She was alive.

She hadn't been able to do it, to throw herself in front of the train. It wasn't fear that had stopped her, if anything that last step would have been the easy option, an escape. It was Alex. Alex wanted her to live. She had died so that Lucy could have a second chance.

A new start.

And no matter how hard it would be, how lonely, Lucy would honour that.

She turned over, her knees curled up in the foetal position with the duvet tucked under her chin. Fresh lavender. That's when she caught a glimpse of him, he was standing in the hallway, watching her from the crack in the door. Their eyes met, a moment shared in silence, before he pushed the door open.

"Can I get you anything?" asked Tom.

"No, I'm fine, thank you."

Tom smiled at her then turned to walk out.

"Sleep well."

"Wait..." Lucy called after him.

He stopped and looked back, the light from the corridor catching on his face.

She stared at him.

"You're not my uncle, are you?" she said.

"No," he replied.

Lucy didn't flinch, her eyes focused on his, her face absent of any expression.

"But I was telling you the truth," he said, "you are family. And I did care for your mother, very deeply."

"I know," she said. "I believe you."

Then she pulled the duvet up, rolled over with her back turned to him and closed her eyes.

She listened to the click of the door as he pulled it closed behind him, the room falling into darkness.

A smile caught on the corners of her mouth.

Just maybe, she thought.

Chapter 86

Fergus Toop.

Two words. Ten letters.

But there was no mistaking the handwriting.

Toop frowned, the residual rain water dripping from his nose and brow, as he read his own name. She must have known, he thought. She knew that he would come back.

He released the Velcro straps from around his wrists, pulled off his wet bike gloves and sat them on the shelf. With bare fingers he lifted the box of matches, retrieved the envelope from underneath them and walked over to the table beneath the window.

The bothy log book.

Toop started to flick through the pages, skimming past multiple leaves of paper at a time, until he found the page that he was looking for. It was there, the last few words squished beneath the final line, the tail of the letter *p* disappearing off the bottom of the page. The comparison was clear. The quote in the log book and his name on the envelope, it was her writing.

He put the envelope on the table, removed his helmet and hung his jacket on the back of the chair. It had been a dark wet cycle up to Coire Fionnaraich Bothy and the insides of his shoes were completely sodden. Letting the envelope settle, he stepped outside, returning with an armful of wood from the coal bunker, and used a few shreds of newspaper to get the fire going. Within a few minutes the warmth from the flames started to penetrate the small room. Toop removed his shoes, extracted the inner soles and placed them in front of the heat.

He padded across the cold floor barefoot and retrieved a hip flask and a shot glass from the pocket of his rucksack. He pulled out a chair and sat at the table. He unscrewed the lid, hovered the flask beneath his nose for a couple of seconds and poured himself a stiff Scotch. He took a few sips before he looked over at the envelope again.

Fergus Toop.

He thought about things, about her, about what she might have written. He considered throwing it unopened into the fire and forgetting about it. But he knew that he couldn't, that he wouldn't.

He poured another drink, downed it with one tip of his throat, and pushed the glass aside. The alcohol had little effect, failing to numb his mind. He poured another glass, opened the envelope and read.

Fergus,

If you are reading this then one of two things has happened.

One, I am on trial for the murder of Jonathan Swan and will most likely spend the rest of my life behind bars. Or, if things have gone to plan, I am dead.

Toop ran a hand through his wet hair, wiping the water from his forehead, and focused on her words.

I want to start with an apology.

I'm sorry that you had to be involved in all of this. Really, Fergus, I mean it. I never wanted to betray you. What happened between us, that wasn't a lie, at least not for me. In fact, it was one of the best things that ever happened to me. And happy, well that isn't something that I did well or at all really. So, I suppose what I'm trying to say is, thank you and sorry.

Sorry for lying to you and thank you for letting me feel loved. How does the saying go, it's better to have loved and lost than never to have loved at all.

Wouldn't you agree?

It was a question that Toop had asked himself many times over the years. A question that plagued his subconscious, causing the anger inside of him to flash in his eyes before it would slowly fade, replaced by a look of resignation and loss.

Second, after everything that's happened, the least that I can do is to leave you with the truth - not all of it I'm afraid, that I can't do. But enough.

I don't know what people will have told you, or what you will have found out, but Jonathan Swan deserved to die. He raped an innocent woman and abandoned an innocent child, a sweet little girl who grew up to be a troubled and broken young woman.

Who grew up to be Eve Stone.

You see, Jonathan Swan was my father. And for as long as I can remember I wanted, no I needed, him to pay for the suffering that he had caused.

So yes, I planned to kill him. I had every intention of putting a bullet in his head.

But the truth is I didn't.

I stood there in the rain, a gun pointed at his body, with one thought in my mind.

This man deserves to die.

But I couldn't pull the trigger. I told him to close his eyes, but I just stood there frozen. The man sitting in front of me seemed so normal, so lonely and small, and he wasn't afraid to die. Even though I wanted to, even though I had imagined the moment a hundred times, I couldn't do it.

When he opened his eyes he looked straight up at me. There was no fear there, no anger. He didn't try to run or to shout out. He just sat still and then very slowly he slipped a hand into the pocket of his jacket.

A yellow rose.

Of all things, he pulled out a yellow rose. He was saying sorry. My father sat there, with a gun pointed at his face, and admitted that he wasn't worthy. He accepted that he didn't deserve my forgiveness.

"Let me". Those were his next words.

He held out his hand, not needing to say anything more. I knew what he wanted me to do, what I had to do. It was then that I realised that I was crying. I stepped forward, lifted the rose from his palm and handed him the gun. He took it and I remember his skin brushing against mine for a brief second. Then he pulled his hand away, wiped the handle clean with the hem of his jacket and held it up to his chest. No fingerprints.

He uttered a single sentence.

Greater love hath no one than this.

Seven words.

Greater love hath no one than this.

With his final words the sky exploded, a loud ripple that sliced through the air. Then nothing, just silence.

A father's final gift. A sinner's gift.

Toop took another drink and read through the last few lines of the letter. He pictured her as she wrote, sitting in the same exact spot. His eyes flickered across the final sentence for a second time before he folded the letter, stood, and walked over to the fire.

He threw it into the blaze, watching as flames grew from the edges of the paper. He closed his eyes as the fire continued to burn. A minute passed before he reopened them.

Her final sentence played in his head.

Before you embark on a journey of revenge, you must dig two graves.

THE
WAKE-UP
CALL

Also by Beth O'Leary

The Flatshare
The Switch
The Road Trip
The No-Show

THE
WAKE-UP
CALL

BETH
O'LEARY

QUERCUS

First published in Great Britain in 2023 by

QUERCUS

Quercus Editions Ltd
Carmelite House
50 Victoria Embankment
London EC4Y 0DZ

An Hachette UK company

A CIP catalogue record for this book is available
from the British Library

HB ISBN 978 1 52941 824 8
TPB ISBN 978 1 52941 825 5
EBOOK ISBN 978 1 52941 827 9

10 9 8 7 6 5 4 3 2 1

Text designed and typeset by CC Book Production
Printed and bound in Great Britain by Clays Ltd, Elcograf S.p.A.

Papers used by Quercus Editions Ltd are from well-managed forests
and other responsible sources.

For my readers.

I treasure every one of you.

December 2021

Dear Lucas,

I have a confession to make, and I'm kind of nervous about it, which is why you're getting it in your Christmas card. (Merry Christmas, by the way.)

Whenever we cross paths at the hotel, something strange happens. I get hot. Jittery. Say weird things like 'good morrow!', and forget what it is I'm chatting to a guest about, and look at you instead of looking at whichever of Barty's menu additions Arjun wants to disagree with today.

I'm not usually the sort of person to get infatuated. I'm more of the slow-burn, warm-and-cosy type. And I DON'T lose my head over a guy — I never have. But when I look at you, I get all . . . flustered.

And when you look at me, I wonder if you might feel the same thing. I've been waiting for you to say something, really. But my friend Jem pointed out that maybe you just think I'm not available, or maybe you're not big on sharing how you feel, or maybe I just need to woman up and make the first move.

So here I am. Putting my cosy warm heart on the line to say: I like you. A lot.

If you feel the same way, meet me under the mistletoe at 8 p.m. I'll be the one in the pink dress. And also the one who is Izzy the receptionist. I don't know why I said the pink dress thing.

I'm going to stop writing now, because . . . I've run out of space. And dignity. See you at 8?

Izzy xxx

Dear Izzy,

Merry Christmas and Happy New Year.

Regards,
Lucas

November 2022

Izzy

If Lucas is doing something, I have to be doing it too, but better.

This has generally been very good for my career over the last year, but it does mean that right now I am grappling with a fir-tree branch which measures at least twice my height and four times my width.

'Do you need help?' Lucas asks.

'Absolutely not. Do you?'

I swing my branch into position and narrowly avoid smashing one of the many vases around the lobby. I'm always dodging those things. Like much of the furniture at Forest Manor Hotel and Spa, the vases come from the Bartholomew family, who own the estate. Morris Bartholomew (Barty) and his wife, Uma Singh-Bartholomew (Mrs SB), have turned the grand house into a hotel, and they've repurposed as many of the old family furnishings as possible. I am all for an upcycle – it's kind of my thing – but there's something urn-like about some of these vases.

I can't shake the thought that one of them might contain an old Bartholomew.

'Is that whimsical?' Lucas asks me, pausing to examine my fir branch.

I'm tying it to the bottom of my side of the staircase. The Forest Manor staircase is famous – it's one of those gorgeous sweeping ones that splits in two midway and just begs you to walk down it slowly in a wedding dress, or maybe arrange your children up it for an adorable Von-Trapp-ish family photograph.

'Is that?' I ask, pointing to the potted tree Lucas has hauled in from the garden and placed at the bottom of *his* side of the staircase.

'Yes,' he says, with absolute confidence. 'It is an olive tree. Olives are very whimsical.'

We are dressing the lobby for tomorrow's wedding – the bride's theme is 'winter whimsy'. Lucas and I have decided that asymmetry is whimsical, so we are each doing one side of the staircase. The trouble is, if Lucas goes big, I have to go bigger, so now quite a lot of the garden is in the lobby.

'They're also Mediterranean.'

Lucas looks at me flatly, like, *Your point is?*

'We're in the New Forest. It's November.'

Lucas frowns. I give up.

'What about my silver fairy lights, then?' I ask, gesturing to the small, sparkling lights woven through the greenery that now runs up my bannister. 'Do you think we need some on your side too?'

'No. They're tacky.'

I narrow my eyes. Lucas finds everything about me tacky. He hates my clip-in highlights, my baby-pink trainers, my fondness for supernatural teen dramas. He doesn't get that life is too short for rules about what's cool and what's not cool; life's for living. In full HD. And baby-pink trainers.

'They're cute and twinkly!'

'They're so bright. Like little daggers. No.'

He unfolds his arms and places his hands on his hips instead. Lucas likes to take up as much space as possible. This is presumably why he is always at the gym, so that he can claim yet another inch of my airspace with his ever-broadening shoulders and his bulging biceps.

I take a deep, calming breath. Once this wedding is over, Lucas and I can go back to alternating shifts wherever possible. These days, things don't go well if we're at the front desk together for too long. Mrs SB says it 'doesn't seem to create quite the right atmosphere'. Arjun, the head chef, says 'when Izzy and Lucas are on shift at the same time the hotel is about as welcoming as my grandmother's house', and I've met Arjun's grandmother, so I can say with confidence that this was a very rude remark.

But Lucas and I are the most experienced front-of-house staff at the hotel, and we're the ones who manage weddings, which means that for the next two days, I have to endure nonstop Lucasness.

'Come up to the landing,' Lucas barks. 'See what I am seeing.'

He's always so *commanding*. When I first met Lucas, I thought his Brazilian accent was so sexy – I forgave his rudeness, called it a translation issue, decided he meant well but things didn't quite come out right. But over time, I have learned that Lucas has an excellent grasp of English – he is just an arse.

I traipse up to the central landing, where the staircase splits in two, and take it all in. Our lobby is huge, with a gigantic wooden front desk along the left-hand side, old-fashioned keys dangling on the wall behind it. There's a worn circular rug over the original brown and cream tiles, and a soft-seating area by the tall windows looking out at the lawn. It's gorgeous. And in the last eight years, it's become a home to me – maybe even more so than the little pastel-coloured flat I rent in Fordingbridge.

'This is a classy hotel,' Lucas says. 'The fairy lights look cheap.'

They *were* cheap. What does he expect? Our budget is – as always – non-existent.

'This is a *family* hotel,' I say, just as the Hedgers family walk into the lobby, right on cue. Three kids, all hand in hand, the littlest one toddling along in a snowsuit with his pudgy fingers tucked inside his sister's.

'Wow!' says the oldest, stopping in his tracks to stare at my sparkling bannister. The youngest almost takes a tumble; his sister yanks him upright. 'That looks so cool!'

I shine my smuggest smile in Lucas's direction. He continues to glower. The children look slightly disconcerted, and then intrigued.

I have noticed this phenomenon before. Lucas *should* be terrible with children – he's huge and scowly and doesn't know how to talk to them. But they always seem to find him fascinating. The other day I heard him greet Middle Hedgers (real name: Ruby Hedgers, age six, favourite hobbies include martial arts, ponies

12

and climbing things that aren't safe) by saying, 'Good morning, how did you sleep? I hope well?' It is exactly what he says to adult guests, delivered in the exact same tone. But Ruby loved it. 'Oh, I slept *all* night,' she told him, with great importance. 'When it was seven on my clock, I got up and stood by Mummy and Daddy's bed until they woke up too, and Daddy didn't think I was there, so he screamed, and it was *so* funny.' To which Lucas nodded, quite serious, and said, 'That sounds like a horrible way to be woken,' and Ruby descended into fits of giggles.

Bizarre.

'The children like the fairy lights,' I tell Lucas, spreading my hands.

'The children also like shoes with wheels in them, and Haribo, and they will eat Arjun's ice-cream sundaes until they are sick,' Lucas says. 'Children cannot be trusted.'

I glance at the grown-up Hedgers to make sure they aren't offended by Lucas's comments, but they're ushering the kids into their room and don't seem to have heard. They're in Sweet Pea, because Mrs Hedgers is a wheelchair user – the lifts have been broken for over a month now, and it's been a nightmare with only five downstairs bedrooms.

'No fairy lights on my side. We should take those ones down, too.'

'Oh my God! Can't you just compromise and say, fine, let's use fairy lights but more sparingly, or something?'

'They hurt my eyes. It's a no.'

'When you work with someone you can't just say *it's a no* and leave it at that.'

'Why not?'

'You have to meet me halfway.'

'Why?'

'Because! It's reasonable!'

'Ah. Reasonable like reorganising the stationery every time you are on shift so that I can never find things?'

'That's not why I do it. I do it because your way is—'

'Reasonable?'

'Crap!' I say, belatedly glancing towards Sweet Pea to make sure the door has closed behind the Hedgers' children. 'Your way is crap. The drawer always gets jammed because you put the hole-puncher in on its side and the Post-its should be at the front because we use them all the time but they're right at the back, behind the with-compliments slips, which we never use, so excuse me for saving you time!'

'Is it reasonable to renumber the rooms without telling me?'

'That was Mrs SB's idea! I was just following orders!'

'Did she order you not to tell me?'

We're squared up now, and somehow I've ended up with my hands on my hips too, a posture I have only ever adopted when pretending to be a superhero (something you do surprisingly often when you work in a family-friendly hotel).

'I just forgot. I'm a human being. Sue me.'

'You didn't forget to tell Poor Mandy.'

Mandy is the other permanent member of the front-of-house team. She is not actually poor in the financial sense – she has just become known as 'Poor Mandy' here at Forest Manor Hotel and Spa because she's always stuck between me and Lucas when

14

we're arguing about something. Poor Mandy doesn't care about the way the stationery drawer is arranged. She just wants some peace and quiet.

'Well, Poor Mandy didn't specifically tell me never to message her outside of working hours, so I probably WhatsApped her about it.'

'I did not say, don't message me outside of working hours. I just said that *bombarding* me with hotel administration at eleven at night on a Sunday is not—'

'Reasonable,' I say, through gritted teeth. 'Right, of course. Well, if you're so keen on *reasonable*, we'll stick to reasonable un-fairy-lit bannisters and we'll host a reasonably good wedding and Barty and Mrs SB will make the reasonable decision to close the hotel because it's no longer viable. Is that what you want?'

'Are you under the impression that you can save Forest Manor Hotel and Spa with large quantities of twinkly lights?'

'Yes!' I shout. 'No! I mean, it's not about the decorations per se, it's about going the extra mile. Forest Manor is *so* perfect for this time of year, and if this wedding goes well, then every single guest will go away thinking the hotel is gorgeous and they should minibreak here, or have their engagement party here, and that means we're that little bit closer to staying afloat in 2023.'

'Izzy, the hotel cannot be saved by a few minibreaks or engagement parties. We need investment.'

I don't respond to this. It's not because I agree with him, or because – God forbid – I'm letting Lucas have the last word. It's because the ceiling has just fallen in on our heads.

Lucas

One moment Izzy is glaring up at me, fierce and spiky, with her hands planted on her hips. And the next, she is on top of me, small and soft and smelling of cinnamon sugar, with half the ceiling on top of her.

I have no understanding of how we got from A to B here.

'Oh my God,' Izzy says, rolling off me in a cloud of plaster. 'Did I just save your life?'

'No,' I say. It is best to say no when Izzy asks you a question. 'What?'

'The ceiling fell in,' she says, pointing at the ceiling. Helpful, as ever. 'And I threw myself over you to save you.'

I lie there beside her. We are both on our backs on the landing. High above us, the ceiling gapes open. I can see the old wall lamps in the first-floor hallway.

This is not good.

I turn my head to look at Izzy. Her cheeks are flushed and

16

her pink-striped hair is all over the place, but she appears unharmed. There is a chunk of plaster behind her head, large enough to have killed one of us. I suddenly feel very cold.

'Thank you, then, I suppose,' I say.

Her expression sours and she stands, brushing her legs down.

'You're welcome,' she says. When Izzy says this to me, it translates as *go to hell, arsehole.* If she were speaking to anybody else, it would no doubt be entirely sincere. But when it comes to me, whatever Izzy's saying, the subtext is essentially always *vai à merda, cuzão.*

Nobody but me seems to notice this. Everyone else thinks Izzy is 'nice' and 'fun' and 'sweet'. Even Arjun treats her like a princess, and Arjun treats our customers in the way that a famous musician might treat his fans – with a sort of fond contempt. But then, Arjun didn't have Izzy yelling *You're not good enough for her anyway, you cold-hearted shiny-shoed robot-man!* at him across the hotel gardens last Christmas.

Izzy does appear to have just saved my life though, so I try to be polite.

'I am very grateful,' I say. 'And I apologise that I did not throw myself over you first. I had assumed you would be able to look after yourself.'

This doesn't go down well. She glowers at me. Izzy has a whole range of glowers and glares. She has big green eyes and very long eyelashes, and always draws little black flicks on the edges of her eyelids. When I think about Izzy, which is as rarely as possible, I see those eyes narrowed at me. Catlike and bright.

'I *can* look after myself,' she says.

'Yes,' I say. 'I know. That's why I didn't save you.'

'Hello?' someone calls from upstairs.

'Shit,' Izzy mutters, craning her neck to look up at the hole in the ceiling. 'Mrs Muller?'

For all her faults, Izzy has an exceptional memory for our guests. If you've stayed with us once, Izzy will know your son's name, your breakfast order and your star sign. Though even I remember Mrs Muller: she stays here often, always upsetting the cleaning team by getting splodges of paint everywhere while she works on her art. She's in her seventies, half German, half Jamaican, with an accent that I find frustratingly challenging, and a tendency to tip the hotel staff as though we're in America, which I don't mind at all.

'Call the fire brigade,' Izzy hisses at me, before returning her attention to Mrs Muller. 'Mrs Muller, please be very careful! There's been a – slight – umm—'

'Accident,' I suggest.

'Issue,' Izzy says. 'There's been a slight issue with the floor! But we're getting it sorted right away.'

We both try to peer through the hole. We need to do something before any of the other fifty guests currently staying at Forest Manor happen to step out of their bedrooms and risk falling down a storey or two.

'Mrs Muller, please step back!' I say, then head down the steps to the lobby – it is just as dangerous for us as it is for her. 'You should move too,' I tell Izzy over my shoulder.

She ignores me. Well, I tried. I eye the damage to the staircase and get my phone out to dial 190, then remember it's not that in the UK, it's ...

'Nine nine nine,' Izzy says.

'I know that,' I snap. I'm already calling.

A shower of plaster comes cascading down from the hole, dousing Izzy in dust. She splutters, her long brown-and-pink hair now covered in white powder.

'Whoa,' says an excited voice from behind me. I turn to see Ruby Hedgers, the six-year-old, in the doorway of Sweet Pea. 'Is it snowing?'

'No,' I tell her, 'it is just structural damage. Hello, yes, fire brigade, please ...'

The hotel is swarming with firefighters. Izzy is being unprofessionally flirtatious with one of the particularly handsome ones. I am in a very bad mood.

It has been a stressful morning. Understandably, the guests are a little disturbed by all this. Several of them did not take well to being posted out of windows and down ladders. One of the firefighters told us that the damage to the ceiling and staircase has 'no quick fix' and said 'this is going to be a big job', and in case that wasn't clear enough, he rubbed his forefinger and thumb together, a gesture that means the same in Brazil as it does here: money, money, money.

This is the root of all our problems at Forest Manor Hotel and Spa. As I understand it, the hotel was thriving before the pandemic, but business suffered badly during the Covid lockdowns, which coincided with the entire roof needing replacing. Now we are limping along, unable to give the hotel the renovation it needs. When I started here two years ago, Forest Manor was already looking tired; it has lost even more of its luxuriousness, and that, in turn, means prices have had to drop, even in our award-winning restaurant.

But the heart of this place remains the same. I truly believe there is no hotel in England quite as special as this one. I knew it the moment I first stepped into the lobby and saw the guests reading newspapers on the sofas in their hotel slippers, looking out at the children playing on the lawns. It was the picture of comfort. We treasure our guests here – the moment I hand them their key, they become part of our family.

'Lucas, right?' says a voice behind me, a hand clapping down on my shoulder.

I steel myself, placing my precious third coffee of the day on the lobby table. Of course, we don't always like *every* member of our family.

Louis Keele is staying in Wood Aster, one of the downstairs suites, for the next two months while he's in the area on business. It is our finest room, and Louis likes the finest things. *People don't appreciate quality any more*, he told a colleague the other day on their way through the lobby. I imagine it is much easier to 'appreciate' quality when your father made several million pounds on the property market in the 90s, but I wouldn't know.

'Yes, Mr Keele. The hotel is being evacuated,' I say.

He knows this, obviously. There are firefighters everywhere, and there is a cordon across the doorway that Louis has just ducked under. Also, a lot of the ceiling is on the staircase.

'I'm very sorry, but you'll need to vacate your room for a short time, just while we get all this sorted.'

He is looking at 'all this' with interest. I clench my fists. Louis puts me on edge. There is something hungry underneath his easy smile – something calculating. He was here last Christmas, and even then he was asking Mrs SB if she would consider selling to his father's company – or, as he calls it, 'the Keele family firm'. She had laughed and told him no, but the situation is so different now. We were in serious financial trouble *before* the ceiling caved in.

Louis whistles slowly, tucking his hands in his trouser pockets. 'This sort of damage, with the broader renovations needed here . . .' He grimaces in sympathy. 'Excuse the crude language, but you guys are in real deep shit, aren't you?'

'Louis!' Izzy trills, appearing from the dining room and shooting me a warning look that suggests my expression is not as obliging as it should be. 'Let me take you outside. We're having an impromptu winter picnic under the pergola, or the pergoda, or the pagoda, I have actually never known what the difference is between all of those, but you know what I mean.'

She has her hand on his arm. Izzy is very tactile for a Brit – with everyone except me.

'Mrs SB called,' Izzy says to me over her shoulder as she leads Louis away. 'Someone needs to phone the already-hysterical bride whose wedding just got cancelled. I told her how passionate you were about the set-up for tomorrow's wedding and said you'd be the perfect person to make the bride feel heard.'

I grit my teeth. Izzy knows I do not enjoy emotional

conversations. The only consolation is that I have already signed Izzy up to help Barty fill in a forty-four-page insurance document which he has definitely downloaded in the wrong format. It will be pure torture for her.

'And she wants to see us both in the office at five,' Izzy adds.

It is only as the front door creaks shut behind Izzy and Louis that I realise what this is likely to mean.

Even if it is safe to use the downstairs of the hotel, that leaves us with five bedrooms instead of twenty-five. They are five of the most expensive bedrooms, which is something, but still, it's a fraction of what we'd usually earn over the winter months, and doesn't exactly require a full front-of-house team. In the average week, Izzy and I would each share the desk with one of the agency receptionists Mrs SB employs, and endure our one overlap day (Monday. The gloomiest of days). Mandy would take most of the evening shifts, when only one receptionist is required.

If I were Mrs SB, I would be looking to cut a member of front-of-house staff. Given the short notice, she will probably have to pay the agency receptionists even if they don't come in, and Mandy is an old family friend of Barty's.

Which leaves . . . me and Izzy.

Izzy

It's five o'clock. I've got my pitch ready. I've had some useful feedback from Arjun, who said I was focusing a bit too much on why I was better at my job than Lucas, which doesn't make me sound like a team player. I disagree, obviously – if anyone isn't a team player, it's Lucas. He's always annoying housekeeping, and he once made Ollie cry when the dishwasher broke. But maybe I don't need the slide about how my booking book is better than his online booking system in literally every way.

Now that the two of us are standing side by side outside Opal Cottage – the old gate house where the Singh-Bartholomews live – I am finding myself feeling a teeny bit sorry for Lucas. He looks as anxious as I feel. It's a freezing cold day, and the grass is still wet from this morning's sleet, but he's rolled his shirt-sleeves up and keeps tugging at his collar as if he's too hot. He catches my eye, and I am *just* considering smiling at him when he says, 'By the way, I reorganised your box for you.'

All thoughts of smiling evaporate.

'My box o'bits?'

Lucas's expression shifts from 'tense and implacable' to a subtle 'I tire of your nonsense'.

'The box that you keep under our desk, filled with your belongings, yes.'

'You can't go through my box o'bits! That's been there for eight years!'

'That was obvious from the contents,' Lucas says. 'It was easy to condense it into a smaller, more sensible container when I removed all the out-of-date packets of sweets.'

'Sweets never go off! Tell me you did *not* throw anything away.'

He regards me flatly. 'I kick that box at least twice per day. I have asked you repeatedly to move it. Rationalising the contents seemed like a compromise. Aren't you always telling me to compromise?'

'Excuse me? You've been kicking my box? There are breakables in there, you know.' Well, my *Teen Wolf* mug. But that is *very* precious.

Mrs SB opens the door and we snap to attention. It's obvious that her day has been a lot more stressful than mine – and mine has been nonstop chaos. She's wearing a cardigan, but only has one arm in a sleeve. The other is just dangling down her back like a bright pink tail. She has a phone trapped between her shoulder and cheek, and her usually flamboyant eyeshadow is an ominously boring shade of taupe. She gestures us inside, cardigan arm flapping, and says into the phone, 'Absolutely, yes, that won't be a problem at all,' while pulling a face.

She flaps her hands at the armchairs in the entrance hall where she seems to have nested, judging by the half-eaten bowl of pasta, the hooded blanket draped over a chair arm, and the important-looking paperwork strewn everywhere. Barty waves at us from the kitchen without looking up – he is literally elbow-deep in ring-binder files, his spectacles balanced on the tip of his long, aristocratic nose.

Lucas sits down gingerly, as though all the chaos might be catching. I settle in with my laptop bag clutched to my chest, trying to remember my opening lines. *In the last eight years at Forest Manor, I have become an invaluable member of the team, coordinating everything from large-scale weddings to . . .*

'Hi,' Mrs SB says on an exhale once she's hung up the phone. 'You two are a sight for sore eyes. Is it still a crime scene over there?'

She waves her hands at the window that looks over the hotel. Lucas and I exchange a quick glance.

'There's a lot going on,' I say brightly. 'But things have calmed now that Barty's sorted everyone temporary accommodation, and I've got four builders coming around for quotes . . .'

'And I have contacted three structural engineers,' Lucas butts in. 'The work is far too extensive for a regular builder to manage.'

Mrs SB's eyes widen at *far too extensive*. I stay quiet. Sometimes Lucas scores my goals for me.

He doesn't know Mrs SB as well as I do. She and Barty opened this hotel as newlyweds, more than forty years ago – the building isn't just where they work, it's the child they never had. They love every inch of this place, from the quaint attic rooms to the big brass door knocker. Forest Manor was made for luxury and romance, for string quartets, slow dances and lavish candlelit dinners. I hate watching Mrs SB grapple with the fact that after all we've been through, they can't afford to keep this magical place from falling apart.

'We're staying open,' Mrs SB says, with resolution. 'The insurers have said we can, as long as the building work is "sufficiently cordoned-off", so I'm adding "buy cordons" to my to-do list. After "googling what cordons are". We've had to cancel all the winter weddings, but we've still got five good suites, and the kitchen is untouched, whatever Arjun says.'

Arjun is very concerned about plaster dust. I gave this short shrift this afternoon, but you do have to manage Arjun's ego quite carefully. I'll send someone around later to do some token dusting around the oven and tell him it's sorted.

'But closing all twenty upstairs rooms . . . and having builders and . . . *structural engineers* everywhere . . .' She rubs her forehead, pushing her glasses up on to her head. 'Will the Hedgers stay?'

I nod. 'Their home insurance is covering their stay – their house is flooded,' I tell her. 'They don't have anywhere else to go, to be honest.'

'Good,' Mrs SB says, then winces at herself. 'Sorry. You know what I mean. And we've got Mrs Muller, she's here until January. We'll need to prioritise the long-term guests, I think. The couple from New Orleans have cancelled and gone to The Pig, so we can upgrade Mrs Muller to their room. Louis Keele has made it clear he's keen to stick around . . .'

I glance at Lucas, curious. He made a little sound when Mrs SB mentioned Louis. A familiar, disgusted snort that generally happens after I say something, actually.

'Who else is here on a long stay?' Mrs SB asks.

'Mr Townsend and the Jacobs,' Lucas and I say simultaneously.

'The Jacobs are a young Belgian couple with a five-month-old,' I say. 'They love everything British, have their bacon well-done and are obsessed with *Fawlty Towers*.'

We all know Mr Townsend, so I don't bother sharing my facts about him. He's here every winter for at least three months, and these days he and I even exchange the odd email in the time he's away from the hotel – he's become a friend, as many return guests do. I know Barty and Mrs SB feel the same.

'Well, liking *Fawlty Towers* is a good sign,' Mrs SB says with a grimace. 'Right. And they're . . .'

'Keen to stay,' I say promptly. 'I've already checked.'

'Good. Well done, Izzy. As for the rest of them . . .' Mrs SB says, staring at the laptop open on her knees. 'I'll deal with them. Somehow.'

She looks up at us with a distressed smile. Mrs SB is the world's nicest boss, and she can't bear to let anybody down, so if she's upset, that almost certainly means bad things for us.

'Now. On to you two,' she says.

Oh, God.

'I must be honest with you both. From the new year, I just can't guarantee anything. We may well . . .' She swallows. 'We're out of money, quite frankly. These next few weeks will be make or break. But I know how important it is for each of you to be working at the hotel this winter.'

I feel rather than see Lucas stiffen at that. For the first time, I wonder exactly why Lucas is working for the whole of November and December, rather than going back to see his family in Brazil like he did last year. And then I immediately stop thinking about this, because any thoughts that involve last Christmas and Lucas are strictly forbidden by order of my friend Jem.

'With only five rooms in use . . . I just can't justify employing you both to work on the desk alongside an agency receptionist.'

There it is. I fiddle with the strap on my bag and feel my pitch drying up in my throat. What was it I wanted to say? Something about being invaluable? I've worked at the hotel for eight years? The stationery drawer is much better when I'm here?

'Mrs SB,' Lucas says, 'I understand your difficulty. May I remind you of the superior digital booking system I introduced when I—'

'Personal notes!' I shout. They both turn to look at me. 'It was my idea to have the personal welcome notes in the rooms, and so many of our good reviews mention those.'

'They mention your terrible handwriting,' Lucas says.

I flush. People are so mean on the internet.

'I am extremely economical,' Lucas tells Mrs SB, who looks wearier by the minute. 'When we need new printer paper, I always order—'

'The fancy overpriced stuff,' I finish for him.

'The quality paper that requires less ink,' Lucas ploughs on. 'Unlike Izzy, I think carefully about cost implications.'

'Unlike Izzy? Excuse me? Who was complaining about my

budget fairy lights this morning? If you had your way, we'd make everything in this hotel out of solid gold.'

'That is ridiculous,' Lucas says, without even bothering to look at me. 'My solution is not solid-gold fairy lights, clearly. My solution is no fairy lights.'

'What next?' I say, my voice rising. 'No sofas? No beds?'

'Stop it, please,' Mrs SB says, holding up both hands in surrender. 'There's no need to battle it out, I'm keeping you both on until the new year. The agency director has kindly released us from our contract, in the circumstances, and will just provide a skeleton staff for front-of-house on Tuesdays and Wednesdays, if the two of you are willing to work five days?'

'Yes,' we both say, so loudly that Mrs SB startles slightly.

Usually, our fifth day is a split shift, so one of us covers the evening for Mandy to have her night off. I won't miss that, though – evening shifts are less fun. All the kids at the hotel have gone to bed, for starters.

'Well. Good. Thank you, both of you. I need responsible, experienced staff here – I can trust you two and Mandy with anything. I know you'll muck in wherever you're needed. I'll be letting half the waiting staff go, and even more of the housekeeping team, and Arjun will have to cope with just Ollie in the kitchen.'

'You're only leaving him the kitchen porter?' I say, unable to help myself. Arjun is not going to take that well.

'Raw talent,' Mrs SB says briskly. 'He can mould the boy in his own image. Now ...' She sniffs, reaching her hands out. I take one first; Lucas hesitates before gripping her other hand in his own. 'That's enough business talk,' she says. 'May I remind

29

you that we are a family here. Whatever happens, that won't change. If Forest Manor has to close, I will do whatever I can to help you. *Whatever* I can. Please know that the two of you will always be very dear to me.'

I'm tearing up. Mrs SB knows exactly how hard it is for me to have a conversation like this, and she squeezes my hand tightly. For a second I actually let myself think about it: drinking my last coffee-spiked hot chocolate with Arjun; packing my box o'bits into my car; hugging goodbye to Barty and Mrs SB, the people who made me feel at home when that mattered more than anything.

'Absolutely,' I say. My voice is a bit squeaky. 'And I'm here for you for as long as you can have me. Just name a job, and I'm on it.'

Lucas nods once. 'Whatever you need.'

'Wonderful. Well,' Mrs SB gives us a small, tired smile and releases our hands, 'we're selling as much as we can. That's step one.'

I widen my eyes. 'And Barty's . . .'

'Very upset about it,' Mrs SB says, lowering her voice and glancing towards the kitchen. 'But if we can't raise funds, we will lose the hotel. So some of those old Bartholomew pieces have to go. Can I put you two in charge of the lost-property room?'

'In charge, as in, of *selling* it all?' I say. The lost-property room started out as a lost-property box, but over the years it grew, and now there are hundreds – if not thousands – of items in there. We're not big on throwing things away here at Forest Manor. 'Can we even do that?'

'I've had a look, and the law is a bit vague, but I think as long as we took steps to return the items – which we always do when something new lands in there – and a reasonable amount of time has passed, then we're entitled to call it ours. And if it's ours . . . then I don't see why it can't raise us some money. It's a bit of a mess in there, but you never know, there might be some gems. Can I count on you two to get it all sold off? I'm sure Poor Mandy will help.'

'Absolutely,' Lucas says. 'I look forward to it.'

My eyebrow twitches. Lucas hates the lost-property room. He calls it 'the bin'.

Mrs SB sits back with a long sigh, then notices she only has her cardigan half on and says, 'Oh, bother. What a day. I'm going to need you two to really step up, now. I hope you've realised this means you'll be working shifts together five days a week.' She brings her glasses back down on to the bridge of her nose and adopts her sternest expression. 'Can you both do that?'

Neither of us makes eye contact with the other.

'Of course,' I say brightly.

'Yes,' Lucas says. 'Yes, I can work with Izzy. No problem at all.'

The next day, I realise what Mrs SB means when she says *mucking in*. We're in the kitchen: I'm suddenly a sous-chef and Lucas has just been enlisted to wait on tables at lunch. There is a gold-trimmed notice on the front desk that reads, *Please ring for assistance and we will be with you in a jiffy!* in Barty's curling cursive. I suspect that note is going to be on the desk a lot in the next few weeks.

'It will not fit,' Lucas says, voice muffled from inside the polo shirt he's trying to pull on. The issue is that Lucas is enormous, and the waiting uniforms are not designed for people who tower over everyone and have those weird extra muscles joining their neck and their shoulders.

Arjun shoots me a gleeful glance over the pot he is currently stirring. Looking gleeful while slowly stirring a pot does make you look a bit witchy, so I try to stay poker-faced on the other hob. Arjun's making his black dal, which has to be prepared in an extremely precise way. He's already yelled at me five times and apologised seven times.

Arjun is a sweetheart, he just *acts* like a dragon. If Forest Manor is my family, Arjun's my overbearing older brother. He always thinks he's right, and annoyingly he often is – he was the first person to tell me Drew wasn't a good friend to me. But he's softer than he seems. Every year, he makes me a special batch of brownies on the date of my dad's birthday, because I once told him brownies were Dad's favourite, and if he clocks I'm having a rough day, he always slips a teaspoon of sugar into my tea.

'You're almost there,' Arjun says to Lucas. This is clearly cheering Arjun up, which is good, because he's been in a terrible mood ever since Mrs SB told him about the cuts to the kitchen staff. 'Just tug it a bit more,' he says.

'It . . . won't . . .' Lucas's head pops out. He clocks our expressions and his face darkens. 'You are laughing at me.'

'Never,' I say. 'Arjun, is it time to add the cream?'

'No! God! No! Do *not* upon pain of *death* add the cream yet!'

'Right,' I say cheerily. 'Not cream time. Got it. Lucas, are you just going to wear that as a scarf, or . . .'

Lucas looks down at the polo shirt currently dangling from his neck. He's wearing a T-shirt underneath, which isn't helping the polo shirt fit, and is doing a relatively poor job of hiding the endless ridges of muscle that make up Lucas's torso. I turn away and start tidying off-cuts of vegetables into the compost bin. Nobody needs to be seeing all those abs.

'We have no other polo shirts?'

'None,' I say, though I haven't actually checked.

Lucas gives me a look that suggests he may have guessed as much. With a weary sigh, he begins the arduous task of trying to squeeze an arm in, just as Louis Keele walks through the swinging double doors, casual as you like, as though guests pop into the kitchen all the time.

'Wow,' he says. 'It smells great in here. Isn't that a bit small for you, Lucas?'

Lucas's irritation radiates from him like the heat from the hobs. I stifle a grin. Louis is a bit entitled, but it doesn't particularly bother me – he's a guest, and I figure if it makes him happy to get involved behind the scenes, then what's the harm? Plus . . . he's cute.

'You shouldn't be back here,' Lucas says.

His tone is borderline rude. Lucas has never been great at the sunny-and-obliging-demeanour thing. I watch him realise he's been inappropriately blunt and reach for something more positive to say.

'Perhaps you would like to go for a swim in the spa, Mr Keele, if you're looking for entertainment?' he says, as he finally yanks the polo shirt down over his torso. It stops just below his belly button, a good three inches of black T-shirt showing out of the bottom.

Louis gives me a conspiratorial smile. He's one of those good-looking guys who can actually pull off a wink: a bit *EastEnders*, a bit cheeky. He wears his mousey-brown hair swept back from his forehead and has very white teeth; he's often in a suit with no jacket or tie. Our vibe has always been a little flirty, which Lucas clearly regards as *deeply* unprofessional on my part. This may or may not provide an incentive to smile back at Louis right now.

'I'll go for a swim if you'll join me?' he says to me. He glances at Arjun. 'She must be due a break soon, surely . . .'

'No breaks for the wicked,' I tell him. 'Arjun has me stirring that pot every two minutes and forty seconds.'

'This is the recipe that the *Observer* food reviewer said brought ground-breaking flavours to a sleepy corner of the forest, am I right?' Louis says, looking over Arjun's shoulder. 'Your trade-mark black dal?'

Arjun straightens slightly. 'Yes, actually.'

'Amazing, wow,' Louis says, clapping him on the shoulder. 'It smells fantastic. Incredible what you can do in this space.'

'Does anyone have *anything* I can take to table five?' Ollie says, bursting in through the doors to the restaurant.

As the only remaining permanent member of Arjun's team, Ollie should really be the one stirring this dal, but I took pity on him and let him fill the waiter job instead. Arjun already looked like he was about to start breathing fire, and Ollie – bless him – would definitely drive him over the edge.

'Bread? Olives? Something poisonous?' Ollie goes on. 'The bloke says it's not his fault you mugs let the ceiling fall in, and he doesn't see why it should be holding up his lunch, and I did say we don't usually serve lunch until twelve but he said this is supposed to be a boutique luxury hotel and he should be able to have lunch whenever he – God, Lucas, what are you wearing? You look like a right twat! Oh,' Ollie says, turning scarlet. 'Sorry sir, I didn't realise a guest was . . .'

'Just leaving,' Louis says, with another easy smile. 'Izzy – rain check on that swim?'

'Sure, looking forward to it!' I say, smiling back and checking the clock. 'Time to stir, Arjun?'

'You're not already stirring?' he says with absolute horror, as Ollie disappears into the restaurant with a bread basket and Louis slips out of the other door.

After the chaos of yesterday, today is eerily quiet.

You can really feel all those empty rooms. We put everyone in a bay window for breakfast, looking out over the lawns and the woodland beyond, but it's still too subdued for my liking. Mr Townsend stays hunched over his copy of *The Times*; Louis and Mrs Muller don't make it to breakfast; the Jacobs are grey with exhaustion, their baby asleep at last in the pram beside their table. It's the Hedgers who bring all the energy, but there's only so much that even three kids under ten can do to brighten up the atmosphere. As I return to the lobby, I vow to figure something out for tomorrow. Background music, maybe? Or will that come across as too corporate?

'Oh, Mrs Hedgers!' I call, as she wheels in with a pile of shopping bags on her lap. 'Let me help you with those.'

She waves me away, gaze landing on my latest innovation: the debris nativity on the staircase landing.

'That's . . . quite something,' she says.

I feel myself going pink. 'I just figured, even if the ceiling has fallen in, until the builders get here, we can still make the most of the space, right?' I say.

'Yes. Yes, I can see that,' Mrs Hedgers says.

I've built a nativity into the rubble of the fallen ceiling. Baby Jesus is lying in a cradle between two chunks of ceiling plaster, and I've spread artificial snow around the scene, even dusting the shoulders of the wise men (three old statues of previous Bartholomew family members from the gardens). My personal favourite element is the sheep, which I created out of an old white footstool and a lot of cotton wool balls. I know it's a bit tacky and over-the-top, but I think it's cheerful – and the hotel desperately needs some cheer right now.

'You're a very creative young woman,' Mrs Hedgers says, turning her steady gaze my way.

For someone with such energetic children, Mrs Hedgers is surprisingly calm. She wears her dark brown hair in a chignon, smooth and neat, and there's never a speck of mud on the wheels of her chair when she heads out of the door. On her check-in notes, she listed her profession as 'life and career-change coach', which is probably why she seems to be so impressively *together*. I guess you can't tell other people how to live their lives if yours is a bit of a state.

'Oh, thank you!'

'Is it hard work, staying switched on all the time?' she asks, tilting her head.

'Sorry?'

Mrs Hedgers smiles slightly. 'Creative people tend to need their downtime.' She looks at the nativity. 'You like to add a little sparkle to everyone else's day, am I right?'

'That's actually why I love working in hospitality,' I say, twisting my fingers together. Mrs Hedgers is making me nervous. She has a headteacherly sort of energy, as if at any moment she'll tell me I'm not allowed to wear clip-in highlights at school. 'I'm a total people-person.'

'And how do you switch off?'

'Umm. Hanging out with friends?'

'Hmm,' says Mrs Hedgers.

'I do yoga too, sometimes,' I find myself saying. I think I last did yoga in the first lockdown, when everyone got excited about working out in our living rooms, as if the lockdown rules were the reason we weren't all bounding out into the woods for fifteen-mile runs every morning.

Mrs Hedgers waits. I can come up with no other down-time activities except 'watching television', which sounds like something Ruby Hedgers would put forward in answer to this question, so I just get gradually pinker and wait in silence.

'Well,' Mrs Hedgers says, hands on her chair's wheels again. 'Perhaps something to think about. It's so important for us to nourish ourselves so that we can continue to nourish those around us.'

'Right! Totally. Oh, sorry!' I say, hopping out of her way. 'Actually, while I have you, I've been meaning to ask – we still need a card for any costs that your insurer won't be covering for your stay. Would you . . .'

'They'll cover it all,' Mrs Hedgers says, and there's steel in her smile. 'Just send the bill their way.'

'Oh, OK,' I say, as she pushes open the door to her suite and manoeuvres herself through.

As the door closes behind her, I stare at it for a while. Nothing about that conversation should have made me feel especially uncomfortable, but I'm all discombobulated. Maybe it's because she didn't really like my nativity scene. Is that why? *Something* has got under my skin, and now I feel as though I've made a mistake, but I can't figure out where.

I whip out my phone and message Jem. She's in the States, but I do some quick maths and decide that even though I can never remember whether it's five hours ahead or five hours behind, as long as it's five *something* I'm not waking her in the middle of the night.

Is this lame? I say, attaching a photo of the nativity.

Umm, no?!! she replies instantly. *It is in fact the best thing I have ever seen!*

I smile down at my phone as she peppers me with stars and Christmas tree emojis. There is nobody in the world with a heart as pure as Jem Young.

Why the self-doubt? she asks. *Are you OK, little pigeon?*

Oh sorry, I'm totally fine! Just 'having a silly moment', as your mum would say. Maybe time for a sugar fix . . .

It's always time for a sugar fix. And please do not quote my mother at me at this hour!!

But Mrs Young has so many excellent one-liners! What about that time she told me I was an abject failure, dragging her daughter to the dogs?

Or the time she told me I was 'a disappointment, fundamentally speaking'?

I press my hand to my heart. We joke about these moments now, but I know how badly they wounded Jem. Even if these days she has *fundamentally speaking* literally tattooed on her arse.

You have never disappointed me, not even when you chose Team Jacob over Team Edward, I type, with a string of hearts.

She writes back, *Love you. Rehearsals now – got to go. Missing you so much x*

I tap out a heartfelt *Miss you more* before sliding my phone back into my pocket. Winter is my Jem time – her being gone has left me feeling a little unsteady. We only do Christmas together every other year – I'm on rotation between Jem and Grigg and Sameera – but even if I'm not actually with her on Christmas Day, we always spend September onwards sending each other fantastically bad new Christmas songs and meeting up for mulled wine after work.

But this year she's so busy that bothering her with the new festive album from a washed-up noughties band feels kind of stupid. Jem's always wanted to be a performer – musical theatre is the dream – and this year she finally got a spot in the ensemble of a brand-new American musical. It's the perfect breakout role for her, after years slogging away in part-time jobs.

It just also means spending six months in Washington DC, where her parents live. Which couldn't be *less* perfect. Jem spent half her childhood living on my street in Surrey, and half in DC – her family moved back and forth twice. When her parents finally settled in the US for good, Jem stayed here. Nice and close to me, nice and far away from them.

Fate, she'd said gloomily to me as we'd drunk cheap wine on my floor and mourned the fact that her dream had come true in her nightmare location. *Or Karma. Or something. Basically, the universe has decided I can't escape my mother.*

I grab a bag of candy kittens from the shelf under my computer screen and let the sugar rush hit as I flick through the booking book. My phone buzzes with a notification: it's from Google, reminding me of a photo from this time last year. I wince. Google is missing some serious subtext: it's a picture of me with Drew, my old flatmate, who I emphatically do *not* want to remember, especially at this time of year. I swipe the notification away and ram in a few more candy kittens.

'Lost property time,' says a familiar voice behind me.

I slam the book closed on the desk and steel myself for an interaction with Lucas. As I turn, I see him regarding the booking book with his usual disdain. One of my favourite activities is to make Lucas say 'the booking book' as many times as possible during a shift, because he hates my cutesy names for things. The trick is to trap him when a guest is there so he can't be a dickhead – or at least not out loud.

'Is it?' I say testily.

I glance at the clock mounted behind the desk. It's another relic from the Bartholomew family. It needs rewinding every morning, and by the end of Poor Mandy's shift, it's always running nineteen minutes behind. Checking the time on the lobby clock involves a combination of maths and guesswork: it's around midday, so the clock is probably already at least five minutes slow, so that means . . .

'It's twelve on the dot,' Lucas says, already sounding exasperated with me. 'I don't know why you even look at that clock. Don't you have a watch?'

I do have a watch. It is mint green and fabulously chunky, and I remember to put it on maybe two mornings out of ten. Today was not one of those mornings.

'I don't need a watch,' I say sweetly. 'I have you here to yell the time at me.'

I do one last sweep of the lobby to check it's all in order and then grab the key to the lost-property room. It's directly behind us – the door is just to the right of the old Bartholomew clock – but I've not been in there for months. The lost-property room was a staffroom, once, with a coffee machine and two comfy armchairs. Now it's just . . .

'Chaos,' Lucas says, as I unlock the door and step into the small amount of available floor space on the other side.

Boxes and boxes of *stuff*. A rocking horse. A collection of broken teacups, once used for afternoon teas here. An old projector. An absolute plethora of umbrellas.

So yes, it's kind of a state. But it's also kind of a treasure trove.

My heart lifts as I cast my eye over it all. If I fixed up that old rocking horse, we could definitely sell it for at least eighty quid. Mending the teacups won't take long, and people will go crazy for that cutesy 1950s pattern on them. We might be able to raise some real money from all this. Mrs SB is a genius.

'We should decide how and where we want to sell each category of item,' Lucas says, rubbing his mouth as he scans over the contents of the room. 'I'll start a spreadsheet.'

I ignore him and dive in. The first box is labelled 'tatty books' and the second 'coats left behind in 2019'.

I hear Lucas mutter something in Portuguese behind me, and choose to believe it is an expression of delight and excitement.

Lucas

After two days of Izzy making everything as difficult as possible, we establish ourselves on various online stores for second-hand goods, and life is suddenly filled with boxes, envelopes and trips to the post office. Mandy volunteers to head up sales via social media, which Izzy and I are very happy about, since sorting the hotel's Instagram presence has been on both our to-do lists for as long as I've been here. Izzy tries to insist on a hand-drawn table to keep track of items, but then she spills her gingerbread latte on it, and has to come crawling back to my Excel spreadsheet.

My days off pass in a blur of studying, and suddenly it's Thursday. I pull my collar up against the wind and step closer to the manor wall as I lift the phone to my ear. Thursday means I ring my uncle. I don't know why I do this. Nobody asks me to, and it always puts me in a bad mood afterwards, but I've discovered that if I *don't* call him at least once a week, I feel even worse.

'Hello? Lucas?' Uncle Antônio answers in Portuguese.

'Hi, Uncle.'

'I'm just heading back into the office after hours of meet-ings – this week has been relentless,' my uncle says irritably.

I grimace. By the end of this call, I will feel stupid for ringing at all, and this is the first hit: the suggestion that he's too busy to talk to me. He's not *said* that, so of course if I mention feeling this way, he will say I'm being difficult.

My sister Ana and I have always been aware that we are a burden upon Uncle Antônio. Our father died shortly after I was born, but his brother Antônio supported our mother in the time when she was off work, and insisted on having a role in our lives after that. I am grateful to him, of course. Endlessly, repeatedly. It sometimes seems there is no end to the gratitude that is required.

'Is now a bad time?' I ask.

'Now is fine. Tell me how your course is going. Are you run-ning that place yet?'

'I'm less than a year into the course, Uncle, and I'm doing it part-time.'

'There's no room for part-timers in this world, Lucas,' Antônio begins.

I cut him off before he gets into full flow. 'I mean, I'm doing it while working at the hotel. I need the practical experience as well as the degree.'

'Hmm, well. I hope they know you'll be their boss one day soon.'

My stomach tightens anxiously. I'm not doing the course out of a desire to take over Forest Manor. But as soon as Antônio says it, that old impulse kicks in: I need to work harder, I need to be pushing for a promotion, I need to do more, do better . . .

'Listen, Lucas, I think you should come home at Christmas.'

I clench my teeth. 'I can't afford it. The flights are too expensive. I've booked to come back in February.'

'February is the worst time to come home. Carnival, all the tourists . . .'

'I've made my decision,' I say again. It's best to be strong with my uncle – if you're anything but assertive, you've already lost. 'I have to go. Speak soon.'

After ending the call, I pull up my banking app, and then I shut it again very quickly, because the only thing guaranteed to make my mood worse is seeing quite how large that minus number has grown in the last few weeks. I'm still throbbing with all those old feelings, sweating them out beneath my thick coat. I can't feel the cold wind now. A phone call with my uncle: the perfect way to warm up in an English winter.

I head back to the hotel entrance, with its rounded privet hedges and its big stone steps. As I walk into the lobby, I eye Izzy's ridiculous rubble nativity scene. For an unpleasant moment, I'm reminded of last year's Christmas party – Izzy had set up a nativity for that, too. I remember walking past it with Drew, just a few moments after she'd introduced herself. *God, could that be more Izzy?* she'd said. *Who else would make the camels pink?* The memory makes me wince.

I approach the front desk. Mrs SB is there with Izzy, their heads bent close together, inspecting something. I am immediately suspicious.

45

'These could be worth a lot!' Mrs SB says.

Izzy looks up, her hand flying to the thin gold chain she's wearing around her throat.

'You want us to sell *these*?'

'Of course. Why not?' Mrs SB says.

'Mrs SB, I get it, I know how important the money is, but . . . These aren't just pieces of jewellery. They're *wedding* rings. *Engagement* rings,' Izzy says, her voice rising. 'These are little love stories, right here in this box.'

I look over their shoulders. There are five rings lying haphazardly on a folded piece of yellowing kitchen paper inside a Tupperware box. One of them is diamond studded; another sports a giant emerald at its centre, framed by two pink stones. Each one has a tiny sticker looped around it with a date printed in different handwriting.

'What is all this?' I ask.

'They're from the swimming-pool lost property,' Izzy says to me. 'I want to return them.'

'*Return* them? Aren't we supposed to be making money, not giving it away?' I ask, and then I catch Izzy's expression.

She's really upset about this. Her eyes are swimming. She blinks fast and looks away again.

'Losing a wedding ring isn't like losing an umbrella,' she says. 'I know the law says you have to keep items for a reasonable length of time – but what's reasonable when it's something with such sentimental value?'

At the mention of the law, Mrs SB looks a little distressed.

'Oh, well . . .'

'Just give me one week. Please, Mrs SB. We're doing brilliantly at selling off the other items already. But do we really want to be the sort of hotel that pawns off someone's *wedding* ring?'

'Yes?' I say.

'No,' Mrs SB says, with a heavy sigh. 'No, I suppose we don't. Thank you, Izzy.' She squeezes her shoulder. 'Our resident angel. You mustn't let us lose our heart here, all right, dear?'

I stare between them, and then back at the rings. What has heart got to do with it? These are just expensive items of jewellery. Who's to say they're more sentimentally valuable to people than their favourite umbrella?

'You can't be serious,' I begin, but Mrs SB is already striding off towards Barty, who has just appeared in the doorway, wearing a panicked expression and holding two laptops at once.

'One week!' she calls over her shoulder at Izzy, who immediately starts checking the dates on each ring. 'And then our duty is done!'

'There is no duty here,' I say. 'These are just the same as all the rest of the junk in there.'

Izzy brandishes an old booking book at me. There was a digital system before I arrived at Forest Manor, though a very bad one – and yet Izzy still insisted on writing things in that book as well as putting them on the computer. She continues this practice now, even with our superior new online system. It is one of the many ridiculous things she does.

'What's the date on that one?' she asks, pointing to the gold wedding ring I've picked up between thumb and forefinger.

'The first of November, 2018,' I say. 'Do you honestly think you can find the owner of a ring that was lost here four years ago?'

She flicks through the book and stabs a finger at the page. 'Ha!' she says. 'Five pool bookings that day, six spa sessions. All noted down in the . . .'

I raise an eyebrow at her.

'Sorry, I just can't quite . . . what's the word . . .' She taps her bottom lip, eyes wicked.

'Izzy. You are such a child.'

She grins at me, and there it is – a traitorous flicker of sensation in my gut. This happens sometimes. Ninety-nine per cent of the time, I think Izzy is the most annoying woman I have ever met, but very occasionally I can't help noticing how beautiful she is.

'This is ridiculous,' I say, looking back down at the rings.

'Tiffany Moore,' Izzy announces, flicking back to check the guest's original booking. 'And here's her landline number.'

'Izzy, this is a waste of your time.'

'OK, well, as you say: *my* time, so . . .' She motions at me to be quiet as the phone rings.

For one childish second, I am inclined to reach over and hang up the phone. I have no reason for this other than the satisfaction of knowing that she will find it deeply irritating. I don't understand how she does this to me, but something about Izzy Jenkins makes me want to behave very badly.

I don't even move – don't even twitch – but Izzy reaches a hand out and clamps it over mine on the desk. There is another twinge in my stomach, a sensation like cool seawater hitting sun-baked skin.

'Don't even think about it, Mister da Silva,' she whispers, and then slides her hand from mine. 'Oh, hello! Is Tiffany there, please?' she says into the phone, all sugar and sweetness again. As though I can't still feel the imprint of her nails tingling on the back of my hand.

I leave her to this ridiculous task and manage at least two hours of jobs before the next crisis hits. You can tell we are at one-sixth of our usual capacity. Generally, at Forest Manor, the crises come at least every fifteen minutes.

I am in Bluebell, the room where Mrs Muller is currently staying. Behind me, Dinah – our head of housekeeping – enters the room carrying a Hoover in one hand and a large bag of cleaning products in the other.

'There is nothing that will get that off. Nothing,' Dinah says immediately, dropping the Hoover with a thump. 'White spirit, maybe, but how will you avoid taking off the paint underneath?'

The wall is splattered in oil paint – red, green, and blue. The apparatus of Mrs Muller's latest form of artistic expression is still lying on a token dustsheet beneath her easel. It looks like a cross between a catapult and a leaf-blower.

'I apologise – when the muses strike, they strike, you see. I'll be needing another room, of course,' Mrs Muller says. 'I can't very well work in all this mess.'

Dinah begins vacuuming behind us. Leave Dinah anywhere for any amount of time and she'll start aggressively vacuum cleaning something. This helpfully masks the sound of me growling under my breath.

'Mrs Muller,' I say, 'you know we only have five rooms at present.'

She stares up at me from the armchair in the corner. I notice a splodge of blue paint on its fabric and am once again grateful for the sound of Dinah's Hoover. Mrs Muller is a regular at the hotel – she is an important guest. She is also a demanding one, but I understand that. I suspect I would be a demanding guest too.

'I will see what I can do, Mrs Muller. Leave it with me.'

'Well?' I ask Izzy when I return to the lobby.

'Well what?' she says, distracted as she sorts through a box of paperback books. 'Could we take some of this to a car boot sale, maybe? Use your car? My boot is teeny.'

I stare at her in horror. 'You want me to put all of this rubbish in my car?'

'It's not rubbish! These paperbacks will make a pound each. Every little helps.'

'We need tens of thousands of pounds of investment, so one pound does not particularly help.'

She dims a little and says something about the quantity of items still to be sold. I watch her counting out books on the floor behind the desk and feel an unexpected twinge of guilt for making her shoulders sag that way. Our endless back-and-forth is built into the rhythm of my day here: I had expected a sharp retort. Perhaps she will take revenge later – she likes to do that sometimes. I will probably find something sticky 'accidentally' spilled on my keyboard again this afternoon.

'So was it Tiffany Moore's wedding ring?' I find myself asking.

Izzy looks up at me, surprised, and then smug. 'Look who's already getting on board with The Ring Thing!'

Of course this mad plan now has a rhyming name.

'I'm not on board. I was just making conversation.'

'Gosh, I wasn't aware you knew how to do that. Well, it wasn't hers,' Izzy says, returning to the paperbacks. 'She said her wedding ring is still firmly on her finger. I've tried a couple more people but I'm hitting the rest of the list after this box. Unless you want to help, and give someone a call now?'

'I'm not getting involved in your childish plan,' I say as I return to my lost-property spreadsheet.

'Oh, of course not,' Izzy says, in an infuriating singsong voice. 'Understanding the concept of sentimental value requires some capacity for human emotion, I suppose.'

I ignore her as she busies herself around me. She's so *energetic*. I would expect her to be exhausted at the end of a shift, but from what I've seen, she always has evening plans with someone – she seems to have huge quantities of friends. They're always dropping in, hugging her over the desk, vowing never to go so long without seeing her again.

I've not noticed a boyfriend around recently, though. Last year there was usually one of those loitering about too, but since we've been working shifts together again, I've not come upon a man in too-tight trousers with a guitar on his back waiting in the lobby, so I'd have to guess that Izzy is currently single.

'Hello, is that Kelly?' Izzy says into the phone, catching it between her shoulder and ear as she sticks together an old teacup with both hands.

I listen as she explains the situation to the woman on the other end of the phone.

'Not mine,' the woman barks.

I can hear every word from where I'm sitting. It is incredibly distracting to have to listen to Izzy's phone conversations in this way. I have long suspected her of turning up the volume on that phone for this precise reason.

'Was I even at your hotel in 2018?' Kelly says. 'Seems unlikely. New Forest isn't really my scene. Not much to do. Too many trees. Very samey.'

I can't help bristling. I love the New Forest, and there are at least fifteen leaflets under this desk that will demonstrate exactly how much there is to do here. This place has become home to me. I'd defend it in the same way I'd defend Niterói, the city where I grew up. It has its faults, but it's mine.

'You came for a long weekend with your husband,' Izzy says.

'Oh, *that* husband,' Kelly says. 'Yeah, no, we're not married any more. But it can't be my ring. I keep my old wedding rings in the loft.'

Izzy snorts out a surprised laugh. 'Right. OK. Well, thank you for your help, Kelly.'

'You really go the extra mile, don't you?' Kelly says.

Izzy lifts her chin. 'Well, yes, I think it's—'

'Listen, a little life lesson for free, from me to you. Don't fucking bother. Nobody gives a shit and you'll just wear yourself out. Bye-bye!'

Izzy stares at the phone for a moment after Kelly hangs up. I can't help laughing. She shoots me a filthy glare and clicks the phone back into the receiver, returning to her boxes. She's made progress since I last looked. Or, at least, things are now in different piles.

'Is there a system here?' I ask.

She rolls her eyes. 'Of course. Unsorted; unsellable; for up-cycling; for Mandy's little putting-pics-on-Twitter scheme; for the car boots; for Etsy; for Gumtree; for washing; for the bin.'

She points at each pile so quickly I'm lost by 'for upcycling', a word I don't understand anyway. I stare at it all, unwilling to ask her to repeat herself.

After a moment, she starts again, more slowly. 'Unsorted. Unsellable. Upcycling – so like, stuff I think I can glam up. This is stuff for Poor Mandy to take pretty pictures of. And this is for the car boot, Etsy, Gumtree ... Then these need washing, and that's for the rubbish bin.'

I follow this time. I hate it when the language barrier slows me down – it's rare now, though it happened all the time when I first moved to the UK three years ago. Nowadays I even think in English most of the time. My *vô* would have been horrified to hear that – my grandfather believed no language is more beautiful than Brazilian Portuguese. But I like English, for all its awkwardness. It is usually worth taking the time to learn something difficult, I find.

I watch Izzy as she taps away at the keyboard, making an

irritated noise when the system takes a moment to load. I can still see the woman I thought she was last year. Independent, stubborn, but kind and funny too.

And then I remember her screaming at me across the hotel lawn last December. The countless times she screwed me over in the last year, the petty point-scoring, the way her humour turns barbed the moment it's turned on me.

I look away to sort the next box. Not *everything* difficult is worth the time.

Izzy

The next few days are a blur of restaurant service, odd jobs and building dust. Lucas and I come to a rare and begrudging agreement on one thing: if we must share shifts, we should be as far away from each other as possible. So one of us gets on with some of the four billion things that need doing around here, and the other covers the desk, even if that just means keeping an ear out from the kitchen and sprinting when the phone rings.

Slowly, items from around the hotel begin to disappear. An antique wooden dresser; several paintings of old men whose importance was long ago forgotten, which they would probably have found very upsetting; and the vases. I never thought I would miss those vases, but every time someone comes to collect another one, I feel a teeny twinge in my chest.

Meanwhile, I am making rubbish progress with The Ring Thing. It's actually a lot harder than I thought it would be, though of course Lucas is under the impression that I'm seconds away from returning every single one. I do get one promising email about the diamond engagement ring from an address that's a garbled string of letters and numbers. It says, *Hold fire, I'll call upon return to UK.* No name, nothing. All a bit weird. But nobody rings, so I forget about it, lost in a flurry of lost-property items, rain and social obligations.

When the phone call comes, I am talking through a new lunch menu with Arjun, who now has a very limited number of people with whom to discuss these things (Ollie suggested we should serve Doritos with Arjun's forty-eight-hour chilli and has been banned from having opinions).

'The bitterness needs offsetting,' Arjun is saying.

'Right, totally,' I say, bubble-wrapping a vintage snow globe that just sold to someone in Northumberland for a satisfying £85. It's a great price, but I hate selling this stuff – especially the festive decorations. I want the hotel to look like it did on my first Christmas here: glowing, gorgeous, its mantlepieces laden with thick fir branches and golden lights.

'I'm thinking salt-crusted parsnip?'

'Salt-crusted,' I say, tearing the Sellotape with my teeth. 'Perfect.'

'Are you humouring me?' Arjun asks, eyes appearing from behind the menu, which is held about two inches from his face. He's so overdue a visit to the optician that I have considered booking one for him and luring him there by pretending I've found a fantastic new deli.

'I'm giving you what you need,' I say, 'which is a sounding board and some validation.'

The menu drops further. 'Will you swap jobs with Ollie?' Arjun asks. 'Please?'

'Ollie's great. He's just new, and you never like new things. You thought I was annoying for at *least* a year.'

'You have always been my favourite!' Arjun says, outraged at the very suggestion. He has a selective memory for his own bad-temperedness.

'Give Ollie a chance.'

'Puh,' Arjun says, as he nabs my pen to scribble down a note about parsnips. 'You give Lucas a chance, then.'

He looks up and laughs at my expression. Arjun is usually the last person to suggest going easy on anyone. I remember the first time Drew popped in to see me while I was at work – she'd been hoping for a free lunch. Arjun had eyed her through the kitchen door and said, *That's the flatmate you're always bending over backwards for? I say cut her loose. She's ordered three sides, Izzy. That is a woman who takes what she can get.*

The phone rings before I can respond to Arjun.

'Forest Manor Hotel and Spa, this is Izzy speaking! How can I help you?'

'Hello,' says a gravelly male voice. 'Full name, please?'

'Umm. Izzy Jenkins? Isabelle Jenkins?'

'And can I ask you to confirm the address of your place of work?'

I blink. 'Am I, like, going through security for something here?'

There is a slight pause. 'I got an email,' the man says. 'And I need to confirm that I'm speaking to the correct person.'

'Was the email about a wedding or engagement ring?' I say hopefully.

'Affirmative,' the man says.

Ooh, I love that. I am going to start saying *affirmative*. When Jem next messages me asking if I'm all caught up on *Strictly*, that is exactly what I'm going to say back.

'I responded to say I would be in touch when I returned to the UK. I'm back now, and I'd like to request a follow-up email with an image of the engagement ring in question,' he says.

'I can do that for you, no problem!'

'I'll be in touch once that has been safely received,' he says. 'Goodbye.'

'The Ring Thing?' Arjun asks as I click the phone back into the receiver, slightly dazed.

'Yeah. Crap. That was all so weird I didn't even take his name. Though I'm pretty sure I know who it was.' I look up at Arjun. 'Am I being ridiculous about these rings, like Lucas says?'

Arjun tilts his head, tapping the pen on the menu. 'You're being an optimist,' he says eventually. 'And a romantic.'

'So . . . Ridiculous?'

'No.' He gives me his full attention – a rare thing from Arjun. 'You're being Izzy, and it's excellent,' he says, as though it's as simple as that. 'Now, excuse me. I have some parsnips to salt.'

I watch him go with a lump in my throat. I have seen Arjun almost every day for eight years. At first we didn't click, but slowly, week by week, we've become more than colleagues, more even than friends. I've cried on him several times, and he cried on me after his awful, toxic divorce. We might never have been mates outside of this place, but now we rely on each other – he's part of my life. For Lucas, losing this job would probably be an inconvenience. For me, it would be like losing a family all over again.

And I just *can't*.

On the last Monday of November, when I am two days away from having to sell that curious Tupperware of rings, a straight-backed man in a razor-sharp suit comes marching into the lobby. Poor Mandy is setting up, gamely creating herself a space amongst all the lost-property boxes, and I'm already on my way out the door – I've got drinks with a couple of temps I used to work with when I first started at Forest Manor.

'Eric Matterson,' the man announces when he reaches the desk. 'I'm here about a ring.'

Mandy's eyes find mine. I dash over.

Eric looks about sixty – he is greying at the temples and has a deep frown-line between his eyebrows. This is *exactly* how I imagined the guy on the phone. He has the carefully pressed look of a military type, and an intimidating air of steeliness.

'A French nineteenth-century rose-cut diamond,' he is saying, 'set into a claw in a D-shaped gold ring of approximately three millimetres in width.'

'Hi,' I say.

He looks at me. 'Hello,' he says, as if humouring me. 'Cushion-cut diamonds around the central stone.'

I already know the one he means – I emailed him the picture

two days ago. It's a beautiful ring. Obviously antique, even to an amateur like me. My stomach flutters with excitement.

'Does it belong to you?' I ask.

He stares at me. 'Yes. Obviously.'

A young man darts through the door behind him, shaking out his coat in a shower of drops like a dog out of water. Poor Mandy heads over to take his umbrella, unexpectedly dousing her own shoes as she pulls it closed. She looks down at her feet, crestfallen, before returning to the desk with the air of a woman who fully expects the universe to give her wet shoes.

'Dad, can you stop doing that?' the young man says, trying to rearrange his hair in the large mirror hanging on the lobby wall. Mrs SB was measuring that up this morning – I doubt it'll be here much longer.

'Doing what?' Eric asks.

'*Slipping off*,' his son says with exasperation. 'Dad was a spy in the Cold War,' he explains to us, joining his father at the desk. 'Some habits can't be shaken off, apparently. I've only just about persuaded him to communicate over an encrypted messenger app instead of using those super hardcore ones that all the terrorists are on, you know?'

'Charlie,' Eric says, face set in an expression of fixed patience, 'please will you stop telling strangers that I was a spy in the Cold War?' His eyes flick towards me, then Mandy, face barely moving. 'I wasn't a spy,' he says.

'No, of course not,' says Mandy, just as Lucas appears behind her, as if from nowhere, Lucifer-style.

For such a big man, he can be surprisingly stealthy. He's still in his uniform, but he's wearing the wrong shoes – trainers instead of his usual shining black brogues – as if he started getting changed and then thought better of it. I don't know what he's doing lurking here. We all know he thinks The Ring Thing is stupid and sentimental. I hope he's not planning to sabotage this in revenge for the pin cushion from lost property that I inadvertently left on his chair yesterday.

'Proof,' Eric says, reaching into his pocket and laying a photograph on the desk between us.

It's old and faded, A5, just like the ones in my parents' photo albums. The man in the image is unmistakably Eric – as straight-backed as he is today – and the woman showing the camera her ring beside him looks just as serious.

'My wife,' Eric says, and for the first time, I catch a hint of emotion from him.

'Thank you,' I say. It hadn't occurred to me to ask for proof, so I'm glad he offered. 'Here, it's yours. I'm so pleased it's found you again.'

Eric clears his throat as I click open the Tupperware and I make a mental note to move these rings into something less conspicuously shabby. This box does not scream 'we have taken great care of your possessions'. The trouble is, Lucas has been needling me about keeping valuable items in a Tupperware, so now if I switch them into something else, I look like I'm conceding.

'Give it to my son,' Eric says, when I hold the ring out. He averts his eyes. 'It's yours now, Charlie, all right?'

Charlie's mouth forms an almost perfect O. He looks between

each of us, even Lucas, who is just standing in a looming sort of way and not bothering to introduce himself to anybody.

'You . . . Do you mean that?' Charlie says to his father.

'Do you need me to say it twice?'

'No, I . . . But as in . . . You understand that if I have Mum's ring, I'm going to . . .'

'Use it to propose to that young man of yours, yes,' Eric says, tone clipped. He looks up at the ceiling. 'Quite right. You've made him wait long enough.'

'*I've* made . . .' Charlie snaps his mouth closed. 'Wow.'

I *knew* this ring mattered. I could just feel it when it first glimmered up at me on that piece of kitchen paper. I let my gaze slide to Lucas. It's generally hard to read his expression – he defaults to a pretty unchanging 'implacable' – but his gaze is very fixed as he watches Charlie tear up in front of us.

'Mum would have wanted that,' Charlie says to his father. 'I really . . . Thank you.'

'Yes, well,' Eric says. 'I may have been a bit . . . picky for you. Hiro isn't *too* bad. I just want you to be happy.'

This last part looks like news to Charlie. He takes it with a slight wobble of his bottom lip.

'There'll be a reward,' Eric says, turning back to us abruptly and pulling out his phone. 'Let me look into the numbers.'

'Sorry?' I say. 'A . . .'

'Financial reward. This ring is worth a large sum. I appreciate the lengths you went to in order to return it to us. It is . . . greatly significant to my family.'

I watch Eric's Adam's apple bob as he swallows, and despite

myself I feel my eyes brim up. My dad was nothing like Eric – he was warm, open, ready to laugh. But I can't help thinking of Dad. The ring he gave me for my twenty-first birthday, now lying at the bottom of the sea after a *stupid* drunk swim in Brighton on my twenty-second birthday. I touch my necklace, the gold chain Mum gave me for my twenty-first – *something different from each of us, you know what we're like, can't agree on anything!*

'That's incredibly kind of you, sir,' Lucas says, when I fail to answer. He shoots me an odd look before returning his attention to Eric. 'Can we invite you to stay for a drink with your son?'

I shake myself. 'Yes! And actually . . .' I look at Charlie as he steps forward and takes the ring reverently from my palm. 'If you're looking for a gorgeous location to propose, you've found the perfect place.'

He looks around the hotel as if noticing where he is for the first time.

'Huh,' he says. 'That would be cute, wouldn't it? Given Mum's ring was here all this time.'

'We can meet to talk about that now, if you wish,' Lucas says, smelling profit, no doubt. 'I'm available.'

'As am I!' I say, already mentally composing a message cancelling my evening plans. I suspect Charlie is going to do his proposal in a big way, and that disposable income is not a problem for his family, which means that right now, I am Charlie's number-one fan.

'Perfect,' Eric says, making his way towards the bar. 'Charlie! A drink before our meeting.'

Charlie follows after his father in a daze.

'You're not getting the credit for this, if that's your plan, muscling in with your "meeting",' I say to Lucas. 'The Ring Thing was *my* idea.'

'You hardly expected this to happen,' Lucas scoffs.

That grates on me, so I smile. I know this smile winds Lucas up. It's my most obliging, most engaging one – the one that always makes guests calm down when they're angry. It has the opposite effect on Lucas. I suspect he knows that when I smile like this, really I'm thinking, *You're an idiot, and I'm going to be so nice to you, you won't even notice that I'm getting my way and you're not getting yours.*

'If you think you can swan in now, and then tell Mrs SB and Barty that *you* got this reward for the hotel . . .'

Lucas pulls his chin back slightly, eyes flaring. 'Is that what you think I'd do?'

I pause. His acts of sabotage aren't generally that dishonourable, admittedly. But if he's not planning to take the credit, why is he helping?

'I care about this place too, you know,' Lucas says.

I tilt my head, like, *Really though?* I know Lucas likes this job, but I'm not sure the man has it in him to really *love* something the way I love Forest Manor.

'Whatever,' I say. 'I need to get changed back into uniform if we're doing this meeting.'

I'm in a white knitted jumper that hangs down to my knees over washed-out jeans and my baby-pink trainers – I love this outfit, but it's not very professional. I hike my bag on to my shoulder and head for the lost-property room. There's space in there now that we've cleared it out a bit – or, as Lucas put it earlier, 'moved the contents of this terrible room into the lobby where everyone can see them'.

I slip out of my jumper and trainers and then bend to yank my uniform back out of my bag. I like the Forest Manor uniform – it's just a simple white shirt and black trousers, with the hotel logo on the left breast, but I feel good when I'm wearing it. It's like slipping into the person I am at work. At the hotel, I'm not overstretched, I'm not exhausted; I'm nobody's tragic anecdote. I'm the one who . . . what did Mrs Hedgers say? The one who brings the sparkle.

'Oh, Izzy, I wanted to ask about this box of – oops!' says Poor Mandy, barging through the door behind me and then clocking that I'm in nothing but my jeans and bra.

I turn. Lucas is standing on the other side of the desk behind Mandy, and for the briefest of moments, before Mandy shuts the door, we lock eyes.

These days, Lucas tends to look at me with a sort of flat, weary regard, as though he's just waiting for me to annoy him. It's grown harder and harder to believe that I ever saw anything more than that in Lucas's gaze when he looked at me. But right now, as our eyes meet, something shifts. He's not completely in control of himself, and what I see makes my skin tingle. For the first time since that humiliating screaming match on the hotel lawns, Lucas da Silva is looking at me like he wants me.

The door slams shut and the moment's gone, but my skin still glows from his gaze.

God. I hand the man my heart, tell him to meet me under the

mistletoe, then turn up there to find him kissing my flatmate. I call him out for being a thoughtless dickhead and he tells me I'm *making drama*. He spends all year making this job as hard as possible for me, refusing to compromise on anything, even after what he did last Christmas.

And *still* he can turn me hot with one single glance.

Lucas

'Explain it to me,' Pedro says in Portuguese, coffee machine whirring behind him. 'You hate her because . . .'

'It's complicated,' I say, eyeing the coffee as it streams out of the machine into my favourite mug, the tall grey one with just the right-sized handle.

I've been frequenting Smooth Pedro's Coffee and Smoothie Bar for almost two years now. Pedro and I met at the gym – I heard his accent across the weights zone, and it was like breathing in and suddenly smelling home. He's from Teresópolis and has been in the UK for a few years longer than me. He gives terrible advice but makes excellent coffee.

'I can do complicated,' he says, and then, at my dubious expression: 'Go on, try me. Allow me to surprise you. Wasn't I right about putting avocado in your smoothie?'

This feels slightly different, but I humour him. 'Last year, we were flirtatious, but she was always seeing someone, and it never really came to anything. Then at the hotel Christmas party, I kissed this woman who turned out to be her flatmate. It was under the mistletoe, not even a real thing. But Izzy got so protective. She dragged me out on to the lawn and yelled that I had behaved like a pig, and that, hang on . . .'

I wrap my hands around the mug of coffee as I try to remember her exact wording.

'*You're not good enough for her anyway, you cold-hearted shiny-shoed robot-man.*'

'Whew. I am seeing some warning signs here,' says Pedro.

'I know.'

'Do you think she was jealous?'

'Izzy? No. And that would be crazy, anyway. We weren't together, we'd never even kissed . . .'

'Hmm,' Pedro says, unimpressed. 'So she just didn't think you were good enough for her friend?'

'Exactly.'

I swallow. I have enough self-insight to know that *not good enough* is something I struggle with. But it's more than that. I liked Izzy. I respected her opinion. Knowing that she thought Drew shouldn't be kissing a man like me had done more than just hit an old nerve – it had reminded me that wherever I am in the world, women always see me the same way. *You don't have a heart, so don't tell me I broke it,* my ex had said on her way out of the door. When she had first confessed to cheating on me, Camila had seemed genuinely surprised to see me crying. *I honestly didn't know you had it in you,* she'd said.

I close my eyes, sipping my coffee as Pedro gets the smoothie bar ready for opening. I'm off today and tomorrow, but I will be working here in my favourite seat at the window – my laptop is already packed in the bag at my feet. I am behind on my course, with an essay due on Friday, and on top of that, Izzy talked Charlie into proposing to his boyfriend on Thursday, and promised all sorts of bespoke elements that we now have to organise on a tight budget. I need to stay focused.

And I absolutely *must* stop thinking about Izzy Jenkins in nothing but jeans and a pink bra.

'I need Izzy,' Mrs SB says distractedly, as she powers towards me across the lobby with several ring binders tucked awkwardly under one arm.

It's Thursday morning. My essay is almost done, and Charlie's proposal is as arranged as I could make it without coming into the hotel or coordinating with Izzy outside of working hours. I watch as Mrs SB dodges a couple departing from the restaurant and gives them a wide, *it's all under control* smile before dropping a file on to the tiles and saying, 'Oh, bugger.'

'Izzy is—'

'Right here!' Izzy sings, sailing into the lobby from the restaurant.

She looks disarmingly pretty in waiting uniform, two strands of silky hair falling out of her ponytail. I try and fail not to think about the pink bra.

'Ah, good,' Mrs SB says, before glancing towards the corridor that leads to Sweet Violet. She lowers her voice. 'Mr Townsend is very upset about the builders.'

As one, we look at the builders, who are currently debating something at the top of a scaffolding tower by the staircase. They are incredibly intrusive. I have asked them to be quiet on multiple occasions, but the only effect has been that they have stopped greeting me when I arrive in the mornings.

Mr Townsend is a particularly special guest here. He's been coming for decades, I believe, at first with his wife and then, when she passed away, he would stay on his own for the winter. I don't usually have personal conversations with guests, but even I feel fond of the man. Every fortnight or so, I give him a lift to the shops, and we have started having a coffee together afterwards. He reminds me of my *vô*, with his spindly reading glasses and slow, thoughtful smile. He has Parkinson's, and every year he struggles a little more with his symptoms, but he is very stoic about it.

'Hmm,' Izzy says, tapping her bottom lip. 'OK. Leave it with me.'

Mrs SB smiles, already on her way again. 'My favourite sentence. Thank you, dear!'

I watch Izzy as she settles Mr Townsend on the sofa by the window, sitting on her haunches in front of him as they talk. How carefully she listens, how gently she explains the situation, how warmly he regards her. They end up discussing The Ring Thing – it seems to be all anyone talks about around here, much to my irritation. *I know why this project matters to you so much, Izzy,* he says, which makes me move a little closer to hear better. But he goes on to talk about his own wife. *I think it's lovely. My Maisie treasured her ring until the day she was taken from me,* he says, settling back into his seat as the rain comes down against the glass behind them. *When we were first stepping out together . . .*

I look away. I understand why Mrs SB wanted Izzy for this job. People love her without her even having to try. They don't see the Izzy I see all day – they don't know how cutting and uncompromising she can be.

To everyone but me, it seems, Izzy is absolutely perfect.

Charlie's plans for his proposal escalate as the day goes on. By the evening, our one remaining gardener is setting up fireworks at the end of the lawns, Arjun is searching the county for a very specific type of champagne, and several members of the Matterson and Tanaka families are gathering in the bar for a surprise celebration after Charlie and Hiro's private dinner out here under the pergola.

I am grateful to be outside for a few moments. I wouldn't say it's peaceful – Izzy is with me. But this afternoon's rain glimmers on the trees around us, and the air is soft and fresh as nightfall presses in.

When I moved here, I never expected to love the forest so much. I thought it would be picturesque, perhaps, but I didn't realise how something so old and so beautiful would make me feel. It is easy to find calm in a place that outdates you by about a millennium.

'I feel like it's not saying *proposal*. We need to dial up the sparkliness,' says Izzy, stepping back to survey the pergola with a critical tilt of her head.

I breathe out through my nose. Izzy offsets all calming

properties of the New Forest. My blood pressure is already climbing.

'Why does a proposal require sparkle, exactly?'

The pergola looks classy – there are candles, tasteful floral decorations and a light sprinkling of fairy lights hanging in loops between the eight oak pillars.

'It's a huge moment! It needs to feel epic,' Izzy says, and then, catching my eye-roll, she says, 'Oh, let me guess, you hate proposals? And joy? And love?'

'I do not hate joy and love. Or proposals. Put those fairy lights down,' I say, exasperated. 'You'll ruin it. We already have lights.'

What is it with this woman and those things? If she had her way, we'd all wander around the hotel draped in them.

'Not *enough* lights,' Izzy says, already mounting the ladder to hang the next set. 'And I don't believe you. I literally cannot imagine you proposing. You'd be like . . .' She trails off. 'OK, I'm not going to attempt a Brazilian accent. But you'd say something really factual. Like, *Why don't we get married, here are all the reasons I think this is a good idea.*'

'Do it in the accent,' I say, moving to stand under her ladder. No doubt if she fell and broke a bone it would be my fault, somehow. 'Then I might tell you how I would propose.'

That catches her by surprise – her hands falter on the fairy lights and she looks down at me. I meet her gaze after a day of avoiding eye contact by every possible means. She has surprising eyes. From her colouring you'd expect hazel or brown, but they're the green of palmeira leaves, and almond-shaped, with decadent long lashes. Izzy is 'cute', that's what men would say – she's petite, with round cheeks and a button nose. Cute, not sexy. Until you meet her eyes, and then you change your mind.

'I'm not doing the accent,' she says after a moment, returning her attention to the string of lights.

'OK.'

'I'm not doing it – it'll be offensively bad.'

'Fine.'

She waits. I wait.

'Oh, for God's sake, fine: *Why don't we get married*,' she tries, and then, when I start laughing, 'That was good! I thought it was good!'

'It started Spanish,' I say, straightening up and sniffing as I compose myself again. 'And then became Australian.'

Even in the half-light I can see that she's red with embarrassment, and I grin, mood greatly improved.

'Shut up, Lucas. Go on, then – how would you propose?' she asks as she climbs down the ladder and shifts it to the next pillar.

'Not like this,' I say.

With all the outdoor heaters set up and the table beautifully dressed, this is technically an ideal spot for a proposal. But there is something tense about it.

'This is too . . .'

'Spontaneous? Romantic?' she says, climbing up the rungs again as the colour subsides in her cheeks.

'I was going to say showy. What if Hiro says no? Half of his family is waiting in the bar.'

'Do you just *enjoy* sucking the fun out of everything? We're

73

helping to create something magical here, and you're standing there talking about Hiro breaking Charlie's heart.'

I ignore this, taking comfort – as I will many times – from remembering Izzy trying to sound Brazilian. She is wilfully naïve about this sort of thing. I am just being realistic.

'Anyway, asking someone to marry you is a question,' she says over her shoulder, standing on one foot to loop the lights a little further along the beam. 'So there's always the possibility the other person will say no.'

'If there's the possibility she will say no, then I wouldn't be asking,' I say. This strikes me as a given, but Izzy pauses as she comes down the ladder, staring at me.

'You would already know she'd say yes? Where's the excitement in that?'

'A proposal is an agreement,' I say. 'It's a lifelong commitment. You don't do it on a whim.'

'Well, that makes sense, at least,' Izzy says dryly. 'I've never seen you do anything on a whim. Turn them on, would you?'

I flick on the lights, a bad mood blooming in my stomach. What's so good about whims? Isn't it just another word for not thinking things through?

'What would you want, then?' I ask her, as we step back to admire the overall effect. 'You would prefer to be blindsided?'

'No, of course not, I'd just want it to be romantic, not some sort of pre-agreed contrived thing, you know? Ooh, they're here!' she hisses, checking the nearest outdoor heater is working with one hand and lighting the candle at the centre of the table with the other.

We've instructed Ollie to come out and wait on the table no more than fifteen minutes after Charlie and Hiro are seated. Charlie wants to propose at the start of the meal, so that he can enjoy his dinner. Or – I can't help thinking – so that he has time for a quick getaway if Hiro says no.

'Go! Go! Go!' Izzy whispers.

She runs off into the woods. I stare in the direction of her flying hair and the white bottoms of her trainers before walking after her. Running is entirely unnecessary. Also, she's going in a completely random direction. I hesitate when I hit the path that will take me back to the hotel, and the evening I had planned for myself: drive home, heat up a portion of *feijoada* from the freezer, and eat it in front of *A Grande Família*. It is what I always do on Thursdays. Every two months I batch cook a huge *feijoada* specifically for this reason.

It is safe and comfortable. A small joy in a stressful week.

If I follow Izzy somewhere into the New Forest, I suspect I will not have a safe and comfortable night. I hesitate, listening to the sounds of Charlie and Hiro settling into their seats: Hiro's murmur of delight, Charlie's nervous laugh.

I step off the path.

Izzy

I'm up a tree by the time I realise Lucas has followed me. He really is surprisingly stealthy.

'Izzy. Are you in a tree?'

His tone is as dry and expressionless as ever. I shift on my branch to get a better view, ignoring the dampness soaking into my clothes. Between the trees, the pergola is lit up in yellow gold, and if Lucas would shut up, I'd be able to hear every word Hiro and Charlie are saying.

This place is so gorgeous at night. If the New Forest seems like a fairy-tale wood in the daytime, in the dark it's all goblins and witchcraft. No matter how wet or cold it is, there's magic in the air. I once saw a white owl drop between the trees right in front of me on my walk home, its pale face turned to mine in wide-eyed surprise. And the night sky here is stunning: reams of stars, as thick and bright as spilled glitter.

'Izzy. I heard something up this tree. Is it you? Or a cat?'

I snort.

'It is you. What are you doing?'

'Will you shush? I'm trying to watch!'

'Did you climb a tree so you could spy on Charlie's proposal?'

'Yes, obviously.'

'This is a private moment for two people you don't know.'

'Oh, please. It's not like I'm livestreaming. Aww, that is *adorable*.'

'What is adorable?'

'He's – oh, oh my God, this is too cute.'

'What is too cute?'

'Will you either shut up or get up?'

'I am not climbing this tree.'

There is a brief, wonderful silence. Between the branches, the light hits Hiro's face as he lifts his hands to his mouth in shock and delight, and I feel myself tearing up. Lucas is such a cynic. This proposal is exactly what Hiro wanted, and they're absolutely going to live happily ever after.

'Tell me what is happening,' Lucas says.

'Are you kidding?'

'Do you actually want me in your tree?'

It is a pretty small tree.

'Fine. He said yes. They're – aww . . .'

'You are terrible at this.'

'What do you want, like, a football commentary?'

'That would be perfect.'

'And he's leaning in, the ring's on Hiro's finger, I don't believe it, Charlie's done it! He's really done it! Charlie Matterson has proposed to Hiro Tanaka, and Hiro has accepted. Here today at Forest Manor Hotel and Spa, Charlie's shown the world what he's made of, and – oh – he's leaning in for a kiss! And it's another winner!'

'Please stop.'

I've given myself the giggles. I wriggle off my tree branch to the one below and then hop down to ground level with a little less grace than I'd like; I stumble and have to grab on to something, which turns out to be Lucas's arm, though it's hard to tell the difference between that and a tree trunk, to be fair.

He pulls away from me in the darkness as if I've scalded him.

'What!' I say, before I can stop myself. 'I'm not contagious.'

It's hard to read his expression – down here the lights from the pergola are blocked by the trees, and he's shadowy, edged in dark gold.

'What did I do wrong this time?' Lucas says, without particular rancour.

The forest floor is wet, its moss soaked through from today's rain. We begin to walk back to the hotel, skirting the clearing with the pergola to give Charlie and Hiro their privacy. Our work is officially done – it's over to Arjun, Ollie and the waiting staff now.

'Do you honestly find me so repellent? Seriously?'

I glance across at Lucas's profile, the hard jut of his brow and jaw, the precise lines of his haircut.

'You once expressed a desire never to come within two metres of me, "pandemic or no pandemic",' he says. 'I am just respecting your wishes.'

I wince. I did say that. It sounds harsh rather than funny when he quotes it back to me. I remind myself that this man read the Christmas card in which I confessed my feelings for him and *laughed*. I do not need to feel bad for offending him.

'That was right after you told Mrs SB on me when I'd broken lockdown rules for that wedding. I was pissed off,' I say, looking down at the path. We're lit by little inset lights – they glow against Lucas's ridiculously well-polished shoes with each step.

'I did not "tell on you". I raised a concern, because if you continued risking the health of everyone at the hotel in order to please a handful of guests, you could have got us closed down.'

'It was their wedding day,' I say, and here's the rising tide of frustration that always comes after prolonged exposure to Lucas. 'They wanted their whole family there and all I did was find an innovative solution to how to get more than fifteen people celebrating *without* technically all being at the same—'

'It's done,' he says, breaking in as we step on to the lawns. 'We have already agreed to disagree on whether it was right.'

I grit my teeth. We're almost at the hotel car park. Almost time to slam the door on my beautiful sky-blue Smart car, get Harper Armwright's Christmas album playing and drive away from Lucas at speed.

My phone buzzes in my hand, lighting up, and we both look down at the screen. An email from Mrs SB. Subject line: *£15,000 reward from Eric Matterson?!?!*

'Holy shit,' I whisper, coming to a halt and flicking the email open.

New plan, it reads. *Return every ring. Even just one more reward like*

that would make this worth every bit of effort. Wow. You're an absolute
star, Izzy – WELL DONE!! X

'Well,' Lucas says stiffly, setting off towards the car park again.
'You certainly got the credit.'

'Yeah,' I say. 'It was me who did it, so . . .' I have to double-step
to keep up with him. 'Don't be jealous. This is a hotel mission
now. You're officially part of The Ring Thing.'

He waits a long moment before responding. 'That *is* a significant reward.'

'I'm sorry, was that an admission that The Ring Thing was
an excellent idea and from now on you're going to help me?'

'You didn't do this in the hope of a reward.'

'I did it because it felt right, and putting good stuff out into
the universe gets you good stuff back.' I spread my arms as we
step between the hedges and into the car park. 'Isn't that kind
of the same?'

He stares at me flatly. 'I hope you don't actually think that's
how the world works.'

I do, absolutely, so I roll my eyes at him. He slows, and I
glance at his car. It's one of those sleek, dark ones with blackout
windows, the sort of car a supervillain would drive. Figures.

'To answer your questions, yes, I will join you in working on
this ring . . . business,' he says. 'Since Mrs SB wants it done. And
no. I don't find you repellent.'

I raise my eyebrows in surprise. Lucas's head is turned away
from me, towards the hotel, with its beautiful eighteenth-
century windows glowing gold. I take the opportunity to really
look at him. His eyebrows are hard slashes, drawn together in

his habitual frown, but his lips are surprisingly full. He has the sort of soft, wide mouth you'd describe as *expressive* on someone who had more than one expression.

'It is one of the many things about you that annoys me,' he says.

I intend to snort a laugh and take my moment to walk away when he's conceded something. But I'm still looking at the light and shadow playing across his face, and instead, on impulse, I find myself saying, 'Vice versa, Lucas da Silva. You are offensively handsome.'

It clearly catches him by surprise, which surprises *me* – I mean, he knows I used to fancy him. Plus he's so objectively gorgeous, it didn't feel like a particularly revealing thing to say – it was like telling him he's tall or bad-tempered. He jangles his car keys in his hand, and I get the sense he's lost for words, which makes me a little giddy. All of a sudden I feel like doing something risky. I've not felt that particular zip of daring go through me for a while, and I'd forgotten how *fun* it feels.

'If you're helping with The Ring Thing,' I say, 'do you want to make it a bit more interesting?'

'Interesting . . . how?' Lucas says, keys still jangling.

I reach for my own keys in my pocket, Smartie's lights blinking in the dark car park as I hit unlock. This is a conversation that feels like it might need a fast exit.

'A bet. Whoever returns the next ring wins.'

The wind blusters through the car park, ruffling the hedges, sending a lone plastic bottle skittering under the cars.

'Wins what?' Lucas asks.

'Well . . . what would you like?'

The keys stop jangling. He is suddenly very still.

'What would I like?'

'Mm.'

It seems colder now, the breeze sharper. Lucas's stillness reminds me of a big cat waiting to pounce.

'I want one day,' he says. 'One day in which you do things my way. I am in charge. What I say goes.'

'You'd love that, wouldn't you?' I say derisively, but my breath quickens.

He looks at me with dark, glinting eyes. 'If you win, you can have the same.'

Lucas at my beck and call, agreeing with everything I say, doing as he's told? It is almost too good to imagine. And I'm confident I can return a ring before he can. This sort of challenge is made for me – Lucas will try to use statistics and spreadsheets, but this is about understanding *people*. I lift my chin, shucking off the strange, hot-cold feeling that's come over me in the face of his steady stare.

'Deal,' I say, and hold out my hand to shake his.

Our palms connect hard. The feeling of his fingers gripping my hand makes my heart quicken, like the moment at the start of a race – you're not running yet, but you know you will be.

Lucas

I arrive at the hotel the next morning to find that Izzy is already here, and has spread a great number of socks across the desk. After a moment, I conclude that this is part of an effort to sort them into pairs, which strikes me as an enormous waste of time – but then, Izzy loves to do what she calls 'going the extra mile'.

'I've sorted your Mrs Muller problem,' she says to me, not bothering with a hello.

One of the builders calls, 'Hey, Izz!' as he strolls in, still vaping, and she gives him a big smile and a wave, all of which irritates me. Despite the two hours I've just spent in the gym, I'm on edge – I have been all week. The stress of working shifts with Izzy Jenkins, no doubt.

'It's not *my* Mrs Muller problem,' I say, very deliberately shifting the clothes heaped on my chair to the already teetering pile on hers. 'Any problem Mrs Muller is having concerns all of us.'

A note from Poor Mandy says that Louis Keele requested a wake-up call for eight fifteen today, so I ring him, hang up as quickly as possible – he is still mid sleepy grunt – and then wait for Izzy to tell me what she's done. She just continues sorting socks, humming Ed Sheeran's 'Bad Habits'. She has stuck a note to my keyboard – something about paint in the store cupboard, but as usual her handwriting is totally unreadable. She has also moved the pen pot to her side of the desk, even though it should live right in the middle. I am disproportionately annoyed by both these things. Maybe I need to go back to the gym after work, too.

'Well?' I say.

'Well what?'

'What did you do about Mrs Muller?'

She smiles in satisfaction and brings out her phone, pulling up a photo of the paint splattering the wall of Mrs Muller's suite. I stare at it, trying to get the point, until she leans forward and zooms in on the bottom corner of the mess. Her hair falls forward, striped in green and blue today, and I make the mistake of inhaling. She smells of cinnamon again.

'See it?' she says.

I lean closer, my head just inches from hers. There is a small sign stuck to the wall. *When the Muses Strike, by M. Muller*, it reads. *December 2022*. It is just like the cards you see next to artworks in a museum.

'She was thrilled,' Izzy says. 'Honoured, she said. She's going to stay in "her room" at the hotel every year from now on.'

'So we have to keep that mess there?'

'It's art!' she says.

A message pops up on the top of her screen. *Sameera says . . . Will you just angry-shag him in a spare hotel room already?* it reads.

She turns the screen black and steps away from me instantly. 'Umm,' she says.

I sit down, directing my attention firmly towards the computer, but my heart is pounding. Who does this Sameera think Izzy should angry-shag? I don't know of anyone at the hotel Izzy is angry with other than . . . me.

'I assume you saw that,' Izzy says, sorting socks with too much enthusiasm – one goes flying over the edge of the desk on to the lobby rug. 'The message.'

'Yes,' I say, scrolling through the hotel's inbox, and then scrolling back up through the unread emails again, because I don't think I absorbed a single subject line.

'It's not . . . My friend Grigg's wife is just super inappropriate. I'm not going to shag anyone. Definitely not in an angry way. Having sex when you're angry is never a good idea. Not that it's any of your business.'

'I didn't ask,' I point out, keeping my voice as dry as possible. I will my heart rate to slow. The message probably referred to someone from outside the hotel. Just because it mentioned a hotel room doesn't necessarily mean it was about one of Izzy's colleagues.

'Morning Izzy. Lucas.'

Louis Keele. I offer him a polite smile and then return my gaze firmly to my inbox. Izzy can deal with him. He wants Izzy anyway. I type out a few emails to possible ring owners just as the rest of the builders traipse in, trailing wet mud across the lobby floor behind Louis. I reach for the phone to call house-keeping, but Dinah appears, as if conjured by inconsiderateness, and scowls after them, mop already in hand.

I like Dinah. She never goes the extra mile – she goes just far enough, and I have a lot of respect for that.

'I wanted to give you a heads up,' Louis says.

I glance up again. Louis is not a large man, or a particularly impressive one, but he is just the sort of guy who would put me on edge if I weren't there already. He's self-assured, and has a warm charm that makes conversation easy. In other words, he is very unlike me.

'Mr Townsend, the sweet guy with the tremor? As I left my room, I heard him muttering about this "miserable place" and how this will be "some Christmas".' Louis pulls a sympathetic face. He is always a lot nicer when Izzy is around. 'Sorry, I just thought you'd want prior warning . . .'

We all turn as Mr Townsend appears. He is visibly upset, his head bowed, his movements jerky. I look away – I suspect Mr Townsend would rather not have everybody in the lobby staring at him – and see Louis' phone, which rests between his hands on the desk. There's a photo of the lobby up on his screen. I frown.

'Oh, God,' Izzy mutters, stepping around the desk. 'Thank you, Louis. I really appreciate that. Mr Townsend? How are you today?'

'She's good,' Louis says, watching Izzy soothe Mr Townsend. He leans on the desk and starts to toss the socks in front of him into a pile. This will annoy Izzy, so I leave him to it. 'A natural.' He side-eyes me. 'Cute, too.'

The bad temper brewing in my chest begins to pick up momentum.

'I'm thinking of investing, you know,' Louis says before I can answer. 'In Forest Manor.'

'Oh. That's great news.' Perhaps that's why he's taking photographs. I should be pleased that he's considering investing, but I can't help wondering what he would do to this hotel if he had a say in how it's run.

'Mm. I think it has potential,' he says, still watching Izzy as she leads Mr Townsend into an armchair, head ducked, listening. 'My dad loves buildings like this, old places, you know, with history.'

'It's a very special hotel,' I say stiffly. I can't help noticing that Louis seems more interested in looking down Izzy's shirt than contemplating his future investment.

'Yeah, absolutely. The building has tons of development potential. Hmm. Great figure, too, hasn't she?' he adds, tilting his head to the side.

The building has tons of development potential? I bite down on my cheek so hard it hurts. That sounds like something you'd say if you were buying a manor house, not investing in a hotel. Is that Louis' game? And might the Singh-Bartholomews sell, now that things have become so desperate?

I look at what I have typed on the draft email to a potential wedding client in front of me. *Hiog[rwJIPR;Wkgk.* Yes. If there were a word for this feeling, it would probably look something like that. Louis sees no reason why Izzy would not want his attention, just as he sees no reason why he shouldn't get to do as he likes with this beautiful hotel, and it makes my blood boil.

'Better shoot. Good chat,' he says, firing me a wink as he saunters off.

He dodges Mr and Mrs Hedgers, who are heading through to their room with the kids behind them, muttering furiously to one another. Izzy would try to figure out what's wrong. I watch them go, thinking they look like they'd rather be left alone.

I look back at my screen as my pulse slows. There's one new email. I click through.

OMG! it says. *That is totally my wedding ring! Can I come in on Monday to pick it up? Hubby will be so pleased!*

'*Porra!*' I mutter, already typing back.

Izzy

I lie back on my bed, pull the laptop on to my knees and reach for my tea. It's a spiced loose leaf tea blend – it's a total faff to make, but I love it, and lately it's become a bit of a ritual for my rare, precious evenings to myself. I open Netflix, looking for something new, even though I already know I'll be rewatching *Charmed*, and then I make the mistake of checking my phone. Sixty-eight unread messages from seven chats.

I am a people person. I've always had a whole gaggle of friends, and that's exactly how I like it, but lately I've started to feel like I'm keeping up with my WhatsApps for the sake of it. Replying just to get rid of the unread messages, not because I really want to hear how my old colleagues' kids are, or how a mate from school is getting on with her new job.

An ex-boyfriend once said that I collect people and don't let them go, and the comment has really stayed with me. At the time I told him you can never have too many friends, and that there's nothing wrong with being loyal, but when everything happened with Drew last year, it made me see things a little differently.

From the moment I met her, I knew we'd get along. She walked into my flat for a viewing with this big, cheeky smile and fabulous square glasses and I was smitten. I was on furlough and needed the extra money, and I knew that whoever moved in to my box room would be spending a lot of time with me – the perils of flatsharing in a lockdown. But she seemed so fun, I instantly relaxed.

And Drew could be really fun when she wanted to. Say, when she was trying to get a room in your flat. But once she was installed there with a twelve-month contract, she was a different person altogether. I tried so hard to rediscover that side of her. I coaxed her into a more positive outlook as she whinged on my sofa about being bored; I bowed to her requests to change my flat's decor because it was 'too childish' and 'too pink' in the background of her video calls. Basically, I was so determined to be friends with my flatmate that I put up with almost twelve months of absolute nonsense. And then she kissed the man she *knew* I liked, and I realised that I was making all this effort for someone who gave zero shits about me.

My outlook has started to shift in the year post Drew. Maybe I don't need to keep people in my life at all costs. Maybe I don't need to be surrounded in the way I did back when my parents died. There are a few people who will always bring me joy – Jem, Grigg, Sameera. But as I scroll through my recent conversations, I ask myself who I am looking forward to catching up with from this list, and the answer is kind of shocking. There's pretty much nobody I actually want to see.

The phone rings in my hand and I let out a yip of surprise, spilling tea on my duvet cover.

'Shit,' I say, dabbing as I answer the video call.

'Hello,' Grigg says, unfazed at being greeted with a swear word.

Not much fazes Grigg: he is the exhausted father of a seven-month-old who wakes up five times a night, and still he remains unflappable. We met when we both spent a summer waiting tables at The Jolly Farmer pub on the edge of the Forest, and, even aged sixteen, he'd had the air of a mild-mannered old man. I remember watching him drop a tray of full pints: he stood there for a moment, looking thoughtfully at the carnage on the floor around him, and then said, *You know, Izzy, I am just not sure I have found my calling, here.* He's an accountant these days, and likes it much better.

His wife Sameera bobs into view in the background, giving me a wave with a slice of pizza in her mouth.

'Hey, sweetness!' she calls through her mouthful.

'How's my favourite godson?' I ask.

'Sleeping! At bedtime!'

'Amazing!'

'I know, right? Did Sexy Scowly Receptionist really see Grigg's message?' asks Sameera, giggling already.

'Not my message,' Grigg says. 'I was merely relaying a message from you, darling wife. I have never said *angry-shag* in my life before.'

'Don't laugh, Sam!' I say, but I'm giggling along with Sameera, who is doubled over behind Grigg. 'It was so awkward!'

'Did he know it was about him, do you think?' Sameera calls, disappearing off-screen.

'I don't know,' I say, reaching for the spare pillow to bury my face in it. 'I obviously tried to make it sound like it wasn't. I don't even want to shag him! That's *you* talking, not me! But now he's going to think I want him.'

'Don't you?' Grigg says. He's gnawing on a pizza crust. In the rare windows of time when baby Rupe is asleep, they tend to do everything at once – I'm pretty sure Sameera is putting on a wash in the background. 'Didn't you write him that love letter last Christmas?'

From somewhere off-screen, Sameera throws a handful of dirty laundry at Grigg. He barely flinches.

'Grigg!'

'It was not a love letter,' I say, 'it was a Christmas card, and yes, I had a crush on him once, but all I said in that message to you was that there was a bit of a *vibe* at the mo – that doesn't mean I want him. We still hate each other.'

'You don't need to like someone to fancy them,' Sameera says.

'Don't you?' Grigg asks mildly.

'I don't fancy him,' I say, but the moment I say it, I know I'm lying. I know, deep down, that I didn't want to cover myself up when Lucas caught me half-dressed through the lost-property-room door, and that if I weren't still attracted to him, I'd have squealed and dashed out of view as quick as a rat. 'Oh, shit,' I say, re-burying my face in the pillow.

'I think this is good!' Sameera says. 'You always go for such . . .'

'Wet-arse men,' Grigg finishes for her.

'Excuse me?'

'Lost causes, guys who live in dimly-lit basements, men with big dreams they're going to get started on some time next summer.' Grigg takes a large bite of his pizza.

'Hey!' I say, though actually this is painfully pitch-perfect. I think about Tristan's flat above his parents' garage, and Dean's start-up plans, and I grimace.

'Grigg's right,' Sameera says excitedly. 'Sexy Scowly has drive and ambition! That's way more you! Didn't you say he lost the job he came here for because the place shut down, and then he got the job at your hotel, like, *days* before his visa was due to expire?'

'Yeah, he did,' I say, chewing my lip.

It's one of the very rare pieces of personal information I've gleaned from Lucas – it came up in a conversation about lockdown rules. Thank God those days are gone. We argued worse than ever when the government guidelines kept changing every few weeks.

'He's driven, sure. He's also a massive knob,' I remind them.

'Does he!' Sameera crows, bounding back into view again with a bunch of laundry bundled to her chest.

'*Is* a massive knob, Sam,' I say, and then laugh at the disappointment on her face. 'I promise you, I'm not interested in Lucas any more, not after what happened last Christmas.' I hold up a hand when they both open their mouths to speak. 'I *will* acknowledge that I still find him attractive.'

'What's wrong with a bit of flirtation, then? You don't need to worry about leading him on or hurting his feelings, given that he hates you as much as you hate him. And if the flirting leads to angry sex, hurray!' Sameera throws a hand up, sending a pair of knickers flying with it. 'If you decide you don't want to sleep with him, then you've wound him up for weeks on end – also hurray!'

'Well,' I say, sipping my tea, 'when you put it like that . . .'

'Hey, what address should we post your Christmas present to?' Grigg asks, turning the camera back to him again. 'I keep meaning to ask – where's Jem living right now?'

'Just post it here,' I say, shifting my pillow behind me. 'I'll take it with me when I go. I can't believe you guys have the headspace for shopping this early, with Rupe still up half the night. You're doing so well.'

'Cried on the sofa for a full forty minutes this morning, sweetness!' Sameera calls. I hear the slam of what I assume is the washing-machine door.

'Oh, Sam . . . Is there anything I can do?' For about the millionth time, I wish they'd not made the move to Edinburgh. If they were still down here in the New Forest, I could be the one putting on that wash, making them dinner, settling Rupe.

'Have a torrid love affair and then tell me all about it?' Sameera suggests, finally flopping down next to Grigg on the sofa. He pulls her in close and kisses her head.

'I love you,' I tell her, 'but not enough for torrid. Torrid sounds messy.'

'Torrid sounds *exciting*,' Sameera corrects me. 'You need a bit of that.'

'My life is nonstop excitement,' I say. 'Right, I'll leave you to the million things you've stockpiled to get done while the baby's down. Bye, loves. I hope Rupe sleeps through.'

'Me too,' Sameera says, with feeling.

I drop my phone on the duvet and settle back in with *Charmed*, sipping my tea and ignoring my WhatsApps. Trying not to mind that when I said my life is nonstop excitement, Grigg and Sameera both laughed.

Usually, winter is a whirlwind at the hotel. Work Christmas lunches, girly spa trips, cosy couples' minibreaks and lavish winter weddings. It feels horribly quiet now. On an average day here, I always play a hundred different roles (public relations manager, kids' entertainer, window un-jammer, whatever the crisis needs) but the roles I'm playing at the moment aren't nearly as fun as usual. Today, for instance, I am spending my Monday deep-cleaning the carpet and sorting umbrellas from the lost-property room. *All* the umbrellas are black. Black reminds me of funerals – I own zero black clothes, and my current umbrella is polka-dot pale blue, though I lose them so frequently it's hard to keep track.

The Ring Thing is keeping me going at the moment. After we phoned the same people within minutes of each other on Saturday morning (awkward), Lucas and I decided we'll each focus on a ring of our own, to minimise the risk of strangling one another in frustration. Lucas's ring is a fancy diamond-studded band – of course he picked that one – whereas I went for the gold wedding ring, battered and well-loved. The other two – the beautiful emerald engagement ring and the stylish hammered-silver wedding band – will have to wait until I've beaten Lucas at this bet.

He seems to be having even worse luck than I am. Yesterday I heard someone yelling at him on the phone for 'bothering them about a wedding ring five days after they'd been jilted'. Oops. I know I should want him to find his ring's owner for the sake of the hotel, and I *do*, of course I do, I just . . . don't want him to find them *yet*.

I smile as I walk back in from my lunch break (leftovers in the kitchen with Arjun) and spot Mr Townsend in the armchair by the lobby window. Now *there's* a success story. It took me a couple of attempts to figure out what Mr Townsend needed from his stay here. At first, I tried to give him a spa session, thinking he wanted peace and quiet – but now I've nailed it.

People come to a hotel at this time of year for all sorts of reasons, and I realised Mr Townsend's reason was exactly the same as mine: because he didn't want to spend Christmas alone.

So I've set him up right here in the middle of things. I've encouraged him to see the builders not as a disruption to hotel activity, but as *part* of it. Now that he knows the tall one hates the one with the ponytail, and the guy in charge is definitely in love with the one woman on the team, he's quite content to sit here in the lobby and watch their antics – and ours.

'Any luck with your ring?' Mr Townsend calls.

'Getting there!' I call back. 'Can I fetch you anything? A tea? A new book?'

'I'm all set, thank you. You missed a call,' he says, nodding towards the desk, 'but they left a voicemail.'

'We're going to have to put you on the payroll,' I tell him, just as Louis strolls into the lobby.

'Hey, Izzy,' he says. 'Up for that swim tonight?'

He's wearing jeans and a wool jumper, his hands tucked in his pockets. I get the sense there's more to Louis than the boyish cheekiness – a bit of an edge, maybe. It makes me curious. He's different from the usual men I go for, and after my chat with Grigg and Sameera, I'm thinking that's definitely a good thing. Maybe I should give this a go.

I try to imagine what my mum would have said about him. She and Dad always told me I should choose someone kind and attentive – 'a man who smiles easily, that's what you need', Mum once said.

That thought swings it.

'Why not?' I say, just as Lucas marches out of the restaurant, looking furious about something.

Louis smiles. 'Excellent. See you when your shift ends – five, is it?'

'Perfect.' I turn my attention to the glowering Lucas. 'What?' I ask.

The two of us have been avoiding each other more than ever since our interaction in the car park. Every time I see him, that conversation leaps into my mind – his intensity, the way he'd looked at me when I'd called him *offensively handsome*.

'You volunteered me to wait on the hen party for lunch?'

I press my lips together, trying very hard not to smile. I forgot I did that.

'Can you not do it?' I ask.

'I can,' he says, with deliberation. 'But I don't want to. You know I hate waiting on the big groups. Especially drunk ones. *Especially* hens.'

'But you always go down so well with the hens!'

'If anyone attempts to undress me, it will be you I'm suing,' Lucas says darkly.

'Well, I'm going to be spending the time sorting coins from the lost-property room and taking them to the post office. You could swap, if you like.'

I gesture to the jars of loose change lining the edge of the front desk. Lucas stares at them.

'Does that actually need to be done?'

'It's money,' I point out. 'Are you suggesting I throw it in the bin?'

He growls under his breath and stalks off towards the restaurant. Then he pauses, turning with his hand on the door.

'How is your hunt for your wedding ring's owner going?'

'Brilliantly!' I say. 'I'm down to my final five contenders.'

Five, seventeen – what's the difference, really?

'Good for you,' Lucas says.

I narrow my eyes. His tone is far too . . . nice.

'How's yours going?' I ask.

'A woman is dropping in to collect her lost ring at three

o'clock,' he says, pushing through the restaurant door and letting it swing shut behind him.

Shit.

I glance at the clock. Two minutes to three. Lucas's ring owner is due any second. Would it be wrong of me to run some intervention? Lock the hotel doors, just for ten minutes or so? Send Lucas off to do something urgent and then tell his visitor that the ring has already been claimed by somebody else?

It would be wrong, definitely. However . . .

'Don't even try,' Lucas says, not looking up from where he's cleaning silver candlesticks at the other end of the front desk.

'I didn't do anything!'

'You are . . . *tramando*.'

'I don't know what that means.'

'Scheming. Plotting.'

'Would I ever?' I say as he turns to look at me. I arrange my expression into the picture of innocence.

'That face doesn't work on me,' Lucas says.

His eyes hold mine, dark and knowing. Something flutters in my stomach. Then his gaze snaps to the door as a woman steps into the lobby, bringing in a blast of freezing air.

'Hello!' Lucas calls, with more enthusiasm than I've seen from him since someone suggested updating the restaurant table booking system. 'Are you Ruth?'

'Yes, hi, that's me!' the woman says, pasting on a large smile.

I am immediately suspicious. Obviously I have skin in the game here, but I meet a lot of members of the public in this job, and I've developed a bit of an eye for the ones who are going to cause trouble. The people who won't pay their bar tab, who will take things from the hotel that aren't strictly toiletries, who will print out the same Groupon voucher twice. And this Ruth has troublemaker written all over her, from her pristine ponytail to the toes of her trying-to-look-expensive boots.

I do not believe that Lucas's ring belongs to this woman. That ring is stunning, but it's not showy: the diamonds are tiny and the design is really subtle. I'd say a woman with a counterfeit designer handbag probably wants a wedding ring that shouts about how pricey it was, not something small and pretty.

'Thanks so much for coming in,' I say, standing up with my best smile. 'As I'm sure you'll understand, we'll have to check a few things to make sure we're giving the ring to the right person.'

To her credit, her expression doesn't change. 'Sure,' she says, pulling her handbag closer against her side. 'What do you need? Some ID?'

'Do you have a receipt for the ring?' I ask.

'Perhaps you could just describe it,' Lucas says, glancing sideways at me.

I look back at him, raising my eyebrows. *Really?* my face says. *You're so concerned about winning our bet that you're prepared to give a valuable piece of jewellery to a potential fraud? What if it causes problems for the hotel?*

I watch his face darken as he comes to the same conclusion.

'I bought it in a jeweller's,' the woman says, patting at her hair. 'So there's no digital receipt. It was years ago! But I can tell you it's a thin gold ring studded with diamonds.'

I shoot another look at Lucas. His grim expression tells me that he said that much in his initial email.

'You'll see what a conundrum we're in,' I say, smile still in place. 'Is there any way you can prove it's your ring?'

'Can you prove it's not?' she asks. There's a sharpness in her tone now.

'Perhaps you could tell us when you stayed here?' Lucas asks.

Her gaze shifts from me to Lucas and back again. She swallows.

'2020,' she says.

'Oh dear. Not quite,' I say.

'2018?' she tries, confidence visibly evaporating.

'I know!' I turn to Lucas. 'We could ask if she knows about the chipped diamond. Oh, crap,' I say, covering my mouth.

'Yes!' she says, relieved. 'One of the diamonds was chipped! How could I forget that? There you go. There can't be many rings that fit that description, can there? And . . .' She waggles her bare hand at us. 'I've definitely lost my wedding ring.'

Well, this is awkward. I turn to Lucas, who is blinking rapidly, his expression fixed.

'Over to you?' I say sweetly, sitting down again. Mentioning the chip was an absolute masterstroke, if I do say so myself. There was – of course – no chip.

This has been super helpful. I've realised what an advantage I have over Lucas in this particular race, because my ring has an engraving on the inside. So even if I have a long list to work through, once I find my owner, I'll know they're the one – and just like that, I'll be the winner, glory shall be mine, and Lucas will have to abide by my every wish.

And, oh, I'm going to make him suffer.

Lucas

I started late today, so I am staying late too. That is only reasonable. And the seating areas dotted around the pool badly need tidying. There are magazines here from a time when all the UK had to worry about was whether a man named Jeremy Clarkson had or had not punched someone.

That is why I'm here: tidying. It's nothing to do with the fact that Louis Keele is currently powering up and down the swimming pool, waiting for Izzy to arrive for their . . . plans. Their arrangement. Their date?

'Fetch me a beer, would you, Lucas?' Louis calls from the pool, twisting to float on his back.

Fetch me a beer. Like I'm a dog. I turn around, ready to snarl, but then Izzy appears in the doorway of the women's changing room and I lose my train of thought entirely.

'Lucas,' she says, surprised. She's wearing a dressing gown hanging open over her bikini. 'What are you doing here?'

I recognise that bikini: it lives in the box she keeps under the desk. I noticed it when I tidied her box, an act I knew would irritate her enormously, and which ended up feeling slightly sordid, partly because of that bikini. You can't see a bikini without imagining the person in it.

And it is very small. Turquoise green with thin straps. Right now, I can only see a few inches of it between the two sides of her dressing gown, along with a shocking flash of smooth, pale skin, but the sight makes my breath catch in my throat. My imagination did not do her justice.

She looks so different. She's barefoot, with her hair unstriped and pulled up in a bun. There's something vulnerable about her like this, and I feel a stab of an emotion that in another context I might call fear. But it's not that, it can't be – there's nothing to be afraid of.

'Hello,' I say, hating how stiff I sound. 'I started late. So I'm staying late.'

Her eyes narrow slightly. We're in a glass building that links the main house to the spa, which was formerly the stables – the space is lit only by a series of low-energy bulbs above the water, so it's shadowy in here. Behind me I hear the slick splash of Louis moving methodically through the pool.

'You're staying late ... in the swimming pool area?'

'I am tidying the spa, yes.'

'Tonight?'

'Yes.'

Her eyes get narrower. 'What game are you playing, Lucas da Silva?' she asks.

'No game. I'm working.'

'Hmm.'

I'm sweating. I don't know what game I am playing, that's the truthful answer. Now that I'm standing between Izzy and the pool, I can't ignore how reluctant I am to step aside and let her pass. I don't want Izzy to spend her evening in a bikini with Louis Keele. I don't trust that man with the future of this hotel, and I definitely don't trust him with Izzy.

Which is ridiculous. I swallow and move aside, returning my attention to the dog-eared magazines in wicker baskets by the chairs. When I glance back at her, she's dropping the dressing gown on to a sunlounger.

Fuck. I look away sharply, heart pounding in my throat, suddenly very aware that I shouldn't be here. She's not wearing that bikini for me. I wasn't supposed to see that smooth sweep of naked waist, her long, bare legs, the tiny tattoo at the point where her bikini top is tied. Seeing her in such a different context is making it harder to remember that this is the infuriating Izzy Jenkins, and without that, she is just a dangerously beautiful woman in swimwear.

'That beer, Lucas, mate?' Louis calls.

I know why he's asking. It's not because he particularly wants a beer. It's because he wants Izzy to see me fetch him one.

'No drinks in the spa,' I snap.

'Damn. Can't you make an exception?' says Louis.

'No exceptions, Louis, not even for you!' Izzy calls as she slides into the pool. 'Race you!'

Louis looks at Izzy with blatant appreciation. I feel another stab of that strange, new fear. As they launch into their race, I watch him gaining on her, his form cutting through the water, and then I turn away, heading into the main spa, because what else can I do? In the same way that the bikini wasn't for me, I don't get to feel anxious when Izzy's on a date.

And I hate her, I remind myself. I hate her and she hates me.

After an hour of scrubbing the spa hall floor, I strip down to the vest top I'm wearing under my shirt. I've been in and out – I've needed various bits of equipment from the main hotel, and you have to walk through the pool to get there. But this time, as I move through to return the bag of cleaning supplies to their usual cupboard, Izzy is climbing out of the pool, and I have to slow down to let her reach for her towel.

'How was your date?' I ask in a low voice as she pulls it around herself, tucking it under her arm.

Louis has just stepped through to the men's changing room. I relax a little as the door shuts behind him.

'You've been here pretty much the whole time,' Izzy says. 'You tell me.'

'You won every race,' I say, setting down the bag and folding my arms across my chest. 'So I'd say he's no match for you.'

'Maybe I'm not looking for a guy who tries to outperform me,' she says, widening her eyes slightly as she tucks the towel tighter. Our voices echo in here, the water lapping quietly beside us.

'Oh, he was trying.' I smirk. 'I know his type. Pushy. Likes to win. Compensating for something, no doubt. He just wasn't fast enough.'

'Really?' She tilts her head. 'He seemed like the perfect gentleman to me.'

'You think that's what you need?'

She raises her eyebrows, incredulous. 'You think I need something else?'

'I think you're getting bored of men who will roll over for you on your command,' I say, lifting one shoulder in a shrug. 'I've seen your boyfriends, hanging around, waiting for you to tell them what to do next, chauffeuring you home in their beaten-up cars . . .'

Her eyes flare with real irritation. 'That'll be your first job,' she says. 'When I win the bet. Chauffeuring me home in your beaten-up car.'

'My car is spotless.'

'Actually,' she says, 'it got a little scratched this evening. Someone in a Smart car is no good at manoeuvres.'

'You wouldn't,' I growl. 'That is . . .'

'Seriously extra,' she says, and she's laughing now. 'No, I wouldn't. But it's got you raging, hasn't it?'

It's true. I am tense; heat is pounding through me.

'Big muscles, fancy car . . . You sure *you're* not compensating for something?' she calls as she walks off into the changing room.

On Thursday afternoon, as I settle back at the front desk after a frantic day sorting lost property, my sister messages me on the family WhatsApp group. *Lucas, saudade! Está gostando do clima de Natal britânico?*

She wants to know if I'm enjoying my English Christmas. Messaging me via the family group is an unsubtle reminder that I've been too quiet, and probably a sign that my mother is worrying.

Uncle Antônio isn't in the family WhatsApp group. I occasionally feel guilty about this, but I can't quite bring myself to set up another space in which Ana and I will inevitably feel inadequate.

I flinch suddenly as something lands on my head, and spin around to find Izzy behind me. I catch the reindeer antlers she just tried to put on me.

'No,' I say.

'It's not festive enough around here!' she complains, adjusting her own antlers. Her hair is pulled back in a bun again, like it was that night at the pool. 'It's December now, and the builders won't let me decorate the bannisters yet, and my nativity is gone ...'

'What about that?' I say, pointing to the enormous Christmas tree occupying much of the lobby.

It took Izzy half a day to decorate that tree. At one point she suggested abseiling down from the scaffolding to get the star on the top, and I don't think she was joking. I stayed out of it, which means that the whole thing is completely overdone, but I am trying to learn when to pick my battles. I can live with too many baubles on the tree.

Though it does annoy me. All the time. A lot.

'Everyone has a Christmas tree,' Izzy says, waving a hand. 'We need to step it up a gear. We may not have a full house, but the restaurant is booked to capacity most nights up to

Christmas – and all the diners will be walking through this lobby, wondering if maybe they should come for a weekend when the renovations are done . . .'

She's right. Despite the building work, we need to be a good advertisement for the hotel at the moment. I look around at all the mess and wince.

'Tidying all this lost property would be a start.'

'Most of this is waiting for buyer collection. Which, by the way, was *all* organised by me. What have you sold lately?'

I scowl. 'Today, I took a whole box of items to auction. I raised almost a thousand pounds. All you do is fiddle around pairing socks and trying to match sets of earrings.'

'Yeah, well, you keep bagsying all the high-value items!' Izzy says, then answers the phone as it rings. 'Oh, hi! Thanks for calling back! Yes, I'd love to speak to Hans about the ring.' She swivels in her chair to direct the full strength of her smugness in my direction. 'Fantastic. Whenever's good for him.'

Merda. I haven't got any further with mine since Ruth's attempted fraud, which was all extremely uncomfortable. There are still four contenders who haven't replied to my calls or follow-up emails. I mentally bump everything else on my to-do list. This is my new priority.

'Ooh, antlers!' coos Poor Mandy as she staggers into the lobby under the weight of her two giant Sainsbury's bags. She untangles them from around her shoulders and they land on the lobby rug with a thud as she digs out her phone – case flap dangling – and starts snapping photographs of us. 'Lucas, dear, put yours on too! This will be wonderful on the Facebook.'

Izzy clicks the phone back in its cradle with great deliberate-ness and then turns to me.

'Antlers on, Lucas!' she says. 'Do it for the Facebook!'

I glare at her, but put on the antlers. I must check what Poor Mandy is doing to the Forest Manor social media pages – this is one of the many things on my to-do list, just underneath creating a woodland play area and persuading someone other than me to deep-clean the fryer.

'Oh, that's a lovely one. I've sent it to you both too,' Poor Mandy says, tapping away at her phone. She has a habit of moving her lips or muttering as she types, so even before my phone pings, I could guess that she has written, *Fab photo of you two, lots of love, Mandy.*

I look down at the photo for a moment. Izzy has leapt in beside me – she's beaming, her antlers already sliding through her hair. She's wearing some sort of pale-pink sheen on her cheekbones today, and the lights of the Christmas tree make her glitter.

After a moment I crop the photo down so it's just me, wearing antlers, glancing off to the side. I send it on the family WhatsApp, telling them I'm getting in the Christmas spirit already.

'Guys, guys, guys,' Ollie says, power walking over from the kitchen. Ollie has been told repeatedly not to run through the hotel, so now he does an odd fast walk that involves a lot of arm movement.

The kitchen door swings behind him, almost whacking Arjun in the face as he follows behind Ollie. The chef's expression is so thunderous I want to laugh.

'Mrs SB is—'

'Crying,' Arjun says over Ollie. 'Ollie, there are five pans on the hob, what are you doing out here? It's dangerous.'

I watch Ollie hover for one tortured moment, deciding whether or not to point out that Arjun is *also* out here, rather than attending to the hob, and that he actually walked out second. Ollie makes the wise choice for his career and dashes back to the kitchen again.

'What? Where?' Izzy says, leaning across the desk as Arjun points towards the window.

Mrs SB passes outside, holding a tissue to her cheek. Izzy is already on her way out. I follow her, just catching the hotel's heavy wooden door in time to stop it slamming in my face. Presumably she got that idea from Ollie.

It's freezing outside, and darkness is setting in across the gardens. Mrs SB steps beyond the beam of the lights on either side of the hotel's entrance, disappearing down the path that leads to Opal Cottage.

'Mrs SB, are you OK?' Izzy calls, quickening her pace.

'Fine, dear!'

Her voice is muffled. Not very convincing.

'Talk to us,' Izzy says as we approach. 'Maybe we can help.'

Mrs SB turns her face aside so Izzy can't see her tears, but I'm on the other side of her. 'Oh, bother,' she says, coming to a standstill between us.

We're in the middle of the rose garden now, lit by the small lights along the borders. The glow catches each puff of Mrs SB's breath as she tries to pull herself together, tissue held to her eyes.

'It's just . . . a little . . . much,' she manages. 'At the moment.'

'Of course.' Izzy rubs her arm soothingly.

'I'm so sorry, both of you. I feel I've let you down horribly.'

'You've not let anybody down!' Izzy says. 'You've kept this hotel running through years of lockdowns and a cost-of-living crisis. That's incredible. It's no wonder the place is struggling – how could it not be?'

I stand, arms folded, feeling painfully awkward. I want to hug Mrs SB, but Izzy's already there, so all I can do is try to project quite how deeply I care – something I know I've never been especially good at showing even when the hugging option is available.

'You take so much on yourself,' Izzy says. 'Can we help more? With the management and administration, maybe? Lucas is really good at this sort of thing – spreadsheets and organisation and stuff.'

I stare at her in surprise. Her cheeks go faintly pink. I open my mouth to say something similar in return – I've long thought that Izzy could be put to better use at the hotel. She should be managing these renovations, in my opinion. She has a good eye for what makes a space work, and she's excellent at coordinating large numbers of people. But Mrs SB is speaking again before I can find the right thing to say.

'Oh, I'm embarrassed to show you the accounts, honestly. I know Barty will feel the same.'

'Don't be embarrassed.' My voice is gruffer than I'd like it to be. I clear my throat. 'I would love to help. I want the same things you and Barty want. I want this place to thrive, and for

112

our . . . the family we have built here to . . .' Why is this so difficult to say? 'I'm happy to help,' I finish abruptly.

Izzy is staring at me like I've just announced that in future I'd rather we deliver all internal communications by carrier pigeon. I avert my eyes, looking up at the sky. The stars are just beginning to blink into life between grey smudges of cloud.

I should be searching for other jobs. This place will almost certainly go under before the year is out. But standing here, breathing in the forest air, with the hotel's grand old bulk behind me . . . I just cannot imagine myself feeling this sense of belonging anywhere else.

I know why Izzy's so surprised to hear me talking about the hotel as a family: she thinks I don't care. That I'm heartless. But if I am, then why does my chest hurt at the thought of letting this part of my life go?

'I suppose I could just send you the accounts. Perhaps you can look for places we can be more efficient.' Mrs SB sniffs, pulling back from Izzy's arms. 'I find it a bit overwhelming, if I'm truthful. I've never been good with numbers.'

My fingers flex at the thought of having access to the sums behind the hotel's decisions. I'll get to see how Forest Manor really works. All the moving parts. I can do more than just raising a few hundred pounds with old lost-property rubbish – I can *help*.

'I like numbers,' I tell her, the ache in my chest subsiding. 'Just send it all my way.'

'Thank you. Thank you.' She squeezes both our arms and heads off towards Opal Cottage.

We watch her go.

'I appreciate what you said,' I tell Izzy eventually. 'About spreadsheets. When I have the opportunity, I would like to tell Mrs SB that you too deserve a chance to expand your skills here at the hotel.'

'What?'

'I mean . . . There's a lot more you could be doing here too.'

She bristles. 'I'm doing plenty, thanks. And you're welcome. Just . . . Go gently when you get back to her on the figures, OK? Some of us are humans, not robots.'

She walks away through the rose bushes, towards the hotel. The word *robot* stings like a slap. *I'm human too*, I want to say. *When you're unkind to me, it hurts.*

My phone flashes up a reply from Ana as I follow Izzy back inside. Ana has sent my photo back with a large red circle around the tiny portion of Izzy's shoulder that is visible in the photograph.

Quem é essa pessoa???

Oh, *porra*. She wants to know who it is.

É uma mulher?? says my mother.

Merda. Now they've clocked it's a woman. But how? It's about three millimetres of white shirt and . . . oh. A telltale strand of long pink hair. Damn.

I hesitate, wondering how to play this. My mother and sister are convinced I need a girlfriend, despite the fact that I have functioned happily for several years without one. And when I *did* have one, I was mostly quite miserable.

??! LUCAS?!

That's from Ana. I rub my eyes with my thumb and forefinger.

É só uma colega de trabalho, I type. *Just a colleague.*

Ela é bonita? Ana asks.

My thumb hovers. If I say yes, she's pretty, then they will not be satisfied until Izzy is flying over to Brazil for a large family wedding. So the obvious thing to do is to say no, she's not pretty. I glance across at Izzy as we step back into the lobby, watching as she tucks her hair behind her ear with a small, impatient hand, her gold hoop earring swinging as she walks.

I write, *She is very difficult to work with. We don't get along*, in Portuguese, and then wait to see if I get away with sidestepping the question.

Então ela é linda! Ana writes. *So she's beautiful, then!*

I click away from the chat. I can't have this conversation right now. I'm meant to be working.

Izzy

I'm just starting to think that my big fat gold ring is a big fat dead end when I *finally* get a hit on Friday.

> Hi Izzy,
> Thanks very much for your email. It reminded me how nice your hotel is –
> I'll definitely be booking another stay soon!

I smile to myself. If you put good stuff out into the universe . . .

> I'm almost certain that ring belongs to my wife. She's actually bought a
> new one since we lost it, but we'd still love to have it back. I've attached
> a photo of the ring on my wife's hand, and the engraving. Does it match?
> Yours,
> Graham

It absolutely *does* match. I lean back in my desk chair, soaking in the feeling as I gaze up at the staircase behind the scaffolding. Winning is the best.

I snap another photo of the ring, then hit reply on Graham's email. I frown – the address he's responded to me from is slightly different from the one I used for him. Just to be safe, I put the other one in the cc line too.

Hi Graham!

Fantastic news! Please do drop in as soon as possible to claim your wife's ring back! I'm so happy it's found its way back to you. And what a lovely picture of the two of you on your wedding day! Here's another snap of the ring itself so you can see that the engraving matches 😃

All the best,

Izzy

After hitting send, I belatedly wonder if that might have been one too many exclamation marks. I've always been partial to an exclamation mark. Full stops just seem so . . . grown-up. When I stop wanting pick-and-mix for dinner, that's when I'll start using full stops. That's real adulthood.

'Golly,' Poor Mandy says, marching in and hefting her bag down into a space between lost-property boxes.

I love how Mandy has taken our lost-property project in her stride and not once complained about the mess – if only Lucas could be more Mandy.

'I just ran into that Mrs Hedgers the career coach outside. She's very . . .' Mandy flaps a hand in front of her face as if to cool herself down, though it's two degrees outside, and not much warmer in here – we're trying to skimp on the heating as much as we can without pissing off the guests. 'She's a lot, isn't she?'

I remember what Mrs Hedgers said to me about switching off and I wince. Last night, after going for drinks with my school friends, I spent two hours trying to work out the logistics of getting to a hen-do in January, concluded it would cost me £380, agonised about whether I could bail on these grounds, and then fell asleep on the sofa in front of the latest series of *Married at First Sight: Australia*, which I'd promised Jem I'd watch so that we can recreate our old MAFSA nights when we next Zoom.

I'm not sure that counts as switching off.

'What did she say to you?' I ask, diving into the next lost-property box. This one is pens. Even I think we probably shouldn't have kept all these.

'She asked if I had trouble asserting myself,' Poor Mandy says. 'I said, I'm not sure, but I don't think so? And then she told me all sorts of information about the value of strong boundaries and now I feel a bit . . .' she plonks herself down in her chair, 'funny.'

I bite my lip, giving Mrs Hedgers a smile and a wave as she passes on her way to Sweet Pea. Mandy *definitely* has trouble asserting herself. She's ridiculously amenable. Does that mean Mrs Hedgers was right about me, too?

When I'm at work, I'm always giving a little extra, going a little further, being a little nicer. But I wouldn't want to be any other way – I *like* being brilliant at my job. I like being the person who brings that sparkle. That's how everyone sees me and that's who I want to be.

If I'm completely honest, though, I do sometimes wish I could dial it down a notch and spend the day with unwashed hair and a bad attitude. Just *sometimes*. And it's not like I really get much of a chance to do that outside of work, either – I'm always with people, and lately, since Jem, Grigg and Sameera have moved away, those people aren't *my* people. They're not the people I can completely switch off with. I have to be nice, bouncy people-person Izzy all the time.

Except with Lucas, obviously.

Mandy leans across to answer the phone. 'Hello, Forest Manor Hotel and Spa.' She glances at me. 'No, Lucas isn't here right now, but I can take a message?'

Poor Mandy writes something down in her usual, painstakingly slow fashion. Is this how people achieve neat handwriting? Not worth it, I say.

I bob up to read over her shoulder.

Call back about wedding ring. Urgent. And then a phone number.

Shit, shit, shit.

'I'll take that to Lucas,' I say, swiping the note off the desk.

'Oh, thank you, dear!' calls Poor, innocent Mandy as I walk away.

All's fair in love, war and petty workplace feuding, right?

I tap the number Poor Mandy wrote into my phone and then crumple the note in my hand. I seem to have ended up in the spa. I was heading in the direction of the restaurant bin, but chucking the note away felt just a bit too unscrupulous. However, if it were to happen to get wet, and the number were to be lost until, say, I had managed to return *my* ring first . . . After all, I'm so close. Graham will drop in any moment now to claim his wife's lost ring.

I sidle towards the swimming pool, note in hand. The water slops and echoes in the still, thick air.

'What's that?'

I spin around and my foot slips on the wet floor. For an awful, teetering moment, I think I'm in danger of falling on my arse on the tiles in front of Lucas da Silva, as if the universe has decided I have not humiliated myself enough in front of this man. I right myself just in time. He folds his arms and a smile tugs at his lips.

I'm still clutching the note.

'It's just . . . a thing,' I say, then pull a face at myself. 'It's a thing Mandy gave me,' I go on, rallying. 'Not important.'

'Is that why you were holding it over the swimming pool?'

I look at his face – all smugness and chiselled jaw – and I narrow my eyes.

'I wasn't.'

'You were. Almost.' He holds his hand out. 'Mandy said you had a note for me.'

'Ugh. Fine. But I wasn't going to drop it in the pool.' I hand it to him, then, without much grace, I add: 'Probably.'

'Playing dirty,' Lucas says. 'Isn't that what that's called?'

I flush. 'It's called playing to win,' I say, marching past him.

His broad shoulders take up so much *space*. I circle by on the pool side, and then, because I'm angry and in a bad mood, and maybe – just a little bit – because I want to see what he'll do if we touch, I pass too close. But he moves at the same moment, leaning ever so slightly my way, as though he had the same idea. And I go glancing off him and . . .

'Shit!' I splutter.

. . . right into the pool. The shock of the fall leaves me gasping. I gulp for air, treading water, mascara stinging in my eyes.

'You arsehole!' I shout. 'You just pushed me in the pool!'

'I did not,' he says, crouching down and reaching a hand to help me out. He tucks the note into his back pocket with his other hand, and as anger surges through me, as my sodden clothes drag at my limbs, I have an idea.

There's more than one way to get that note wet.

I lunge for Lucas's hand and pull hard. He's squatting, balanced on the polished toes of his shoes – I overbalance him.

He descends into the water like a giant rock. Just tumbles in, slow motion, still curled up with his knees to his chest. Despite the anger swirling in my belly, I find myself laughing – more at the surprise of it than anything. I can't believe I actually just pulled him into the pool.

He bursts up through the surface and his eyes find mine immediately. They're *sparkling* with anger. I let out a nervous *eep*. He's actually pissed off now. I've seen Lucas annoyed more times than I can count, but I've hardly ever seen him really raging. It's kind of . . . God. Is it bad that it's kind of sexy?

He says something long and presumably very insulting in Portuguese. I swim backwards to try to create a bit of distance between us, but he's a lot bigger than me, and it only takes one swipe for him to grab my leg.

'You,' he says, voice low and furious, 'are not going anywhere.'

He actually lets go of my leg the moment I kick it, but I don't swim away again, I just bob there, trying not to grin. The rush of anger has gone as quickly as it came; now I am having to work very hard not to nervous-giggle.

'You push me, I push you,' I say. My shirt snags at my skin as I move – it is *not* comfortable swimming in clothes. 'If you're going to do something, Lucas, you need to live with the consequences.'

'I did not push you.'

'Well, OK, technically I didn't push you either,' I say, and I know my grin is winding him up, which just makes it even harder not to smile.

'You are so *childish*,' he spits, swiping at his eyes and advancing on me.

'What are you going to do, dunk me?'

'Something like that, yes,' he says, and then, with both hands, he sends a huge wave splashing down over my head.

I splutter, gasping. 'Oh my God!'

I splash him too. He splashes me back. We're soaking and the water's churning and my back has hit the edge of the pool now, my shirt slick as silk against my body. When the water settles, Lucas is right in front of me, arms braced on either side of mine, hands gripping the ledge. His chest is heaving. His eyes still have that spark in them, but as we face each other, dripping, his cheek twitches ever so slightly.

'You can smile,' I tell him, leaning my elbows back on the pool's edge, my soaked shirt pulling taut. 'It's not dangerous.'

He smiles. I take that back. This wet, dark-eyed Lucas is a different beast from the uniformed man who stands beside me at the front desk. With his white shirt clinging to the muscles of his chest and droplets gleaming on the skin of his neck, he's not just offensively handsome, he's *hot*.

'I'm going to win our bet,' he promises me, his voice low. We're so close I can see the flecks and tones in his brown eyes. 'You know I am. That's why you do things like pull me into swimming pools and try to destroy phone numbers.'

'I didn't . . .'

I stop talking. His gaze has dipped, eyes moving over me. I feel a droplet of water chase another over my collarbone, down to my sodden shirt, and I watch him catch that tiny movement, pupils flaring.

'Yes?' he prompts.

He looks at my lips. And for a wild, daring moment, I think I might kiss him – snake my arms over his shoulders, pull our wet bodies flush . . .

I take an uneven breath.

'I saved the number in my phone. You know I'd never do something that might actually harm the hotel. Not even to piss you off.'

Lucas studies me, unreadable. 'Why are we like this?' he says, after a moment. 'You and me?'

'Like what?'

The chlorine has made my throat ache; I swallow. His eyes are on mine now.

'Always fighting.'

He pauses, taking a small breath, as if he's hesitating over what to say. His eyes slide away from me, and I breathe out, as if he's let me go.

'Well,' he says. 'Since last Christmas.'

And there it is. I turn my head aside. I don't want to look at him now, not while we're talking about this.

'I think you just answered your own question,' I say. 'You know why I hate you.'

He flinches slightly when I say *hate*, and I almost wish I could take it back, though I don't know why – he knows it, I know it. I take another breath, steadier now, and meet his eyes again.

'I've always figured you hate me because I'm everything you don't like all wrapped up in one human being,' I go on. 'And you know you were a dick last Christmas and don't like that I'm right about it. How'd I do? Is that it?'

Lucas lifts a hand off the side of the pool to wipe his eyes. That tension between us is sluicing away, replaced by something much more familiar.

'You think you are everything I don't like? All wrapped up . . . in one human being?'

'Aren't I?'

He looks back at me. 'No,' he says eventually. 'Not at all.'

I shift, discomposed. 'You find me strange, though.'

'A little.'

That hurts more than it should. I thought I was past Lucas's insults getting to me – but then, I did just hand him the very one that could do the most damage.

Lucas shifts to the side so he can rest his back against the pool. 'Is strange that bad?' he asks.

Clearly that whole thought played out right across my face, then.

'No. I'm proud of being a bit strange now.'

'Now?'

'Let's just say, at school I was the weird kid.' I shrug, swallowing. 'It wasn't that great. Kids weren't always super nice to me. Strange isn't cool when you're thirteen.'

'You were bullied?' he asks.

I stare out at the gardens, fogged and hazy through the pool windows. I thought I could tell him about this without feeling pathetic – to justify why I'd reacted that way when he called me strange, so he knows it's not really him that's got to me, it's old stuff. But this is harder than I thought it would be, especially when my body is still tingling. I'm on edge, exposed; I hate this feeling. I hope he didn't realise how close I came to kissing him.

'A bit, yeah,' I say, kicking my legs slowly through the water. 'It probably sounds stupid to you, but these things do stay with you.'

'Did anyone help? Your parents? Teachers?'

I shake my head. 'They didn't know.'

'Not even your parents?'

'Nope. I'm very good at looking cheerful when I feel like crap.' I've not got the tone quite right – he side-glances me, and I'm too afraid to look at him in case I see pity on his face.

'It doesn't sound stupid,' he says quietly. 'Do they know now? Your parents?'

Ugh. Not this conversation too. I'm starting to feel worryingly emotional – this has been a lot.

'My parents both died when I was twenty-one, so, no! We didn't get the chance to have that chat,' I say as I drag myself up on my arms and out of the pool.

'Your parents died?' Lucas says.

'Yep.' I'm swinging my legs around, yanking off my dark, soaked trainers and peeling off my socks. I want to get out of here. The pool room is too warm, and my wet clothes feel suffocating.

'I'm very sorry.'

He sounds so formal. I wish I'd not told him. People always change when they know. If he starts being nice to me just because I'm an orphan, I will *not* be able to handle it.

'How did they die?'

I blink.

'I'm sorry. That was a bit . . .'

'Yeah. It was,' I say, shooting him a look over my shoulder as I tuck my wet socks into my equally wet shoes.

The pool water slops and slooshes. I'm just getting up to leave when he says, 'My dad died when I was still too small to remember him. My mum didn't tell me what happened to him until I was a teenager. So I always used to make up how he died. Tiger bite. Skydive gone wrong. Or – if I was feeling anxious – then I'd imagine it was some hereditary disease, and my mum knew I had it too, and that's why she wouldn't tell me.'

I turn my head slowly to look at him. There's not a hint of how he's feeling in his posture – he sounds as emotionless as he would if he were discussing the hotel restaurant. But what he's just told me ... I may not like Lucas, but that makes my heart *ache* for the little boy he was.

'I'm so sorry, Lucas, that's awful.'

'It was a workplace accident, actually. He was a labourer. But yes. I'm sorry I asked about yours. It's just ... habit.'

After a moment's hesitation, I settle cross-legged on the tiles, squeezing the pool water out of the bottom of my trousers.

'My parents were always into sailing – these madcap adventures all around the world,' I say. My voice barely carries above the sounds of the water. 'It was never my thing, really, but after I left home, they bought a new boat and took it all over the place. America, the Caribbean, Norway. And one day ... their boat sank.'

I watch Lucas; he's still expressionless. I wonder if that one was on his list. It's just the sort of death a kid might imagine for the parent he doesn't remember. To me, though, it had seemed absolutely impossible. My parents were such experienced sailors – I never considered their adventures dangerous. It was just what they always did.

'It was so sudden,' I say. 'People act like that's better, but I don't know. It was like the world fundamentally changed into a horrible place in a split second and I was completely unequipped to handle it.' I can hear how odd my voice sounds as I try to keep it breezy. 'Anyway, now you know why I'm so "childish", as you put it. Life is so short! You can be gone just like that.' I click my fingers as I stand, looking down at the gigantic puddle I've left on the tiles beneath me. 'You've got to live every moment and enjoy it.'

Lucas tilts his head, saying nothing. I head for the towels, then pause as he says, 'No, you don't.'

'Pardon?'

'You don't have to enjoy every moment. Nobody can do that. It would be . . . exhausting.'

I'm thrown. I don't think I needed to worry about Lucas being more tactful with me on account of my dead parents.

'Well, I do,' I say, a little defensively. 'That's how I live my life.'

'No,' Lucas says.

He turns to look back at me, droplets sliding along the hard line of his jaw.

'You don't,' he says. 'You have bad days too. Everyone has bad days. As you so often like to remind me – you're a human.'

'You know what? Most people do not use the news of my parents' death as a chance to tell me I'm not living my life right,' I snap. But it's hard to muster my usual frustration – I can't forget his steady, low voice saying *I always used to make up how he died.*

'I'm not saying that,' Lucas says. 'I'm saying, you're not being honest.'

He pulls himself up on to the side of the pool, and even in the midst of this conversation I can't help but suck in a breath as the water paints his shirt to his skin. I can see every steely muscle, every contour. After a moment it makes me wonder what *he* can see, and I look down at myself to notice that my own shirt is clinging to my bra as if I'm in some sort of noughties frat-boy comedy film. Shit. I spin and reach for a towel from the basket by the wall.

'You are very positive, especially given what you've been through in your life,' Lucas says behind me. 'But you are still a real person. You swear when you drop things, and you think certain guests are idiots. You play dirty to win a bet.'

'Well, yeah, but . . .' *Only with you*, I almost say. Nobody else in this hotel would ever say that I swear or think badly of guests. If you asked Ollie whether I'd play dirty to win a bet, he'd go, *Izzy Jenkins? No way. She's a total sweetheart.*

I pull the towel around me, but all it does is bring the cold, soaked clothes closer to my skin – I need to strip off and get in a hot shower. I'm starting to shake, and I'm filled with the mess of emotions Lucas always seems to stir up in me: frustration, uncertainty, and the shadowy hurt that's been lurking there since last winter.

'So neither of us is perfect, then,' I say.

'Precisely,' Lucas says with satisfaction. He strolls off towards the men's changing room – not bothering with a towel, shirt clinging to the muscles of his back. I am left with the irritating sense that somehow, I've just managed to prove his point.

The ink didn't smudge. Poor Mandy must have used some kind of magical Team-Lucas pen. On Saturday morning, I listen morosely as Lucas conducts a second conversation with the owner of his diamond-studded wedding ring. I'm trying to work out exactly what the complexity is here – because there's definitely *something* complicated.

'Ah, I see,' says Lucas. 'Today will not be possible, but . . .'

He glances at me. I make sure to look extremely busy.

'Yes,' he says. 'I'll be there.'

After he hangs up, I don't ask. I continue not asking for as long as it is humanly possible to do so, and then I give up, because we've been coexisting in frosty silence ever since I arrived this morning and I am just not a person who can handle silence.

'Well?' I say.

'I will be returning the ring to its rightful owner tomorrow.'

'Returning it to them? As in, leaving the hotel?'

'Why not? This is hotel work. Top priority.'

I suppose it is, technically. I frown.

'And you're sure it's her ring?' I ask.

'No,' he concedes. 'But I will find out tomorrow.'

'Then I'm coming too,' I say, pushing my chair back from the computer and spinning to face him. 'I don't trust you.'

He raises his eyebrows slowly, still sorting through old receipts. 'Who will manage the front desk?'

'Ollie will do it. He owes me a favour.'

'Arjun will kill you if you take Ollie from him for a day.'

'Let me handle Arjun. I'm coming. I want to see the ring reunion anyway – this isn't *just* about the bet, remember?' I say, though I have definitely forgotten this myself of late. 'Where-abouts is this woman based?'

'London,' he says. 'Little Venice. I'll be booking an advance for the . . .' He checks his computer screen. 'Nine thirty-three.'

'OK, great,' I say. 'See you on the platform.'

'Great,' he says dryly, carefully stapling a collection of receipts together. *Click*, goes the stapler. As precise and meticulous and inexplicably irritating as ever.

Lucas

Mrs SB has forwarded me the last five years of accounts, and I've spent four hours poring over them.

I cannot remember the last time I felt this happy.

Everything I've learned on my course is coming to life now that I am looking at a real hotel's numbers – it is completely different from the test cases we've studied. This isn't theoretical. This is a place I truly care about, and as I sift through all our expenditures, noting areas where we could economise, I realise how powerless I've felt sitting here at the front desk while the hotel falls apart around me.

'All right, Lucas?' says Louis Keele, dinging the bell a few times, despite the fact that I am right here.

Well, there goes my good mood.

'Izzy about?'

'I don't know.'

That sounded rude. I look up and try to seem polite and

professional, but Louis hasn't noticed my bad manners. He's looking at a printout in front of me.

'Are those the hotel accounts?' he says.

I cover them with an arm, trying to make it look as though I'm just reaching for my mouse. I'm not sure what to do. Do potential investors see all these numbers? Or should I keep them hidden? I didn't need four hours to discover that they are not very favourable. If Mrs SB hasn't shared this information, I certainly don't want to.

'Why did you need Izzy?' I ask. As much as I don't want to talk to Louis about Izzy, some distraction is required.

'I'm thinking of asking her to dinner,' Louis says, eyes still on the paperwork.

Maybe I should show him the accounts.

'Actually,' Louis says, finally looking up at me. 'You might be quite useful. You know her better than I do. What's my best angle? Red roses? Impromptu picnic? Funny limerick?' His face turns a little sly. 'What would *you* do if you were trying to date her?'

Despite myself, I think about it. Izzy likes things that other people don't look at twice. Cheap second-hand jewellery; those awful teen dramas nobody else admits to watching; cocktails with silly names. I once caught her googling whether you could keep a wild rat as a pet. She will not want red roses. She would prefer a bouquet of interesting weeds.

Impromptu picnic is slightly better. She likes surprises. But it's freezing weather and she does feel the cold – when she leaves the hotel in the evening, she's always wrapped up as if she is heading out to the Antarctic.

A funny limerick could go either way. She's quick to laugh, but she is very funny, too, and I am not convinced Louis can match her sense of humour.

I should give him an answer along these lines. There's no reason not to help him. But then I see the calculating look in Louis' eye – the same expression he wore when he first saw the damage to the hotel ceiling all those weeks ago. And there it is again: the sensation I felt when Izzy slipped into the swimming pool with him.

'I would go for a classic date,' I find myself saying. 'Red roses and champagne at an expensive restaurant.'

'Yeah?' Louis says, frowning slightly. 'She doesn't seem that traditional to me.'

'Deep down she is highly conventional,' I say, returning my attention to my computer screen.

'Right, well, thanks, mate,' Louis says, and even though I'm not looking, I can still sense that charming, easy smile which has no doubt got him very far in life.

I look down at my phone as he walks away and see a new message from Uncle Antônio. He has sent me a link to an article with no message accompanying it. The article is called *Ten Signs You're Not Fulfilling Your Potential (Even If You Think You Are)*.

I turn my phone over and take a deep breath, trying to remember what really matters to me. My mother, my sister. Their happiness, and – increasingly – my own. All the small ways in which I make a difference to people's lives here.

But with Louis' expensive cologne still in the air, it's harder than ever to remember that the life I've built here is more than good enough for me.

On Sunday morning, it is so cold my breath is snatched from my throat. The forecast predicts heavy snow, though the British forecast is always promising extreme weather which usually ends up as drizzle, so I'm not too alarmed.

Izzy is at Brockenhurst station before me, dressed in fur-lined boots and a hooded, padded coat that reminds me of a sleeping bag. She is video-calling someone – no doubt one of her countless friends. As I approach, I recognise this one: Jem, a tall, smiling woman with box braids, multiple face piercings and a small, yappy dog. She used to live nearby and visited the hotel regularly, carrying the dog under an arm. The last time I saw her was a couple of months ago, when she came to say goodbye before she moved away. She and Izzy had hugged for so long that I'd wondered if the dog was still breathing in there.

'Have Grigg and Sameera got a big Scottish Christmas planned?' Jem is saying.

'Yeah!' Izzy says. Her voice is a bit too bright. 'Yeah, can't wait. And you're going to have a . . . have a . . .'

Jem starts laughing. 'Even Izzy Jenkins cannot put a positive spin on Christmas with my family. I am fucked.'

'You're going to have a . . . Christmas!' Izzy says, laughing too. 'And then it will be done, box ticked, and next year you'll spend it here with me.'

'Yeah,' Jem says, smiling. I glance at her over Izzy's shoulder. She is wearing a furry hat that I'm sure I've previously seen on

Izzy, her eyebrow piercings glittering beneath it. 'That's more like it. I'll be so jel of you getting buzzed with your buddies all Christmas.'

Izzy catches sight of me behind her. 'Got to go! Give Piddles a cuddle from me. Love you so much!'

'Love you too, little pigeon,' Jem says, blowing a kiss at the screen before she disappears.

I come to stand beside Izzy.

'Piddles?'

'The dog. Yappy and nasty. Unless you're Jem, in which case, adorable and misunderstood.'

'And little pigeon?'

'It's an inside joke. An affectionate nickname. You wouldn't understand.'

I just raise my eyebrows at that. There is something scrappy about a pigeon that suits the version of Izzy I have come to see this winter – perhaps I understand better than she thinks.

We join the nearest queue as the train pulls in. I pre-booked my seat, but Izzy didn't, and after I tut about this, she looks very smug to find an available seat directly opposite mine.

I plan to spend the train journey working on a draft budget for Mrs SB, but it's hard to concentrate. Izzy has removed her many layers and is playing solitaire with a set of battered playing cards, wearing a baby-blue top with no straps.

'Want to play something?' Izzy says.

I've been staring at her cards in an effort not to stare at the smooth white skin above that blue top. I think for a moment.

'Poker?' I say.

'With just two of us?'

'It can be done. Texas Hold 'em? Though . . .' I suddenly wish I'd not suggested it. 'I don't want to play for money,' I add, embarrassed.

'Of course not,' Izzy says, like the very thought is ridiculous. 'Though we're on a train, so strip poker is out.'

The idea that strip poker might otherwise be in throws me. She digs around in her rucksack and produces a small box of raisins, the sort you might give to a child as a snack.

'Chips,' she says, opening the box. 'Whoever's up by Waterloo gets to choose how we decorate the lobby?'

'I don't want to decorate the lobby any more than it is decorated right now,' I say, frowning.

'Exactly. Whereas I think we are seriously lacking in tinsel.' She smiles at me and I swallow.

'You up for a challenge?' she asks.

'Of course,' I say, reaching for the cards.

I try to be magnanimous for the journey from Waterloo to Little Venice. I knew Izzy would be terrible at poker. Everything is always written all over her face. She takes losing extremely badly, just as I would expect, and sulks the entire way to Shannon's flat.

The woman who greets us when we arrive is wearing a large hat that reads, *Thank u, next.* I look beyond her to the open-plan living area to find that everyone inside is wearing the same. The music is pounding already, though it's only lunchtime.

'I don't know you,' says the woman in the doorway. 'Did he send you? If so, tell him Shannon has every fucking right to—'

'Nobody sent us,' Izzy says quickly. 'Shannon invited us. We're here about a ring?'

'Oh!' The woman's face lights up. 'Come on in, she's in the kitchen working on the cake.'

Izzy's sulking expression has been replaced with the bright, fascinated look she wears when she's truly enjoying herself. She is a bad loser, but she is also very easily distracted.

Shannon is a tall blonde woman wearing a sequinned dress with an apron over the top. My first impression on entering the pristine kitchen is that she looks like a housewife from an American TV show. However, the cake she is icing is shaped like a penis, which does throw this image out a little.

'Hello,' she says, putting down her icing pen and wiping her hands on her apron. 'You must be Lucas! Did you bring your girlfriend?'

'Not girlfriend,' we say in unison.

'Even better,' Shannon says.

'I'm Izzy,' Izzy says, holding out her hand. 'Congratulations!'

It seems this is the correct thing to say, because Shannon gives her a wide smile.

'Thanks so much! I've been so excited for today. I wanted to give it as much energy as my wedding day. Isn't it amazing that they all took annual leave? We're going for a long weekend in Madeira for my unhoneymoon.' She gestures towards the people in the living area. 'You know what I did for my actual honeymoon? Hiked in the Alps. Did I like hiking? Did I like snow? Did I fuck! You know what I do like, though?'

She has the icing pen back in her hand, and is pointing it at us.

'Sunshine and cocktails with people who have stood by me.'

'*That* is my sort of holiday,' Izzy says. 'I love this. Can I have a hat?'

'Oh, hats are obligatory,' Shannon says, pointing to a stack of them on the kitchen counter.

Izzy looks at me. 'Perfect! Lucas *loves* novelty headgear.'

'I've brought the ring,' I say to Shannon. Someone needs to get this conversation on track. Though I can't help thinking that we aren't as likely to get a fifteen-thousand-pound reward for a ring representing a marriage that's ended. 'We will need some way to confirm that it's yours – that is, if you still want it.'

'One step ahead of you,' says Shannon, still icing as she pulls her phone out with her other hand. 'Here, my wedding photos.'

I glance from the screen to Shannon's face.

'Don't worry,' she says. 'They don't make me sad any more. I'm where I want to be right now. It doesn't matter how I got here.'

'God, that is such an amazing mentality,' Izzy says, mouth already full of a cupcake she's picked up from somewhere.

With her *Thank u, next* hat on, Izzy looks like everyone else at the party – already quite at home. I was so surprised when she told me that she had been bullied at school. Everybody loves Izzy. But I can see it now – the way she just fits in. I suspect that is a skill she picked up because she needed it.

'Are you sure that's your ring?' she asks Shannon. 'Could it be . . . a similar ring?'

Shannon looks at her in surprise. Izzy pulls an apologetic face, cupcake pouched in one cheek.

'Sorry. We have a bet,' she explains, swallowing. 'If it's your ring, I lose.'

'Ah. Well, sorry,' Shannon says. She spreads her hands. 'But if it's any consolation, every loss can be a win, right?'

Izzy absorbs this, then turns to me.

'Can I have a word?' she asks, tugging me into the corner by the drinks trolley. 'She hasn't *proven* it's hers,' she whispers.

'This is very undignified, Izzy,' I say, enjoying myself immensely. 'Perhaps you should learn to lose with grace.'

'She could have just ordered the same ring from the same jeweller!'

'And stayed at the hotel at the same time as someone else with that ring, who also lost it?'

'Yes!'

I fold my arms and look down at her. Her hair is mussed beneath her ridiculous hat, and for a moment, her relentless competitiveness doesn't seem irritating – it seems charming. She just cares *so much*.

Then her shoulders sag. 'Shit,' she says.

She looks genuinely gutted. I look away. Winning doesn't feel quite as good as I thought it would.

'Today is about fresh starts,' Shannon says, as we return to her side. 'Wiping that slate clean. If that means anything to you two, you're welcome to stay for the party.'

I check the time on the clock above the kitchen door. We

should be getting back. Ollie is on his own at the desk, and technically our work here is done.

'We should go,' Izzy and I say to each other in unison.

There is a pause. And then I find myself saying, 'Perhaps we could stay for a short while. An hour or so.'

Izzy stares at me, mouth slightly open. I feel a small flash of triumph at having surprised her.

'You want to stay at the party?'

'We can leave if you would prefer,' I say, as Shannon puts the finishing touches on her cake.

'No. I want to stay. Ollie's expecting to cover the whole day anyway,' Izzy says, and then stands on tiptoe to plonk a hat on my head. 'I need cheering up. And I'm pretty sure anyone we work with would say that you and I could do with a fresh start.'

I now see why Shannon was so keen to get the ring back today. We are gathered around a man wearing goggles and heavy-duty gloves, setting up mysterious pieces of equipment on the floor of Shannon's living room. In the centre is a large slab, on which rests the wedding ring.

'Shannon, if you would like to say a few words first,' the man says, gesturing for her to take his spot.

'Thank you,' she says, stepping forward in a pair of Perspex goggles. 'We are gathered here today to celebrate a union, not of two people, but of a whole community.' She smiles. 'You have all been here for me for every step of the last five miserable years. You are the ones who told me that it's not failing to give up on a love that isn't healthy – because that's not love. Without you all, I wouldn't be standing here today.'

Everyone claps. A small, curly-haired woman beside me wipes away a tear with the back of her hand. There are couples here too, and they seem just as moved as everybody else.

What a strange event. I don't know how I feel about this. I want to believe that marriage is for ever. When *I* choose to marry, that's what it'll be.

But there is something undeniably special about this, too, and as I glance at Izzy, I see how completely this has captured her. By nature, she is much more open-minded than I am. Usually that tendency strikes me as over idealistic, but right now I feel a little envious of the way she meets new things.

I look back at Shannon and try to see her the way Izzy would: without judgement. I try to imagine what that ring means to Shannon now, and I can see that there is something beautiful in what she's saying. We are all misled and misdirected from time to time. Perhaps there really is no shame in that, as long as we wake up to it before it's too late to change.

'Today, I want to let go of the past,' Shannon announces. 'I want to always remember the fact that if you burn a diamond . . . it only gets tougher.'

With that, she kneels and blasts the blowtorch at the wedding ring resting on the slab.

The gold melts fast – faster than I would have expected. With some careful support from the man in the goggles, Shannon splits the ring down into a heap of diamonds and a small ball of gold.

Everyone is whooping and cheering. I glance back at Izzy, who is deep in conversation with two strangers; she's laughing behind her hand. Lately, looking at Izzy has made me feel such a tangle of things. Fearful, lustful, wary, possessive. But watching her now through the anonymity of the crowd, I see a bright, bold young woman whose parents would be very proud of her, and the thought makes my chest feel tight.

She finds me in the spare bedroom some time later. I'm on my laptop in an armchair, going back over Mrs SB's spreadsheet. Izzy stops short, a champagne glass in hand, her bare shoulders now dotted with red and gold glitter. Through the window beside her the snow is coming down in thick, feathery flakes.

'Oh my God,' Izzy says. 'No way are you working.'

I am instantly defensive. 'We are *both* meant to be working.'

'Oh, please! You were the one who said we should stay. Besides, there is literally no work I can do remotely. Come dance. They're playing noughties tunes with eye-wateringly misogynistic lyrics. Half the room's raving, the other half is deconstructing the problematic songs. Basically, this is a fantastic party.'

She's reaching a hand towards me. I've never held Izzy's hand before – except when she pulled me into the pool.

'Fresh start?' she says, voice dropping a little. 'We could try it? Just for a few minutes, until we go home?'

I meet her eyes. I can see mischief glimmering there – just like when she met my eyes through the lost-property-room door in her pink bra. Just like when her back was pressed to the side of the swimming pool.

I am a careful man by nature. But Izzy makes me feel reckless.

There is a physical attraction between us, that is becoming increasingly obvious. But she doesn't respect me. There's nothing to stop her taking what she wants from me and leaving it at that.

Which should be fine. It *would* be fine if I hated her as much as she hates me. We would be on the same level, and there would be no danger of anyone hurting anybody's feelings.

Very suddenly, I see the problem. I don't hate Izzy Jenkins at all.

'I'm Izzy,' she says, when I don't answer. 'Pleased to meet you.'

I stretch my hand out slowly and shake hers. It's cool and small in mine. My heart beats harder, too hard.

'Lucas da Silva,' I say. 'Pleased to meet you too.'

We dance. There's distance between us at first – as there would be, I suppose, if we really were the strangers we're pretending to be. But the gap closes slowly from song to song, until my hips are bumping hers and her hair paints a trail across my arm each time she tosses her head. The music is bad American pop, but I don't care. I want to dance with Izzy. I want to give in to the thump-thump of desire that courses through me when I see her. I want to ignore real life for once and just pretend that I'm a guy, at a party, dancing with a beautiful girl.

'You're good,' she says, raising her voice over the music. 'You can dance!'

'So can you.'

'Well, yeah,' she says, as if this should have been obvious. 'But I thought the whole thing about Brazilians all being great dancers was a cliché.'

'It is a cliché. We are not all great dancers,' I tell her, thinking of my sister, who often cheerfully proclaims that she's about as good at keeping time as she is at keeping boyfriends.

'But if any Brazilian was going to be bad at dancing,' Izzy says, 'I feel like it would be you.'

I glare at her. She laughs.

'And how do you know I'm Brazilian?'

She pulls a face at the break from character. 'I mean, ah, where are you from?' she asks.

'Niterói,' I tell her. The song shifts and I watch her body shift too, finding the new beat. 'It's in Rio de Janeiro, Brazil.'

'Brazil! What's it like there at this time of year?'

'Hot,' I say, holding her gaze. I take a sip of my beer.

That thump-thump of desire gets louder. She's closer, looking up at me, the glitter on her shoulders sparkling under the light of Shannon's chandelier.

'How about you? Where are you from?'

'Surrey,' she says, her leg brushing mine as she dances. 'Way less exciting. Though I loved growing up there.'

Something passes over her face – a memory of her parents, perhaps.

'And what do you do?' I ask, to bring her back to me.

She stumbles slightly as someone moves past us and I steady her with a hand on her waist. Somehow it feels right for the hand to stay there, and now we're not just dancing, we're dancing *together*. Her hands come to rest lightly on my shoulders and her hips twist in time with mine.

'I work at a hotel.'

I try to imagine what I would say next if I didn't stand beside her at the front desk every morning. It's getting hard to concentrate. Her body moves with mine and there's just the soft fabric of her baby-blue top between my palm and her skin. She's warm and a little breathless. I can smell her cinnamon scent every time I inhale.

I settle for the question I often get asked. 'Are people always checking in under fake names to have affairs?'

She gives me a small, knowing smile. 'That or turning up naked under trench coats. Yeah. Nonstop.'

I let out an *ah* of recognition as the song changes to Anitta's 'Envolver'. Izzy clocks it and lifts her gaze to mine. We're body to body: her arms aren't just resting lightly on my shoulders now, they're wound around my neck, and my hand is at the small of her back, keeping our shifting hips in sync.

'Can you translate this song for me? What's it actually about?' she asks me.

'Well, it's in Spanish, so . . .'

'Oh.' She blushes. 'Sorry. I thought it was in Portuguese.'

For once, I'm not interested in embarrassing her.

'My Spanish isn't bad, so I can try . . . But, uh, the song is a little rude.'

'We just danced to "212",' she says, tilting her head back far enough that her hair tickles my hand on her waist as she looks up at me. 'I think I can handle some sexual undertones.'

I take a swig of my beer. 'She's saying something like . . . Tell me what we're supposed to do when we want each other this much. She's saying, if we go to bed together . . . you won't last five minutes.'

Izzy laughs at that, still dancing. 'What else?'

'She's saying that she won't let this guy get involved with her. Whatever happens there stays there.'

I think we're dancing close until Izzy closes those tiny centimetres between us and I realise what *close* actually feels like. Her stomach pressed to my hips, her breasts against my chest. The contact sends desire snapping through me. I'm hard, and she must be able to tell, but she just keeps dancing.

'What an interesting idea,' she says, looking me right in the eyes.

I feel her phone buzz in the same moment she does. That's how close my hand is to the back pocket of her jeans. She looks down and pulls away as she tugs the phone out.

'It's Ollie,' she says, and just like that, we're back. Standing in the middle of a makeshift dance floor in a stranger's living room when we ought to be at work. The room seems smaller, the music wincingly loud.

I can't hear the phone conversation, but I follow her off the dance floor and watch her body language. The way she stiffens and pulls her hair up in a one-handed ponytail, then lets it drop again as she talks.

When she hangs up, she turns and finds me immediately.

'We have to go back,' she says.

'What's happened?'

'It's . . .' She tugs her bottom lip between her teeth. 'Graham's wife has arrived at the hotel.'

'Your ring owner?'

'No-o,' Izzy says. 'Graham's *other* wife.'

Izzy

It seems that Graham has two different-but-similar email addresses for a reason. Because he has two different-but-similar lives.

And when I copied the other address into my email exchange . . . I gave Wife 1 access to a thread about a wedding ring that belonged to Wife 2, creating some understandable drama. Wife 1 turned up in our lobby, screaming and shouting, demanding answers from poor Ollie, who had absolutely no idea what she was talking about. Apparently, she is now refusing to leave the premises until she 'gets some answers from whoever sent that email'.

'We can get as far as Woking.'

Lucas is pacing back and forth along Shannon's upstairs corridor, oblivious to the people popping up to use the bathroom and having to dodge past him like he's the Big Bad Boss in an old GameBoy game. He is staring fixedly at his phone, National

Rail app open on the screen. I can't believe that half an hour ago I was grinding up against this man on the dance floor. The thought is completely surreal.

'Right, great,' I say, chewing my thumbnail.

I've really messed up here. Well, Graham did most of the messing up. But I've brought this whole bigamy drama into the hotel, and now I'm not even there to sort it out – I'm here, sexy-dancing with Lucas. What am I *doing*?

'Maybe from Woking there will be a bus,' Lucas says, furiously tapping away at his phone.

I look out of the window over the staircase. The snow is coming fast, caught up in itself, whirling and swooping like one of those Van Gogh paintings of the stars.

'UK roads can't really do snowstorms,' I tell him, leaning back against the wall as someone emerges from the bathroom and hesitates, then dashes past in the moment before Lucas pivots on his heels to pace back again. 'I think the odds of buses running in a couple of hours' time are pretty low.'

'It is a bit of snow! It is a little bit cold!' Lucas snaps.

'Well, OK, I'm not the bloody transport secretary, am I?' I snap back, nettled.

He's behaving like all that dancing never happened. Gone is the loose-limbed, half-smiling man who circled his hips against mine half an hour ago; here's grouchy, uptight Lucas, taking things out on me that aren't my fault.

'Why did we stay so late?' he says, swiping his thumb down to refresh the outgoing trains again. I watch as the red text blinks, the delays lengthening.

'Because we were having fun. Before you switched back to the usual Lucas, who is incapable of fun, and just snaps at me about everything.'

He looks up at me at last, surprised. 'I'm not snapping at you.'

I pull a disbelieving face, spreading my arms out. 'Hello? You literally just yelled at me about it being only a little bit cold.'

'I wasn't yelling *at* you about it being cold. Why would I yell at you about that? It's not your fault, is it?'

He seems genuinely nonplussed. I stare back at him in silence, trying to figure him out.

'Sorry, is this a queue for the toilet?' says a small man in chinos, bobbing up at the top of the stairs.

I wave him through. 'So you were just . . . yelling?'

'This is frustrating,' Lucas says, looking back at his phone to refresh the page. 'I want to be back at the hotel. And I hate . . . this situation. I'm not frustrated with you.'

'Right.' I pause, fiddling with my necklace. 'Actually, no. I don't think that's OK.'

He blinks at me, taking this in.

'You didn't need to raise your voice,' I say. We're in new territory here – I've never called him out on this before, but as I say it, I realise how much it pisses me off. He does it all the time at the hotel. I wonder how often our arguments start because he raises his voice and that in itself just winds me up. 'I'm frustrated too. I'm not yelling.'

'You're just saying unkind things instead,' he says. 'Is that any better?'

'Excuse me?' I'm genuinely staggered by this. I have been

called many things over the years – weird, stupid, ditzy – but I've *never* been called unkind.

'I am *incapable of fun*, you said.'

'Oh, I . . .' I did say that. I guess when it comes to Lucas, I've always just given him shit like that, and he gives it right back to me, so it never occurred to me that it was unkind. I can feel my cheeks getting pink. I press the backs of my hands to my warm skin. 'I thought . . . That's just sort of . . . what we say to each other. It's kind of . . . jokey.'

'Is it?' Lucas resumes pacing. 'Neither of us seems to laugh very much.'

I don't know what to say. I feel quite ashamed of myself.

'You two OK?' Shannon calls up the stairs. 'Our flight's delayed, so everyone is heading home for tonight – can you get back all right?'

We glance at each other.

'I'm sure we'll be fine!' I call. 'Trains are a bit ropey, but we'll get there.'

'Great,' Shannon says, sounding relieved. 'I'd offer you our spare room, but a few friends who live further away need somewhere to crash, so . . .'

'We'll get going, then,' I say, looking at the trains on Lucas's phone screen. Another one cancelled. Yellow exclamation marks in triangles everywhere. 'Thanks so much for having us, Shannon!'

'Safe travels!' she calls, heels already clip-clopping back to the kitchen again.

If this were a Christmas movie, she'd have put us up in her

spare room, and we'd have stayed up all night talking. It would have been cosy and gorgeous. But it's not a Christmas movie, and so Lucas and I end up sitting outside WHSmith at Waterloo, staring morosely at the departure boards, still stewing from our latest argument.

Back there under Shannon's chandelier, I'd come so close to kissing him. He's infuriating and short-tempered and there are a hundred things I don't like about him, but I can't deny that I'm almost *painfully* attracted to him. I kept thinking of Sameera and Grigg saying there's no harm in having a fling with him – nobody can get hurt if you don't even like each other.

But is it normal to want to have sex with someone you hate? Is that something I need to look at? I did a few years of therapy after my parents died, and I learned enough about healthy thoughts to suspect this is a topic my old therapist would probably have wanted to discuss.

I glance at Lucas. He is eating a sandwich angrily, which I didn't know was possible, but he's really managing with aplomb. I roll my eyes. He's so dramatic. So broody and moody and *rude*.

And he thinks I'm unkind. I press my hand to the base of my ribs as the thought hits, accompanied by a quick flash of shame. My parents used to have a sign dangling above the oven in our kitchen that said *No act of kindness is ever wasted* – it was important to them that whatever else I became in life, I'd always be kind, and I'm suddenly terrified that I've let them down. The thought takes the wind out of me.

'There! Platform seven!' Lucas yells, exploding up from his seat.

His sandwich packaging goes flying as we race each other to the snow-topped train. He's a fast runner, but I'm craftier – by the time I jump on, he's still floundering around between two tourists and their luggage.

'Ha!' I say, sticking my tongue out as he eventually hops through the door, breathing hard.

I'm expecting a comeback about how infantile I'm being, but when he looks at me, for a moment his face is unguarded. He's smiling.

'What?' I say, suspicious.

His smile smooths away. 'Nothing,' he says, moving past me, angling – of course – for the only available seat.

Mrs SB texts an update when we get to Woking. *I've given Mrs Rogers no.1 our spare room in Opal Cottage for the night, and invited Mr Graham Rogers and Mrs Rogers no.2 here for brunch and a civil conversation in the morning. Amazing what the promise of a free meal can do.* The message ends with a thumbs-up. Mrs SB only ever uses a thumbs-up without irony, so she must be calmer than she was when Ollie called. Still, I feel awful for causing her all this trouble. It's the last thing she needs right now – and even though she was super nice about us both being off on this trip, I do feel *very* guilty for leaving the hotel on a job that really only needed one of us.

Woking station is packed with pissed-off travellers, all alternating between staring at phones and departure screens. It's too cold; my nose hurts. I just want to go home and crawl into my bed.

'Replacement bus service cancelled,' Lucas growls, not looking up from his phone. He mutters something in Portuguese, and then says, 'What do we do now?'

I'm surprised he's asking me. Lucas usually likes to plough on, making his own decisions and expecting me to trot along after him.

'Cab?' I say, already wincing.

'I *can't*,' Lucas says, and there's real anguish in his voice at the very thought of it.

I get it – I'm not rolling in it either, and a taxi from here would cost us at least £200. I get my phone out and hit up Google. A cheap hotel right by the station has rooms available for £40. I doubt they'll stay at that price for long – other people will have the same idea as me soon enough.

'Look, it sounds like everyone's fine at Forest Manor now, and we can't afford a cab, so . . .' I hold out the screen to him.

He stares at it for a moment. His eyes flick up to mine.

'We can get two rooms,' I say quickly. 'If you want.'

'I would rather . . . Well, it's up to you,' he says.

'One's fine for me. I'll just sleep on the floor.'

He looks irritated. '*I* will sleep on the floor.'

'I don't know if there'll be enough floor for you,' I say, nodding at the size of him.

His lip lifts ever so slightly. 'Book it,' he says decisively. 'Before it's too late. I'll transfer you my share now.'

He's already back on his phone when I open my mouth to say don't worry, it can wait. I swallow it back. I know Lucas is skint, but he's also very proud.

'Thanks,' I say instead.

A few clicks later, and it's done. Unbelievably, incomprehensibly, I am about to spend the night in a hotel room with Lucas da Silva.

The first thing that strikes me about the room is that nobody will be able to sleep on the floor in here. Every spare inch is taken up with a desk, a chair, side tables for the bed, and a footstool that's way too big for the space. Plus that ridiculous thing they put out for your luggage, like a small hammock for your suitcase. Who uses those, and why?

We have no suitcases, obviously. I don't even have a toothbrush. I try to give my teeth a particularly vigorous lick, which achieves nothing other than hurting my tongue, and then I throw myself down on the bed with a long, loud *ugh*.

At least it's warm. There's an air-conditioning unit whirring away over the bathroom door, blasting out hot air. Everything in here is a very washable shade of dark grey. It's completely impersonal – the opposite of Forest Manor Hotel and Spa. This hotel isn't a place where people go the extra mile, it's a place where colleagues go to bed with each other when they shouldn't.

I lift my head to look at Lucas, who is still examining the room with his arms folded. We're not doing that, obviously.

Except a few hours ago I really did want to have sex with Lucas, and that thought hasn't *completely* gone away.

'You did a good thing today,' he says abruptly.

My thoughts immediately go to the dance floor. The sound of Anitta, the feel of Lucas's hand pressing the small of my back . . .

'It's better for both those women to know the truth.'

Oh. Graham. Yes. Graham the bigamist. The other major event of the day.

'That wasn't a good thing for the hotel, though,' I say. 'I've made Mrs SB and Barty's life even more stressful.'

Lucas shrugs. 'Some things are important enough to cause a little drama.'

I raise my eyebrows. It's not like Lucas to be in favour of drama.

'It's early for bed,' Lucas says, checking his watch. 'I think I'll go for a walk.'

'A walk? In central Woking? In a snowstorm?'

Lucas turns his attention to the window, as if remembering the problem.

'We could go to the bar?' I suggest, sitting up on my elbows.

Lucas grimaces. Ah, right – no spending unnecessary money. I reach for the remote control and turn on the telly. It lands on *Love Actually*. I let out a delighted yip and shimmy up the bed so I'm propped up on the pillows.

'You've seen this, right?' I say to him.

He watches for a few moments. 'No.'

'Oh my God. Sit down. That's a crime against Christmas right there. Is this not a thing in Brazil? There's even a super-hot muscly Brazilian guy in it and everything.'

His lip quirks. 'Do you think us super-hot muscly Brazilian guys seek each other out?'

I flush. 'No, that's not – whatever. You have to see it.'

He looks slightly fatigued by this, but perches on the bed beside me, and then after a moment swings his legs around.

'It's *Love Actually*? My sister does tell me I must watch this all the time,' he says. 'What have I missed? Who is that man?'

'Just watch,' I say. Because of course Lucas is one of those assertive males who talks over crucial dialogue.

On screen, David meets Natalie for the first time. Lucas settles in beside me, fingers linked on his chest.

'So he is going to fall in love with that woman?' he asks, as Annie appears on-screen.

'No, that's his chief of staff,' I say, laughing. 'It's Natalie he falls in love with. Your romance radar is terrible.' Then I pause. Is that unkind? 'Sorry,' I say, just as Lucas says,

'So they're colleagues – that means they can't be anything more?'

I keep my eyes on the scene playing out on-screen and give up on actually hearing anything.

'Well, I guess . . . the Prime Minister sleeping with his chief of staff would maybe be a no-no?'

'Hmm,' Lucas says, taking this in.

'What's the deal with office romances in Brazil? Is everyone cool with it?'

'It depends,' Lucas says, 'on how you conduct yourself at work. You have to be appropriate.'

'Yeah, kind of the same here.'

I think of me and Lucas, fully clothed in the swimming pool, splashing each other wildly. Not sure anyone would accuse us of conducting ourselves appropriately.

We watch the film in silence. I wonder why Lucas asked about colleagues being romantically involved. I wonder if it's about me. I wonder if we're about to cross a line that cannot be uncrossed, and whether I care about that, and I already know that I don't.

Lucas turns on to his side, facing me. I shift my head to look at him. I let myself really take him in: the serious brown eyes, the straight brows, the faint hollow beneath his cheekbone. We're close enough that I can feel his breath ghosting over my cheek.

'You have always told me what you think of me,' he says eventually. His voice is low. Behind it, the telly chatters on. 'You've always been honest.'

'That's true.' I shift so I'm lying on my side too. I tuck a hand under my cheek. He echoes the gesture, other hand tapping restlessly at the covers between us.

'Will you tell me what you think of me now?'

I'm not expecting that question. I don't know *what* I think of Lucas these days. I think he's too stern and doesn't know how to laugh at himself; I think he's pedantic and rude. I think last Christmas he behaved like a dickhead. But I also think he's sexy and complex, and that there's a warmth somewhere in there, behind all the scowling.

'I think maybe I don't really know you at all,' I say slowly.

His expression shifts infinitesimally. I wouldn't have noticed it if we hadn't been so close. All of a sudden I'm hit with an urge to just . . . shake him. He's so controlled. I want to make him let go.

I lift one hand to rest against his jaw, framing his face, the heel of my hand against his neck. His stubble is rough under my palm. I feel his jaw clench, but he stays very still, just watching me with dark, liquid eyes. The heat I felt on the dance floor starts up again deep in my belly, a low, wild beat.

The decision I'm making is a bad one – I know it even as I lean towards him, eyes on his parted lips. But I don't care. I don't *care*. I want this, and I'm sick and tired of trying to work out why.

I kiss him. That heat grows tenfold inside me, like I've blown on a flame, and for a second, maybe two, Lucas kisses me back.

Then he's pulling away, spinning to sit with his back to me. I stare at his hunched shoulders, how they rise and fall with each breath. I'm breathing hard too, and my cheeks are hot.

'Shit,' I mutter. 'Sorry. I thought . . .'

'It's fine.' Lucas's voice is sharp. 'I just . . . That wouldn't be a good idea.' He glances over his shoulder for an instant before returning his gaze to the carpet. It's too fast to read anything into his face.

'I'm not looking for a relationship, if that's what you're worried about,' I say, stung. 'I know you're not going to be flying someone like me back to meet your mum.'

He turns at this, shifting to see me properly. *Love Actually* rattles on between us and I reach impatiently for the remote, switching it off.

'What do you mean, *someone like me*?'

'I'm just saying, your type is probably women who work out with you in tiny gymwear and drink green juice. But also like serious films with subtitles. And football. And have really long legs.'

I'm floundering, hot with desire and embarrassment in equal measure. I need to get control of this situation again. At last his expression is one I recognise: he's wearing the faintly exasperated face he uses when he's humouring me. Fine. At least that's not pity.

'You know nothing about my type,' he says. 'Evidently.'

'Well, I know a little bit, don't I?' I sit up and shift to the edge of the bed. 'It doesn't matter. I don't like you, you don't like me, I thought maybe we could just have some fun for a night, you didn't want to, the end. I'm going for a walk.'

'In central Woking? In a snowstorm?'

I glare at him for parroting my words back to me.

'Yes,' I say, lifting my chin as I grab my coat and head to the door. 'See you at bedtime.'

God, that's going to be awkward.

Lucas

It is hard to imagine how that could have gone worse.

Why would she kiss me right after saying she doesn't know me at all? Why then, of all the moments? It was a sentence that simultaneously hurt and gave me hope: she has never *tried* to know me, but perhaps if I could get her to try, she might . . .

I press my hands to my eyes. This has been an unpleasant day. Like a train bearing down on me, a great truth has been rolling in, and as I lie here in this embarrassment of a hotel room, I have no choice but to acknowledge that I want Izzy Jenkins to like me.

Because I like her. I like her stripy hair and the way she plays dirty. I like that she challenges me. I like that she's so much more interesting than she seems at first glance. I want to be the one person who knows every inch of the real Izzy.

My phone beeps: another message from the family WhatsApp, which has turned into a long-running game of let's-annoy-Lucas, with a detour into a series of rapid-fire questions about barbecue marinades from my sister.

Hey Lucas, how's your date going?? Ana asks, with a GIF of a giggling elephant whose significance I couldn't possibly begin to understand.

I hesitate for a moment and then, on impulse, I tap on her name and click *video call.*

She answers after three rings, with her ringlets pinned and enormous fake eyelashes swooping up to her eyebrows.

'Well, hello,' she says, cocking her head.

'It isn't a date,' I say. Whenever I call family, it feels a little strange slipping back into Portuguese again. I am a slightly different man in my mother tongue. Bolder, firmer, louder. I don't think either English Lucas or Brazilian Lucas is the truer one, but the two languages bring out different sides of me, and right now I want to remember the version of myself who breathes through his Rs and goes after what he wants.

'But you wish it was,' Ana says. She's looking at herself in a mirror, adjusting her eyelashes.

'Where are you going?'

'An actual date,' she says, pouting at her reflection. 'He's coming here.'

'Isn't it the middle of the afternoon?'

'It's nap time. I have a two-hour window and a guy who is very open-minded. Don't deflect, you called me for a reason – what's up?'

'Oh, I won't take up your window of—'

'Lucas.'

'Fine. I'll be quick. I think I like her. Izzy. My co-worker. She tried to kiss me and I blew her off because . . . she hates me. I don't want to kiss her like *that*, you know?'

Ana inhales between her teeth. 'And she got upset about it.'

'Mm. Now she hates me more than ever.'

'Her pride is bruised. There's a reason it's harder for women to approach men than the other way around – when the world tells you your worth is about men desiring you, it's hard to take it when they don't, and we're scared to be rejected. You've given her a knock-back. You need to work extra hard to make her feel better again.'

'How do I do that?'

Ana puckers her lips. I'm not sure if this is lipstick-related or something to do with me.

'What's she like? What makes her feel good about herself?'

'She's very independent. And she has a lot of friends. And she likes second-hand things, and pick-and-mix.'

Ana's face suddenly warms into a smile. 'Oh, you are smitten.'

I growl.

'You'll know what to do. If you really like her, it'll come to you, because if you're made for each other, you're made to heal her when she's hurting. I have to go, but I'm glad you called. I'm so proud of you over there, studying, working, going for what you actually want. I miss you.'

'Miss you too. I love you,' I say. Something else that's much easier to say in Portuguese. 'Enjoy your date. I hope—'

The door opens and a pink-nosed, snow-covered Izzy pokes her head in.

'Oh, sorry, are you on the phone?' she says, pausing mid step.

'Is that her?' Ana asks, thankfully in Portuguese.

'Bye,' I say, before she can say anything incriminating and easily translatable. 'Don't worry,' I tell Izzy as I hang up, 'we were finished.'

'Look,' Izzy says, 'it's extremely cold outside and I just got sprayed with slush by a passing bus, so I really need a hot bath. Can we just agree to coexist in silence and forget that . . .' she points at the bed '. . . ever happened?'

I will not be forgetting that kiss. Yes, it came at the wrong moment, and yes, my mind was racing, but the feeling of Izzy's lips against mine – her hand on me, her tongue, that cinnamon-sugar scent . . . My body just lit up, as if that kiss was a match thrown on a fire, and it took all of my strength to resist her.

'Fine,' I say, clearing my throat. 'Whatever you want.'

She marches into the bathroom and closes the door. I think about what Ana said: if I'm meant for Izzy, I'll know how to make her feel better. I'm pretty sure that whatever it is she needs, I'm not giving it to her right now. I stare at the ceiling and try to think. She will want to make it clear that she doesn't need me. Izzy doesn't like to need anybody. She will want to feel attractive, because I'm an idiot and probably made her feel as though I didn't want her, even though the woman haunts my dreams and has done so for much longer than I'd like to admit.

And she will want to get one up on me again, because that's how we operate.

Maybe that's the answer. Maybe, as painful as this thought is . . . Maybe I need to let Izzy win something.

She comes out of the bathroom in a tantalisingly small towel, her feet bare, her hair wet. The stripes are gone. It never occurred to me that she must take them out when she washes it, but she didn't wear them at the pool either. I had never seen anyone with stripy hair before I met Izzy. It should look tacky, but it doesn't. Izzy has that effect on things.

True to her word, she doesn't speak to me. She just grabs her handbag and then heads back into the bathroom, closing the door with an emphatic *click*. When she re-emerges, she has dressed, dried her hair and pinned the stripes back in. Meanwhile I have finished *Love Actually* and am feeling highly sentimental.

'Listen,' I begin, and she holds up a hand.

'That sounds like the start of a sentence about the incident we agreed not to speak about.' She walks around to sit on the footstool, picking fluff off her jeans.

'I just wanted to say that—'

'Lucas.'

'I don't want you to think that—'

'Have I not made myself clear?'

'It's not that I—'

'Oh my God, are you incapable of listening to me, or—'

'It's not that I don't find you beautiful.'

I almost bellow it in the effort to be heard, but as soon as I've said it, she goes quiet. She looks at me at last. I shift up against the pillows, folding my arms over my chest.

'You are very beautiful,' I say, more quietly. 'And the kiss was . . .'

'Lucas . . .' Her warning is weaker this time.

'It was a beautiful kiss, too. But . . .'

'Yeah. It was stupid. People who don't like each other shouldn't kiss, that's . . . weird and messed up,' she says, looking out of the window beside her. 'I reminded myself of that on my nice scenic walk just now.'

I choose my words carefully. 'My type isn't women in tiny gymwear who watch complicated films. Right now it is a small, irritating Brit with wicked green eyes who is occupying all of my thoughts, even though my brain knows she shouldn't be. Do you understand?'

Her eyes widen.

'But we're not going to kiss.'

'You're being very commanding. You know that annoys me.'

She doesn't precisely *look* annoyed.

'Kissing is off the table,' I say.

She lifts an eyebrow.

'Too dangerous,' I say.

I sit forward, watching how her body responds to my movements – she leans closer a fraction after I do, like I've pulled her in. Like we're still dancing.

'You're right, it would be stupid,' I continue, letting my voice drop lower. 'But – whatever you say – I do know how to have fun. Which is why I would like to propose another game of poker.'

*

166

If I was in any doubt about my feelings for this woman, then every triumphant hand she wins would clear it up for me, because it is agony letting her win at poker. *Agony.*

'You actually suck at this,' she says gleefully, claiming her chips (still raisins). 'You got seriously lucky winning earlier, didn't you?'

'Yes,' I say, through gritted teeth. 'It seems I did.'

'Shirt off, then,' she says, lifting her gaze to me as she deals the cards again. Her eyes are full of mischief.

Strip poker. I am either a genius or an idiot for suggesting this. On the one hand, it has definitely cheered her up, but on the other, I have just committed to fully undressing in a room with Izzy without so much as touching her. This feels like a particularly brutal form of self-torture.

I take my shirt off slowly, sitting up on the bedspread. She's down to her blue strapless top and jeans, and I don't plan on letting her get further than that. As much as I want to undress her, this isn't how that's going to happen. If I ever get to see Izzy naked, it won't be about anything but us.

Her gaze shifts over me. I breathe out, trying not to tense too much. I like how it feels, just watching her watch me. Letting her take without trying to win anything back for once.

'What's with all the muscle, then?' she asks, dealing the cards on the duvet between us.

I'm about to respond with something sharp – *all the muscle* feels so dismissive. But I swallow it back. What she said about me raising my voice struck me hard, because that's how discussions happen at my uncle's house. Everyone is always snapping and shouting. I hadn't realised quite how much of that I had absorbed.

'I get wound up sometimes. The gym is where I go to lose the heat.'

She gives me a quick grin. 'You get wound up sometimes? Who knew!'

I'm glad to see that grin again. I check my cards – ace of diamonds, jack of diamonds. *Ah, cara . . .*

'I started exercising hard when I was a teenager.'

I swallow, wondering how much I can give her. Remembering Camila walking out of my flat saying I didn't have a heart.

'It was about my dad, I think. The fear that I had some fatal disease inside me too. It made me feel safer, knowing I was healthy and looking after my body.'

Her eyes widen. 'I'm sorry, Lucas. That's so horrible. I wish your mum had told you what happened to your dad.'

I shake my head. 'She struggled to talk about it. It wasn't her fault. Anyway, it made me realise how good exercise feels. How it helps you calm down. So – not all bad.'

'Hmm,' Izzy says, still frowning. 'Fold,' she says, setting her cards down. 'That was a rubbish hand.'

'What do you do to cool off when I've wound you up, then?' I ask her. 'No, let me guess. You ring a friend and complain about me?'

She smiles slightly. 'Yeah, sometimes. Or curl up with something wholesome on Netflix if I'm not seeing anyone. Remind myself that the world is full of warmth and fuzziness as well as grumpy Brazilians.'

I let her have that one. She deals the cards again. For a while we just play poker, only speaking when the game requires it. I should fill the silence, but I don't quite know how to talk to her now. Too much has happened today. Everything feels *esquisito*, as if someone's knocked my life askew.

'Is this how it's going to be now?' Izzy says eventually. 'If I'd known all I had to do to make you go quiet was kiss you, then I'd have done it earlier.'

She looks down at her cards, letting her hair shield her face. I want to push it back and lift her chin. Tell her not to hide from me.

'I called you grumpy and you didn't even snap at me,' she says, still looking down at her cards. 'It's weird.'

'It's not the kiss,' I say. 'I am trying to be less ... short-tempered. After what you said about shouting.' I take another deep breath. 'My uncle raises his voice a lot. I don't want to be like that.'

Opening up like this feels as if I'm bending something the wrong way – it's not natural. My body grows more and more tense with the effort. She watches me through her eyelashes, uncharacteristically still.

'He's not *bad*,' I say. I suddenly feel a lot more naked than I did twenty seconds ago. 'He's just . . . forceful. He only respects strong people who stand up to him. He was a big part of my childhood, so I got strong.'

'And your mum?' Izzy asks quietly. 'What's she like?'

'She's strong too.' I smile. 'But strong like you. She holds her own but still gives a lot to other people.'

Izzy swallows. I've surprised her, I can tell. Her eyes dropping to my chest for a moment, gaze hovering over my tattoo, the single word just below my heart.

'I didn't expect that,' she says, nodding to it. 'You don't strike me as the tattoo type.'

I'm not, really. But when I made the choice to move to the UK, I suddenly understood the impulse people have to mark something permanently, to say, *this will never change.*

'What does it mean?' Izzy asks. 'Sow . . . da-day?'

'*Saudade.* Sow-da-dee.'

Izzy has another go. She doesn't quite get the final syllable right, but still, I like the sound of Portuguese on her tongue.

'It means . . . missing. Longing. There's no English word like it. I got the tattoo when I knew I would be moving away from my family – my mum, my sister and my grandmother. And my grandfather, too, who passed away not long before. That side of my family are very close, and I knew I would miss them so much. I wanted to mark how important that is to me – how important they are.'

She tilts her head. 'Why did you move?'

It's such a complicated, layered question. The reasons I wanted to live in England as a child are different from the reasons I moved here as an adult; the reasons I've stayed are different from those, too. And I don't want to tell Izzy about the course, which was a huge factor in why I moved to this part of the UK.

The only people who know I'm studying for a degree are my family. Even Pedro doesn't know. He thinks when I am working at the smoothie bar, I am doing hotel business. I always thought

I would feel comfortable talking about it once I got into the course. Then I thought I would feel comfortable once I passed my first term. But the moment I think of telling a friend or colleague about it, I imagine having to confess that I've failed or dropped out or couldn't afford this term's fees, and my mouth just snaps shut.

I know I'm too proud – I shouldn't care so much what others will think if I can't complete the course. But it's hard to shake my uncle's voice, even after all these years, and he has never tolerated failure.

'I've always had a fascination with the UK,' I say. 'And staying at home didn't seem right for me. Working in hospitality, I felt it even more – everyone was travelling from somewhere exciting, and I was just where I'd started. I never felt I was in quite the right place.'

'And now?'

I run my fingers across the backs of my cards. 'I don't know. I think maybe it wasn't a place that I was looking for. But I like it here. I like the job. I like the countryside.' I like that I'm doing my degree at one of the best places in the world to study hotel management, and that I'm doing it for *me*. 'What about you? The tattoo on your spine?'

Her eyes snap to mine, searching my face. 'Umm . . . When have you seen my tattoo?'

I go hot. I've just confessed to looking at her in a bikini when her back was turned.

'When you were . . . When you swam with Louis.'

She raises her eyebrows. 'Oh?'

'You turned around when I was . . . I just . . . saw it. Accidentally.'

She smiles slowly and lifts a hand to her back, tracing the spot in the centre of her spine where I saw the tattoo. 'And how long *were* you "accidentally" checking me out in my swimwear? Did you see anything else of interest? Shall I quiz you on freckle locations?'

'It was a very brief moment,' I say, immediately thinking about the perfect little mole on the curve of her hip.

'Mmhmm. Well. It's a treble clef.'

I wait.

'For my parents. It was always just the three of us. My dad was estranged from his family and my mum was an only child, so we didn't have that big aunts-and-uncles, loads-of-cousins type vibe – it was just us three. Trouble trebled, Dad used to say. Hence . . . treble.' She shrugs. 'It's a stupid play on words. I was twenty-one and thought it was clever.'

'I don't think it's stupid. It's creative.'

She gives me a small smile at that. A different sort of smile from usual.

'I cannot imagine how hard it was for you to lose them.'

'No,' she says simply. 'It changed me completely.'

'What were you like before?'

She pauses as if she wasn't expecting that question. 'Quiet, actually,' she says. 'I held myself back a lot. Now I go full-out because – like I said – life's too short for having regrets.'

I hesitate before answering. I'm not sure Izzy *does* go 'full-out'. She's certainly spontaneous, and she works hard. But her life does not seem to me to be built on taking chances. Just look at the inferior men she dates. The job she's been in for eight years without promotion. The friends she has all over the world, and how rarely she takes time off to visit them.

'Do you feel like you don't hold anything back now? That you *really* go full-out?'

She looks at me shrewdly. After a moment, she snorts. 'Lose the trousers, Lucas. Don't think you can distract me by Mrs Hedgers-ing me.'

Remarkably, for a moment, I had almost forgotten I am sitting here topless.

'Mrs . . .'

'Mrs Hedgers, the career-change coach in Sweet Pea? Has she not got you yet? She did a number on me and Poor Mandy. Told Mandy she's not assertive enough.'

Izzy is breezy and bright again, as though we never spoke about her parents. I'd like to push and ask her more, but I know I'll get nowhere.

'In the time I have known Mandy,' I say, 'she has never once asserted herself.'

'I know, right?'

'What did Mrs Hedgers say about you?'

Izzy shifts so her feet are tucked underneath her on the bed. Her socks are gone, lost when she played a bad hand at the start of the game.

'She said I don't know how to switch off.'

Interesting.

'On Thursday, you'll try some of the ways I unwind and switch off.'

'Oh, will I, now?'

I raise my eyebrows, lying back against the pillows with my hands behind my head.

'Have you forgotten? Thursday is my day. I'm in charge.'

'Oh, shit, yeah.' Something passes across her face. I wonder if it's worry.

'I won't . . . If you want to change your mind about the bet . . .'

'Are you kidding? Please. I'd never have given you that opportunity if I'd won.'

'But it's different. I'm a man. We are always in charge, so . . .' This doesn't come out the way I intended – she's glaring at me. I grope around for the right words, remembering how succinctly Ana put it when she was explaining why it's different for a woman to approach a man than the other way around. 'No, I just mean, it's not the same because of the way society always puts men in control anyway, so me telling you what to do, it just feels like it could be . . .'

'Oh.' Her face clears. 'Yeah. A bit loaded. Well, actually, oddly enough I do trust you to be a gentleman about it. You want to have a safeword or something?' She laughs at my expression. 'If I say, *fuck right off, Lucas*, then you have to back off. Agreed?'

'It is a good safe phrase,' I say solemnly, and I can tell from her face that she doesn't know whether I'm joking.

'Trousers,' she says, pointing at my knees.

'Ah. Yes.' I shift to the end of the bed and stand to take them off.

The atmosphere in the room shifts the moment I start unfastening my belt. Izzy is quiet, watching me as I unbutton my jeans, rolling her bottom lip between her finger and thumb. I thought stripping off would make her feel like she was in charge, but she's not laughing or humiliating me, she's just watching me, and I shiver under her gaze. It's been a while since I've stripped down for a woman, but they're normally touching me by this point. The distance between us should make this less intimate, but somehow it's the opposite.

I lie down on my back again, my head on the pillow. Laid out for her, with the cards and that silly little heap of raisins between us. I hear her breath catch and the sound sends something turning over inside me.

'If I win the next hand, you'll be naked,' Izzy says.

'Mm.'

'I was going to make you run out into the car park in the snow,' she says, 'but now that feels kind of cruel.'

'How were you going to make me do that?' I ask, amused.

She shrugs. 'I'd dare you.'

The room is very small and very quiet. Izzy has her bottom lip between her teeth now, biting down. My breath is catching too.

'But I think maybe dares are a bad idea now too.'

I think we're in one of those sliding-doors moments. Balancing on the edge of a decision we won't be able to unmake. I am struggling to remember why I shouldn't lean across the poker cards and pull her down into a kiss – not the kind of kiss she gave me, sweet and slow, but a fiery, electric-shock of a kiss, the kind that gets you hot in half a second.

'I'm getting ready for bed now, Lucas,' Izzy says. Her voice is low and quiet.

'OK,' I say.

She doesn't move. 'I don't get you,' she says. 'At all.'

I tip my chin, and she sighs out a breath, unmoving.

'You would strip naked for me, but you don't want to kiss me?'

'I never said I didn't want to kiss you.'

Her eyes move over me. 'Kiss me, then.'

I grit my teeth. She's within reach. I could grab her with one arm and have her body against mine before she'd caught her breath. I haven't forgotten how she looked in that bikini at the pool – the soft curve of her breast, the dip at the small of her back. I know how she'd fit against me.

I've got good self-control, but even I have limits. The moment stretches, testing me.

'Right,' Izzy says, moving at last. 'God, I'm a glutton for rejection when it comes to you, aren't I?'

The moment breaks. She slams into the bathroom, and I lie there, breathing hard, reminding myself that what's true in the gym applies here too: holding it a little longer always pays off.

It is perhaps the worst night's sleep I have ever had, and I have slept on airport floors, on many tiny sofas, and, once, at a terrible party I was dragged to by my sister, in the bottom of a closet.

Izzy is a quiet sleeper. She lies curled towards me with her knees tucked up and her hands pillowing her cheek. Even in the darkness, I notice things I have never noticed before. I see how her brows arch to a point, and how a very fine line brackets the corner of her mouth like the blueprint of a smile.

For a dangerous few minutes somewhere between two and three in the morning, I imagine what my life would look like with Izzy in it. I catalogue what she'd think of my flat, wonder which side of my bed she'd claim as hers, imagine how it would feel to lift her against my bedroom wall and wrap her legs around my waist.

And then I spend at least another hour wondering if I've made a terrible mistake by choosing not to kiss her. What if she'll never see me as anything more than the emotionless 'robot-man' who gets in her way all day? Then all I've done is lose my one chance of having any part of her at all. At three in the morning, a kiss with the wrong intentions feels much better than trying and failing to change Izzy's mind, and ending up with no kiss at all.

I manage a few hours of sleep before the winter sun sears through the threadbare curtains and wakes me again. Izzy hasn't moved, but her hair has shifted, laying two strands across her cheek. I get as close as lifting my hand to smooth them back before remembering how inappropriate that would be.

I slide out of the bed quietly and grab my clothes before slipping into the bathroom. I want to get back to Forest Manor. This room feels like a trap – if I spend much more time with Izzy here, I'll kiss her.

She lifts her head as I emerge from the bathroom. 'Oh,' she says, rubbing her face. 'I remember. Woking. Snow. Ugh.'

I straighten my pillow. I don't know where to look. She slept in her top and knickers – her jeans are folded on the footstool.

'We should go. The trains are running again.'

'Yeah? Has it settled?' she asks. 'The snow,' she clarifies when I look blank.

She slides her legs out of the bed and pads over to fetch the rest of her clothes. I turn away with a sharp breath as she bends to pull on her jeans.

'Wow,' she says, opening the curtains.

I step around the bed and look over her shoulder. Outside, the town looks like a different place – it's blanketed in snow, every hard edge softened, every block of flats now capped in white.

'A blank slate,' Izzy says, and the small smile she shoots over her shoulder gives me hope.

Izzy

We travel home in a silence that is only broken twice: once by Lucas saying, 'Please stop kicking the table leg', and once by me objecting to Lucas manspreading, though the moment he moves his knee out of my space, I find to my alarm that I kind of want it back again.

I feel totally panicked by last night. The kiss. The strip poker. Lucas in nothing but boxers. It's hard to even know where to begin with processing it all, so instead I just stare out at the snowy countryside and listen to an upcycling podcast, fully aware that I am forgetting everything the podcaster says in real-time.

When we get back to the hotel, there is a dark-haired woman sitting on the front steps, doubled over, shoulders shaking with sobs. A thin layer of snow dusts the stone around her, but her navy coat is hanging open, as though she hasn't noticed the cold.

Lucas and I exchange a glance and accelerate.

'Madam?' Lucas says. 'Can we help you?'

She looks up at us through blue-rimmed glasses clouded with tears.

'*You*,' she says, with venom. 'You're the ones doing this ring thing, aren't you?'

Shit. Is this Wife 1? Wife 2? Or someone else entirely whose life I have managed to ruin?

'Yes,' Lucas says calmly, ducking down to sit on the step beside her. 'That's us.'

This is kind of him – I think we all know this is *my* pet project. I was quick to remind him of that when it was earning us a fifteen-grand reward.

'You've ruined everything. Graham is – was – he *was* a good husband. We were *happy*.'

Her make-up is scored with tear tracks. She's beautiful, in that classic, statuesque way that always ages so well – I find myself thinking, *How could anyone cheat on someone like her?* As if beautiful people are immune to the damage a screwed-up man can create.

My stomach twists. I feel terrible. I never, ever imagined that The Ring Thing could cause any harm. I just thought about how desperately I would want someone to return the ring my dad gave me if they ever found it. But maybe some things are better off lost.

'Mrs . . .'

'Rogers. Actually, that's his name, so – Ms Ashley, I guess.'

'I see,' Lucas says. 'Ms Ashley, I am very sorry for the pain this has caused you.'

She's sobbing again. I twist my hands together, sitting down on the other side of Ms Ashley, then biting my lip as the freezing cold snow soaks through the backs of my trousers.

'But Graham was *not* a good husband.'

Lucas's voice is firm. I glance at his face, surprised – I thought he would just listen and make some supportive noises, but he's gone in pretty hard there.

'Someone who can lie to you so easily, and give his love to somebody else when he promised it all to you . . . that is not a good husband.'

Ms Ashley drops her face into her hands. 'Oh, God. But Graham is so *nice*. Everyone says it.'

She lifts her gaze to me. I almost recoil at her expression.

'Don't listen to people,' she says. 'You hear me? People are stupid. Listen to your instincts. Yours. Nobody else's. Everyone said I should go out with Graham because he's a good guy and *now fucking look at me!*'

I try not to jump as she starts shouting. I glance up – a car is pulling in to the car park.

Ms Ashley shoots to her feet. 'That's them. *You wanker!*' she screams at the car.

I widen my eyes at Lucas, standing up and brushing the snow off my legs.

'Ah,' comes Mrs SB's voice from behind us, in the hotel doorway. 'Everyone's here very early for brunch! How nice. Mrs Rogers . . .'

'Ms Ashley,' Lucas and I correct her in unison.

'Ms Ashley,' Mrs SB says, not missing a beat. 'I wondered where you'd got to. Won't you come back inside and warm up?'

'I don't think I can do this,' Ms Ashley says, staring at the four-by-four currently parking up, with a serious-faced couple inside: Graham, presumably, and the other Mrs Rogers. 'Look at that car. Is that his car? He would never drive a car like that, but he's driving that car right now. How is that possible?' Ms Ashley fixes her gaze on me again. 'He was always too good to be true,' she whispers, gripping my arm. 'I should have known.'

I grip her hand right back, feeling a bit desperate. I want to give her a hug, but I am pretty sure she doesn't want one from me. 'You couldn't have known. Ms Ashley, it's not your fault.'

'I can't do this,' she says. 'I can't sit in the same room as them. I thought I could yesterday, but I can't do it. Oh, God.'

They're climbing out of the car. The other Mrs Rogers looks as though she is vibrating with rage. She slams the door hard and stalks past her husband. She's younger, curvier, with orange-blonde hair in a crown braid.

'Darling,' says Graham, racing after her. 'Please. Talk to me. I love you.'

He *does* look like a nice guy. A bumbling British type. All tweed and good intentions. He's not seen Ms Ashley yet, I realise – she's hidden behind one of the round box hedges. She steps out now, her arms folded, her whole body trembling.

'Which darling would that be?' she says.

It's extraordinary to watch Graham make his decision. In one second, then two, it all passes over his face: indecision, cunning, deliberation. Not so well-intentioned now. As the other Mrs Rogers falters at the sight of Ms Ashley, Graham picks the life he wants to live.

'The truth is, darling,' he says to the blonde wife he drove here. 'This is all a terrible mix-up. I knew this woman once. I'm sorry to tell you . . . she's quite mad.'

Ms Ashley's mouth drops open. The blonde Mrs Rogers narrows her eyes, keeping her gaze fixed on the woman in front of her.

'Tell me,' she says.

Ms Ashley doesn't hesitate. 'He married me eight years ago in Godalming. We live together in New Milton. He stays away a lot for work. We've had two cats, a miscarriage, eight holidays in Spain, and three days ago he told me he'd never loved me more.'

'All nonsense,' Graham says immediately.

Mrs Rogers nods once. 'In that case – no brunch,' she says, redirecting her attention to Mrs SB. 'We're calling the police instead.'

Ms Ashley tenses. We all wait, wondering exactly which *we* Mrs Rogers means, until she turns slowly and looks at her husband.

'Bigamy is a serious crime, *darling*,' she says.

When the police car pulls up the hotel's sweeping gravel drive, most of the hotel staff, Mr Townsend and even the Jacobs (their cheerfully waving baby included) have come to watch the drama unfold.

The two former Mrs Rogers stand at opposite ends of the crowd, stony-faced, as Mr Rogers gawps in the face of the policeman currently reading him his rights.

'This is ridiculous,' he says, looking back at us all. He is giving off odious these-sorts-of-things-don't-happen-to-men-like-me vibes, which makes me want that policeman to use the handcuffs currently dangling from his belt. 'You're having me *arrested*? Are you quite serious?'

'I think they're pretty serious, mate,' says the policeman. 'I know I certainly am. Get in the car.'

'This is all a terrible misunderstanding,' Graham implores, in the general direction of his wives.

The policeman taps on the roof of the car. 'In. Now.'

'Now, see here,' says Graham, and then – to whoops from the crowd – the policeman places one hand firmly on his head and shoves him in the back seat.

The car door slams shut. Ms Brown flips Graham the bird as the police drive away, and Ms Ashley yells an insult so colourful that Mr and Mrs Hedgers immediately scoop up the children and flee the scene before Ruby asks anyone to repeat it.

'Is it too early to get drunk?' Ms Brown asks Barty and Mrs SB.

'I leave that to your judgement,' Barty says. 'But I will mention that we have a twenty-four-hour licence.'

'Perfect,' says Ms Brown, heading inside. 'Come on,' she says to Ms Ashley, without looking at her. 'I think you and I need to chat.'

As the two of them settle in at our grand, mahogany bar with a Bloody Mary each, I notice my hands are shaking on the menu I'm carrying over to them. It's just . . . I always try to see the best in people. To think that everyone is fundamentally quite nice really. And then someone does something this awful and it makes me wonder how the hell you're meant to know who to trust.

I play with my necklace, the one my mum gave me. It's times like these that I miss my parents the most.

'I really hate you right now,' Ms Ashley is saying as I reach them at the bar.

'Oh, same to you, love,' says Ms Brown. 'Maybe we'll get to the solidarity part later.'

'If we drink enough alcohol,' Ms Ashley says, taking a vicious bite from her stick of celery.

'Can I interest you in some breakfast to go with that ...?' I ask, my voice a little squeaky.

'You,' Ms Ashley says, zeroing in on me as she sucks up half her cocktail through the straw. 'The ring meddler.'

'I really am so sorry,' I say wretchedly. Today I seem to have done the exact opposite of adding sparkle. I've made everything significantly gloomier.

'Not your fault, love,' says Ms Brown, already waving at Ollie for another drink. 'A lot of men are shits. You do your best to dodge 'em, but ...'

Ollie shrinks into himself, shaking up the next cocktail as quietly as possible.

'Izzy!' Arjun calls. 'There's something for you at the front desk! Ask me how I know!'

I spin to look at him. His hair is a mess and he's not wearing his apron, which always makes him look a bit weird, as if he's not wearing his shoes.

'How do you know?' I say obligingly.

'Because you are here, and Lucas is off somewhere else, and

Ollie is behind the bar ballsing up that Bloody Mary, and so *I* had to leave the kitchen to answer the reception bell!'

I glance at the two women, but they don't seem to mind someone else doing a bit of shouting.

'No food, love,' Ms Brown says to me. 'Just keep the booze coming.' This is directed at Ollie.

I move to go after Arjun and then remember something. 'Oh! Do you want the ring?' I blurt, patting my pocket.

Ms Brown stares at me, then looks down at her hand, and across at Ms Ashley's. They are both still wearing their wedding rings.

'I think we've got enough rings here, don't you? Just sell it. Keep the money. Looks like this place could use it,' she says, nodding after Arjun. 'Get that man some help, eh, love?'

I mean, I don't think this ring is worth quite enough to employ a sous-chef for Arjun, but I appreciate the intention, and I'm glad we're getting *something* out of this disaster. I thank them and leave the Mrs Rogers to it, heading to the lobby as Arjun flounces back into the kitchen again.

Louis is waiting for me at the front desk. There is a gigantic bunch of red roses beside him. They look unreal – as in, they genuinely look fake, so perfect is every petal and upturned leaf. They're tied with a thick white ribbon and there's an embossed note beside them. My heart sinks. This is really not my sort of thing.

'Open the card,' Louis says, tapping it against the desk.

I flick the envelope open. *Join me for dinner at The Angel's Wing tonight*, it says.

'Louis . . .' I begin.

The Angel's Wing is a super-posh restaurant near Brockenhurst – it's the sort of place London types go to when they want to be in the countryside but still eat like they're in the city. It's got a dress code and everything.

'Too much?' he says.

I can't precisely say why I don't want to go. I was up for it when we had our swimming date, and there are plenty of reasons to give things a try with Louis: he's good-looking, he's attentive, and he's definitely got the drive and ambition that Sameera thought I should look for in a man.

'The Angel's Wing is really expensive . . .' I say.

'It's on me,' Louis says. 'I should have mentioned that.'

'Izzy!' Lucas barks from the direction of the kitchen. 'Arjun needs you!'

Seriously? I just *saw* Arjun. I don't know where Lucas has emerged from, and it is completely typical that he is now insisting on my presence despite being MIA for at least an hour himself.

Louis nods to the flowers and card. 'I just thought a romantic gesture would be the right thing to go for, given . . .'

'Isabelle!' Lucas shouts.

Isabelle? Excuse me? Only Jem gets to call me Isabelle, and that is because she was my friend when I was eight years old and has earned the right over the last two decades to call me whatever she likes.

Lucas comes marching out of the kitchen. As his eyes move over the bunch of roses, his face flickers.

'Am I interrupting?' he says, in a tone that suggests he knows very well that he is, and feels strongly that there should be no moment for him to interrupt.

'Just give us a minute, would you?' Louis says, with an uncharacteristic touch of irritation.

Lucas's cheek twitches. 'Izzy is needed. She is working. She will be available to discuss personal matters at five p.m. when her shift ends.'

I gawp. Honestly, the cheek of him. Suddenly he's Mr Not In Working Hours after spending yesterday dancing to Anitta in a flat in Little Venice. Part of me is glad he's being his usual self now we're back – it's easier to forget the man I saw laid bare in that hotel room, or dancing with me in Shannon's flat. It's easier to imagine that the last twenty-four hours never happened.

It's also easier to make this decision.

'Thank you, Louis,' I say, turning to him with a smile. 'I'd love to go for dinner tonight. See you at seven thirty.'

I've not lived with a friend since Drew, and this is the first time I've regretted the decision to live alone. I can't decide what to wear, and nobody is replying to my frantic WhatsApp requests for outfit advice. I'm trying to focus on the date ahead, but instead I keep thinking about Lucas's judgemental face as he said, *Am I interrupting?* Eventually, after getting mascara on the bridge of my nose for the third time, I figure out why it's bothering me so much.

I think Lucas was jealous. Not just judging me for being unprofessional – *jealous*.

But what the hell am I supposed to make of that?

As I fasten three of my favourite necklaces, I realise my hands are clammy. I haven't been on a date for a while. It wasn't a conscious decision to stop dating, I just got sick of trawling through Bumble and shaving my legs for men who wouldn't prove worthy of seeing them.

I look at my reflection and the memory shoots up yet again: Lucas's lips against mine, and then that awful, awkward silence as he turned his back on me.

So humiliating.

At least I won at strip poker. Though is it really winning if the consequence is having an image of Lucas looking unspeakably sexy in nothing but his boxers seared to the inside of your eyelids?

When I arrive at The Angel's Wing, Louis is waiting outside in a suit with no tie. He opens the door for me, then the next door, and then he takes my coat and pulls out my chair for me. I say 'thank you' too many times and end up a bit flustered.

The date itself is ... nice. Louis is fun to talk to – there's nothing not to like. And the food and drink is amazing. Arjun's a fantastic chef, so I'm used to good food, but he doesn't really go in for the cream-laced French stuff they do at The Angel's Wing.

But by the time our desserts arrive, underneath all the wine and dairy in my stomach is a low feeling of dread. I can't stop thinking about what Ms Ashley said. *Listen to your instincts.* And even though Louis is totally the right sort of guy on paper, and even though I'm sure my mum and dad would've loved how much of a gentleman he is ... there is just something telling me this isn't right.

It *should* be right. But it's not.

'Louis ...'

'You're not feeling it?'

His voice is light and casual, the same tone he was just using a moment ago to discuss his love of golf.

'I'm so sorry. You're a really lovely guy ...'

He waves that away. 'I get it, I get why you're hesitant this time around.'

I frown slightly. I told him about my last couple of relationships, but now I wonder if I've overplayed the general rubbishness of Tristan and Dean, because otherwise this comment seems a bit odd.

'I put too much pressure on things with the flowers and all that,' Louis says, reaching to top up my wine as the waitress delivers our chocolate puddings. 'Let's just ease off the gas.'

'I'm not sure we're a good fit,' I try.

He shakes his head. 'Come on, don't shut this down before you've even got to know me, Izzy. Let me take you out again in a few days. We can just go for a walk with a coffee, maybe – something low-key. Let's hang out a bit, see how it feels, see where it goes ...' He takes a spoonful of pudding and closes his eyes with a moan. 'Try that, oh my God.'

'I mean, we can go out again if you want,' I find myself saying, 'but I need to be honest and say I don't think I'm going to change my mind. Sorry. I don't want you wasting your time with me when ...'

'My choice what I do with my time. I can handle myself, Izzy,' he says with a wink. 'Just have fun and relax, OK? There's no pressure from me.'

I'm not sure how to argue with that. And this date has been lovely, technically speaking. Was it actually any lovelier than this with Tristan or Dean? I don't remember being particularly swept away by either of their first dates, and both of them became my boyfriends.

So why not Louis?

I text Jem when I'm home to fill her in on how I'm feeling, and she replies with a voice note.

Pigeon, I hear what you're saying, but . . . Your parents wanted you to date a guy who seemed sweet and kind – eight years ago. You were so young when they said that to you, Izz. You're an adult now. You're wiser. I know it hurts so bad that your mum and dad aren't here to give you advice, but for what it's worth, I think they'd tell you that you know best now. If something in your heart says this guy's not quite right for you, they'd want you to listen to that.

It makes me cry. I play it twice more. She's right: it *does* hurt that Mum and Dad aren't here to advise me on what to do. It hurts that I'm having to figure out how to be an adult on my own, and that all the wisdom they've given me is at least eight years out of date. I'll never be able to bring a guy back to the house I grew up in and close the kitchen door to say, *So, guys? What do you think of him? Be honest!*

Louis has messaged me while I've been listening to Jem:

Fancy a stroll around Winchester Christmas market on Friday eve? he's written. *Don't think too hard about it* 😊 *No pressure, just give it a shot!*

Hmm. Now it's an *evening* stroll, and will probably involve food – that seems like a step up from a walk with coffee.

I make a decision then and there: I'll go to the Christmas market with Louis, and if it's still not feeling right, I'll draw a line under things with him. He may say he doesn't mind wasting his time, but life's too short for me to waste mine.

Another message pops up from Jem. *Here for you always*, it says.

I clutch the phone. It's been hard not to feel a little abandoned over the last year, as each of my favourite people have left to another part of the world. I know it's not about me, but I can't help wishing that we could still be here for each other in the way we were before.

But there are different ways of being *here*. I play Jem's voice note one more time and feel so grateful for the friends who still make space for me in their whirlwind lives; the people who know exactly why something will hurt, and who know just what to say to make it better.

Thank you. And you – always, I reply, and then I choose my favourite pyjamas, boil the kettle for my hot-water bottle, and curl up in bed. I've got an unusually quiet few days ahead, and I think I might just spend them on the sofa. It's been such a mad week, even by my standards – I need to re-anchor myself. By the time I'm back at work, I'm sure I'll be full-on Izzy again, ready to face anything.

Even though right now that idea feels kind of exhausting.

Lucas

It's Thursday – my day. Lucas Day. My chance to change Izzy's mind.

I arrive at her flat at six a.m. It takes her quite some time to open the door.

'Oh my God, what is wrong with you,' she says, already walking back inside.

I take this as an invitation to follow, but she turns on her heels and holds out a hand.

'No crossing the threshold,' she says.

'It's Thursday,' I tell her, stopping in the doorway, holding the door open with one arm.

'Yes, I'm aware.'

She's in pyjamas – pink ones with spots. Her hair is pulled up in a topknot and she has the same adorably ruffled look she had that morning in Woking. She fetches herself a bowl of cereal and starts eating, standing in the middle of her flat in a lost sort of way, as if she can't figure out how she's ended up there.

'My day,' I prompt her. 'Because I won.'

'But why are you here so early?' Her tone is slightly plaintive.

'We're going to the gym.'

'The *gym*?' She spins. 'Why?'

'Because I say so.'

Her stare turns into a glare. I suppress a smile.

'Do you have any sportswear?'

'Of course I have sportswear,' she says, looking slightly embarrassed. 'I'm not – I do exercise *sometimes*.'

I think about her comment about my type of woman – their 'tiny gymwear' – and realise I am being an idiot.

'We are going to the gym because it's how I unwind,' I tell her. 'It's not about you. You don't need to exercise. I'm not saying you need to exercise. I'm not trying to say that.'

Her expression warms a little as I squirm in her doorway.

'Stay there,' she says, turning her back on me. 'I'm not inviting you in. I've watched way too many episodes of *The Vampire Diaries* to fall for that.'

I lean against the door frame as she closes the bedroom door. Her flat is the top floor of a converted house. She's styled it in calm pastels: a fluffy cream rug, a pale-blue throw over the back of the mint-coloured sofa. The decor reminds me vaguely of an old-fashioned British sweetshop.

Izzy emerges from the bedroom. She's in gym gear now. Tight grey leggings and a pale-yellow crop top, with red and orange stripes in her hair.

She looks gorgeous. For a moment I wish for the feeling I had before our trip to London – the way I used to be able to look at her and think, *Yes, she's beautiful, but she's a pain in the arse.*

I still think those things, but suddenly I also think about how badly I want to hold her. Sling my arm over her shoulder as we head out the door. Kiss her like it's something we do all the time.

She bends to pull some trainers out from behind the door and hauls an oversized bag over her shoulder. At my enquiring look, she says, 'I've packed for every eventuality. I have a feeling you have some odd activities lined up for me.'

'We're just going to work,' I say, amused. 'This isn't a stag do.'

'Mmhmm,' she says, locking the door to her flat behind her. 'Well, since we've been working together five days a week, I've been dunked in a swimming pool, danced with strangers at a divorce party and fallen on my face in the snow outside a Papa Johns in Woking.'

I raise my eyebrows as we make our way down to the street. 'I didn't know about that.'

'Oh. Right. Well, yeah, my walk in Woking wasn't that fun.'

There is a stocky New Forest pony nibbling at the hedge by the side of the road. Neither of us remark upon it. When I first moved to the New Forest, I was astonished to find myself caught in a traffic jam caused by a gaggle of unfazed ponies, but I'm used to them now. They roam wild around here – it's no stranger than seeing a pigeon.

'God, your car is so shiny,' Izzy says, as we approach it. 'Do you polish it?'

I do, actually, but I know Izzy well enough to realise I'm better off not confessing to that. This car is my pride and joy. She's third-hand and has seventy thousand miles on the clock; I fixed her up myself, painstakingly, with help from a friend who lives on my road. Now she looks as good as new. As a child, I always dreamed of living in England and having a car like this. Back then, it had been because I wanted to be James Bond, and didn't know the difference between a two-hundred-thousand-pound Aston Martin and a fixed-up 55-reg BMW. Now, it's because of what it means: the freedom to live and work in this strange, wet, awkward little country that I have fallen so unexpectedly in love with.

I open the passenger door for Izzy. She looks surprised, and then wary.

'Why are you being nice?' she says.

'It is all part of the grand plan to torture you for a day,' I say, slamming the car door behind her. Her expectations of me are so low. But I can hardly blame her. We have baited each other for months on end – I've been petty, difficult, argumentative.

I've been just like my uncle, in fact. The thought is painful to swallow.

As I drive us to the gym, Izzy looks at something on her phone, biting her bottom lip. I glance across at her.

'Yet another no for the emerald ring,' she says. 'These last two are so tricky.'

'You haven't given up, then? After Graham Rogers?'

'Absolutely not. One bad egg does not make a bad egg box, you know?'

I don't know if this is an odd Britishism or an Izzy-ism, but best to just nod.

'I still believe we're doing something important. Maybe that emerald ring really meant something to somebody.'

I almost say, *And how does that help the hotel, exactly?* But I snatch it back in time. This matters to her. I don't understand why, but I'm trying to be more open-minded, and that means accepting that people aren't always logical. After all, I've not been particularly logical myself lately. For instance, I am currently trying to win over a woman who has spent the last year making my life as miserable as possible, including spending two months trying to persuade Mrs SB and Barty to do 'bagpipe Fridays' in the lobby because I happened to mention a dislike for the instrument.

'The other one looks valuable too, you know,' she says, rubbing her bottom lip between her forefinger and thumb as she stares out of the window. 'There *might* be another reward.'

'I hope so,' I say as I pull in to the car park. 'We need it.'

Izzy nods, saying nothing. She hasn't seen the spreadsheets. She doesn't know how big a hole there is in the centre of the hotel's finances – how the amount we've raised from selling items has sunk into that pit without even touching the sides. But she's not naïve. I can see from her frown that she knows the truth: without a small miracle, there will be no Forest Manor Hotel and Spa by the new year.

When we enter the gym, I get worried. Izzy's shoulders have crept up, and she's fiddling with the bottom of her crop top, shifting on the toes of her trainers. I hadn't expected this. The moment I walk into a gym, I feel comfortable. Even the smell relaxes me – that mix of air freshener, clean sweat and rubber.

It's clear I have work to do here. I steer her towards the gym mats first. No intimidating equipment, and nobody else there at the moment.

'Some stretches, first,' I tell her.

She brightens. 'OK,' she says. 'I can do stretches.'

She is not lying. I watch her touch her toes and try to think pure thoughts.

'Why don't you like the gym?' I ask her as I stretch out my quads. They're tight from yesterday's run, but my arms are feeling good. I skipped upper body on Tuesday so that I would be well rested for today. It is critical that Izzy does not find out about this.

'Everyone here is just very . . .' She looks around, still folded over on herself with her hands on her feet. 'Like you. Like superpeople.'

I realise this is not intended as a compliment, but I can't help feeling a glimmer of pleasure at it anyway.

'They're not,' I say. I look around, seeing what she's seeing, and lift a hand to wave at a few people I know. 'Everyone is welcome at a gym. And if you *talk* to the people who come to the gym a lot, we aren't as bad as we look.'

Her expression is dubious, but I'm no longer worried, because my trump card has arrived.

Kieran, the first friend I made in the New Forest, and the best personal trainer I have come across anywhere. He is a small, scrawny white man with no hair and too many tattoos, and he is that very rare thing: a person I liked straight away.

'Lucas!' he bellows, beaming at me and waving with both

arms, as though he is directing an aeroplane. 'Wow, hi!' he says to Izzy, as she straightens up.

'Hi!' she says, slightly taken aback.

A common response to Kieran's arrival. He treats every day as though he is on set at a children's television show.

'We're going to work out!' Kieran says, already bouncing on the spot. 'But in a fun way! A *really* fun way! Do you like beating Lucas at things?'

'Yeah, I do, actually,' Izzy says.

I may have given Kieran some background before booking this session. It cost more than I could afford, but I can already tell that it'll be worth it.

'I'll never beat him in the gym, though. Look at the man,' Izzy says, waving a hand in my direction.

'Oh-ho-ho,' Kieran says, rubbing his hands together. 'Just you wait and see.'

Izzy

It's undeniable: I feel amazing. Kieran insisted that I take at least fifteen minutes in the shower after our session and now, dried off and dressed in my work uniform, I feel like I'm walking several inches off the ground. I can't remember when I last exercised really hard – did it always leave me feeling like this? It's as if someone's just given me a massage, but like, inside my brain as well as every muscle of my body.

Obviously when the exercise was happening it was largely quite horrible. But Kieran assures me that it gets better as you do it more, and the after effects *are* delightful.

Beating Lucas was pretty great too. Kieran wasn't wrong – there were things I could do better than Lucas. I was better at the skipping rope skills, and I could sprint faster than him on the running machines. And even when we were doing things that were clearly more his ballpark than mine, Kieran never made it feel like losing. Nor did Lucas, to be fair.

It's been interesting seeing him here. He's a different man in this context. Everyone seems to know him – they all come over and hug him, and tell me things like 'couldn't have moved house without this guy', or 'you know what, when my cat died, Lucas was a hero'. I'd like to say I'm shocked to know that there are people who rely on Lucas, but I'm not, actually – I can imagine he'd be a big help if your cat died, or if you needed to move house. If he wasn't your arch-nemesis.

The main issue I've had this morning is Lucas's unrelenting *muscliness*. It's so unavoidable here. The exposed biceps, the impossibly broad shoulders, the sweat. (Why is it that when men sweat, it's sexy, but when I sweat, I look like I've been crossbred with a tomato?) I've never been attracted to big, hench men, and actually, if I look at some of the others in here, it doesn't do it for me at all. It is a Lucas-specific problem. The worst kind.

The only consolation is the fact that I caught Lucas checking me out too. I looked up when we were doing the warm-down and found his eyes on me in the mirror, low-lidded, appreciative. He turned his head away sharply when he saw me looking. No surprise there. After all, he's rejected me three times now. Lucas may want me on some level, but he's got cast-iron control, and his brain's decided he's not interested, so that's that. I mean, my brain has decided the same thing.

But it is quite nice to see that it's not *just* me who's struggling to stick with that decision.

He told me to meet him in the gym lobby, and he's already speaking to the receptionist when I arrive, buttoned up in his work clothes, looking as pristine as usual. Dangerous biceps safely sheathed.

'Let me pay for the session,' I say, coming to join him.

His face takes on the fixed look it gets when he's embarrassed. 'No need,' he says stiffly.

Hmm. This is clearly a lie. As the receptionist holds the card reader out to him, I lean across and tap my card before Lucas can get his wallet out.

'Izzy,' he snaps, exasperated.

I give him my sweetest smile. 'Oops.'

I watch him struggle. He can't *stand* the idea of me doing him a favour, but I can see that deep down, he knows he can't really afford to pay. Something twinges in my chest.

'Thank you,' he says, without meeting my eyes. 'We are having breakfast next,' he tells me, already heading for the door. He forgets to hold it open for me, so I guess the whole chivalric opening-the-car-door thing isn't going to be sticking around.

'No, sorry,' I say, as I clock where we're going for breakfast. 'Juice? That is not food.'

'Smoothies,' he says, and puts a hand on my elbow to steer me firmly inside. I go hot where he's touching me, then everywhere else, too. We've very rarely touched – the odd glance of a hand here or there, but that's mostly it. Apart from when we danced. And when I kissed him, obviously.

Ugh. In pops the memory again. Will that ever stop feeling so awful?

'Smoothies are just juices you aren't sure whether to chew or not.'

Lucas looks slightly horrified at this. 'Well, it's free, because Pedro is a friend. So it's what you're getting. He does excellent coffee, too,' he says, nodding to the man behind the bar and gesturing to a seat for me to take. It's actually the exact spot I would have chosen – one of the shiny pink bar stools that looks out of the front window to the street outside.

'A gym friend?' I guess, taking in Pedro, who just *glows* with good health. Sickening, really.

'Yes. He's from Rio too.'

'Oh! That must be nice.'

I give Pedro a tentative smile. He grins back. His dark hair is wavy and carefully styled, and he's wearing a T-shirt that clings to every muscle – he looks like he might be the breakout star of this year's *Love Island*, that one the whole nation falls in love with.

'Hello,' says Pedro, wiping his hands as he emerges from behind the bar. 'Are you Izzy?'

'Yes,' I say, with slight suspicion. 'Why, what's Lucas said?'

'Only how beautiful you are,' says Pedro, beaming as he pulls up a bar stool next to me.

Lucas pulls the stool back again just as Pedro is about to sit on it. Pedro manages to save himself from ending up on the floor by making a wild grab for Lucas, who then almost goes down with him. I burst out laughing, as does Pedro; Lucas brushes himself down and remains expressionless.

'I didn't say that,' Lucas says, sitting down on the stool Pedro had wanted. 'Ignore Pedro. Ignore anything Pedro tells you.'

I look back at Pedro with renewed interest.

'Well, you *are* beautiful,' Pedro says. 'So Lucas should say it. What can I get you? It's on the house. May I recommend the Sweet Peach Party?'

He leans over the menu with me, talking me through it, eyes flicking between me and Lucas. A naughty smile grows on his face as Lucas's expression gets darker and darker – I get the sense I'm part of an attempt to wind Lucas up that I haven't fully understood, but that's fine, I'm on board with it – until eventually Lucas grabs the menu and stalks over to the bar.

'Hey!' I say, turning around. 'I haven't chosen yet.'

'My day,' he reminds me. 'Can I get service here?'

Pedro stands with a chuckle.

'Don't order me one of those protein ones!' I call to Lucas. 'I don't want to get all muscly like you.'

I watch Lucas's grip tighten on the menu as he turns back towards me. 'You don't build muscle just by drinking . . .' He stops as I start laughing. 'Pedro!' he snaps. 'Make her something with broccoli in it, please.'

'Ah, I've found my kindred spirit, I think,' Pedro says to me as he skips back to the bar, pristine trainers bouncing on the polished wood floor. 'Someone who knows how to annoy Lucas almost as well as I do.'

We drink our coffees in the bar, and then have our smoothies on the walk back to the car. In defiance of Lucas, Pedro cheerfully made me something delicious, spiked with fresh ginger and stuffed with tropical fruit. It's admittedly quite refreshing, but I maintain that this is not breakfast. Coco Pops: now *that* is breakfast.

Mrs Muller passes us on her way from the dining room as we enter the hotel. Her hair is in a silk wrap and she has a paintbrush tucked behind her ear.

'Morning, Mrs Muller!' I call.

'Muses striking!' she calls back, with a languid wave. 'Don't talk to me!'

I nod. Fair enough. Mr Townsend smiles up from his armchair, folding his newspaper on his knees as we approach.

'Lucas!' he calls. 'May I call upon you to take me to Budgens tomorrow?'

'Of course.'

This is a fortnightly tradition – Mr Townsend likes very particular snacks in his room, and Lucas likes any excuse to drive his car.

'Coffee afterwards, yes?'

I glance at Lucas in surprise. It's not like him to socialise with a guest, but Mr Townsend said that as though it's become a regular feature.

'I'd like that. Now, if you'll excuse me,' Lucas says, with a nod of his head, 'I must speak to Arjun.'

'How was the night?' I ask Mr Townsend as Lucas disappears into the kitchen. We don't have an overnight receptionist at the moment, but Mr Townsend usually knows exactly what's been going on – he goes to bed late and wakes up early.

'The young 'un slept like a log,' Mr Townsend says, nodding

towards the Jacobs family's room. 'Just one two a.m. feed. Those blackout blinds you ordered have worked like a charm.'

'And you?'

'I got more than enough rest,' he says with a smile. 'Maisie used to say we're better with a little fatigue in our systems. It keeps us fighting.'

I pull a face, scanning the lobby for jobs that need doing. 'She sounds hardcore.'

'She was an actress,' he says. 'Theatre. I think she just wanted an excuse to stay out even later than she already did. That woman could dance the feet off a caterpillar.'

'Sounds like a girl after my own heart,' I say, rearranging the fir branch on the mantlepiece. Though actually it's been ages since I've danced. Except for that day in Shannon's flat, which I am now having to try very hard not to think about.

'So, what's he got planned for you?' Mr Townsend asks, nodding in the direction Lucas went.

'Sorry?'

'It is Lucas Day, isn't it?'

'Who told you that?'

Mr Townsend tries looking mysterious for a moment, and then gives up and says, 'Ollie.'

'Who told *him*? No, don't tell me, it was Arjun. So does everybody know?'

'I don't think Barty does,' Mr Townsend says. 'But Barty never seems to know what's going on around here, does he?'

I manage not to laugh at this, and give myself a rare full marks for professionalism. A family pass on their way to brunch in the dining room, and Mr Townsend and I pause politely before launching back in.

'It may be Lucas Day officially, but I think it's an Izzy day really,' I say. 'After all, you're happy . . .'

'Perfectly,' Mr Townsend says, reaching for his glasses.

'The muses are striking away at Mrs Muller . . .'

'The housekeeping team are no doubt thrilled to hear it.'

'And I got Baby Jacobs to sleep!'

'Certainly an Izzy day,' Mr Townsend says gravely.

I lift my chin, putting the finishing touches on the mantlepiece decorations. Lucas needs to up his game, I'd say.

'Oh my God. No.'

'No?'

'*No!*'

'Is that, *Fuck right off, Lucas, no*?'

I grimace. 'Well, no, it isn't. But I don't want to do this. I thought you'd make me do gross stuff, like scrubbing bathrooms! I didn't think you'd make me' – I wave my hands around the computer screen – '*digitalise*.'

'If you become more familiar with the system, you will learn how useful it can be. Even Poor Mandy likes it now.'

'She likes it if you're asking. When I ask, she says she prefers the booking book.'

'Of course she does. But what happens if there's a fire and the booking book burns? Everything will be lost for ever.'

I do *know* that the online system is more sensible. I'm not a total Luddite. I just love the ritual of the booking book, and guests do too – signing in with the fountain pen, flicking through the thin pages, the heft of that leather cover as it thuds closed on the desk . . . It's all part of the hotel experience, like the gold bell they ding if they need us and we're not there. We could have an intercom-type system for that, but we don't, because dinging is fun.

'I'm updating guest profiles this morning,' Lucas says. 'Which means you are, too. Here,' he says, pushing one of the old booking books my way. 'You can have 2011. Your ring was lost the summer of that year – maybe you'll find something useful.'

Reluctantly, I reach for the book and drag it towards me. Lucas gives a satisfied nod and returns to his computer screen, tapping away.

'How long am I doing this for?' I ask, logging in.

'Until I say so.'

I can *feel* his smile.

He keeps me at the desk like this for an hour and a half. This might actually be the longest I've ever sat still at work, and it's definitely the longest I've sat next to Lucas without one of us speaking to a guest or running off to do something else.

It's oddly companionable. Mostly we don't talk, but occasionally Lucas makes an idle remark, and at one point, astonishingly, he makes me a cup of tea. We coexist, basically. I'm quite surprised we have it in us.

Infuriatingly, Lucas is right: I *do* find something useful for my ring. As I transfer everything to Lucas's system, I notice that a few of the guests on extended stays were missed when

I made my list of people to contact, because they'd checked in several weeks or months before the time when the ring was found.

I scribble down their names, pen pausing when I hit *Mr and Mrs Townsend*. It's sort of happy and sort of sad to think that Maisie was with him back then. I make a note to speak to him – the ring can't be Maisie's, since she wore hers until the day she died, but he might remember someone losing their engagement ring during one of his stays at the hotel.

Eventually Lucas checks his watch, clicks his pen and declares we're done. He sets Barty's sign on the front desk – *Please ring for assistance and we will be with you in a jiffy!* – and leads me to the store cupboard. It's tidier than when I was last in here – he's sorted the shelves and pulled out all the different paint tins, dusting off their lids.

'That one,' he tells me. 'Can you carry it?'

I give him a withering look and then realise he's teasing me.

'I've seen you in the gym now, remember,' he says, picking up two paint tins of his own. 'You will never be able to pretend you need me to do heavy lifting for you again.'

Damn. I can never be arsed shifting the garden furniture, and guests *always* want it in a different spot. One of the very few upsides of being on shift with Lucas is that I can usually rope him into doing it.

I follow him through the bar to the conservatory at the back of the hotel. It's carpeted and filled with a motley collection of too many armchairs, and it's always been a bit of a wasted space – it's usually where the elderly folk gather at a wedding party to get away from the noise. I've not been back here for a while, and I pause in the entrance, mouth dropping open.

'Lucas!'

'What do you think?'

I look around, taking it all in. He's cleared the room completely and pulled up the carpet, and he's scrubbed the place down too – the windows are sparkling, showing the expanse of frosty gardens outside. It's no longer an old conservatory, it's more like an . . .

'*Orangery*,' I say, clapping my hands. 'We'll call it the orangery! People can eat bar food out here. Or even get married! For small ceremonies, this would actually be beautiful!' I spin on my heels, admiring the space. 'And the paint is for the floorboards?'

Lucas nods. His eyes are warm when they meet mine; he's glad I like it, I think. I look away.

'A thin coat,' I say, tilting the paint tins to check the colour. 'A kind of washed-out white?'

He nods. 'This is your job until lunchtime.'

I roll my sleeves up and start levering open the paint tin. This is *way* better than digitalising. Little does Lucas know, he's just handed me a task that I'd choose over pretty much anything else. I smile as I dip the brush and get to work. Definitely an Izzy day.

Lucas

It is satisfying annoying Izzy. I like getting her to rise to the bait; I like making her eyes flare and narrow, and I like how her humour comes out when she's snapping back at me.

But it turns out that making Izzy happy is a hundred times more satisfying.

'Finished. It looks *great* in there,' she says, bouncing her way back to me across the lobby. 'What's next?'

'Lunch,' I say.

We usually ask for a plate from Arjun for lunch, but today I've requested something special. He regarded me with great suspicion when I said I needed a favour, but when I told him it was for Izzy, he complied without complaint. It was a rare and enjoyable experience.

'We're having it upstairs,' I say, nodding to Irwin, the builder who gave me permission to use the newly reconstructed staircase. *Skip the fourth and eighth step* was his first instruction.

His second was, *And if you fall through the ceiling while flirting upstairs, make sure you're too dead to sue me.*

I take her all the way up to the turret room. This is the second most expensive room in the hotel, after the one Louis is staying in. It is half the size but twice as impressive, in my opinion. It's split over two levels, and one wall is curved. Up on the top level there is a sitting area that looks out over the garden and the forest beyond, and that's where I've set us up for lunch.

'Oh, no,' Izzy says, slowing as she approaches the chairs.

This is not the reaction I had expected to the spread I've set up on the table. We have *moqueca*, rice, *feijão tropeiro*, and *farofa*, of course – there are few meals my mother will serve without *farofa*. It is a beautiful selection of some of my favourite Brazilian foods. As much as Arjun frustrates me, he is an exceptional cook, and he listened to the advice I passed on from my mother when he was preparing all the dishes. They don't smell *exactly* like they do at home, but they're the closest thing I've had since coming to the UK, and my mouth is already watering.

'Fish,' Izzy says grimly. Her gaze shifts slowly to me. 'Well played.'

Merda.

She looks slightly green. Did I know Izzy doesn't like fish? I panic, sifting back through all the times we've raced through a quick plate of food together in the middle of a hectic day.

'God, the smell ...' she says, covering her nose with her sleeve. 'Do I have to eat it?'

I sit down, swallowing my disappointment. 'No,' I say. I hear the sharpness in my voice and hold still for a moment. It's not

Izzy's fault I've made her a lunch she doesn't like. I didn't ask her if she liked fish stew. *Don't snap*, I tell myself. *You're better than this.* 'But it might surprise you.'

It doesn't surprise her. I watch her try to swallow down the *moqueca* and immediately pour her a fresh glass of water, which she downs in one.

'There,' she says, wiping her mouth. 'I tried it. Can I eat this sausage and bean thing now? Oh my God,' she says, already taking a mouthful. 'Now *that* is delicious.'

Well. That's something.

My phone rings just as we're finishing eating. Ana.

I glance at Izzy, who is scraping up the last of her *farofa*, carefully avoiding the tiny amount of fish stew still sitting untouched on her plate. Is this a good idea? The phone is ringing out – I need to decide now.

'Lucas! It looks like you're eating good food for once!' Ana says in Portuguese when she answers.

Izzy's eyes go wide as she realises what's happening. 'Shall I . . .' she says, gesturing to the door.

A twinge of nerves moves through me as I turn the screen to bring her into shot.

'Oh, hello, who's this?' Ana says, eyes turning as wide as Izzy's.

The mention of another person on-screen brings my mother to the phone at remarkable speed.

'Hi!' Ana says in English. 'You must be Izzy!'

I wonder why I'm doing this. The only answer I can dredge up is that I want Ana and my mother to meet Izzy. And I want

Izzy to realise that my family are good, kind people. Maybe that will make her see me differently.

'Yeah!' Izzy says, sitting up a bit straighter. 'Hi. Nice to meet you.'

'We've heard so much about you,' my mother says, and Ana rolls her eyes beside her. 'I'm Teresa, Lucas's mother. This is Ana.'

'Tell us everything, Izzy,' Ana says. 'What is Lucas like when he's at work? Do all the guests complain because he is so grumpy?'

Izzy laughs. I give thanks for my sister, who can be relied upon to smooth over the trickiest moments. Still looking after her awkward little brother even from five thousand miles away.

'No. They mostly love him, actually. It's me who complains,' Izzy says.

Ana smiles at that. 'I bet the kids love him. Kids always love Lucas.' She pulls a face, pretending to be me. 'Hello, small person, how are you today? Shall we discuss politics? It's like he turns into Uncle Antônio.'

I flinch. Ana clocks it.

'Sorry,' she says. 'That was a stupid joke. You're nothing like him, Lucas.'

'This Izzy is very pretty,' my mother says to Ana in Portuguese, moving the conversation on. The way Izzy's cheeks redden makes it obvious that it was a fairly easy phrase to translate.

'How are you both?' Izzy says, smiling tentatively and glancing sideways at me. 'Are you looking forward to Christmas?'

They both answer at once, in a mix of English and Portuguese, just as Bruno starts crying somewhere very close to the phone. Izzy looks like she is both fascinated and overwhelmed.

'Yes,' I summarise. 'They are. And they're fine. And they miss me.'

'Nobody said that,' Ana says, just as my mother says, 'I miss you so much!'

I smile as I clock Izzy recognising the word *saudade* in there.

'That fish stew looks dry,' my mother adds in Portuguese, peering at the screen. 'Did you make that, Lucas?'

'I should go,' I tell them, keeping to English so Izzy doesn't feel excluded. 'But I'm glad you caught us.'

'It does look dry,' my sister says, scooping Bruno up in her arms. 'You should come home and have Mum's *moqueca* instead.'

My throat aches. 'Soon,' I promise them. '*Em breve.*'

'Oh, who's this!' Izzy says, smiling at Bruno.

Ana introduces him with pride, holding Bruno up to the camera, which he does not particularly enjoy, judging by his indignant expression.

'He's gorgeous,' Izzy says.

The moment I see her face as she looks at my nephew, I know why I answered the phone. This is what I wanted: to bring together these things that matter to me so much.

'Oh, wow,' Izzy says once we've said our goodbyes and hung up. And then, to my horror, her eyes fill with tears.

I'm beside her before I've realised what I'm doing, ducked down, my hand on her shoulder.

'I'm fine!' she says, patting her eyes with her sleeve. 'Sorry, God. This is embarrassing.'

I fetch her the box of tissues from the coffee table, and she dabs at her face, trying not to smudge her make-up.

I crouch beside her and curse myself. I hadn't thought about how throwing Izzy into my family would make her feel. She has no family – not a single person who she knows without question would tell her that they miss her in the same breath they criticise her fish stew.

'I'm sorry,' I say. 'It was thoughtless of me to answer the phone to my family.'

'I don't know why I'm so upset.' She blows her nose. 'Seeing people in super happy families used to always get me, but I've not been like this for ages. It just creeps up on you sometimes, I guess. And . . . I don't know. I'd got a bit complacent. Didn't brace myself.' She smiles ruefully. 'I haven't been looking after myself well enough, maybe? That always has an impact on how I can handle things like this.'

I try to come up with the right thing to say, but all I can think is, *I want to look after you. So that you don't have to do it all, for once.*

'Anyway,' she says, wiping her eyes decisively. 'Today is your day, not mine, isn't it? So I'd better put the self-care on the backburner.'

This lunch has been a disaster. I pause for a moment, wondering if I should just send her home to have a long bath and watch a film. But . . . I think my plan for the afternoon will make her smile. I think I can fix this. So I just straighten up and say, 'Take a few moments. Then I'll meet you downstairs.'

Izzy stands with her hands on her hips and surveys the product of my days off.

'If you thought I wouldn't be able to hack this,' she says, eyes sparkling, 'then you seriously underestimated me.'

I had planned to have the adventure playground finished by Christmas, but once Izzy and I settled on Thursday as Lucas Day, I knew I had to get it done sooner. I called in all the favours I had, irritating Pedro more than ever before with my *chatice e perfeccionismo* (fussiness and perfectionism). While it's far from finished, it is certainly serviceable. With Poor Mandy kindly covering the front desk for a couple of hours, we have nothing to do but scale ropes and tackle monkey bars.

I know Izzy. She has the open heart of a child – she loves an adventure. An afternoon of zip wires and climbing trees will surely make her happy. And if she has to jump into my arms during any element of this afternoon, then that will be fine too.

'You are my test case,' I tell her. 'We're doing the full route.' I point at the sketched map I drew up late last night, which shows the order in which each element of the playground should be tackled.

Her grin is infectious. 'Bring it on,' she says.

She brightens with every step she takes up the ladder and along the hanging bridge. I don't get the chance to pull her close, or help her over one of my towers built of pallets, or even squeeze into the treehouse with her, because the moment she steps into it, she's already launching off on the zip wire. But that's OK. Maybe it's better. We know there's chemistry between us. Today is about showing her that we can be *happy* together. We can squabble instead of fight. Sit side-by-side in a comfortable silence instead of a frosty one.

And it's also about showing her I'm not a dickhead. Though this seems to be harder to prove than I had expected.

'Ha! Done! Take that, Lucas da Silva,' she says, throwing down her helmet as she hops off the rope net and on to the grass. 'You thought I'd chicken out, right?'

'No,' I say mildly.

She shoots me a knowing look. 'Confess. You wanted me hanging off the middle of that zip wire like Boris over the Thames.'

This allusion passes me by, but I get the idea.

'This wasn't intended to embarrass you,' I begin, but the last two words are drowned out by the arrival of the Hedgers children, with their father running several metres behind them, his thin grey hair flying.

'Mrs Izzy!' shouts the eldest Hedgers. 'I want a go!'

'Oh, shit,' I mutter. 'This area is not yet open!'

'Sorry, sorry, I did see the sign . . .' Mr Hedgers says, scooping up the youngest of the children and grabbing Ruby by the hand on his way to the eldest one. 'No, Winston, not on the . . . Oh, God. Don't worry, I promise we won't sue you,' he says to me and Izzy as Winston tackles the tower of pallets.

'Thanks,' Izzy says, eyeing Winston and reaching for her helmet again. 'I'll just . . .'

She heads over to help Winston.

'I actually did want to speak to you,' Mr Hedgers says to me, watching Izzy adopt a wary squat beneath his son with her arms upstretched, ready to catch him if he falls.

'Of course.'

I let Ruby transfer herself from Mr Hedgers' hand to my knee, where she hangs, monkey-like, gazing up at me with glee.

'One of the things I love most about my wife is her absolutely unshakeable belief that she can do anything,' Mr Hedgers says. He looks tired. He is a tall, thin man, naturally stooped, but his shoulders are more rounded than usual. 'But she can't. Frankly. And we need help. The insurers said they'd pay to put us up here because of the flooding, but there's a cap on the amount they'll cover. Turns out we'd have to pay ourselves from the twenty-third of December onwards. Annie has been fighting as hard as she can, but even she can't talk them out of it. It was in the contract – we signed it.' He shrugs wearily. 'Pages and pages on those things, of course we only skimmed over it all . . .'

'Somebody should have flagged it to you.'

'I know. But they didn't. And the kids are so excited about spending Christmas here. We don't want to have to move out and go to a budget place just in time for Christmas Day.'

I swallow back a sigh, looking out over the playground. The Hedgers are a lovely family – the children have brought much joy to the hotel in the last couple of months. They deserve a beautiful Christmas, but . . .

'I'll speak to the owners,' I promise. 'But I should tell you that the hotel is struggling at the moment. We may not . . . Well. Let me speak to Mrs Singh-Bartholomew and her husband.'

Mr Hedgers gives me a tired, grey smile. 'Thank you,' he says. 'And if you wouldn't mind not mentioning to Annie that I asked . . . She hates the idea of charity.'

Once we've removed Winston from the playground – a process

that reminds me of levering a barnacle from a rock – I update Izzy on the situation with the insurer. She looks incensed as we make our way to Opal Cottage, her fire-streaked hair bouncing on her shoulders.

'Why are they being such arseholes? It's not like the insurers don't have the money.'

'It's just business to them,' I say, and then swallow back any further insights on this topic in the face of the furious glare she shoots my way.

'Well, it's real people, not just numbers. Those poor kids. This is all so unsettling for them anyway. And we've made the hotel so homely for them!' Izzy tears up slightly. 'I chose Ruby's favourite star to go on the top of the tree!'

How did I ever, ever hate this woman?

'The finance spreadsheets you've been working on,' Izzy says, looking up at me. 'Is it – is it *very* bad?'

It was bad before the ceiling fell in. In an attempt to recover from the losses of the pandemic, we've accumulated debts, we've skipped essential maintenance, and we've cut room prices to try to stimulate demand – a move that hasn't paid off. We have very few bookings, which in turn makes it hard to secure investment. Mrs SB and Barty often say they are not 'numbers people', and it is obvious that the hotel was not run economically even when it made a healthy profit. The result is that now we are in real, serious trouble.

'Yes,' I say quietly. 'It is very, very bad.'

Izzy sighs as she knocks on the door of Opal Cottage, pulling her coat closer around her.

'Oh, perfect!' Mrs SB says.

She is already turning around by the time the door is open, walking back into the cottage. We step into the warmth, shedding our coats and hanging them on the wonky iron hooks beside the door.

'I'm baking!' Mrs SB says.

Izzy and I exchange a glance. We have never known Mrs SB to bake. When we step into the kitchen, it becomes clear what this actually means: Barty is kneading bread in an apron and Mrs SB is reading him instructions from an AGA recipe book.

We explain the Hedgers' financial situation as Barty slaps away at his dough and Mrs SB tells him he's not put enough yeast in. He takes this well. I watch them as Izzy talks. How they just slot together, even when they're quietly annoying one another. I've never looked at other couples like this before, but suddenly – now that I've realised how I feel about Izzy – I'm seeing everyone in a different way. I want to sit them all down and ask them, how did you do it? How did you get from strangers to this, where you're like one person split in two?

None of my relationships have ever been like this. And as much as I think my ex was wrong to tell me I have no heart . . . as I stand here in the warmth of the Singh-Bartholomew kitchen, I do wonder if I ever really gave that heart to Camila.

'Normally I would say yes without even thinking about it,' Mrs SB says sadly. 'You know I'd love to help the Hedgers. But I have to look after all of you, first and foremost. That's my job, and I've not been doing it properly.'

Barty reaches a floury hand across to hold hers for a moment, and then resumes kneading.

'Mrs SB, that's not . . .' Izzy begins, but Mrs SB waves her to silence.

'Don't,' she says. 'You'll make me cry. Let's talk business, please.' She sniffs. 'The Christmas party.'

Izzy and I both freeze.

The Christmas party is a topic we do not discuss.

'What?' Mrs SB says, staring at us both.

'Nothing,' I say, collecting myself first. 'What was it you wanted to say?'

'I'm just wondering how you're getting along with planning it for this year?'

'You want a Christmas party this year?' Izzy says, doing a very poor job of hiding her horror.

'Of course. It might be a last hurrah, after all,' Barty says, dabbing his damp brow.

Mrs SB looks at us expectantly. Last year the party happened in mid December, partly because I had my flights home booked for December seventeenth, and I had led on organising the event. But it's already December fifteenth.

'Since you're both here for Christmas, shall we do it on the twenty-fourth?' Mrs SB asks.

In Brazil, the twenty-fourth is the focus of Christmas celebrations – this will be perfect for me. I have no plans for the day, and a party at the hotel will be an ideal way to stop me missing my family so much.

I glance sideways at Izzy. Her face is set. No doubt she is

remembering that argument on the lawns at the last Christmas party. How I'd snapped at her, how she'd screamed back. How Drew had hovered in the hotel entrance, watching, and then said to Izzy, *You know, you don't actually own either of us, though?*

Which was true. But it had hit Izzy like a slap in the face.

The more I get to know Izzy this winter, the less I understand the way she reacted that night. I always assumed she'd been protecting her friend, but Drew seems to have disappeared from Izzy's life without trace. I'd imagined they were very close, but if they were, there is no way Izzy would have let Drew go – she never seems to let *any* friends go.

So why was she so furious with me for kissing Drew?

I want to believe Pedro's suggestion – that she was jealous. But even if she was . . . her reaction was so unreasonable. All year I've told myself that it is classic Izzy – always unreasonable, and nobody else seems to see it. But that doesn't fit with the Izzy standing beside me now.

'Twenty-fourth is great,' Izzy says, voice strangled.

'Oh, I suppose I need to check with the builders about where we'll have got to with renovations by then . . .' Mrs SB glances distractedly at her phone.

I pounce. 'If you are looking to delegate the work with the builders and decorators, Izzy would be an excellent choice.'

The look on Izzy's face is one I want to see every single day. I have to look away.

'Izzy?'

'I'd love to. Absolutely. I can handle it from now on, if you just forward me everything you've got in terms of quotes and so on, I can just . . . take that off your plate.'

'Delegating,' Barty says, pointing a doughy finger at his wife. 'See?'

'Well, thank you! Both of you. And how are you getting on with your rings?'

We exchange a glance.

'Oh,' Mrs SB says, smile falling. 'Tell me we aren't due another showdown on the driveway. No more bigamists, please.'

'No, no,' Izzy says hastily. 'Just . . . we've stalled a little. But don't worry. Lucas and I are on it.'

'Good! Now, put your heads together and get to work on the party,' Mrs SB says, waving us off. As we walk out, we hear her scolding, 'Barty! You'll knock *all* the air out of it if you do that!'

Izzy

Lucas tells me to meet him at the car at five fifteen. I'm there at ten past, shivering in my teddy coat and woolly hat.

Lucas arrives at quarter past on the dot. He's changed into his casual clothes again, and under his open coat he's wearing a soft, dark-grey jumper and jeans – he looks like a celebrity caught stepping out for a coffee on a winter morning. He's that kind of handsome, the kind that makes you famous.

'Thanks for the lift home,' I say as we get in the car.

'We aren't going to your flat,' he says.

'What?'

'It is still my day.'

'But it's the end of the *working* day,' I wheedle. Today has been confusingly enjoyable, but it has also involved a *lot* of Lucas – I'm not sure how much more I can take.

'I'm not done with you yet,' he says, with the hint of a smile.

'Where are we going?'

'*My* flat,' he says, pulling out of the car park.

I've never seen where Lucas lives. I imagine it is extremely tidy, and that lots of things are made of very well polished wood. The thought of stepping into his private space makes me a little nervous and *extremely* curious.

We sit in silence for the drive. I hold my rucksack on my lap and cling to it like it's my support animal. Lucas lives about a fifteen-minute drive from the hotel, but it feels like hours.

He fiddles with the radio and 'Last Christmas' sings out through his car speakers. I snort, turning my face to the window. This song always makes me think about him, and not in a good way. I can feel him looking at me, questioning, but I keep my gaze on the grey slush lining the road outside. The song is a useful reminder that no matter how gorgeous he is, no matter if he speaks up for me with Mrs SB, he's still the man who kissed my flatmate on the day I'd confessed my feelings for him and then acted like I was crazy for caring. Red flag after red flag, basically.

His flat isn't like I'd imagined it would be at all. It's surprisingly characterful and homely. The sofa is battered old leather and the wooden coffee table looks handmade. There's an impressive number of books on the shelves, a mix of Brazilian and English titles – I didn't know Lucas read books. Most of them are non-fiction, so I suspect I'm some way away from persuading him to tackle my Sarah J Maas collection, but still, I'm impressed.

'Would you like a beer?' he asks, opening the fridge.

'Oh. Sure. Thanks.' I take the lager he offers me. 'So what are we doing? What brand of torture have you lined up for me next?'

'You're doing my evening,' he says, grabbing a collection of vegetables from the fridge. 'Nothing special. Though I am sure you will find a way to make it torturous.'

He points with a knife to a chopping board hanging on the kitchen wall.

'Ginger root, please. Finely chopped.'

A predictably rubbish job. I get to work peeling the nub of ginger, watching him covertly as he slices a pepper.

'You know, you got a couple of things wrong today. I loved the adventure playground. And the floorboard-painting was right up my alley. As in, just the sort of thing that I like,' I say, as I see his brow furrow, the way it does when he doesn't quite understand something I've said.

'Why do you like painting floorboards?'

'I love making stuff better,' I say, after a moment's thought.

There is something intimate about cooking together like this. It's unsettling. I'm missing the solid, reassuring presence of the front desk, the familiar hum of voices from the restaurant.

'Before my parents died, I was doing an interior design course,' I go on, filling the silence. 'I had this idea of setting up a business that redecorated spaces, only without any new materials. We'd use as much recycled stuff as we could, and where possible we'd use what was already there, just dressed up.'

'Upcycling,' Lucas says.

'Yeah!' I say. 'That's exactly it. Anyway. Obviously it's fallen to the wayside a bit but maybe I'll go back to the course if we lose our jobs.'

I feel him stiffen at that as he reaches for the ginger, combining it with the garlic on his board and adding them to the sizzling oil in the pan. His eyebrows are drawn in a tight frown. He's stressed about the job, I realise – I don't know why this hasn't occurred to me before. I guess it's that I'm sad rather than stressed. Losing the family we have at the hotel is what guts me – I haven't thought much about having to find other work, because I'm relatively confident in my CV, and I know there are a few jobs going around the area. But I guess the stakes are higher for Lucas. I don't know how long he would be able to stay in the UK if he lost his job, and I know money is tight for him.

'It might all just be fine. I think Louis is really considering investing,' I say.

'Hmm,' Lucas says. 'Louis is considering something, certainly.'

I frown. 'What does that mean?'

'He wants the building. I am not so sure he wants the hotel.'

My eyes widen. 'You think he wants to *buy* the place? Take it off the Singh-Bartholomews?'

Now he mentions it, I remember Louis jokingly offering on the hotel last Christmas, and Mrs SB laughing him off. *Could* he? I'd never considered the idea of Forest Manor as anything else, but I guess it would make a beautiful set of flats, or offices, or . . .

'No,' I say, shaking my head. 'Louis would have told me.'

Lucas stiffens at this. 'Food's ready,' he says, shoving a knife and fork at me.

We eat on the sofa. I expect Lucas to turn on the TV, but instead he grabs a pile of yellow cards from the coffee table and sets about reading them while he eats. I snoop over his shoulder – they look like revision cards.

'Are you studying?' I ask, surprised. He's never mentioned it.

He nods, chewing. I wait for him to say more but he doesn't, and he won't meet my eyes, either. I lean forward for the pack of cards that sits on the table and start flicking through. *Modelling consumer decision-making . . . market segmentation . . . perishability vs stock . . . hotel service delivery . . .*

'Hotel management?' I say. 'You're studying hotel management?'

He nods again, flicking to the next card. Like this is no big deal at all.

'Is that your plan, then?' I say, heat rising up my chest. I stab at my stir fry with my fork. 'Take over Forest Manor one day?'

'No. Not at all.'

'Then you'd be able to boss me around and I wouldn't be able to do anything about it.'

'Actually,' he says, 'my degree is not about trying to beat you at something, Izzy. It is something I'm doing for me.'

'Right,' I say. I'm flustered and miserable and I'm not sure why. I wish I hadn't mentioned the interior design course I failed to complete. 'Well, good for you.'

I've always known that Lucas thinks he's better at the job than I am, but I've also always thought he's wrong. Only now he's going to go and make it official, getting a degree and everything. Not that any of this matters – he and I will likely part ways in the new year anyway. He can manage some swanky hotel somewhere and I'll take that waitressing job they're always advertising in the window of Tilly's café in Brockenhurst – which is *fine*. I'd be perfectly content with that.

Lucas stands suddenly, pacing to the French doors opposite us and throwing them open. He's in just a T-shirt and jeans – he took his jumper off while we were cooking – and it's freezing outside. I raise my eyebrows as the cold wind hits me a few seconds later and he says, 'It's too hot in here.'

I can't help it: I think about him in the gym, a bead of sweat running down between his shoulder blades. Christ. How can I find this man so obnoxious *and* so sexy? Even now, as he steps out on to his little balcony and leans his forearms on the glass barrier, I'm noticing the muscles rolling in his shoulders, the bare, pale-brown stretch of his neck.

You'd think all the rejection would make me want him less, but it doesn't. I don't know what that says about me. At least I'm consistent. Not easily swayed by, you know, reality.

He just stays there, saying nothing, so I pull the blanket off the back of the sofa and tug it over my knees – a literal comfort blanket. I need it: I feel so unsteady, like there's a tremor going through the flat, sending everything trembling.

'Izzy,' he says.

That's it. Just *Izzy*. He doesn't even turn around. It's raining now, that faint, drifting rain that sparkles when it catches the light.

'You don't like me, do you?'

The question takes me aback. It's kind of a given, isn't it? Lucas and I hate each other – everyone knows that. He's pig-headed and surly and has a temper; he's deliberately difficult with me at work, and he's rejected me enough times that even if I had no pride, it would be hard not to bear a *bit* of ill feeling towards him. And ultimately, fundamentally, he will always be the man who kissed my flatmate on the day I handed him my heart.

'No,' I say slowly. 'I don't like you.'

'You *used* to like me,' Lucas says, glancing over his shoulder for half a second before returning his gaze to the rain. 'And then I kissed your flatmate.'

I tuck the blanket tighter. We don't talk about that. The one instance when we did talk about that, we ended up screaming at each other across the hotel lawns, and he flew back to Brazil the next morning.

I think of that card all the time. Now that I know Lucas better, I can imagine him cringing at the soppy bits. *My cosy warm heart.* Ugh. Writing that in his Christmas card felt brave and bold, the sort of thing a woman in a rom-com would do. Jem had been so sure it would end in romance, and I'd got caught up imagining our kiss under the mistletoe, the way he would scoop me up against him and tell me he felt the exact same way.

Damn Jem and all her romance novels.

'And that's . . . gone?' Lucas looks down at the beer bottle in his hands.

'Well, you kind of wrecked it, yeah,' I say, feeling it all again: the shock, the embarrassment, that awful conversation with Drew when we got home. She'd *known* how I felt about Lucas, and still kissed him. And maybe mid argument wasn't the time for me to ask her for the overdue rent, but when she walked out she literally threw a Christmas bauble at my head, so I think I win in the game of who-behaved-better.

'I *wrecked* it?' He turns at last. 'What was I supposed to do?'

I stare at him. 'Oh, I don't know, *not* kiss my flatmate under the mistletoe?'

'Izzy, come on. I have never understood why that was such a crime.'

I look away. 'Obviously you are and were entitled to kiss whoever you choose.'

'Thank you.'

That *thank you* sets my teeth on edge. I put my beer down on the table a little too hard.

'Am I still required to be here?' I snap.

He recoils. 'Oh. No. Of course not.'

'Right. Well, I'll leave you to your evening, then. Night, Lucas.'

'Izzy.'

Just *Izzy* again. I move to step away and then breathe in sharply. He's right behind me, his hand on my arm. He moved so fast; the contact is unexpected, and I'm not steeled to it. I'm hot with anger, remembering the way it all felt last year, and the sensation of his skin on mine sends me burning even hotter. He spins me around with a tug of my arm and I look up at him. My breath is cold on my parted lips.

His expression is thunderous. I've seen frustration in Lucas's eyes a hundred times, but there's a new depth to it tonight, and I know – I *know* he wants me.

'You drive me crazy,' he says. His voice is hoarse and his gaze is on my mouth.

I say nothing. We're both breathing heavily, our bodies close, but I'm not letting him lead me into another proposition that he'll knock back. If he wants something tonight, he's going to have to make the first move.

'I've tried,' he says. 'I've really, really tried. And still . . .'

He moves even closer, forcing my chin higher if I want to meet his gaze square-on. He's so huge, all muscle, tightly coiled.

I can't resist. It's something about the way he holds himself back – it tugs at the part of me that can't turn down a challenge. I can feel that he's a breath away from giving in.

I brush my chest against his. He breathes in roughly and that's it, that's *it*. Whatever it was that kept Lucas hemmed in, it snaps. He kisses me.

And it's pure fire. He tilts me back and kisses me so deeply I lose my breath and my footing all at once; he's half lifted me, half thrown me to the sofa cushions, one hand on my thigh as I wrap my legs around him. It's messy and fierce, the way you'd kiss if kissing was fighting. His tongue stokes mine and I dig my nails into his back. I've never felt a tide of desire like this – never gone under so quickly. If he wanted me now, I'd be his.

But he slows the kiss – not breaking away, just easing. Slow, languid kisses instead of hungry ones. I whimper in my throat and then turn my head aside, embarrassed by the need he'll hear in my voice. He turns my head back with one finger and looks me right in the eye.

'If we do this,' he says, voice rough, accent strong. 'Then you don't look away from me.'

I swallow. I'm lying here, breathless, raw, and it's *Lucas* looking down on me. I don't know if it's habit or pride, but I feel a sudden, powerful need to take the upper hand again.

'If we do this,' I counter, 'then we need some rules.'

We're sitting at either end of the sofa, eyeing each other warily. He has a cushion in his lap, like a teenage boy, and I've got my arms looped around my knees so he can't tell they're trembling.

'Why didn't you kiss me before? In the hotel room?' I ask, clearing my throat. 'Why now?'

He looks towards the French doors. They're still open, but I don't think either of us is feeling the cold.

'It's like you said. Two people who hate each other, kissing . . .' He swallows. 'It's weird and messed up.'

'Right.' Did I mean that? Do I think that? Right now all I can think about is how good that felt, and how badly I would like to do it again. 'And what's changed, then?'

He looks down at his cushion. 'What's changed is I have stopped caring about "messed up". I want you.' He looks up. 'You want me. We're adults, we can make our own choices as long as nobody is getting hurt.'

I nod. 'That's what I think. And that's why I think we need some rules. Do this in a sensitive, sensible way, and just get each other out of our systems once and for all.'

He flinches.

'What?' I say, already tense. I do know Lucas wants me – that's fairly undeniable right now – but after putting myself on the line so many times, part of me is waiting for him to walk back out on to the balcony and turn cold again.

'So this happens just once?' he asks.

'Of course,' I say, slightly horrified. 'God, I didn't mean – I'm not asking you to date me or anything, I'm just suggesting one night.'

His face is unreadable. After a moment, he nods. 'Fine.'

'So, first rule,' I say, shifting myself up straighter. 'This doesn't change anything. You don't have to pretend we get along because you've slept with me.'

He stares at me levelly. 'You want us to behave as we always do at work?'

'Exactly.'

'So you will still rearrange the stationery drawer and make me say *booking book* all the time?'

'What, you thought you could kiss me into being nice to you?'

One corner of his mouth lifts. 'No,' he says. 'Not exactly. OK. So what is your next rule?'

'No telling anyone at work.'

His expression darkens. 'Are you so embarrassed of me?'

'No!' I say, frowning. 'It's not that, it's just . . . We're colleagues.'

'Hmm.'

'It won't be good for the hotel if everyone's gossiping about us. You know what people are like.'

His face returns to its habitual stoniness. 'Fine. I wouldn't tell anyone anyway.'

I'm annoying him by trying to take over here, I can tell. This is familiar ground – I don't particularly mind. My body is still thrumming with the force of that kiss, and I *like* this. I like the way we push each other.

'Last rule,' I say. 'It's *just* sex. I won't sleep over tonight. There will be no cuddling. That way it's . . .' the word that springs to mind is *safe*, but I say, 'simple.'

His jaw is clenched. 'Simple,' he says.

He stares at me for so long that I start to shift, my confidence waning a little. I've taken so many knocks when it comes to Lucas. I know he doesn't like me. He's made that abundantly clear. I'm just relying on the attraction between us overruling that, and there's always the threat of his brain kicking in at any moment, reminding him of all the reasons we shouldn't do this.

And I can tell he's thinking. Which is not good.

But the moment passes, and quite suddenly, as if a decision has been made, Lucas throws the cushion on to the floor and reaches for my ankle. He circles it with finger and thumb. His expression hasn't changed, but I can see his chest is rising and falling faster than usual.

'Any more rules?' he says, sliding his hand up my calf. 'Or are you finished?'

I can't think of any more rules. I can't think of much at all with him touching me.

'No more.'

'So,' he says, his hand reaching my thigh. 'What happens now?'

His fingers climb slowly, slowly. The tension in my body rises too, spreading like kindling catching light.

The very tip of his finger stops at the seam of my jeans. I am perfectly still, my eyes fixed on his. I have no idea how to do this. I've imagined having sex with Lucas countless times, but I always thought it would start explosively, the way that kiss did a moment ago. I never thought it would begin with eye contact and the slow path of his fingers; I thought we'd fall into one another and I wouldn't have to make the leap.

His gaze shifts across my face. I'm a tumultuous mix of turned-on and terrified. I want Lucas so badly, but I don't trust him at all. Can I do this? Sleep with him without getting attached, without letting my walls down? For all my rule-setting, I've never actually had sex with someone I don't like before.

Lucas's hand slides down my leg again, pausing on my ankle, where he began.

'There is something in consumer rights legislation,' he says, 'called a cooling-off period.'

I blink. 'Oh. Right?' We've gone from hand-on-upper-thigh to consumer rights legislation at breakneck speed; my body is still thrumming with desire.

'Yes. There is a time when you can change your mind. I think that is what we need.'

'What? No,' I say quickly, sitting up. 'I'm good. I've made my mind up.'

I shift closer on the sofa, and he smiles. It is a slow, languid smile I've never seen on him before. It's *extremely* sexy. The smile says, *I know what you want, and I know I can give it to you.*

'Still,' he says, sliding his hand from my leg. 'I think . . . we wait a day or two.'

'What? No. No!'

'One day or two?'

I stare back at him. Is he crazy? He wants me to leave this flat right now?

'We don't need to wait.'

He raises his eyebrows ever so slightly. 'One, or two?'

Oh my God. Why is he so, so annoying?

'Lucas . . .'

'One or two?'

For fuck's sake.

'Do you not want this?' I say, pulling back, drawing my knees up again. 'Because—'

'Izzy,' he says, 'I am trying to be a gentleman. Today is my day, remember? I don't want you to feel any . . . pressure.'

'Well, I don't!' I say. 'I've made it pretty clear what I want.'

'Mm.' He tilts his head. 'Then it will be clear tomorrow too. We can wait one night.'

I swallow, running my hands through my hair, trying to pull myself together. My body feels boneless. All I want to do is melt into him.

'Izzy,' Lucas says, and his voice is gentle now. 'I want you to think about this. I want you to be sure.'

'I *am*,' I begin again, but I trail off in the face of his determined expression. I know that face. Lucas has made up his mind.

'All right,' I say, standing up. 'Tomorrow. After work.'

I feel the traces of the last half-hour everywhere: the warmth of his hand on my ankle, the roughness of his stubble on my cheek, the frustrated ache at my core. Looking down at him on the sofa, I'm struck afresh by how different he is here. At work he's so buttoned-up and serious, but now he's in a crumpled

T-shirt, loose and hazy-eyed. There's something so sexy about seeing him like this. I want to climb into his lap and kiss that insolent slope of his bottom lip.

'Just so you know,' I say, 'if you're really making me wait until tomorrow night, I'm going to make your day as difficult as possible.'

The corners of his mouth turn up just a touch. 'It is an opportunity to torture me,' he says. 'I would expect nothing less.'

Lucas

Izzy assumed the cooling-off period was just for her, and I didn't correct her. But I need this.

'The whole thing is a great idea,' says Pedro in Portuguese, over the noise of the coffee machine. 'Didn't I say you should have slept with her from the start?'

'That's probably why I've come to see you this morning instead of ringing my sister,' I say wryly, glancing at the customers waiting to be served in Smooth Pedro's. I've pulled a bar stool up by the till. I did consider offering to help with the breakfast rush, but last time I helped, Pedro kept whipping me with his dish cloth, so I decided against it. 'I'm hoping you are going to tell me I'm not out of my mind.'

'Absolutely not out of your mind! Oat milk mocha single shot?' he says, switching to English and flashing his most flirtatious smile at the woman at the front of the queue.

She smiles back, flicking her blonde curls over her shoulder. 'Thanks, Pedro,' she says. 'You're actually the best.'

'Damn right,' he says to her and then he winks.

I sigh.

'What?' he says.

'You are making it harder for me to think you're sensible. Sensible men don't wink,' I say, thinking gloomily of Louis, who winks at least once a day, and is definitely an idiot.

'Why the hell would you want to be sensible? You want this girl, don't you?'

I nod into my Yowsa smoothie (ginger, rocket, orange, carrot).

'So take her!'

'Pedro . . .'

'I just mean – she is offering you something. Not everything you want, sure, you want the marriage and babies . . .'

I glare at him. He grins.

'But it's a start.'

'It's a start.'

This is what I told myself last night. Izzy seems programmed to think the worst of me – the reason everything I did yesterday backfired was because she assumed at every point that I was trying to make her as miserable as possible. By the time we got to my flat, I was so defeated, and then she was walking out on me, and I *knew* she'd kiss me back if I kissed her. Resisting any longer just seemed impossible.

'Her rules are a good idea – they'll stop you catching feelings,' Pedro says. He wipes down the coffee machine and throws the cloth over his shoulder.

Those rules. They infuriated me. But I know Pedro is right: I'm developing dangerous feelings already, and if there aren't any boundaries when I spend the night with her, I am at real risk of harm.

'You're a big boy, Lucas,' Pedro says. 'What is it you're afraid of?'

I close my eyes. 'I think I was holding back the only card I had, and now I'm playing it,' I say eventually. 'I have one thing she is interested in and I'm about to give it to her.'

The next woman in the queue is ordering. Pedro ducks his head to listen to her, then spins on his heels to start conjuring up a white chocolate latte.

'You're talking like an American girl about to give up her virginity, *cara*,' Pedro says, and then realises he's speaking English and laughs as the entire queue turns to stare at me.

'Thank you for that.'

'Sorry. I'm just saying, you're not giving anything up. Sex with her means closeness. It means pillow-talk and all those hormones that women get when they have sex with you.'

'Pedro,' I say, rubbing my forehead.

'OK, if you want to be romantic about it, you're showing her how it could be between the two of you if you were together. So many great love stories started in the bedroom. My brother's wife was his one-night-stand rebound girl! And now they have a horrible number of children.'

This is actually quite helpful. 'Thank you, Pedro,' I say.

'No problem! Now remember, be safe, *cara* – condoms are your friend!'

This, of course, is in English. I drink the last of my smoothie, shoot the sniggering Pedro a filthy glance and head for the door.

When I arrive at Forest Manor for my shift, I realise that this feeling in my stomach is actually quite familiar: getting to work and wondering what Izzy will throw at me today. But it's new, too. The excitement, the anticipation for tonight. Thinking about her body, and knowing I *can*, because within a matter of hours – unless she's changed her mind – I'll be holding her.

But it's not Izzy who walks in next, it's Louis. He's wearing an open-necked white shirt under an expensive wool coat, looking every bit the modern Englishman.

'Lucas, hey,' he says, tapping a hand on the front desk. It's strewn with old cigar cases – Mandy was photographing them for 'those little Instagram videos with songs on them' at the end of her shift. 'Izzy about?'

'Not yet. Would you like a table in the bar for a coffee?'

I hate that I have to be polite to this man. I hate that he gets to buy Izzy flowers and I don't.

'No, I can't stop. Just wanted to see if she's still on for this evening.'

I take too long to answer, and he tilts his head, eyebrows raised. Reminding me that he's a customer, and ignoring him isn't an option.

'I don't know,' I say. 'But she didn't mention having plans this evening.'

'I'm taking her to the Winchester Christmas market. Parking's a nightmare but I've got a friend with a space in Fulflood, so we're set,' he says, with a little smile, as if to say, *Aren't I the lucky one?*

She can't be seeing Louis tonight. Tonight is *our* night.

'Would you like me to give her a message?' I snap out.

'No, don't worry,' Louis says, tapping the desk again and pushing away. 'I'll just WhatsApp her.'

All the tension that left me in the gym is surging through me again. My phone rings; I answer too quickly, desperate for the interruption, and the person on the other end of the line says, 'Oh, hi,' taken aback.

Louis gives me a small wave as he heads for the door, and I resist the temptation to return this with a rude gesture.

'It's Gerry,' says the man on the phone. 'My son said a woman rang about a ring?'

I sit up straighter. 'Yes, sir,' I say. 'Can I help you?'

'It was a long, long time ago, but I actually do recall a lady losing an engagement ring while I was staying at your hotel. She asked for my help looking for it. In the end, we never tracked it down. She told me she'd get a replica made so as not to upset her husband, who was a lovely bloke, loved her to distraction. Sorry, I don't remember their names.'

I jot this down. 'Can you tell me which ring it is you're referring to, sir?'

'An emerald one. Izzy Jenkins emailed me?'

'Thank you so much for calling,' I say. 'It's all written down – I'll let her know.'

She walks in just as I tuck the note I've written under her keyboard, beside her to-do list. My whole body tightens at the

244

sight of her, and I smile – I wouldn't be able to stop myself even if I wanted to. She looks beautiful. She's in her uniform, rucksack slung over her arm, gold rings glinting on her fingers and her ears.

'Lucas,' she says, with a quick arch of her brow.

'Izzy.'

I watch her as she comes around behind the desk, slinging her bag under her chair and turning her computer on. She side-eyes me, ponytail bouncing. Her hair is still striped in red and orange, and beside the fine gold necklace she always wears is just one more, with a tiny broken heart pendant. I wonder why she made those choices – the fiery hair, the heart.

She reads my note and frowns.

'What?' I ask.

'Nothing, it's just . . . this makes things more complicated with the emerald ring. If half the couple don't even know it was lost, because the woman kept it a secret . . .' She purses her lips. 'Never mind. I'll get there.' She widens her eyes slightly at her to-do list. 'So much to do today. Chat through the snag list for the bannisters with Irwin, negotiate some deals we can actually afford for staff at the Christmas party, torture you interminably until the evening comes . . .'

She meets my eyes, and her expression is pure wickedness. My heart lifts: she isn't seeing Louis tonight. She's got plans with *me*.

'It's going to be a long day,' she says.

She makes me wait until eleven before she plays her first move. I return from a trip to the post office to find her looking up at

me from the desk with a quick, devious smile that hooks something in my chest and pulls it taut. She stands, reaches for my
desk chair, and wheels it away towards the lost-property room.

'Am I using your chair today, or . . .?'

'This way, Lucas!' she calls.

I humour her. I'd follow her anywhere these days – maybe
I always would have. When I step into the lost-property room,
I pause. There's a trestle table set up in here, and an array of
face paints on its surface.

'My skills are a little rusty. I need a subject to practise on
ahead of the Christmas party,' she says, pointing to my desk
chair, now positioned in the centre of the room.

She walks to the door and clicks it shut. The sound sends a
shiver across my skin like the trail of a fingertip.

'Sit,' she says, when I don't.

'Did someone make this Izzy Day?' I ask, raising my eyebrows
at her.

'Sit, *please*?' she tries, and this time I do as I'm told.

She dips a small, pointed brush into a rectangle of blue paint,
moistens it with water and dips again. I watch the way she
frowns when she concentrates, how she brushes her hair away
from her eyes with the back of her hand. Everything about her
is suddenly acutely fascinating.

I wonder when it happened. If there was one single tipping-
point moment when I began to fall for her. Did I ever truly hate
her? It seems unthinkable now.

Izzy touches the brush to my temple, stepping close enough
to skim her thighs against my knees. The paint is cool – I flinch

246

slightly, and she tuts, brush still moving, tickling against my skin. Dab, paint. Dab, paint. Each time she leans in towards me, I have to fight the temptation to look down her shirt.

'So,' I say, as she works her way down the side of my jaw. 'You have me at your mercy. What are you going to do with me?'

'I'm thinking a sort of Jack Frost vibe,' she says, but the quirk in the corner of her mouth tells me she knows what I mean.

The next time she returns to me with the paint, she stands even closer. Heat unfurls along my spine, and on impulse I shift my knees to trap her leg between mine. She breathes in sharply, brush stilling on my cheek. I give in and let my gaze flick to that triangle of pale skin where her shirt falls open at the neck. I can see the edge of a white lace bra, and the soft curve of her breast.

I shouldn't have looked. That has not made this easier.

'Have you changed your mind, then?' she asks, twisting away to reach the paint, but keeping her thigh between my knees. 'About tonight?'

The brush whispers against my cheekbone. Izzy licks her bottom lip. I could have her in my lap in half a second. I want to. She knows I want to.

'No. I've not changed my mind. Have you?'

'I told you my decision was made.'

I incline my head in acknowledgement as she moves away to top up her brush. This time, as she turns back to me, she presses a thumb under my chin and forces my head up, then to the side, baring my throat. She takes the brush to the sensitive skin beneath my ear and I inhale, closing my eyes. She's not even touching me and this is turning my blood to fire.

'You could have had me in your bed last night,' she says. 'One message.'

I knew that. I felt it for every slow minute of the evening.

'You really do have ironclad self-control, don't you?'

She has no idea.

'I want to know what happens when you let go,' she whispers, leaning in. 'I want to make you lose your fucking mind.'

Pelo amor de Deus. My heart is pounding.

'All done,' she says brightly, pulling back, her thigh slipping from between my knees. 'Want to see?'

I open my eyes. She's looking down on me with an infuriatingly familiar expression: the self-satisfied smile she wears when she's beaten me at something.

She holds a small make-up mirror out for me to see myself. I have no idea what I'm going to find – it could be reindeer, or snowmen, or possibly *Lucas is a dick* written on my jawline. But it's amazing. A tumble of white and blue snowflakes running from my right temple to the left side of my neck.

'It's good,' I say. 'Now can I do it for you?'

'You? Paint my face?'

'Mmhmm.'

The reception bell dings. As one, we look towards the door.

'Saved by the bell,' she says, already bouncing away towards the lobby. 'You might want to . . . wait a minute.'

'Yes,' I say, shifting in my seat. 'Perhaps you had better get that one.'

*

We both end up having to wait tables over lunch. Izzy changes into her waitressing uniform in the lost-property room, leaving the door ajar, taunting me, tempting me to follow her inside. When she steps out to see me frozen in my seat, determinedly not looking, she gives me a smug look, as if to say, *Couldn't take the heat, then?*

I imagine I'll be safe waiting tables, but we pass so often, always close enough to brush arms, always locking eyes. I never lose her in that room – I know exactly where she is. At one point, as she moves past me into the kitchen, she whispers, 'Slow day, Lucas? I've never *seen* you check the time so often.'

I am openly staring at her across the dining area when Mr Townsend walks in. By the time I manage to redivert my attention to the specials board, he is regarding me with amused interest. I swallow.

'Can I help you, Mr Townsend?' I ask. 'Has there been a phone call?'

We've come to rely on Mr Townsend this winter: he is the only person ever guaranteed to be in the lobby.

'It's Budgens time,' he says.

Merda. I glance at the Bartholomew clock through the dining-room door, which is propped open so that Izzy and I can see the front desk. After some quick maths, I realise Mr Townsend is right.

'Lunch service ends in half an hour,' I say. 'I am all yours after that.'

'Lovely.' Mr Townsend pauses. 'Why don't you bring Izzy?'

'We can't spare her, I'm afraid.'

'I'd like her to come.'

I eye him with suspicion. He looks back at me with an expression of innocence that brings Izzy herself to mind.

'I might insist upon it, actually,' Mr Townsend says. 'I think stepping out of the hotel together would do us all some good.'

'Excuse me,' says a woman whose toddler is currently drawing shapes on the tablecloth with pea soup. 'Please can I get the bill? Like, as soon as you can? Ideally right now?'

'Half an hour,' I say to Mr Townsend. 'In the lobby.'

'With Izzy.'

The man has more backbone than I'd expected.

'It's up to her,' I say. 'And Mrs SB. And,' I add, as an afterthought, 'Barty.'

Mr Townsend smiles. 'I'll speak to Uma,' he says, planting his stick and setting off into the lobby. 'She can never say no to a guest, that one.'

'Isn't this nice?' Izzy says from the back seat of my car. 'A team trip to Budgens!'

Things have escalated. I'm not sure Mr Townsend is very pleased about this – his aim, I suspect, was to get Izzy and me together outside the hotel, having observed the way I looked at her in the dining room and decided to play matchmaker. But Ollie overheard us talking about the trip during lunch service, and was so determined not to be left manning the front desk again that he made up an obscure ingredient he had to get – himself – for Arjun. And then Barty overheard *him* and said he was coming to get some doughnuts. I believe Mrs SB is managing the front desk, which she hasn't done for approximately forty years. I wonder if she knows how to work the computer.

'Are you all right, Lucas?' Mr Townsend asks me kindly from the passenger seat.

'Absolutely,' I say, though there is sweat prickling between my shoulders.

Right now, in this car with me, I have Izzy, plus one elderly guest, one kitchen porter, and my boss. And yet every time I glance back in the mirror, all I see is *her*. The wicked heat in those palmeira green eyes. The way she seems to know every time I'm looking at her. How her gaze meets mine fast, hard, like we're crossing swords.

She said she'd torture me today, but she's hardly had to – it's the day itself that's torturous. Every slow minute that stands between me and a night with Izzy.

Upon our arrival at Budgens, things go smoothly for an impressive ten minutes. I feel calmer here, away from the hotel. It is easier to think about something other than Izzy Jenkins – even if she is in the same aisle.

We select a box of doughnuts after a long discussion about which of the available flavours is best (all are overrated. Doughnuts are just *bolinhos de chuva* with too much sugar and no personality). Mr Townsend chooses the first of his snacks (shortbread biscuits of a very specific shape). Barty shouts 'Mrs SB likes it rough!' across the chilled aisle (he was referring to puff pastry). And then Izzy opens her rucksack and pulls out the Tupperware of rings, right there by the fridges.

I breathe in sharply.

'Why do you have those here?'

'I wanted to talk to Mr Townsend about the emerald one when we go for coffee after this,' she says, trying to unclip the lid. She presses the box to her stomach, hunching over, nails working at one corner. 'He was staying at the hotel when it was lost, and he might remember something, but I'm just going to check that one's definitely in there, because I did take it out to have it cleaned, and . . . Argh!'

The lid pings off. The two remaining rings go flying.

'Shit. Shit!' Izzy drops to the ground, as though under enemy fire.

'What? What?' Barty yells, looking around wildly.

'Nobody panic!' says Izzy, commando-crawling across the floor of Budgens. 'I've got the silver wedding ring! It's just the emerald . . . one . . .'

She lifts her head slowly. The ring is between Mr Townsend's sensible brogues. He is staring down at it with open astonishment. A member of the Budgens staff pauses behind him, clearly contemplating asking questions about Izzy's position, and then makes the sensible decision to move on and pretend he didn't see anything out of the ordinary.

I am also trying to pretend that there is nothing out of the ordinary about seeing Izzy in this position, mostly by staring fixedly at the ceiling.

'Mr Townsend?' Izzy says.

'That ring,' he says, voice shaking.

252

Izzy stands and holds it out to him. The bright supermarket lights hit the ring's emerald and it sends green light scattering across the vinyl floor.

'That's Maisie's ring,' Mr Townsend says, almost breathless. 'That's it, right there. She was buried with that ring. What the devil is it doing in your Tupperware box?'

We all make our way to the café, sitting around a circular table, eating our Budgens doughnuts with our café-bought coffees. I feel quite uncomfortable about this, but Barty has no shame, and he was the one who paid for it all.

Izzy explains what Gerry told her over the phone. How the woman who lost that emerald ring had a replica made so as not to upset her husband. How much she'd loved him, and how she hadn't wanted to hurt him by admitting she had lost his precious ring.

'I'm not sad,' Mr Townsend says. His tone is thoughtful. He turns his face to the rain outside, blinking slowly behind his glasses. 'It's very typical of Maisie, actually. She never could stand to upset anybody. It used to drive me up the wall, the lengths she would go to to avoid causing anyone else any bother. And she was always wearing fake jewels onstage, so I suppose she knew how to have something like that made.'

'I think it's romantic,' Izzy says.

'Yeah,' Ollie pipes up. 'She went to *loads* of effort so you wouldn't be upset. That's nice, isn't it?'

'Yes. It is.' Mr Townsend opens his hand, looking down at the ring. It is beautiful. It's Izzy's favourite from the box, I think – she's always fiddling with it. 'Maisie and I were never straightforward. On and off like a light switch, she used to say.'

'You broke up?' I ask.

I don't know whether it's because Mr Townsend is old, or because his wife passed away, but I had always imagined them having a very sweet, sedate relationship. In my head, Mrs Townsend was probably a kind-hearted older lady who wore florals and baked.

But then, I always have idealised the dead. See my father, bitten by a venomous adder while saving a small village, or killed in a high-speed car chase while serving in the Agência Brasileira de Inteligência.

'Oh, all the time,' Mr Townsend says wryly. 'But we always found our way back to each other. That was just our story.' He shrugs. 'Our friends didn't understand. But I've always said that love takes a different shape for everybody. Some of us fall in love the straightforward way, and some of us have a more . . . winding path.'

Mr Townsend is giving me a significant look. I stare down at my Americano as Izzy's phone bursts to life beside her coffee cup.

'Excuse me,' Izzy says, standing. 'Mrs SB's calling. I'm going to guess that . . .' She taps her bottom lip. 'Dinah's bleached something antique.'

'Ruby's climbed something dangerous,' I counter-offer.

She bites back a smile. 'Closest guess wins?'

I nod once as she answers the call.

'Hi, Mrs SB! Ah, Baby Jacobs has peed on that eighteenth-century rug, has he . . .'

Izzy mouths *I win* at me as she heads outside, and I raise my eyebrows. I would say that's debatable.

'Refill?' Ollie asks. He's got himself a bottomless coffee. I am not sure he should be allowed this much caffeine.

'I'll come with you, stretch the legs,' Barty says, getting up.

'It never occurred to me that one of your special rings could be mine,' Mr Townsend says as they make their way to the till. He closes it in his trembling palm. 'All that dashing around and making phone calls. I'm sorry I didn't save you the bother.'

'It's not your fault,' I say. 'And Izzy's enjoying the search, I think. It seems to matter a great deal to her.'

'Well, of course,' Mr Townsend says, eyes still on his closed fist. 'Given the ring she lost.'

He looks up when I say nothing.

'Ah,' he says. 'Was that a secret?'

'She doesn't . . . share personal things with me,' I say, slightly pained. 'She lost a ring?'

'She told me a few years ago, when we were discussing her family. It was a twenty-first birthday present from her father – she lost it while swimming in the sea in Brighton,' Mr Townsend says. 'Very sad.'

I remember how she'd looked in that first conversation we'd had with Mrs SB – how her eyes had shone with tears.

I am struck by an entirely ridiculous urge to trawl the ocean. Perhaps Izzy's ring washed up somewhere? Perhaps I could . . . learn to scuba dive . . .?

'It was years ago,' Mr Townsend says gently. 'It's gone for good, that ring.'

I clear my throat, looking down at my coffee, embarrassed. I had not realised I was quite so transparent.

'So that's why she cares so much,' I say, taking a sip as I try to compose myself.

'Partly, I imagine,' Mr Townsend says. 'But I think Izzy likes anything with a story attached. And rings are objects we give a lot of value to, us humans. Symbols of eternity, dedication, you name it. They were always going to catch her eye.' He looks at me levelly. 'Lucas . . . Do you care for her?'

I am so taken aback, and so overrun with the emotions of the day, that I almost answer him honestly. But then, as I open my mouth, my uncle pops into my head, and I imagine what he'd say if he knew I was spilling my romantic troubles to a guest. And just like that, I clam up. My whole body responds to the thought. Stiff back, chin up, face blank.

'She is a very talented colleague,' I say.

I hate that I'm still like this, even with Antônio so many thousands of miles away. Even with my own car, my own flat, my own job, my own degree – almost. But these traits are so deeply engrained, I don't know how to unlearn them.

In my embarrassment, I almost miss something important that Mr Townsend says: that Izzy likes things with stories behind them. It only comes to me on the drive home, with everyone chatting away in the back seat. Izzy has looked at me – really *looked* at me – just a few times in the last few weeks, and every single time it's been a moment when I've let her see something that I don't necessarily want to show her. Telling her why I exercise. Sharing why I raise my voice sometimes, and why I so badly want to change that. Moments when I showed her there's a story to me.

It's an uncomfortable realisation. I don't like to share personal matters with anybody – it's not how I was raised. But I don't want to be that way. I would like some of Izzy's courage, her openness. I would like to believe that I can let a person see me, and that once they have, they might think more of me, not less.

Izzy

I am so glad Mr Townsend took that well. I'm not sure I could have handled it if The Ring Thing backfired again. I'm frazzled enough today as it is. Torturing Lucas has been fairly torturous for me, too – I *really* hoped he'd cave and follow me into the lost-property room when I was getting changed.

'Never leave again,' Mrs SB says when we return. She gives Mr Townsend a stern look. 'And you, sir, have used up your I'm-a-guest privileges.'

'I only requested two of them,' Mr Townsend points out, making his way over to his armchair. 'Don't blame me for the stowaways.'

'You rascal,' Mrs SB says to Barty as he swoops in to kiss her across the desk. 'You'd better have saved me a doughnut.'

Barty looks guilty. I'm pretty sure he ate at least four.

'Another ring down, then!' Ollie says.

He's crossing the lobby with a specific, bent-kneed dash that means he cannot be seen through the window on the restaurant door. Arjun-dodging has become a habit for anyone who has had to play sous-chef this winter, but Ollie is particularly good at it.

'No reward, though,' he says as he joins us at the desk. 'Yesterday Mrs SB told me we're probably going bust and losing all our jobs. So could you crack on and return a really expensive one, maybe? Save the day a bit?'

'Ollie, that is a very abbreviated version of our sensitive employee–employer chat. But yes,' Mrs SB says, holding out a pile of post to me, then turning it upside-down so the FINAL NOTICE is on the bottom instead of the top. 'Just one more reward like the Mattersons gave us could make all the difference now.'

'The last ring does look fancy,' I say, trying not to laugh as Lucas notices that Mrs SB has adjusted his desk chair, and makes a visibly painful effort not to object to this. 'Maybe it'll be fifth time lucky.'

The final ring is a stylish band, beaten silver, slightly askew. I love it. It's not as beautiful as Maisie's ring, but it's clearly designer, and I bet whoever owned it was interesting – you can just tell.

Arjun pops up in the window of the restaurant door. 'Ollie!' he barks.

'Balls,' says Ollie, trying a belated duck.

'I can still see you!'

'He's had me dicing on and off since Tuesday,' Ollie says miserably, dragging his feet as he turns towards the kitchen. 'If you do get a massive reward for that last ring, will you buy me an invisibility cloak?'

'You told me yesterday that you were loving the chance to help prepare the food,' Mrs SB says.

'Yes, but I've got *blisters*,' Ollie says mournfully, as he walks into the kitchen with the air of a man tasked with saving the planet against his will.

'He really dons that chef's hat with a flourish now, doesn't he?' Mrs SB says dryly as we watch him through the door.

'He's doing brilliantly, to be honest,' I say.

'I know. He's a star. You're all stars. This is good for him,' Mrs SB says, with a nod towards the kitchen. 'He likes to be pushed. Whereas *you* two . . . You like a little healthy competition.' She smiles at us, and for a moment I catch a glimpse of the woman she must have been when she and Barty first fell in love: a few years younger than him, and much less conventional. 'I happened to hear that you had a bet running on two of those first rings. Shall we introduce another?'

'Another bet?' I say, as Lucas looks up slowly from the computer screen.

'Yes. You see, this year, I'm giving Poor Mandy a break from being the Christmas elf,' Mrs SB says.

'No!' I say.

Mandy is a *brilliant* Christmas elf. She delivers all the hotel cards and presents – I write every guest a card, and Mrs SB and Barty get everybody a small gift, and Poor Mandy distributes them in this absolutely ridiculous elf costume that must date from about 1965. It is a staple of the Forest Manor Christmas.

'Yes,' Mrs SB says firmly. 'The poor woman never complains,

but that costume simply doesn't fit her any more, and it's not right. I was going to ask one of you to do it.'

Lucas's head turns slowly towards me.

'So perhaps ... Whoever fails to return the ring gets elf duties.'

'Absolutely not,' says Lucas.

'That's a great idea,' I say.

This is perfect. I have no problem with wearing an elf costume and delivering presents, other than the fact that I like my Christmas to be *exactly* like the Christmas before, and I would prefer Poor Mandy to have to do it on those grounds. But Lucas having to dress up as an elf? Yes please.

'The costume won't fit me,' he tries.

Mrs SB is on the customer's side of the desk now. She leans on her forearms, looking slightly gleeful.

'Mandy is an excellent seamstress.'

'But she can't adjust it for herself?'

'Come on, Lucas,' I say. 'What are you, scared?'

'What are you, five?' he says, eyes locking on to mine.

'It'll be fun.'

'This is serious. All of this. I'm not looking for *fun*.'

His tone has shifted; his eyes are dark. I swallow, looking away, conscious of Mrs SB standing on the other side of the desk. We've been like this all day, Lucas and I – even when we're bickering like normal, there's an undercurrent there, the reality of the night ahead never far away. Every time I remember what we're planning to do this evening, my stomach dips like I'm on a plane that's just hit turbulence. Teasing him has been an easy way to feel in control, but the truth is, I have no idea what'll happen the moment the clock strikes five.

'I do know that the situation is serious, OK? I'm aware of the stakes,' I say, keeping my voice light. 'But Mrs SB is right. We work better with a bit of competition.' I pull out one of the waiting lost-property boxes – I need something to do with my hands. 'I think a bet really would be best for the hotel.'

'And you feel the same?' Lucas asks Mrs SB.

'Oh, entirely,' says Mrs SB.

Lucas sighs. 'Fine,' he says. 'I will enjoy seeing you in those elf boots, Izzy.'

That undercurrent again. That edge to his voice, even now, when we're talking about bloody elf costumes.

'I'm not losing this one,' I say. 'Also, I would rock those boots, and you know it.'

Lucas's eyes flick over me.

Mrs SB chortles, drumming her hands on the desk for a moment. 'Excellent,' she says. 'Excellent!'

Lucas's face remains implacable. I imagine him in that elf costume, and discover, quite disturbingly, that Lucas da Silva can make literally *anything* sexy.

Finally, finally, the Bartholomew clock strikes five.

Lucas stops typing instantly. He turns his head to look at me. After a day of teasing Lucas at every opportunity, I have a feeling I'm about to get my comeuppance.

'I'll drive,' he says, picking up his bag and heading for the door.

I scramble to catch him up, wriggling into my rucksack straps as I step outside.

'You're not driving me,' I call, and he slows slightly, not turning around as he crosses the gravel towards the car park.

'Ah. You're seeing Louis tonight instead,' he says.

'What? No. No.' I've caught him up now. 'How do you even know Louis wanted to hang out tonight?'

I only remembered my plans with Louis this morning. I messaged him earlier to cancel, to which he replied, *Tomorrow night instead?*

His persistence is admirable, if slightly exasperating.

'He told me.' Lucas glances at me, eyes dark. 'In detail.'

'I rescheduled him to tomorrow, since we have . . . plans tonight. I just meant you can't drive me because I'm not staying over at your place,' I say. 'Afterwards. I can't just leave Smartie here.'

He looks at me properly now. I shiver. I'm excited, nervous, thrilled, and a little bit disbelieving, because that *afterwards* I'm talking about seems like a world I just cannot imagine. What will it be like, seeing him naked? Touching him? Letting him touch me?

'Ah yes,' Lucas says slowly. Almost a drawl. 'That was one of your rules.' He reaches into his pocket for his car keys and begins to walk again. 'I will pick you up at your flat and drive you in tomorrow morning.'

He climbs into the driver's seat, throwing his satchel into the back. I hesitate, glancing towards Smartie.

'Let's just go in two cars,' I say.

'That is ridiculous.'

It *is* ridiculous: petrol is so expensive, the planet is dying, and driving along after Lucas in convoy makes the whole thing feel a bit seedy.

I get into his car, breathing in the smell of clean leather and Lucas. It's *so* tidy in here. My car is filled with bits and bobs: hair bands, CDs (Smartie is old-school), water bottles that roll around under the seats if you take a sharp corner. Lucas's car is pristine.

My legs jitter as he drives, knees bouncing. I meant to get changed before we left – my uniform is extremely unsexy. At least I'm in good underwear. It's been digging in to numerous body parts all day but I'm grateful for it now. I'm hot with anticipation, cold with nerves.

Lucas lays a hand on my knee.

'You can still change your mind, *meu bem.*'

My breath seems louder, everything else quieter.

'I don't want to.'

'But it's always true. You can always change your mind.'

I relax back into the seat. I knew that, of course, but it's calmed me to hear him say it out loud. Something's shifted since that car door closed. Everything's different. For instance, Lucas's hand stays on my knee as he drives. I stare down at it: Lucas da Silva's hand on *my* leg. The mind boggles. How did we get here? And what does *meu bem* mean?

'You have driven me mad today,' he says, taking his hand away to shift gear and then setting it right back there on my knee.

'Don't I drive you mad every day?'

'Yes,' he says, voice almost silken. His eyes stay on the road. 'But not quite like this.'

'No?'

'No. You have been particularly irresistible.'

I've never been called irresistible before. I reach tentatively for his hand on my leg, and trace my fingers over his, listening to the way his breathing changes at the contact. It is so strange to touch him like this. So strange to see him as a man I *can* touch.

'This is weird, isn't it,' I whisper. 'Weird but . . .' *exciting*, I want to say, because there's a giddy, drunken thrill moving through me now, like I'm a teenager again.

'Weird but good,' he says, his voice low and soft.

'Can I . . .' My throat is dry. I swallow, turning my body towards him within the confines of my seat belt. His hand shifts on my thigh, and that tiny movement pulls all of my attention to that one spot, as if suddenly the heat of his palm on my leg is the only thing that could possibly matter.

'Yes,' he says calmly. 'You can. Whatever it is you want.' He turns to look at me for a split second and his eyes are as dark as the sky outside. 'I'm yours.'

'For the night,' I whisper, and his eyes flicker.

'Yes. For the night.'

I want to reach across to touch him, but before I can, the car jerks and I'm thrown forward. His hand grips my thigh tightly then flies to the steering wheel. The engine chokes, chokes again; the car stutters along, and Lucas is steering us to a lay-by on this dark country road and suddenly we're stationary, handbrake on, both breathing hard.

'Fuck,' I say. 'Is your car . . .'

'I'm not sure,' Lucas says, sounding much calmer than I feel.

'Do you think we should . . .'

He's trying the engine. It makes a sound a bit like a steam train. We both wince. I wonder how long it'll take us to walk back to Smartie from here. We've been driving for almost ten minutes on fast roads. Maybe . . . an hour and a half on foot.

Fucking hell. I'm way too turned on for a hike.

'I'll call my breakdown provider,' he says, pulling his phone out of his pocket. He opens his door as if to step out of the car, realises how freezing it is out there and slams the door shut again with a quiet Portuguese swear word.

The conversation is brief – classic Lucas – and the conclusion is that they'll be here in an hour or two.

'I should wait for them to arrive,' he says. He sounds calm, but his shoulders are tense, and he mutters something else in Portuguese before unclicking his seat belt and turning my way. 'If you . . .'

He trails off. I stare back at him, watching his eyes shift from cool concentration to something slower and hotter. We look at each other for so long that it starts to feel like a dare – like a challenge to the other to glance away first. I draw my bottom lip in between my teeth, just slightly, and it does the trick – his gaze drops to my mouth. I win.

'If I what?' I whisper.

I watch him try to pull himself together.

'If you want to go, you don't have to wait with me,' he says.

'I can wait,' I say, but the truth is, by now, I can't.

He kisses me first, hard, fast. It's exactly like last time – zero to a hundred in seconds, all fierceness and fire, and we're twisted awkwardly and battling to touch each other over the gearbox and the space between us until we break apart in frustration, chests heaving, and he says, 'Come here.'

He pushes his seat as far back as it goes. I climb into his lap. He looks up at me, smoothing my hair back from my face, running his hands down my sides.

'We obviously won't . . .'

'Not here, no,' he says, smiling, and tilts his chin up to invite another kiss.

I've kissed plenty of guys. I know what it feels like to get caught up making out with someone, how the world seems to fade and it's just your bodies and your breath. But this is . . . bigger. Brighter. I didn't know kissing could feel like this – as though it's clearing my mind until there's only sensation.

Lucas kisses with absolute assurance, commanding even when he's trapped beneath me, with one hand urging my body closer to his and the other tangling in my hair, tilting my head so he can kiss me more deeply. I want him so badly it's an aching, desperate urge – I have to get closer, take more of him, give more of myself.

Within ten minutes, we're breathless and beyond reason. *We obviously won't* becomes *we probably shouldn't*, and then after twenty minutes of making out in the driving seat like teenagers, without a single car passing us down this dark country road, it becomes *we could just* and *quero você, I want you* and *God, Lucas* and *please* and *please* and *yes.*

*

'Oh my God. You had sex with him in *his car?*'

I rest my head on Smartie's steering wheel for a moment. I'm held at some lights and Jem is on speakerphone on the passenger seat. 'I actually cannot believe myself,' I say. 'We were on a public road.'

'Izzy! I didn't know you had it in you!'

'Neither did I! But he got me so het up.'

Jem laughs. '*Het up*. You are adorable. Well, I'm happy for you. Assuming it was great? Was it great?'

I swallow, switching into first as the lights change. It *was* great. Dizzyingly, disconcertingly great. We were squashed into a car with the steering wheel digging into my back, still half dressed in our uniforms, but I had never been less aware of my surroundings. I could have been anywhere. And every sensation was amplified, dreamlike. My forehead to his, his hands gripping my waist, the way he shifted underneath me as if he knew precisely what I needed, even if I wouldn't have been able to tell him myself.

'It was intense,' I tell her, exhaling as I speed along to the hotel. I'm early. I'm never this early, but I just couldn't sleep. 'I guess because we hate each other so much, it kind of multiplied everything? That's such an intense feeling, right, and there's always been that fire between us. Maybe angry sex is actually the best sex?'

'Uh-huh,' Jem says slowly.

'You don't think so?'

'Well, no, actually, but it's more that . . . I'm not sure you really hate each other, do you?'

That pulls me up short – I notice I'm going seventy and make a face, braking.

'Course we do. He was such a dick to me last Christmas, don't you remember?'

'I remember,' she says. 'But maybe you've forgiven him for it.'

'What! I have *not*.' I'm quite affronted. 'He's not even apologised – or offered any sort of explanation!'

'OK, well I know you tend to hold a grudge like Gollum with something shiny . . . but have you actually asked him what happened, pigeon? Maybe he didn't get your card.'

I have wishfully considered this option many times in the last year. In the immediate aftermath of the mistletoe incident, I was so sure this was the explanation that I hunted Poor Mandy down at home to ask her again – was she *certain* she gave my card to Lucas? Did he *definitely* read it?

And she'd said yes, he read it. And laughed.

'He got the card,' I say, swallowing. I don't like thinking about it, not when my body is still soft and sore and satisfied from last night. 'Anyway, I've not even told you the worst part. The breakdown cover turned up early . . .'

'Oh, *no*.'

'Not that bad. I was back in my seat.' I'm wincing at the memory of the woman's face, how amused she'd been by my ruffled hair and red cheeks. 'But she offered to give me a lift back to my car as they'd be a while fixing Lucas's, so I just said bye to Lucas and left with her.'

'How did you say bye to him?' Jem asks.

'Oh, weird wave.'

'Little pigeon.' Jem's voice is infused with warmth, and it makes me miss her more than ever. 'You are too cute.'

'Embarrassing, you mean. It was great though: I just went home and had a bath and did my own thing! I think casual one-time sex is the way forward for me.'

'Really?'

'Yes! Why not?'

'Well, maybe I'm not the best person to ask . . .'

'You're always the best person to ask,' I say.

'You are well aware this would never happen to me,' Jem says, amused. 'I cannot even *conceive* of it, Izz.'

Jem is demisexual, as in, she's only attracted to people when she's formed an emotional connection with them first. Great sex with someone you hate is a total contradiction in terms for her, I guess.

'Do you think I've been really stupid?' I say. 'Do you think I shouldn't have had sex with him?'

'Of course not! I'm not judging, not ever, you know that. I'm just not convinced you're getting what you want from a relationship, here. You're . . . *cosy*, Izzy. You've always wanted a partner who wears woolly jumpers and has a nice smile and a lovely family.'

I wish she'd not said *cosy*. It takes me right back to that bloody Christmas card again.

'Well, it's not a relationship anyway, so no need to worry,' I remind her. 'Now . . . speaking of lovely families,' I say, dodging a pothole.

'Don't. I'm actually on the sidewalk outside the house with

Piddles, in the very spot where I used to smoke as a teenager and dream of running away. Some things never change.'

'You know, you *can* run. You're a grown-up now. You don't have to spend the holidays with them just because you've ended up back in Washington. They make you miserable, Jem.'

'Oh, but they're my family,' Jem says, and I can hear that she's rubbing her forehead, the way she always does when she's feeling guilty or sad. 'I'm lucky to have them.'

I know what she means. *When you don't have yours.*

'They're lucky to have *you*,' I say. 'I would so love it if you could walk into that house and own the woman I've always known you to be. So what if you're not a doctor or a lawyer or a super-rich businesswoman? You're chasing a different dream, and you're doing brilliantly. They should be proud of you.'

'I'm a backing dancer who's got her first break aged twenty-nine, Izzy,' Jem says dryly. 'I get paid like, twelve dollars a month after tax.'

'Who cares! You have a gift, and the kindest, purest heart, which I personally think matters a hell of a lot more than whether you're a "success". Which you are. So you win on all counts. Not that we subscribe to the idea of it being a competition. God, it's complicated rising above other people's expectations, isn't it?'

'It really is.' Jem sniffs. 'Thanks, Izz. Damn, you've made me cry.'

'I have many rambling pep talks up my sleeve,' I tell her. 'Would you like one every hour, on the hour, just in case you need it?'

'You want me to sob my way through the holidays?'

'Only in a nice way!' I say, turning in to the hotel car park.

Lucas

There was a plan. It involved good red wine and candles. Slow kisses and pillow-talk.

My car in a lay-by was not the plan.

'Isn't this the sort of conversation you should be having with one of your gym buddies?' Ana says in my ear.

I am actually in the gym right now. It is the only place where I feel sane at the moment. I'm on the treadmill, jogging and panicking.

'What about that Pedro guy?' Ana asks.

'Pedro got me into this mess to begin with,' I say, swiping a droplet of sweat from my chin.

There aren't many people here yet, and the morning gym crowd is more serious and subdued. Which suits me just fine.

'Unless you are now using "Pedro" as a codename for your penis, I don't think that's true,' my sister says.

I wince. 'I've messed up, haven't I?'

'Does it feel like you've messed up? Did it not, you know, go well?'

It was the hottest and most intense experience of my life. I have never, ever wanted somebody so badly. Every moment we spent together in that car, I could feel myself drowning in the euphoria of it, even as I begged myself to wait and remember everything, because this was precious.

But I had one shot.

I wanted Izzy to take me seriously. I wanted to tell her my story, to show her that I do have a heart, whatever she's always thought. And instead, I behaved like a thoughtless teenage boy. I should have waited until the breakdown truck arrived. I should have driven her back to my flat for a late dinner, kissed her slowly on the sofa, and told her how beautiful she was.

'It was amazing, but not how it should have gone. I had a plan.'

'Oh, a *plan*. I know how much you love a plan.'

Every time Ana says *plan* it is loaded with sisterly scorn. I scowl, upping the tempo on the running machine.

'It's not that. I just wanted it to be special.'

'Wasn't it?'

It was. But it wasn't *right*. This was my chance to show Izzy there's something real between us – everything had to be perfect. Instead, I'd been almost panicked with desire, desperate for more of her, and then those people had come to fix the car, and . . .

'Hello? Lucas? It is very, very early here, and Bruno has finished his feed, so I'm actually only still awake because I'm being an amazing sister, but if you don't say something soon, I'm going to fall asleep.'

'Sorry. Go back to bed,' I say. 'Love you. Kiss my nephew for me.'

'Love you too. And no chance,' she says. 'I am not waking that baby unless something very big is on fire.'

I smile as I reach for my phone to switch back to my workout playlist. I can't wait to see Bruno again in February. As soon as this thought crosses my mind, I imagine Izzy there with me: charming my sister, tickling a giggle from Bruno, laughing with me as we get the barbecue going in the garden. The image is so potent I lose my footing and have to grab at the treadmill.

I don't want to get Izzy out of my system. That is clearer than ever after last night. I want all of her. Her kindness, her commitment, her technicolour hair and the way she always puts me in my place. I want to take her home and call her mine.

As soon as I arrive at the hotel, it becomes clear that Izzy is still taking her rules extremely seriously.

'Lucas,' she says, giving me a bright smile when I get to the desk. 'I've got a lead on the final ring. Better up your game if you don't want to be dressing as Santa's little helper. Oh, and I've sorted a magician for the party, and Irwin says they'll be done with the staircase just in time.'

She's so ... brisk. Cold, even. But she still smells of cinnamon sugar and I know what the curve of her waist feels like. I've dragged my tongue along the inch of collarbone I can see through the collar of her shirt.

'You OK to cover the desk this morning so I can get on top of all the renovation work?'

'Yes, fine,' I say. 'But, Izzy . . .'

She whizzes away, hair flying.

I spend my morning posting out lost-property items we've sold and trying to decipher Izzy's to-do list. I move mechanically, getting things done, and all the while I'm thinking, *Was that all the Izzy I get?* That thought, the very idea . . . It hollows me out.

And then there's the knowledge that Izzy is going out with Louis tonight. That is making everything considerably worse.

I've never been jealous like this with another woman, but then, I'd never been cheated on before Camila. Izzy is the first woman I've cared about since that relationship ended. Maybe this is what Camila's done to me – for all her protestations that she couldn't change me at all.

I take a pause in the lost-property room, pressing my fingers to my eyelids, trying to gather myself. I *hate* the idea that my relationship with Camila made me weaker. I remember the way I felt when Izzy slipped into the pool with Louis – that feeling I was so convinced shouldn't be called fear – and I wonder whether I *had* been frightened after all. That's what jealousy is, isn't it? Fear of losing someone?

'This is stupid,' I whisper under my breath as I step back through into the lobby. The images play out at the back of my mind: Louis walking Izzy through the crowds of the Christmas market, lacing his fingers through hers, turning to her under the mistletoe . . .

The bell dings.

'Sorry to bother you, Lucas,' Mr Hedgers says when I startle. 'You look like a man with a lot on his mind.'

I was actually imagining Louis slow-dancing with Izzy on an ice rink under the stars, but hopefully Mr Hedgers can't tell how quickly that all spiralled.

'What can I do for you, Mr Hedgers?' I say, settling down in my chair. It's not been quite right ever since Mrs SB sat in it. I shift a little from side to side, but nothing improves matters.

Mr Hedgers gives me a baffled smile. 'I have something of a mystery on my hands, and I'm hoping you can help me with it. Mrs Singh-Bartholomew let us know yesterday that we can stay. That we're covered until the new year. But my wife says the insurer hasn't backed down – in fact, she was just eviscerating them on the phone this morning,' he says, pulling a face. 'I can't understand how Mrs SB made the mistake?'

I frown. It seems unlikely that Mrs SB has changed her mind. I emailed her just yesterday with a summary of my suggestions for budgeting at the hotel, and there is *not* room for random acts of charity, as much as I want to help the Hedgers.

I promise to investigate, and send Mrs SB a quick email, asking to meet her later.

Then I just . . . work.

That's it.

I don't see Izzy all day. She flits in and out of the lobby but is gone before I can speak to her. I can't decide if she is avoiding me on purpose. I hope not. Or perhaps I hope so. What would avoiding me *mean*?

When I do eventually collide with her, it's outside Opal

Cottage, just when I'm due to meet with Mrs SB. The rain is coming down in thick, steady droplets, and she's under a spotty pale-blue umbrella. I'm using my large black one, big enough for two, and it keeps us at a distance, as if we're each walking in our own bubble.

'Hi,' she says, and immediately turns pink.

I relax slightly. Those flushed cheeks tell me she hasn't forgotten about yesterday at all.

'Hello,' I say. I hold her gaze, and her cheeks grow pinker.

Mrs SB opens the door and Izzy flees inside. I follow more slowly, watching her, how fast she's talking, the way her hands keep reaching around as though she needs something to fiddle with. She glances sideways at me, then her gaze slips away again.

'Let me put the kettle on,' she says, voice tipping higher.

I smile as she dashes off. I'm feeling a lot better now. An unsettled Izzy is an Izzy who is feeling things she didn't expect to feel; an unsettled Izzy means *change*.

'Mrs SB, the Hedgers,' I begin, as Izzy clatters around in the kitchen.

Mrs SB's face lights up. 'Wonderful, isn't it?'

'Well, yes, I am glad they are staying, but . . .'

I look at Izzy. She's not going to like this, and while that wouldn't have bothered me a few weeks ago, now I hate the thought of upsetting her.

'We can't afford it.'

Izzy glances over, frowning.

'Oh, I know,' Mrs SB says, sounding puzzled. 'That's why I was so pleased when the donation came through.'

'The donation?'

'On the hotel's Kickstarter page.'

I stare at her.

'Poor Mandy set it up,' she says, laughing at my shocked expression. 'She's been doing all sorts with the internet on her shifts.' She sighs, settling back into her armchair as Izzy returns with cups of tea. 'We're making a little money on there. But it won't be enough. We need real investment. I've seen your email, Lucas, and I've not replied, because frankly it's far too depressing for words. I've tried everything, every loan, everyone. Louis Keele is our last hope.'

I notice that I am grinding my teeth, and hope that it isn't audible. I don't trust Louis' intentions with Forest Manor one bit.

'Izzy, I know you've formed a friendship with Louis – of course I wouldn't want to ask you to do anything you weren't comfortable with . . .'

It's definitely audible now.

'But could you just get a sense of whether there's any hope, there? Whether he *might* . . .'

'Of course,' Izzy says, squeezing Mrs SB's shoulder. 'I'll ask him, OK? I'm seeing him tonight.'

'Perfect,' Mrs SB says, closing her eyes.

No, not perfect. Not perfect at *all*.

As we leave Opal Cottage, Izzy walks ahead of me, and I catch her up in a few strides, putting a hand on her arm. She jumps, turning. The rain has eased a little, and neither of us has put up our umbrellas for the short walk back to the hotel. Izzy folds her arms to pull her coat close around her.

'Yes?' she says. 'What is it?'

'Hello.' I try to hold her gaze, but it slides away from me again. 'So we are not going to talk about it? At all?'

'That's what we decided, wasn't it?'

'We decided to remain professional at work.' I dig the point of my umbrella into the grass, my knuckles tight on the handle. 'I only see you at work. Does that mean we never speak of it again?'

'We can speak about it, if you think we need to.' She glances up at me. 'Do we need to?'

I don't know. I want to apologise to her for not making it more romantic, but she never wanted romance from me. She'll get that from Louis tonight, presumably. I swallow, glancing back towards Opal Cottage. Its chimney is smoking, the Christmas tree visible in the left-hand window. We're standing just outside the front garden, beneath the old oak tree.

'So I'm out of your system now?' I ask, looking back at her. I shift the handle of my umbrella to and fro between my palms, and she watches my hands.

'Mmhmm,' she says. 'Yeah, all sorted. Same for you?'

Something in her voice gives me pause. Carefully, deliberately, I try stepping closer. She stays where she is, eyes flicking to mine. Wary, but also excited, I think. I recall how pink-cheeked and fidgety she was when we first arrived at the cottage, and I let myself wonder if Izzy has been thinking about me as much as I've been thinking about her today.

'No, Izzy. You're not *out of my system.*'

It's raining more heavily again, pattering at the branches

above us. I reach out to brush a raindrop from her cheek with one slow swipe of my thumb.

She inhales at the contact, gaze fixed to mine, but she doesn't move away, so I keep my hand there, framing her face. My heart starts to beat in the low, stubborn, insistent tempo it always hits when I'm close enough to kiss her. I watch for those small shifts that tell me what Izzy's body wants. How she straightens a little, as though pulled towards me, and how her pupils dilate. After just one frantic evening in a car, I can already read Izzy's body better than I've ever read her mind.

'But you're done with me, are you?' I ask.

'What did you think would happen? We'd have sex and I'd suddenly find you irresistible?' she says, but her voice catches in her throat, and my confidence grows. She didn't answer my question.

'You've found me irresistible for some time,' I say, then I smile as her eyes flare with irritation. With me and Izzy, there's always been a fine line between pissed off and turned on. 'That was the problem, wasn't it?'

'I wouldn't say . . .' she begins, and then she trails off.

I've stepped closer, and she's backed up against the bark of the oak tree, her hair sparkling with rainwater, her chest rising and falling fast.

'Lucas,' she whispers.

My heart is thundering now. I lift my hand from her cheek and brace my forearm against the tree above her head to hold a few inches of distance between our bodies. She looks up at me, lips parted. I can see the shift in her eyes, the moment she relaxes. She's letting go. Forgetting about real life, remembering about me. I'd expect it to make me feel triumphant, but instead I feel an unexpected clench of emotion – I love that her body trusts mine.

'Tell me to *Fuck right off, Lucas,* and I'm gone,' I whisper, dipping my mouth to hover above the soft, secret place on her neck that I learned about last night. 'Tell me you're done with me.'

'I'm . . .'

She doesn't finish. I reward the admission with a hot kiss to her cold skin, and she moans.

'What did you think would happen?' I repeat her question back to her, my mouth against her skin. 'That we'd have sex and suddenly we'd be able to resist each other?'

The door to Opal Cottage slams and we move as one: she twists away from me as I push back from the tree, lunging for my umbrella when it slips from my hand.

'You tell Barclays they can shove it up their arses!' Barty shouts as he makes his way up the path. 'Oh, hello, you two,' he says, rounding the corner and finding us hovering guiltily beneath the tree. 'Off back to the hotel?'

'No, I'd better . . . I'll . . .' Izzy's cheeks are as pink as I've ever seen them. 'I'm going that way,' she says, and heads off into the woods.

'Is she all right?' Barty says, as we begin making our way back to the hotel.

I clear my throat, the heat in my body simmering down again. I don't know quite what that was, underneath the oak tree, but there's excitement singing through me now. Because it definitely wasn't nothing. And after a day thinking I'll never kiss Izzy again, not-nothing feels pretty incredible.

'She's fine,' I say. 'We were just arguing again.'

'Oh, you two,' Barty says, shaking his head. 'Always at each other, aren't you?'

I cough again. 'Something like that, yes.'

Izzy

What is wrong with me?

The whole point of last night with Lucas was to stop stuff like this happening. By the time I get back to the hotel – via a cold, unnecessary detour into the woods – I am soaking, and Lucas is at the desk. He looks up at me, heavy eyed, amused. Despite the sobering walk in the forest, I'm warm again the moment his gaze meets mine.

'Shall I fetch you a towel, Izzy?' he asks.

'No,' I say stubbornly, dripping on the lobby carpet. 'I'm fine.'

His lip quirks. He returns his gaze to the computer screen. 'As you wish,' he says, as though he didn't just pin me up against a tree and kiss my neck and make me *melt*.

Infuriating, bewildering robot-man.

I get changed in the spa area and manage to dodge Lucas for the rest of the day, but it does require ingenuity. At one point I have to pretend to get a cramp, and when Ollie asks me to take some tablecloths to Lucas, I end up asking Ruby Hedgers to do it for me. She informs me that this is child labour and tries to extort me for a lot of money; I only avoid a trip to court by giving her a packet of my candy kittens.

At least I'm getting somewhere with my ring. There's one name on the list of guests that jumped out at me this week: Goldilocks. When a celebrity visits the hotel, they usually choose a pseudonym to check in under – only a few key members of staff will be aware of their identity. Goldilocks has pseudonym written all over it. Grilling everyone around the hotel about this takes up most of my afternoon, and is the perfect distraction.

'If I remembered who stayed here in 2019 under the name Goldilocks, Izzy,' Arjun says in exasperation, after I pop into the kitchen to ask for a third time, 'I would tell you purely to shut you up. You are like Izzy-on-crack today. What's got you so wired?'

'Nothing!' I yelp, sliding down off the countertop and wishing my colleagues didn't know me *quite* so well.

Once I'm home and drying my wet uniform on the radiators, everything feels a lot simpler. I had a momentary relapse at Opal Cottage, that's all. It was never going to be a clean-cut thing: find Lucas irresistible one moment, find him repulsive again the next. There was going to be a period of transition. I'm just in that. It's no big deal.

Helloooo, comes a text from Sameera. *We are wondering if you and Sexy Scowly Receptionist are going at it like rabbits now you've 'broken the seal'? Hahaha! x*

I chuck my phone across the room to the sofa and get back to drying clothes. *Breaking the seal* is not the thing here. It's about *getting it out of the system.* Honestly. What's Sameera on about?

As I walk through the Winchester Christmas market with Louis later that night, I take a deep, calming breath and pull myself together. The market is so cute that my cosy heart is about to explode. Warm spiced cider, the smell of dried oranges and eggnog, the sound of children laughing as they race between the stalls . . . It is one hundred per cent, double-shot cosiness. My perfect second date.

So why am I wishing I was somewhere else?

'It's not as simple as whether I have the money to invest,' Louis is saying.

He keeps putting his hand on my back as we move through the crowd. It's not at all gropey or anything, but it's annoying me.

'The money's there, of course, but I have to think about the breadth of my portfolio,' Louis says. 'Think with my head, not my heart.'

'Well, that's not really my forte,' I say brightly. 'But I can tell you that we have so much planned for Forest Manor.'

I try to pep myself up again and focus on the nice things about Louis. How he ticks every box. How I said I'd give this a proper chance. But ever since The Angel's Wing, I've been going off him, and once that process starts, it's so hard to backpedal. Suddenly his slicked-back hair looks greasy rather than stylish, and he winks *way* too often. I'm not even convinced that his gentlemanly listening face is all that genuine, actually.

'Oh, I've been meaning to ask – what's Arjun's deal?' Louis says. 'How long has he been at Forest Manor?'

'Arjun? Oh, for ever. He trained under some super-fancy Michelin-starred chef up north somewhere, though. Why?'

'Just curious. How's his wine knowledge?'

'Amazing, actually. Our wine cellar is legendary. If you want to sample something in particular, you can always just ask me.'

'And why's Arjun stayed at Forest Manor so long, do you think?'

I frown, thinking of what Lucas said about Louis' plans for Forest Manor. I wrap my aching fingers around my gingerbread hot chocolate.

'I think he loves the hotel. Same as me.'

'Right, but . . .' Louis seems to realise that this is more inter-rogation than conversation. He laughs. 'Sorry. Just making sure he'll be sticking around. He's such an asset, and if I'm going to be investing in Forest Manor Hotel . . .'

I relax slightly. If he wants Arjun, he can't be planning to turn the place into flats.

'Why *do* you guys love Forest Manor so much?' Louis asks. 'It's almost certainly going under in the new year. But none of you have left for a new job. What's that about?'

I reach around for the words to capture it. The magic of Forest Manor at its best: sconce lights glowing, live music playing, the warm hubbub of a happy crowd in the dining room. All the weddings: those love stories that found their happily-ever-after against the backdrop of our beautiful sandstone walls. And, for me, the coffees and heart-to-hearts with Arjun after dinner

286

service has ended and neither of us wants to go home; the slow-growing friendships with guests like Mr Townsend who come to the hotel year after year; the sense of being part of something that brings joy in a harsh, frightening world.

'You know when people say somewhere is a home away from home?' I say. 'I think it's that. For all of us. So when we're talking about losing our jobs . . . we're also kind of talking about losing our home.'

'Right, wow. That's cool.'

He doesn't get it, I can tell. Suddenly, I can't be bothered with much more of this. I planned to wait longer, but as we walk slowly between the stalls, I find myself saying, 'Louis, I don't think we should see each other like this any more. I'm just not feeling a spark.'

'This again!' he says, nudging me. 'Izzy, you said you'd relax and give this a proper shot.'

I frown. 'I am. I have.'

'All right, sure,' he says easily. 'I hear you loud and clear. You want a mulled wine?'

'What? No, Louis, I want to head home, OK?'

'You certain?'

'I'm certain,' I say, with emphasis.

'OK.' He smiles. 'Let's head back to my car, then.'

He's just the same all the way home, chatting away. At first I assume it's an act – he was so keen at The Angel's Wing – but he seems genuinely fine. Maybe he was losing interest too, or maybe he just doesn't want me to feel bad about calling things off. Whatever the reason, I'm relieved: I'd worried he might get petty, or even let it affect his potential investment in the hotel, but he asks more questions about Forest Manor as we hang around outside my flat, and then hugs me goodbye like we're friends. It's nice to wave him off with absolutely zero regrets.

Once I get inside, I settle in on my sofa with a bowl of Krave and an episode of *The Vampire Diaries* that I know so well I can reel off half the lines from memory. Everything I could possibly need.

Except I keep checking my phone. Opening WhatsApp, closing it again. If I'm honest with myself, I'm thinking about Lucas. I want to know what he's doing tonight.

For some reason.

Ugh.

I stare at the TV. The trouble is, last night was just so . . . memorable. I feel like every inch of it is traced across my skin – as though instead of getting rid of Lucas, I've tattooed him there. The rasp of his breath, the solid muscle of his shoulders, the words he whispered in low, quick Portuguese . . .

I swallow. Maybe the problem is that it was all so rushed.

Maybe it's not really getting it out of your system if it's a snatched hour in a car. Maybe I just need a bit . . . more.

And then, just as I'm about to cave and open WhatsApp, a new message appears. From Lucas. Who has not messaged me since 2021.

How was the market?

I scrunch up my nose. Since when does Lucas ask me how my evening is going?

It was gorgeous, I reply after a moment. *So festive.*

I pause, and then I do something very bad. I type, *I was kind of preoccupied, though.*

Preoccupied with what?

Thinking. About last night.

His next reply doesn't come for fifteen minutes, and I feel as if I am quite possibly about to die of embarrassment. I fidget on the sofa, trying to concentrate on the television. I'll just quit my job, I think to myself. I'll just never go back to work, so I never have to see him again after sending that message and not getting a reply.

When he finally writes back, the message is infuriating.

How was Louis? is all it says.

I type my reply before I can think better of it.

Are you jealous?

His response is instantaneous this time.

Yes.

I knew it.

Was it a date?

What's it to you? I type.

Can you just tell me that he was respectful?

I roll my eyes. *Lucas.*

Yes?

Is it any of your business what happens between me and Louis?

There's a knock on the door. I slurp the last of the cereal on my way to answer it, sliding the empty bowl on to the kitchen counter.

It's Lucas at my front door, messaging. He must have left his flat the moment I said I was thinking about last night.

He doesn't look up when I open the door; my phone pings in my hand. He's wearing his usual black coat open over loose, low jogging bottoms and a long-sleeved tee, with a duffel bag by his feet. The idea of him right there in my hallway seems as strange and impossible and exciting as the sight of him tipping his head back against the driver's seat, muscles pulling taut in his shoulders, eyes piercing mine.

After a long moment facing each other across the threshold, I glance from Lucas to my phone screen.

No. But can it be my business to check you're OK?

'No,' I say out loud.

'Why not?'

I narrow my eyes at him, but I'm tingling. I've spent all day avoiding that tingle.

'You don't get to be jealous,' I tell him. 'You don't even like me, Lucas. In fact, I'd say this isn't about me at all. It's about another man. It's a stupid macho possessive thing and it's a total red flag for me, if you didn't have enough of those already.'

'I can assure you,' he says, 'I am not thinking about Louis right now. I am thinking about you.' His tone is clipped, and his eyes are all darkness. 'Are you going to let me in?'

'Why would I let you in?'

He doesn't answer that. Not as if he doesn't know, more as if he thinks it's obvious.

'You're being completely obnoxious,' I tell him. 'We had rules. You're breaking them.'

'Tell me to leave, then.'

We face off on either side of the threshold. Slowly, slowly, his gaze shifts. Taking me in. My jumper dress, leggings, the woolly socks I slipped on when I got in the door. Back to the neckline of my dress, the only place where I'm showing skin. As he lifts his eyes to meet mine again, I feel like he's stripped me bare. The tingle is a buzz now, insistent, like the giddy rush of a tequila shot hitting your stomach.

'We said one night,' I say, but even I can hear the lack of conviction in my voice.

'Then I'll leave,' Lucas says, not moving an inch.

I say nothing. He waits.

'Is that what you want, Izzy?'

It absolutely isn't. We made those rules for a reason, though. One night felt safe – I could do that without getting hurt. But to give him more than that, this man who drives me mad all day, who goes out of his way to make my life difficult, who *laughed* when I told him I had feelings for him?

That would be dangerous.

'Tell me to go,' he says, his voice low and rasping as he stands there in my hallway, one step away from coming in.

But I don't. Despite all the reasons I should, that low hot buzz has set in, and no part of me wants to send Lucas away. I know what it feels like between us now. He's not just some abstract fantasy. He's real, and that's even harder to resist.

I cross the threshold between us and kiss him hard, pulling him inside, letting the door close behind us with a short, sharp slam.

*

He doesn't stay over, he just . . . doesn't leave.

We doze for stretches at a time, but the whole night, we're in bed together. From the moment he crosses into my flat and hitches me up against him, he barely says a word in English. He whispers Portuguese against my stomach, my thighs, the back of my neck, but we don't talk.

I wake again at seven, lying flat on top of him, my ear pressed to his chest, my legs falling on either side of his. I can't believe I slept like this – I can't believe *he* did. His body is warm beneath mine, but I'm cold – the duvet is on the floor somewhere. I lift my head, resting my chin on his ribcage, looking up at him. He shifts beneath me, and the feeling of his nakedness sends a ripple through me, tired and distant but there.

He opens his eyes and lifts his head to look at me. We say nothing. I wonder if I should feel embarrassed, or shy, but I don't – I can't muster the energy.

He rubs my arms. 'You're cold,' he says. His voice is throaty and warm.

I twist to the side, rolling off him, reaching over the edge of the bed for my duvet. He pulls it up for me and makes sure my feet are tucked in. I settle on my side, and he does the same, his hand finding its way back to my hip. That casual touch doesn't feel strange, which is strange in itself.

'Sorry,' I say, my voice a little hoarse. 'I didn't mean to fall asleep.'

He regards me steadily, brightly lit under the bedroom light we never turned off last night.

'It doesn't have to be just one night,' he says. 'Or just two.'

I can already feel how much I'll crave him when he's gone. The idea that I could dial down the desire with a night in bed feels so stupid now that I know his body like this. I know the sounds he makes, the way his hands shift over my skin, the casual confidence with which he drives me crazy.

I should shut this down. It's a bad idea on so many levels I've lost count.

Instead, I say, 'We'll piss each other off so much.'

'Maybe.' His eyebrows twitch. 'But we have your rules to help with that.'

'Right, the rules.' I bite my bottom lip. 'Yeah. But . . . I think we'd need one more.'

'More rules,' Lucas says. 'Oh, good.'

'No talking about the past when we're together. If we're fighting, it'll only get toxic.'

His eyes rove over my face, as though he's looking for the answer to a question. I turn over, staring up at the ceiling, my body suddenly too warm under the duvet. I mustn't forget that Lucas has already shown me who he really is. I have to hold on to that.

For an aching moment I wish I could just phone my mum, tell her that I've slept with someone I shouldn't have, and then let her tell me what to do. Let *her* protect me from a broken heart. Just give myself one morning off from always fighting to look after myself.

'All right. But I have a rule too.'

I turn back to him. He's hazier this morning: there's a brush of stubble on his jaw and a tired glaze to his eyes. His hand dropped from my waist when I shifted, but he places it back there, one thumb sliding up and down my bottom rib.

'No seeing other people,' he says.

This doesn't entirely surprise me.

'You mean no Louis?'

He says nothing, just watching me. I am struck by the total bizarreness of having him in my bed, and it sends a shiver through me. He feels it and tightens his grip on my waist for a moment, as if to steady me.

'You are so weird about Louis,' I tell him, trying to gather myself.

'Do you like him?'

I hesitate. I know precisely why I've held back on telling Lucas that there is nothing between me and Louis. For all my talk about red flags, a little, guilty part of me likes that he's jealous.

'No,' I say eventually. 'I've been clear with Louis that there is nothing romantic between us and there never will be. Happy?'

After a long moment, Lucas gives me the ghost of a smile. 'Happy,' he says.

I look away, reaching for my phone to check the time. 'We should go to work,' I say, and another shiver goes through me, because I'm going to have to stand side-by-side with Lucas at the desk, and he's going to be pedantic and rude, and all this – this slow hot dream of a night – will be gone the minute we get out of this bed.

I watch him get ready. How he changes from the man who unravelled me to the man I see every day: shirt perfectly tucked, jaw perfectly shaved, back perfectly straight. As he pulls on his waistcoat, I open Instagram on my phone, looking for distraction, and scroll past a dog video, a book recommendation, and a post from Drew Bancroft.

I pause. Scroll back up again. She's different. Her hair, once long and bouncy, is now cropped short around her ears, and she's changed her big, square glasses for a pair of round ones. *Can you believe this face can't find work rn?!* the caption reads. *If you've got a job going, hit me up please, I promise you I'm fabulous and NEVER late (lol no but really I am working on that).*

Looking at her makes it a *lot* easier to remember the humiliation of that night. Seeing Lucas's hand on her hip as they kissed in the very spot where I'd dreamed of kissing him, screaming at him across the lawn and watching his face turn disdainful . . .

'You'll be late,' Lucas says, looking at me in the mirror.

I switch off my phone screen. 'I won't.'

He glances at his watch. 'You will.'

'I *won't*.'

I pull the duvet up to my chest and try to slow my breathing. I can't believe he stayed here all night. I can't believe I've agreed to doing this again. I can't believe how badly I *want* to.

I'm freaking out a bit. Understandable, maybe, but I'd rather do it when Lucas *isn't* standing right there in front of my bedroom mirror.

His face is blank as he turns to look at me over his shoulder.

'Izzy. It's quarter past. *I* am going to be late. You are still naked under that duvet.'

'Just go, Lucas, OK?'

He frowns, reaching for his duffel bag. 'Fine. If that's what you want.'

As he walks out of my bedroom, I tell myself I'm an adult. I can do this, if I want to. And there's no denying I want to.

I just have to keep my walls up, that's all.

Lucas

Every night we spend together, I learn something about her. The small formation of freckles on her ankle; how she's ticklish there. The way her voice lifts when certain people ring her – Sameera, Grigg, Jem – and how it tightens for anyone else. The photograph of her parents on her bedside table, and how she touches it absently sometimes, the way you might stroke a cat.

By the week before Christmas, I am gone. I am out of my own control. Every time we touch, I feel myself tumble a little further, and every time she gives me a bright, professional smile at work it hurts a bit more. I had imagined the danger in this arrangement would be Izzy losing interest in me after we had sex. But it seems the real danger is me falling in love.

We stick to the rules, but as far as I'm concerned, they're no protection at all. We may not fall asleep together – aside from that first extraordinary night at her flat. But we still hold each other, move together, wrap each other up almost every night.

She shows no sign of getting me out of her system, and I'm more addicted to her than ever.

One night she messages me at three in the morning – she's woken and can't get back to sleep. I suggest a change of location. She's outside my flat within twenty minutes, in my bed within another two, and when dawn breaks, she's naked in my arms, dozing, satisfied. I watch the sky lighten in the gap between my curtains and savour the feeling of her body against mine.

'Can we talk?' I say.

I feel her go still. 'What kind of talking?'

'I want to say that I'm sorry for being jealous when you went to the Christmas market with Louis.' My heart quickens. I've wanted to tell her this for days. If I want Izzy to see me as a human being, to take me seriously, then she needs to know my story. 'He makes me . . . You make me . . . I *am*,' I say, correcting myself in frustration, 'I am on edge when you're with him. My last relationship . . .'

She stiffens in my arms. I keep talking, faster now.

'Camila cheated on me.' It is *painful* saying this out loud. 'Then she acted like – like it was my fault, because I didn't give her enough. So she said she went looking for that love elsewhere. I know it's no excuse for my possessiveness. But I wanted to tell you that there's something behind the jealousy other than just, you know, that I am a man with so many red flags, as you called me. I want you to understand that I'm working on this. I want to be better.'

'Lucas, I . . .' Izzy pulls away from me, reaching for the

overnight bag she brought with her last night. 'That's . . . Thank you. For telling me that. But . . .'

This is not going how I hoped it would. She's tense, avoiding my gaze entirely.

'Izzy?' I say.

She looks upset. I reach for her, but she steps away from the bed.

'I'm just conscious of the time,' she says, and I watch as she pulls herself together, pasting on the Izzy that I see at work: bright, smiling, ready for anything. It's amazing. It takes her less than five seconds.

'We have half an hour. You can stay for a coffee if you want,' I say, feeling a little desperate.

She frowns at me as she ducks down to pull on her socks. 'You don't have to do that.'

'I want to. I'd like to.'

I have to choke it out, and the moment I do, I regret it: her eyes flare wide with alarm again. It's the closest I've come to saying *I like you* out loud. Between Izzy and me, that phrase probably feels as significant as *I love you* would to any other couple.

'You want to have coffee with me?'

'Is that so strange?'

'Yes?' Izzy says, frown deepening. 'A, you hate how I make coffee, you always say I get the milk-to-granule ratio wrong—'

'I would make the coffee. This is my apartment, clearly I will make the coffee. And we will use a cafetière.'

'Oh, of course we will,' she says, and I can't tell if she's amused or irritated. 'B, you go to great lengths never to spend more time than necessary with me every single day, so why would you want to keep me in your flat when you could get me out of it?'

'Because – it's not like that now. I don't do that any more. Haven't you noticed?'

'C,' she says, shoulders creeping higher, voice getting louder. 'We have rules about this stuff.'

'Yes,' I say tightly. 'We have rules. Of course.'

'Lucas, I can't do this if you start – if you start being all nice to me and making me coffee and . . .' She swallows. 'There's a reason we have the rules.'

I cannot think of a single good reason for her fucking rules and I wish I could tell her that, but I can see in her panicked eyes that I'll lose the tiny amount of Izzy I get as soon as I say those words out loud.

'You enjoy your coffee,' she says, yanking her jumper on. 'I'm sure it will be very strong and manly with nary a drop of milk.'

I just stare at her. I have no idea what to say to that. She flushes.

'Maybe we should . . . stop this,' she says. 'It's so – we shouldn't . . . I don't think I can do this.'

'What? No. No, Izzy, wait,' I say, scrabbling out of bed, but she's already slipping away towards the door, doing the awkward wave she does when she's feeling flustered.

'I have to go,' she calls. 'I'll see you at work, OK?'

I stare at my bedroom wall as I hear the front door slam. Fuck. I knew this thing between us was fragile, but I didn't realise I could break it with a single cup of coffee.

*

By the afternoon, I have moved through panic, irritation, frustration and despair. Now I have landed on resolution.

I have a plan.

We had been getting somewhere – she'd messaged me in the middle of the night when she couldn't sleep, and I'd held her as she dozed. Those are small acts of trust. But then I opened up about Camila, and it was too much too soon, and she fled.

If I'm going to change Izzy's mind about the sort of man I am, I suspect I need to take a step backwards before I can move forwards again. I need her to feel comfortable, and there is one dynamic that always works between us.

I finally track her down as I'm leaving the spa. She shoots past me in the corridor, avoiding my gaze, and panic rises through me again. I want to do what I did outside Opal Cottage: test her, move closer, seek out those signs that she still wants me. Instead, I let her go, and then, as she reaches the doors to the spa, I call over my shoulder, 'Just so you know, I've almost found the last ring owner.'

This is an exaggeration. But I have spent two hours on the phone to lots of publicists about whether their clients lost a wedding ring, and various people said they would call me back.

Izzy stops short and swivels to stare at me. 'You mean . . .'

'Goldilocks.'

I can understand her surprise: I have given this contest very little of my attention over the last week. But this morning, I got to work. I found the name I suspect Izzy found days ago – or rather, the fake name.

'You can't have almost found her,' Izzy says. 'I've spoken to *everyone* and nobody can tell me who she is.'

'Well, then. I hope you are practising your elf voice,' I say. I fold my arms, leaning against the wall of the corridor, watching her. 'Poor Mandy always does such a good one.'

Izzy's eyes spark. 'Please,' she says, scathing. 'You're bluffing.'

I shrug. 'OK,' I say, pushing off the wall and heading back towards the lobby.

'Wait,' she says. 'Wait.' She glances around as I turn to face her again. 'This morning,' she says tentatively. 'When I . . .'

'Ran off?' I say, keeping my eyebrows raised.

Her eyes narrow. 'I did not run off.'

'Why were you so scared to have a cup of coffee with me?'

'I was not *scared*.'

'Were you afraid you might enjoy it?'

'Oh, come on.' She straightens up. 'I'm *definitely* not afraid of enjoying a morning coffee with you. God. Do I need to remind you that we have coffee behind the desk most mornings, and it usually ends in an argument about whether or not you are a snobby arsehole about my choice of Starbucks syrups? Spoiler: you absolutely are.'

My lip twitches. Her eyes are sparkling again. Izzy can fake a smile, but she can't fake the way her eyes light up when she's really having fun.

'So you called things off this morning because . . .'

She hesitates for just a moment before saying, 'You weren't sticking to the rules.'

'Ah,' I say. '*Not* because you were scared to have coffee with me.'

'I am *not* – ugh,' she says, throwing her hands in the air. 'You are so infuriating.' She points a finger at me. 'And you are not going to see me in that elf costume.'

I give her a slow smile. 'We'll see,' I say, and walk away.

My smile stays in place as I wind my way through the guests beginning to arrive for the early dinner sitting. I dodge a couple gazing up at our Christmas tree, and two of the Hedgers children, who are fencing with Mr Townsend's walking stick and my umbrella, which I am sure I put behind the front desk.

It's handover time. Poor Mandy greets me with a confused frown as I approach her.

'Izzy says I need to get you a bottle of the 2017 Sauvignon?' Mandy says, immediately getting distracted by several loud *dings* from her phone.

'What? Why?' I ask, moving around the desk. Already my mind is racing. What does it mean? Is it an apology for this morning? Would she like us to drink it together? Is it a gift? What for? 'Oh,' I say, as I look over Mandy's shoulder at Izzy's handover notes. 'That says Louis, not Lucas.'

And suddenly I am no longer thinking of all the reasons Izzy wants me to have a bottle of good wine. Instead, I am thinking of why she would give Louis one. Perhaps she would like *them* to drink it together. Perhaps it is a gift for *him*.

Mandy finishes typing frantically on her phone and squints at the page, pulling her glasses up from her chest, where they dangle on a chain. 'Does it?' she says rather plaintively. She is far too loyal to admit to struggling with Izzy's handwriting. 'Are you sure?'

'I'm certain,' I say.

If my voice is short, Poor Mandy doesn't seem to notice. Her eyes are widening.

'*Does* it?' she says. 'That says Louis? Not Lucas?'

I frown at her. 'Is there a problem, Mandy?'

'No!' she squeaks, still staring down at the word *Louis* on Izzy's notes. 'No, no problem at all! Just . . . me . . . being my usual daft self. Off you go, now, it's your home-time.'

She shoos me away from the desk, her phone dinging loudly again. I collect my bag, reluctant to leave. I would like to stay here for the arrival of Louis' wine. But then my phone buzzes in my pocket, and I find a message from Izzy.

Did you actually put a toy elf on my car?

I smile. So she's going home, then. And if I'm fast, I'll catch her in the car park.

Izzy

Honestly, the man is a child.

The elf is sitting on my wing mirror, and it is giving me the finger.

This is a family hotel. Anyone could have seen this elf. As Lucas strides over to me with that smug half-smirk on his face, I fold my arms and glare at him, but the truth is I'm having to fight not to smile. I feel better than I have all day.

That conversation at his flat this morning really freaked me out. As he'd talked about his ex, this weird surge of emotion had come over me, almost like a hormone hit, like PMS. I felt kind of *vulnerable*.

I never give this man anything – that's how we operate. Both of us are stubborn; neither of us budge an inch. But there he was, naked, telling me about his past, and suddenly I was feeling . . . something. I thought of Jem saying I'm too *cosy* for a relationship like this, and I wondered with panic if she might

305

be right. Lucas was starting to look like a flawed, complex, gorgeous man, when it's absolutely imperative for my well-being that he remains an emotionless arsehole.

Because that's who he is. No matter how he touches me, or what his story is, he's still the guy who laughed at my Christmas card, kissed Drew, and spent all year acting like I'm totally unreasonable *all* the time. He's not one of Jem's romantic heroes, misunderstood and just waiting for the right person to unlock his inner nice guy – he's a regular, thoughtless, competitive pedant who happens to be very good in bed.

But now that we're at work, and he's back to himself, I feel better. All is well. Lucas is still impossible, my walls are still firmly up, and I'm still perfectly safe.

'I thought you might want a – what's it called?' Lucas says, nodding to the elf. 'A sidekick.'

'We have a million things to do, the hotel is falling apart, and you have time to buy a toy elf?'

'I am very good at multitasking,' Lucas says gravely. 'It is part of what makes me so excellent at my job.' His eyes glitter in the darkness. 'For instance, I have managed to spend all day looking for Goldilocks, arranging music for the Christmas party, manning the phones, *and* thinking about you naked.'

I swallow. I was so determined never to sleep with him again after the conversation this morning, but now the suggestion sets something alight deep in my belly, and suddenly my evening plans – *The Princess Switch*, spiced tea, mince pies – feels way less interesting than the idea of driving Lucas home.

'Get in,' I tell him. 'And that elf is riding in your lap, not mine.'

*

The next day should be my day off, but I'm in anyway because we've organised a huge jumble sale at the hotel. It's all-hands-on-deck this morning. Poor Mandy is 'live-tweeting the event', apparently; Barty is polishing everything in sight; even Arjun is carrying an old set of chiffon curtains out on to the lawn. I down a second coffee, trying to look like I wasn't up half the night with Lucas. Arjun already knows something is going on – he saw us pulling in together in Smartie, and gave me a look that said, *Do you know what you're doing there, Ms Jenkins?*

Which I don't. At all. Obviously. Last night with Lucas was breathtakingly hot, and this morning I woke up in his arms, which was a) against the rules and b) extremely risky. We barely made it in on time.

I take a deep breath. It's an absolutely stunning winter morning – with the sun just beginning to scorch through the mist, the gardens are glowing.

'Your friend Grigg is trying to get hold of you,' Lucas says, coming up behind me.

His voice is a dangerous shade of conversational. Lucas playing it casual means he's plotting something, generally. I turn away from the crockery I'm arranging on a picnic blanket to find him holding a large coffee table in one hand in the way that I might hold, say, a large coffee.

'Over there,' I tell him, pointing. 'And what do you mean, Grigg's . . .' I check my phone. Three missed calls. 'God, is he OK?'

'He's panicking about your Christmas present,' Lucas says, showing no signs of carrying the table off to the correct area of the lawn. He's wearing a black scarf over his coat – who owns a plain black scarf? 'He rang reception.'

'Oh.' I have a bad feeling growing in my stomach now. I turn back to my crockery. Would it look better if I put all the teacups together, or . . .

'He wants Jem's address, since you're spending Christmas with her.'

'Right,' I say, unstacking saucers as loudly as possible without breaking anything valuable. Maybe I can just drown this conversation out and then I can pretend it's not happening at all.

'When we went to Shannon's divorce party, at Brockenhurst station, Jem said that you were spending Christmas with Grigg and Sameera.'

'Is that what you choose to remember about our trip to London?'

I can feel the steadiness of Lucas's gaze on the back of my neck.

'Izzy,' he says, with great deliberation. 'Where will you be celebrating Christmas this year?'

'I'm working Christmas.'

'Yes. You are. And do your friends know that?'

'Umm.' I squint down at the picnic blanket. I'm concerned that I might cry if he asks me any more about this.

'I know what it feels like to be away from your family at Christmas,' Lucas says.

I glance over my shoulder at him. Very few people really get that my friends are my family now, just like the team at the hotel. Lucas looks back at me, unreadable, and for a frightening moment I find myself wondering whether he might actually know me really, really well.

I turn back to the teacups. 'I would usually be with Grigg and Sameera this year, but they're spending it in the Outer Hebrides with Grigg's parents.'

Grigg's parents have never taken to Sameera – they have this stupid thing about how me and Grigg should have got together, and it's always awkward when the three of us are with them, mainly because I get so irritated I'm at risk of saying something tactless and that makes Sameera nervous. Now that they've got baby Rupe, it's extra important for them to bond as a family.

So I just told them I'd be with Jem for a second year running, as otherwise she'd be solo for Christmas. They knew she'd got a job in Washington for six months, but I was always a bit vague on the when, so it was all very simple.

'Why don't you tell them the truth?' Lucas asks.

'They'll feel sorry for me.' I look out at the activity on the lawns, the racks of old coats backdropped against the misty grey trees, the cars already pulling up in the car park. 'They all have a lot going on right now. I don't like being a burden on them.'

'I very much doubt they see it that way.'

'Coffee tables are in the corner by the holly bush,' I say. 'You can put that one next to the mahogany one.'

He waits so long I sigh in frustration and straighten up, spinning to look at him.

'Don't feel sorry for me,' I say. 'I'm fine.'

He just looks back at me, and for a moment I have to fight not to tear up. This is stupid. I *am* fine. I've known about this

Christmas business for months – it's just a logistical problem, that's all, and it's easier to keep everyone in the dark so they don't worry about me. I've not cried about it once, so I've no idea why I'm feeling so emotional now.

'Would you put that table down?' I say, exasperated. 'It must weigh about twenty kilos.'

Lucas glances at it, uninterested, shifting its weight slightly in his hand. 'Christmas will still be special, even though they're all a long way away,' he says.

'I know. I *know* that.'

'Ooh, are these teacups a set?' asks a woman behind me.

I spin, never so grateful for an obvious question. 'Yes! They all match. Saucers are just here . . .'

I chitchat until I feel Lucas move away. The woman is just the sort of customer I like – an over-sharer in a fabulous bobble hat – and by the time we've finished talking, I've managed to push all the Lucasness of the morning out of my mind. I'm back to bouncy Izzy again. Smiley, sparkly, and firmly in control.

The next day is the 20th of December, which means I'm off work for the day. It's my mum's birthday, and – even in the days when I couldn't bear to be alone for a moment – I've always spent it solo. The year before Mum died, we'd had a girls' day, just the two of us, and I like to do the same now.

I wake up late and have coffee and cereal in front of *Nativity!*, which my mother always staunchly declared was the world's best Christmas film, though my dad was *Die Hard* all the way.

At first, after the accident, I missed my parents with an

awful, gulping pain. The sort of pain that scoops all the breath out of you. It's not like that now – the ache is duller, and I've adjusted to the emptiness, so it rarely catches me off guard. But as I watch the kids of *Nativity!* dance their way across the stage for the finale, I let myself sink back there for the first time in years. I double over, head on my lap, and remember the day when my life tore in two.

Maybe Lucas did have a point when he said nobody can live life to the fullest all the time. Sometimes it's good to curl up under a blanket and wallow. Afterwards, I pick myself up, chuck the tear-and-snot-soaked blanket in the wash and wipe my face. I shrug on my mum's old denim jacket, pin back my hair and head to Southampton for some Christmas shopping.

I'm just browsing through the rails in Zara when I spot Tristan. My ex-boyfriend.

Tristan and I lasted about three months. I ended it with him, but it could have gone either way – in a matter of weeks, he'd gone from writing me lengthy WhatsApps about how much he loved me to the occasional *Hey, sorry, work's so busy!*, despite the fact that his job was reviewing tech products and he hardly ever seemed to be sent any. He was very defensive about the job. He was defensive about a lot of things: his receding hairline, the fact that his parents bought him a flat, the way he sometimes texted his ex-girlfriend when he was sad or drunk.

He has a new woman in tow now, someone petite and pretty. I watch her fetch Tristan the shoes he wants in a different size, and from over here behind the dresses I feel as though I'm watching the scene play out on TV, with Tristan in the role of 'very average man'. He's so *small*, and I don't mean that physically, I just mean he's . . . blah.

Tristan will no doubt continue to flop through life, eventually marrying one of these women and letting her support him as he pursues some far-fetched ambition he'll be very sensitive about. I can't believe I ever wanted this man.

Really, I'm not sure I *did* ever want him much. He was sweet, at first, and I've always gone for sweet guys – they're safe and comforting, like milk chocolate or boots with a two-inch heel. Nothing remarkable, but no risk of breaking an ankle, either.

But there's no *fire* in Tristan. No grit. Tristan would never stand up for me; he'd never dunk me in a swimming pool fully clothed or dirty dance with me in a divorcee's living room. In the entire time I was with Tristan, we never did anything more exciting together than start a new show on Netflix.

I turn away, abandoning the dress I'd considered buying, and head blindly for the car park. I can't start comparing Lucas to my ex-boyfriends. I shouldn't even be *thinking* of him in those terms. The man has already hurt me once, and everything I've seen of him tells me that he's capable of doing it again without so much as blinking. He's an emotionless, uptight perfectionist, and yes, we have great sex, but that's *all* we have. And it's very, very important that it stays that way.

But I can't stop thinking about wishy-washy Tristan. Playing out scenes from our relationship. Imagining those moments with Lucas, and then trying very hard not to notice that if Lucas had been there, they wouldn't have been *blah*, those moments. No single moment with Lucas ever has been.

Lucas

I am stuck. I don't have a clue how to move things forward with Izzy without scaring her off, but I can't go on like this for much longer, having her without having her. I know it's exactly what I agreed to – but it's also torture.

Surprisingly, it's Pedro who finally gives me an idea. He comes over for a beer in the evening and he tells me that if you want to change the way someone sees you, sometimes all you need to do is change the background. This is actually a comment about optimising Smooth Pedro's Instagram page, but wisdom can come from the most unexpected of places.

So on the night of December 21st, I tell Izzy that we aren't going back to my flat, we're going to Pedro's caravan in the woods.

'Pedro lives in a caravan?' she asks.

'A very nice one. He needed someone to look after it while he's away.'

(Staying in my flat.)

'And it's in the middle of the woods?' Izzy asks with suspicion.

'What, do you think I am leading you into these woods to feed you to the ponies?'

'Well, no,' she allows. 'But I'm not really in the right footwear for this.'

I stop and crouch in the middle of the dimly lit woodland path. It's a beautiful, sharp winter evening. I can smell pine and moss: the deep, ancient scent of these English woods.

'Are we doing squats?' Izzy asks.

'No,' I say, as patiently as I can manage. 'You are climbing on my back.'

'Oh!'

She jumps aboard without hesitation, and another fragment of my heart goes tumbling. Her body trusts me now, even if the rest of her doesn't. I shift her slightly so we're both comfortable; she laces her hands around my neck and settles in.

Pedro's caravan really is very nice. He's strung lights around his porch, and they dangle over the bed inside too, tracing tracks across my eyelids as I lie back in the sheets and close my eyes. I wonder if I will ever be able to see a string of fairy lights without thinking of Izzy Jenkins.

'Oof.'

She lands right on top of me. Knees on either side of my hips, and – I open my eyes – no trousers on. She snuggles in, doubling over to lay her head against my chest.

'Mm. Good duvet.'

I close my arms around her and hold her like she's mine, but she's not mine at all. She starts to kiss my neck and my body responds instantly. I put my hands on her upper arms, holding her back.

'The lasagne will be done in ten minutes.'

She pulls back. 'Lasagne?'

'It's just a pre-made one,' I say. 'I thought we should eat.'

We never eat together, usually. But there isn't a specific rule against it.

'Well, I guess . . .' She frowns. 'I *am* hungry.'

'We could wait for it outside on Pedro's porch. You can see the stars.'

Her frown deepens. 'Umm,' she says. '*Or* we could . . .'

She presses a slow kiss to my neck. My breath hitches. I brush my hands up and down her arms, trying to ignore the way she wriggles in my lap, making this plan significantly more difficult.

'Come on,' I say, closing my eyes for a moment and then rolling her over, pressing a kiss to her lips as I shift off the bed. 'There's a heater out there.'

She pulls her trousers back on and follows me slowly. It's beautiful out here. The caravan sits in a carefully mown patch of lawn bordered by the forest on all sides. Pedro has laid some pale wooden decking, with two chairs facing out to the trees. I bend to switch the lights off as Izzy settles in her seat.

I have to walk with my arms out in front of me to find my chair. Slowly, my eyes begin to adjust. The moon is half full, bright white above the trees, and the stars are extraordinary. It's as if someone has sown them like seeds across the sky.

'Oh, wow,' Izzy breathes, looking up. 'I've actually never seen them looking so clear. I guess . . . less light pollution here than at the hotel.'

'It's beautiful, isn't it?'

I can barely see her nod in the darkness. I sit back in the chair, trying to find calmness in the star-soaked sky.

'How was your day?' I try.

She pauses. 'You have literally never asked me that before.'

'No?'

'Nope. Never. Anyway, you know how my day was. You were there.'

It's a rare acknowledgement of real life outside of our evenings together. I pounce on it.

'You seemed irritated with Poor Mandy this afternoon.'

'She said she'd help me find out who Goldilocks is, and then got distracted doing a reel for Instagram. I love that woman, but she gets scattier by the day, and introducing her to social media means she's pulled in even more directions at once.'

I hear Izzy sigh. An owl hoots in the forest and another answers. Through superhuman effort, I manage not to point out that asking for help to find the owner of the last ring could *definitely* be regarded as cheating. The bet was between me and Izzy. But I suppose I should have known she would play dirty.

'We're all stressed, with New Year looming, I do get that,' she continues. 'I feel pretty scatty too, to be fair. The renovation work is just so . . . consuming, but in a really good way, like I feel as though I'm doing something *me* and . . .' She pauses. 'Sorry. I shouldn't be talking about work.'

'I don't mind.'

'No, it's . . . It's better that we keep it separate.' She pulls her knees up underneath her, face upturned, pale in the moonlight.

'I'm glad you're enjoying work on the renovations. Is it what you'd like to do, longer term?'

'Lucas . . .'

I am prepared for this.

'We said no talking about the past. I'm talking about the future.'

I can feel her hesitation. This conversation is making her uneasy. I wish I knew why. She's so determined to keep me out of her life – I can't understand it. What's the risk? Why can't she just try?

'Well . . . yeah. I still have a bit of a yen to do the upcycling business thing. I would never want to leave Forest Manor, though, if it still existed. It's my home.'

'You could work part-time at both.'

'I guess.' She reaches down to pull a blanket out from under the chair, tucking it over her knees, hair swinging across her face so I can't even see what little the moonlight gives of her expression. 'But starting my own business feels so risky. It'd be safer just to get a waitressing job if the hotel goes under.'

I frown. Izzy never particularly enjoys waiting tables at the hotel.

'Time sometimes feels like it's . . . I don't know,' she says. 'It's just streaming by and I'm happy, obviously, I'm so content in my life, but, like, I haven't even *thought* about the upcycling project for months, and it's been years since I first came up with the idea, and I've just . . .' She rubs her face. 'Anyway.'

'Go on.'

'No, it's fine, I'm all good. Ignore me.'

The oven dings.

'And there's the lasagne,' Izzy says, with audible relief.

She flicks the light on as she heads back inside, and the stars blink out, washed away by the artificial glare. I stay where I am, running over what she told me. *Content*, she said. As though it means the same thing as happy. But I don't think it does.

'Oh, you burned it!' she calls from the kitchen.

I sit bolt upright, horrified. 'Did I?'

I hear her snort with surprised laughter. 'Oh my God.'

'What?'

I look over my shoulder as she appears in the doorway, over-baked M&S lasagne on a tray in her hands.

'Sorry, I just had to see your face, Mr Perfectionist.'

She's grinning. Her hair is half tucked into the neck of her jumper. Izzy always seems at home wherever she is, but right now she looks particularly comfortable. This is good. This is progress. When we're in bed together, Izzy relaxes, but when we're not, she's usually wary, as if I'm about to sprout devil horns.

'What?'

'You just cannot handle messing anything up, can you?' she says, teasing.

I eye the lasagne. It is very dry and brown at the edges. Pedro's oven must be more powerful than mine. Izzy starts to laugh.

'You are ridiculous. It's a lasagne! Nobody cares.'

'I care,' I say. 'I want you to have the best things.'

She sobers at that, looking at me, round-eyed.

'Lucas,' she says, softly now. 'You can relax. It's just me.'

It's just me. Like she isn't fucking *everything.*

'After all, what's the point in having a fling with someone you don't care about if you can't let things hang a bit, you know?' she calls over her shoulder as she heads back inside. 'Just enjoy the fact that you give no shits about what I think of you, and try *not* being perfect for once.'

I look back at the sky and then close my eyes as the caravan door swings shut behind her. *Ah, porra.* We're getting absolutely nowhere.

She doesn't stay over at the caravan. I spend the whole next day fearful that I've scared her away, but then, at one minute past five, my phone buzzes, and my heart leaps in response, like Pavlov's dog salivating. A message at this time almost always means the same thing. *Come to mine later?* it says.

I wolf down my dinner at home and check my reflection on my way out, trying not to notice the tension in my jaw. Every time we do this, things get better and worse all at once. There's no way to argue that this is anything other than foolishness – I am clearly going to get hurt. I'm getting hurt already. And still I knock on her door, feeling that double kick in the gut when she opens it dressed in delicate, pale-pink lingerie.

'You look incredible.' My throat is dry.

She blushes at the compliment; it touches her shoulders and throat, and I lift my hand to trace the heat on her skin, feeling her pulse quicken under my touch. She pulls me inside and into the bedroom, on to the covers, under them, into her, and just

like every time, I let myself believe that she'll ask me to stay
the night.

Her phone rings when she's close, almost there, sweat beading
on the skin between her breasts. Her head is tipped back so I can
see the full bareness of her throat. These moments are always
the ones when I am most hopeful. When she comes apart in my
arms, she's absolutely herself, hiding nothing. If she's ever going
to really *see* me then I sometimes think it'll be in a moment like
this, as we teeter, eyes locking, bodies letting go.

'Look at me,' I whisper.

And she does. The phone rings out, and she gasps against my
lips just as I gasp against hers. She grips me so fiercely, and I
hold her just as tightly, and for a moment I wonder if she might
not want to let me go.

The phone rings again, and this time she groans, loosening
her grip and rolling away to answer it.

'Grigg,' she says, reaching for her dressing gown. 'Do you
mind if I answer? You can just chill here if you want.' She hesitates. 'Or go, if you'd rather . . .'

'I'll wait,' I say quickly.

She disappears into the living area, then I hear the door to
her spare room closing behind her. I look around her bedroom.
I've never been in here without her before. The colour scheme
matches the living area, and matches Izzy: soft pastels, faint
polka dots and fluffiness.

I catch sight of the bath through the bathroom door and
wonder. There is no specific rule about baths, but running her
one would feel like a step up from leaving the minute we're

done, and she did say I could stay here. What was her plan for afterwards?

I head into the bathroom. There is a gold-edged mirror above the basin, and make-up cluttered across the surfaces. I'm just turning on the taps when I hear her voice.

'The sex is *incredible*,' Izzy is saying.

It is almost perfectly clear through the bathroom wall, even with the water running. I retreat to the door after a split second's hesitation, but then she says, 'But I'll never be his girlfriend, will I?'

I freeze. I can't hear Grigg and Sameera's response, just a tinny rattle of voices.

'I mean, the sex doesn't really change anything. He's still . . . Lucas. *That* guy.'

I should leave. I don't. Horror settles quietly in my stomach.

'Who, Louis?' she says.

I bite down on my lip.

'Oh, yeah, I guess so.'

More echoing, indistinct voices.

'Yeah, he's still a contender,' she says. 'Still in the game. That's how he'd put it,' she says, and there's something in her voice I can't identify – a sort of fondness, maybe, or wryness. 'Ugh, it's been such a mad couple of weeks. Anyway, how are you two? How did Rupe manage the journey?'

I withdraw, clicking the bathroom door shut.

I leave her flat, walking blindly to my car. I think about all the ways I've tried to show her the sort of man I am. How I've treasured every moment with her, and tried to make her feel treasured too, and yet still I'm '*that* guy'. Good enough to take to bed but not a *contender*. Not like Louis.

Before this winter, she would just have been proving everything I already felt about myself. But these last few weeks have changed me. *I've* changed me. Now, through the chorus in my head telling me I'm not good enough, there is a small voice saying, *actually . . . I deserve better than this.*

Izzy

What the fuck?

I stare down at the bath, water still glugging down the over-flow pipe, and then around at my empty flat.

He just . . . left?

I know I was gone a while chatting to Grigg and Sameera, but surely he'd pop his head in to say bye if he had to shoot off?

I call Grigg back. He looks unperturbed.

'What did you forget?' he says.

'Lucas left.'

'Left?'

'He's . . . gone. Without saying bye. He left the bath running . . .'

Grigg blinks a few times and then says, 'Maybe he's passed out somewhere?'

'God, maybe,' I say, heading out of the bathroom to check for collapsed Lucases behind sofas and doors. My flat is small – this doesn't take long. 'Nope. Just not here.'

'It must have been an emergency. Have you rung him?'

'No,' I say, feeling stupid. 'I rang you.'

'Call him, then call me back, OK?'

He's gone. I flick to my WhatsApp with Lucas. Above our last exchange – *Come to mine later? I'll be there at eight* – is this:

You left your pink socks with fairies on them here.

Are you sure those aren't yours?

. . .

Ha OK bring them next time you come over. Or wear them to work? Good conversation-starter?

I actively avoid starting conversations. Conversations find me more often than I would like as it is.

You are so ridiculously grumpy for a man in hospitality.

I warm up sometimes. For some people.

I swallow. It looks . . . flirty. Coupley, almost. That's exactly what Sameera and Grigg said on the phone, too. *So are you dating, now?* Sameera had asked, nose wrinkled. *When does having non-stop sex become a relationship?*

But it's not a relationship – it can't be. There are rules.

I gnaw the inside of my lip as Lucas's number rings and rings. No answer. I hang up and message Grigg, and then sit down on the edge of the very full bath.

I am more unsettled than I would like to be. Lucas and I are . . . a fling. We're flinging. I shouldn't care if he's acting like a dickhead, walking out without saying goodbye. But I do, and that's scaring me a *lot*, and the overfull bath is making the whole thing feel especially dramatic.

I message him.

Are you OK? Where did you go?

He sees it but doesn't reply. I can't decide whether I'm worried or angry, but I hope it's angry, because if I'm worried, that means I care, and I *mustn't*. I've put my heart on the line for Lucas da Silva before and it was such a disaster. I am not a person who lets someone burn her twice. Life is too short for wasting time with people who don't deserve you.

I'm fine. I just needed some space.

I stare at the message, baffled, until another pops up.

Apologies about the bath.

Ugh. This man. He is *bewildering*. I chuck my phone on to the bathmat and strip off. If I'm going to mope around about Lucas, I might as well make use of this bathwater. I sink into the water, my heart thumping hard, and I tilt my head back as the heat begins to relax my muscles. *You don't care about Lucas*, I remind myself. *He doesn't care and you don't care.* But as I close my eyes, I can still feel my heart thudding in my ears, and it's not slowing down.

'Sweetie, I only have five minutes, max,' Jem whispers into the phone. 'It is *so* cold out here. I may die of frostbite, and Piddles definitely feels the same way. But I have so much I want to say to you. I feel like I'm going to have to be Mean Jem.'

Jem is standing outside her parents' house – if she takes a call inside, she'll wake everybody up. It is so good to hear her voice. It's the middle of the night and I am foraging in my fridge, because after lying awake for hours you really start to realise how long it's been since your last meal. I don't normally go this long without eating when I'm awake, so why start now?

'You know what I think your mum would say to you right now?'

Oof. Jem is one of the few people who will throw my parents into conversation without flinching. She lived on my road when we were at primary school, and was around at our place all the time – my dad used to joke that they'd only wanted one kid but it seemed this extra one came with the house. She's the only person who could guess at what my mum would say and actually have me listen.

'She'd say you're being stubborn as a mule and blind as a bat. How can you not see how much you love this boy?'

I stare wordlessly across my kitchen. I can hear Jem blowing on her hands to warm them up.

'Hello? Can you hear me?' she says.

'Yeah, hi, I can hear you, I just . . . *What?*'

'Izzy . . . I'm pretty sure you've loved him all year.'

'I have not! I hated him until about five minutes ago!'

'OK, so, let's try this,' Jem says. 'Tell me the other people you've really hated in your life. People who give you that icky, skin-crawl, what-an-asshole feeling.'

I think about it. 'Obviously evil dictators and stuff.'

'People you know, I mean.'

'Oh, Mr Figgle!' I say, grabbing a bottle of milk and heading for the freezer. Milkshake. Milkshake is the answer. 'Our old PE teacher, remember? He was so horrible to the kids who didn't play sports, and do you remember he laughed at Chloe when she said it wasn't fair that only the boys got to have a football team?'

'Anyone else?'

'Kyle from my interior design course,' I say. 'He gaslit like, six girls on the course. A total sleaze.'

'Gross. Go on.'

I think I'm already out. Hate is a strong word and generally speaking I quite like most human beings. Except Lucas, obviously.

'So . . . did you want to have sex with either of those people?' Jem asks.

'No, eww,' I say, peeling a banana and splitting it into the blender.

'But *Lucas* . . .'

'Yeah, it's a bit different, he looks like a Brazilian god,' I point out, whirring the blender. 'Sorry, milkshake. Mr Figgle looked like a meerkat.'

'Do you think . . . maybe . . .'

'It's OK,' I assure her. 'You can be Mean Jem.'

'Sometimes you can be a tiny bit stubborn? And sometimes . . . you like to take the easy option.'

I pour out my milkshake in silence.

'Sorry, I love you,' Jem says. 'I love you, I love you.'

'Yes, I love you too,' I say tetchily. 'What do you mean, take the easy option?'

'Well, committing to a relationship with a man who's hurt you before? That's hard. Having sex with him and insisting that you don't want anything serious? Much easier.'

This blows my mind a little. It feels terrifyingly true.

'Shit.'

'Truth-bomb?' Jem says apologetically.

'Yeah, kind of. I felt like doing it this way would be safe,' I say, testing the thought out, chewing my bottom lip. 'But when I realised he'd left the flat I felt . . .'

Jem waits patiently. But I do feel the pressure of her impending frostbite.

'I felt scared.'

'Ooh, OK, now we're getting somewhere!' whispers Jem. 'Scared of what?'

My voice keeps getting smaller and smaller.

'. . . Having lost him.'

'This guy you hate, you mean?'

'Fine, hate is over dramatic, I know that. But we don't get on. We disagree on everything. We argue all the time. He behaved like a twat last Christmas and never apologised!'

But even as I say it, a hundred other things come to mind. How fiercely he stands up for what he thinks, even when it would be easier to back down and agree with me. How his eyes go soft when he talks about his baby nephew. How he pulls me against him when I turn up at his door, like he can't stand another second of distance between us.

'What would happen if you talked to him about last Christmas, little pigeon?'

I recoil at the very thought. My whole body shrinks inwards as though someone's doused me in cold water.

'No,' I say firmly. 'No, we have a rule about talking about the past.'

'Do you think . . . maybe . . .'

'Go on, just say it.'

'Do you think this is why you made that stupid rule in the first place?' Jem says in a rush. 'Like, *why* don't you want to talk to him about last Christmas?'

'Argh. Because – Jem, it's so humiliating.'

'And why's that?'

'Because . . .'

'Without wanting to put the pressure on, I have lost all sensation in my feet.'

'Because it actually *hurt*,' I blurt. 'I didn't think it would. I thought it was fun and brave when I wrote it, but knowing he laughed at that card? Tossed it aside and made out with Drew, of all people? It makes me want to curl up in a ball.'

'And why's that?'

'Because . . . Because . . .'

'Even my *hair* is cold right now.'

'Because I *really liked him*.'

'Yesss,' Jem says. I hear a creak down the line – I suspect she just did a small hop on the porch. 'It wasn't a casual "hey, I fancy you", that card. It was you handing him your heart. And you've never done that with a guy before.'

'I've had loads of boyfriends,' I say. I can hear how defensive I sound. This whole conversation is making me squirm.

'Ye-es,' Jem says. 'But men like Tristan and Dean.'

I scrunch up my nose. 'Yeah?'

'They're sort of, umm . . . nothingy? Like, they're safe options. You're OK when it ends because you never really cared about them in the first place.'

'Can we do you now?' I say, getting a bit desperate. 'Are you having a crisis, at all?'

'We can do me tomorrow, when I can feel my extremities again. Lucas isn't safe and nothingy, right?'

He's not. He's fire and steel and ice. When I'm with him, whether we're in bed or in the hotel, I'm always feeling *something*.

'I have a really horrible feeling about how this conversation is going to end,' I say.

'I think you have to talk to Lucas about last Christmas,' Jem says.

I make a sound somewhere between a wail and a growl. 'No! No, you're wrong, I can just keep that in a box for evermore and keep having lovely sex with my annoying colleague!'

'OK, so, none of that is happening. But I really love you. And I'm sorry. Can you forgive me for being Mean Jem?'

'Don't be ridiculous, you've been a massive help,' I say. 'Thank you for risking frostbite for me.'

'Always!' she says, and then she shrieks. 'Piddles! Oh, shit.'

I wince at the cacophony on the other end of the line. There is definitely a cat yowling over there. And possibly a dustbin falling over.

'Anything I can do?' I say, sipping my milkshake.

'Unless you can catch Piddles remotely, no,' says a breathless Jem. 'Bye, pigeon.'

'Good luck!' I call, just as the barking begins.

Lucas

When Izzy walks into the Forest Manor lobby in the morning, I'm braced. I'm sure my face is wearing the wary expression I've seen so often on hers over the last year.

I was up until three a.m. and still I have no idea what I want to say. I walked out of her flat and left the bath running. That is ridiculous. I don't *do* things like that, but then, around Izzy, I do all sorts of things I thought I would never do.

And I can't stop hearing the words she said. *I'll never be his girlfriend, will I?*

Every time I remember how good it feels between us, I come back to that, and the anger flares up again. The worst part is that I've led myself right here: I went into this situation knowing that she disliked me and wanted nothing more than a physical relationship. She has been extremely clear about that. So I *can't* be angry. Which only makes me feel more furious.

331

'Hello,' Izzy says. Her tone is perfectly cool. 'As you can see, I have not drowned. No thanks to you.'

If she wants to rile me up, she's done it. *That's* how she wants to start this conversation? Flippancy, finger-pointing, childishness? It's everything we used to be, and I hate it.

I jerk my head towards the lost-property room and spin away from the desk. There's nowhere to sit in here except on a box, so I stand with my arms folded, and after closing the door behind her, she does the same.

'I apologise about the bath . . . situation.' I can hear how stiff I sound. I'm being the Lucas she used to know, the one I've been working so hard to help her forget. *That guy.*

'Thanks. And how about the disappearing act?'

'I heard you on the phone. I had to leave.'

Her eyebrows fly up. 'You were listening to my phone call with my friends?'

'No! No. I went to run you a bath and the wall . . . I just heard it.'

'Right.' Her gaze is level. 'And what exactly did you "just hear"?'

The air crackles between us. It always does. I'm furious and scared, but I still want to walk her back against the wall and kiss her.

'What you really think of me. That's what I heard.'

She frowns. 'I don't remember exactly, but I don't think I said anything about what I *really think of you* except maybe . . .' Her cheeks are turning slowly pink. 'How good it is between us. The sex.'

There's a knock at the door just as she says *sex*. We both jump as if we've been caught half-dressed.

Izzy opens the door. It's Louis Keele. The way my body reacts is shameful. A rush of adrenaline, my fists bunching, muscles flexing. It's pure, animal jealousy and there's no place for it – but the way he looks at Izzy makes me want to hit him.

He's still a contender, she said. *That's how he'd put it.*

É, com certeza . . .

'Can I grab you for a sec, Izzy?' he says. Ignoring me completely.

They walk out into the lobby. I follow. Louis clearly wants to have Izzy to himself. I hover within reach, looking busy, making it obvious I'm in earshot. Louis stays on this side of the desk, crossing that line, because he's just the sort of man who doesn't respect a boundary.

'Listen, I'm still weighing up the investment,' he says. 'My dad suggested getting another tour from someone who really knows the *heart* of the place. And who does heart better than Izzy Jenkins? What do you say – could you spare some time this afternoon?'

'Sure!' Izzy says. 'Whatever you need.'

They chitchat. Izzy pats his arm when he says something about his father, and I remind myself that she is like this: tactile by nature with everyone but me. Even now, she still won't touch me like that at work.

I'm exhausted. I scan over the hotel's Kickstarter page and am unable to register whether the sum has gone up since I last hit the button. Someone drops by to pick up an item they saw for sale on our Facebook page, and says 'Totally love you guys!' on her way out, which strikes me as a sign that Poor Mandy is selling things far too cheaply. Then Arjun leans his head through from the restaurant and calls for Izzy, finally pulling her away from Louis.

'Are you all right, Izz?' I catch Arjun saying as they walk through to the kitchen.

He glances back at me. I wonder how much she's told him.

'I'm fine! It's chopped parsley you want, right?' Izzy says brightly, because of course she already knows exactly what he needs.

'I'm shooting my shot with Izzy today, you know,' Louis says to me. He leans forward on the desk, watching Izzy disappear through the restaurant doors with Arjun. 'Got high hopes.'

'Have you?' I snap, not even bothering to veil the dislike in my voice – I don't have the energy. 'I thought you two were finished.'

He gives a coy smile. 'This thing with Izzy's been slow-building since last December – we've had the odd setback, but . . .'

I grip the back of my desk chair, breathing too fast.

'Last December?'

'Yeah. When I first came to the hotel.' He fiddles idly with the cord on my telephone. 'She told me how she felt about me then.'

My whole body flinches, knuckles turning white on the back of the chair.

'I had a girlfriend at that point, so I didn't act on it, but I kept the card she sent me.' Louis pats the back pocket of his trousers. 'I'm going to whip it out today. Win her round once and for all. Nothing says romance like holding on to a love letter for a whole year, does it?'

334

I don't know what to say. I am staring at Louis' back pocket, desperate to read this card, playing the words Izzy said over and over as my heart races. *I've been clear with Louis that there is nothing romantic between us and there never will be.*

Louis must be mistaken. He must be.

'What did . . . What did her card say?'

Slowly, with deliberation, Louis pulls out a battered Christmas card from his pocket. He waves it at me with a cheeky grin. This fake heart-to-heart we are having makes my skin crawl.

'Says she's *infatuated*. Gets hot every time we cross paths at the hotel. Wants to kiss me under the mistletoe.' He shrugs. 'I get why she's colder this year – we need to build the trust. I didn't reply to the card, did I? Probably hurt her feelings. But there's been that spark between us once, and that sort of thing doesn't just go away. She's single, she's made that clear, so . . .'

I know why he's telling me this. He's marking out his territory, playing his move so I know there's no use me playing mine. We may be standing here in smart shirts talking politely, but really we're fighting like stags.

'Anyway. Wish me luck, lad,' Louis says with a wink, and then he claps me on the arm.

I twitch. I am one scrap of self-control away from spinning around and punching him in the stomach.

'See ya,' he says, strolling away with a smile.

That's it. It's finished. If there's even anything to finish. I was never hers and she was never mine, so I suppose there's no break-up here. Just me, opening myself up to someone who's chosen someone else.

And why wouldn't she? Despite everything I've done, when she looks at me, she sees a man who's not good enough. And for all the effort I've made to fight those feelings, for all the times I've hung up on my uncle and told myself *you're doing great*, it's really fucking hard to believe I'm worth something when the woman I love thinks a *cuzão* like Louis is a better man than me.

I look up to find Mr Townsend watching me. I turn away sharply, aware of the tears in my eyes.

'Son,' he says, 'are you all right?'

I breathe out slowly, trying to get control of myself. 'No,' I say. 'I'm not. I want to go home.'

Izzy

No. No no no no no no.

Louis and I are in the turret room, at the window where Lucas gave me Brazilian food and introduced me to his family. The sun is setting above the trees, gorgeous in powder pink.

I have the card in my hands. *The* card. It has two cute penguins on the front, both wearing Christmas hats. I never thought I would see this card again.

It's a lot smaller than I remember. I am holding it with my fingertips, as though at any moment it might explode.

'Louis.'

I open the card and in comes a wave of shame and humiliation as I remember writing it, how brave I'd felt. Putting myself out there. Being bold. Living life to the fullest, just like my parents always wanted.

Dear Lucas, it says. *I have a confession to make.*

'Louis . . . This wasn't your Christmas card.'

For the first time since I've known Louis, he looks unsure of himself.

'Pardon?' he says, ducking his head to look at it with me.

'Lucas.' I press my hand to my forehead. *Oh my God.* 'I wrote this for *Lucas.*'

'Then why does it say . . .' He trails off. 'You have really bad handwriting,' he says after a moment, and there's an edge to his voice now.

'I am so sorry, Louis.'

'So it's Lucas you want, then,' Louis says, stepping back slightly. The sunset bathes us in rosy light; it's a very romantic setting. I suppose that's why he got the card out. The perfect moment. 'It's always been him?'

The question floors me. Because . . . well, yes, it has, really. I've cursed him and crossed him and kissed him, but yeah, it's always been him, hasn't it? Nobody has ever made my cosy warm heart beat the way he does.

I was infatuated then, and if I am entirely honest with myself, I'm infatuated now.

And he never knew. He *never knew.*

'I really am so sorry, Louis. But I need to go, I've got to . . .'

He frowns, interrupting me. 'Your colleague, that sorry-for-herself one, she gave the card to me. She said it was for me.'

I wince. Poor Mandy has never complained about my hand-writing, but Lucas always says she gets him to translate half the stuff I write down. I thought he was exaggerating. It's always perfectly clear to *me.*

'I guess she must've read it wrong too. I'm sorry.'

Louis' expression shifts. He seems to go from affable to calculating in a flash.

'Does Mrs SB know you and Lucas have been getting off with each other on company time?'

I stare at him. 'What? No, she . . . But we haven't been . . .'

I trail off. Because, well, we have, a bit.

'What are you going to do?' I ask. 'Dob me in?'

I'm kind of joking, but Louis just looks at me appraisingly for a moment.

'Do you know how many women would kill to have me take them to The Angel's Wing?'

'Excuse me?'

'You think you're really special, Izzy, with your multicoloured hair and your cute "mission" to save this hotel. But the truth is you're just a mousey little nobody in a dead-end job. It's kind of sad.'

My mouth drops open. Louis' nastiness is so sudden and so unexpected that his words don't really land at all – in fact, as he slicks back his hair and adjusts his expensive jacket, I find myself wanting to laugh at him.

'A mousey little nobody? Oh, Louis.' I shake my head, shoving the card into my back pocket. 'You know what's really sad? The fact that you seem to think you're somebody.'

I spin towards the door, already moving. I don't have time for this slimeball – I need to find Lucas. I need to explain. God, what's he been thinking all this time? What was he thinking when we had that screaming match after the Christmas party last year? What was he thinking when I said I hated him, couldn't trust him, never would?

I want to cry. It's as if the last year has shifted like an optical illusion, and suddenly I'm seeing a completely different picture. I just – I just *have* to find Lucas.

Poor Mandy is settling in at the desk, Mr Townsend is in his chair, the motley collection of builders are mostly on ladders, and three restaurant guests are making their way to the door. But no Lucas in sight.

It's half four – I've never known him leave early before. Typical. I hover in front of the desk for a moment, craning my neck to look for his car in the car park, but it's not in his usual spot – he'll have gone home, to the gym, or to Smooth Pedro's. My money is on the gym, and I'm itching to get into Smartie and chase him down, but . . .

'Mandy,' I say, turning to look at her.

'Oh, God, Izzy, I'm so sorry!' she blurts instantly.

She covers her face with her hands. I stare at her.

'You know, don't you?' she says, peeking out between her fingers. 'I promise you, I only figured out what happened the other day when Lucas told me I'd misread Louis' name on your handover notes. I *swear* it was an accident.'

'You knew this had happened and didn't tell me?' I say, voice rising. I clutch the edge of the desk. 'Mandy!'

'I'm so sorry! I just couldn't – I couldn't . . . What good would it do now?'

'A lot, actually,' I say, closing my eyes. All those times I worked so hard to keep my walls up . . . All those times I assumed Lucas was being an arsehole . . .

'If it helps, I've paid for the mistake every day, working with you and Lucas while you're at each other's throats, the two of you kicking me back and forth between you . . . Not that I'm complaining!' she says hurriedly.

I place my palms flat on the desk and look at her, hunched over the keyboard, her glasses trembling on their chain. I remember what Mrs Hedgers said about Mandy, how she struggles to assert herself, and suddenly – despite all of the frustration coursing through me right now – I want to give her a hug.

Poor Mandy. It can't be easy.

'Mandy,' I say, 'you have every right to complain.'

'Oh, no, I . . .'

'No, listen to me. Speak *up*. If Lucas and I drive you nuts, tell us. If you prefer the online system to the booking book, say so. If you realise you've made a mistake handing out my Christmas cards and have given some bellend the card in which I declare my love for someone else entirely, *tell me*. This isn't even your fault, Mandy, it's my stupid handwriting, but you have made things so much worse by sitting on this!'

'Have I? Have I really?' She looks wretched. 'I've thought about this nonstop, you know. That'll be why he didn't mind kissing that friend of yours under the mistletoe, won't it?'

'Yes,' I say, my toes literally curling at the thought of all the times I've told Lucas he was a dickhead for kissing Drew. I scrunch up my eyes, wishing I could take back every time I tried to make Lucas feel small this year in an effort to make myself feel bigger.

'Excuse me, Izzy,' Mr Townsend says, straining to stand.

I shoot over to help him out of his armchair, ignoring the teeny flutter of irritation I feel at the diversion. Mr Townsend has sat here so often we just leave his reading glasses on the side table now, and there's a Mr Townsend-shaped dip in the cushion. If anyone else sits in this armchair, everyone in the lobby tends to look alarmed until the encroacher feels uncomfortable and leaves again.

'I think I may have done something rather unhelpful,' he says, leaning on my arm. 'I couldn't help but overhear . . . As I understand it, the Christmas card that Louis received last year *wasn't* intended for him? And your . . . unique handwriting . . .'

'Yes. The card was meant for Lucas.'

'Ah,' Mr Townsend says, holding his fingers delicately to his lips. 'In that case, you might want to sit down for this, dear.'

I let him transfer his hand from my arm to the back of the armchair, and I take a seat, though sitting down is the last thing I want to do. I'm absolutely buzzing, desperate to find Lucas, desperate to apologise and kiss him and tell him – God. I don't know. Hopefully I'll know when I see him.

'Louis told Lucas,' Mr Townsend says, 'about the card, that is. And . . . Well, Lucas was rather . . .'

'No,' I breathe, gripping the chair's arms. '*No*. Was he really upset?' I stare up at Mr Townsend. This is a *disaster*.

'Devastated, actually. I think he cares for you very deeply, my dear.'

342

I whimper. When I think of everything I've put Lucas through this year, I can hardly believe he cares about me at all. No wonder he's always snapped back at me when I've given him attitude. He must have thought I was completely unreasonable, hating him without ever offering an explanation. I press the heels of my hands into my eyes, liquid eyeliner forgotten, and curse my stupid pride. Why didn't I just have an adult conversation with him about that Christmas card? Why didn't I just suck up the embarrassment and say, Hey, why *did* you laugh at me for saying I was infatuated with you? And why did you kiss my flatmate under the mistletoe instead of me?

'He said he wanted to go home,' Mr Townsend says.

I glance at the Bartholomew clock above the front desk and do my usual calculations. Lucas will probably be back at his flat by now. At least I know not to waste time going to the gym first.

'Thank you,' I say, moving to stand.

Mr Townsend lays his hand on my shoulder. 'He said he wanted to go *home*,' he says.

I look up at him.

'I explained to Lucas that I am lucky enough to have accumulated a lot of money in my life, and that every Christmas I like to find ways to spend it that bring the world a bit of joy. It's something my wife started with me – we'd sit at our front window and watch the world go by all year, and then by December, we'd have an idea of everyone who needed a helping hand. The little girl who yearned for a bike like her brother's, the lady who wished she could afford to visit her new grandchild . . .'

I reach up and squeeze his hand on the armchair, and he smiles down at me.

'The family whose insurance company won't pay for a few more days at the hotel.'

My eyes widen as the penny drops.

'And the young man who is heartbroken and homesick at Christmas, who can't afford to go back to Brazil.'

Oh. *Oh. Oh, shit.*

I shoot up out of the chair. 'When's his flight, Mr Townsend?'

Mr Townsend looks at the clock. I wait while he does his own calculation – he's been at the hotel long enough to know the drill.

'It departs for Faro from Bournemouth airport in an hour and a half,' he says. 'I'm so sorry, Izzy. I thought it was a good deed.'

I'm already running to the door. 'Don't worry, Mr Townsend! Not your fault!' I yell over my shoulder, and then I stop short at the exit, spinning to look at him. 'When you say lots of money . . . You don't have a spare hundred grand to save the hotel, do you?'

He smiles. 'I'm afraid that is rather too much for me.'

I sag. 'That's OK. It's such a nice thing you do. You've made the Hedgers' Christmas.'

'And ruined yours,' Mr Townsend says wryly.

'Not if I drive very fast!' I call, pushing through the door, wincing at the blast of freezing air. 'And I always drive very fast!'

As far as I can tell from googling while driving (do not recommend, extremely dangerous) – Lucas's flight boards in thirty-eight minutes.

'Move! Move!' I hoot my horn. 'Oh my God, Jem, there's a fucking pony in the way!'

'Ride it?' Jem suggests.

She's on speaker. She rang for entertainment and distraction – she's currently hiding in her parents' spare bedroom with the disgraced Piddles, feeling (as she put it) 'about the size of a frickin Borrower' after a lunch with her overachieving cousins. She was *delighted* when I told her I was actually chasing a man down at an airport, rom-com style.

'Don't be ridiculous, they go at twenty miles an hour, max,' I say, hooting the horn again. 'Oh my God, I'm going to have to get out.'

I yank on the parking brake and tumble out of the car, shooing the horse aside and then running back to Smartie.

'I'm on the move again!' I yell.

Jem gives me a little supportive *whoop*. I slam the brakes on as a pheasant trundles across the road.

'Argh, pheasant! Bloody New Forest wildlife!' I shout. 'These animals have no respect for an epic love story!'

'Maybe that bird is on his way to his one great love,' Jem says. 'Always remember you never know what kind of day someone else is having.'

'Can you not be sickeningly nice, just this one time?'

She laughs. 'You'll make it, little pigeon.'

'I really won't! He'll already be through to departures, I don't know *how* I'm going to find him – how do people do it in films?'

'I dunno, actually,' Jem says thoughtfully, as I climb up the gears, the pheasant having finally reached the other side of the road. 'It involves a lot of running . . . And ducking under things. Or jumping over things.'

'I wish I'd gone to the gym more than once in the last six months,' I say, speeding up. 'He won't answer the phone, so that's out. At least he's tall. He'll be easy to spot in a crowd. I'm just going to have to wing it when I get there. Oh, God, what if he never forgives me for being such a knob?' A wash of fear moves through me. 'What if he doesn't like me any more? What if he's just going to reject me all over again, in front of an airport full of people?'

'Then it'll hurt,' Jem says. 'But you'll handle it.' Her voice softens into its lowest key. 'You can cope with so much more than you think, Izzy. You've coped with the very worst thing in the world.'

I screech around a corner. 'Do you think losing my parents has made me too scared of risking things? I always try to live life to the fullest, you know, but am I not actually doing that at all?'

'You are in so many ways – you're so brave! But letting someone in, loving someone, that's hard for all of us. And you've got the extra challenge of knowing what it feels like to say goodbye to the people you love most. So . . .'

'I'm going to do it, though,' I say, the adrenaline soaring. 'I'm going to tell him I— I'm going to tell him I'm in love with him.'

'Go seize the day, my little pigeon. My romance-loving heart could really do with a happy ending right now.'

I can hear the smile in Jem's voice.

'I'll do my best to deliver,' I promise her, 'and kill as few pheasants as possible in the process.'

'Atta girl.'

In all my wild imaginings of how this airport chase is going to go, I've been envisaging it like *Love Actually* or *Friends*. Sprinting through crowds, shouting Lucas's name, desperate to find him.

I had forgotten what Bournemouth airport is like.

It's basically one room. There's no queue for security – it's all very calm. Slightly wrong-footed, I approach the woman checking tickets and passports.

'Hi! I don't have a ticket! I'm here to tell a man I love him!'

She eyes me. 'Roger,' she calls, without looking away. 'We've got another one!'

Roger appears from somewhere, hitching up his belt. He is very large and looks very bored.

'May I start by saying, do not try to push past me,' Roger says. 'I will catch you immediately and escort you to Bournemouth police station.'

If asking politely doesn't work, pushing past the security guard is my Plan B, so this is a blow.

'Now, which flight is this gentleman on?'

'To Rio de Janeiro!' I say breathlessly.

'Via Faro, then,' Roger says. He checks his watch. 'You're very late,' he says, displeased.

'I know! But – can I just go through and speak to him?'

'No,' says Roger.

'Please?'

This does seem to placate him slightly. Maybe the romantic-declaration types aren't usually big on pleases and thank yous.

'You can't go through without a ticket.'

'Can I buy a ticket to somewhere? Where's cheap?' I say, looking around wildly at the self check-in machines.

'Do you have your passport?' asks the woman at the desk.

'Oh. No.'

'Then no, you can't buy a ticket,' she says.

I shift from foot to foot. 'What can I do?'

They both regard me steadily. They are ruining my momentum here. That flight is boarding right now, and they are talking so *slowly*.

'Look,' I say, pulling the Christmas card out of my back pocket. 'Here. Last year, I wrote this card for the man I love, to tell him how I feel about him. I really put my heart on the line. And then I *thought* he read the card and laughed at it and kissed my flatmate under the mistletoe instead. But he didn't! The card went to the wrong person, because people are really crap at reading handwritten notes, and I've been torturing this lovely man all year because I thought he was a dickhead and he *wasn't*.'

'Your handwriting is awful,' Roger observes. 'Is that supposed to be a C?'

'Aww, *cosy warm heart*,' says the woman. 'That's sweet.'

'Right?' I say desperately. I'll take whatever wins I can get. 'Can I go through? Explain the whole thing to him before he flies off to Brazil and never comes back?'

'No,' Roger says.

I just about refrain from screaming in irritation.

'Do you know what you want to say to him?' the woman asks.

'No,' I say. 'Not at all. But I'll know when I see him.'

The woman sucks her teeth.

'That won't do,' she says.

'What do you mean?'

'Well, there's one way we can put you in touch with this gent,' she says. 'But you'll really need to know what it is you want to say.'

Lucas

'*Attention all passengers for flight 10220 to Faro . . .*'

I try to eat another mouthful of my WHSmith sandwich. It makes me think of Izzy, and our trip to London together, when we had bought food at Waterloo before our train journey to Woking. How I'd realised what she meant to me that day – how obvious it had seemed.

I find it very sad that I am triggered by WHSmith, especially as there is nowhere else to buy a good sandwich right now.

'*We have a message for Lucas da Silva.*'

I freeze, sandwich halfway to my mouth.

'*Dear Lucas.*'

Que porra é essa?

'*I have a confession to make. Last year, I wrote you a Christmas card.*'

Is this some sort of cruel joke?

'*I told you I was infatuated. That every time we crossed paths in the hotel . . .*'

It must be. I set down my sandwich, heat rushing to my face.

'*I felt hot and jittery. I asked you to meet me under the mistletoe at the Christmas party.*'

This is her card to Louis. It's all the parts he quoted to me, with that sly smile on his face. I want to press my hands to my ears, but it won't block out the woman reading the message over the tannoy – it's too loud. There's no escaping it.

'*You were there when I arrived. Under the mistletoe. But you were kissing someone else.*'

The woman beside me tuts. I look around – everyone is doing the same, looking for Lucas da Silva, presumably. I have a creeping sense of strangeness, as though everything I think I know is shifting, but I'm not there yet – I still don't understand.

'*I was heartbroken. Humiliated. And I took it out on you. I thought you were heartless and cruel. I spent a whole year avoiding you, one-upping you, making your life as difficult as possible. But Lucas . . .*'

I jump at the repetition of my name. I was just beginning to think this message must surely be for someone else. Because if it's from Izzy – if that card was meant for me . . .

'*You didn't deserve that. Any of it. Because you never got that card – it went to the wrong person.*'

I drop my head into my hands. It can't be. Surely it can't be.

'*So this time around, I'm going to be completely upfront. I'm still jittery every time I see you. I'm still infatuated – more infatuated than ever. In fact, there are a whole lot of things I want to say to you that I don't think you should hear via Lydia on the tannoy – that's me, by the way.*'

A few people around me laugh. There are smiles, now, and someone is filming this on their phone.

'So meet me under the Airport Security sign right now, Lucas da Silva. It's not quite mistletoe. But it will have to do. Yours, Izzy.'

I'm running. Jumping suitcases, hurdling over people's outstretched legs, dodging my way through duty free. As I sprint back through security, a guard gives me a nod and a smile, but I'm looking for Izzy, Izzy, Izzy, my heart thumping her name.

She's there. A little bedraggled, still in her uniform, her bag at her feet. Something soars in me at the sight of her.

She runs the moment she sees me. We both come to a stop as we hit the belt barriers, dithering; I move to zigzag my way through them but Izzy ducks under, scuttling through, and I laugh, opening my arms to her.

She throws herself at me. I'm almost knocked backwards.

'Lucas, oh my God.'

I hold her, breathe her in.

'I'm so sorry.'

'That card . . . It was meant for me?'

She pulls back for long enough to tug it out of her back pocket and hand it to me.

'Merry Christmas,' she says. 'Sorry it's late.'

I kiss her. Without thought, without question, without wondering how to play this or whether it's the right move – I just scoop her into my arms and press my lips to hers. I can feel her shaking against me, the slight chill of tears on her cheeks. We've kissed so many times, but not once have we kissed like this, with neither of us holding any part of ourselves back.

There's applause around us. We break apart, sheepish, and find a man and woman in uniform watching us like indulgent parents. Lydia and a colleague, I presume. I look back down at Izzy. She's so beautiful, with her hair striped in pink and her make-up all smudged from kissing me.

'Hi,' I whisper to her.

'Hi,' she whispers back. 'There is so much I want to say to you right now.'

'Izzy,' I say. 'There are so many times this winter that I've wanted to tell you I . . .'

I trail off. She is pressing her finger to my lips.

'Me first,' she says, with fierceness. 'I love you. I am completely, helplessly, undeniably in love with you. And I am so sorry about the stupid card. Poor Mandy said you got it and laughed at it. I really thought you didn't give a shit about my feelings. I thought you'd had every opportunity to apologise for the way you'd acted, and you genuinely didn't think you'd done anything wrong. It all just seemed like such a red flag that I . . . I wrote you off completely. I decided you were an arsehole and I didn't want to let anything change my mind, because . . . I think it's because I try to be – I want to be *strong*, and look after myself . . .' She buries her face into my chest and holds me tightly as she cries. 'I am so, so sorry.'

'Izzy, shh, you're OK. It's OK.'

I sit with what she's said as I press my lips to the top of her head, the airport bustle resuming around us. What would I have thought, in her position? I would have trusted Mandy's word too. I would have assumed the worst of Izzy, because it's easy to believe someone would laugh at you. Easier than believing they'd love you back.

And was I all that different? I never gave Izzy the opportunity to explain why she was so upset by my kiss with Drew. I returned from Brazil to find her cold and argumentative; the way she treated me confirmed everything I already thought of myself, so I snapped back when she snapped at me, and suddenly that was all the two of us did. I decided Izzy was unreasonable, difficult, over dramatic. I wrote her off too.

'You thought I chose to kiss Drew under the mistletoe instead of you,' I say slowly, piecing it together.

'Mmhmm,' she says into my coat. Her sobs have calmed, and her shoulders are steady now, but she won't lift her gaze to mine.

'Izzy,' I say, pulling back and raising my spare hand to her cheek, nudging her to look up at me. I don't want her to spend a single second thinking I'd want anyone but her. 'That kiss meant absolutely nothing. We met, we flirted a little, and then she said, *Hey, look, mistletoe*, and I thought, why not? If I had received that card, I would never, ever have kissed her.'

'Well, it doesn't really matter,' Izzy says through her tears. 'Because I fell in love with you anyway. Even though I tried *so* hard not to.'

Someone clears their throat behind us, and we pull apart, turning to look.

'You want that exchanged?' Lydia says, pointing to the ticket I'm still clutching in my right hand. 'Because a . . .' She consults the note in her hand. 'A Mister Townsend just rang and said if you don't take this flight, he'll be one good deed down, so he'd

354

like us to exchange it for an extra ticket for your February trip instead. Made no sense to me, but we'll do it if you want it.'

'An extra ticket for . . .'

I glance down at Izzy. She wipes her cheeks with hands that are red with cold.

'Would you like to come to Niterói in February?' I ask her, ducking so my nose brushes hers, my arms still looped around her.

'You want to take me home to meet your family?' Her hands tighten around my waist.

'Izzy – of course I do.' I swallow, fighting the urge to shut my emotions down. 'I want you to be *part* of my family.'

Her face breaks into a wide smile – a genuine one, a smile that makes her eyes bright.

'Oh my God. I'd love to come.'

I kiss her again. My heart is pounding. For a moment it feels too frightening to say the words I want to say out loud. But then I open my eyes and look at Izzy, tear-stained and windswept, her face upturned to mine. After weeks of holding herself back, she's all here. I want to be the same.

'I love you, Izzy Jenkins.'

'Even my tacky pink trainers?' Izzy asks, through a tearful laugh. She clutches my arms.

'I love your pink trainers.'

'Even my messy little car?'

'I love Smartie. She's yours.'

'Even my handwriting?'

I start laughing, pulling her into my chest again. 'Hmm,' I

say, kissing her forehead, her hair, every part of her I can reach. 'Maybe give me a day or two on that one.'

We can't stop touching each other. Izzy suggests car sex again, and tries to argue that there'd be a 'symmetry' to this. We bicker about whether this is or is not romantic from the airport to the edge of the forest, and I love it. In one dizzy rush – like that moment in Shannon's flat – I realise I want to squabble with Izzy for the rest of my life. Except this time, when that emotion hits me, there's nothing ruining it. She doesn't hate me. She doesn't want Louis. She wants me.

'Wait,' I say, and she brakes slightly. 'No, I mean . . . On the phone. You said Louis is still a contender. Still in the game.'

'Well, he is, I think,' Izzy says, then she pulls a face. 'If I haven't put him off.' She turns to me in the silence that follows this. 'What? Why are you giving me your arch-nemesis face?'

'I thought . . . me and you . . . Are you my girlfriend?' I blurt. My heart is pounding again, those old feelings never far away.

'Yes! Aren't I? After the unbelievably romantic airport I-love-you thing?' She looks panicked. 'Have I misunderstood?'

'Have I?'

'Hang on,' Izzy says. 'This is always where we go off the rails. Tell me what you think is going on. I'll tell you what I think is going on. We will continue to talk about it until we are both on the same page and everything is sorted out. This is how we do things now, OK?'

'OK,' I say, loosening my clenched fists and taking a breath. 'What did you mean when you said Louis is still a contender?'

'I meant he's still thinking of investing in the hotel. Grigg and Sameera had asked for an update on the job, so . . .'

Oh.

Understanding dawns on Izzy's face.

'No, you didn't! Lucas! This is why you shouldn't listen in on phone conversations. God!'

'Noted,' I say, clinging to the door handle as Izzy pulls in for a car coming the other way.

She's not an *unsafe* driver, but she does go very, very fast. Her phone buzzes, screen lighting up.

'Would you mind checking that for me?' she says, nodding to her phone. 'It might be Jem. She'll be wanting her happy-ending update.'

I can't help a smile at the gesture of trust – yesterday, Izzy would never have let me look at her phone. I take it from the cup holder between us. There's one message, from Louis.

Hi Izzy. I've just let Mrs SB know that another investment opportunity has come up and my dad and I think it's a better fit for us. Good luck, no hard feelings. Cheers, Louis.

I read it out to Izzy.

'No hard feelings?' she says. '*What a*—'

'*Merda.*' I clap a hand to my mouth. Thinking about the hotel has reminded me of something important. '*Eu pedi demissão.* I resigned!'

'What?' Izzy stares over at me in horror. 'From the hotel?'

'Yes! I emailed Mrs SB my letter of resignation at the airport.'

'Well, unresign!' Izzy says. 'How am I meant to do my job without you getting in my way all the time? Call her! Call her!'

She points at her phone in my hand. I dial Mrs SB's number and switch to loudspeaker.

'Izzy!' Mrs SB shouts. 'Are you with Lucas?'

We exchange a glance.

'Yes, actually,' Izzy says. 'How did you—'

'Louis told me you're a couple!'

Both our eyes narrow in unison.

'Louis?' I say, incredulous.

'That can wait!' Mrs SB yells. 'Lucas! Barty and I are racing to the airport to stop you. You can't leave, Lucas, you mustn't. If I could offer you a pay rise, I would, or some job security of longer than two weeks, frankly, but – please! It's not over yet!'

'You're racing to the airport?' I repeat, checking the time on the dashboard. 'My flight departed forty minutes ago.'

'What? Did it? Barty!'

'It's the time difference!' Barty protests in the background. 'It's very confusing!'

'He's not leaving, Mrs SB,' Izzy says, with a smile in her voice. 'I'm bringing him home.'

'Izzy, you *angel*. If there's a Forest Manor Hotel in the world, it needs you two in it, do you hear me?'

Both our smiles waver at the reminder of reality. The likelihood is there will be no job to return to within a matter of days.

'Stop thinking negative thoughts!' Mrs SB says. 'I can hear them from here. We still have *days* left to save the hotel. It's not too late. We've not sold some of the larger antiques yet, and there's your last ring, too . . .'

Izzy pulls a face. Clearly she's doing no better than me at finding the mysterious Goldilocks.

'Forest Manor Hotel is a survivor,' Mrs SB says. 'She sheltered sixty children from the Blitz in her day. She's weathered storms and pandemics and more expensive structural damage than this, let me tell you. We *will* be open in the new year.'

'What was it you said about Louis, Mrs SB?' Izzy asks.

'Oh, yes. He came in and told me you were romantically involved. He seemed to be under the impression that I'd fire you both,' Mrs SB says. 'He was most disappointed when Barty and I cheered loudly enough to bring the ceiling down all over again. I don't know *what* that young man thinks he's up to, but since this afternoon, he's also contacted the local press with a story about our front desk going unmanned and sent the food safety inspector around.'

'What?' Izzy says, startled. 'That vindictive little . . . *weasel*!'

'Don't worry,' Barty shouts. 'Even *The Forest Local News* didn't think that story was worth printing. And you know the inspector has a soft spot for Arjun's truffles. He's been installed on table sixteen for hours.'

I can't resist. 'I told you Louis was a dickhead,' I say.

'Brace yourself, Lucas, because I'm only going to say this once,' Izzy tells me. 'You were *absolutely* right.'

Izzy

Lucas's flat is so familiar now – the creak of the leather sofa, the smell of his shower gel from the morning, the hum of the electric heater he puts on for me because I feel the cold more than he does. But as we turn to face each other on the sofa, so much is different. Now that I know the truth about last Christmas, I can see how tightly it was always holding me back. I'd never given myself over to him the way I am now – I've never *relaxed* like this, guard fully down.

'Do you think it will be different now?' I ask quietly, taking one of his hands and pulling it to my lap. I run my fingers over his, tracing his knuckles, then the lines of his palm. 'Between us?'

'Maybe. More intense.'

I flick my gaze up to his. *More* intense?

'Mm,' he says, with a small, slow smile. 'I know.'

'Can I ask you about something?' I run my nails lightly back and forth across his forearm.

He watches my hand. 'Of course. Anything.'

'Your ex. Camila.'

He stays still. I slide my hand back to lace my fingers through his.

'I'm listening now. Will you tell me about what happened with her?'

'It's nothing big,' he says, and his eyes flick up to my face as I shake my head.

'I think maybe it is.'

'She just ... It was my fault, really. I found it difficult to open up to her. She read it as lack of feeling.' He shrugs. 'Lots of people see me that way.'

Including me, for the last year. I swallow, my throat suddenly dry.

'But actually, you feel *big*,' I say, lifting my hand to his chest. 'But it's all stuck in there. Right?'

He snorts lightly but doesn't deny it.

'And she cheated on you?'

'Yes. That's how it ended. She said, *You don't have a heart, so don't tell me I broke it.*'

I inhale sharply. Not because it's cruel – though it is – but because I could imagine myself having said it once. Lucas *can* seem heartless: he's so logical, and so inscrutable, and so bloody *muscly*, and for some reason all those things in combination read as a certain kind of guy. The uptight robot-man. The guy you sleep with but nothing more, because that's all he's got to give you.

But Lucas is the man who makes Ruby Hedgers laugh until

she snorts. He's the man who heard my Christmas plans and said, *I know how it feels to be away from your family at Christmas*, because he understood that my friends *are* my family now. He's made my blood boil, and my body burn, but he's also made me laugh and challenge myself and have real fun. He is a hell of a lot more than he looks.

'Deep down, I think you're *all* heart,' I whisper, shifting closer.

He gives me a small smile at that.

'And I get that it's made you a little prickly about cheating. But I do need you to trust me. Even if I'm chatting with a guy.' I laugh as he winces. 'Lucas.'

'Yes, I know. I do trust you. I do. I'm sorry.'

'And I know I've jumped to conclusions more times than I can count in the last year – I've always assumed the worst of you,' I say, looking down at our twined hands. 'I was horrible when you told me about your hotel management course, and then when you tried to open up about Camila . . . I just couldn't fit it together with the guy I was so sure you were. It freaked me out that you were . . . I don't know. I needed you to be a dickhead, so that I could stop myself from falling in love with you. But you kept being lovely and interesting.'

He squeezes my hand for a moment and then lets go, letting me explore him, my fingers tracing up to his elbow, his bicep.

'I promise to think the best of you from this moment on. To ask you if I think you've done something hurtful. I promise never to be unkind.' I smile slightly. 'Though I kind of like that you've seen that side of me. The worst of me. People tend to think I'm super nice, and I do try to be, obviously, but . . .

Sometimes everyone's a bit of a bitch, aren't they? I get a bit exhausted trying to keep it up nonstop without ever slipping up and swearing at bad drivers or complaining about guests, you know?'

'Ah, yes,' Lucas says, and his bicep flexes under my palm. 'Angelic Izzy. I never thought you were that, by the way. Not even when you were nice to me.'

I laugh. 'No?'

'No. You have . . .' He reaches for my other hand, the one that isn't working its way over the muscles of his arm, and pulls me closer, until one of his knees crosses over mine. 'You have too much bite to be an angel. Too much sting.'

I take the invitation and lean forward to press my teeth to his neck, then suck – not hard enough to leave a mark, but hard enough to make him chuckle and pull me against him until I climb up into his lap. He wraps his arms around me, and I feel something new. He's held me like this before – my legs framing his, his face buried in my neck – but this time having his arms around me settles something that I didn't know needed settling. I feel safe.

'*Meu amor*,' he whispers, his lips against my ear. 'My love.'

I close my eyes and move against him. It still feels frightening to tell him I love him, even with his arms locked around me, holding me tight, urging me forward, back. But I've made my mind up. No more easy options – I want this, the bright, explosive joy of it. I want to say those words every day.

'I love you,' I whisper.

'*Eu te amo*,' he whispers back, and then he lifts his mouth to mine, and I have to still my hips for a moment, because the kiss is almost too much with the taste of those words on his tongue.

He's right. It is more intense. He takes me to his bedroom and we whisper it all night: *eu te amo. I love you.* By the morning I feel changed. Lucas has always shaken me up, leaving me furious, frenzied, weak with wanting, whatever it might be. But now it's different. Now he holds me steady, too.

As much as I wish that card hadn't gone astray, I can't regret the last year. We know each other so well now. This isn't the culmination of a few stolen glances at work, it's a relationship that's been twisting and turning for over a year, and I know it'll be stronger for it.

He makes me coffee and brings it to me in bed, naked, slow, letting me look. I pull him to me, and he settles his head against my chest, watching the rain come down through the window.

'We have so much to do,' he says, without particular intent. His fingers find mine, lacing over my stomach. 'Christmas party tomorrow.'

'And just over a week until it's all over. New Year's.'

He sighs. 'I don't know what I'll do. I've applied for some receptionist roles nearby, but . . .'

I sit up, looking down at him. 'You and I pretty much run Forest Manor. You can't go back to receptionist work now – you deserve something in management.'

'Then I would have to look further away.' His hand tightens on mine. 'And I don't want to. I like it here.'

I squeeze his hand back.

'And you're right: you and I *do* pretty much run Forest Manor,' he says, looking serious. 'And you hate waitressing.' He raises his eyebrows.

'Yeah, I've thought about that a lot.' I bite my lip. 'Honestly, I don't want to take a waitressing job. But I don't want to move either. I just *wish* we could find a way to keep the hotel going. Maybe if we find Goldilocks . . .'

His stubble rasps against my bare skin as he lifts his head to look at me. 'We will keep trying,' he says. 'Maybe we can do it together.'

'Excuse me?' I say, pulling back in outrage. 'You may be my boyfriend now, but that bet is still on.'

He winces. 'Really?'

'You want to concede and wear the elf outfit?'

'. . . No.'

'Well then.' I kiss him on the nose. 'In that case, I'm still planning to kick your arse at this.'

Lucas

It's Christmas Eve: party day, and my second day as Izzy Jenkins' boyfriend.

I am the sort of happy I would have previously considered unobtainable – and I am very close to making today absolutely perfect.

'If you could just try to remember . . .' I say, glancing up towards the hotel's main entrance.

'Are you actually calling me at eight in the morning on Christmas Eve to ask me if I remember a celebrity staying on my floor at your hotel in 2019?' says the woman on the other end of the line.

It is a refreshing and necessary reminder that I might be trying a *bit* too hard.

'My apologies,' I say. 'If anything comes to mind, please do get in touch by email.'

'Right,' the woman says, and I wince at the *click* as she hangs up.

'No luck?' Poor Mandy says sympathetically, popping up from the front of the desk, where she is doing what Izzy refers to as 'festooning'. Everyone is either festooning for Izzy or chopping vegetables for Arjun right now.

'No luck,' I say.

Poor Mandy pats my arm. She has been patting me a lot since the Christmas-card debacle was cleared up. I think she feels responsible for Izzy and me torturing one another for a year. Which she is, a bit.

'Do you know what, dear?' Mandy says, beginning the arduous process of checking her phone: glasses coming down from her head, hand going into her pocket, a lot of wriggling and bouncing up and down in her chair as she eases the phone out from her jeans, the case flipping open, her glasses dropping down her nose and up again . . . 'I may be able to help you.'

I appreciate Poor Mandy – she is always reliable, she's very popular with the guests, and she works all the worst shifts. But I am almost certain that her idea will involve tweeting to our 112 followers, and I simply cannot see that helping.

'Thank you,' I say. 'Feel free to try.'

'Any luck?' Ollie calls as he dashes past with a tray of jellies.

'Not yet,' I call after him. 'Do you know if Izzy is having—'

'I'm Switzerland!' Ollie yells over his shoulder. 'You're getting nothing out of me!'

'Anything on the ring?' Barty calls down the newly functioning stairs as he dashes along the landing. Everyone is dashing today. It is giving the hotel a faint buzz, as though someone has dialled all the appliances up at once.

'Not yet,' I call. Everyone's support is appreciated, but also, when I have no updates, slightly irritating.

'Lucas! Anything on the—'

'Not yet!' I snap, and then look up to find the cool gaze of my girlfriend.

'—Christmas party menu that's vegan?'

'Oh.'

I soften instantly. Izzy looks amused.

'Yes. Here.'

I show her Arjun's latest scribbled version of the menu. She scans over it and I watch, hungry for the sight of her. All that time I spent thinking I could do without Izzy Jenkins in my day, and now I truly cannot have too much of her.

'Have we—'

'Yes. They're set up in the orangery.'

She taps her bottom lip, still scanning the menu.

'Does Arjun know about the—'

'Yes. He swore a lot, but we got through it.'

Izzy nods. She looks up at me.

'And—'

'Yes.'

'I didn't actually—'

'I am confident that it is already done.'

'It's not, because—'

'Have a cup of tea. Stop thinking so hard.'

'I was going to say, have I told you that I love you today?'

'Oh. No. You haven't.'

'See?' She looks smug as she turns away. 'Told you it wasn't all done yet. Mr Townsend! How can I help you?'

Mr Townsend is making his way over from his armchair. He is doing a remarkably good job of dodging various members of the housekeeping team, as well as a small chihuahua that arrived with Dinah today. 'Doggy daycare problems,' she announced as she walked in with it on a lead. 'Do not give me shit about this.'

'It's Lucas I need, actually,' Mr Townsend says. 'Will you join me in the orangery? I'd like to try out those new sofas.'

He smiles as he takes my arm.

'Oh, fine!' Izzy says, shooting me an arch look, as if to say, *So you're the favourite now!*

I raise my eyebrows back at her – *Of course I am.* Then my phone buzzes in my hand, and I look down to see *Antônio calling.* My breath hitches. It's Saturday. I didn't phone him on Thursday. I didn't forget – I just didn't want to.

And I don't want to speak to him now, either. I have noticed that the more I value myself, the less grateful I feel to my uncle, and the more I wonder why I put myself through these conversations at all. For now, for a while, he will have to wait until I feel ready to talk to him.

The call rings out as Mr Townsend and I make our way through to the orangery. I exhale slowly.

'I have something for you,' Mr Townsend says, as I settle him on a sofa.

Izzy found this sofa on Gumtree, being sold . . . by us. It's an old one from Opal Cottage – once a bold shade of red, it is now russet and faded, but somehow it has come to life again under the patterned cushion covers that Izzy created from an old set of hotel curtains. She has such a gift for this: bringing out the best in things.

'Here.' Mr Townsend opens his palm. The emerald ring sits in the folds of his hand, circling the point where his lifeline splits. 'It's for you. Or rather, it's for her.'

Ai, meu Deus.

'Mr Townsend . . .'

'I've been carrying it around since we went to Budgens, not knowing what to do with it. The fact is, it doesn't quite belong to me any more. That's how it feels. Because Maisie lost it and replaced it. The ring she wore on the day she died was hers, and this one . . . It was lying in wait for someone else to find it, perhaps.'

'I can't possibly . . . And it's far too soon . . .'

Mr Townsend looks up at me shrewdly. 'Is it? I only met my Maisie a dozen times before we were married.'

'But these days . . .'

'Oh, yes, these days, these days.' Mr Townsend waves his other hand. 'Some things change, but love doesn't. When you know . . .'

You know. I understand why people say that about love now: there's no quantifying this. It is too enormous – too dizzyingly deep.

And it's true that I've thought of marrying her. If I could, if this world were perfect, I'd dredge the ocean for that ring from her father, the one she lost, and I'd get down on one knee and hand it to her. But this world isn't perfect, and neither am I.

Sometimes things are lost, and you grieve for them, and they change you, and that's OK.

It might not be perfect to propose with the emerald ring, but it *would* be beautiful. It has a story – a legacy. It's part of the family she found here at the hotel.

'I can't possibly accept this from you,' I say, but even I can hear that my voice is a little less convincing now.

'Keep it in your pocket until you need it,' Mr Townsend says, just as Mrs Hedgers enters the room, trailing tinsel behind her.

'Sorry to interrupt,' she says as she leans to tape one end of the tinsel to the edge of the window frame. 'Izzy's orders.'

Mr Townsend presses the ring into my hand and cups it in his own. I shake in his grasp, and we stay like this, both holding that ring; for a moment it holds two messy love stories inside its loop. Then Mr Townsend removes his hands, and it's just one love story. Mine, for a while. Until I give it to Izzy, and it becomes hers.

For an unpleasant half-hour, it seems nobody will come to the Christmas party. Our invitations suggested a start time of 2 p.m. – Izzy wanted the children to be part of the celebration. The plan was that people would come and go when it suited them.

But it doesn't seem to be suiting them to come at all.

'They'll turn up,' Izzy says, adjusting yet another candle.

She has done a beautiful job in here. We've made the lobby the centre point of the party – it's where the face painting and the magician are set up, along with the live band, a collection of jazz musicians who once played a wedding here and have been kind enough to help us out with a cut-price performance. The buffet is through in the restaurant, and our bar is filled with comfortable seating. Ollie is in charge of cocktails in the orangery, a role that he accepted with much grumbling and thinly disguised delight.

I doubt Izzy can tell, but I am even more nervous about this party than she is. My Christmas present for her will be revealed tonight, and I am having sudden terrors that I didn't get it right. After all, I planned it before the two of us got together. And I've taken a bit of a risk.

'Rather quiet, isn't it?' Mr Townsend says, shuffling over.

Izzy looks irritated, then melts when she realises it's Mr Townsend speaking.

'They'll come,' she says. 'Where are the Hedgers? They always bring the fun. Lucas, will you give them a knock?' On seeing my expression, she adds, 'It's not intrusive, it's helpful! I promise they won't mind.'

I shoot her an unconvinced look and get a tongue-out face in return. I head to Sweet Pea. Mrs Hedgers opens the door: she looks completely different from the woman I saw just a couple of hours ago, in the orangery. Her hair is loose around her shoulders for the first time since I've known her, and there are tear tracks on her cheeks.

'Oh, I'm so sorry,' I say, already backing away, but she beckons me in and wheels herself back inside. I have no choice but to catch the door and follow her or let it shut behind her.

I step inside, feeling uneasy. I don't enter rooms while guests are present, generally – it feels like I am doing the same thing Louis did when he stepped behind the front desk.

'Lucas,' she says, reaching up to the dresser for the tissues and neatly blowing her nose. 'I was hoping to catch you, actually. The children are in the gardens with my husband, burning off some energy before they're expected to socialise with people who may not appreciate the degree of barging that takes place on a regular Hedgers-family Saturday.'

'I don't want to intrude,' I say, already backing towards the door.

'Stay,' Mrs Hedgers says.

It's more command than request. I do as I'm told, holding my hands behind my back, hovering in front of the door.

'My husband finally told me what Mr Townsend did for us. And do you know what I felt? I felt irritated. Irritated that we'd had to accept charity and irritated that I hadn't *won*. I hadn't beaten the insurance company. It hadn't gone my way.'

'I'm sorry,' I say. 'I can understand that.'

She smiles, sniffing. 'I know you can. You like to get things done and you like perfection.'

I incline my head. 'Thank you.'

'It wasn't precisely a compliment,' she says, patting at the cushions on the settee until they're lined up just right. 'I'm the same. And I'm brilliant at what I do. But I'm not brilliant at everything, and I find that very hard. Is this ringing any bells?'

I believe I am being Mrs Hedgers-ed.

'Yes,' I admit. 'I'm . . . I can be . . . uncompromising.'

This time her smile is smaller. 'The perfection you're always chasing, Mr da Silva – no amount of hard work will get you what you want. Trust me. I've worked very, very hard.'

She wheels towards the mirror, beginning to fix her make-up. It's a surprisingly intimate gesture for a woman I see as so put-together, and I'm sure it's very deliberate.

Mrs Hedgers catches my eye in the mirror. 'The ring Mr Townsend gave you. May I give you some advice about it?'

I watch my own expression shift ever so slightly in the mirror: eyes a fraction wider, eyebrows flinching. Today has been the strangest day. The hotel has been a meaningful part of my life since my very first shift here, but this winter it seems to have woven itself through every element of me – I am hardly surprised to find yet another guest involving themselves in my personal life. Perhaps because I've spent all winter involving myself in theirs.

'A ring can make a good thing stronger and a bad thing weaker. You need to be as whole as you can be before you put one on your finger. So all I'd say is ... don't ask the question until you feel sure of her answer.'

This is precisely how I described my ideal proposal when I first spoke about marriage with Izzy all those weeks ago, under the fairy lights: I thought I would ask the love of my life to marry me, and I'd know she would say yes. But Mrs Hedgers is right to suspect that I'm running away with myself. Since yesterday, my mind has been playing out the future, already thinking of all the ways I could lose her, and suddenly the idea of securing Izzy Jenkins in marriage is extremely appealing. I want her to be *mine* before she realises she's far too good to be.

I'd considered this February, when we go to Brazil together. Or summer at the latest.

'When you know she loves you, and you trust it – ask her then. That's my opinion,' Mrs Hedgers says, flashing me a freshly lipsticked smile. 'For what it's worth. Which, by the way, is a lot. Hard work doesn't get you everything, but it does help with the pay cheques, I find. Now, I must go and find my better half, and then I must thank the man who has saved my Christmas.' She swallows. 'Please remind me that there is no shame in accepting help.'

'There is no shame in accepting help.'

She nods, pulling her hair up and clipping it in place. 'Sometimes you do need someone else to say it,' she says. 'I don't know why, but you do. Right. Shall we?' She gestures towards the door.

Izzy

I'm dotted in face paint. The band is playing Harper Armwright's 'December Kisses', and a group of tipsy ladies are dancing an unrelated Scottish reel by the front desk; Charlie and Hiro are here, our very first success story of The Ring Thing, enjoying a glass of mulled wine by the fire with Mr Townsend. Arjun has finally stopped laughing about the fact that I'm now Lucas's girlfriend ('I am never going to let you live this down, Jenkins, you know that, right?') and has even taken a short break from the kitchen to enjoy the festivities.

I am full to the brim with happiness. For a bright, freedom-filled moment the future of the hotel doesn't seem to matter, because right now we're at our very best. Forest Manor Hotel is glowing with festive joy, and if you squint a bit, the sleet coming down outside the windows might even pass for snow.

And it's almost time for Lucas's Christmas present. Planned and pulled together late last night, in whispered phone calls taken while hiding in his bathroom, because until yesterday I was genuinely planning to buy him a lump of coal.

I just have one last thing to do before the clock strikes six, and it's going to be unpleasant, no matter how joyful the mood in here.

Last week, I decided that unfinished business is bad for the soul, so I offered Drew Bancroft a job.

Well, only three hours' work, making cocktails with Ollie. I'm not *that* nice. But I thought an olive branch was overdue, and I kept thinking of her Instagram post about how she couldn't find work. Before I knew it, I'd DMed her.

And now she's here, filling a punch bowl with eggnog in the orangery. She's rocking a serious-New-York-journalist kind of look which I can't help admiring. It's so weird seeing her in the hotel again. I hope this wasn't a terrible idea. I was feeling very secure and loved-up when I reached out, but now I'm remembering seeing Drew at the *last* Christmas party. Which was . . . awful.

I'm briefly waylaid greeting guests – the Jacobs, and Lucas's friend Pedro, and a couple of the temps I've worked with this year – so by the time I get to her, she's fully prepared to face me.

'Oh my God, *hi*,' she says, as if she had forgotten my existence until this very moment but is delighted to have been reminded. She reaches a long-nailed hand out to touch my arm across the bar. 'I appreciated you reaching out.'

And finding me some work, I wait for her to say. She doesn't.

'Hello, Drew,' I say, trying to sound olive-branchy. 'How are things?'

'Listen, I've been thinking,' she says, entirely ignoring the question. Drew has always worked to her own script. 'I want to tell you . . .' she pauses dramatically, 'that I forgive you.'

I stare at her. Beside her, Ollie freezes midway through zesting an orange, his eyes going wide.

'*You've* forgiven *me*?'

'For kicking me out the way you did.'

'For . . . Drew. I did not kick you out.' My heart is *pounding*. I think of all the times I bit my tongue with Drew and tried to be a 'good friend', and I think of all the times I snapped at Lucas about something meaningless, and I can't believe I got this so twisted. 'Let's recap: you knew how I felt about Lucas. You knew I wrote him that card. You kissed him under the mistletoe. I got upset. I asked you to give me the month's rent you owed me and move out by the end of January. And then you threw a bauble at my head and stropped off.'

She rolls her eyes, and suddenly she looks exactly like the woman I lived with last year, despite the new hair and glasses.

'Izzy, please. The bauble thing was an accident.'

'How?' I ask, genuinely bewildered.

'I think you need to let stuff go?'

'Right,' I say, because there is definitely some truth in this. I am a grudge-holder. I can be petty. I know this. It has caused me some bother this year. 'Well, if you say sorry, I am happy to let it go.'

'Say sorry?'

Ollie has stopped even pretending to make cocktails. He is just watching this unfold, half of a squished orange segment in his palm, a drop of juice trickling down to his elbow. Around us, the crowd mills and hums, and beyond them, the garden stretches out in frosty whites and greens through the orangery windows.

'Why would I say sorry when you were such a bitch about it?'

I take a deep breath, and I smile. My favourite smile, the one I reserve for the very worst guests.

There are times for olive branches, and then there are times for the sort of childish pettiness that a year of baiting Lucas has really helped me hone.

'Drew . . . you're fired,' I say.

Her mouth drops open. 'Excuse me?'

'Yes. You're fired. I am firing you. You need to leave now.'

Ollie's expression turns aghast, but he'll manage solo. He's good under pressure. He's also sensible enough not to object.

'This is three hours of bar work, cash in hand. You can't *fire* me. It's not a job.' She looks around, suddenly aware of the interest of the crowd around us.

My smile stays in place. 'If I could have fired you from being my friend, Drew, I'd have done it, but that's not a thing, so I'm taking what I can get.'

Then I catch the time on her watch: three minutes to six.

'Argh!' I jump.

Drew looks at me as though I am unhinged.

'Bye, Drew! Off you go! Have a nice life!' I say, spinning on my heels and sprinting away. I will not be wasting one more minute on Drew Bancroft – especially when I barely have one minute to spare.

I get to the lobby just in time. Dinah is wheeling the old projector in from the lost-property room, and up on the landing Kaz, Reese, Raheem and Helen throw white sheets over the bannisters so that when the projector starts up, the video should line up *just* right.

Well, we're out by about a metre. But it'll do!

'Surprise!' shout Lucas's family, their image projected on the sheets, just as I spin around to hear a different chorus of voices yell, 'Surprise!'

Lucas is standing in the doorway to the hotel, framed by Grigg, Sameera and Jem.

I can't compute it. They don't quite look real. But then they descend on me, burying me in one big hug, and behind us on the makeshift bedsheet screen the da Silvas are yelling *Feliz Natal!*

'Oh my God!' I say, emerging from the middle of the huddle and swiping my hair out of my face. 'How are you all here?'

'Lucas,' Jem says, wearing her widest, warmest smile.

Sameera tucks my hair behind my ears and kisses me on the forehead as my eyes fill with tears.

'You! You!' she says. 'Lying to all of us about where you were spending Christmas! This is not the time or place, but as soon as the festivities are over, I am going to have a right go at you. Oh, God, it's so good to see you!'

'Lucas told on me?' I say, wiping my eyes as Grigg pulls me in for another hug. 'You guys! You should be in the Outer Hebrides! And *you* should be in America!' I say to Jem.

'We fly back tonight,' Sameera tells me, grinning at Grigg. 'His mum would kill us if we missed Christmas lunch, and I can't be away from Rupe any longer or I will literally explode. But Jem is staying, right?'

'Absolutely,' Jem says. 'As soon as Lucas messaged me, I thought ... What am I doing here, being told it's not too late for me to turn my life around, when I could be with people who love me *and* the life I've chosen? So Piddles and I jumped on the next flight.'

I squeeze her arm. I know that will have been a lot harder than she's making it sound. Behind her, Lucas's sister is yelling at him in fast Portuguese; Grigg and Sameera move aside so I can see Lucas's expression, and it's like going back in time and seeing what Lucas would have looked like as a little boy. His face has just *lit* up. Pure, stripped-back, childlike delight.

'Izzy!' Lucas's mum calls. 'Izzy, thank you for having us!'

'Oh my gosh, thank you for being here!' I shout up at the giant image hanging above the crowd, all of whom are staring at these goings-on with delight and/or bewilderment. 'With *very* little notice! I know the twenty-fourth is the big day over there, and you're right in the thick of Christmas, so thank you for taking the time.'

'Always, for Lucas,' she says, looking down at her son. 'Love you. Miss you.'

'*Saudade*,' Lucas says, and he holds his hand to his heart, where the word is tattooed on his skin. '*Tô com muita saudade.*'

'Tell them about the flights,' I say, coming to stand beside him.

'*Feliz Natal!*' shouts a little girl, popping up in the corner of the screen. One of the cousins, presumably, and totally adorable.

Lucas laughs. 'Helena! *Feliz Natal!*'

'What flights?' says Ana. She was the one who set this up for me – I found her on Instagram last night. She loved the idea. It was Ana who came up with using the bedsheets.

'We're coming home in February,' Lucas says, face breaking into another boyish grin.

'*We!*' Lucas's mother shrieks in delight.

Lucas laughs and takes my hand. 'Yes, both of us,' he says.

'That is, if you'll have me,' I add.

'We've wanted you since that first photo, *amiga*,' Ana says. 'Anyone who annoys Lucas that much belongs in this family.'

They stay for almost an hour. Helena and her brother learn how to say 'I want more sweeties' in English, thanks to the potentially quite dangerous influence of Ruby Hedgers, and Ruby learns how to say 'I want to go to Rio de Janeiro!' in Brazilian Portuguese, which might be a problem for Mr and Mrs Hedgers, given the cost of flights. But having the da Silvas hanging out over the party takes everything up a notch. By the time Arjun declares the evening buffet open, complete with an array of desserts in the orangery, everyone is very loud, very happy and – for the most part – very drunk.

'Your friend, she's so beautiful!' Pedro shouts at me as we dance.

He's here as a guest, but spent at least an hour helping Arjun in the kitchen, and doubled up as a magician for a while when our actual magician had to take a phone call. We are not afraid to call in a favour here at Forest Manor Hotel, and it turns out Lucas's friend is way too generous for his own good.

'Jem, you mean?'

I look back at her – she's dancing with a few of the women from housekeeping, eyes closed, hips swaying. She's in her favourite dress, the red velvet one with a sweetheart neckline, and her dark-brown skin is sprayed with fine gold glitter. All her piercings are gold today too, shining under the Christmas lights. She *does* look gorgeous.

Pedro is already angling to dance her way.

'Pedro sleeps with women and never calls them back,' Lucas says in my ear, dancing behind me. 'I'm sorry. I thought I should say.'

I laugh, turning to wind my arms around his neck so we can dance the way we did on that strange, snowy day in London.

'That won't work with Jem,' I say, half to Lucas, half to Pedro. 'She's demisexual. She has to form an emotional connection first – she would never sleep with a guy she's only just met.'

Pedro stares at me, abruptly abandoning his dance moves. 'Demi . . . sexual?'

'Uh-huh.'

'So she won't want to sleep with me?'

'Not unless you've built an emotional relationship, no.'

'*Emotional?*' Pedro says, looking positively panicked.

'It's nice, Pedro.' I'm trying not to laugh. 'You should try it some time.'

A tap on the shoulder distracts me from Pedro's wide, anxious eyes.

Ugh.

Louis Keele. I tighten my arm around Lucas's waist as we

both turn to look at him. Louis is wearing a casual smile, a crisp shirt, and a little too much cologne. I glance up at Lucas. He's wearing a familiar glower.

'Hey, you two, I was hoping to catch you,' Louis says. Very relaxed and friendly. No suggestion that last time he saw me he was viciously unpleasant, but I suspected he'd play it this way after his 'no hard feelings' text. 'I thought I should give you a heads up about my new investment,' he continues, his smile beginning to look more like a smirk. 'Only fair. An old school-house in Fordingbridge came on to the market and I just . . . Well. I couldn't resist. It's going to make a beautiful hotel.'

'You . . . are opening a hotel?' Lucas says.

'Oh my God,' I say, before Louis can answer. 'Is that why you were asking so many questions about Forest Manor?' My voice rises. 'Were you *ever* considering actually investing? Or were you just trying to steal all our best ideas?'

'I was considering investing,' Louis says, extremely insincerely.

'You wanted to poach Arjun, didn't you?' I say, advancing on Louis with a pointing finger.

Lucas tightens his grip on me. 'Easy,' he says, but I can hear the smile in his voice.

'Who wouldn't want to poach Arjun?' Louis says. 'He's the best chef in the New Forest. He wouldn't budge, though. You lot really have your claws in him.'

'And what insults did you have for Arjun when you failed to seduce him?' Lucas asks politely. 'Is *he* a small, mousey nobody, too?'

Louis' eyes flick to mine. I smile, as if to say, *Yes, of course I told him everything. Yes, we are mutually deciding not to destroy you. No, I am not confident I can prevent him from breaking rank and beating you to a pulp if he so chooses.*

Louis swallows. 'Look, like I say, I just wanted to give you the heads up. There's a bit of competition on the horizon.'

I pull myself up as tall as I can, and only wobble slightly in the process – not bad three cocktails down.

'Well,' I say, in my sweetest voice. 'That won't be a problem. Lucas and I love a bit of competition.'

Lucas

'The thing about true love, right, is that sometimes you have to really push yourself out of your comfort zone to find it?' Ruby Hedgers tells me, from the top of the frame of a four-poster bed in one of the newly refurbished upstairs bedrooms (closed off to party guests, discovered by Ruby when the clock hit bed-time). 'Like, Hamza from my class at school fancied Sophie, and everyone said she was sooo out of his league, but then he gave her the cake his mum made him for his lunch and she said he could be her boyfriend.'

'Ruby,' I say, 'aren't you six?'

'Yes,' she says, with great solemnity. 'Yes I am.'

'Isn't that a bit young for boyfriends?'

'Totally,' she says, in the same tone. 'But Sophie doesn't know that. Which is lucky for Hamza.'

'There you are,' Mrs Hedgers says, entering the room behind me. 'Lovely to have your lifts back in order, Lucas. I particularly enjoyed the slow jazz and gold-embossed wallpaper – hello, Ruby, I bet you can't climb down that post like a fireman's pole, can you?'

Ruby promptly begins climbing down to prove her mother wrong. I give Mrs Hedgers an impressed look, which she takes with the nod of a woman who knows her own talents.

'Lucas,' she says. 'There is a young couple trying to—'

'*There* you are,' says Izzy's friend Grigg, bursting into the room behind Mrs Hedgers. His wife Sameera runs in behind him, coming up short, slightly out of breath.

'Oh, look. Everyone has been looking for us,' Ruby says with delight, pausing mid descent.

'Lucas,' Grigg says.

I have never seen a man with such bulging bags under his eyes – but the eyes themselves are steady and kind. Grigg is one of those people who would manage to make something look crumpled even if it were very recently ironed, while his wife is just the opposite: she exudes the sort of effortless glamour that makes her stained white T-shirt look vaguely iconic.

'We don't want to bother Izzy, because she's talking to the project manager of the building team about a local property looking for someone to coordinate a redesign for them . . .'

He smiles as my eyebrows shoot up.

'But I think one of your colleagues may be having a minor panic attack in the swimming pool,' he finishes, and my eyebrows drop into a frown again.

Merda.

'Have you . . .'

'Go. I'll take it from here,' Mrs Hedgers says, as Ruby clings to the post of the bed like a koala, contemplating her path down.

I don't run, of course – that's against hotel policy. But I do walk very, very fast.

The swimming pool should be locked to guests today – much like the upstairs bedrooms. But when we get there, the door is ajar. Poor Mandy is sitting on the edge of the pool, trousers rolled up to the knees, feet dangling in, with Pedro and Jem on either side of her and a mobile phone in each of her hands.

'I just wonder if keeping all these expensive phones *directly* over a body of water might not be the smartest move, sweetie?' Jem is saying, reaching tentatively for the phone nearest her.

'Mandy?' I say.

Her head snaps up. Her eyes remind me of a horse that has been startled and is likely to stand on your foot.

'Lucas,' she breathes. 'There's just . . . so much to do. So many people.'

I look around. The spa area is an oasis of calm, the noise from the party a low background hum behind the sound of the water.

'Mandy . . . why do you have two phones?' I ask, approaching.

I catch Pedro's eye. He mouths *No sudden movements* at me in Portuguese.

'What? Oh.' Mandy looks from one to the other. 'I thought if I put Twitter on this one and Instagram on this one then all the notifications wouldn't be quite so overwhelming. But then I couldn't get Twitter *off* this one and Facebook wouldn't update on this one so now I've got everything everywhere and . . . it's just . . . so . . . *much.*'

'I'm thinking maybe you've had enough screen time . . . Mandy?' Jem says, looking at me for confirmation.

She eases the nearest phone from Mandy's hand and tosses it to me. I catch it. Thankfully. That was a very confident throw, and while I'm quite pleased that Jem rates my catching skills, I would also prefer her to never do that again, particularly this close to a swimming pool.

'Oh, wow,' Pedro says. He's bent over Poor Mandy's other phone while Mandy stares listlessly at the garden through the window opposite, eyes glazed. 'You guys have ninety thousand Instagram followers?'

'*What?*' I say, starting forward and crouching down beside him.

'Hashtag The Ring Thing,' Jem says, looking over Pedro's other shoulder.

I watch Pedro breathe in at her proximity and try not to smile. It looks like Pedro decided to introduce himself to Jem, then. Fascinating. I wonder if he has *ever* formed an emotional connection with a woman before. I am very much looking forward to my next morning coffee at Smooth Pedro's – there is almost too much to tease him about.

'Hashtag save Forest Manor Hotel. *Both* trending,' Jem says.

'You need to use hashtags,' Mandy says faintly. 'They're good for engagement.'

'This photo of you and Izzy arguing over a Tupperware box has two hundred thousand likes,' Pedro says, mouth hanging open.

'You need to add a personal touch,' Mandy says, in the same vacant tone. 'It makes your brand much more relatable.'

The last time I checked our social media profiles, they did not look like this.

'Mandy,' I say, 'when did this happen?'

'Oh, sort of all the time, really, over the last few weeks,' she says. 'The more pictures I posted about Izzy's Ring Thing, the bigger it got.'

Pedro swears. 'You have a direct message from someone with fifteen million followers here. And . . .'

'*There* you are,' Arjun says, barging into the spa with his chef's hat in hand and some tapenade on his forehead. 'There's a Harper Armwright outside the hotel with a six-piece band. What the fuck?'

'Oh, yes, Harper,' Poor Mandy says dreamily. 'She'll be here to collect her wedding ring.'

I've heard of Harper Armwright. She did a duet with Michael Bublé; Izzy has one of her old CDs in her box o'bits. But I'm not a fan, particularly – I would choose Los Hermanos over Harper Armwright any day.

And yet even I feel somewhat starstruck when I see her out-side the hotel. She carries herself like she's special. It's in her every move: the slow turn of her head, the set of her shoulders, the thoughtlessness with which she leaves the car door for some-body else to close. And it's in the warm, well-practised smile she gives us, with an extra special moment of eye contact for

Sameera, who is hopping on the spot and whining *Oh my God it's Harper actual Armwright* under her breath.

'You must be Lucas,' Harper says to me, with a voice like honey. She holds out her hand for me to shake. 'One half of my Christmas miracle.'

We manage to smuggle her in under Izzy's woolly hat and a pair of sunglasses I keep in my glove box. It's her security team who draw attention. I glower at them when they refuse to look less conspicuous, and they glower right back. I have the vague sense that I may have found my people.

'I must have lost it when the paparazzi turned up – we left this place in such a hurry,' Harper says, sliding the ring slowly on to her finger and breathing out. 'All those years it was just sitting here? It's like . . . Wow.'

We're in the lost-property room. It seems to pale around Harper's glow. This woman belongs on stadium stages and in penthouse suites – as much as I am proud of Forest Manor Hotel, this is not the part of it I would most like her to see. Izzy shifts a couple of steps to her left, covering the sun-bleached section of wall where a large box sat for many years.

'My wife was gutted. She made it herself, did you know that? It's *completely* unique, and it slots perfectly beside hers.' She smiles down at the ring on her hand. 'When a friend sent her your Instagram post about this cute mission you're on? To return all those lost rings? And then you put up a pic of this one earlier today and I just thought, *No way.* But there it was.' She shakes her head in wonder. 'It's literally priceless, this ring.'

We all wait with bated breath. Mrs SB is gripping Barty's arm; Izzy has her bottom lip between her finger and thumb. Poor Mandy is staring at a fixed point on the wall, fingers tapping at her sides as though she is still subconsciously responding to direct messages.

Nobody has said the word *reward* yet. But everyone is thinking it.

We wait. Harper keeps smiling. One of her security guys checks his watch.

'Now, since I'm here,' Harper says, looking between us and dialling her smile up a notch, 'how about a little set?'

'A set! Right!' Mrs SB says brightly. 'Lovely.'

Izzy and I exchange a glance. *No* reward? But Harper Armwright must be worth about half a billion pounds.

Ollie!' Mrs SB calls suddenly.

I turn to see Ollie standing open-mouthed in the doorway.

'Is that . . .' he begins, voice hoarse.

'Yes, dear, Harper Armwright,' Mrs SB says briskly. 'I'm going to need you to help her get set up for a performance.'

'Per . . . formance . . .' Ollie whispers, clutching at the door frame, as though perhaps he might otherwise not be able to remain standing.

'My fans will be so excited – we'll do a reel, yeah?' Harper says to one of the members of her team, who nods enthusiastically, whipping her phone out. 'I've already told them how super-cute this place is. It'll be perfect. *So* Christmas.'

Barty's phone sings out the old Nokia theme tune. Harper

jumps slightly and then stares in fascination as he pulls out his 1990s mobile phone.

'Sorry,' Poor Mandy says, coming to life and snagging her glasses down from the top of her head. 'You told your fifteen million followers that our hotel is super-cute?'

'Yuh-huh,' Harper says, as she waits for her security guy to declare she's safe to leave our lost-property room. 'Can I get one of those?' she asks a member of her team, pointing to Barty's phone.

'Apparently our website has stopped working,' Barty says, phone still at his ear as the security guard looks left, right, left again, and then gestures Harper through after Ollie, who seems to have remembered how to be a functional human being.

We all turn to stare at Barty.

'It says there is "too much traffic". Apparently, we've had one hundred bookings in the last six minutes.'

Mrs SB lowers herself slowly on to a box. Harper beams around at us from the doorway.

'Oh, that's so nice!' she says, then waves goodbye over her shoulder, her hand just about visible behind the gigantic bald man in sunglasses who follows close behind her.

Slowly, as one, we turn to look at Poor Mandy. The lights on the tree shine through the door from the lobby, alternating red and green, flashing in Mandy's glasses.

'Sorry,' she says. 'You said do the social media. Did I go too far?'

'Mandy,' Mrs SB says, voice choked. 'Dearest Mandy. I am so sorry.'

Poor Mandy looks baffled as Mrs SB pulls her into a hug, and then Barty and Izzy join them, and then, because it's Christmas, and because Izzy loves me back, and because Mandy has just saved my job, I pile in too.

'What are you sorry for?' Mandy asks, from inside the hug.

'When someone doesn't value themselves, dear,' Mrs SB says, pulling back and wiping her face, 'it's far too easy to take their word for it. But you're absolutely *brilliant*. So brilliant, in fact, that you've saved Forest Manor Hotel from oblivion.'

'Oh, I'm *so* glad to have helped,' Mandy says, looking overcome. 'I did wonder . . . but I didn't want to get anyone's hopes up, and . . .' She breathes on her glasses and then wipes them on her reindeer jumper. 'Anyway, it was all Izzy and Lucas, really. It was all The Ring Thing. I just spread the word. I have to say, I'll be very glad to delete Twitter now,' she says, just as Mrs SB cuts in to say, 'I'll be promoting you to Head of Social Media Marketing with immediate effect!'

'Oh,' Poor Mandy says, looking stricken. 'Really?'

'Well, you have such a knack for this!' Mrs SB says, waving her phone.

'Right,' Poor Mandy says forlornly. Then, after a deep breath, she lifts her chin and says, 'Actually, I'd rather stay on reception, if I may.'

'Oh!' Mrs SB looks at Mandy with surprise. 'Yes! Of *course*.'

Mandy draws herself up. 'But I am very happy to train whoever you recruit to work on our social media,' she says, voice wobbling slightly. 'And I look forward to the pay rise that will be forthcoming once the hotel is back on its feet in the new year.'

There is a shocked, admiring silence, and then, behind us, the lobby fills with cheers as Harper hits the opening notes of an acoustic 'December Kisses'. It feels like an appropriate response.

I don't think Mandy will be called *Poor Mandy* any longer. That name doesn't suit her at all.

Izzy snuggles into me, shifting up the bench. It's four in the morning, and we're in the pergola, lit by the fairy lights. The trees reach above us, their branches criss-crossing the star-sprayed sky. My muscles ache from hours of dancing on the lobby rug with Izzy in my arms.

'So, I guess ... Mandy won the bet,' Izzy says, resting her head against my shoulder. 'She found Harper.'

'Does that mean we both have to dress up as elves tomorrow?' I ask, kissing the top of Izzy's head.

'Yep,' Izzy says. 'Looks like it. Good old Mandy. I'm so proud of her.'

'We have not made Mandy's year easy,' I say.

'God, we were a nightmare, weren't we? Do you remember that week back in January when we refused to communicate directly, and she ended up as the go-between?'

I snort. 'Do you remember the time you moved the location of every single icon on my computer home screen and pretended the temp did it?'

'It *could* have been the temp.'

'Was it the temp?'

Izzy waves a hand, as if this is beside the point. 'Do you

remember the time you told Arjun that I thought his mousse was too floofy?'

'You did say that,' I point out.

'Not *to Arjun*.'

'Do you remember the time you glued my mouse to the desk?'

'That was actually an accident,' Izzy says, grinning.

'Do you remember the time we almost kissed in the pool?' I say, my voice quieter now.

'Do you remember the time I chased you down at the airport?' she says, her voice dropping too, her fingers winding between mine.

'Do you remember the time I let you win at poker?' I whisper.

She gasps, spinning in my arms to look at me. 'You did *not*.'

I'm laughing now.

'Lucas! That is honestly the worst thing you've ever done to me. Worse than pushing me into the swimming pool.'

'I did not push you into the swimming pool,' I say.

Then she gasps suddenly, raising a hand to her mouth. 'Oh, my God. I've just remembered.' She grips my arm. 'I put Christmas cracker jokes in all the guests' cards last year, didn't I?'

I smile. 'You did.'

'So the Christmas card you got from me . . . the one I wrote for Louis, the one you laughed at . . .' She covers her face with her hands.

'It said, *Why does Santa have three gardens? So he can "hoe hoe hoe"!*'

'Fucking hell,' she says between her fingers. 'I can't believe you even laughed at that, to be honest.'

396

'Well, I thought it was cute,' I say as she settles back against me. 'Remember, I liked you back then.'

I hold her as she laughs, looking up at the stars between the leaves. After a few moments, I start to smile. My eyes are adjusting to the darkness, and I can see what's growing in the branches above us.

'Izzy,' I whisper, and she lifts her face to mine. 'Look up.'

It takes her a moment too. She laughs.

'Shall I go get Drew, or . . .'

'Shut up, Izzy.'

She's still laughing when I lay her back across my lap and kiss her under the mistletoe.

December 2023

Izzy

'Good morning, Ms Jenkins. This is your four forty-five wake-up call.'

I squint at the time blinking on the hotel clock, shoving my new fringe out of my eyes and feeling blindly behind me. Nothing, just empty sheets. What the hell? Is he pranking me? This would not be the first time, but a wake-up call pre five a.m. is particularly cruel, even by our standards.

'Thanks,' I manage. '*Obrigada*. Did I . . . request this wake-up call? Like, did I ask you to call me?'

'I'm sorry,' the receptionist says, sounding a little stressed. 'I'm not sure I understand.'

'Don't worry about it,' I say, rubbing my eyes hard with my free hand and rolling over. 'Thanks. And happy New Year.'

I press the button by the side of the bed to lift the blinds, and there he is, being predictably ridiculous: my boyfriend. Doing push-ups on the hotel balcony before the sun is even up.

'What exactly am I doing out of bed at this hour?' I ask him as I slide the balcony door open.

Lucas looks up at me, a faint sheen of sweat on his forehead and chest. His gaze shifts up my bare legs to the sight of me in his white shirt from the night before, and his eyes smoulder. Even after twelve months, he just *melts* me when he looks at me like that. I scowl at him, like, *Don't distract me*, and he smirks, like, *I make no promises*.

'We're going swimming,' he says, standing up. He is already in his swim shorts.

'*Now?* No. That's disgusting,' I say, turning back towards the bed. 'Goodnight.'

I flop forwards on to the cool sheets of our king-size bed. He grabs me by the ankle and I shriek as he tugs me back.

'Come on,' he says. 'You will love it.'

'It's night time.'

'It is about to be daytime.'

I turn my head to look outside. With all the lights in our room turned off, I can see the sky turning from black to deep indigo; the sea is a shade paler, the sands ghostly white. The majestic Pão de Açúcar – Sugarloaf Mountain – is already visible, rising dark above the horizon. Excitement flutters in my stomach.

'Swimming like, in the sea? At sunrise?'

'Precisely,' Lucas says.

I spin just in time to catch my bikini when he throws it my way.

OK. Maybe I don't mind getting up early. We've splashed out on three nights at this luxury hotel in Rio de Janeiro for

New Year's, at the end of our Christmas with Lucas's mum in Niterói. Do I really want to spend any more of my hours here unconscious than absolutely necessary?

Once we're down in the lobby – with a wave for the receptionist – it's only a few steps from the hotel to the beach. The air is already warm with promise, as if the sun barely left last night, and as Lucas and I run to the water's edge the sand shifts feather-soft beneath my bare feet. Lucas goes under first. I swim hard to reach him, the seawater cool enough to make me suck in a breath. I lunge for Lucas just as he spins to lunge for me. We pull each other under, laughing, snorting, spluttering, and end up tangled up with my legs around his hips just as the sun begins to draw a single bright line on the horizon.

He kisses me hard. I realise he's shaking a little around me, his hands balled in fists – it must be cooler than I realised. I wrap my arms around the familiar solidity of his shoulders and kiss him back just as hard, my fingers in the short stubble of his hair, my knees tightening at his sides. We're kissing as if we're saying something we don't have words for. And that's what gives me the idea.

Because lately, when I feel like this – that there's no way to show him how much I love him, that there just aren't words or kisses fierce enough for this – a question pops into my head. And with the vast, beautiful sky turning pink around us, it suddenly feels like the perfect moment to ask it.

'Lucas,' I say, pulling back from him. 'Will you marry me?'

For a long moment, he just stares at me, the droplets on his skin catching silver-pink in the sunrise.

'Lucas?' I say after a moment, gripping his shoulders tighter. 'Should I not . . . Do you not . . .' I glance at the skyline. It's an artwork of pink and purple and orange. 'This just seemed like a totally perfect moment to propose.'

'I know,' Lucas says, voice catching slightly in his throat.

He shifts, one arm letting go of me in the water as he moves to show me something in his closed hand.

A ring.

I know that ring. It's Maisie Townsend's ring. My hand flies to my mouth.

I saw Mr Townsend just a couple of weeks ago, before we left for Brazil; I'm still working part-time at Forest Manor while I launch my business. We'd caught up over Arjun's new afternoon tea, and as I'd walked him back to his room, Mr Townsend had said something that now makes a lot more sense. *Have a good Christmas*, he'd said, and then, as the door was closing behind him, he'd added: *And happy New Year from Maisie and me.*

My knees go loose with shock, and I almost go under. I grab Lucas, spluttering, as he says, 'Why do you think you're in the sea for the sunrise?'

'Oh my God,' I say, clinging to him, reaching for the ring.

He closes his hand again.

'Izzy Jenkins,' he says, 'have you really just one-upped my proposal?'

I throw my head back and laugh.

'Do you know how much planning went into this? There is a picnic breakfast waiting for us on that beach. I had to bribe the receptionist to do a wake-up call – in English – because the hotel doesn't even offer them. I had to get this ring out of the hotel safe while you were brushing your teeth, and you *kept* wandering out of the bathroom.'

'Give me that ring!' I say, reaching for his hand.

'Do you even have a ring for me?' he asks, a smile tugging at the corner of his mouth as I try to peel back his fingers.

'Well, no,' I admit. 'It was kind of a spontaneous thing.'

'So . . . no ring,' he says, counting off on his other hand. 'No picnic breakfast waiting.'

'Great setting though,' I say, gesturing to the dramatic sky. 'You have to give me that.'

'One-all on setting,' he agrees.

'And a point to me for actually asking the question,' I add, still trying to open his hand. Even the man's fingers are ridiculously muscular – there's no budging him. 'You haven't technically asked me anything yet.'

'My apologies,' Lucas says, and he stills my hand with his, catching my gaze. 'Izzy,' he says, and now I'm not laughing. 'Izzy Jenkins. My love for you grows stronger every day. I want for ever with you. I want to find out how big and bright this love will be when we're old and grey.'

His bottom lip trembles ever so slightly. I've long since learned that I was wrong to think of Lucas's expression as implacable: the emotion is always there if you look closely enough.

'I've known I'll ask you to marry me since that moment at the airport last Christmas, but I wanted to wait until I truly believed enough of myself to trust that you would say yes. I still think this isn't a question you should ask because you need to know the answer.'

'Oh my God,' I say, beginning to cry.

Lucas's hand tightens over mine, and then he extracts his fist, unfolding his fingers and holding the ring out to me over the water.

'Mr Townsend gave me this ring to give to you when the time was right. He knew you had lost a ring that mattered to you, and he wanted to start a new story for you with this one. I wish I could have found the ring your father gave you. But I think this one holds its spirit, maybe.' He smiles. 'There's something I would have never said before I met you.'

I'm all tears and seawater. I swipe at my cheeks with trembling hands.

'Izzy, will you accept this ring, and do me the honour of becoming my wife?'

'Yes. Yes.' I sob as he slides the ring on to my finger. 'Oh, my God. I can't believe . . .' I clench my fist. 'Let's get out of the sea. I am *not* losing this one.'

Lucas laughs. I love that laugh – it's his lightest one, unselfconscious and full. I want to make him laugh like that a hundred times a day for ever.

'OK, so now I have asked the question . . .' he says.

I grab his hand as we find our footing on the sand and begin to walk to the shore. Rio de Janeiro stretches before us, waking up, if it ever truly slept. Apartment windows blink bright in the sunlight, and the fierce blue mountains rise behind it all, just waiting for us to explore them.

'Yes,' I say, looking over at the man I hated, the man I love, the man who makes me burn my brightest.

'I win? At proposing? I win this one?'

I laugh. 'You win this one,' I say, and he scoops me up in his arms, whooping, dancing up the beach.

I feel the ring pressing into my palm, carrying so much within it. I'm crying, laughing, clinging to Lucas as the December sky lightens above us. What an honour to wear this ring. And what an honour to call this difficult, wonderful, obstinate, generous man mine.

Acknowledgements

This is a book I wasn't supposed to write – I had no publication scheduled for 2023. Essentially, *The Wake-Up Call* was created through the sheer stubbornness of Izzy and Lucas, who refused to shut up even when I told them to. Now that you've read the book, this probably won't surprise you.

A lot of brilliant people came together to bring this story out into the world, people who said, *sure, that wasn't the plan, but let's do it anyway.* I'm grateful to be surrounded by such innovative and creative talents.

Tanera Simons, my partner in crime (or should that be partner in rom-com?): thank you, as always, for your patience, care and clear-headedness. You're a wonder. Cassie Browne, Emma Capron, Kat Burdon, Cindy Hwang, my super-creative editors: thank you for giving me the nudge I needed to let this book fly, and for all your help shaping the story. Helena Mayrink: thank you so much for your brilliant insights, ideas and support on the Brazilian aspects of this novel, as well as all the Portuguese translations, and thanks also to Pedro Staite for your help – and for letting me borrow your name!

Jon Butler, Stef Bierwerth, Hannah Winter, Ellie Nightingale, Ella Patel, Hannah Robinson, Angela Kim, Hannah Engler, Lauren Burnstein, Tina Joell, Chelsea Pascoe and everyone at Quercus and Berkley: thank you for all your creativity, passion and hard work. To Georgia Fuller, Mary Darby, Salma Zarugh, Kira Walker, Sheila David and all at Darley Anderson Agency: thank you so much for continuing to share my books with people around the world.

Thank you to my parents for all the sage advice while I navigated writing this book. Thank you to Gilly McAllister for too many things to name, but primarily for being the other (better) half of my brain. Thank you to Caroline Hulse and Lia Louis for listening to many rants and providing much wisdom. To my sister, Ellen: thank you for being my rock.

Sam, my love. Thank you for treating these stories of mine with such respect – so much so that you took a pause in your career so that I could tend to mine. You are a rare, extraordinary man, and the most wonderful father. To my little bug: thank you for filling my life with the purest, brightest, most profound joy.

Lisa, Lucy, Beth, Hannah, Rhianna, Kate, Carly, Alison, and all the amazing team at my son's nursery: thank you for looking after my little boy with such love and care while I am writing these stories. Without you, this book would not exist.

Finally, dearest, dearest readers . . . I dedicated this book to you, which perhaps feels a bit redundant (I mean, of course the book is for my readers) – but I felt it needed saying for this one. I will never stop feeling lucky to do this job, and I only get to do it because you read the stories I write. Thank you for the faith you put in me every time you pick up one of my books. I mean it – I truly treasure you.